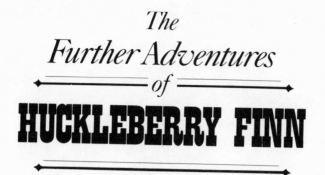

The
Further Adventures
— *of* —
HUCKLEBERRY FINN

The
Further Adventures
of
HUCKLEBERRY FINN
by
Greg Matthews

Crown Publishers, Inc.   New York

Published in the United States of America by
Crown Publishers, Inc., One Park Avenue, New York, New York 10016
and in Great Britain by Macmillan London Limited
Manufactured in the United States of America
Library of Congress Cataloging in Publication Data
Matthews, Greg.
The further adventures of Huckleberry Finn.
I. Title.
PS3563.A847F8   1984   813'.54   83-2051
ISBN 0-517-55057-1
Book design by Camilla Filancia
10 9 8 7 6 5 4 3 2 1
First American Edition

For Jane

Contents

✦ 1 ✦

Back to School—The Miracle—Whiskey by the River—The

Fire—At the Judge's

There was another book I writ before this one which give the story about how me and Jim went down the river on a raft, him looking for freedom on account of he's a nigger slave and me looking to get away from the Widow Douglas who's trying to sivilize me, and you could say we both wanted the same thing. I reckon most people don't read but one book in their life so if that warn't the one you read I best tell what happened at the end of that story, which is this: Jim got set free by his owner Miss Watson that died and give him freedom in her will, and Jim tells me he seen a dead man on the river and it was my own Pap, so now I'm a true orphan. Tom Sawyer says him and me and Jim should go for howling adventures among the Injuns out west and I figured it was a good plan.

Well, it never worked out that way, not at first. Things run along smooth enough after everything got put back like it was before me and Jim run off. Jim was a free nigger now and he never stopped bragging on it. That was all very fine for him, but I never felt like hoorahing about Pap. It was kind of a relief knowing he's dead and gone but at the same time I felt sorry too; I can't explain it. Jim says as how we're both free men now with a big rosy future full of freedom ahead of us. But it never made all that much difference. I moved back in with the Widow Douglas same as before and Jim, he stayed on with her doing all the usual chores he done before for Miss Watson, only now he got paid two dollars a week for it which is more money than he ever had in his life.

I laid out a thousand dollars from Injun Joe's loot to get Jim's wife and boy and girl out of slavery and they come to live at the widow's till Jim could build a house with the money he earned, which would be when he's around ninety. I offered him the cash so's he could do it

1

straight off but he says I done enough for him already, so his wife done the kitchen chores and such around the place and Jim was happy having his family under one roof.

Along at the tail end of summer, school started again and I drug myself along to the schoolhouse mainly to show the widow I was sorry for having run off with her sister's nigger, atonement as they say. Tom Sawyer made it tolerable easy at first but pretty soon he took to mooning and spooning around Becky Thatcher in spite of her calling him a low-down friend of a nigger thief (me).

So you could say I warn't none too happy about things, and you would of been right. After them free and easy days on the raft with Jim it was like being cooped up in prison, wearing all them clothes the widow give me, stiff and new and discomforting, and eating regular with a knife and fork and a napkin across my knees to catch the stuff that never made it as far as my mouth and which I warn't allowed to scoop up and give it a second try. It was godawful dull. Nights when sleep never come I just stared at the ceiling and recollected the good times me and Jim had drifting along down the river with nobody to tell us what to do. They was the best days of my life so far, and it seemed like they warn't ever going to come back. A body might just as well die after times like that because the rest of his life just won't measure up. It was like hauling a cannonball around inside of me, all heavy and mournful feeling, and it made me walk slow and think slow, like being only half awake all the time.

Here's what I mean. I come down the street on a Saturday with my eyes all glassed over and staring at the ground. Someone says "Hey, Huck," Jo Harper or Ben Rogers maybe, only I don't even look around, don't even say "How do," just keep on walking, sliding my boots along the sidewalk, too tired and heavy feeling to lift them proper. Pretty soon I come to the edge of town and I take myself off into the woods and flop under a tree like a rag doll. There's cool shade on my face and it feels good, but at the selfsame time it makes me want to cry. How can you figure behavior like that? So I'm sitting there flopped under the tree and the shade moves across the ground nice and slow and I'm staring at it while it moves and thinking nothing at all, which is possible I can tell you. Then I see the snake, a puff adder gliding along smooth as silk. This is the queer part I'm trying to tell. I don't shoot off like a rocket and lam out of there, I just lay quiet watching it come along the ground till it reaches my foot where it stops, surprised I'm still there, not scared or nothing. It slithers over my boot, curious-like, and comes up to take a closer look at me. I never budged, I never sweated a drop, just looked him square in his slitty eyes, and when his tongue flickers in and out rapid I done the same, returning the compliment. We stayed like that flickering our tongues at each other for some considerable time, then up comes my arm real slow, and my hand come to a stop a couple inches away from the puff adder's head. I offer him the back of my hand to bite. He ducks his head sideways and back again, back and forth like a dance, and I keep my eyes on his. Then he stops bobbing side to side and turns and slithers away. It was a perfeckly good hand he could of bit but never did. He slithers off into the leaves and then he's gone.

I knowed right off it's a sign, but the meaning of it was a mystery. I stayed sat down and turned it over good, and finally after I give up trying to puzzle it out the answer hit me. It was Pap. He come back to let me know he forgives me for hating him and being scared of him the way you are with a snake. The devil must of give him time off to come up and do it. Pap must of done one good thing in his life to get parole that way, but whatever it was he never done it while I was around. I would of remembered. Anyway, I felt a whole lot better now I understood. It was like coming through fog into open water and seeing everything bright and clear and I made up my mind to have a snake for a totem like the Injuns do.

I felt pretty good for about a week, then the blue devils come back to plague me again worse than before. The widow seen the way of it and dosed me up on castor oil so I spent a fair amount of time in the outhouse, which is not such a bad place to be when you want to get away from the entire world. I sat in there and considered things. I had my share of Injun Joe's loot being took care of by Judge Thatcher, five thousand dollars of it left after buying Jim's family into freedom, but somehow I never got happiness from it. I had a friend, Tom Sawyer, but he never bothered coming around nowadays on account of always being with Becky Thatcher. I had a full belly (before the widow dosed me) and clothes on my back and a soft bed and a roof over my head, but none of it mattered worth a damn. I could feel the whole shebang coming down slow and steady, squashing me under, and it seemed there warn't nothing I could do about it besides kill myself.

Then comes a thundering and knocking on the outhouse door and Jim's voice come through the half moon cut in the planking.

"Huck, is you in dere, Huck? I'se brimful to bustin' wid somethin' to tell, Huck."

So I pulled up my britches and come out, and he's hopping from one foot to the other with a big grin on his face and I say:

"Well, what's so important you had to disturb my function?"

"It's 'Lisbeth, Huck! She kin hear! She done took a tumble down de steps an' bang her head on de groun' an' now she kin hear good as you an' me! She ain't deef no more, Huck!"

Without you already read my other book about me and Jim you won't know he had a deaf and dumb daughter about five years old that could never talk or hear even a cannon if it went off right beside her. Jim and his wife give up hope long ago she'd ever be like her little brother who was a normal nigger boy, so now Jim's all aglow with the miraculousness of it, telling me the story three times over.

"I seen her fall down de outside steps, Huck, an' rushed on over fast as I could a-bawlin' her name out loud an' Lawd if she don' turn aroun' an' lookit me when I bawls it! She's sittin' all of a daze feelin' de bump on her head an' I calls out her name an' she turns aroun'! She done it perzacly one second after I calls it, Huck, so I knowed right off she kin hear! De Lawd must of give her de push down dem steps so's to loosen de cobwebs in her head!"

The long and the short of it is Jim and me took his little girl to Doc Crabb, who's the only one in town that'll touch a nigger, and he pokes around inside her ears with a little stick and goes behind her and claps his hands and suchlike and ends up deciding she can hear good as gold, only he can't explain why. But he does say maybe she ain't dumb neither, and just never spoke words on account of not knowing what words is, being deaf, and now she can hear talk being spoke all around her she'll know people ain't just breathing when they open and shut their mouths, and she'll listen and get the hang of it and start in talking herself.

Jim come out walking on air with Elizabeth perched on his shoulders looking around at the sound of folks jawing and buggy wheels squeaking and a blue jay on a picket fence warbling away. You never seen the like of her face, all full of wonderment. It made me feel kind of lighthearted too, the way you get when someone else's happiness rubs off on you. Jim was the best nigger I ever met and if anyone deserved a piece of good luck I reckon it was him. We went on home and told the widow and she declared it was a miracle and give Elizabeth a hunk of sugar to suck and Jim the rest of the day off.

"Leave the chores Jim; you must celebrate this blessed event," she says.

And he did, with whiskey, which was maybe not so smart seeing he never had but a mouthful before in his life. But his wages was there to buy it and his little girl was there with two good ears to give him a reason for it so he went and got the whiskey, only it was me that went into the store to fetch it for him.

"You do it, Huck," he says. "I never went into no store to get liquor befo'. I don' have no 'sperience of it. You go on in an' get it for me. Here de money. If 'n dey got big bottles an' little bottles you be sure an' get de bigges'."

So I done it, in two minds about the whole thing, but doing it anyway. When I handed over the bottle Jim tucked it under his arm like it was a treasure and walked extra careful so as not to jog it loose and smash it on the way home. When his old woman seen what he had she got kind of snotty and went at him about the demon drink and such. She's a big woman with a voice to match, but Jim stood firm.

"It only for de celebratin' of de chile's bran' new ears," he says, getting his dander up. "Don' you get tonguewhippin' me, woman. I'se de boss in dis here place an' if 'n I wants to celebrate wid a couple snorts das my priv'lege an' no woman goin' to tell me diff 'rent."

And he hauled out the cork and tilted the bottle right there and then in front of her and his adam's apple bobbed up and down like a monkey on a stick. About five seconds later the taste hit him and he gasps and gags and his eyes come near to bugging out of his head. His old lady throwed back her head and brayed like a jackass.

"De drinker," she says, scornful. "De genulman wid de top hat an' walkin' cane an' de glasser whiskey in his han' fixin' to cut de dash. Huh! Mo' like de boy takin' de firs' puff on de pipe an' comin' near to puke on it! Well, if 'n you wants to look ridickerless you kin go somewheres else an' do it. I ain't havin' no chiler mine watchin' her daddy make de fool an' pukin' all over de flo'. You git right now, an' you, Huck, you watch over him good. Now he a free man he thinkin' all de time he kin do what he want, but it ain't so. He still a nigger an' niggers don' go buyin' no bottler whiskey, not in dis town."

So we went down by the river and settled in a shady spot where we

could hear the water sliding by and took turns pulling at the whiskey.
It went down slow but regular till the bottle was near three-quarters
empty and the sun was setting. Sometimes we chinwagged about this
and that, but mostly we just sat and sucked on the bottle. Soon it come
on toward dusk and the bats and owls begun to flit around. Jim give a
sigh and shook his head and I could see the white of his teeth and the
whites of his eyes, considerable crossed by now, and he says:

"Huck, you is sittin' wid de happies' man in de worl'."

"Why's that, Jim?" I ask, knowing the why of it already but not
wanting to stop him talking it all out.

"On account of I got ever'thin' a man need. A woman dat look after
me fine an' two chillen dat both kin hear real good. Dat Johnny, he a
chip off'n de ol' block, a-tearassin' aroun' an' gettin' in trouble all de
time. I'se goin' to hafter wallop him good perty soon, an' learn him
some respec' an' manners. He a free man too, an' he goin' to get brung
up right. Das de mos' impo'tant thing, Huck, dat freedom. A man ain't
a man nohow lessen he got freedom. You an' me is lucky. We got a
whole amounter freedom an' de brains to enjoy it. Ain't dat so, Huck?"

I disagreed with him about the enjoying but never spoke it. I just let
him rattle on about freedom and happiness and how his cup runneth
over. Meanwhile his bottle runneth low and the moon come up and
the bullfrogs got to croaking at one another and pretty soon Jim commenced to snore. I sat peaceful and pie-eyed listening to the frogs and
the crickets and Jim sawing wood, a nice easy feeling. Along come a
steamboat all lit up with smoke belching from her chimneys and blotting out the stars. There was an orchestra on her playing a tune that
come to me clear as a bell across half a mile of water, then she's gone
around a bend and the sternwheel slapping the water fades and dies.

It warn't no good. Them blue devils was back, bottle shaped, and
there ain't a meaner kind than that. Maybe this was how Pap got
started on drinking, feeling good at first then bad later on. I tried keeping him out of my head but he kept peering around a tree and laughing at me, his face all fishbelly white and his long hair hanging down
in his eyes, then at last he ducks back out of sight and he's gone. I got
out my pipe and smoked awhile to steady my nerves. What right did a
nigger have to be happy when a white man was miserable? It never
made no kind of sense, but it warn't Jim's fault so I never held it
against him. He's my friend after all.

Right about then I decide to lower the level of whiskey inside me and raise the level of the mighty Mississippi, only it was hard work to stand up straight and I had to crawl on hands and knees down the bank, steepish hereabouts so I ended up sliding head first into the drink, which give the bullfrogs something to croak about for days, I bet. It was cool in the water, so I stayed there floating in the shallows and sobering up some. Then I seen the fire, not the flames on account of the trees, but the glow in the sky overhead. Something in St. Petersburg was burning.

I swum ashore and tried to wake Jim, but he's dead drunk so I left him there and legged it back to town quick as I could, thinking how he'd be sorry in the morning he missed all the excitement. Finding the fire was easy enough; I just followed everyone that was streaming along toward it, but the closer I got the sicker I felt. The fire was in our street, and it was the Widow Douglas's house. The flames was licking the boards from the ground on up to the gables, crackling and roaring and throwing red light over everything. I looked at the windows but there warn't nobody there waiting to jump down. The town fire engine come clanging along the street and come to a halt and the brigade whipped out the hose and pumped away, playing the water onto the front porch where it done as much good as a gnat pissing on a stove. I run back and forth like a fretful dog trying to get close but the heat turned me away. Finally the roof give way with a crash and the whole place come down like a house of cards and shot sparks and flame high up in the air, then the walls fell in and it never even looked like a house no more. All the brigade could do was play the hose on the place next door so it won't catch light too. People around me was saying how no one come out of the house after the fire got started. The widow was dead and Jim's family too, all of them crisped. I pushed through the crowd and run hard as I could away into the dark.

Next morning when Jim opens his eyes the first thing he seen was me sitting right by him. He pulled himself up onto his elbows and give me a bleary look.

"Lawdy, Huck, I got all de chillen of Israel trampin' in my head dis mornin'. Dat whiskey's mighty fine for celebratin', but I'd sure hate to do it regular. Reckon I'd get de Philistines too."

He laughs at his joke, which is middling witty coming from him, then he catches the look on my face.

"Say, Huck, you lookin' awful troubled 'bout somethin'. You tell your ol' frien' Jim. You got a pain in de gut from celebratin'?"

"No," I say.

"Well, what den?"

"The widow's house burned down last night, Jim. They're all dead."

He looks at me, then across the river, then back at me.

"Mus' be dem trampin' Israelites makin' me hear dat 'bout de widder's house burnin' down," he says, and shook his head and clouted his ears a few times.

"Now you kin tell me it again, Huck, what you tol' jest now."

"You heard it right, Jim. I'm real sorry."

"You ain't playin' no joke on ol' Jim is you, Huck? I mind a couple other times you done that jest for laffs. I don' mind if'n you wants to play a joke, only this'n ain't funny. You tell me straight now 'bout what it was you said."

"It ain't no joke. I told you already, the house burned down and they're all dead."

When it sunk in he got up on his feet and stood there swaying side to side like a tree in a storm, his eyes empty and his jaw all slack, then he got down on his knees and picked up every pebble and stone he could lay hands on and dumped them in his pockets till his clothes was all lumpy and he couldn't hardly straighten up again. Then he went down to the river and waded in. I figured his mind must of gone so I stayed quiet, waiting to see what he done next. It was real interesting. He went in about chin deep and ducked under and stayed there. Up come some bubbles, then nothing, and it come to me he's trying to kill himself. I dove in and swum hard for where he's squatted on the bottom. I couldn't hardly see him so I had to do it all by touch, pulling the stones out of his pockets and hauling at his jacket to make him come up. He broke the surface real sluggish and started back down again, so I took a breath and followed and pulled out more rocks and hauled him up again. It was pitiful to see. I drug him into the shallows then up onto the bank. He spit some water and moaned and made to go back in the river but I stopped him.

"Whyn't you let me die, Huck? What I got to live for now?"

"Why, plenty, Jim. There's lots of things to live for still."

I can't think of even one offhand, but talking him out of killing himself seemed like the right thing to do.

"Po' little 'Lisbeth. . . . Now she ain't ever goin' to talk."

"Look at it this way, Jim, now she won't have the bother of learning."

But he never listened to sense, just went on moaning nigger fashion till he had to stop and puke. After that he calmed down some and sat all glassy-eyed and silent as the grave. I smoked a couple or three pipes meantime, staying close in case he made a break for the water again, and while I smoked I got to thinking about the widow and how she done her best to sivilize me. She was stiff-necked and tiresome in her ways sometimes but she was a good old bird for all that, and I reckoned I'd miss her. That happened with a pet raccoon I had once. The fool animal got snagged in one of Pap's rabbit snares and I had to kill it. I mourned for that coon a week or more till I got over it. The least I could do for the widow was give her a fortnight's worth of full-strength mourning, starting right now. So I concentrated real hard and managed to squeeze out a tear or two but pretty soon got drowsy and nodded off.

When I woke up it was noon and my clothes was dried out. I looked around for Jim but he warn't there. Then I see a bubble come up in the water a few yards from shore. Quick as a flash I jumped in and thrashed around trying to find him, but no luck. Maybe the current got him this time. Then I see him standing on the bank watching me like he's wondering what I'm doing, so it must of been a catfish bubble I seen. I come out feeling sheepish and sat in the sun to dry off again. Jim stood around like a lost soul and I figured he needs distraction, so I hauled out my totem stick that I whittled after the snake business I told about and give it to him.

"Here, Jim, what do you make of this?"

He studied it close a minute or two then says:

"Das a stick."

"Right enough, but I done things to it. See the snake head I carved at the top."

"Is dat a snake? It look more like a fish."

"Well, it's a snake. This here's a totem like the Injuns have. They pick an animal for their totem and carve it up on a tree trunk and plant it in front of their tepees for good luck. They generally have all kinds of animals carved one on top of the other, but it's the one on top that counts."

"Is dat a fac'? Den how come dis totem got a snake on it? A snake ain't no animal."

"What is it then if it ain't an animal?"

"Huck, you knows more'n anyone 'bout most ever'thin', but even a nigger know better'n to call a snake a animal. Animals got fur an' claws an' such."

"Well all right then, what is it?"

"Why, a insec', Huck. Ain't nothin' else for it to be I reckon."

"Whatever it is it's my totem. It come to me in a dream so it has to be right. This little stick's just a model, see? What we have to do is make a full-size one, then we'll have us a genuine totem and our luck'll pick up."

"I don' believe I got no luck nohow. I got no luck an' no fambly no mo'."

And he started moaning and crooning all over again. I tried to talk him into coming back to town with me but he says he ain't going nowhere near the widow's house on account of his family would be flitting around thereabouts as ghosts waiting for him to show up. He felt terrible guilty about not being there when the fire started and dying with them.

"All right then, Jim, but I'm going to have to tie you up while I'm gone."

"What you wanter do dat for, Huck?"

"It's for your own good. You might get the sorrows again and throw yourself in the river."

"I won' do dat again, Huck, I promise. I don' know what come over me befo'."

"You ain't in your right mind just now, Jim, so I got to take steps on your behalf."

I took off my belt and made Jim do the same, then joined them together and made him sit with his back to a tree. I passed the belts across his chest and buckled them around back of the trunk where he warn't able to reach, then tied his ankles and wrists with his bootlaces. When I finished he was trussed up like a turkey and looking just as miserable.

"You sit tight an hour or so, Jim. I'll be right back."

"But looky, Huck, supposin' you drops dead? Ain't nobody goin' to know I'se here."

"Well if it happens just holler good and loud and I guess someone's bound to hear you and set you free."

I left him there and went back into town. The widow's house was just a pile of hot cinders and the chinaberry tree in the front yard had all the leaves scorched off one side. There's a fair crowd there still and

Jo Harper come up and says everyone's looking for me, so I went along to Judge Thatcher's house and knocked on the door. The nigger maid let me in and showed me into the parlor and pretty soon in come Becky Thatcher, kind of hard to reckernize without Tom Sawyer draped all over her, but I picked out the curls and the frilly dress and the smug look easy enough. Soon as she seen me she whips out a handkerchief that never had a speck of snot on it and dabbed away at her eyes trying to make them red.

"Oh, Huckleberry," she says, looking forlorn. "What a tragedy to befall you. What a grim jest fickle fate has played upon you. You have my deepest sincerest condolences in your hour of ill omen. If I can be of assistance in any way during your ordeal . . ."

I played up to her real good, turning my mouth down at the corners and snuffling like a bloodhound.

"Can I borrer your handkerchief?" I ask.

"Why surely you may," she says, and near broke her arm in the rush giving it to me.

"Thank you kindly, Becky. You're a samaritan, I reckon."

I blowed my bugle hard into it, bringing down a wad of softies and a fair collection of crusts, then I give it back. Her jaw dropped about three feet like I'm giving her a dead spider or something. Then she gets her wits together and smiles gracious-like and says:

"You may keep it."

"Thanks. I'm short on wipers momentarily."

Then the door opens and this time it's the judge, looking sad and worried. Becky seen her chance to slide out, and the judge come over and put a hand on my shoulder, man-to-man-like.

"Huckleberry, words cannot express my sympathy. I know you held the widow in fond esteem, as did we all. The loss must be a heavy burden for you."

"Yes, Judge," says I. "Me and Jim are all broke up about it."

"Jim also survived?"

"Yessir. Him and me went fishing last night."

"Well, that is some consolation. I know you are good friends with the nigger."

"That's so, Judge. There's just him and me now."

The judge took me into his office and offered me the plushest chair and drug another over so's he could look me in the eye.

"Huckleberry," he says, "we must have a serious talk. The widow's untimely death has precipitated events somewhat, but I believe you are mature enough to be given certain confidential information."

And he goes on to say how the widow made out her will in my favor so now on top of Injun Joe's five thousand dollars I can add maybe two thousand more, which makes a considerable mountain of money. But here's the clincher. Except for my dollar-a-day allowance I can't lay a hand on it till I reach twenty-one, the selfsame arrangement as with the other loot. It was like having an apple tree and being told you could only pick oranges off it. Not only that, the widow's money was tagged for getting me educated in some fancy eastern school called Harvard. That shook me some I can tell you.

"So then," he finishes up, "you are an extremely wealthy young fellow. You have prospects, as they say. I have no doubt that the future holds great promise for you. With sound investment your nest egg will make you a man of considerable means by the time you attain your majority. I assume you wish to leave your capital in my hands until then?"

"May as well, Judge. I reckon I can trust you."

"I appreciate your trust, Huckleberry. Now, what plans do you have for the immediate future?"

"I got none."

"None at all?"

"Maybe I'll move into Pap's old cabin for awhile."

"My boy, you can't be serious. What about your schooling?"

"I'd just as soon let it go hang, Judge."

"But the conditions of the widow's will state quite clearly that your education must be continued."

"Well, maybe I'll go back next year. Right now I don't feel much like pushing pens and learning history and such."

So because there warn't nothing he could do to stop me he hemmed and hawed and said he understands the way things is, and we parted company cordial. Then I went back to untie Jim.

2

The Old Cabin—The Totem—Hibernation—Gold in

California!—The Plan—Murder in St. Petersburg

And that's how it started. Pap's cabin was about three miles upriver on the Illinois shore, tucked away in a stand of trees so thick you couldn't spit without hitting one or other of them. Jim and me stocked up with a heap of supplies and rowed up there in a skiff. We never included no whiskey in the supplies. It took a few days to clean the place out but we soon put it to rights and settled in cozy. Living there with Jim was surely a different thing to living there with Pap. We got along fine, just like being back on the raft, easy times with fishing and trapping and lazing around trading yarns. Sometimes Jim got blue when he recollected his family but them times got further apart and he got to be his cheerful self again.

We only went back into town one time early on, and that was for the funerals. I went along to the white folks' graveyard and Jim went along to the nigger graveyard and we watched everyone get buried. I spied Tom Sawyer in the crowd by the widow's graveside and we spoke a few words but he warn't hardly interested in talking over old times and was forever looking around to see where Becky Thatcher is, and so we parted kind of stiff and formal. I never seen anyone change so fast for the bad. After the preacher done his piece about the ashes and dust and it was all done, the judge asked me back to his place for a bite to eat, but I said no thank you and went along to fetch Jim.

The nigger graveyard had but a few people there to see Jim's family put under but they hollered and moaned enough for ten times the number, so that made up for it. It seemed like a lot of trouble to bury a handful of charred bones, and they was mighty particular about them bones too. Doc Crabb got called in to check all

13

the human remains that got raked out of the ashes so as to tell
which was white bones and which was nigger bones. Blamed if I
know how he told the difference, but he sorted through them right
fast and told which was the widow's and which was Jim's wife's.
The children was no problem on account of the size. It seemed like
a waste to put them all in full-length coffins when a couple of hat-
boxes would of done, but folks is very reverent about them that's
dead, even if they never liked them when they was alive. We went
back to the cabin and I kept a close eye on Jim for a few days after
that, but he never had no symptoms of the mournfuls so I relaxed.

Then all of a sudden he did start behaving queer, going off into
the woods each day with the axe. I heard him hacking away from
sunup to sundown but all he ever come back with was a few scraps
of kindling. He never breathed a word about what he's up to, so one
morning I made to tag along with him and find out, only he stopped
me.

"You cain't come wid me, Huck. I'se got to go alone."

"Why, Jim? Are you doing something shameful you don't want
me to see?"

"I'se doin' somethin', but it ain't shameful. I'se sorry, Huck, but
you cain't come."

"Well, that's good. That's a fine way to treat a friend. I figured you
and me never kept no secrets."

"This'n's a secret jest for now, Huck. When I'se done you kin see
all you wants. Meantime you got to promise you won' go traipsin' in
de trees over yonder an' spoilin' de surprise."

"First it's secrets, now it's promises. You're stretching the friendship, Jim."

"Please, Huck, do like I say."

"Well I ain't all that interested anyway. For all I care you can
build a gallows and hang from it."

"Dat ain't no way to talk, Huck. We'se friends still, ain't we?"

"That depends. This surprise better be good."

"It's a real dandy, honest."

So he kept on working and I kept on wondering. Once or twice I
got tempted to sneak along and take a peek, but I give him my
promise after all, so the secret stayed that way. I had a notion he was
building a raft like the one we had before.

Time slipped along and the leaves come down thick and fast and the nights got colder. Then come the day Jim announces the secret is ready for looking at. There was frost on the ground and we crunched along through it into the woods. Jim points and says:

"Dere she be, Huck. What you think of her?"

It's a tree with all its branches hacked off and the top section gone altogether, also the bark was stripped away clear down to the ground and there's chunks hacked out of the trunk all the way up. It looked like a twenty-foot-high peeled finger pointing at the sky. Jim stood there with a big grin waiting for me to say something. A few minutes went by and his grin started to slack off.

"Don' you like it, Huck?"

"Why, sure I do, Jim. It's . . . magnanimous."

"You means it, Huck?"

"I ain't ever seen another like it, and that's the truth. It's one of a kind, Jim."

"I ain't surprise' to hear it. Makin' one is a powerful heaper work I kin tell you."

So we stood looking at it awhile longer, then I can't hold back no more.

"Say, Jim, what do you call it?"

"What I calls it? Do it have to have a name, Huck? I didn' know dat."

"Everything has to have a name."

"Dat seems a pecul'yer notion, givin' it a name. What kinder name you reckon'd suit her, Huck? It got to be a big 'un cos she's awful big. Alexander 'bout de bigges' name I knows."

"Not that kind of name, Jim. What's that there I'm pointing at?"

"Das a axe, Huck. You knows dat."

"And what's that over yonder?"

"A bush I reckon. Is we goin' to give dat a name too, Huck?"

"What do we live in?"

He scratches his head in perplexion.

"A cabin?"

"Axe, bush, cabin. All them are names, not people names, de-scriptual names."

" I don' foller you, Huck."

"I mean what the dangblast is it?"

"You don' know what it is?"

"No I don't, and I bet the smartest man in the world wouldn't know neither."

He hung his head and says sullen-like:

"It a totem."

"A what?"

"A totem, like de one you whittled an' showed me."

"An Injun totem?"

"I reckon."

"Well why didn't you come out and say so? I can see it now."

And we looked at it awhile longer, taking it in. Then I say:

"Start at the bottom. What's that first part?"

"A bear," he says.

It looked more like a fat dog.

"And what's the next bit?"

"Das a eagle wid de wings folded in."

It looked like a bat, and an ugly one.

"How about the big knobbly bit up on top?"

"Das de snake. You sayin' as how you wantin' a snake totem, so das what I done. 'Pears to me you ain't impressed, Huck."

"I'm impressed, Jim. It's a real work of art. I can see the snake now. It gives me shivers just looking."

It was the most boggle-eyed snake I ever seen, more like a fly, but I never let on.

"Well, Jim, I appreciate what you done for me. This must be the grandest totem east of the Mississippi. All we have to do now is put it where a totem's supposed to be."

"Where dat, Huck?"

"Why, directly in front of the tepee."

"We ain't got no tepee."

"Then we'll put it in front of the cabin."

"It goin' to be some kinder job movin'. De roots under it go ever' which way."

"Then we'll have to chop it down."

And that's what we done. I showed Jim where to lay to with the axe and he worked like a demon. Pretty soon down come the totem with a crash. I sent Jim to fetch ropes from the cabin and we tied them around the snake's head, which was even more repulsive close up than I figured, and we commenced to hauling. But it never budged an inch.

"Jim," says I, "we're going to have to amputate. It's too blamed long."

"We goin' to cut her short, Huck?"

"Have to. It can't stay here."

So I showed him where to cut and he chopped off the bottom ten foot or so. It would of been easier with a crosscut saw but we never had one.

"Well, that's shortened her considerable, Jim. Let's try again."

So we hauled on the ropes and it still never shifted.

"Lawd, Huck, dere ain't no way to tote dis totem."

"I reckon we'll just have to cut more off it."

"Dere ain't but ten foot lef'. What kinder totem it goin' to be if'n we cut her down more?"

"It has to be done, Jim."

And so it was. But even a five-foot totem turned out too heavy. Finally I made Jim cut off the snake head bit, which was about three foot long, or tall when stood up, and we hauled it successful to the cabin.

"Now we need a hole to sit her in so the wind don't blow her over, Jim."

"But de wind don' hardly blow here, Huck. De trees too many keepin' it out. An' how de wind goin' to blow over somethin' jest three foot high?"

I explained to him about how Injun totems is sunk into the ground traditional.

"You wouldn't want it to fall down and get your enemies' scalps all over dirt would you?"

"Scalps, Huck?"

"A totem ain't a totem without it's got ten or fifty scalps hanging off it."

"How we goin' to get 'em? Ain't no one around here to scalp 'cept you an' me."

"We'll raid St. Petersburg and lift some hair off the population."

"Dat soun's awful risky, Huck. Dere's a lotter folks in town. Who you got in mind?"

I could see Becky Thatcher's curls dangling off the snake's nose clear as day, but I told Jim to forget about scalps for the while and get a hole dug for the totem. Which he done, two foot deep. We rolled the snake over to it and stood her upright and filled in dirt around the neck. It looked like a frog poking its nose out of water.

"Das de shortes' totem in de worl', Huck. It don' amount to hardly nothin'."

"Never mind, Jim. It'll bring us good luck."

"I hopes you right, Huck. Dat totem costed me a heaper sweat."

Next day the snow come and buried it. And it kept on coming, dropping down soft and white and silent, and pretty soon everything was knee deep. It's a fine sight but awful hard to slog through. We started sleeping twelve and sixteen hours at a stretch, only getting up to eat and smoke and stoke up the stove with wood till it was going full blast and the air around the flue shivered with heat. Jim says:

"I reckon de bears an' squirrels got de right notion, Huck, shuttin' theirselfs away in de hibernation. Dis winter livin' jest a waster time an' food. Ol' Jim'd rather be rolled up in a cave somewheres sleepin' cozy till springtime."

"You've hit on something, Jim. We'll try it."

"How you mean, Huck?"

"We'll make a hibernation experiment. It'll be the first one in history."

"How we goin' to do it?"

"It's simple. There's the meat hut outside with nothing in it right now. I reckon you could just about squeeze in there and pretend it's a cave."

"Me, Huck?"

"One of us has to stay awake and go out every once in awhile to check up on you and take notes. That's how experiments are made."

"But why do it have to be me as goes in de meat hut?"

"Because you can't write notes, Jim. It's obvious."

"I ain't sure 'bout dis, Huck."

"Just think, Jim, if it works you'll be famous. Don't you want to see your name in the newspapers? I bet we get invited to give scientifical lectures in England and Europe and them places."

"An' what if it don' work? Das what I'm askin'."

"Faint heart never won famousness, Jim. You can take a blanket with you."

"But Huck, I'se four foot from de stove an' I got three blankets aroun' me now an' I'se jest tol'able warm. Ain't no way I'se goin' to keep warm out in de meat hut."

"The trick is to fall asleep fast as you can, then you don't feel the cold."

He never wanted to do it, not having the adventure spirit, but I got him out of bed in the end and pushed him outside, where it's bitter cold with more snow floating down. I hauled open the meat hut door and Jim crawled in and sat himself crosslegged. I give him a blanket and he got it across his shoulders after considerable twisting and turning and skinning his knuckles on the roof and walls. He's none too happy, so I told him again about being famous then shut the door and dropped the latch. Then I went back in the cabin and dozed off. When I woke up I wondered where Jim was, then I remembered the experiment and went out to the meat hut.

"Did you fall asleep yet, Jim?"

No answer. I opened the door quiet in case he was hibernating and looked in. His eyes was open still and his teeth chattering away in his head, so it ain't happened yet.

"I'll come back later when you're asleep," says I.

He never spoke so I figured he was agreeable. I went inside and dozed some more then come out and checked again. His teeth was quiet now but his eyes had kept open and his face and hands turned a shade of blue, hard to detect in a nigger, but there it was.

"You got to close your eyes, Jim. It won't work otherwise."

He give a kind of moan and rolled his eyes, telling me he's sorry I guess. I made to close the door again when he give a strangled sort of cry and throwed himself through the doorway, still all huddled up and crosslegged, like one of them little Chinaman statues that's gone and fell on its face. It was pretty clear he never wanted to keep at it. Some folks won't take a chance for fame even if it's give to them on a silver plate. So I turned him on his back like a turtle and slid him across to the cabin on the blanket, which has gone stiffish, and rolled him through the door. He still never uncrossed his legs or talked. I figured he was peeved at me over something so I propped him against the wall and left him alone till he come out of the sulks. After a pipe I nodded off and when I woke up it was night and Jim was back in bed same as before with all the blankets piled on top of him. I decided next time he come up with an idea I'd ignore it.

Thanksgiving and Christmas and New Year come and went but we never paid them no heed. I figured 1849 would be a year just like any other. It turned out I was wrong, but I never knowed it then. Our supplies run low so we took the skiff and headed for town. The river was dark and mean-looking with chunks of ice floating along here and there so we had to work our way across to the Missouri shore real careful. When St. Petersburg come into view it's looking pretty as a picture under all that snow. We tied up at the wharf and Jim says he'll go visit some nigger friends while I collect my back allowance from the judge. We agreed to meet at the store in a couple of hours and I headed for the Thatcher place. The judge took me through to his office and counted out the money, looking stern while he done it. Then he says to me:

"I'm concerned for you, my boy."

I seen a lecture coming plain as day.

"The people of St. Petersburg are concerned for you," he says, driving it home.

"How so, Judge?"

"You have seven thousand dollars in trust, which places you in an enviable position. It is my hope and the hope of other leading citizens that you will in due course assume the mantle of responsibility that awaits you. Certainly you have the wherewithal to achieve this end. But . . ." and he points his finger right between my eyes, "you are not behaving in a manner suited to your station. With all this money, with all the opportunity it represents, you still choose to live in a ramshackle cabin out in the woods. It will not do. You are building a reputation for eccentricity, and that is a stigma no sane man should bring upon himself if he can avoid it. I'm aware of the difficulties that have dogged your footsteps since you came into the world, Huckleberry, and I understand your inability to cope with a style of living to which you are unaccustomed, but you must be able to see that living as you do will only result in your becoming as useless as was your wretched father. You must adjust to your new-found position in society, for your own sake."

"Maybe I have got seven thousand dollars, Judge, but I may as well not have seeing as I can't touch none of it. I'm still a long ways from twenty-one."

"Quite so, but as trustee of your estate I am empowered to release capital for your needs, so long as I deem them worthwhile."

"Like for fancy schooling and such."

"Correct, and while we're on the subject I should add that the land on which the widow's house stood is now an eyesore. I would cheerfully arrange for an allocation of funds should you decide to rebuild on the site and move back to St. Petersburg."

"Well, I'll think about it."

"There is one other matter."

"Yes, Judge?"

"Jim. People find it hard to understand why he is with you. As a freed slave he is not part of your legacy."

"We're friends."

"That is exactly what disturbs me. You are living on a level with the poorest white trash and supporting a nigger to boot. I realize Jim is a good man but the fact remains you are treating him as an equal."

The way he said it made me feel guilty all right. He rattled on for another few minutes about presenting the right face to the world, then he relaxed and got chatty.

"Living a life of isolation as you do, I suppose you have not heard the news."

"What news would that be, Judge?"

"Why, the gold strike in California. The entire country is buzzing. President Polk has announced that the rumors of a bonanza are perfectly true. According to reports it's possible to make your fortune in a matter of days. There are even stories of men striking it rich within minutes, but these are probably exaggerations. At best a gold rush will provide an incentive for Americans to go west and populate the new territories. At worst it will mean a disastrous loss of manpower in the east. Thousands have left their homes and families already, and the figure will rise dramatically in the spring. Gold fever has a way of drawing men from all walks of life."

Listening to him I felt a funny kind of tingle come tiptoeing up my spine and I swear the hairs on the back of my neck stood out. I can't hardly breathe and there's a drumming in my ears that drowned out everything he says except "gold." Then he stopped and give me a queer look.

"Are you all right, my boy?"

"Yessir, Judge. The room's a mite warm I reckon."

"Would you like a glass of water?"

"No, thank you, Judge. I have to be getting along now."

"Very well. Promise me you'll think carefully on our little talk."

"Yessir, I'll do that. I'm already giving it ponderation."

"Good," he says, and give me a fatherly smile.

I took myself to where the widow's house used to be. It looked kind of sad and forlorn with just the chimney bricks poking up through the snow. I stayed there awhile stamping my feet to keep out the cold and thinking hard, then I went to the store. By the time Jim come along I had all the stuff we needed and he helped me load it in a couple of gunny sacks and we went back to the wharf. All under the piles was sheet ice going out a few yards to where the water got deeper and faster. We had to rock the skiff to break her free, then we rowed four miles upriver staying close to the Missouri shore, then swung across and let the current take us back a mile to the cabin. It took that whole mile to get across to the Illinois shore, dodging ice all the way. By that time it was coming on to dusk and we fired up the stove to thaw out. I was still thinking. I ate thinking and fell asleep thinking.

What woke me was a cold wind coming through the doorway and Jim moaning and babbling and pulling at my shoulder.

"What is it, Jim? What's wrong?"

"She come for me, Huck. . . . She down by de river waitin'. . . ."

"Who is? Who's down there?"

"My ol' woman. She come for me like I knowed she would. Don' let her git me, Huck!"

"Your old woman's dead, Jim. She can't hurt you."

"She come back an' she down by de river right dis minute. I wen' out for to take a leak an' I seed her ghos' all over white an' starin' at me. She call out my name, Huck, I swear. . . ."

"I never seen a ghost before. Show me."

"I ain't goin' back out dere, Huck, not for a barr'ler money."

"Well I aim to see it. Tell me where it is."

"Don' go, Huck! De ghos' an' goblins git you for sure!"

"I ain't afraid of no goblins nor ghosts. I want to see it, Jim. Tell me where it is."

We argued back and forth and finally he give in and come back out with me. We tiptoed a way till we could hear the river grumbling along then Jim points with the axe he brung for protection.

"Dere she be, Huck, my ol' woman."

And my heart skipped a beat when I looked. There she was, all in white like he told me. We froze still as statues, waiting for her to say something or beckon mysterious the way ghosts do, but she just stood there same as us.

"Le's go, Huck," Jim whispers.

"Wait on. Maybe she's got a message for you."

But she stayed silent, which was vexing. I figured seeing she's a beginner she ain't yet got the hang of spooking, so I say:

"Have you got a message for Jim and what is it?"

But she stayed quiet. Then the moon come out from behind the clouds and I seen the way of it.

"Why, she ain't but a little tree covered in snow."

"No, Huck, she jest look dat way to fool you."

"I'm telling you, Jim, it's a tree."

"It a ghos' come to harnt me, Huck."

So I went over and shook the snow off the branches, and underneath it's just a plain fir sapling. Jim says:

"Huck, she done use magic an' turn herself into a tree."

"It was a tree all the time, Jim."

I snapped off a branch and brung it over to him and when he finally got up the bravery to touch it he says full of amazement:

"Ain't dat rare, Huck. . . . It feel jest like de real trees."

I seen another way is needed, so I say:

"Jim, did you ever wonder why ghosts is white?"

"I reckon cos dey ain't got no blood in 'em, Huck."

"Well that's true, but why does having no blood leave them white?"

"Das de color of de skin das lef' behin'."

"Are you trying to tell me your old woman had white skin?"

That stumped him good for a moment, then he says:

"Well, Huck, it muster bin de widder's ghos' come back to harnt *you*, steader my ol' woman come to harnt me."

I give up on it after that. He just warn't prepared to reason straight. We went on back to the cabin before the cold got into our bones and I figured now was as good a time as any to tell Jim about my plan, so I done it, starting with what Judge Thatcher told me. When I finished Jim slapped his knee, real pleased about it.

"Das a dandy plan, Huck. Is we truly goin' to do it?"

"I made up my mind on it, Jim. We need adventure. This old cabin is stagnatering us."

"Dis Californy, how far away is she perzacly?"

"Why, it's a fair step I reckon. That's why the plan has to work. We're going to need that cash to get us there."

"Huck, if'n it don' work I'se goin' to know for sure dere ain't no justice in de worl'."

So we waited a few days for a break in the weather then moved back to St. Petersburg. I got a room at the Wharf Hotel and Jim went off to stay with a friend. Then I went to see the judge and told him I'm turning over a new leaf and wanted to build a house on the land the widow left me and go back to school and generally get myself ready to be a certified grade-A citizen. He was mighty pleased and says I could move in with him until the house gets built, but I say I want to stay at the hotel so's not to be no trouble. He was agreeable and told me about a man in town that drawed up plans for houses and says I should go see him, and I promised I would, which was about the only truthful thing I told that day.

The town was in a flurry about gold and there was dozens already leaving to go west without even waiting for spring, steaming down to St. Louis then up the Missouri to St. Joe, which is the jumping-off place for the California trail. It near tore my heart out watching them go and me having to stay behind. But I kept on telling myself about the plan and how it was working smooth so far. The house planner whipped up a drawing and I took it along to a house builder and got told exactly what I wanted to hear, namely that he generally never worked over winter on account of the cold and never had but a few feet of lumber in his yard out back, so he needs payment in advance to get the timber before he can start, plus extra for working in the cold.

I told the judge about it and he says he'll fix it up with the bank. Then I went to see Jim and find out how his end of things was coming along. The week before I give him eighty dollars from my back-allowance to get mules for us, and he done well with the help of his nigger friend who's a fair judge of horseflesh, so there's two mules in a rundown stable on the edge of town being looked after by a friend of the friend. Niggers is always mighty obliging to one another. So we was all set.

I sweated ice worrying about snags I never thought of till now.

Then the judge give me a slip of paper signed by himself and told me to go get the money. First I went back to the hotel and changed the $1,000 writ on the slip into $2,000 then legged it for the bank. I made it in double quick time and handed over the slip. The teller says:

"Would you like the bank to arrange the transfer of funds?"

"No thank you. I'll do it myself."

He went away and come back with a piece of paper and give it to me.

"What's this?" says I.

"That's a bank note for the amount. You give it to the party concerned and he can either cash it or bank it."

"But . . . he wants to be paid directly in cash. He told me so."

"I'm sorry, Mr. Finn, but the judge's slip is not made out for cash."

That shook me down to my boots, but I soldiered on.

"He must of made a mistake then. I told him it had to be cash."

"All I can do is give you a blank cash slip. Take it to the judge and have him make it out again."

I grabbed it and run back to the hotel and used up the next half hour doing the judge's scrawly signature on a scrap of paper till I got it right, then I filled in the new slip, still $2,000, and signed his name on the bottom. When I got back to the bank my legs was like jelly. I wobbled up to the teller and give him the forgery. He looks at it casual-like and went off. It seemed like he took forever, then he come back with a wad of money and hands it over. He says:

"Would you like someone to go with you for safety?"

"I can manage fine, thank you."

"Well, keep it under your coat."

"I will."

And I staggered out. Back at the hotel I got out a brand-new money belt I had hid in the back of a drawer and put the bills into it, then strapped it around myself under my shirt and walked out past the desk clerk casual and cool. That was the last the Wharf Hotel ever seen of me. I got Jim and we lit out for the stable, but when we got there the wife of the nigger that's looking after the mules says they got loose and wandered off and her husband and eldest boy was out right now rounding them up, so we had to wait around doing nothing and fretting something awful at being stopped before

we even got started. Time marched along and still they never
showed. The nigger's wife fixed us some food but we warn't hungry,
and finally I can't stand it no more. There's a letter in my pocket for
the judge explaining things, and it was part of the plan to have Jim's
friend deliver it one night a couple of days after we left, but now I'm
so restless I figure I may as well slip it under the judge's door beforehand seeing as there's nothing in it to tell which way we went.

"Jim," says I, "I'm going back into town on unfinished business. I
won't be no more than an hour at most."

He says as how he'll stay on and wait for the mules and I set off
back to town, pushing along through the snow and wind. It's evening by now and there warn't a soul around so I had no trouble
getting to the judge's house without no one seeing me, and when I
come up the walk to the front door I pulled out the letter. I done that
letter a fair few times to get her how I wanted, and this is how she
read:

Dear Judge, This is to let you know I am sorry for what I done. I
do not think it is a crime. But some people would. Please do not
come after me. I am not telling where anyway. I had to do it or bust.
yours truly,
Huck Finn

I got to say it, book learning and schooling come in mighty handy
sometimes. So I'm all set to put the letter under the door when I
seen something in the snow on the front step. It's a footprint, but
not just any old kind. There's a cross on the heel made by nails to
keep off spells and devils. There's only the one print, crisp and clear
and fresh, and it made me break out in a flood of sweat. I never
knowed but one person ever had such a cross on his hoof and that
was my own Pap which Jim swore blind he seen dead on that house
floating down the river all that time ago. But there it is, large as life,
and I come near to an attack of the fan-tods just looking at it.

Then I seen something else. The door warn't shut like you'd expect on a winter's day but open maybe six inches, and the hairs on
my neck got stiff as porcupine quills. I could of run off right there
and then but I never done it, which they call a missed opportunity.
No, I pushed the door open all the way and stepped inside where it's
dark and cold with no lamps lit, and the wind is blowing snow onto
the hall carpet. I closed the door and listened awhile, but there

warn't no voices nor knives and plates banging in the kitchen, not a cat's *me-yow,* just a grandfather clock tick-tocking slow and solemn and the wind blowing outside, low and steady. So I went in further, going from room to room, but there's no one around and every step took give me the shivers that little bit more. When I got to the back of the house and I'm stood outside the judge's office I had the jitters so bad my knees can't hardly bend.

Then I'm through the door and in the office and the curtains was drawn so it's dark as a whale belly. I blundered around the furniture some, then struck a lucifer and lit a lamp near to hand. And there's the office all of a shambles around me, the chairs and desk turned over and away in corners they warn't in before and papers and legal files just scattered all over, with a big splash of red ink across the wall with drips running down, only dried, so I reckon it all happened awhile before I come. And there's the judge with just his legs showing behind the roll-top desk which is smashed open, on his back so I knowed even before I seen the rest of him he's dead as a wedge. I took a closer look and there's a pool of blood under his head from where his neck was sawed open. Whoever done it was the kind to make certain because the knife is sticking out of his chest too. The judge's eyes must of stayed open all through being murdered; they're staring right at me where I froze to the floor.

I seen dead men before but nothing like this, done deliberate and for gain, which is why the desk and drawers is smashed open so: robbery and murder. Maybe the judge seen the robber at work and it was someone he reckernized and he had to be killed so he won't say the name. Pap's been dead all this time but I knowed it was him, don't ask me how. It come to me like a bolt from the blue, the sure and certain knowledge as they say. Pap was alive and come for revenge on the judge, who never gave him the money he figured was his on account of being my Pap, which they call the motive. It was clear and plain, and I recollected the widow's house burning down and how no one could figure how it happened, and how before that Pap was made to feel small by the widow with lectures about this and that, mostly to do with him being a drunk and general good-for-nothing, which wounded Pap's pride some I can tell you, because even drunks as low as Pap can't take no more camel straw on their back, and from a woman too.

I run this kind of stuff through my head over and over, trying to get it straight, but it was forever coming unstuck, nothing I could give the proof of except the hoofprint outside. Right about then the front door slammed and footsteps come along the hall, two sets, and Becky Thatcher's voice says all peevish:

"Why are the lamps not lit?"

The nigger maid says:

"We only jest come in, Miz Becky."

"Well get them lit straightaway. A body could have an injury in all this dark. Papa must have fallen asleep at his desk."

The door come open and there I was, and there they was, and there's the judge, the only one that took it all calm and composed. The nigger maid screamed and run back out into the street hollering loud enough to get heard in St. Louis and Becky had a fit of the vapors and sunk graceful to the floor without giving herself a knock on the head or nothing hurtful. I figured the best thing to do is fan her face like I seen ladies do on a hot day, so I done it with the hem of her dress which is located convenient and was still doing it when there come a tramping of feet through the front door and the nigger maid's back with half the town and still hollering. She points and says:

"Lookit! Now he done lif' her dress! Murder an' molesterin' on de same day! Lawd, lawd, how dere be so much sin insider one chile?"

"You best be explaining yourself, Finn," says Jo Harper's old man, looking mighty grim, and someone else grabbed me by the neck and hauled me up and give me a shake that set the teeth rattling in my head.

"Well, boy? Speak up! What're you doing here?"

It sounded mighty lame when I told them I only come to deliver a letter.

◆ 3 ◆

A Prisoner's Life—Religion on a Plate—Conversations

with Tom Sawyer—Desperate Plans—Failure

Things moved along swift after that. They drug me down to the jailhouse on the edge of town and Sheriff Bottoms put me in a cell and there was more people crammed in there than peach preserves in a mason jar, all talking loud and telling me to come clean and give out the whole truth, which would be better for me in the long run. They already had it but it never fit what they wanted to hear, namely Huck Finn went and slit the judge's throat and lifted his daughter's skirts, which is something I never would of felt like doing even drunk. There was such a babbling of noise Sheriff Bottoms ordered everybody out so he can talk with me peaceful and find out what truly happened. Well, they hated to go, thinking maybe they'd miss out on a confession full of gore, but he made them and they grumbled some and went, but I could still hear them outside along with the rest of St. Petersburg except them that's crippled or deaf.

The sheriff set himself down and rubbed his jaw awhile, then says:

"Now then, Huckleberry, they say you went and murdered the judge. Is it so?"

And I told it all over again, about the letter and the footprint with the cross on the heel and the open door and all of it, and he hummed into his fist looking serious and stern and says:

"This letter, have you got it with you still?"

"No, Sheriff, and I disremember what I done with it. I had it in my hand up until I seen Pap's footprint. I reckon I must of dropped it on the front porch without knowing."

"What's in the contents of it?"

"It was private. I can't say."

"Son, this could be important. You've got to tell me."

"I'll go this far. It was apologizing for something."

"I've got to know more, Huck."

"I can't do it."

You proberly guessed it already. It's the money belt still tied around my belly. If it got around I forged the judge's signature on top of the murder I never would of stood a chance. If they found the letter it would of explanated me being at the judge's house, but like I say, shoved me in deeper. And I never wanted to get Jim mixed in with it neither. If a nigger gets snagged up in something where folks is peeved, he'll get blamed faster than a fox with chicken feathers in his mouth. So I stayed shut about the letter, thinking I never should of let on about it but it's too late now. Sheriff Bottoms went on at me about it some more but I never budged, so then he says:

"About this footprint story. You know your Pap's dead, Huck. The whole town knows. It's the flimsiest kind of make-believe."

"No it ain't, I swear. Pap's alive, I just know it."

"Very well, son. I see you're a reluctant witness despite your best interests. You're hiding something I reckon. My advice to you is think again on your story before tomorrow."

He left me alone and went into the other room that was part of the jailhouse, a little office with a desk and a stove that had a flue which come through the wall between to keep the cell warmed before going up through the roof. So I was snug enough with the blankets he give me too, in spite of the itty-bitty window having no pane in it. I give that window a careful looking over, but it's too small to squeeze through and barred anyway. Sheriff Bottoms's wife come along after the crowd outside got cold and went home, and she brung food for us both. The sheriff can't go home at all on account of having to guard me and keep an escape from happening. She come through into the cell with a heaped plate and set it down along with a Bible, for spiritual comfort, she says. I got more comfort from the plate. She watched me eat, shaking her head and tut-tutting away like the Widow Douglas done when she caught me at wrongdoing. Then she went away again. It was late by now so I bundled myself up in the blankets and got set to try and sleep when there come a tapping at the window bars and a soft *me-yow* and I knowed it was Tom Sawyer giving our old sign from the pirate gang days. I clumb up on a stool and there he is outside the window along with Jim.

"Well," Tom says, "I never thought someone with your criminal background would be fool enough to get nabbed red-handed. I'm disappointed in you, Huck. Why didn't you do the dastardly deed with a smidgen more carefulness, the way I would of?"

So you see he never changed all that much after all, still with all his superior smart-lip ways like I remembered. It was like old times.

"I never done it, Tom. I'm innocent as a lamb."

"That's the right spirit," he says. "Deny everything and let your crime be a matter betwixt yourself and your conscience. It's much more noble that way instead of blatting it to all the world. Why, if you live to be a hundred you'll never forget the bloodiness of it and the suffering will make you wise as Solomon."

"But I never *done* it."

"Huck, your closest bosom companions alone can share the burden of guilt with you. Me and Jim are safe to be given all the details, even them that wrench your heart to tell of."

"There ain't nothing to wrench my heart nor any other part. I'm a victim of circuses got catched in place of the true murderer, honest."

"Do you swear on your soul it's the absolute truth?"

"Both feet, Tom. I'll walk on stumps if it ain't."

"Well all right," he says. "I'll believe it, but it's a mighty poor showing. Being the innocent accused don't have half the shine of being a genuine murderer. I wouldn't brag on it if I was you."

Then Jim gets his chance to slip a word in edgeways and he told how the news run through town like floodwater and when he heard the trouble I'm in he legged it to Tom Sawyer's place to let him in on it, and they both come on the trot to see if they can render their assistance, as Tom puts it. How can a body not be gratified at something like that? It made me feel right humble and I out and say so, and Jim says:

"What we goin' do now, Huck? De plan ain't no good, not wid you in de pokey."

"Did the mules get found?"

"Dey was fetched back jest after you lef', Huck."

So if the letter had of been delivered regular I never would of landed in the spot I'm in, but it's too late to spill tears over crocodile milk as the saying goes. Tom says:

"What plan? What mules?"

So I told him how Jim and me was going to run off to California and he says what a grand idea it was and how he'd come along too if that was agreeable. Well it warn't, not by a long haul. Tom Sawyer is the bossingest person I ever met. If he come along he'd have me and Jim jumping through hoops and telling us what to do every hour of the day and night like he done on the Phelps's farm that time trying to get Jim free. But I never said it out loud, being brung up polite. What I say instead is:

"That's a dandy idea, Tom. We'd be proud to have you along only we can't none of us go while I'm locked up in here."

"Then we'll have to get you out," he says.

One thing for sure about Tom Sawyer, you hand him a problem and he'll give you the answer right quick.

"How we goin' to do it?" asks Jim, and Tom says cool and breezy-like:

"I'll have a selection of strategies ready in a day or two."

And I believed it. Why, he practickly had brains oozing out his ears. He goes on:

"Have they searched you yet for hidden weapons and such?"

"They never bothered, seeing the knife was still planted in the judge, just took my belt so's I won't go and hang myself with it."

"How about your bootlaces?"

"I still got 'em."

"Then you can plait them together and make a passable decent hanging rope. Won't they look foolish come morning when they find you dangling."

"But I don't plan on hanging myself. What I want is to escape."

"It's a perfect opportunity to prove how clever a prisoner can be, Huck."

"Dang it, Tom, you ain't thinking straight. Here, take this and look after it for me."

And I hauled out the money belt and shoved it through the window.

"There's two thousand dollars there," I say. "You can use some of it to help me escape if it costs money, only don't use more'n you have to."

"That much'll get you at least a dozen regular escapes, or just three or four of the history-making type. Which kind do you want?"

"I'll just be needing the one, I reckon, and a regular at that. I can't afford to make no history."

"Money's a small price to pay for immortal fame, Huck. Anyone can escape on the cheap. What you need is something with real style that'll get talked about up and down the river till kingdom come, maybe even over in Europe where all the expert escapers live."

"I ain't concerned about fame or nothing, just to get free."

"Well don't fret. A simple thing like a jail escape is easy organized, but first you've got to stand trial and get convicted. That way they'll raise twice as much whoop and holler when you cut loose and run."

You can see how Tom Sawyer for all his considerable brains still come out with some of the foolishest notions. He would of gone on for hours with such talk but I cut him off sharpish, getting my dander up, explainable when a body's in jail for a murder he never done.

"Lookit, Tom, just you get me out and never mind no waiting for trials and convicts, nor fame and whoop and holler neither. I never killed the judge only there ain't a way I can prove it. They'll hang me for sure if I don't slip the leash and soon. I mean it."

He seen I warn't in no mood for nonsense and promised he'd give it a good thinking over and come up with a way out, then they got set to leave, but before they done it Jim reaches his hand through the bars and give a grip to my shoulder and says:

"You hol' on, Huck, an' don' give in. I ain't forgot what you done for me dat time on de river. You bin a frien' to me, Huck, an' I ain't goin' to let you get hung."

It brung on the chokes, the way he done it, serious and grim-faced, and I just nodded to show I understand. Then they was gone and I had the night ahead of me to ponder on things, none of it cheery, but I pretty soon fell asleep anyway.

Next morning Sheriff Bottoms come in and says he looked all around Judge Thatcher's house but never found the letter nor the footprint, the snow on the front step being all trampled underfoot. It never come as a surprise to me. He says:

"Are you keeping your story same as before or do you want to change it?"

"I'll keep it," says I, and he tugged on the end of his nose awhile and says:

"I sent a message to Judge Walsall down in Pikesville to come up for the hearing. He'll likely be here in a day or two. You'll just have to wait until then. I'll make things comfortable as I can for you meantime. Is there anything you want special?"

"No thank you, Sheriff."

He was a decent man, not used to murder and such, which never happened in St. Petersburg since the night Injun Joe killed Doc Robinson in the graveyard and Muff Potter got blamed. Mostly he just had to handle river men that got drunk and hurt each other down by the wharf. It was plain he warn't happy about having me there in the cell. He says:

"You must be cold in here with that window. I'll put up the outside shutter again. I took it down to give the place some air after a drunk spilled his supper in the corner."

That give my heart a flutter. I needed that window to talk with Tom and Jim through, so I say innocent as I can:

"Please don't bother none about it, Sheriff. The stovepipe gives off a power of heat and with the shutter up I'd feel awful penned in. Also I can still get a whiff of that drunk's supper now and then. I'd prefer to be airigated if it's all the same to you."

So he left the window like it was and my heart quieted down again. I recollected how me and Tom used to pass extra food to Muff Potter through that selfsame window when he was here. It was guilt made us do it, knowing he was innocent same as me. But maybe you know that story already.

In the afternoon Ben Rogers come tapping at the bars and we started jawing. The sheriff was in the office so he never heard. First off Ben says I'm famous and he asks can he have a lock of my hair or maybe a thread from my coat, or better yet a handful so he can sell them ten cents apiece and split the profit with me half and half. I seen right away Ben would be a big success in the world so I was agreeable, and he passed a knife through the bars so I could saw off a hank of headstraw followed up by some few dozen threads frayed off my sleeve. I say he can keep the profits entire if I can keep the knife, a bargain since he stood to make maybe five dollars and the knife warn't the best I ever seen, the blade all over rust. He jumped at the offer and stuffed the trade in his pockets.

"Thank you kindly, Huck," he says. "You're a friend I reckon. I'm proud to know you, never mind what the town's saying."

I ask what that is and he says:

"Why, they say it's a disgrace the way you tried to shift the blame onto your poor old Pap that's dead and can't answer to it. They're calling it a low-down act and typical of you."

So there you see how a town won't ever forget a body's past, even if he's made the attempt to be sivilized. And while Pap was around they never called him poor old Finn, more like dangblasted old Finn and other things even hotter. They made up their minds I done the deed and warn't about to think different. I hoped Tom Sawyer was squeezing his brain for plans, without which I was already hanged. Then Ben says:

"Well, if there's anything else I can bring you, just give the word."

I let on a hacksaw would do fine but he just give a twisted kind of grin and says he don't know where to lay hands on one. So we give each other a "So long" and I'm alone again. I stood awhile looking out the window. No houses thereabouts, so I stared at the trees all covered in snow, real pretty and seeming a long way away. There was flakes coming down slow and fine like powder, swirling some here and there in the wind and not a sound. I come near to a fit of the mournfuls at the way things was, but never let myself give in to it all the way, hope springing eternal, as the saying goes. But it never sprang very high.

Mrs. Bottoms brung me more food, cooked decent too, even if I'm a murderer, and asks if I been reading the Bible any.

"Yes, ma'am," says I, "it's a sturdy staff in my time of torment. Them stories and sayings is a comfort all right, and I'm glad you give it to me."

"It's just a loan," she says. Until I'm hung, she means. "And which of the stories have you found to be most inspiring?"

The one that come to mind is Samson bringing down the temple, which is the kind of talent I could of used right now to bust out, but what I say is:

"I'm partial to the one about Daniel in the lion's den, ma'am. It's a real treat to read."

She give a satisfied smile at that and says:

"Can you tell me what it was that protected Daniel while he was in that terrible place?"

"It . . . well . . . I reckon it must of been something that come in right handy."

I seen a circus once with lions and they was awful broken down and mangy and never seemed interested in nothing, so maybe Daniel met some of that kind. Mrs. Bottoms says:

"It was the power of the Lord that done it. His all-embracing Love filled that den with divine light and rendered the beasts docile and tame, all because Daniel was beloved of the Lord."

Pap fell drunk in a hogpen once and everyone knows hogs is the meanest most temperamental critturs that come out of the ark, and will eat a baby or the leg off a man if they get the chance, but they never went for Pap, so unless he was beloved of the Lord too I figured Daniel's trick warn't such a miracle. But you can't say that to a church-going woman like Mrs. Bottoms, so I nodded and smiled while she rattled on about repenting and forgiving and turning cheeks and such. After a time her breath give out and she left, but not before giving me the news that God is the world's greatest forgiver. Why, He'll forgive just about anything if you get on your knees and ask Him nice with plenty of groveling. I give her my promise I'd pray for guidance that very night and she went off happy, just running over with holy spirit. It don't take a lot to make her kind satisfied, so I reckoned the lie was worthwhile. Payment for the food is how I seen it.

Sheriff Bottoms come in awhile later to see if I'm still a prisoner, which I was, so he went out again. Then Tom Sawyer is at the window, and he shoved in a brick of yeller soap.

"What's this for?" I ask.

"It's obvious, Huck. There's only one thing to do with soap in prison."

"But I don't have no water except to drink."

He shook his head exasperated and says:

"It's for whittling. You have to whittle a gun out of it and when the sheriff comes in you tell him to let you out or you'll shoot him dead."

"If he's dead he can't let me out, and I'm a double murderer on top of it."

"You *can't* shoot him. It's a soap gun, see? It's all bluff."

"It won't work. Who ever seen a yeller gun?"

"I planned for that," he says, and shoves a tin of bootblack in. "Just you smear it with that and it'll look deadly as the real thing."

"Couldn't you of got me a real gun?"

"Too easy," he says. "Where's the challenge? The whole point about escaping is to outwit the enemy with your superior cleverness. Without a strong helping of that it's just an ordinary getaway."

"One of them'd do me fine right now. Ain't you had no other plans? You promised a parcel of good ones."

"Course I have. I organized a whole slew of what they call contingencies. If the first one don't work you move right along to the next. One of them's bound to do the trick. I'm worried you don't have the right kind of escaper's attitude, Huck."

Well, that got me irritated, you can see why, so I say:

"There ain't the time for this brand of foolishness, not any more. I got to be out of here tomorrow at the latest before Judge Walsall gets here from Pikesville. I sunk my trust in you and all you done so far is play games. I'll give the soap a try, seeing as you went to the trouble of planning it, but I don't count on it working, not by a mile, so you better think of a way to bust me out before it's too late. I always reckoned you was smart but now I'm in two minds about it."

"Well there's no need to be huffy," he says, upset by the talking-to I give him, not usual for me so it hit him unexpected. We sort of glared at each other, hot under the collar, then he says:

"All right then, we'll dump the contingencies and concentrate on the one and only plan that's bound to work for sure."

"And what plan's that?" I ask.

"I don't have it ready to hand as yet," he admits, then goes on. "But it'll be a real sock-dolager, foolproof and certified. This time tomorrow you'll be free. It's a promise."

And he put his hand through to shake on it, serious and mannish, so I wrung his fingers hard to show I was sorry for what I said and he went off looking thoughtful like Napoleon planning the Hundred Years War, which must of needed considerable pondering.

I hid the bootblack under the mattress, then set to with the soap and Ben Rogers's knife and pretty soon had a fair-sized pile of shavings around me. Then in come the sheriff sudden-like and catched me on the hop. I whipped the stuff behind me quick and he asks if I'm hungry again seeing as his wife left food warming on the office stove.

"No thank you, Sheriff. I reckon I've lost the habit of appetite lately," says I. It warn't true but prisoners is allowed to stretch the facts as part of the job. Then I seen it was a good way to make him leave so I could stash the soap and knife under the mattress and the shavings too, so I say:

"Now you come to mention it I'm hungry. I could eat a panful."

Then he seen the mess around my feet. It was a clean cell before, so he noticed it.

"What's that there?" he says, and points.

"Where?"

"Right there on the floor. And what's that you're hiding behind your back?"

I seen there warn't no use to pretend so I fished out the soap on its own and kept the knife behind me still.

"What is it?" he says, suspicious.

"This? Why, it's . . . taffy candy," says I, and bit off a hunk and started chewing.

"Where'd it come from?" he wants to know, and I say:

"I had it with me, Sheriff. A boy my age gets peckish once in awhile. It's the crumbling kind and I reckon I've spilled some on the floor."

He watched me chew awhile. I've had medicine tasted better than that soap. Then he says:

"I'm partial to taffy myself. Care to share a piece of it?"

"I'd just as soon not do it, Sheriff. It's the awfulest taffy I ever et. You'd likely choke on it."

He's got a little smile on his face now, and he says:

"Maybe there's too much soap in it. Most recipes say not to put in more'n a pinch."

"Soap?" says I, and my eyebrows lift innocent-like.

"Smells just like it," he says. "Are you sure it ain't soap?"

I took another bite and my eyebrows lifted clear into my hat.

"Gosh sakes, Sheriff, you're right! That explains the taste."

He's grinning open now, watching the foam creep out from behind my teeth. He says:

"What else have you got hid there, gumdrops maybe?"

I brung out the knife reluctant and he says:

"Where'd that come from?"

"It's my own that I had in my pocket all along."

"It warn't handed to you through the window?"

"Why, who'd do a thing like that? Prisoners is out of bounds to everyone. The whole world knows that."

"Well you better hand it over. It's against the regulations for you to have a knife, even a puny one like that. You can keep the soap."

So I had to give it over, and there was the plan busted wide open before I ever truly started on it. I never had trust in it anyhow. I stood there kicking the shavings around and feeling foolish while Sheriff Bottoms went out back of the jailhouse and hammered the shutter in place, which proves he never believed me. The cell was darkish after that and it suited my mood. If Tom Sawyer come up with a plan that needed something passed through the window it was a goner. Then the sheriff come back in with a broom and says I have to sweep up the soap I shaved off. His wife won't like it, he says, and never lets a speck of dust in their own place. So I swept it up neat. It was easy chores but it come close to making me set down and weep, which I don't ever do as a rule.

That night I never slept a wink.

✦ 4 ✦

Escape!—A Rough Ride—Bad Signs on the Arkansas—
Goodbye, Mississippi—Heading West

Next morning Sheriff Bottoms told me it looks like Judge Walsall could be delayed getting here by snow on the road. He'd be coming up by coach, not steamer, on account of all the ice in the river. Big chunks have stove in riverboats before now. The news cheered me up some, but not much. I hoped Tom Sawyer never heard it or he'd maybe slack off on his plan hatching. I was in the grip of devils all morning and past noon, just itching for the plan to happen and get free, walking in circles like a dog on a chain. I was in a distressful state.

Then I heard the office door slammed open and Tom Sawyer's voice come through to me, shouting and excited.

"Sheriff! Sheriff! There's awful screaming going on over at the Wilsons' place! Someone's being murdered for sure! You got to come quick and stop it! Bring your gun!"

It was the best playacting I ever heard. There's a bang as the sheriff's chair legs hit the floor and then his boots clumping about and I seen the plan clear as day; the sheriff would rush off to stop the murder Tom invented and Tom, he'd say he was too winded to rush on back with him and when the sheriff was out of sight he'd grab the keys and set me loose. Then I heard the clinking of keys and my heart went into my boots. The sheriff's taking them along with him! And then Tom's voice says he'll come too and the sheriff never stopped to argue. Crash! bang! goes the office door and then nothing. I near tore my hair out with the frustrativeness of it. If that was Tom Sawyer's best plan he's a sap-head. Any fool could of seen beforehand the sheriff would take the keys with him. Sheriffs is paid to remember stuff like that. I set to cussing with all the words I learned off Pap, the briskest kind of language, and kicked over the latrine bucket, a mistake since it warn't empty.

Then come a voice at the window, and it's Jim.

"Huck, stan' away from de wall," he says, and something thumped hard against the bricks outside, then again and again, and pretty soon bricks come flying into the cell followed by a sledgehammer swinging in and out. First there's just a little hole then a bigger one as Jim beavered away at it. The mortar was old and them bricks never needed much persuasion to part company. In as long as it takes to tell what happened there's a hole big enough to scramble through and I'm outside on my knees in the snow. Jim slung the sledgehammer off into the trees and hauled me onto my feet and we churned our legs away from there fast as we could, Jim leading the way and giving me the story between puffs.

"Dat Tom, he stay up all night jest thinkin' on how to get you outer de jail, but he don' have no luck on it till he recollected ol' man Wilson goin' to slaughter a hog today, Blossom dat won de prize a couple years back, an' it give him de bes' plan yet. When him an' de sher'ff gets to de Wilsons' Tom kin say he never could tell de diff'- rence of a hog screamin' an' a body gettin' murdered. Tom, he a smart boy an' das for sure."

"But the sheriff's going to know it was a decoy when he comes back and sees I'm gone."

"Das what he'll be thinkin', only he cain't prove it. Ain't goin' to be nothin' he kin do 'cept cuss."

So Tom Sawyer went and delivered the goods after all, and I'd just a minute ago been calling him a sap-head when all along he's a genius.

"But how's he going to join us for California, Jim? Is it part of the plan to meet up with him later on?"

Jim shakes his head and says:

"He ain't goin' to be comin', Huck. Runnin' off after dis'd put de finger on him for sure, so he goin' to stay put in town. He give me a message for to give you. He say to get aholder plenty gold nuggets so's you kin buy a ship an' send for him an' go a-tearin' 'roun de seven seas together."

I made up my mind right there I'd do it. I'd find enough gold to be a millionaire and own the grandest ship on the ocean, painted all over red and gold and called the *Injun Princess*. There'd be an Injun girl for a figurehead on the bows with her hand up shading her eyes, on the lookout for snags and such, and me and Tom would be captains both, and Jim the first mate.

"Where we running to, Jim?"

"De river, Huck. I got de skiff waitin' hid on de bank. If'n dey puts hounds on de trail de water fool 'em good."

"Then where do we go?"

"Downriver 'bout ten mile. I got a frien' waitin' for us wid de mules an' supplies nex' to Rocky Point. Tom say de sher'ff goin' to figure we kep' on downriver far as St. Louis or somewheres an' he won' be lookin' for us 'cept on de river. Mighty smart, dat boy."

It was a good plan, up to Sawyer standard like the escape, so I never doubted it. As we run, Jim untied the money belt from around himself and give it back to me to put on, and I got more comfort from it than the fanciest silk sash.

Pretty soon we come to the river and followed her downstream to where Jim had the skiff hid, and we hauled it to the water and got in. Jim pushed off and then we're rushing along at a fast lick away from the bank so no one can see us in the snow, still falling thickish, but not so bad we won't see Rocky Point when we come to it. All the steamboat pilots use it for navigation, it stands out so. The river was iced up worse than I seen it any winter before, flat chunks all gray and brown and dangersome, but we was going the same way as them so it warn't such a risk as plowing upstream against the current. The river swept us along rapid, grumbling and rumbling the way she does, the ice chunks grinding one against the other and sliding off again. A skiff in fast water is light as a leaf so we went faster than the ice. Jim stayed in the bows with a pole to keep us off the worst-looking ones and I done my best to hold us straight and steady with a paddle at the stern—mighty hard on the wrists, I can tell you.

After awhile the snow started coming down harder than ever, lashing along sideways in the wind with white curtains and veils twisting and swirling and blotting out the shore. Jim bawls out:

"How far you reckon we come, Huck?"

"Maybe six or seven mile! We better get closer in or miss the Point!"

But it warn't so easy. The current boomed along deep and swift and we near busted ourselfs trying to break free of it. We made a mite of progress inshore, then I seen something ahead, big and dark, and for a second I figured it's the Point, but it's squarish not rounded, and then I reckernized her; it's the *Arkansas* that run hard onto a snag last year and got stuck fast, and now she's looming up dead ahead, high and wide like a cliff. Jim poled frantic to keep us clear of the ice wedged along her deck and I skulled hard with the oar, but too late. The skiff run straight up onto the ice and slid along till the hurricane deck was overhead then come to a stop sudden. Jim and me both took a sprawl but never got hurt, not even very wet, and we looked around to get the lay of things.

The *Arkansas* was side-on to the current and you could see the snag where it poked up through the bows just for'ard of the firebox. When it happened she must of slewed around and fetched up on others just under the water. She settled some, and her main deck was awash, tilted maybe fifteen degrees, the side facing upriver all tumbled with ice and her deck cargo swept away. There's just the hurricane deck and Texas deck and wheelhouse high and dry, all frosted with ice and snow like a big lopsided wedding cake and her tall chimneys leaning over like old dead trees waiting to fall. I seen her go by once when she was the proudest boat on the river and it's a shame now she ain't nothing but a wreck. Every timber was creaking and trembling with the water and ice trying to pull her under, and the wind whistled shrill through the guy wires between the chimneys, a mournful sound.

"We bes' be gettin off, Huck," says Jim. "She li'ble to break up perty soon. Feel her shake."

He was right, but I wanted to look her over before we shoved off. I never met nothing curiouser than me unless it's a cat. Says I:

"Take the skiff along to the stern, Jim. Maybe there's some stuff aboard her we can use."

"It ain't worth it, Huck. She be strip' clean by now."

"I'll just be a minute or three," says I, and stepped careful across to the stairway and went on up to the hurricane deck, slipping and sliding. I went along through all the cabins and Jim's right again;

she's empty, just a shell with all the walls frosted. The Texas deck was the same, with doors and shutters banging in the wind. Then I come to the main cabin and straight away felt something different. There warn't nothing to catch my eye first off, but then I seen a pile of rubbish over in the corner where the deck tilt had it gathered, and when I come closer I seen it's old empty cans of food mainly and other trash too. Now that was mighty strange up here where the high-class passengers used to sit and jaw and smoke, and it means someone lived here awhile after she hit the snag and was left to rot, only why would anyone do it except maybe a hermit? It was the lowest kind of living. I give the cans a poke with my boot and they rattled around some, hollow and sad, and I stood there trying to figure it out with the whole *Arkansas* shaking and straining under my soles. Finally I give up and turned to go, and then I seen it. Pap's footprint.

There's dust on the floor from the summer, all froze over now and made hard, and there's the print with the cross on the heel and another not so clear. I got down on all fours and looked at them close. The edges was rounded over, and it means the prints got made before the frost come in through the broken windows, back before winter set in. Back when the Widow Douglas's house burned down. It would of been a made-to-order hideout seeing no one ever come here. I had that same feeling I had on the judge's doorstep, kind of like getting throttled and wanting to puke at the same time. I scuffed the print away with my hand, but it stayed firm and true in my head. Now I knowed practickly for sure Pap's alive and killing them that stood in his way in the past, which means me as well. I signed away my share of Injun Joe's loot to the judge for safekeeping and it got Pap awful riled when he found out there warn't a way he could get his dirty hands on it. He must of carried a grudge ever since, and not just the usual kind. Only a crazy man would of near sawed the judge's head off that way, and I'm next if he can find me.

I went back to where Jim's waiting and we pushed off, heading around the stern clear of the paddle wheel. The current grabbed us and we scudded along same as before, working our way gradual across to the shore. Jim says:

"You fin' any kinder stuff back dere, Huck?"

"No."

I never wanted to talk about it.

Pretty soon we come in sight of Rocky Point standing out sharp and high through the snowfall and run the skiff onto the bank a hundred yards below. Soon as we set foot on shore Jim pushed her out into the flow again and she was whisked away out of sight. That way if they find her they'll figure we drowned. Then we trudged along to the Point and went around to where the rocky part turns into trees, and there's Jim's nigger friend waiting with our mules and another mule to take him back to St. Petersburg. It never took but a minute. The nigger give Jim a hug like they was related and wished us both good luck. Then he offers me his hand, the first nigger apart from Jim that ever done it, and says all the niggers in town know my name and have got respect for it ever since I helped Jim run off that time, and how none of them reckon it's me that murdered the judge and they all hope I get away. I near sat down with the surprise of it. I never give niggers no mind but for Jim, and all of them is on my side when everyone white wants to see me hanged. It never made sense. I give him my thanks and shook his hand warm, then he got on his mule and rode off.

I looked at the river grumbling along past the Point and felt a wrench inside of me. She's the first thing I ever recollect when I was small. I lived on her all my life and now I'm leaving, maybe forever. She never cared about me or no one, only wanting one thing and that's to get down to the sea, and it come to me I'm leaving home for the first time, not St. Petersburg which is only where I lived, I mean the river, which is where I belonged. East of her there's sivilization, just farms and towns and cities even bigger than St. Louis they say, and I was never tempted to see none of it. West is different. I seen a map in the judge's house once and it showed the plains stretching all the way to the Rocky Mountains, and then there's desert and after that come the Sierras, after which comes California, and where that ends there's a whole world of ocean till you get to China. All of a sudden I felt mighty small, and I never wanted to go out and get lost among all that distance and emptiness. Jim says:

"De snow lettin' up some, Huck. We bes' be goin'."

And the scaredness inside of me went away. Hereabouts I'm wanted for a murder I never done, and I never was too popular even before it. Out west there's Injuns and gold and adventure waiting. I

give the river a silent goodbye and we clumb on our mules and
pointed them away into the trees and kicked our heels till they got
moving.

"Jim," says I, "we're going from Rocky Point to beyond the Rocky
Mountains. Don't you think there's poetry in it?"

"I don' know 'bout po'try, Huck. I jest knows we goin' away somewheres we ain't knowed of. Das po'try 'nough for me, I reckon."

And that's how we started off for California.

♦ 5 ♦

Knights and Dragons—Shelter from the Storm—A Slew of

Lies—Lady Luck—Pipe Smokers of History

We headed due west, which is where St. Joseph is, two hundred miles and more away. About a mile from the river we hit a westbound road and followed her, easier than riding through trees. The mules was plodders but steady. I seen horse-collar galls on my nag's neck and Jim's was the same, so we're making our desperate getaway on farm mules, but I never minded. Soon there warn't no wind or snow to speak of and we was both tolerable warm, with heavy blankets tied around us and over our heads, and we had foodsacks and bedrolls slung over our saddles, all a body could need. Says I:

"Jim, don't you just feel like a knight in armor setting off on a quest?"

"What kinder night's dat, Huck?"

"It ain't a night like you get after daytime, it's the name they give to a soldier, and the armor's his clothes, made out of tin."

"Dat soun's perty much of a discomfort. How dey ben' over an' walk all shut in like dat?"

"I don't know, but they do it, and have swordfights by the dozen and slay dragons and such every other week, but mostly they go on quests."

"I never hearder no ques', Huck. What it be?"

"That's a journey someplace, looking for something, just like us going off to look for gold. We're on a quest, Jim, and it's a prideful thing."

"Dese knights, dey lookin' for gold too?"

"Sometimes. Dragons live in caves that are just brimming over with it, and when the knight slays the dragon and lets out buckets of steaming blood he can walk right in and claim it all, but first he's got to free the lady tied up outside."

"What she doin' dere, Huck?"

"The dragon keeps her there all the time, right by the cave so's a knight passing by don't think it's just empty and not worth the bother of getting off his horse to looksee. Soon as he spots a lady tied up though, he knows there's a dragon lurking there in the dark and he's obliged to go in and kill it."

"'Pears to me dem dragons ain't too smart. Tyin' up de women outside jest bring de knights down on 'em like a candle do wid insecs an' such. Whyn't dey jest sit tight in de cave an' count de gold quiet-like?"

"It ain't in the rules, Jim. The dragons has got to let the knights know they're at home, otherwise there wouldn't ever be no killing done, and what's a knight going to do with his time if he can't find dragons to kill? Why, he'd sit around all day polishing his armor and getting fat, and he'd be the poorest kind of trash without any dragon gold to pay his way, and he'd never get married neither. They mostly marries off with the rescued ladies and buy a castle to live in forever after."

"Ain't nothin' else dey do 'cept for killin' dragons?"

"Just one, and that's when they go on the biggest quest of all, to find the Holy Grail."

"I ain't ever hearder dat neither."

"It's a cup, only not just ordinary like you and me drink out of. It's made of silver and pearls and rubies and it's filled to the brim with Jesus' tears. He drank out of it at the last supper and afterwards it got lost when they washed up the dishes. The knights give plenty of time to searching for it, riding up hills and down again and asking around if anyone's seen it. They use up about a hundred horseshoes a year tramping around trying to find it, and while they're away their wives just sit at home knitting and feeding the dog and pining away with lonesomeness. It's awful hard on everyone, but they just got to find it. Them tears is the most valuable thing in the world to knights on account of they're so religious."

"Why'd Jesus go an' fill his cup wid tears, Huck?"

"I don't rightly know, but there was twelve of them at the supper besides himself. He likely got landed with the bill at the end, and he warn't a rich man."

"Wait on, Huck. How come he payin' de bill when he kin rustle up loafs an' fishes by de bushel outer nothin'?"

"Maybe it was a Roman eating house they were at. Them Romans liked hard cash every time and never set much store by miracles. That's how they come to rule the world hundreds of years ago, by only trading in dollars, not trusting to miracles that maybe wouldn't show up when the bills had to get paid. They was mighty practical folk."

"You reckon de Grail out west, Huck?"

"You might have hit on something, Jim. There's people out there but scattered far and wide, so there's a heap of space for it to be lost in, and the Injuns wouldn't ever reckernize it if they seen it, proberly use it for a cook pot."

"Ain't dere been no knights out west to give her a look?"

"Not as I know of. They stick mostly to Europe and Arabia and such places. King Richard, he spent years in the Holy Land looking for it, lifting up stones and riding up mountains, but he never found it, and it made him so mad he started a war out there against the Ayrabs, trying to make them tell where they hid it, but that come to nothing too. I reckon if King Richard can't find it then it must be out west."

We kept on going all afternoon till dusk come down around us. It takes a considerable time to leave sivilization behind; there was farms set back off the road every few mile with lights in the windows and smoke coming out of the chimneys, cozy and warm, but we never seen a living soul. Then it started in to snow again and I had to figure where to spend the night. I picked the wrong time of year to start out, but now there's a hangman's noose over my shoulder so I never had the choice. Our teeth chattered away in our heads and there's ice on our eyebrows and we shivered so hard we near fell off the mules. Then I seen a light winking in another farmhouse and I made up my mind.

"Jim, we're going to have to ask for shelter over yonder. If we don't we'll freeze."

He nodded his head and chattered some so I reckoned he's agreeable, and we followed a rutty little track off the road to the farm. When we come up to it I seen it's a tumbledown place, just a two-room house and barn and yard. I slid off my mule and knocked on the door and waited, then it opens and there's a little woman about as tall as me with her hair pulled back tight in a bun and a face all pruned with wrinkles and little beady black eyes and the tiniest mouth all sucked in like a cat's rear end. She give me a look then says:

"Well?"

"Please, ma'am, me and my nigger are froze and don't have nowhere to stay the night. I'd be obliged if you could see fit to let us use your barn just till morning."

She give me another looking over then stands aside and says:

"Come in. The nigger can put them mules in a stall and stay there too."

So Jim led them away to the barn and I went inside, where it's just as poor-looking as the outside, but there's a stove giving out heat that set me steaming away like a leaky boiler.

"Take off that blanket and sit," she says, and I done it.

"Have you et?" she wants to know, and I say no, and she set out two china plates and a tin pan and dollops out three portions of stew bubbling on the stove, a mountain for her own and miserable rations for Jim and me. Jim gets the tin pan.

"Take it out to the nigger," she says, so I did, and come back fast before the food got cold and scooped it inside me, two or three mouthfuls. The lady gummed away at her pile, looking at me with them beady little eyes.

"That was fine eating, ma'am. Thank you kindly."

"You kin call me Mrs. Aintree," she says. "That's my name. What's your'n?"

"Jack Thomas, ma'am. Me and the nigger are on our way to my uncle's place near Wellstown."

"Where's that?"

"Out near Independence," says I, lying.

"I never heard of it."

"Well it's a mighty long way, and kind of small to be on the map."

"And what might your uncle's name be?" she says, suspicious.

"Brewster Thomas, ma'am."

"He'll be on your Ma's side of the family."

But I seen the trap there and say:

"No, ma'am, on my Pap's. That's how I come to have the same name."

She chewed on, still watching me with them snake eyes. It give me a shiver the way they never once blinked. She says:

"What's your business in this Wellstown?"

"Pap died and there's only Uncle Brewster left in this world to take me in, ma'am. Pap died awful, got drunk and fell off the back of a steamboat and got mangled in the wheel. Every limb got broke they say, and pulped as well. I warn't allowed to look at him, only his face to make sure it's Pap, and it was. I cried and cried. He was the finest Pap in the world."

"Where's your Ma?"

"She's gone to heaven too, ma'am. She give up the ghost the day I got born. Pap brung up me and little Sis all on his own. He loved Ma too dear to marry again."

"How kin you have a little sister when your Ma died the day you was born?"

It's a good question and I should of seen it coming. A trueborn liar like me never lets himself down as a rule, but them eyes had me rattled so I warn't lying at full strength.

"She warn't really my little sister, not the way you mean, ma'am. She got born two years before I come along. I got in the habit of calling her little on account of she's a dwarf."

"A dwarf? One of them little punkin heads?"

"Yes, ma'am. She was just twenty-nine inches tall without no shoes on. She could stand right under a table and you'd of never knowed she's there without you looked. She had a fondness for tables, especially them with cloths that come down to the floor so she could hide herself. She was right playful. Pap give her one of them midget ponies to ride and she called him Jewel. They looked a picture trotting around the yard with Jewel's little bitty hooves prancing up and down and Sis's punkin head going up and down in time. Me and Pap used to just stand there watching. She was the happiest little girl I ever seen. It was tragical the way she died. Pap never got over it."

"Well how'd it happen?" she says, hooked firm.

"It was like I say, ma'am, with Sis mounted up on Jewel and cantering around in circles, going over the little jump Pap made so's to make it more interesting for them both, and when Sis had enough of it she got down off Jewel onto a bucket turned upside down she used, and she's patting Jewel on the neck saying what a good little horsy he is, and then it happened. I can remember it yet."

I give a few sniffs on a blob of loose snot up my nose for the right effect and crinkled up my eyes some and blinked rapid like I'm holding back a regular flood of tears. Oh, it was prime lying, and she's all open-mouthed waiting to hear the rest of it.

"Well, ma'am, there she was stood right by Jewel and reaching into her pocket for a sugar lump to give him when the awful event took its toll, right in front of my eyes. . . ."

"Well? Don't stop, boy. What happened then?"

"All of a sudden little Jewel give a kind of hiccup and keeled over on top of her. The horse doctor said later he had a jittery heart in him that just stopped, and down he went with Sis underneath."

"My Lord, ain't it awful," she says.

"Yes, ma'am. Sis's eyes practickly bugged out of her punkin head with the shock of it and then she's dead too, squeezed all out of shape. If it had of been a regular-size horse she would of been squashed flat, so we got to be grateful for small mercies I reckon."

"Why, that's the saddest story I ever heard."

"Yes, ma'am, it surely is. Sis and Jewel was devoted to each other in life and they both met untimely death together. Pap reckoned as how it was only fittin' to have them buried in the same plot side by side, and that's what he done. After that he took to the bottle for comfort and things warn't ever the same again. We had to sell the house and every-thing to pay for the drinking till there's only the nigger left. Pap would of sold him too only he fell off the steamboat."

She tut-tutted away and shoveled in more food which she'd forgot while I was lying, and shook her head sympathetic, then she starts in on her own piece of misery.

"My boy Albie, he's run off to find gold in California, my only boy that I held next to my heart. Just upped and went a week ago Friday. What kinder son would do a thing like that? He was brung up correct and taught to fear God and was give plenty of hard work to quieten him down so's not to give in to temptation, and he just upped and left, chasing rainbows."

I judged it was mean rations at the table that sent him off, but never spoke it, just let her rattle on around mouthfuls.

"We done our best, Hollis and me, always tried to give our boy the guidance a young'un needs in life, and it's all wasted now he's gone. How kin we run a farm without no one to help? Is it right? The Lord'll pass judgment on Albie once he gets out there with them painted heathens. It's my opinion God created this gold in California to suck all the trash west and leave sivilized parts the cleaner for it. Them that's headed for gold is headed for perdition. If the Injuns don't get ahold of 'em they're bound to starve in the wilderness, and there won't be no manna from heaven to save their sinning hides. You wouldn't ever think of going out there would you, boy?"

"No, ma'am. It's too dangersome and too far I reckon. I'm content to stay with my kin and lead a blame-free life the way the Book says to."

"I'm right glad to hear it. There's boys no older'n you with sin in their hearts and the devil on their shoulders. You take that Huckleberry Finn that lives over in St. Petersburg. Why, just the other day a neighbor told us he cut the throat of the respectablest man in town, just a half-growed river rat piece of trash that never had guidance from a mother in the way of the Lord. It goes to prove without you get raised by the Book you're surely doomed to eternal fire."

"Yes, ma'am. This cutthroat Finn must be the lowest kind of sinner. Did they catch him?"

"They surely did, standing right over the corpse with a knife still dripping blood in his hand. They're fixing to hang him next week."

"Well it's no more'n he deserves."

"My Hollis, he's gone into town for supplies. I reckon he'll come back with the exact day of the hanging and we'll both of us go into town to see it happen. It's always a blessing to see a criminal sent on his way down to Satan. It makes a body feel right clean after."

My face started to crawl and twitch, and I say:

"When's your husband due back, ma'am?"

"The weather's likely too bad for him tonight. If the Lord sends us clear skies he'll be back tomorrow."

If he's in town he'll know I busted out of jail, and maybe they've gone looking for Jim and found he's gone too, and now they're after the both of us, a boy and a nigger, and Mrs. Aintree, she's seen us both. We should of kept going, snow or not. Now my face is twitching like a fish on a line and I give it a slap to settle down.

"What in the world did you go and hit yourself for?" she says.

"Moskeeter on my cheek, ma'am."

"There ain't no moskeeters this time of year. Are you feeling poorly, boy? Do you want a spoon of tonic?"

"No thank you, ma'am. I reckon it's time I turned in. I'm mighty weary after a day's traveling."

"You're a peculiar child, Jack Thomas, but you've lost kin and suffered some, and it's understandable. You go along to the barn and take a good night's rest. That'll do you a power of good."

"I hope so, ma'am. Thank you again for the food and hospitality."

She says goodnight and I scuttled for the barn. The mules was there in the stalls alongside some cows but Jim warn't around.

"Jim, where are you?" I call, and there's a rustling up in the hayloft and his head pokes out.

"I'se up here, Huck. It de warmes' place wid all de hay."

I clumb up the ladder and burrowed in with him and told the danger we're in.

"We could leave now, Jim, and be miles away by morning when he gets back."

"She still snowin' perty bad, Huck. Das why we come here in de firs' place. Ain't no sense in goin' back out again till she stop."

He's right, so we agreed to get some sleep and move on soon as it quit snowing. It's maybe fifteen miles to St. Petersburg so it was fair to reckon Hollis Aintree warn't going to get back till tomorrow evening earliest. If it was still snowing come morning we'd light out anyway and put some distance between us and the Aintree place, and the snow would cover our tracks too. Figuring it all out made us rest easier and we settled down for shuteye, but before we done it I say:

"Jim, put your mind back to last year when we was on the raft and seen that house come bobbing along on the flood. We went in the upstairs room and you seen a dead man you reckon was Pap."

"Das right, Huck. What you wantin' to know?"

"Was it him for sure?"

"I reckon so. He had dat same white skin like he's sick, an' long hair like yo' Pap had, an' he 'bout de same reach top to toe, but de clincher be de bottler whiskey in his han'. Soon's I seen dat I knowed."

"But are you really truly certain sure? Did you look at him up close so's there warn't no mistake?"

"No, Huck. I gets res'less roun' dead folk."

"So it could of been someone with just a passing resemblance."

"Maybe, but I reckon not. Soon's I seen him I says to myself, das Huck's Pap an' he better not get tol' 'bout it, not yet awhile. So I never tol' it, not till later. Why you askin', Huck?"

So I told him about seeing Pap's hoofprint on Judge Thatcher's doorstep, and he says:

"De whole town know 'bout dat, I reckon. Ever'body sayin' you made it up out'n yo' head in de panic, tryin' to blame a dead man."

"It warn't made up, Jim. I seen it, and I seen it again on board the *Arkansas*."

I give him the full story and his eyes got wide.

"You sure 'bout dis, Huck?"

"Certain sure, Jim."

"Maybe yo' Pap come back from de dead to harnt you," he says.

"Ghosts don't make no footprints, Jim. I reckon it's Pap. He's flesh and blood still, come back for revenge on the Widow Douglas and the judge for the way they riled him that time, and maybe me as well."

"I hopes you wrong, Huck. Dat man got de devil workin' in him."

We chewed the fat awhile longer then got sleepy and give a visit to the land of Nod, then I'm awake with Jim's hand over my mouth and he whispers soft in my ear:

"Huck, dere's someone down in de barn. He jest come in."

I wriggled over to the edge of the loft and took a peek. There's a man under me and he's looking at our mules and scratching at his head, and I figured it's got to be Hollis Aintree come back from St. Petersburg ahead of time. Then I seen the barn doors are open and it's daylight outside, clear and sharp with no snow falling. We got so comfy in the loft we must of practickly set up house in Nod. Mr. Aintree unsaddled his mare and stalled her and give her some oats, then he went out and closed the doors behind him.

"Jim," says I, "we're in a peck of trouble. He must of stayed overnight at a farm between here and town and he's back early. Get the mules saddled and I'll keep a lookout."

We slid down the ladder like it was greased and Jim set to with the mules, getting it all done in record time. I looked at the house through a gap in the door and sure enough, here comes Hollis stamping his way back to the barn, only now he's got a gun and looking mighty nervous. He stopped halfway, maybe asking himself if he's got the gumption to tackle Huckleberry Finn the bloodthirsty judge-killer, then he thinks about the reward money I bet Sheriff Bottoms put out on me and he starts coming again, looking determined this time.

"He's coming, Jim. Get on the other side of the door. When he comes through we'll both have to jump him."

"I cain't do dat, Huck."

"You got to. I'm too light to do it all alone."

"I cain't do it," he says again, looking forlorn.

"Do you want me to go back to jail and you along with me? Well it'll happen if you don't give a hand. There ain't time to argue, Jim."

He come over to the door reluctant and we took up position and

waited, hardly breathing, my skin all crawling with the suspense of it.
Tom Sawyer, he would of loved it. We waited and waited and I reckon
old Hollis must of started thinking again about how he'll get his throat
cut if he comes inside. Then he mustered up the courage to open the
door a little way and poke his gun barrel through. The barrel never had
its throat cut so he poked the rest of it in, and it never come to harm
neither. I seen his hands, then his head. It's dark in the barn so he
never noticed us both sides of the door. He opened it a couple inches
more, chewing his lips when it creaked, then he's inside. He took a few
steps, eyes watching the loft, then he seen the mules is saddled so we
ain't up there no more, and he swung about all terrified and seen
me and aimed the gun. Jim flung himself like a lightning bolt and
knocked him sideways and the gun went off harmless through the
wall, and Hollis dropped it and babbles away fast as he can:

"Don't kill me," he says, begging, and I'm ashamed to be the cause
of him acting that way. "Don't kill me please! I got a wife and son!"

He's so scared he forgot Albie run off a week ago Friday for California, and I spoke to him gentle to get him calmed.

"Mr. Aintree, sir, we ain't going to hurt you nor Mrs. Aintree. What
you heard tell about me is all a lie. I never killed Judge Thatcher, only I
can't prove it and had to bust out of jail."

"Take anything you want," he says, not listening. "Take the horse,
take the gun, only don't, please don't do us no harm. . . ."

"I already told you, Mr. Aintree. We don't intend no harm to no one,
only to get away to St. Louis and . . ."

Here I clap my hand over my mouth like I let out something I never
should of, and there's a silence, then I rush along talking fast:

". . . up north where they don't know me. You don't have no need to
worry. We'll take your horse so's you can't ride to give the alarm, and
we'll have to tie you up as well to give us time for our getaway. I'm
sorry but we got to do it. Jim, fetch a rope."

We tied up his hands and feet, but not too tight, then I say:

"Mr. Aintree, sir, we're going over to the house now. Is there any
guns except for the one you brung over?"

"No. That there's the only one. You kin take it if you want."

"Thank you, but I reckon we'll leave it. We're both of us peaceable.
We'll be over at the house some considerable time getting food and
such, so please don't go yelling or nothing."

"I won't," he says. "I'll stay quiet."

"I'm awful sorry about all this that's happened," I say, but he never believed it.

I put twenty dollars in his pocket for the horse, then Jim and me led the mules and mare outside. But we never went over to the house. I never could tie up a woman. I counted on her being so scared after she heard the shot she'd stay clear of the barn for awhile till she got more curious than scared and went out to look, and by that time we'd be miles away. We got on the mules and set off down the farm track for the road, Jim leading the mare on a rope. He was awful quiet and miserable looking so I say:

"Well, Jim, has the lockjaw got you?"

"I'se thinkin', Huck, an' it's troublin' me some."

"Why don't you share it out?"

"What I done back dere I ain't never done befo'."

"Tied a man up?"

"Dat too, but befo' dat I went an' knock a white man down. I ain't never done nothin' like dat befo'."

"You had to do it, Jim. He would of captured us, maybe shot us dead."

"I knows dat, Huck, an' das why I done it, but I don' feel good 'bout it. Dat man jest a no count dirt farmer, but white. I'se scared. Yestiddy bustin' you out I warn't scared, but now I got de shakes on accounter knockin' down a white man."

"You never hurt him, Jim."

"It don' matter. I went an' knock him down. I don' wanter talk no mo' 'bout it."

So we rode along silent for awhile and reached the road and turned west along it. By and by Jim says:

"Huck, how come you let on we's headed for St. Louis? You layin' a wrong trail for de sher'ff?"

"That's the plan, Jim. I hope I acted it good enough so's Mr. Aintree was fooled. There's just one thing that's bothering me and that's our tracks. The sheriff just has to set eyes on them and he'll follow right along behind."

But I never needed to worry. Pretty soon down come the snow again, thick enough to bury tracks even left by a herd of elephants. It lasted for hours and we near froze, same as yesterday, but we had to keep going. We ate in the saddle and never passed a soul on the road. When dusk come the snow stopped, and it turned out later that was the last snowfall of winter, so the worst was over. We stayed the night in a barn that was empty and ramshackle and next day went on. With no snow we made good time. We come to a small town in the afternoon and skirted around her, cutting through the woods, then back onto the road. All the time I had an itchy feeling in between my shoulders, and it's from waiting to turn around and see Sheriff Bottoms behind us with a bunch of men with guns. But it never happened. Lady Luck was riding along with us, maybe on Mr. Aintree's mare. That night we slept under a wood bridge over a creek, and mighty cold and damp it was, but better than the open. When I woke up next morning I seen the mare has broke her halter and gone, and I wondered if Lady Luck went with her. It was mighty discouraging.

With the weather fining up at last, we had company on the road, but no one give us a second look. Proberly they never heard of Huck Finn's jailbreak this far from the river, not yet anyhow. So we ambled along bold as brass, like we had a right to be there, not sneaking through the trees like outlaws, but still with the blankets pulled up around our heads to hide our faces. Nobody suspicioned us for it; the air was cold as Pap's heart. And that's how the days went by, sleeping in barns that was set away from houses and not used, or sometimes in woods where the trees was close together and the branches thick overhead to give us shelter. We never went into a town, always around, and when I judged we was eighty mile or more from St. Petersburg I got to feeling relaxed again. Then come trouble. Jim's mule one night chewed a hole in both foodsacks and et everything that warn't in a tin, so we was near out of supplies. The next town we come to I say:

"Jim, take both mules and go around and wait for me on the other side of town. Stay hid in the trees till you see me coming along the road."

"You askin' for trouble, Huck. We bin lucky so far."

"We don't have no choice. We got to eat. Nobody's going to take no notice of me. I'll just walk into a store and get what we need and walk out again."

He warn't happy but he seen the sense of it, and pretty soon I'm strolling down the only street in town, which is called Hedleyville. You never seen a littler town, with three buildings and a cabin or two. There's a store like there is in every town and I stepped up onto the porch and knocked snow and mud off my boots and went in. There's maybe six or eight men sat round the stove smoking and chewing and jawing. Seeing I ain't a man, they give me no notice. I went up to the counter and rattled off a list of supplies to the storekeeper and he started fetching it down off shelfs and out of barrels. There's a fair pile so I ask for a sack, and he give me one and I loaded it.

"Fourteen dollars and twenty-seven cents," he says.

I handed over two ten-dollar bills. They was new and flat and crisp like they come straight off the press, and he looked at them suspicious, holding them up to the light and sort of snapping them in his fingers. Them around the stove was watching now. There ain't nothing like the sound of money to make heads turn.

"It ain't counterfeit," says I, "Pap just sold our farm and got paid in new bills. If you like I can crinkle 'em up for you."

Someone give a hoot and they all joined in except the storekeeper.

"Danged if you ain't the suspicionest man in the state, Ed Sykes," says one. Another with whiskers says:

"You boys heard about the time old Ed figured he'd get himself one of them mail order brides? He goes to the post office and sends away the letter and two months later there's a woman turns up on his doorstep and says she's the one. Well, Ed looks her up and down and says she cain't be no mail order bride. 'Why not?' she says. 'On account of you ain't wrapped up in paper and string,' he says, and slams the door."

That set them haw-hawing and slapping their legs. The storekeeper frowned at them through his little round spectacles and give me a look that says I'm to blame.

"That ain't the end of it though," says Whiskers. "That woman raised such a holler Ed had to let her into the house, and right away he's suspicious and wants to know if she's a virgin. 'I ain't about to marry me a bride that ain't a virgin,' he says, and she says, 'Well then you kin put your finger up and feel for yourself if you really got to know.' So Ed gets down on his knees and fumbles under her dress and finds what he's after and runs his finger up . . . and up . . . and up . . . and still cain't feel no cork so he says, 'Ma'am, you ain't no virgin,' and she looks real upset. 'Mr. Sykes,' she says, 'you have got your finger up my ass.'"

That one had them braying like jackasses and stomping the floor. The storekeeper give me my change and I headed for the door with the sack over my shoulder. I'm almost there when one of the stovers says:

"Wait on there, boy. What'd you say your name is?"

"I never did, but it's Ben Rogers."

"Whereabouts is this farm your Pap sold? I ain't heard of no sale around here."

"No, sir. It's back near Independence. We're moving east to Illinois to be with the rest of the family."

"Well you must be the only ones. The rest of the country's heading for California to look for gold. Ain't you tempted, boy?"

"No, sir. Ma says gold is the devil's metal."

"Where's your Pap now?" says another, squirting tobacco juice into a spittoon.

"He's up the road a little," says I. "The wagon busted an axle and he sent me into town to get supplies. He reckons we'll be stuck there a day or two."

"Well you tell him to come see Hank Mophett. He's the best man for fixing things hereabouts. Don't you forget it."

"I won't, sir," says I, and turned to go.

"Wait on," says Whiskers. "What'd you say your name was again?"

"Ben Rogers, sir."

"You sure it ain't Huckleberry Finn?"

"No, sir. I'd be mortified to have a name like that."

"I just figured I'd make sure. This Finn, he's wanted clear across Missouri for murder and he's on the run with a nigger. You sure you ain't slit no judge's throat lately?"

"No, sir. Shot a bank teller last week, but I reckon that don't count."

That tickled them. They set to hooting and stomping again and I slid out the door and up the road with legs all gone to jelly under me. It never took but a step or three to leave a town that size. I followed the road around a bend out of eye-reach of Hedleyville and pretty soon Jim give a holler. He brung the mules down onto the road from a stand of trees and I clumb aboard. He says:

"You get ever'thin' we needs, Huck?"

"I did, and bad news besides. They know about us even way out here, Jim. We got to go careful and not get seen if we can help it."

"How we goin' to do it, Huck? De sky gettin' bluer ever' day. De snow turnin' to slush an' folks soon be gettin' aroun' on de road. Ain't no way to stop 'em lookin' at us I kin figure."

"There's got to be a way around it."

"How 'bout de same trick we done on de river, when you dressed up like a gal?"

"What kind of family'd let their daughter travel with just a buck nigger? We'd stand out even more that way."

"How 'bout I dresses up too?"

"Women never travel alone, Jim, black or white. Anyway, your beard's growed out and we don't have a razor. A bearded nigger woman's bound to bring the whole state down on us to gawp. No, it has to be something else."

"Dere's dat trick we done one time, paintin' me up to be a sick Ayrab wid disease bustin' out all over."

"They don't get sick Ayrabs out here, Jim, nor healthy ones neither. You'd get talked about all to blazes. Think on it some more."

"I reckon I run outer possibles, Huck. You give her a try."

So we rode along with me thinking furious hard, but nothing come to me that warn't foolhardy and bound to fail. Jim was right about one thing, the season was on the turn for sure. Three days now we had bright sunshine most of the time and the road was getting muddier and slipperier as the snow got trampled on and melted. Soon Jim says:

"You figured somethin' yet, Huck?"

"Not yet. I'll smoke a pipe and see if it helps any."

We both got out our pipes and filled them and puffed away, but a pipe smoked on the move somehow don't give the same gratifaction of a pipe smoked when you're rested. I say so and Jim agreed.

"De bes' time for smokin' be de end of a weary day when you knows you kin rest up an' not hafter do another lick till mornin'. Das when a man gets to thinkin' on dis an' dat, quiet an' peaceful."

"It's true, Jim. Why, the world's greatest thinkers is all pipe smokers."

"Is dat a fac'?"

"A well-knowed fact, Jim. It's practickly commonplace, that fact."

"What's some of dese big thinkers' names?"

"I reckon Solomon was about the first to take it up, and he goes back thousands of years. Whenever he had troubles, and kings do get them, he'd out with his pouch and pipe and fill her up and puff away till he untroubled things, only his wife called Ruth used to get upset something terrible whenever he done it. Soon as she seen that pipe come out she's out of the house and down to the fields to mow

the barley and chop the cotton like all the folk that warn't royalty,
just so's she could get some fresh air. Old Solomon, soon as he
knocked his pipe out he'd climb in his chariot and go fetch her
back."

"Women is mighty funny 'bout smokin'. Seems to me if dey took
up de habit like us we wouldn' get so much complainin' an' speechi-
fyin' 'bout de smoke an' stink."

"It's a good point, Jim, but women reckon it ain't feminine to
smoke, so they'll always raise the roof when we do it."

"Who else famous for smokin' an' thinkin', Huck?"

"The next one'd be Moses. He was such a deep thinker he
smoked all the time and his pipe never went out except when he's
asleep, and even then he had a servant keep feeding it and fanning
it. You remember how he led the children of Israel out of Egypt with
a pillar of smoke by day and a pillar of fire by night? Well that was
Moses' pipe, just blazing away and giving off sparks and smoke like
a steamboat's chimneys."

"Don' dat beat all. An' I was all de time thinkin' it's God Almighty
sent dem pillars along."

"That's because it got translated wrong when King James was
putting the Bible in English, Jim. The King James version is just
riddled with mistakes. To get the accurate truth you got to read the
Queen Anne version, which is different and a whole lot shorter."

"De queen done translaterin'?"

"She surely did. Queens generally has a lot of time on their hands
so that's what she done most days. In the evenings she made tables
and chairs in a little carpentry shop behind the throne room and got
famous for that too."

"She a pipe smoker, Huck? I reckon a queen dat does carpen-
terin' kin do mos' anythin'."

"The pages of history is blank on that, but Aristotle, he was a
smoker definite, and what's more he done most of it in the bath."

"Why he do dat, Huck?"

"He was the cautious kind, Jim, and wanted plenty of water
around so he'd never set fire to the house. He was a deep thinker
too. He figured out that if you take a triangle and step on it and run a
wagon over it and beat it out of all shape it's still a triangle."

"I don' unnerstan' dat, Huck."

"No one can, Jim, and that's why Aristotle is held to be the deepest thinker of them all."

Later on in the day we come to a crossroad and there's a bunch of wagons like I never seen before, and that's how we come to meet the McSweens.

✦ 6 ✦

A *Church on Wheels—High Times— God's Work—Coin*
and Paper—The Facts of Life

There was five wagons, not iron-
hooped and canvas-covered but with walls and roofs painted all over
with pictures in the brightest colors, angels mostly, in pink night-
gowns flying up and down and around corners with light coming out
of their heads, whitish gold where it touches their long hair and rainbow colored further out. It hurt your eyes to look, they was so grand.
There's ruts in the ground where four of the wagons went catty-
corner across from one road to another to miss the mudhole in the
middle of the crossroads, but the fifth never made it and was bogged
down axle-deep and leaning over to one side. There's about ten people
stood around, all women except for two men, one tall and lanky and
lantern-jawed dressed all in black, and the other short and fat and
bearded with a fancy silk waistcoat brighter even than the wagons.
Waistcoat come across to us and give us a beaming smile and says:

"Hail, fellow wayfarers. Are you perchance bound west along this
here road?"

"We are," says I, and he beams all the wider and says:

"I beg leave to request Christian assistance in the matter of getting
our wagon unbogged. We'd be purely grateful for it."

"I reckon we can oblige," says I, and we got down and went over to
the wagon. It's axle-deep like I say, and the team never could of pulled
it out alone. Waistcoat says:

"We struggled and strained with her but to no avail. She is sunk
deep in the slough of despond awaiting the arrival of sinew and muscle
and Christian charity, and lo, it has come in the person of you and your
nigger."

It's flowery talk all right, but I seen through it. There warn't none of them covered in mud which they would of been if they struggled and strained like he says, but I let it pass and say:

"What you got to do is dig a trench in front of the wheels with a slope to it, then fill them with brush so the wheels can grab on it and come free. Is there a shovel in your rig?"

"There surely is," says Waistcoat, and turns to the women. "Constance, fetch the shovel from the calliope."

Away she went and come back from the first wagon with a shovel that's considerable blackened with soot like a steamboat shovel that's used for feeding the firebox. She give it to Waistcoat who give it to me and I handed it to Jim and he got digging. Says I:

"It'll be a heap faster if you give a hand to fetch the brush."

He clapped his hands together and I see they're gloved, soiled but not real dirty, and he hollers:

"Faith, Hope, Charity, Constance, Mercy, Grace, Chastity, give the young man assistance in the gathering of the brush! May it be a plentiful gathering!"

And the girls started gathering hither and yon, picking up dead brush and breaking off twigs from the trees and piling it all in a heap, so there warn't much for me to do. Waistcoat beamed away at the females then offers me a glove and says:

"I am Phineas McSween. This here gentleman is my brother the Reverend Mordecai and over yonder is my good wife Harriet, but we call her Ma."

She's a right big woman, bigger than any three of the rest, and she give me a little nod but never spoke and the Reverend done the same. Pa McSween says:

"The young ladies are all the proud fruit of my loins, every one. I call them the seven virtues. No man ever had a finer family nor more close-knit than we. May I know the name of our kindly benefactor?"

"Tom Sawyer," says I.

"Tom, you have delivered us from the depths of despair. We are behind schedule and due for arrival in Slocombe tomorrow. The populace awaits us with eagerness due to passing through last year with great success and making a solemn vow to return. It is a typical show of thanks, which we generally get in every town on our winding way."

"Is it a circus?" I ask, and he looks at me scornful.

"A circus?" he spits. "We are the minstrels of the Lord, just as

brother Mordecai is his minister. You see before you the McSween
Traveling Church of Christ the Lamb."

He points at the nearest wagon which has got a picture of Jesus
squeezing a lamb next to him and staring at you with big lonesome
eyes. He's wearing white so's you can pick him out from all them pink
angels, and McSween goes on:

"We are the Lord's attendants, spreading the gospel far and wide
through the towns west of the river where men and women, Godfear-
ing hardworking citizens all, are starved of the Word. It is our beholden task and duty to bring enlightenment and salvation to these
worthy souls that they may profit thereby and rejoice in the blood of
the Lamb. We are the shepherds of His farflung flock, and mighty
proud to be so."

And the Reverend and Ma both give out with "Amen."

Then McSween wants to know where I'm bound and I give him the
story about going to join Uncle Brewster Sawyer out near St. Joseph,
and he looks thoughtful for a minute then says:

"Strange are the ways of the Lord. That is the very location we are
aimed at, with minor diversionation along the way. The Lord has whispered in my ear and told me your nigger there has a strong back and a
willing heart and the road betwixt here and St. Joseph is plagued with
mudholes aplenty that will be needing backbone and gristle to get us
out of. The Lord reckons it'd be a fine proposition if I offered you a
place among our happy throng, you and the nigger both, so you can
help in His holy work. Seeing as how man does not live by bread alone
I'll cross your palm with a dollar a week and you can feed along with
the rest and sleep comfortable in a wagon at night. How do you figure
it appeals, young Tom?"

It appealed a heap. Traveling along with the church Jim and me will
blend right in and not be a boy and nigger on their own. I had my mind
made up on it faster than a kingfisher scoops his lunch.

"Mr. McSween," says I, "it's a handsome offer and me and Samson
is proud to join up with you."

We shook hands all over again and Ma beamed and the Reverend
Mordecai's lip give a twitch to show he approved.

The seven virtues gathered in a mountain of brush and I give Jim a
hand with the shoveling, then we filled the trenches with it and Mc-
Sween whipped up the horses and out come the wagon with a sucking
and a squelching. The seven virtues give a cheer and patted me on the

head and one or three even kissed me. They was all passing pretty but one, which is Chastity, and she's a pinhead without hardly room enough in her pointy little skull for a brain which accounts for her ways, jumping up and down and goo-gooing like an overgrowed baby. It's sad to see but I reckon she's happy in spite of it.

The whole tribe portioned theirselfs out among the first four wagons and Jim and me got to drive the last one with our mules unsaddled and tied on behind. Then we set off, bumping and bouncing along. There's a little window behind the seat and Jim peeked inside the wagon and says it's full of canvas and poles and ropes, so it's their meeting tent like most Bible-thumpers use everywhere.

When evening come the lead wagon pulled off the road and the rest followed and got arranged in a square. Jim and me unhitched the teams and got them tethered to a rope between the trees and fed and watered them and give them a rubdown and last of all put a blanket over each. It was hard work but when we finished Ma McSween and the girls had food ready over a campfire and it was cheery to stand around watching the flames and eating plenty. The girls ain't hardly shy at all and wanted to know all kinds of things about me, so I had to lie fast and free to keep up.

The Reverend et his food and went off somewheres and Faith or Hope, or maybe it's Charity tells me Mordecai ain't sociable like the rest and prefers to keep himself to himself. He's a holy roller and don't like to mix too much with ordinary folks in case some of his holiness rubs off and makes him impure. He don't even sleep under a roof at night even in winter, just makes up a bed of brush for himself on the ground with a blanket for cover and a stone for a pillow. He done it for the mortification of his soul and to keep him in mind of how puny and weak he is in the sight of the Lord, only a human being after all, and God is partial to the humblest kind. I figured he's a truly religious man or else a fool.

"Daughters," says McSween, "why don't we fire up the calliope and have us a rehearsal."

They scampered about with a will fetching armloads of kindling, and McSween got me and Jim to give him a hand with one of the wagons. It's got walls that unbolt and can be lifted down and there she is, a steam calliope. There's a whole forest of tall pipes with valves up and down them that little tin angels open and shut when you hit the keys, all covered in silver and gold and mighty pleasing to the eye.

There's a firebox underneath in the wagon bed that you feed from behind through a little door and a chimney for the smoke.

McSween stoked her up and pretty soon she's hissing away like a bag of snakes and little wispy puffs of steam come leaking out here and there among the angels. He topped up the water tank from a barrel with a hand pump then sat himself down on a velvet stool and brung his gloves down hard on the keys. All them chubby angels flung back their arms and out come a blast of steam and sound from holes all over the pipes. He done it a few more times, clearing the tubes he calls it, then starts to play, and can't he just! Them gloves fairly flew along the ivories like little animals, jumping and landing and leaping away again, galloping along up one end then turning around and haring back down to the other. The angels batted their arms in and out like they're trying to fly and let free music that swooped and rolled like it's alive, the thrillingest thing I ever heard. I reckon he could of played in one of them big sympathy orchestras.

Then he settled down some and done a regular church song, "Bringing in the Sheaves" and the seven virtues except Chastity started singing along, and their voices was sweet and harmonial and a treat to listen to. They followed up with "Rock of Ages" then "Come to Jesus" and finally let rip with "How Blessed Is Thy Face." It's just perfect the way they done it and McSween looked mighty pleased with the show.

Then the girls went and got a fiddle and harmonica and squeezebox and set to with more music and singing, not religious, the kind they play whenever folks want to dance and have a high old time. They played them insterments like a real music band, as good as McSween on the calliope, and right lively tunes they hammered out too, "Skip to My Lou" and such, and Ma and Pa McSween clapped hands along with it and Chastity too, only she kept getting it wrong, going too fast or slow, but nobody minded. Then Mercy or Hope or one of them grabbed ahold of me.

"Dance, Tom Sawyer," she says, and I done it, bashful and clumsy at first, then the others joined in and flung me back and forth between them like niggers loading flour sacks, back and forth and spinning around till I don't know which way is which and things is swirling around me and the blood goes rushing through my head with a roar and I staggered off away from them still spinning like a top and fell down in a tangled heap. They played on, faster and faster, and Jim all of a sudden jumped into the firelight and kicked up his heels and danced like he's barefoot over hot coals. Them that warn't playing danced around Jim with their skirts and hair flying they're so frantic and fast, then even Jim got tuckered out and had to lean against a wagon. The McSween girls just went on flying around the fire till Grace or Hope or Constance went leaping over the flames with her petticoats showing and the rest followed on, laughing and whooping and landing nimble-footed and dancing on till they one by one give out and stood with their breath heaving in and out, enough to set a blacksmith's forge aglow.

"Now then, daughters," says McSween, "it's time for bed. Say goodnight to Tom."

They all sung out goodnight and I give it back to them and they trooped off into the wagons. Me and Jim and McSween bolted the walls back on the calliope, then he says to me:

"Young man, you will sleep in the tent wagon. Samson can do the same or sleep underneath if that's your preference. Goodnight to you."

"Goodnight, Mr. McSween, sir."

Ma and Pa shared a wagon with Chastity on account of she's still a baby in spite of being full growed, and the Reverend flung himself down on some brush all opened to the stars so's he can talk personal to God. Jim and me clumb in among the canvas and spread ourselfs out on it for a mattress, lumpy but not too bad, and got wrapped up in our blankets snug and warm. Jim says:

"Huck, I'se mighty glad we run inter dese folks. Dey sure knows how to have fun. I ain't felt dis good since befo' de widder's house burn down."

"Me too, Jim. Our luck's holding true."

But there's a voice inside of me that says our luck ain't going to hold if the McSweens hear about Huck Finn the murderer. Jim started snoring right off but I lay there all restless and worried till I wore myself out with it and slid off into dreams. But even that never give me peace because here's Pap stood over me with his hair hanging in his face and his tobacco breath stinking and he leers all crooked at me and says:

"You're thinkin' you seen the last of me, but it ain't so. I reckon I'll get you yet, same as I done the widow and the judge. They figured they was might clever, but I showed them who's smart."

"Please, Pap," says I, "go away and let me be. I never done you no harm."

"No harm!" he thunders. "Only made me look small in front of folks with your prissy ways and book learnin'! You ain't no Finn, you're the widow's boy, and I made a vow I'd take my revenge on her kin, and it's *you*. You better be watchin' over your shoulder at night, boy."

And he cackles and takes a swig from his bottle and vanishes. It warn't the pleasantest dream I ever had.

Next morning McSween hammered on the door to wake us. Breakfast got dished up, hot and plenty of it, and afterwards the girls sung stretches of song while they tidied up the place. I never come across such a happy crowd in one family, except for the Reverend who never spoke a word nor tested his face with a change of look now and then. Proberly the happiest was the pinhead, chasing around after birds that come down for scraps, but birds is hard to catch and she tripped and started blubbing till Ma give her a pat on her pointy head and a biscuit to chew.

I seen Reverend Mordecai watching me close, staring direct with his eyes, the kind that bore right through you. It made me nervous and edgy the way he done it, just standing and staring, and I wonder if God told him I'm wanted for murder.

Everything got packed away and the teams hitched and the wagons rolled out. There was more people on the road with us, all heading west in wagons and buckboards and light rigs, some just on horseback and others on foot, and we never needed to get told why they was all on the move; each and every one was headed for California. A man on horseback went along a little way with Jim and me, just jawing casual, and he wants to know if we're going to California too.

"No, sir," says I. "We're the McSween Traveling Church of Christ the Lamb."

"Don't you want to get rich?" he says. "All you need to do is get to California and the hard work's done. You just sit down on a rock to catch your breath after crossing the mountains, then when you're rested up you just turn that rock over and there's your gold waiting to be picked up. You can make a million dollars in a month, they say. I can't hardly wait to get there and start turning them rocks over."

He whipped his horse up and galloped on down the road and I seen he's the foolishest kind of person that don't know beans from bacon. Says I:

"There goes a prime idiot, Jim, and I bet he ain't the only one, but it's all to the good far as you and me's concerned. Why, if there's thousands of folk heading along the same route we'll just slide in among them and get lost in the crowd."

"You figure we goin' to be safe when we gets past St. Joe, Huck?"

"I'm counting on it, Jim. They say there ain't no law once you cross the Missouri. It's just wide-open country and every man has to carry a notion of what's right and wrong inside of him, and if you get in trouble you just have to get yourself out of it again. It's total and positive freedom, which is good or bad depending on who you are and who's along with you."

"You an' me gets along jest fine, Huck."

"That's true, but you got to take into account all them that's alongside you, so we got to pick and choose who we let come with us. It's a long way to California and poor company makes a journey longer. I wish the McSweens was going west. They're about the finest company you could want."

"You right 'bout dat, Huck."

I warn't at all, but that revelation come later.

Soon it come on to rain and poured down till the snow by the roadside got turned to slush. Even out in the fields it's melting away fast, just patches left now. One of the virtues come back with rain slickers for us so it warn't so bad seated out in the wet. A body's face and hands got cold but it ain't unbearable. Jim says:

"Is dere niggers out west, Huck?"

"I reckon not, just redskins."

"How dat come to be?"

"On account of Missouri's the westernest slave state. The country beyond that don't belong to no one unless it's the Injuns."

"Ain't dere no slaves?"

"Nary a one, Jim. You don't need slaves where there ain't no farms."

He pondered on that awhile then says:

"Huck, I'se a free nigger. Miz Watson done it befo' she died, an' you paid de cash to get my fambly outer slavery too, an' I reckon I bragged on it some at de time. Dat freedom got a pow'ful strong taste. But den it come to me I still ain't free. I walk down de street an' folks lookit me same as always. Freedom don' make you white, an' lessen you white you ain't goin' to get no respec' from folks. So I still ain't free. I'se hopin' when we ain't in Missouri no mo' I'se goin' to get a new kinder taste, real an' true freedom, even if I'se de only nigger das aroun' to taste her."

Jim's a nigger with high hopes all right.

Around noon we stopped and et and McSween come up to me and says:

"Tom, I'm going to trust you with a task of importance. Slocombe is only ten miles away now but the wagons will not reach there before night. What I want you to do is ride ahead on your mule and go see Mr. Trask that owns a farm on the north edge of town and tell him we're on our way and can we have the same field as last year. If he says yes you give him this." And he handed over two ten-dollar coins. "Then you ride into town and start nailing up these here posters anywhere there's a wall, but first you have to pencil in 'Trask's Field, 8 P.M. Friday' in the space at the bottom. Can you write?"

"Yessir, I write real good."

He give me a canvas bag with a shoulder strap and inside there's dozens of printed paper sheets and a hammer and twist of nails and a pencil. He made me repeat what I got to do then says:

"I'm giving you my trust, Tom. Don't you go sliding off with my twenty dollars now. Remember, your nigger's still back here with us."

"I'd never let Samson go for just twenty dollars, Mr. McSween. He'd fetch eight hundred for sure."

"Well that's all right then. You saddle your mule and get along, and may the Lord go with you."

I put the money in my left pocket to keep it apart from my own small change which is in the right, then got the mule ready. I slung the bag over my shoulder and cantered off, giving the wagons a wave when I passed. All the girls and Ma and Pa give me a wave and a cheer except Mordecai, who just stared. I could feel them eyes in my back till I rounded a bend. That man give me the uncomfortablest feeling.

A mule don't want to gallop as a rule, but he'll do it if you switch his rump with a stick and dig your heels considerable, which is what I done.

Slocombe is a big town compared to some, and I asked around for directions and pretty soon I'm knocking on Trask's front door. It's a rundown farm and I figure he'll need that twenty dollars. A skinny woman opens the door and wants to know my business.

"I'm here for the McSween Traveling Church of Christ the Lamb, ma'am, and wanting to see Mr. Trask."

Her face opened up a little and she says:

"Come in and I'll fetch him directly. You can wait in the kitchen."

I took a chair and she went out back hollering for him. It's the miserablest kitchen I ever sat in but I never had to tolerate it long before Trask come stamping up the back steps. He come in and says:

"Where's McSween?"

"He sent me along, Mr. Trask, sir. The wagons is too slow."

"He tell you about the arrangement we got?"

"Yessir. Is it the same place as last year?"

"Tell him yes. You brung the money I hope."

"Yessir, I did."

I fished in my left pocket and there ain't nothing there but a hole. McSween's twenty dollars is lost in the mud somewhere along ten miles of road. I done some fast figuring and say:

"Excuse me, Mr. Trask, sir, could I make a visit to the outhouse?"

"It's out back," he says, and I went out there and sat on the board awhile then opened my shirt and hooked two ten-dollar bills out of my money belt. Then I went back inside and handed them over.

"There it is. I reckon I'll be going now."

"Wait awhile," says Mrs. Trask. "Don't you want a cup of coffee and a bite of food? You look mighty cold."

Trask went out again and she fixed coffee and started in to fry eggs. I took out all the sheets and penciled in what McSween told me, still worried about them coins. If Trask lets on I paid in bills he'll smell a rat, definite. Mrs. Trask dished up and watched me chew and swaller.

"What's your name?" she says.

"Tom Sawyer, ma'am."

"You wasn't with the church last year, was you?"

"No, ma'am. I just joined up a little while back. They're real nice people."

"Yes," she says, but half-hearted, and there's a worried look on her face. Then she says:

"So you ain't acquainted with the running of things."

"No, ma'am. I reckon I'll see how it works tomorrow when they put on a show."

"Don't you let Mr. McSween hear you calling it a show. It's a meeting."

"Yes, ma'am, I'll remember it."

She's quiet for a spell, then says:

"How old are you, Tom?"

"I was thirteen or fourteen last year, ma'am, so I figure I'm fourteen or fifteen this'n."

"Well I'm going to give you some advice. Tomorrow night when the meeting's on you go straight to bed after the singing stops."

"Why, ma'am?"

"Never you mind, you just do it."

"Yes, ma'am. A body gets up easier in the morning if he's rested longer."

"I can see you're a sensible boy, Tom Sawyer. You mind my words and you'll be the better for it. Do you want more coffee?"

"No thank you, ma'am. I'll just finish the penciling and go. These all got to be nailed up around town before dark."

"It's gratifying to see a boy take his duties serious," she says.

"Yes, ma'am."

The way she talks is considerable mystifying, but I'm too minded about the money to try and figure it, and pretty soon I'm back in town and hammering away on walls everywhere. If it was wood and stood up straight it got a poster, sometimes two. They was eye-catchers all right, with big printed words that say:

Have YOU been SAVED?
Where will YOU spend ETERNITY?
GOD loveth ALL men
Even them that hath SINNED
For whoever shall wash in
THE BLOOD OF THE LAMB
Shall be SAVED from the
FLAMES OF HELL
And be MADE PURE again
COME to the MEETING
And ye SHALL be SAVED ! !
Rev. MORDECAI McSWEEN officiating
Music and hymns rendered by
THE McSWEEN HEAVENLY ANGELS CHOIR
Trask's Field 8 pm Friday

People was talking about them posters while the nails is still warm from hammering. There's only a couple or three left when I seen a wall that already had paper stuck on it so over I go to give it some more. Then I seen what they are and my blood run cold: wanted posters.

$500 REWARD
for information leading to
the arrest of
HUCKLEBERRY FINN
murderer & forger
escapee & horsethief
description
hair: dark
eyes: brown
height: 5 feet
age: 14 yrs
approach with caution
THIS MAN IS DANGEROUS
also
a nigger by name of JIM
description
6 foot nigger
Send all information to
Sheriff Wade Bottoms
St. Petersburg, Missouri

There it is, in black and white. They proberly papered the whole state with them. I tried tearing them down when there warn't no one looking, but they're pasted on, so no luck. What I done was nail the McSween posters over them; it's all I can do. I collected my mule and rode out of town just on dusk, back along the road. There was fires all along it where the California-bounders was camped for the night, and I met up with the wagons still plodding along about two miles out of town.

"Well, my boy," says McSween, "did you accomplish the Lord's work?"

"Yessir, I done all of it the way you wanted. Mr. Trask says it's the same place again."

"Fine, fine. You go on back with the nigger. We'll keep going till we reach Trask's place."

"Yessir."

I hitched the mule behind the tent wagon and clumb up on the seat with Jim.

"Ever'thin' go easy, Huck?"

"No, it never."

I told about losing the money and then the wanted posters, and he looked grim.

"Dey takin' you serious, Huck. We mus' be a hunnerd mile away by now. How far you reckon dey goin' to chase you befo' dey gives up?"

"Far as St. Joe, that's for sure. After that it's like I told you, free and clear till we get to California."

"Dey got sheriffs an' such out dere?"

"They got a big town called San Francisco so there's bound to be laws. We got to make sure and leave a cold trail across the country between here and there. It's a heap of territory so we got a chance. St. Joe's where we can start breathing easy I reckon, but we still got another hundred mile to go."

"We's mighty lucky to be wid dese McSweens."

Maybe we was, but I never shook the notion Reverend Mordecai has already suspicioned us.

McSween knowed the way even in the dark and we skirted around the north side of Slocombe and fetched up at the Trask place sometime before midnight. The wagons went through a gate that's been left open ready and we pulled up over by a stand of trees next to a creek, then the girls and Ma got food ready while Jim and me tended the horses. Trask come over from the house to pay his compliments and him and McSween went off together jawing about I don't know what, only I hope it ain't about me and that money.

He come back just before everyone turned in and never looked at me so I figure we're safe for the moment, then he's heading my way and my knees knocked hard enough to break. He come up to me and says:

"Tom, you and Samson had better get a good night's rest. First thing tomorrow we'll put the tent up, and it's powerful hard work even for Christian souls."

"Yessir, Mr. McSween. We'll both of us pray for extra strength before we turn in."

"That's sensible thinking, my boy. I believe I did the right thing hiring you."

"I'm glad you done it too, sir. It's real exciting and it's all for Jesus."

"Your attitude is commendable and well worth a dollar a week. Why, it occurs to me you might just have the makings of a preacher yourself. Did you ever pause and reflect upon that blessed prospect, Tom?"

"I been praying for guidance some considerable time now, sir. It always seemed like too grand a dream for just a small unimportant person like me to have."

"Mighty oaks from tiny acorns grow," he says, solemn and wise.

"Deuteronomy?" I ask, and he frowns.

"You have much to learn, Tom, but your heart is true. Good-night."

Away he goes, and there's just the littlest whiff of whiskey left in the air, but maybe I'm wrong about that. I'm all set to join Jim in the wagon when along come one of the virtues and it's Grace, who was last born but for Chastity. I reckon Ma and Pa give up childbearing after that. Grace is just seventeen and the prettiest of them all. She looks around to see if there's anyone watching us and there ain't, but she grabbed my arm tight and pulled me away into the shadows anyway.

"Tom," she says, "how old are you?"

There was two big questions on the lips of the nation that year; how much gold is there in California and how old is Huck Finn. I told her what I told Mrs. Trask and she got that same worried look. I never knowed a body's age is so important to women but there it is, twice in one day. She says:

"Did you ever have any sisters?"

"No, ma'am, just five brothers."

"There's no need to call me ma'am. I'm just a few years older than you. Call me Grace."

I would of called her anything she wanted if she'd only let the blood back in my arm. Says I:

"Was there something you wanted, Miss Grace?"

"Just plain Grace will do fine," she says.

"You ain't plain. You're right pretty I reckon."

Tom Sawyer says if you pay a female a compliment she'll appreciate it even if it's a lie, but I warn't lying. She's a real looker, as they say.

"Thank you," she says, and never simpered or nothing like Becky Thatcher would of done, then there's a silence. Finally she says:

"So you never had the experience of sisters?"

"No, ma'am . . . Grace. Just a heap of brothers. Ma always wanted a little girl to balance things out but one never come along. The last boy, Cecil, he had a hard time of it. She kept him in pinafores and never let no one cut his hair. He looked mighty cute but Pap put a stop to it when he turned four years old. He reckoned it warn't manly and cut them curls off Cecil himself, and Ma cried and cried when he flung them in the stove. You could smell it for hours, the hair I mean."

"Do you know about . . . the facts of life?"

"I reckon I do. Ma told me it's all a vale of tears but we get our reward in heaven."

"No, I mean about men and women."

"Well, there's maybe a million people in the world and half's men and half's women, or thereabouts."

"And why did God make it so, do you think?"

I pondered over that one awhile then say:

"Variety."

"But what's the reason for it?" she says.

"Question not the ways of the Lord," says I, quick as a flash, but it ain't what she wants to hear.

"Tom," she says, "do you know where babies come from?"

"I surely do. They come in black bags the doctor brings. That's why they're small I guess, so's all them doctors don't have to go out and buy bigger bags."

"That's not the way of it at all. I always thought country folk knew about the natural order of things."

"Well I do. There's the four seasons, day and night, low water and high . . ."

"Bulls and cows," she says.

"Pardon me?"

"Stallions and mares," she says.

Now, you can't call me backwards or slow. I seen right away what she's harping on. Says I:

"You mean . . . roosters and hens?"

"That's it exactly. People do it too, and pretty much the same way."

It warn't news to me. Tom Sawyer explained all of it one day when we never had nothing better to talk about. When it's done right it's called fornicatering, and when it's done wrong it's cornholing. He give me a long description on how he'd go about it, with Becky Thatcher say, and it was the most ridickerless thing I ever heard, but he swore it's all natural. I made up my mind then and there I'd never do nothing so undignificated, but Tom reckoned I'll change my mind someday. So now I say to Grace:

"Everyone knows that. I don't see why you bothered with asking."

"It's just . . ." and she got all flustered. "It's just . . . well, so long as you know," she says, and flounces off directly, and I'm left with another mystery and a tingling arm. There's something about females that's entirely different to men I reckon.

I went on back to the tent wagon and the last thing I seen before I clumb inside was Mordecai over by the fire, just staring at me long and hard.

✦ 7 ✦

The Role of Religion—Messing with Jesus—Saving Souls—

A Sad Discovery—Reflections on Friendship—A

Handy Theory

We started work on getting the
tent up at first light. McSween and Trask give a hand hauling it out
and spreading it across the ground. The field was grassy so there
warn't no mud to dirty the canvas, which has got a fair amount dried
on it already. It's a considerable size and the virtues and Ma got called
in to help with joining the poles together and poking them up through
little holes ringed with iron to support the weight. Them first few poles
was the hardest part, but after they was up it all got simplified. The
guy ropes was stretched and pegged and more poles went up inside to
lift the roof some and by noon it's done. Reverend Mordecai never
lifted a finger, just studied his Bible, learning his lines. There was last-
minute fiddling with the ropes to get them just so, and there she
stands looking mighty impressive. I seen circus tents that was bigger
but this'n can cram maybe two hundred people inside her, long as they
stay stood. There ain't no chairs anyway, just a pulpit for the Reverend
and a wood platform for the virtues to stand on.

There's a section at the back that lifts up and the calliope had its
walls and roof took off and was rolled inside with just the smoke-
stack poking free. Then it's all set. The pinhead got all excited and
run about like a chicken with its head off till Ma got her calmed with
a biscuit. Grace tells me there's a special tin of them biscuits that
Chastity's partial to and nobody can have any except the pinhead,
and they're called Ma's Helpers. I reckon if Chastity was religious
like the rest she'd figure God is a giant biscuit on a throne with little
winged oatcakes fluttering around.

Ma herded the girls into the wagons and says they got to rest through the afternoon so's they'll be in prime shape for the meeting tonight. Soon they're snoring and Mordecai's nose is still buried in the Book and McSween's off somewhere with Trask, which leaves Jim and me free. We lazied around and smoked our pipes, taking things easy after all the strain this morning. Jim says:

"Huck, I bin thinkin' on dis here travelin' church. Why you reckon dey does it?"

"Humans got a basic need for religion, Jim. It fills in all the holes that can't get filled in with just thinking and pondering. There's questions that's just too big for understanding, so folks put it all down to God and His workings. That way they can sleep at night and not have to worry about not finding the answers to the questions."

"What kinder questions, Huck?"

"I reckon the biggest is why we got to die. Philosophers has been asking it for hundreds of years and they ain't got the answer yet."

"Why you reckon we has to die?"

"It's obvious, Jim. If we never died the whole country would get cluttered with people just getting older and older, and you know how cussed and cranky old folks is. They'd be three or four deep everywhere, just complaining and snapping their gums and getting in the way of everyone, so they got to die to make room for them that's young. We get our parcel of years and when they're done we wing it up to heaven. That's the theory of it."

"How 'bout Methuselah, Huck? He done live nine hunnerd years. How come he got de extra portion?"

"It must of been his holiness. If you're real holy God gives out another hundred years or two as a reward. But there's another of them old Jews that lasted even longer than Methuselah."

"Who dat be?"

"He's called the Wandering Jew and he don't ever die. He's near two thousand years old already."

"He mus' be de holies' man alive, Huck."

"That's where you're wrong, Jim. He got that way through getting Jesus riled."

"How it happen?"

"Well, he's called Cartaphilus, and he lived in the Holy Land around the time Jesus was preaching thereabouts, and one day Jesus come up to Cartaphilus who's stood at a crossroads and asks

the way to the Mount of Olives. Cartaphilus points down the road
and says, 'Follow that and you'll reach her,' and Jesus done it, only
it's the road to the wrong place, Damascus proberly, and he goes
back to Cartaphilus and says, 'You give me the wrong road,' and
Cartaphilus says, 'Pardon me,' and points down another road and
says, 'That there's the positive route.' Jesus follows it and finds himself in Baghdad, which is miles from where he wants, so back he
goes to Cartaphilus and says, 'You done it again. Ain't there a map
or something?' Cartaphilus says he don't have one, but he points
along another road and says, 'Just you follow that'n and you'll get
there for sure.' Jesus says he'll do it, only he's getting mighty footsore by now, but there he goes down the road again, and danged if
he don't find himself in Sodom and Gomorrah, which decent folks
don't ever go near. He's mad as all creation about it and drags himself back to the crossroads where Cartaphilus is still waiting and
says, 'That's the third time you done it. Are you the village idiot or
what?' Cartaphilus apologizes all over again and points down the
last road and says, 'I reckon we got her this time, friend. There ain't
but four roads all told,' and Jesus says, 'You just better be right
about this'n. I got a speech to give the assembled multitudes and
I'm behind schedule,' and off he staggers down the fourth road, and
so help me, he fetches up at Nineveh or Tyre, one or the other,
and that just finishes it for him. He crawls back to Cartaphilus and
croaks, 'How can a body be so danged hare-brained? I never met a
stupider fool than you,' and Cartaphilus says, 'Where was it you
wanted again?' Jesus says in a whisper, 'Mount of Olives,' and Cartaphilus says, 'That place? Why, it's just over yonder, about two
minutes' walk,' then he cackles and slaps his belly and pulls out a
calendar and yells, 'April Fool!' Don't Jesus get mad then! He points
a finger at Cartaphilus and works up his wrath and says, 'It's people
like you that give country folk a bad name. Seeing as you played
such a mean trick on me I reckon I'll do the same. You can wander
around the way I just done and see how you like it, and I ain't about
to let you off till I come back for the Puckerlips!' And off he goes,
and Cartaphilus had the curse that's kept him alive all this time, and
he has to wander and wander, never spending two days running in
the same place, and I just bet he kicks himself every April Fool's
day."

"It don' pay to mess wid Jesus, Huck," says Jim.

McSween come back later on and give us orders to polish up the calliope, so that's what we done the rest of the day, rubbing them little angels till they shone.

Then it's evening and we hung lamps in the tent and started a fire under the calliope's boiler and filled her tank with water. About that time people from town started to show, just a small handful to begin, then they come by the wagonload and the place livelied up. Ma stood by the flap where you go into the tent next to a sign that says: ADMISSION 50¢ and took the money. McSween give the calliope a quick blast to make sure she's working then told me to go hurry up the virtues.

By now the whole field is packed with wagons and rigs and there's fires lit here and there to keep the cold off, and bottles passed to and fro between the men for the same reason. The women was jawing together and showing each other babies and young folks was sneaking off down by the creek to spark on the sly. It's a clear night with all the stars winking far away and sharp, and there ain't enough wind to stir the breath that hangs in front of your face.

The McSween wagons was behind the tent and I heard the virtues all talking and singing and laughing together before I knocked on the door. The top half opened and Mercy put her head out.

"Is it time?" she says.

"Yes, ma'am, he's asking for you."

Faith pokes her head out and asks:

"Is it a big crowd?"

"I reckon so."

"Is everybody ready?" asks Constance from inside, and they all say yes. "Then forward march," she says, and the bottom half of the door opened and out they trooped, all in long white gowns that go down to the ground with a big red cross stitched on the fronts. They walked in line across to where the calliope is sticking out of the tent, lifting their gowns out of the wet grass so's I can see their little white slippers. I lifted the flap and they filed inside and stepped up onto the platform so everyone can see them, and there's a kind of sigh from the congregation; they look so pretty and pure and sweet in their gowns with their hair let down and brushed long and free over their shoulders, just like angels.

McSween run his gloves along the keyboard and started into a slow and dreamy piece of music, just passing time till the tent gets

filled, and soon as them that's still outside heard it they quit chin-
wagging and paid Ma their money and hurried on in. Pretty soon
the tent's packed to splitting except for a space down the center
that's roped off, and I knowed it's for the part at the end when them
that wants to be saved will come flooding forward to the pulpit. I
seen this kind of thing before, but that don't stop me being excited
as all the rest. Jim's outside feeding more wood into the firebox to
keep up a head of steam in the calliope.

Then things got started. McSween give a nod to the virtues and
brung his hands down to make a big swelling ripple of sound that
builds and builds then turns into a tune which is "Three Kings of
Eastern Lands." The virtues opened their mouths and out come the
song, clear and true, and everyone drunk it in it's so lovely to hear,
and when it's done they slid right into "Shining Star of Bethlehem,"
then followed up with "The Old Rugged Cross." It ain't like other
meetings where folks join in and sing along. Here they just stood
and listened all openmouthed at the beautifulness of it, not wanting
to drown out the virtues with their own voices, but I reckon that'll
change later on when they get loosened up. They done a couple
more hymns then finished up with "The Walls of Jericho."

There's silence after the calliope dies away, then the flap got lifted
and in come Mordecai and started up the pulpit steps. He's all in
black as usual and his hand is chalk white against the Bible he's
carrying. His jaw is smooth and white from shaving and his hair's
all slicked back over his collar. He took up his place and laid his
Bible down slow and deliberate, then he looks out at the congregation, just boring into them with his eyes. They was all atremble with
eagerness waiting for him to start, but he let them wait till you could
of heard a mouse break wind.

Then he lifted his hand up slow till it's high as he can reach, then
clenches it and bang! down it comes onto the Book, and I learned
where that name Bible-puncher comes from.

"Who among you is without sin!" he roars.

No one owned up and he leaned forward and glared at them,
swinging his head left and right, then he hollers:

"Nay, not one, for you are all accursed in the sight of the Lord!
Each and every miserable sinner here is vile and corrupt and putrid
with transgression and digression from the paths of righteousness!

Let no man deny it lest he bring the wrath of God down upon his shameful head!"

"Amen!" shouts someone in the crowd, and Mordecai goes on:

"You that are tillers of the earth! You that are dwellers in the town! You that are travelers-by! You are each and every one without exception bound for the flames of Hell! Not one will escape Satan's fiery grasp unless . . ." and he stops with a finger raised, "unless ye do repent! Repent of your sins! Repent of your godless ways! Repent of the times without number you have turned your head from our Lord and Savior Jesus Christ Almighty!"

"Amen!" from the crowd, this time louder.

Mordecai points his finger and sweeps his hand across them.

"You are all fallen from virtue! Lost to the sight of the Lord! Loathsome and vile! Rudderless ships upon a sea of Satanic darkness! Blind worms writhing in torment of your own making! You have chosen to ignore the teachings of Jesus! Turned your backs upon His divine message! Fallen into the arms of imps and demons! You have wallowed in the mire of greed and corruption and fleshly lusts! You have embraced the doctrine of the devil! You have tarnished your immortal souls and followed the left-hand path away from the shining light of the Lord! You tremble at the very brink of the fiery pit! Before you is pain everlasting lest you turn back to Jesus!"

"Amen!" they shout, and there's a woman whimpering somewhere, getting in the mood. Mordecai lifts both arms and stares at the roof.

"But all is not lost! For if you turn away from darkness and heed the light that beckons, ye shall yet be saved!"

"Amen!" they howl, and there's a sprinkling of "Hallelujahs!" in there too. Their heads was bobbing around and their shoulders twitching, and Mordecai knowed he's got them on the hook.

"Reach into your hearts and cast out the demon that lurketh within! Turn upon Satan and smite him with all your strength! Pray for salvation! Beg the Lord's forgiveness for your sins! He will take you unto His bosom and bathe you in the blood of the Lamb! He will heal you! He will give you strength to resist the odious gifts of Satan! He will bind your wounds and make you whole! He will forgive your godlessness and take you under his mighty wing! He will deliver you from the hopeless torment and misery in which you dwell! He will render you as newborn babes if you will accept His divine will and repent! Now is the time! Now, while Satan's grasp is weakened! Come to the Lord! Let Him wash away your sin and transgressions! Come out of the darkness and into the light! Come, you that have drained the jug of alcoholic indulgence and found only sorrow therein! Come, you who have blighted the Lord's name with profanity! Come, you that have lusted after another man's wife! Come, you who have lain with the beasts of the field! Come to Jesus and be saved!"

McSween starts in with the calliope and him and the virtues flung theirselfs into "Promised Land of Jordan." This time the whole congregation joined in, and you never heard such a braying and bellowing, but the virtues held their own, jacking their voices up a couple of notches, and McSween near jammed his fingers through the keys he's so caught up in the music. Mordecai waved his arms around in time with the tune and when the song was done he went right back tonguelashing the flock, kind of grinding them down to mush so's to scoop them up again into the arms of Jesus. It was a powerful sight to see. He done things with his eyes and voice that would of took an army otherwise. He could make them shout and sing and weep and wail. He could make them howl like dogs. I reckon if he told them to go set fire to their homes for the glory of the Lord they would of stampeded to do it without no hesitation. Finally he tells anyone that truly wants to be saved to come on out front and get it done here and now, and they just swarmed to the pulpit, on their knees mostly and trampling over each other in the rush to get there first, screeching and crying for salvation and forgiveness. McSween and the virtues kept on pumping out hymn after hymn while Mordecai come down from the pulpit and took hold of the nearest sinner by the hair.

"Do you repent of your sins and accept Jesus as your savior?"

"I do!" shouts a farmer, and Mordecai draws back his hand and slaps him hard across the cheek and hollers:

"Out with you, Satan, in the name of Jesus Christ!"

He flung the saved sinner to one side and went on to the next and done the exact same thing then moved on again. He even done it to the women, slapped them just as hard as the men, and they never flinched. There's one lady I seen come back three times just to make sure Satan's well and truly cast out of her. Mordecai slapped and hollered his way across the tent and back again. He slapped all of them and it took some considerable time, and when he's near done and his slaps was getting weakish the virtues brung the last hymn to a close and snuck out under the flap, but McSween played on. There's wisps of steam coming out of the pipes and drifting across all them redeemed sinners on their knees till there's a regular fog in there, with all the music and screaming running through it jumbled up and making you feel like the end of the world is come at last like the Book says it will.

Then I seen the men was leaving in ones and twos, but not the women; they're singing along with McSween as he lets fly with "Shall We Gather at the River," all of them redfaced from slapping and walking on their knees. The men kept on leaving and pretty soon the tent was only half full, all of them women. It was mighty peculiar and I got a burning curiousness on it. No one seen me whip around outside the tent to the front, where I'm just in time to see the last man leave. I followed him around the field to where there's a bunch of men stood between the wagons tilting a bottle, maybe looking for the sorrow that lurketh within.

"Are them first few done yet?" says one.

"They're gettin' done fast as they can," says another.

"I'm the impatient kind," says the first.

"Well there's a knothole in this here wagon you kin put it to."

They all laughed and tilted the bottle some more, then someone says:

"Which one you wanter have, Ray?"

"I reckon any one 'cept for that peabrain," says Ray.

"Whyn't you just cover her head with a sack," says another, and they laughed some more. None of it made sense but it give me a notion the virtues is part of it, so I legged it over to the McSween wagons. There's at least fifty men stood around and Ma's kind of standing guard over the wagons and taking money off anyone that come near. Then I seen a man come out of one wagon and a second or three later another man come out of another wagon and they both walked away. Then a man come out of Ma and Pa's wagon, and three men that just give Ma their money strolled over and went one apiece into the wagons, and a minute later other men come out and others went in, just like you see them do in public relief places

where there's three and more holes to use, only they can't be going
in the wagons for that on account of there's a whole field to get
reliefed in.

I circled around cautious and come up on the wagons from the
other side, and this close I can hear noises and voices inside. More
men come down the little steps at the end of each wagon and their
places got took inside by them that's waiting. I never did hear good
enough to know what they done in there; McSween was still playing hymns and the women in the tent still singing along, but whatever it was it never took very long because here's more stepping
down and stepping up, and I wonder where the virtues are, seeing
as there ain't hardly enough room in there for all of them men and
the virtues too.

There's a rustling beside me and it's the pinhead. She's spying
too, with a big idiot grin on her face. Then she giggled and it give
me the feeling we was doing something wrong, so I went back to
the tent where Jim is still tending the calliope's firebox and told him
what I seen. He wiped his brow and put his hand on my shoulder
and says:

"Huck, you looks up to dem girls, ain't it so?"

"I reckon I do. They're friendly as can be."

"Das it, Huck. Dey real friendly, an' not jest wid you. I heard men
talkin' das walkin' by an' I knows how come dey goin' insider de
wagons."

"Well, why?"

"De girls is in dere too, Huck."

"They can't be. There ain't room enough."

"If'n you stacks cordwood one on topper de nex' you kin make
room."

"I just wish I knowed what it is you're saying, Jim."

"Dey whores, Huck, all 'cept de pinhead chile."

"Whores?"

"Ain't nothin' else to call 'em, Huck. Dey jest whores."

"But they're real religious, Jim," says I, and he shakes his head.

"Fac's is fac's, Huck. De men payin' money an' goin in de wagons
to do fornicaterin'. Ain't no way you kin get aroun' it."

"But Reverend Mordecai's in there preaching about how big a sin
it is to lust after the flesh and such, and he's down hard on drinking
too, and them that's waiting is all liquored up. And don't them

women wonder where their husbands got to? It don't make no kind of sense, Jim."

"I cain't hardly figure it neither, Huck. I only knows we workin' for a cathouse on wheels."

I never wanted to believe it so I snuck back over to the wagons and watched some more, and now Jim's explanated it to me I can see he's right. The McSweens treated me and Jim fair and was generally fine company, but now I know the true way of it, and it's like reaching into one of them fancy ribboned candy boxes to pull out something sweet and your fingers wrap around a dead rat full of maggots.

I went over to the trees and lit my pipe to give the matter consideration, and by and by I got to smiling on it, one of them crooked ones you smile when you see the joke's on you. It's a feeling I reckernized from other times before this, when big expecterations come crashing down and all you can do is ask why you was sap-head enough to have them expecterations anyway.

I stayed over there till the last man was done and Ma went over to the tent, I reckon to give Pa McSween the nod. He finished the hymn he's on and the meeting was over. The women come out and went to the wagons where all the men was waiting for them and there was noise aplenty as they all went home, with one fight when two wagons locked wheels and the drivers both blamed each other for it. Then the last one rattled across the field and away down the road and it's quiet again. Ma got a fire started and the virtues come out for food. I felt ashamed to be with them, then my belly growled some so I swallered my pride as they say, and followed up with stew and fried bread. The virtues stood around kind of weary looking, back in their regular clothes and their hair all mussed. Hope says:

"Did you enjoy the meeting, Tom?"

"It come as a powerful surprise," says I, not lying.

That got them started on which songs went over best and who hit the wrong note in "Jerusalem the Golden" and such, never a mention about what they done after. You would of thought they was all sweet and innocent and not whores at all, and Ma looks like a Ma should, big and warmhearted, and McSween don't look like no cruel whoremaster, and Mordecai looks thin and wasted and stern enough to be a saint just back from forty days in the wilderness. But it's all counterfeit.

I helped Jim dump the ashes from the calliope, then we turned in.
It's kind of empty in the wagon with no folded up tent to lie on and I
must of tossed and turned considerable because Jim says:

"How you feel, Huck?"

"I'm poorly, I reckon."

"You got de misery?"

"A heap of it. Why do folks always let a body down, Jim?"

"I don' rightly know, Huck. 'Pears to me dey's mostly made dat
way. It don' do no good to wonder why. Ain't nothin you kin do 'cept
let it roll off 'n you."

"I just wish sometimes there was things I can depend on and
never get into disappointment over. I reckon there ain't one solid
fixed thing in the world. Even them things that look it is quicksilver
underneath."

"I reckon you kin depend on me, Huck, an' me on you."

There's quiet for a spell, then I say:

"You're right, Jim. We'd never have nothing at all without we had
each other."

And knowing it let me give myself over to sleep.

Next day was a late sleeper for everyone, and the tent was all took
down and folded and stowed away in the afternoon. When it's done
McSween come over to me and says:

"Tom, let's you and me go for a stroll together. There's things to
discuss between us."

So we walked a little way and he put his hand on my shoulder like
he's my uncle or something and started off the talking.

"Tom, I guess your mind is filled with questions. You must of
seen things last night that have started you thinking. Would I be
right?"

"Yessir, I reckon so."

"This will need understanding beyond your years, Tom, but I'll
take the chance you've got just that. It all began many years ago
when our baby daughter died. Yes, for a brief moment of time there
was an eighth virtue. Modesty was her name. She died of diphtheria
and Ma and me were terrible sad about it, coming hard on the heels
of Chastity, who's a retardee. We prayed for enlightenment, but it
was Mordecai who gave us the answer. He had suffered a recent
loss himself. His beloved church in Deer Falls, Ohio, was taken

from him after he was accused of a crime he did not commit. Can you imagine the effect that would have upon an innocent man?"

"I reckon I could."

"Well, there we were, the most miserable family on the face of the earth. I was in disemployment too, you understand, being the organist in the aforementioned church. Mordecai led us all in prayer and gave us the answer, and it was to travel across the country as a family devoted to the word of God. We used up our last cent to buy wagons and off we went. But it was awful hard, Tom. There are tent meetings by the score, and why should folks flock to one rather than another? You must have something which makes you stand out from the rest. You can't feed a family on an ailing business. The Lord's word can only rise up from your throat if there's food going down. Then Ma, who had a checkered career before I married her, came up with the answer, the answer you witnessed last night. And lo, we prospered! There was only Faith, Hope and Charity at first, then Mercy, Constance and Grace got old enough to join in. We prospered so much I bought us the calliope to round out the choir singing and after that nothing could hold us back. That is how we came to be where and what we are today. The Lord has seen fit to bless our little enterprise, proof positive that we have chosen the correct way to spread the gospel among His flock."

"Do Faith and Hope and them like being whores?" I ask, and his face clouded over.

"Never, never use that word," he says. "My beloved daughters are Brides of Christ, no less, and devoted to his service. You see, Tom, it is easy to get women into a congregation since they have a natural need for comfort and solace, their lives generally being filled with hardship and pain. One of these burdens is the attentions thrust upon them by their husbands at night. Any relief they can get from that particular burden is welcome, only it must not come from the kind of person you just now mentioned. No indeed, it must come in the guise of holy work, and the McSween Brides of Christ provide such relief. The topic is never discussed openly by either spouse, but after any tent meeting it's natural for men to go outside on their own and drink to the glory of the Lord, and this is what their wives have agreed among themselves to believe, that their men are outside simply drinking. Not one woman dares speak the bald truth to

her neighbor since the neighbor would then be obliged to call her a
lying troublemaker, or else agree and admit to turning a blind eye
herself. It's a mighty fine arrangement for all concerned, the perfect
all-round solution, and there are long-term benefits too. Since the
men are happier for having lain with a woman other than their
wives, and the women are happier for having been spared their mar-
ital duty, the marriage, which—who knows—may have hit upon
stony ground, is rekindled anew in this time of mutual happiness.
Yes, I sincerely believe we play our part in holding together the
sacred institution of marriage. Have I made things clear to you, my
boy?"

Well, he had. I seen how it's possible to take things and twist
them into whatever shape you want and see them another way entirely that don't have no resemblance to the truth. But there ain't no
real wickedness in McSween so I just nodded, then back we went to
the wagons and pulled out of Trask's field and onto the road again,
heading west.

✦ 8 ✦

Suspicioned?—The Dead Return—The Arm of the Law—

Unsatisfied Customers—Grace to the Rescue—

The Plan Misfires

Four days we traveled, and I got more and more worried over Mordecai. Every time I turned around there he was, just staring. He must of suspicioned about me being a murderer and he's just waiting to be sure on it, then he'll turn me in. Jim says maybe we should light out and be rid of the McSweens, but we needed them for disguise at least until St. Joe, so we had to tolerate things only it warn't easy.

There was good parts too, plenty to eat and a dry place to sleep but mainly Grace. She stuck to me on account of being the youngest, I reckon. Sometimes she rode on the tent wagon with Jim and me and mostly we had a grand time of it with plenty of laughing, but there's times she went quiet and sad, which made me feel the same. She's a puzzlement, Grace.

The next town was called Torrence, and it's the same as Slocombe. Everywhere in Missouri is the same. This time we set up the tent in a clearing just off the road half a mile from town, and when it got done McSween sent me into town with posters and nails same as before with directions penciled on the bottoms. The meeting won't be till tomorrow night so everyone in Torrence has got plenty of time to read them.

I hitched my mule in the main street and started papering the town, and whenever I come across a Huck Finn wanted poster I peeled it off the wall or else covered it with one of McSween's. It was easy chores and I took my time on it.

Along toward dusk I seen another of them Huck Finn posters across the street but there's someone stood in front of it reading, so I

had to cool my heels till he left. I sat myself in an alley and waited.
That man was an uncommon slow reader. He just stood and stood
looking at it, and I sat and sat looking at his back. He's thin and dirty
looking from behind, and he pulled a bottle from his pocket and
swigged every once in awhile, which proberly never helped with the
reading. Then he's done with it and turns away, and if I warn't
already sat down I would of done, because it's Pap!

He walked off along the sidewalk and turned a corner and I hared
along after him and peeked around. There he is, wobbling some,
and I followed him to a saloon which he went inside of. Now, some
saloons will let a boy in and some won't. I never wanted to bring
notice on myself so I waited till I seen a boy younger than me go in
with a bucket, then a minute later he come out again with it full of
beer, proberly fetching it for someone that's too drunk to fetch it for
himself. In I went with my hat pulled down, sneaking peeks under
the brim, and it never took long to pick out Pap. He's over at the bar
looking like he growed out of the floor, and he's jawing with a big
man dirty like himself and with a beard. It's crowded in there so I
snuck up close without they seen me, just a few foot away. I kept
my eyes on a spittoon and listened hard. The beard says:

"You oughter be grateful. It means they ain't looking for *you*."

"He's still my own boy," says Pap. "It ain't right that someone
young as him is on the run."

"Well, it's happened now. There ain't a thing you can do, not
unless you want to turn us both in to take the blame, but I reckon
you won't do it," he sneers.

Pap squirmed some then took a drink and says:

"They proberly won't catch him anyway. He's real smart for a
young'un, just like his old Pap."

It give me a thrill to hear Pap say that, even if he's the reason I'm
a wanted man. He never give me praise when we was together, not
once. But then I figured he's only saying it to cover up his guiltiness, and I'm back to normal. If I ever get catched, you can bet Pap
won't turn himself in and say he done the murders. He ain't that
kind. Now the beard is talking again and I leaned in close to hear it
over the other talk and laughing going on around.

"He better be smarter than that," he says. "You ain't so all-fired
clever. Who was it says there's a thousand dollars and more in that

safe, and it turns out there ain't no safe at all? It warn't me, so don't give me no big talk about how smart you reckon you are."

"Hell and damnation, Morg," whines Pap. "It was just bad luck. The whole town always figured he had a safe in there."

They're talking about the judge's office, and I see now that Pap warn't alone when he done it, which I never suspicioned before. Morg just sneered some more and sunk his nose in his glass then says:

"Come on. I ain't about to stand here all day listening to you make excuses."

They downed their drinks and left, and I followed along behind but not too close. They went down the street, Pap walking hard to keep up with Morg who just strode along like he owned the world. They went around a corner and I turned it too and run smack into the belly of a man with a big mustache and a sheriff's badge on his lapel. I jump back quick and say:

"Pardon me, sir, I never looked where I was going."

He stared at me and I started backing away slow, then he seen the bag over my shoulder with posters sticking out and says:

"Are you the boy that's been hanging them posters around town?"

"Posters, sir?"

"The McSween family. You work for them, don't you."

"McSween?"

"Let's see that bag you got there," he says, and before I can spring away he's reached over and pulled it off my shoulder and hauled out a handful of sheets.

"Let's you and me take a little ride together, boy. You mounted?"

"I got a mule up the street," says I, and that's where we headed, then to the livery stable where the sheriff got his horse, and we rode out to the camp, side by side. It's the longest ride I ever took. I'm already shook on account of seeing Pap, and now the sheriff is going to see Jim and ask how long we been with the McSweens and figure who we are. He hardly ever spoke on the way, just puffed on a cigar.

"Nice evening," he says, casual.

"Yessir," says I, and that's all till we got to the camp. McSween come across in a rush soon as we got unmounted.

"This is an unexpected pleasure, Sheriff," he says, showing all his teeth.

"No it ain't," says the sheriff, and grinds his cigar butt out under his boot. "It ain't a pleasure at all, it's business. Like as not you expected to find the same sheriff that was in office last year. Well, there's been a vote since then and I'm the new man. They brung me in on the Legal and Decent ticket. I reckon you know what I'm talking about."

"Maybe you should explain, Sheriff. I just don't know what you mean."

"I'll spell it out for you then. You can hold your meeting but the entertainment's got to stop with the preaching and singing."

He jerks his thumb at the virtues, all stood around listening, and says:

"You keep them whores under lock and key till you're in the next county or I'll run the whole shebang into court and impound your tent and wagons. Am I talking clear enough for you?"

"I believe you are, Sheriff," says McSween, going all stiff and dignificated. Then the sheriff says:

"You should be ashamed having a boy this age working for you. Is he kin like the rest?"

"No," says McSween.

The sheriff turns to me and says:

"Where are you from, boy?"

"Deer Falls, Ohio, Sheriff."

"Did you run away from home?"

"No, sir, I'm an orphan. Mr. McSween had pity on me and took me in. He's real kind."

"You're a fool, boy. This bunch is doing evil work. You take my advice and find yourself a respectable job and take up with decent folks. If you want to stay in Torrence and lead a useful life, I'll help you do it."

"Thank you, Sheriff. I'll give it some serious thinking."

He turned back to McSween and says:

"You've had the one and only warning you'll get, McSween. Preaching and hymns, nothing else."

Then he turned and strolled back to his horse and rode away. Ma come over to McSween, and they argued some on what to do, then Mordecai joined in and all three went into a wagon to thrash it out while the virtues just stood around quiet-like, looking at each other.

Jim come out of the shadows where he's been hid all along, and we went away out of ear-reach. He says:

"What you reckon de McSweens fixin' to do now, Huck?"

"I don't know, and maybe I don't care. Jim, I seen Pap in town."

And I give him the whole story, which set him frowning.

"You goin' to de sheriff an' turn him in, Huck?"

"I can't do it, Jim. There ain't any proof he done it and he'd never say so to get me off the hook. He's too cowardly, I reckon. Anyway, he's my own Pap. I can't do nothing to get him hanged. We'll just have to keep on going the same as we are and hope the whole mess gets left behind after we pass St. Joseph."

"You sure 'bout dis, Huck? Could be you ain't ever goin' to get a chance like this'n to get cleared."

"I just can't do it. Don't ask me no more, Jim."

"You made de choosin', Huck. I ain't about to argue on it."

At mealtime Ma and McSween give me dirty looks, like I'm to blame for the sheriff saying what he did. Mordecai just give me the usual stare and I got to wondering if he'll turn me in to the sheriff as a trade-off so's they can do the meeting the way they want. That night I played with the notion of saddling the mules and leaving, but we're still forty mile from St. Joe so it ain't worth it.

Next day it was like a black cloud hung over the camp. No one spoke a word. Chastity picked up the mood like a dog does and scampered about whimpering and whining and munching on her biscuits to give herself distraction from it. Jim and me was mighty uneasy and stayed out of the way. I kept an eye on where the horses was tethered to see if Mordecai don't take one and go for the sheriff to tell all, but he never did, and I figure he's biding his time for now, just playing with me like a cat and mouse. I can't hardly keep my food down, my belly crawled so, and Jim warn't no better off.

Then it's sundown and pretty soon people started coming in from the town and farms roundabout. It's a big turnout, maybe three hundred, and they paid their money and crammed theirselfs into the tent. Jim stoked the calliope like before and the meeting got started. They done it the exact same way as in Slocombe, but it warn't the same kind of success. McSween never had the fire in his playing nor Mordecai in his preaching, and the virtues sung off-key. The congregation got restless and fidgety and only a half dozen wanted to get saved. McSween says the next hymn is the last and all the men joined in louder than before, figuring pretty soon they can slip away and visit the virtues. The girls left on schedule, then McSween messed everyone's plans by saying goodnight and God bless them all, and it's clear there ain't going to be no calliope playing to keep the women inside the tent while the men go visiting. For a minute the congregation was all confused, then angry, and started hollering for more music till McSween got scared and sat down at the calliope again and started playing. That settled them some and the men trickled away and headed for the wagons, but Ma stood there in front of them with her arms folded, big and stony-faced. She says:

"You men get away. There ain't nothing to stay for. We ain't allowed by the sheriff."

That got them riled and they shouted and jeered, but Ma stood firm. Then they started ripping up clods and heaving them at the wagons, and Ma stooped and picked up a length of two-by-two that's lying hid at her feet and swung it casual in her hands, where it looks about as big as a walking cane. That set them back on their heels some, but then they got courage from bottles and swarmed in again, shouting and throwing clods. Ma fetched one or two a crack over the head before she went down, and then they're trampling over her to get to the wagons. They tried the doors but they're locked. It got them madder than ever and they started rocking the wagons back and forth on their wheels till the virtues started screaming inside, but that only made them laugh and rock even harder.

I run into the tent and whispered into McSween's ear but he just went all tight-lipped and kept on playing so I told it to Mordecai, but he's peeved about there being hardly no one that wanted Satan slapped out of them and turned his back on me. It won't do no good to ask Jim for help; they would of killed a nigger that stood up to them. The women knowed something is wrong and stopped singing and went outside, and when they seen what their men was doing some of the bravest ones waded right in and hauled their husbands out by the ear and give them such a tonguewhipping for it. Ma was stood off to one side, breathing heavy and dabbing a cut on her jaw. She seen me and says:

"Go fetch the sheriff!"

But there ain't a need for it, because here he comes with his cigar glowing hot in the dark. He took one look at the mob and hauled out his pistol and fired three times in the air. That brung things to a halt right quick and every face turned to him. He just sat on his horse and puffed smoke awhile then says:

"You people are the most misbegotten I ever saw. Go on home out of my sight."

That's all he spoke, but it done the trick. All the men got to looking sheepish and the women drug them away and there's a heap of activity for ten minutes or so while they got in their rigs and went off. Then it's quiet again, and the sheriff looked at the McSweens gathered around and shook his head.

"I hope this is some kind of lesson for you," he says. "Religion and whoring are separate things. You've had a fair run at it these past few years and I bet you made a pile. You can try it again somewhere else, I reckon I can't stop you, but you better do it outside of my county. I want you packed up and out of here by noon."

"We intend doing just that, Sheriff," says McSween.

Then the sheriff seen Jim and his eyes narrowed down.

"Who owns that nigger?"

No one owned up. I'm too scared to breathe, waiting for the axe to fall.

"Well? Does he belong here or don't he?"

Still nothing from no one.

"Come here, boy," he says to Jim, and Jim slowfooted till he's by the sheriff's horse.

"Who owns you, boy? Are you a runaway?"

"Nossir," says Jim. "I'se free."

"No you are not," says Grace, stepping forward. "I told you before, Samson, if I hear you spouting that freedom trash again I'll whip you for it!" Then she turns to the sheriff and says:

"He's my nigger, but awful proud and contrary. Pa gave him to me for a present. He thinks he's free just because I'm easy on him and don't give him the thrashing he deserves. Well, all that stops right now," she says to Jim. "There'll be no more coddling till you mend your ways, you idle nigger you. Now go clean this place up."

Jim shuffled off acting browbeat and ashamed, and I could of kissed Grace for what she done. It was brave and quick thinking and saved Jim and me both. Then the sheriff's looking at me again.

"Son, is it your intention to stay with these hypocrites? They're bad company for a boy your age."

"I reckon I'll stay on," says I, wishing he'd just ride off.

"You ain't kin to them, boy. You ain't beholden to them just because they fed you."

"I know it, Sheriff. I'd just rather stay."

"It's your choice," he says, but I can see he's disgusted. Then Mordecai chimes in and my heart missed a parcel of beats.

"Sheriff," he says, "this unfortunate child has a terrible secret."

All eyes turned on him and my legs got set to run.

"What secret?" says the sheriff.

"He is the bastard offspring of my second cousin who died giving birth. I feel I have a responsibility for his upbringing."

"Well I can tell you right now you've failed, preacher. With you and the rest of this bunch for examples he'll end up hanged for sure. You McSweens are the lowest kind of degenerate and if there was a law I could use against you I'd do it. Noon tomorrow," he says, and reined his horse around and ambled away just as relaxed as when he come.

McSween jumped right in and says we ain't going to wait, but get the tent down right now and be gone by sunup. We worked like demons, the virtues too, and got everything packed away and the teams hitched while it's still dark. I reckon McSween is worried some of them unsatisfied customers will come back and burn everything down. Soon as we was ready he took the lead, and the McSween Traveling Church of Christ the Lamb went rumbling down the road with its holy tail tucked firm between its legs.

Jim and me talked things over in the hour or so till daylight. We're both mystified by the way Grace and Mordecai lied to save us. Grace, I could see why she done it being a friend, but not the Reverend. Maybe he's still playing cat and mouse, only he's a smarter cat than I judged and he wants to keep me out of jail till the reward money goes up.

One thing I felt good about; we're leaving Pap behind. Him and Morg are thieves both, by what I heard in the saloon, and I never wanted to get tied up with that kind. Pap's steaming full speed ahead to the hanging tree. He's a pitiful man that never had things go right for him, not even in the beginning. When I was little Pap had work cutting cordwood for the steamers. We lived right there in the yard, just a step away from the water, and morning till night he chopped wood and piled it up at the end of the wharf so's the river-boats can nose up to it and the deckhands would sling it one to the next and stack it around the boiler, then they'd back off in a flurry of foam and keep on going upriver or down.

I only recollect one memory of my Ma, and it must of been when I'm mighty small on account of she's so big, and she's pointing up the river and saying, "Here comes the *Andrew Jackson*." She must of died pretty soon after that, Pap never told me what of, just got sick and died. Then it's just me and Pap, and he started in to drink regular. He cut less wood and the steamboat captains complained there was never enough waiting for them, so the man that owned the yard give Pap and me marching orders. Pap set himself up as a trapper in the old cabin on the Illinois shore but he never catched nothing worth real money and kept right on drinking. Them were the days I spent considerable time in town, sleeping in a hogshead and getting acquainted with Tom Sawyer and Jo Harper and such. I warn't unhappy except when I'm with Pap, and even that warn't so bad when he's sober, but that warn't often. It was all downhill for Pap long as I can recall, and it's only natural he's a thief and murderer nowadays.

The teams plodded along all day and when we stopped at dusk the McSweens was too tired to do nothing but crawl inside the wagons and sleep, but before Grace turned in I give her a thank you for what she done. She says:

"I know about you, Huckleberry Finn. I knew it was you and Jim the first time you came along the road. We passed through a town the day before and I saw a sheet that says you're a murderer and other things, but when I saw you I knew it wasn't so. You're a good boy and Jim's a good nigger."

When I took all that in I ask:

"Do the others know?"

"Of course not. I never tell them anything that's important."

The way she spoke I can see she ain't all that proud to be a Mc-Sween.

"I'm obliged to you, Grace," says I, and told her everything from the time the widow's house burned down. She was mighty sorry for me and put her arms around me sisterly and says:

"Poor Huckleberry. Life has given you punishment you never deserved. At least you have a friend in me."

"I'm glad of it, but see here, Grace, if you're the only one that knows, how is it Reverend Mordecai's always staring at me strange?"

"Oh, him," she says, scornful, "he was thrown out of his church in Deer Falls because of unnatural affections for the choirboys. He thinks you're handsome I suppose, but then he's kind of shortsighted. Just don't let him get you alone in the dark or he'll have your britches down before you can say Amen. I hate him. It's thanks to him we're all homeless wanderers and whores."

It give me a shock to hear that kind of brisk talk coming from her lips but she warn't ashamed to speak so, and she goes on to say how miserable the virtues is underneath the singing and laughing except Chastity, who's too pinheaded to understand nothing anyway, and how Hope was all set to be married when Pa McSween decided they was all going to be a traveling church and made her finish with the man she was fixed to wed, and she ain't ever got over it even if it was years ago, and how Ma used to be a whore before Pa married her and don't think nothing about making her daughters do the same. There's time enough later for marriage and such but not yet, Ma says.

"The other girls are so miserable," says Grace, "but they're under Ma and Pa's thumb and daren't do what they want. Well, I don't intend they should keep *me* a whore forever. It's awful the things men do to you, hurtful or just plain tiring. I don't ever want anything to do with men the rest of my life, but first I have to get away and be free. Can I come with you to California?"

That'll complexify things, thinks I.

"It's an awful long way, Grace. It's understandable you wanting to escape like you do, but why go west? Things is easier back east."

"No, I want to go where there's no one that'll know who I am. This side of St. Joseph is just filled with men that did things to me. Across the Missouri I'll be virgin again."

I seen it's going to be uphill work to argue with her. Says I:

"But Jim and me are wanted men. You'll be asking for trouble if you come along. There ain't a grain of sense in it I can see."

"If you don't help me there's no one else who will. I did you a favor with the sheriff so now you can repay it. I won't be a burden on you. Please, Huckleberry."

She flung her arms around me and it was mighty hard to refuse, pressed up against all that softness, which I seen is why she done it. But she's right on one thing; when a body does you a favor you got to pay it back, even if you got doubts about the way to do it.

"Well, all right then," says I, kind of muffled. "You can come too."

She whipped the hat off my head and kissed my hair then jammed it back on, all excited. She even clapped her hands a time or two.

"When can we go?" she wants to know.

"I'll have to think on it awhile and work out a plan," says I.

"Will it take long?"

"That depends. It's got to be a plan that won't go wrong, and that kind takes longer to hatch than the regular."

"Bless you," she says, "you're my salvation. Promise you won't go off and leave me behind."

"I promise."

"Swear on it."

"There ain't a need for that, is there?"

"All the most solemn promises have got to be sworn upon. It's customary."

Tom Sawyer told me that too, so I reckon she's right.

"Well, I'll do it then. I dangblasted sonovabitchin' promise."

That suited her and she says goodnight and went off. Then I had to tell Jim all of it and he's considerable upset.

"You goin' sof' in de head, Huck. How kin we take a girl wid us? I bet she cain't even ride. It's de mos' ridickerless plan I ever heard."

"I ain't all that happy myself, Jim, but I don't see a way around it. She could of turned us in but she never. We're obligated, I reckon."

"I don' like it. When we got dis Grace along we goin' to stan' out a mile."

"But we'll be across the river by then, Jim. There'll be thousands streaming along the trail for us to get lost among. One girl won't make no difference."

"I jest hopes you right, Huck, das all."

"I'm positive on it."

I warn't at all, but I never wanted him to worry more than he is already.

Two days dragged along, and gloomy and dismal is what they were. The McSweens was all sourfaced and silent and painful to be with come mealtimes. The closer we got to St. Joseph the more the road come alive with people heading the same way, gold fever just burning in their eyes. They was stepping quick and eager, all kinds of folk, mostly men but there's a scattering of women too in some of the wagons.

When we're only ten miles from St. Joe Grace brung me the news that McSween wants to swing away south and go down toward Arkansas. St. Joe's too big a town, he figures, and bound to have sheriffs and deputies crawling all over, and he's running shy of lawmen since what happened back in Torrence. So I come up with a plan and it's this: we just wait for dark and when everyone is snoring Grace sneaks out and meets up with Jim and me and we saddle the mules and go. Simple plans is best, that's what Napoleon reckoned and Tom Sawyer agreed with him, so I got confidence in this one. I give Grace the word and she give me a hug in return and vowed she'd do it. I was hoping she'd of changed her mind by then but no, she's all fired up over California, so we still have to take her along. I swore a promise on it.

We made camp same as always beside the road but there's plenty of people that kept right on going even after dark, just itching to be out of Missouri and truly begin the trek west. I never seen the sense in it myself. Ten miles is a small bite out of two thousand, but on they went with lamps swinging from the wagons and bunches of perfect strangers talking to each other like they growed up together. They say a war does the same thing.

I never had no appetite on account of the nervous squirts that kept me running into the bushes, but it never mattered all that much; Ma's cooking nowadays ain't a patch on what it was before Torrence. Jim and me lay awake just listening to the tramp of feet and creaking of wheels on the road, then when we figured the McSweens must be asleep we snuck out and saddled up our mules. One of them started braying till Jim give it a fist between the eyes. If you get a mule that don't behave, just punch it between the eyes and it'll quiet down immediate, or else bite your arm off. We waited for Grace, but she's a long time coming.

"I reckon she still snorin', Huck. Ain't no sign of her."

"She'll be along. She won't of gone to sleep at all, same as us."

"I don' like dis waitin' aroun'."

"Me neither, but we got to."

But she never showed.

"Wait here," says I to Jim, and went to find out why. The doors on the virtues' wagons was all shut and I never knowed for sure which one is hers, so no luck there. Then I heard a voice nearby and it says:

"Tom. . . . Tom. . . . Are you there?"

It's soft and whispery and come from the back of the tent wagon, so it has to be Grace looking for me, proberly so excited she forgot to call me Huck. I went back there and near jumped out of my skin because it ain't Grace at all. It's Mordecai in his nightshirt peering into the tent wagon, and he's as perplexified as me.

"What are you doing?" he says.

"Taking a leak," says I. "How about you?"

"I must talk with you," he says, all urgent and turning around to see if anyone is listening. They ain't, so he grabs my elbow.

"Tom, you are in serious danger," he hisses, and I figure he's catched wind of a batch of sheriffs sneaking around the camp.

"What kind of danger?" I hiss back, worried now.

"The minions of Satan threaten your immortal soul," he says, rolling his eyes. "His pernicious imps are everywhere."

"I know. I heard a couple talking devil talk under the wagon and come out to see if I can catch one. If you put him in a bottle he'll give you three wishes."

"Listen to me, boy. There are forces at work in this world beyond our pitiful understanding, horrible creeping things designed by the Black Master to crawl inside a man's soul and devour it from within. The Satanic worm has found its way into your young body and is writhing inside you at this moment."

"It's just the squirts, honest."

He give me a shake and put his face close to mine so's I can smell his awful stinking breath.

"Tom, only a true servant of the Lord can save you from the terrible fate awaiting you should the worm release its deadly venom. The pain will be excruciating. I have experienced its awful pangs myself, and there is only one way to avoid catastrophe. The poison must be sucked out before it can overwhelm your fine young limbs with hideous palpitations and loathsome boils. Only I can perform this service for you, Tom. I beseech you to place yourself in my hands and submit to the necessary exorcism. Together we will cast out the worm. Let me grant you blessed relief in the name of the Lord. I must pray. . . ."

And down he goes on his knees and flung his arms around me. It give me a scare on account of the money belt he's bound to feel wrapped around me so I pulled back, but he locked his hands behind me.

"Oh, Tom . . ." he moans. "Oh, God. . . ."

I can feel the money crinkling and crackling as he mashes his nose into it, and it called for desperate measures, as they say. I lifted a lamp that's hanging unlit off the back of the wagon and brung it down hard on his head.

"Oh, Tom," he blubbers. "What . . . what are you doing? . . ."

"Hold still, Reverend! There's one of them imps on your head! I'll get him this time!"

Down come the lamp again. It's only tin so it can't truly hurt him, but the glass smashed and spilled oil over his shoulders and hair. Then he started giggling and I knowed he's a lunatic for sure.

"Tom, you're not cooperating, you naughty mischievous child. . . ."

And he grabs me even tighter. I got panicky then and swung that busted lamp hard as I could, but it done no good so I kicked frantic to get free, but only stomped his legs some.

"Oh, Tom . . ." he keeps on moaning.

I seen it ain't no use to fight my way out so I figured another way in about a second and give her a try.

"Reverend! Look out! Satan's right behind you!"

It never would of worked with no one else, but Mordecai took the bait right up to the rod. He unhooked his hands and flung himself around to catch a look at Old Scratch, and danged if he don't throw up his arms and screech like a trod-on cat.

"No! . . . No! . . . Get thee behind me! . . ." he hollers, and I cut and run for the mules, only before I went five steps there's Grace with a bonnet on her head and a little tote bag in her hand and a startled look on her face.

"Huckleberry. . . ." she says as I go flying past, right smack into McSween in his nightshirt.

"What is happening here? . . ." he says, then sees Grace all dressed up to travel. "What are you doing?" he yells at her, and Grace don't know which way to turn.

Then Mordecai come blundering around the wagon backward, arms whirling like windmills to keep the devil off him and little groans coming out of his mouth. He headed straight for the fire and tripped and his shoulder went into the embers. His nightshirt and hair catched alight just like that and he's up and running in circles, screaming for the Lord to save him from the flames of Hell. The rest of the family spilled out of the wagons and the pinhead went mad and run in circles too, screaming just as loud as Mordecai. Grace seen her escape fall to pieces in front of her and starts howling along in chorus, and I figured now is the time to put distance between me and the McSweens.

While they was trying to douse Mordecai with water I snuck off back to Jim. He's already on his mule and I swung onto mine.

"What happen, Huck? Soun's like a body's gettin' killed."

"I'll tell it all later. We got to go."

We went off into the woods away from the road and swung around in a half circle and come back to it further down, then waited for a gap in the travelers so's we don't get seen coming out of the trees like outlaws on the run. When I figured we're safe I told Jim everything and he wagged his finger at me.

"I done tol' you, Huck. Messin' wid dat girl jest boun' to give us a heaper trouble. Maybe nex' time you goin' to listen."

Leaving Grace behind that way warn't right. I give her my promise then never done what we agreed, but I reckon it ain't no use to whale myself over it. I done my best but fickle fate went and sat on the plan. At least Jim and me got away, and that ain't no mean thing.

✦ 9 ✦

St. Joseph—A New Partner—An Interesting Article—Short
Tempers in Tent City—A Long Rifle—Across the Missouri

Just before dawn we come over a little rise and there's St. Joseph laid out before us with lighted windows in houses spread far and wide. Between them and us is a tent city, just canvas and wagons and campfires, hundreds of them, and you can see there's people moving around among them by the way the fires flickered. It's a mighty impressive sight and we soaked it all in, then nudged the mules and went ahead to be part of it.

When the sun come up behind our backs we seen pieces of the Missouri behind the town, then we're too close to see anything except all them wagons and tents. Folks was cooking breakfast over the fires and the smell set our bellies rumbling. Says I:

"Jim, if I don't get food inside me directly I'll fall down in the road and get tromped into the mud."

"I'se kinder peckish too, Huck. What we goin' to do?"

"It's simple. Did you see the way people all along the road been acting, all brotherly and friendly? Well, all we got to do is ask for some food and it'll be handed over gladly, but I'll offer a quarter for politeness' sake."

I seen a woman frying up bacon and bread in a pan and steered over and got down off the mule, then took off my hat and sidled up next to her. Says I:

"Pardon me, ma'am. Me and my nigger got no food to eat. I'd be obliged if you'd give us breakfast for a quarter."

She looked up, not old but plenty wrinkled, with a wart on her nose.

"You'd be obliged, would you?" she says. "I'll do it for five dollars and not a cent less."

"Five dollars for breakfast, ma'am?"

"You heard right."

"I reckon that's too steep for me."

"Well, you can try somewhere else, but you won't get a better offer."

"I reckon we'll try anyhow. Thank you, ma'am."

"Just got in, ain't you," she says.

"Yes, ma'am, right this minute."

"Well you got a lot to learn. Did you bring cash with you or just the nigger?"

"Only a few dollars," says I, not wanting to tell about the money belt.

"Then you may as well turn right around and go back where you come from. You can't do nothing in this place without you've got money to burn. See if I'm wrong."

She turned away and pointed her wart at the frying pan, and Jim and me went on. I tried two other women that's fixing breakfast, and the first wanted seven dollars and next wanted ten. We went back to the wart. She seen us coming and stood with hands on hips and a look that says "I told you so" on her face.

"Where's the five dollars?" she says, and I give it to her.

"Set yourselfs down if you don't mind mud. Stay stood if you do."

She give us a plateful each and we stayed stood to gobble it down.

"Are you headed for California, ma'am?" says I, wanting to be friendly.

"I'm headed for the grave, same as everyone," she says, waspish.

"Oh, I figured seeing as you're in St. Joseph you must of been aiming to join in the rush."

"That was the plan," she says. "Now there ain't one. You see that wagon over there and the one horse beside it?"

"Yes, ma'am."

"Well, when I come here there was two horses and a husband as well. Last week he got drunk and fell down and a wagon run over his back and killed him. I had to sell one of the team to pay for a decent burial. Now I can't go backwards nor forwards. I'm stuck in this mudhole with all these other fools that want to find a pot of gold same as my Ephraim done. I reckon you'll be wanting the same thing."

"Yes, ma'am, we're going to California."

"What's the nigger for, to do all the digging?"

"No, ma'am, I plan on doing my share."

"Where's your folks?"

"They're all dead. There's only me and Goliath."

"You ain't but a boy. Why, you ain't even begun to shave yet. They won't take you, not a boy and a nigger."

"Who won't take us, ma'am?"

"The wagonmasters. Are them mules all you got?"

"Yes, ma'am. They're my inheritance along with Goliath."

"Then they for sure ain't going to take you. You got to have a wagon and on top of it you have to pay twenty dollars to join a train. They don't allow no one afoot or on horseback that can't carry six months' supplies at least. That's the rules."

"You mean we ain't allowed to do it on our own? Who's going to stop us?"

"Nobody, but you'd get killed by redskins if you ain't part of a big train, and big trains don't want no hangers-on that can't feed theirselfs and just be a burden to others. You got no money and no wagon so you can turn tail and go back home."

"Is that what you aim to do, ma'am?"

"Are you deaf, child? I just got through telling you I'm busted flat with only one horse. I'll take root here before my problems get fixed. Drat that Ephraim and his gold fever. He couldn't of found his way to the outhouse without a rope to lead him, and he wanted to go clear across the country to find gold. All it got him was a pine box. He was just a pure idiot, even if he's my own husband."

"I'm sorry about the tragedy that befell you, ma'am. It's a bitter blow I reckon."

"Well I asked for it, letting him talk me into selling up and coming out here. We had a fine farm and now it's all gone."

"Ma'am, do you believe in the scriptures?"

"What's that got to do with it?" she says. "I can get all the consolation I need from the Book without you putting in your ten cents' worth."

"No, ma'am, I mean God moves in mysterious ways, his wonders to perform."

"Horse apples," she says.

"What I mean, ma'am, is if you want to keep going to California there's a way you can do it, and me and Goliath too."

She give me a look that says "Where's the catch?" and I rattled out the plan that come into my head just that instant.

"Ma'am, we need a wagon and you need a team to pull the one you got. These mules is good pullers both. You just tie that horse of yours behind for a spare and we can all join the train together."

She pondered it a moment then says:

"Are you serious, boy?"

"I was never more serious-minded in my life, ma'am."

"What about the twenty dollars and supplies?"

"I reckon I told you a white lie just to be cautious. I got twenty dollars and some more that'll buy supplies."

"Why would I want to go to California now?" she says. "I don't have a notion to dig for gold."

"No, ma'am, that's men's work, and it looks like there's going to be a heap of men out there. I heard tell it's fifty men to one woman, and the first thing a miner does when he strikes it rich is rush off and get married to a respectable lady."

"What are you saying, boy? If it's what I think it is you got the biggest amount of gall I ever come across."

"No offense, ma'am, it's just that you're young still. They say the trip takes six months. That's about regular mourning time I reckon."

"You say one more thing like that and I'll warm your ears. You're the brazenest boy that ever lived."

"No, ma'am, just practical. Maybe you want a little time to think it over."

She never spoke, just started frying up second helpings of bread and bacon, and I seen it's the answer I wanted. When she dished up she says:

"You can call me Mrs. Ambrose."

"Jeff Trueblood, ma'am, and I'm proud to know you."

She give me her hand and I took it and pumped it a time or two. It felt like a chicken foot, hard and thin and cold. That's how we come to be partners, me and Jim and Mrs. Ambrose.

She took me off directly to a wagonmaster's office, just a wood hut in a field of mud, and I paid over the twenty dollars and she put our names down. The wagonmaster's clerk give her a slip of paper with a number on it, and it's sixty-seven.

"That's your place in line," he says. "There's still too much ice coming downriver to cross and we don't know when it's going to let up. When it does and it's safe to use the ferry there'll be a notice put up outside so you'll know where and when your wagon has to be ready for the crossing. Is all that clear?"

"Clear enough," says Mrs. Ambrose, and we left. Says I:

"It'll be a fair-sized train if there's sixty-six ahead of us."

"Safety in numbers," she says. "Come on and we'll get supplies."

"Yes, ma'am."

We went into town and she ordered the stuff, four big sacks full, and we tied the necks and slung them over the mules and walked back to the wagon. The streets was stiff with men and horses and wagons, and everyone was talking about the ice coming downriver from the spring thaw, which is early this year. On every street corner there's hucksters selling patent gold-washing machines and doing fast trade too, but we never bought one. When we got back the supplies was loaded into the wagon, which is only small with homemade hoops bent over it and canvas that never fitted correct, but it's rainproof and not too heavy for the mules to pull so we was all satisfied about it. Then I told how me and Jim never got no sleep last night, leaving out the details of why, and Mrs. Ambrose says we can get in the wagon and take forty winks. We done it and around evening woke up feeling mighty gay about the way things is organized at last, with only the ice holding us back from California.

Mrs. Ambrose fixed more food and after it Jim and me reckoned we'll go for a stroll through town and take a look at the river. She says not to get in no trouble on account of St. Joe is filled with rough men that's drinking too much and fighting while they wait for a crossing. I told her we'll be careful and off we went on foot.

There's just as many people around as in daylight and it took some considerable time to reach the river. It looked mean and dangersome with them big chunks of ice booming along all gray under the stars. We watched it for awhile then walked along the bank till we seen a big post sunk in the ground with a heavy chain tied around it and leading off into the water. A bunch of men was jawing close by so I ask one of them what the chain is for, and he tells me the Missouri is so deep a river that folks is scared the whole west half of the country is going to break free and drift away into the ocean, so they run a chain across and staked it on the other side to keep America in one piece.

All the men laughed plenty even if they heard the story a hundred times before, then the joker tells me it's the ferry chain that they use to haul wagons and such across, only they let it slack off some so it's hanging below the ice and won't get snagged and the posts pulled out and the chain lost on the riverbed. It's the longest chain in the state, he says. Right now the ferry, which is just a biggish raft, is over on the far shore, stranded there till the ice has all gone by.

"That's a powerful big nigger you got there," he says. "Is he yours?"

"No, sir, he belongs to my Pap. We aim to take him to California."

"You tell your Pap to watch that nigger close when you get across the river. West of here is like the free states so he'll likely run off."

"Not if he wants to stay alive he won't," says someone else. "The Injuns'll get him for sure. I bet they never seen a nigger before. They'd reckon he's some kinder animal and kill him." To Jim he says: "You mind what I say, nigger. Don't you run off from your master or you'll get roasted alive by redskins."

"Nossuh," says Jim.

They all laughed and Jim and me went back into town. I looked at all the walls but there warn't one Huck Finn poster, so it looks like we're too far west already for people to bother, and it cheered us considerable. St. Joseph was the nicest town in the world without no posters papered around, even if the streets was churned to mud. We passed a newspaper office and it's still open even at night, so I went in and got a copy. It's a day old and I reckoned I should only have to pay half price for stale news, but the man there says they only print a new edition twice a week anyway, so I had to be satisfied.

We went along the street to where there's light spilling out a saloon window and I read all the interesting portions to Jim. Most of it is about the gold rush and how men was flocking to California by sea. There's thousands going all the way by ship down near the South Pole and up the other side, and others is crossing the skinny part under Mexico and getting on another ship that sails them up to San Francisco. But there's plenty more doing it like us, heading along the trail blazed by the Oregon pioneers seven or eight years back. The writer calls it "the greatest mass migration since Moses led the Israelites out of Egypt." And Jim and me is both part of it.

There was other news too, mostly about the ice which is stretched all the way down to where the Missouri and Mississippi meet at St. Louis. There's steamboats on both rivers been crushed by it, just squashed to flinders against the banks. It was a bad winter, but now it's coming to the end. When the weather warms up the paper says there'll be thousands more trekking west. Jim says:

"You reckon dey got gold out dere for all dem thousan's, Huck?"

"I expect so, Jim. They say there's whole mountains of it."

I turned a page and there's a small piece catched my eye and I read it out:

HUNT FOR YOUTHFUL
MURDERER CONTINUES

All eyes in Missouri and surrounding states are ever watchful and alert as the search for Huckleberry Finn and his nigger accomplice goes on. Finn, the murderous stripling who slew Judge Caleb Thatcher on February twenty-seventh last is still at large among a frightened populace after his daring jailbreak. Sheriff Wade Bottoms of St. Petersburg has told your correspondent that all efforts are being made to apprehend the bloodthirsty juvenile following his wanton assault upon farmer Hollis Aintree and his wife, a woman of frail constitution. Finn and the nigger, known as Jim, made off with Mr. Aintrees' horse after ransacking his home and inflicting torture upon the occupants. Mrs. Aintree suspected Finn of evildoing from the moment she laid eyes upon him but was too greatly in fear for her life to resist his demands for food and money. The Aintrees' meager savings were appropriated along with the horse. It is believed the murderous duo are hiding out in wild country, but just where no one is as yet able to determine. Outlying farms are advised to take all necessary precautions to prevent a repetition of the Aintree outrage. Sheriff Bottoms maintains it is merely a matter of time before the felons are captured and charged, but the murdered man's daughter has stated publicly that ordinary measures are insufficient to snare such a cunning animal, known for his ability to live without discomfort in primitive surroundings. To this end Miss Becky Thatcher, a plucky fifteen-year-old, has instructed her father's attorney to contract the services of Chauncey Thermopylae Barrett, the famed detective and resident of Boston, Mass. Mr. Barrett was recently successful in bringing to justice the notorious bank sneak and

safecracker Wylie Croft after a dramatic shootout in a St. Louis
warehouse, in the course of which Croft sustained serious inju-
ries. It is expected that he will survive to face trial next month.
Your correspondent has been unable to question Mr. Barrett
regarding his involvement in the Finn affair, but does not doubt
that this Galahad of the North will find the challenge irresist-
ible. Readers will not be unaware that the gentleman has oft
times succeeded where the orthodox forces of law have failed.
Sheriff Bottoms deplores the action taken by Miss Thatcher, but
her decision has met with popular approval from the townsfolk
of St. Petersburg, who have to a man mourned the sad demise
of their most respected citizen. Master Thomas Sawyer, erstwhile companion of the notorious Finn, has captured the hearts
of many by vowing he will not cut his hair until the youth who
so sorely betrayed the friendship has been hanged. Master
Sawyer and Miss Thatcher are rumored to have "linked hearts."
The young lady will have need of such tender ministrations until the callous murder of her parent has been avenged.

I tipped my hat to Tom's haircut vow; that was real style, but I
reckon he'll need a ribbon or three off Becky because I don't aim to
get stretched. Jim says:

"Soun's bad, Huck. Who dis Chauncey Thermoply Barrett?"

"The greatest detective in the world, Jim. They call him Bulldog
Barrett like the English hound that chomps his teeth in whatever
he's after and don't let go regardless. He always gets his man, and
I'm the man he's after. I'm right peeved about the Aintrees. We
never done those things they say. Why'd they go and pour oil on the
fire like that?"

"Dat Aintree put up a perty poor show in de barn. Reckon das his
way of lettin' folks know how brave he acted 'steader shakin' like a
leaf. You got to 'spect it, Huck."

"I reckon I'm disgusted with it. Why, he never mentions the
twenty dollars I give him for the horse. It warn't even worth that
much, and we never got no real use from it before it run off. The
whole thing is just danged lies."

We slogged our way back to the wagon, both of us mighty put out
by things. Mrs. Ambrose says we got to sleep underneath on account of she ain't about to share no wagon with a boy and a nigger,
but the ground warn't so bad, not wet or muddy seeing as the
wagon's been stood in the same place a week or more, and we made
a blanket bed and turned in. The last thing I wished before I went to

sleep is for the ice to quit coming down the Missouri so's we can get started on the real journey away from sivilization.

But the ice kept coming, and so did more westbound travelers till St. Joe was ready to bust her seams. The tent city just growed and growed. It was the fine weather done it, bringing out gold rushers like it brings out flies, and they swarmed for the sweetest honeypot in the world which is California, only they can't get past St. Joe, not yet. Time drug heavy for everyone and tempers got short. It'll happen every time you get folks living crammed up close together like we was. Even if it's only wagons or tents they live in, folks will start looking at the mud roundabout like it's private property with a fence around it. It's *their* mud, and just you try to set foot on it. Not all was like that but plenty were, and it made life more miserable than it had to be.

Mrs. Ambrose got into argument with the men in the next wagon, maybe five yards away. They kept on taking a shortcut past her back step, as she sees it, when they could of just as easy gone around the other side. They never seen it that way and called her a horsefaced hag, which was real insulting. Myself, I figure she looks more like a turkey.

She got riled and says they never would of sassed her if she had a man with her and not just a nigger and a boy, but they just laughed and told her to go stick her head in a bucket where it'd look better and not frighten the mules so much. She fumed and fumed till she near blowed steam out her ears, but there warn't nothing she could do. They was both big men and the other neighbors turned deaf and blind whenever she had a fight with them.

The final straw come when they brung back a painted whore one night and lifted her into the wagon, all drunk and laughing. They made a heap of noise, and not just laughing neither. Jim and me heard all of it, and Mrs. Ambrose thrashed about restless and distracted a few feet above us. She stood it long as she can, then clumb down and went and hammered on the end of their wagon with a frying pan.

"You quit that!" she yells.

There's silence in the wagon, then a bushy head pops out from the canvas flap.

"What'n heller you upter, woman?" says he.

"Just you quit that racket this instant or I'll quit it for you!"

"What damn racket?"

"Don't you dare use that kind of talk in front of a woman! You know damn well what damn racket! There's a whore in there and it's just disgusting the noise you're making!"

"I reckon you're just jealous," he says, and Mrs. Ambrose swung that frying pan full circle and crowned him hard. His head kind of swayed left and right then pulled back inside, and there warn't no more noise after that.

Men was all the time talking about hostile Injuns and how every wagon has got to be armed, so I went into town to a gunsmith and paid out forty dollars for a secondhand Hawken, which is a real famous gun, and plenty of shot and a powder horn and ramrod and gun oil. She's old-fashioned but reliable and stood taller than me, and I made a sling to carry her over my shoulder on account of she weighs near fifteen pounds. There's initials carved into the stock, JF, and I reckon that's who owned her before me. She's the first gun I ever owned with money I paid from my own pocket, and I took her away from town and set up rocks and bottles and such and blazed away till I could fire and reload right quick, and I was a fair shot, too.

Around that time I seen my first Injun. He was right there in the main street of St. Joseph, skinny and dirty and lying in the gutter drunk. No one come to take him away. He could of been dead but folks just ignored him and stepped over like he's a log or something. I give him a poke to see if he needs a hand but he only groaned into the long hair plastered over his face. He's wearing white man's clothes with a blanket around them and he's a pitiful sight to see. It was a powerful disappointment to me; even Injun Joe on a bad day used to look better than that.

Time hung heavy on me. Somewhere back across Missouri Chauncey Thermopylae Barrett is most likely sniffing around looking for signs and clues where I went, and it give me a troubled mind to know such a famous man is on my trail. But there ain't nothing I can do except wait around with everyone else that's burning to go west. I had a dream one night and there's a hand comes down on my shoulder and a voice behind me says: "Huckleberry Finn, your time of freedom is over," then the hand turned into teeth and sunk in deep. I never needed to ask who the voice is. I woke up in a sweat and it's only the sharp part of my rifle breech sticking into me, but it shook me some, that dream, and it warn't easy getting back to sleep.

Another fretful week rolled by, then word ran through tent city like wildfire. The ice is gone! There was a rush to the river and sure enough, there she is sweeping by with only a little chunk now and then, and there was shouting and hoorahing and a pistol got emptied at the sky. People hugged each other and men danced around till they fell in the mud. Then there's another rush to the wagonmaster's office to see the notice nailed up outside. It got tore off so they nailed up another. That went too so they had a hundred or so printed up and handed around so everyone can read the schedule and get ready.

Mrs. Ambrose's number was set to get ferried across two days from now, or maybe sooner on account of a whole slew of ferries got built real fast and rope lines was rowed over to the other side and staked, so the schedule warn't nothing but a waste of time and ink. The longest chain in the state got pulled tight till it's just under the water out in midstream and the first wagon and team rolled on board the ferry in the afternoon and got a send-off from the crowd like it was Columbus setting out in the *Mayflower*. The men hauled on the chain and away she went, swinging downstream some halfway across, then pulled back on course when they got closer to the shore. The team was whipped up and the wagon rolled off onto real western soil, and there was more cheering and gunshooting. The new ferries had lines of wagons waiting too, and pretty soon was crossing the river every five minutes or so. We never wasted no time. Jim and me hitched up the mules and I put a saddle on Mrs. Ambrose's horse and led the way down to the riverbank.

Nobody give a hoot what number they was, just first come first served, and you had to pay the ferrymen five dollars for the trip. When night come the ferries set lamps on their corner poles and it was a fine sight to see them going back and forth with the lights shining and reflecting in the water. Then one of the wagonmasters come down to the bank and tried to make the ferrymen quit on account of there might be an accident with folks drowning in the dark, but they told him he's just an old woman and kept right on working, and them in the wagons never paid him no mind neither so he give up.

Around midnight it got to be our turn. Jim led the mules by the bridles and they clattered aboard and pulled the wagon after, prancing and skittish. There's plenty of room so I rode on board too and got down so the horse don't throw me overboard. The ferrymen heaved and across we went. The mules got panicky when they felt the current under their feet but Jim got them calmed. In a little while the ferry bumps onto the shore and we're out of Missouri.

There warn't no sudden change. There's a few cabins over on this side of the river and the wagons was all trying to get assembled a half mile away, but it's a shambles and they ended up scattered all over. Some of them wanted to get started right then in the dark, but the smart ones say to wait for daylight and the wagonmaster. There was near a hundred wagons brung over before word reaches us that the sheriff got called in to make the ferrymen stop. The plan is to let the first batch which is already over get a day or two start on the next batch so they don't get all bunched up together. There's three or four different wagonmasters and each has got his own train to look after, so we're lucky to be with the first. There's people with us that was supposed to be with other trains but it all got scrambled in the rush to the ferries, and even if they paid their money to a different wagonmaster they warn't bothered by it, and everyone settled down to get some sleep.

✦ 10 ✦

The Wagon Train—A Mountain Man—An Unpaid Debt—

Conjures and Crows—A Hex Is Planned

At first light our wagonmaster
come over and joined us, and his name is Colonel Naismith. He's tall
and dignificated and from Tennessee, and you could tell just looking
at him he's used to getting his way, only this morning he's mean-
tempered over what happened last night. He went around the wagons
on his horse, which is a thoroughbred, and told everyone to get assembled. When there's a big crowd around him he says:

"We have begun badly. Last night was a disgrace, and if such a
breach of discipline occurs again the perpetrators will be singled out
and punished in no uncertain terms. I mean what I say. A wagon
train must operate as a unit, a family, and there can be only one
head of that family. In future I expect all of you to do as ordered, for
your own good."

No one spoke up, just looked sheepish, and the colonel turns to a
man stood beside him. He's forty or so, small and wrinkled and
wearing buckskins with fringes and beads all over and broken-down
moccasins. His hair is done in two long braids and his beard was salt
and peppered. There's a feather stuck in his hat and in his hand
there's a long rifle same as mine. Colonel Naismith says:

"I introduce you to our guide for the long journey ahead. Mr.
Winterbough has wide experience of the western terrain. He has
worked for the famed Missouri Fur Company and is one of the original Green River men. The money each of you has paid constitutes
his fee for services about to be rendered, and I regard it as sound
investment. I have total confidence in his expertise and have placed
him as second in command of this enterprise. Mr. Winterbough, do
you wish to say a few words?"

"I reckon not," he says.

"In that case," says the colonel, "please return to your wagons and prepare to move out. Do not crowd together and do not lag behind. The heavier wagons will be first in line, especially if drawn by oxen. They will set the pace for us all. There will be no racing or overtaking. That is all."

It took an hour or more till everyone was strung out in a line and started moving. Jim drove our wagon with Mrs. Ambrose sat next to him and I stayed on horseback and rode alongside, just ambling slow. It was tiresome and dull, so I rode back along the train to the end, where the last in line is a two-wheeled buggy with one horse and a driver. He's dressed neat with a waistcoat that matches up with his jacket and britches and a necktie and porkpie hat. He looked like he's on his way to church, and was mighty upset about being tailender.

"I just don't see the point," he says to me. "Why should I be last? For that matter why do we have to travel in line when the country is wide open?"

"I don't rightly know. It's just the way they do it," says I.

"Well I can't see the sense, not a scrap. I'm a businessman and I don't believe it's right that I should have to trail behind farmers and ne'er-do-wells just because I had the intelligence to invest in a lighter vehicle than them. I made a close study of the exploits of the pioneers and from it drew one firm conclusion; heavy wagons will be unable to cross the mountains. Those idiots at the front with their tons of weight will find themselves in trouble when we reach the Rockies, believe you me. If any of them could read they would have drawn the same conclusion and planned things the way I've done. My rig will sail over those peaks like a cork riding the waves. There is no doubt in my mind I will be among the first to reach California, if not *the* first. I'm just biding my time back here, young man. Before journey's end I will have taken my rightful place at the head of the column."

"Yessir, I expect so."

He warn't pleasant company so I rode to the head of the train counting wagons on the way, and there's ninety-seven of them stretched out over maybe a mile. The pioneers never seen such a train. It just went on and on and was a mighty uplifting sight, and every turn of the wheels took me and Jim further away from St. Petersburg and Pap and Bulldog Barrett. I got to the head of the line

and there's Colonel Naismith and Mr. Winterbough plodding along
on their horses fifty yards ahead of the rest. Mr. Winterbough's
horse showed poorly next to the colonel's thoroughbred, just a runty
pony sprinkled with black and white and brown with a shaggy mane
that hung in his eyes and a tail that's all over knots. I reined in a
little way behind, then the colonel looked back and seen me and
waved me to come ahead, so I rode up alongside them and he says:

"Well, youngster, how does it feel to be heading west?"

"It feels mighty fine, sir. I never went further west than the Mississippi before in my life. I'm from Illinois."

"How many of your family are with you?" he asks.

"Just my aunt on my ma's side, Mrs. Ambrose, and our nigger
Goliath."

"You mean there are no adult men with you?" he says, looking
concerned.

"No, sir, unless you count Goliath. He's full growed."

"What is your name?"

"Jeff Trueblood, sir."

"Well, Jeff Trueblood, the weight of responsibility must rest upon
your young shoulders for the duration of the journey. You must play
the part of a man and render your aunt every assistance."

"Yessir, that's what I figured when we started out. I'm all prepared for it."

"You have the right spirit," he says. "The way ahead is fraught
with dangers both anticipated and unforeseen, and we will all need
stout hearts and steady hands to win through, but with God's help
we will surely do it. Mr. Winterbough, I shall ride back along the
train to see if there are any teething troubles. Good day to you,
young Trueblood," he says polite, even if I ain't but a boy, then
turned his horse and gallops away.

I rode along with Mr. Winterbough awhile and he never spoke a
word, just smoked his pipe and spit occasional at the ground. Finally he says:

"Mighty fine rifle you got there."

"Thank you. It's a Hawken."

"Mine too," he says, then a few hundred yards on he follows up
with: "There ain't finer than a Hawken."

"Yessir."

"Don't call me sir. I ain't no gentleman."

"No, sir, Mr. Winterbough."

"No need to call me that neither. I got give Thaddeus for a name."

He coughed a little and spit a gob and I seen he's got as many spaces between his teeth as a picket fence, and them that's left is all snaggled and brown. It felt like we was almost to the Rockies before he spoke up again. He's the silentest man I ever come across outside of a deaf and dumb person. He says:

"That rifle of your'n has got a familiar look to it."

"Yessir . . . Thaddeus. It's the same as you got. I recollect discussing it a few mile back."

"I mean I seen that very one before. Give it over so's I can see her good, if you don't mind."

I handed her across and he looked at the stock, going straight for the little letters carved there, and nods his head.

"I knowed her soon as I seen her. This here gun was Jed Frazer's."

"Is that someone you're acquainted with?" says I.

"Was," he says. "He's been dead a fair number of years."

"How did he come to die?"

"Crows," he says.

"Pecked to death?" I ask.

"Crow Injuns, boy, the hostilest there is."

"Why?"

"That's just their way. Some Injuns is friendly and some's hostile. Take Mandans f'rinstance. They're right glad to see a white man generally. They'll feed him and trade with him and be glad of his company, but Crows is different. They just hate to see a white face in their territory."

"Are we going to pass through there?"

"Nope, a ways south. Jed and me was up in Crow country after beaver back in 'thirty-six. Skinned a heap of 'em."

"Crows?"

"Beaver. Crows skin *you* if they catch you settin' traps. That's what happened to Jed, catched and skinned. He was alive at the time. Heard him clear across the Rockies. Had a powerful setter lungs."

"Did you try and rescue him?"

"Nope. Too risky."

He never give no excuse for it the way a man that felt guilty would of done, and I seen that Thaddeus is the kind of man that only says the truth no matter what. Says I:

"And you never seen his gun again from that day to this?"

"Nope. Must of passed through a heap of hands these last few years. Where'd you get her?"

"Off a gunsmith in St. Joe. Forty dollars."

"Worth every cent," he says. "I know for certain that there rifle accounted for three grizzly bears, two wolves, a panther, a couple dozen deer and a handful of Crows too. If it ain't been stomped on meantime she'll throw a ball true across a quarter mile."

He give her back to me and we rode on awhile, then he says:

"This aunt of your'n, is she a sensible woman?"

"I reckon so. She don't go in for fancy thinking."

"She ain't brung no tables and chairs and picture frames along?"

"Nothing like that, just supplies."

"I seen some of the truck these people got with 'em. Practickly a whole houseful. They'll heave it away later on. They always do. You take the pioneers now, they ended up with nothin' but their plows and seed left aboard."

"Did you guide them too?"

"I done it just one time. The fur trade went downhill when beaver hats warn't the fashion no more. There was a heap of mountain men without no livelihood after that, and some took to guiding green- horns west. Others went back east and some stayed put and done their best to turn into Injuns theirselfs, but it ain't easy."

"Why? I reckon it must be a real simple thing to do, living like Injuns."

"You ain't ever tried it. You can marry an Injun woman or just live with her and give her sprouts, but it don't make you Injun. You can't be what you ain't. A white man don't get satisfaction from just living simple like the Injuns. There's something inside of white men that don't allow it. Likely they'll set up a trading post way out yonder just so they still got connections with other whites. A white man can't let well enough alone wherever he's at. He's just got to change things to please himself. If a man jumped high enough to reach the moon the first thing he'd do is set up a trading post and do business with the moon people. A white man can't be no Injun. I know, I give it a try. That's how come I done guiding for the settlers back in 'forty-two."

"What happened between then and now?"

"Nothin' I care to speak of," he says, and went quiet again. It's clear he's talked himself out for now so I went back to Mrs. Ambrose's wagon. She seen me coming and hollers:

"You! Jeff Trueblood! Don't you go galloping the flesh off that horse!"

"I warn't, ma'am."

"Don't you lie. I seen you going by like the devil was behind you. That animal's got to carry you two thousand mile, so don't you run him to lather like that."

"Yes, ma'am, I'll walk him all the way from now on."

The colonel never let us stop to cook up food around noon, and says we ain't going to do it any other day neither. It wasted time to stop and light fires and such, and the whole train has to get the habit of eating cold food through the day. I warn't bothered at all. I never et no hot lunch outside of the widow's house so it just seemed natural to go without, but there was plenty that grumbled. It's the first lesson in getting toughened up for the trail.

The sun dipped ahead of us as the day wore on and slid down the sky toward evening. The colonel called a halt and the lead wagon turned in a wide circle and the others followed on. Pretty soon the lead oxen was nose to tail with the businessman in the light rig that wants to be first in line. Well, he was mighty close, and you could even say he's ahead of the rest, but he never looked happier for it. When all the wheels stopped turning there's a circle two hundred yards across. The teams got unhitched and gathered inside so no Injuns can sneak up and steal them, but there ain't going to be Injuns for miles yet, someone says; it's only for practice.

Campfires got lit here and there and it was real friendly with folks stood around jawing and cooking and enjoying the adventure of it all. After I filled up on food I strolled around smoking my pipe and feeling peaceful, then there's a voice from behind a wagon and it froze me dead in my boots.

"Hello, Huckleberry."

I spun around and there's Grace with a tight little smile on her face and firewood she's fetched under one arm.

"Why, hello yourself," says I, swallering smoke and hacking it up again till my eyes flooded.

"You act surprised to see me," she says.

"Well, I'll admit to it. How'd you come to be here?"

"No thanks to you," she says, snippy. "You were about as much help in getting away as a club foot. That was a feeble thing, running off just when I was ready to go too."

"It warn't my fault, Grace, honest. Mordecai went and woke everyone up. I done my best. What happened after we went?"

"It was awful funny. Uncle Mordecai's hair burned off before Pa could roll him on the ground and smother the fire. His head's all over blisters and he has to wear a bandage full of poultice till it's mended. He swears it was the devil set fire to him, and he says you're Satan's imp that was sent to tempt him. I was so furious with you for running off I nearly told about you being a murderer. Don't look at me that way. I never did it, and you can thank me for it to make up for the betrayal."

"Thank you, Grace," says I, wanting to keep on the right side of her. "What happened then? Did you sneak off?"

"Not till next day. Pa saw I was fixing to do just that, with my clothes and bag and everything, so he locked me up and says he won't feed me till I told the whole story. He knew there was something strange about you when he found out you paid Mr. Trask in bills instead of coin, but he was waiting to see just what it was, and he wanted me to give him the truth. Well, I wasn't about to tell that old hypocrite a word, so I just stayed in the wagon all day without eating a bite. Then I heard Chastity playing outside and I whispered to her to unlock the door. Silly old Pa went and left the key in the lock, and she had it open that instant. I just picked up my bag and ran. Ma saw me and let out a yell, but I'm the fastest runner in the family. I stayed off the road for awhile just in case Pa came after me on horseback, then I walked all the way to St. Joe. I never needed your help after all," she says, kind of scornful and superior.

"I'm glad you got away, Grace, truly. Which one's your wagon?"

"That one over there. It's a real boneshaker. I never knew Pa's wagons were sprung till I rode in that old rattletrap."

"Who owns it?"

"Mr. and Mrs. Shaughnessy. He used to be a printer till he sold his press and shop to join the rush. Mrs. Shaughnessy is none too happy about it. She wanted to stay behind but he made her come. If I had of been her I would of run off from him years ago, he's so stupid and boring and full of himself. Still, I never met a man that wasn't."

"Me neither," says I, still wanting to keep her sweet.

"She's taking her revenge, though, pretending to be sick. She lies on a mattress in the wagon and every time it goes over a bump she groans and says her insides are being shook out of place. She never lets up, just keeps on and on at him about how they should never have left home. She'll nag him clear to California. Who are you with?"

I told her about Mrs. Ambrose and she says:

"You're lucky. I saw you riding up and down on your horse. I wish I had one so I could get away from Mrs. Shaughnessy's tongue. She's driving me to distraction."

"I reckon you can borrow him from time to time," says I.

"I should just hope so. After all, I know something that's worth a thousand dollars."

"You do? What is it?"

"Why, the secret about who you are, you little idiot, what else?"

"But I'm only worth five hundred."

"Not any more. Didn't you see the posters that went up in St. Joe the day before we left? The reward got doubled. You're mighty valuable for someone so skinny."

"I can show you the horse right now, Grace. You can pat him and feed him a sugar lump."

"Don't think you can get around me that easy, Huckleberry Finn. I'll call in the debt whenever I please and not before. You just better be nice to me, that's all."

"Anything you say, Grace."

If she got me any more under the thumb I would of had a hole in the top of my skull, but there ain't nothing I can do except smile and be polite. Tom Sawyer says a woman with a grudge against you is a fearful thing and you got to be careful how you tread. Maybe if I'm lucky she'll fall off the wagon and get squashed by the wheels. Says I:

"How did you come to be with the Shaughnessys?"

"Mr. Shaughnessy hired me for a dollar a week to tend his wife, even if he knows she's not truly ailing."

"If he knows, then it's a pure waste of money. It don't make sense."

"Oh, yes it does," she says, patting her hair into shape. "He never intended to hire a nursemaid, but when I came along, why, he just changed his mind."

"But why?"

"Oh, fiddlesticks. Can't you guess? Are you stupider than you look? He thinks I'm pretty is why. I just had to bat my eyes a little and he made me an offer on the spot, just like I knew he would. Men are so predictable. Mrs. Shaughnessy never liked the idea at first, but then I sung her a song and looked all innocent the way Ma taught me and she says how sweet I am and I can sing her to sleep at night so she won't feel the pain in her gizzard. They're both so blockheaded. Still, it's the only way I'll ever get to California."

"I reckon I'll be getting back now," says I. "They'll be expecting me."

"Well you just run along like a good little boy, but don't forget I'm watching you. If you play any mean tricks like the last time I'll tell all. Maybe I'll tell all anyway, I just haven't made up my mind," she says.

"Did I tell you before how pretty your hair is, Grace? It's a real picture."

"I know it is, now scat, you little judge-murderer."

And I did, all meek and humble and doggish. It made me squirm inside to do it, but when your leg's in a bear trap you got to walk with a limp. I hunted out Jim and give him the details and his face went all slack.

"She de las' person we needs on dis trip, Huck. We ain't goin' to get no peacer mind wid dat girl aroun' our necks. Someone put a hex on us for sure. Das de onlies' way I kin figure we gettin' so mucher de bad luck."

"What do you know about hexing, Jim? Maybe we could put one on Grace to make her drop dead or get struck by lightning."

"I knows a fair amount I reckon. Dere was a conjure woman I knowed one time an' de niggers was all scareder her on accounter she had a tame crow sat all de time on her shoulder, an' was uglier'n sin too."

"Well, crows ain't generally held to be handsome except to other crows."

"De woman de ugly one, Huck. De crow was a mighty fine bird, de bigges' I ever seen, an' he talked some too."

"What kind of things did he say?"

"I rec'llect he was pow'ful fonder sayin' 'Pass de peas,' an' 'Sweep de flo',' an' suchlike."

"That don't sound too devilish to me, Jim."

"I reckon he got it off'n de woman when she's givin' her husban' orders aroun' de house. He was all de time watchin' his step so's she never put a hex on him an' turn him into a cockroach, or maybe a bat. He was de miserablest man I ever seen. It don' do no good to marry a conjure woman, Huck. Dis one done run her man downter a shadder."

"But what did you learn off her?"

"Dere was a time I had a bad pain in de belly an' she tol' me how to get it fixed. You got to take a leaf off'n a willer tree das hangin' over still water, an' a blader grass das been stomped on by a bull, an' a wood splinter from a house where someone died jest recent, an' a hunker beeswax from a tree das got two forks, an' you ties it all up in a hair off'n a virgin's head, den you puts it under your piller an' sleeps on it."

"Did it work?"

"It sure did, Huck. I slep' wid dat charm five nights an' de pain went away."

"Well Grace don't have a bellyache that I know of. What we need is a hex that'll give her one so bad she dies of it. Can you remember anything like that?"

He rubbed his hand along his jaw and the beard he's growed rasped away, then he says:

"She tol' me one time de certaintest way to kill a body outside of a gun or axe is to get holder a piecer cloth from de person you want dead's shirt or britches, an' a coupler hairs off de head, an' jest a smidgin of shit dey dropped, an' you mix de turd an' de hair wid clay an' make a doll, den you wraps de cloth aroun' it an' say de spell an' poke a pine needle in it an' bury it on de nex' full moon."

"I reckon it's possible to do all that, but the turd's a problem. Does the spell work without it?"

"It's de prime section, Huck. You got to get holder some."

"Well, I'll work on it and get the rest meantime. Do you recollect the words to the spell?"

"Le's see now. . . . It's comin' to me. . . .

> *Doller clay, doller hair*
> *Make your owner soon beware*
> *Shinin' moon, full an' bright*
> *Kill dis man at dead of night"*

"We'll do it soon as we can, Jim. I don't trust Grace not to tell. She's awful changeable and contrary."

"You sure you wants to do it, Huck? I reckon it's murder."

"No it ain't. Where in the Bible does it say 'Ye shall not hex a body to death'?"

"Nowheres I kin rec'llect."

"Well there you are."

"It do say 'Thou ain't allowed to do de killin'.' "

"So it does, but *we* won't be doing no killing, Jim. It's the hex that'll do it for us."

"If you reckon so, Huck."

"It's her or us as I see it. Don't the Bible say 'Thou shall not allow thyself to be delivered into the hands of thine enemies'?"

"Do it? I don' rightly know dat piece."

"Well it's in there somewhere, and if I had a Bible I'd look it up for you. I never killed the judge and I got to protect myself."

That night the bulldog come chomping his way into my dreams again.

11

The train got settled into ways that never changed from one day to the next. Get up at dawn, cook breakfast, hitch the teams and travel all day except for a break around noon, but you kept the teams hitched while you fed and watered them a little, then on again till near dusk, pull the wagons into a circle, unhitch, feed and water, gather in dead brushwood for fires, feed yourselfs, talk some, then sleep. It was godawful dull. Colonel Naismith worked out a schedule for guard duty to get the men used to it by the time we reached Injun territory, which is any day now. Thaddeus says they'll be Pawnee hereabouts, and most likely friendly, but the colonel says we got to be prepared anyway.

All the while I planned for the hex doll, and it was hard work. First I got the hair, which was the easy part. I just stayed around Grace in the evenings till she got used to me being there like a faithful dog, which is how she treated me anyhow, and one night I said her hair is looking kind of snaggled and dirty and she got huffy and took out her brush and give it a good going over till it shone. Then when she was putting ribbons in it, I snitched a few hairs out of the brush behind her back and shoved them in my pocket.

The piece of dress was harder, but I figured a way. I knowed now what time the Shaughnessys went to bed, and what time Mrs. Shaughnessy finally quit using her mouth for talking and just used it to snore through, about an hour later generally. I had to wait till it's all silent and safe. Grace slept in the tail end of their wagon behind a blanket partition Shaughnessy set up for the sake of maidenly modesty, as he puts it. What I done was I hooked a pair of shears out of Mrs. Ambrose's sewing box and snuck through the camp and climbed up into the back of the Shaughnessy wagon quiet as an Injun, which Thaddeus says don't make no sound at all when they're fixing to sneak into the enemy camp.

The tailboard creaked some when I hauled myself up and over it, then I'm inside and stood over Grace, only it's so dark in there I never seen a thing, only heard her breathing. I felt around careful so's I don't wake her, then I can feel dress material under my fingers and whipped out the shears and cut off a chunk. There still ain't no sound except for Grace breathing and the Shaughnessys snoring over the other side of the blanket. Then I snuck out again and went back to our wagon and whispered to Jim I got the stuff we needed.

"Das good, Huck," he whispers back. "Now we halfway done an' only needs de clay an' de turd. You figured a way to get it yet?"

"I been thinking on that, Jim, and I reckon we got to make do with horse or oxen turd. It ain't dignificated to mess with the human kind."

Jim says he ain't sure the hex works without the genuine makings but he's agreeable, and next day I stole a handkerchief off Mrs. Ambrose and got a pile of oxen flop and took it down into a little gully to mix it up with clay and dirt. I rolled it into a ball and tied all of it in the handkerchief, then stuck it in the back of the wagon and waited for night to come.

About the time everyone went to sleep Jim and me snuck off with the handkerchief, which was round and heavy as a cannonball. We took it away from the train past the guards strolling around and off over a rise. The moon was three-quarters full so there's plenty of light to see what we was doing, and I untied the knot and rolled out the turdball.

"Well, Jim, there it is. Just you go ahead and make the doll and I'll keep a lookout."

He sniffed and looked at it kind of doubtful and says:

"I reckon you got more cleverness in de han's, Huck. You kin make it."

"That ain't right, Jim. It was your idea in the first place."

"No it warn't, Huck. It was you sayin' we got to put de hex on Grace."

"But we never would of had the chance if you hadn't of remembered the mixture and the words."

"Dere's somethin' else, Huck. I been meanin' to tell you de las' few days now. I'se startin' to get de rheumatiz in my han's. Dey gettin' to be awful hard to move. I cain't hardly ben' my fingers at all. See here," he says, and shows his hands all clawed up like a dead bird's and knocked them together like they was made of wood.

I seen there warn't nothing for it but to make the doll myself, so I set to and begun it before I had a change of mind. It never took but a little while. I mixed the hair in with the rest and there she was, legs and arms and everything, only the head's kind of small so it looked more like Chastity than Grace, but Jim says it don't matter. We wrapped the cloth around it, then come the needle sticking part. There warn't no pine trees in hundreds of miles so we used a knitting needle I snuck out of Mrs. Ambrose's sewing box. Then it was done, all except for the burying at full moon which is two days off yet. It's the ugliest, stinkingest doll you could ever see, and I wrapped it up careful in the handkerchief.

After I wiped my hands clean on grass we headed back to the wagons, but when we're still a ways out there come a challenge out of the dark.

"Halt! Who's that out there?" hollers a guard.

We never wanted to get catched with the doll so we ducked low and run for the train.

"Halt!" he yells again, and followed up with a shot. I felt the ball go humming past my head and heard it smack against one of the wagons, then there's people yelling and more shots and general noisification through the whole camp. Men come tumbling out of the wagons in their nightshirts with guns in their hands, all wanting to know who's attacking us. By then Jim and me was inside the circle and just mingled in with the rest. I grabbed a man by the arm and say:

"Is it Injuns? Oh, Lord, I'm scared. . . ."

He flung me off and aimed his rifle out into the dark, where there's voices calling in all directions wanting to know who fired the first shot, and we snuck away under our wagon to let them argue it out between them. We got our own problem, which is where to hide the doll till the time come to use her. Inside the wagon is no good on

account of the smell, so we wrapped it around in bunches of grass
and tied it to the axletree underneath. Then Mrs. Ambrose stepped
down and she's got my Hawken in her hands.

"What's all the ruckus?" she says.

"Injun attack I reckon, ma'am," says I.

"Well what are you hiding under the wagon for? Here's your gun,
go kill a couple."

"Yes, ma'am, I'll do it directly."

I took the Hawken and pointed it out into the dark like the others
was doing, but it never satisfied her.

"Don't just lay there," she says. "Go on out and get 'em, sneaking
heathens."

"It's safer this way, Mrs. Ambrose ma'am."

She give a snort that says I'm a coward and got herself armed and
ready with the frying pan, all set to sell her life dear if the Injuns
take a run at us. We stayed like that till the guards finally settled it
warn't nothing but a wild animal that started the scare, and everyone went back to bed with a lot of cussing about trigger-happy
guards that's blind in one eye and deaf in one ear. Jim and me fixed
our bedding so our feet was close to the doll and not our noses and
pretty soon was asleep.

Next morning after the train was rolling for awhile I reined in and
let it pass by till the last man in line come along, and he's still miserable about it. This time he give me his name, which is Connelly,
and he started in moaning again same as before, but I only give him
half an ear on account of when I looked back along the trail I seen
there's men on horseback following us. The country was wide and
open without trees, just runty brush here and there, so I seen clear
for miles. The riders was still a fair distance off, too far to tell if
they're Injuns or white. Mr. Connelly seen where I'm looking and
spied them too and went all pale, changing fast from his usual color
which is red.

"Is it Injuns?" he says, his voice all shaky.

"I can't rightly tell," says I. "I best let the colonel know."

I give my horse some heel, and off I headed for the front of the
train, just cantering, but when I turned around I seen Mr. Connelly
whipping his horse and following along quickish behind me and
yelling loud as he can:

"Injuns! Injuns behind us!"

He flied past me like the wind and the people in every wagon he passed got scared too and swung out of line and whipped up the teams and joined in till there's thirty or more all rushing along. I had to get out of the way or get stampeded over in the rush, then I kicked my horse into full gallop and passed all of them again, and got to the front of the train just in time to see Mr. Connelly's buggy hit a rock with one wheel and go bouncing off sideways and flip right over. The shafts snapped and he got flung through the air and come down in a tangled heap while the horse dashed on past where Colonel Naismith and Thaddeus was reined in and looking back to see what all the noise is. The colonel's jaw dropped a mile when he seen the way everyone is racing to get away from the end of the train and he pulled out his pistol and fired in the air a few times, but it never stopped a thing. The wagons kept right on going past him, at least half the train by now, and they kept going all of three miles till the teams got winded and brung it all to a halt.

I give the colonel my story about the riders following behind and how Mr. Connelly started things off. He fumed and raged at the stupidness and sent Thaddeus off to fetch them back, then rode along the first half of the train that's still in place telling everyone not to panic. Mr. Connelly's arm was broke and he's howling with the pain of it, but the colonel just ignored him and we went on back to where we can see the riders. He pulled out a telescope and trained it on them and says:

"White men, about a dozen I should say. God's teeth, what a shambles! You have witnessed a perfect example of herd instinct. Take note, my boy, and never ally yourself with any kind of mob when faced with a crisis, real or imaginary. A mob will inevitably worsen any situation by their behavior."

It took an hour to get the wagons back in line, and after it got done the colonel called a meeting and tonguewhipped everyone that panicked and laid into them so hard they hung their heads. He never mentioned Mr. Connelly by name, but he made it clear who was to blame for the whole thing and says if "the person responsible" tries to load the blame off onto Jeff Trueblood then that person would be a liar, because Jeff Trueblood acted alert and sensible over the whole business. It was enough to make a body blush.

When the riders that begun it all reached us it turned out they're just gold rushers the same as us, only they can't be bothered trailing along slow with wagons and lit out with just horses. The colonel had his dander up by then and called them fools to their faces for starting out with no supplies and says he won't be surprised if we find their corpses one day dead of hunger or killed by Injuns. They took it all good-natured and say they aim to be the first forty-niners to reach California overland. That's what the newspapers back east are calling the rushers now, forty-niners. They say they passed other trains behind us and all of them has got cholera striking people down, and there's cholera back in St. Joseph too, which is where it started. It's heading west along with the trains, which is another reason these men never wanted to join up with one. The news spread fast and you could see the fear on people's faces when they heard of it, and everyone backed away from the riders like they was covered in cholera too. Some even pointed guns and told them to keep their distance, so they moved on.

After they left the colonel had to give another speech about not panicking.

"The cholera is behind us," he says. "So long as we keep moving and maintain distance from those following behind there is no reason why the contagion should spread to our train."

"What about them that just passed through?" says someone. "They might have given it to us already."

"They seemed hale and hearty enough to me," says the colonel. "They did not dismount, and no one here laid a hand on them. I believe we can consider our train safe. I say to you once again we must keep calm no matter what dangers face us. Now that it is essential we preserve our lead over the other wagons, there must be no more delays such as the one that has occurred today. We are one hour behind schedule, therefore one hour closer to those stricken with the disease."

That sent everyone scurrying back to their wagons and we moved off again, but not before Mr. Connelly's rig got broke up into firewood. Some kindly folks give him a ride in their wagon and a man who was a horse doctor set his arm in splints, and the splints was made from pieces of the busted rig, which struck some as mighty funny. His horse was rounded up and tied behind and I told him soon as he's able he can use Jim's saddle to ride with. He never thanked me for the offer, just glared like it's all my fault. Some people is just naturally mean-spirited.

The train kept moving later than usual to make up for time lost and we had to gather brushwood in the dark. I come across Grace doing the same as me and asked how things was with her. She says:

"Mrs. Shaughnessy thinks she's got cholera already, silly old biddy. Mr. Shaughnessy thinks she's got bats in the belfry. Just yesterday she says someone cut a piece out of one of her dresses she keeps in the back of the wagon, but it's obvious she did it herself when her mind was unhinged. I have to sing her to sleep every night and she always wants to hear 'Abide with Me,' nothing else. It's just so awful living with them. I think I'll try and find someone else to share a wagon with."

She rattled on about how Mr. Shaughnessy keeps making sheep's eyes at her and touching her hair and such, but I warn't truly listening. If the cloth we used was from Mrs. Shaughnessy's dress and not Grace's, maybe the hex is bound to fail. It was bothersome. Then Grace says:

"What do you want to be when you grow up?"

"I ain't given it no deep consideration yet. Maybe a sea captain if I find enough gold to buy a ship."

"Oh, pooh," she says. "That's what all boys want. Don't you have anything original in your head?"

"I reckon not, if that's how you put it. How about you, Grace?"

"I want to be rich. I want to have diamonds and emeralds and rubies and pearls all heaped up in a bathtub of gold with little lions' feet underneath, and I wouldn't ever bathe again, just wash myself with precious stones the rest of my life."

"That's original all right," says I. "How do you aim to get it?"

"I don't know yet, but it'll have to be through men, since men have got all the money in the world. I guess I'll have to marry a rich man."

"But you told me you never even *liked* men, never mind marrying one."

"Don't be such a sap-head. You don't have to like someone to get married to them. It's all a kind of arrangement. Men want you for something and you want them for something. You just have to tolerate not liking each other for the sake of what you want. It's what sivilization is all about, and if you were older and smarter you'd see the sense in it."

"I thought you wanted to be virgin again this side of the Missouri."

"And so I am," she says. "At least until I find a rich man, then he can pop my cherry after the wedding. He'll never know I'm not a true virgin. Ma passed me off as a virgin for close on two years. It's all just acting."

I reckon Grace's cherry must of been popped so many times if they was laid nose to tail it would of sounded like a string of firecrackers. She had mighty fanciful ideas did Grace, and it's kind of interesting to listen to her, but she ain't trustable so she's got to be struck down by lightning. It's a shame, and I hope she don't feel no pain when it happens.

When I got back to the wagon, Mrs. Ambrose was scratching around inside and looking vexed.

"Drat that pesky smell. Where *is* it coming from? Jeff Trueblood, your eyes are younger than mine. Climb in here and see if you can't find something bad that's making it so odorsome."

It's the turd-clay doll smell coming up through the boards from where we stashed it. I clumb in and sniffed and it was ripe and prime, but I say:

"There ain't nothing in here smells bad, ma'am. The supplies is mostly drygoods that don't turn bad except for the bacon. Did you take a sniff of it?"

"Of course I did. It ain't that at all. Are you sure you can't smell something . . . well, like you can get on your shoe?"

"On my shoe, ma'am?"

"Dogs," she says. "Cattle. You know what I mean."

"I don't believe I ever stepped on any livestock, ma'am. My feet don't lift up that high."

"Don't play the fool with me. I'm talking about dung."

"Dung, ma'am? You can smell dung?"

"A power of it."

"Well, it ain't surprising. There's hundreds of animals right outside."

"This is inside. Are you sure you can't smell nothing?"

"No, ma'am, it smells right nice."

"Fetch the nigger in here. They got keener noses than whites."

So I went and fetched Jim and he went in the wagon and sniffed and says there ain't no smell as he can see, and it made Mrs. Ambrose madder than ever.

"There's got to be a reason for it," she snaps. "Go under the wagon and look."

"We already spread our blankets under there, ma'am, and we never smelt nothing."

"Well look again."

So we done it, acting the part, and say there ain't nothing under there. But she warn't satisfied and wanted to fetch a neighbor in to sniff around. Says I:

"Is that wise, ma'am? If they *do* smell something it means they'll figure you ain't houseproud, and if they *don't* smell nothing, why, then they'll think . . . no, I better not say it."

"Say what? What are you hiding, boy?"

"Nothing, ma'am. I just don't want to upset you. Please forget I ever mentioned it."

"Mentioned what, for gosh sakes? Do I have to beat it out of you?"

"It's something I daresn't speak out loud, ma'am, not with other wagons so close."

"Well whisper it then, only quit mystifying. It gives me the irrits."

"It's . . . well, you made me say it, ma'am. It's disease."

"Disease? What's disease? Stop talking riddles."

"Smelling things that ain't there, ma'am. It's the first symptom. My Uncle Silas is a doctor and he seen a case once, but it's mighty rare. Only one in ten thousand gets it, he says, and he's a disease expert with a sign on the wall to prove it."

"Symptom? . . ." she says, looking worried.

"Yes, ma'am, the first symptom of the worst disease there is."

"Not . . . cholera?"

"No, ma'am, worse. Bubolitis."

"Bubolitis? . . ."

"I reckon so, but there ain't no need to worry. Some folks get over it without losing hardly any parts of their body, but them that gets the full measure of diseasification, well . . . they're better off dead. There ain't much point in being alive if your legs and arms has all fell off."

"Fell off? . . ."

"Yes, ma'am. They just wither away like old fruit and drop right off. First it's the fingers and toes, then the whole limb. But it ain't fatal, even when it's bad as it can get. Why, there was one man who lived to be ninety-three, and he was struck down by bubolitis before he was thirty. They just fixed him up with a baby's pushcart and trundled him around to see the sights and he was happy as can be. Maybe that's on account of it does considerable harm to the brain too. There was cruel people who reckoned this man warn't nothing short of a total idiot, but Uncle Silas says it warn't so. He never dribbled and drooled from idiotness, just had trouble feeding himself without no arms. It all began with him smelling bad smells that warn't there, ma'am, but look on the bright side. It ain't catching, so you won't give it to no one else. Do you still want us to look for something rotten?"

"No," she says, "just tie the flap back and let some air in."

I done it and she give a twitching kind of smile and says:

"There now, that's better. Why, the smell's practickly gone already, in fact it warn't nearly as bad as I figured. I just can't abide smells is all. Well, it's gone at last and we can get some sleep."

"Yes, ma'am. Goodnight."

Me and Jim bedded down with the blankets over our faces to keep out the stink, and before we nodded off we heard Mrs. Ambrose saying her prayers long and loud, which is something she never done before.

12

We was jumpy all next day on account of tonight is the full moon when we bury the doll and say the spell and wait for the lightning. It made us feel just awful. I turned it over and over in my mind about Grace. She ain't the nice person I judged her to be first off, but then she ain't the worst person in the world neither. There's Pap for one that's way ahead of her; she's a saint alongside of him. But if I don't act like her slave, she'll spill the news about Huck Finn. I was in two minds over the whole thing, but what decided me was the way she treated me that very day. I come riding along the train and passed the Shaughnessy wagon where Grace is sat up front between them, and she called me over and give me a smile and says:

"Jeff, I've got a powerful yearning for a bunch of flowers to pin on my dress. Would you be so kind as to fetch me some?"

Mr. Shaughnessy give me a mean look, jealous I reckon.

"Flowers?" says I. "Where?"

"I'm sure I don't know," she says, smiling still. "Just you trot along and find me some like a good boy."

"But there ain't any. It's all grass and nothing but."

She give a little pout and says peevish:

"I'll be ever so upset if I don't get a sweet little posy before sundown. *Ever* so."

"Well, I'll try," says I, and off I galloped.

I galloped here and I galloped there and then I galloped back again, but there warn't no flowers except little budding things that ain't opened out yet. Thaddeus was at the head of the line same as always so I ask him about it and he says:

141

"Too soon. Maybe in a week or so. What you want with flowers anyway? You got a sweetheart?"

"No, but I got to have the flowers urgent."

"Well you can't have 'em, and nor can she. Whyn't you give her a kiss instead?"

"She ain't the kissing type."

"Never fool with a woman that ain't the kissing type," he says. "She'll make your life a pure misery. You can get more joy out of a rock than a woman that don't like to kiss."

Two mile further on he says:

"You can believe me because I done it."

"Done what?"

"Fooled with that kind. But only the once. A moron might do it twice."

"What happened when you fooled with her?"

"Nothin'. Then we got hitched. Nothin' happened after, neither. You take my advice and point your affections somewheres else. Whose idea was these flowers, hers or your'n?"

"Hers, I reckon."

"Well tell her to look for 'em herself, and when she finds 'em she can eat 'em."

"She won't take kindly to getting told that."

"It ain't none of my business. You do what you want."

Awhile later he says:

"You got wide experience of women, boy?"

"I reckon not."

"Well you're young still. Sooner or later you'll get the call and won't know which way to turn. If I was you I'd turn in the direction of dusky maidens."

"You mean Injuns?"

"That's who I mean all right."

"Do Injuns kiss and such?"

"They ain't discovered kissing, that's a white custom, but they do everything else besides. You find yourself a young one that ain't all run to fat, and she'll work you till you're trimmed down to nothing and won't have the strength to swat a fly."

"Did you find one like that, Thaddeus?"

"I surely did. How old would you say I am?"

"I don't rightly know. Maybe forty."

"Well I ain't. I'm twenty-three. This Injun gal run me ragged and aged me overnight, but I never regretted it."

"That's just amazifying," says I. Then: "How old would you say I am?"

"You? I reckon around eighty-five or -six."

Dang him, he stole my joke right out from under me. He's sly, is Thaddeus. I never had the bravery to go back to Grace without no flowers, and after we made camp I slunk around in the shadows feeling jittery and low, but she found me anyhow.

"Where are the flowers?" she wants to know.

"There warn't any. They ain't in bloom yet."

"I call that a mighty poor showing, Huckleberry Finn."

"Pardon me, Grace, would you mind not talking so loud. I'm Jeff Trueblood."

"You're Huckleberry Finn that's got a thousand dollars on his head for murder and other criminal things."

"I know, but it's our secret, ain't it?"

"For now it is," she says, all breezy and stuck up. "The trouble is, I'm just hopeless at keeping secrets from my friends."

"I'm the only friend you got, Grace."

"Well aren't you just the ignorantest little boy. It so happens I made a new friend today."

"Who?"

"None of your business, but I'll tell you this much, you're not fit to lick his boots."

"I warn't aiming to. He can lick 'em himself."

"Sometimes I think you're a pain, Huck Finn. Yes indeed, you give me a pain right in the belly."

Thinks I, it's the needle we poked through the hex doll. It's already working and we ain't even buried it under the full moon yet. I reckon when we speak the spell over it she's going to get considerable more pain than she's got.

"I'm real sorry to hear it, Grace," says I, looking concerned. "Can I get you some castor oil to fix it?"

"No, you can't. Just remove yourself from my sight," she says, lifting her nose like the Queen of Sherbert.

"If that's what you want, Grace, I'll do it and feel gratified."

After that we went our different ways. It was just humilerating the way she made me eat crow, but I took comfort from the full moon riding along above the camp.

Later there was a jamboree around the fires. Everyone that brung an insterment along with them hauled it out and strummed or squeezed or sawed away at it full strength. It warn't the best music I ever heard, but it's good and loud and folks started dancing. There's only one woman to every thirty or so men and them that's female never got a minute's peace, even Mrs. Ambrose. They was flung around in circles till they dropped, then the men danced with each other till the music players dropped. Then Grace stood up on a barrel and sung "In the Sweet Bye and Bye." It brung a lump to the throat and a tear to the eye. Then she done a couple more songs, her voice just as sweet and lovely as can be till the water run down their faces in floods and there warn't a man there that never fell in love with her for being so saintly and pure. It was the funniest sight I ever seen. Even Mr. Connelly disremembered his broke arm and blubbered away with the rest, so you can see how powerful a distraction Grace is. Well, her days was numbered.

Later still when it got quiet again we untied the doll from under the wagon and took it away, which proberly made Mrs. Ambrose give a special thank you to God for saving her from bubolitis now the smell is gone. We snuck past the guards and went a little way off to bury it. Jim brung along a shovel and I picked a spot and he dug a hole, then we took the doll out of the handkerchief and laid it to rest a couple of feet down. I shoveled dirt over it and patted it down and waited for Jim to say the spell, but he only looked at me queer. Says I:

"What are you waiting for, Jim? Say the spell and we can get some sleep."

"I can't do it, Huck," he says, and hung his head.

"Did you forget the words?"

"I got 'em in my head still, Huck, but I ain't goin' to say 'em."

"Why not? Do you want Grace to tell on us and finish your days on the end of a rope?"

"I don' want dat, Huck, but I reckon we cain't rightly kill Grace jest on accounter she knows 'bout us. It ain't right."

"Well tell me the spell again and I'll do it."

"I ain't goin' to, Huck."

"I can't let her ride roughshod over me no more, Jim. It ain't dignificated. She's got a hold on me she don't deserve to have. I just got to break it or never hold my head up again."

"Das true, Huck, but dis ain't de way to do it. Usin' de hex doll ain't no diff'rent to usin' a knife like dey say you done wid de judge."

I turned it over some and he's right; hexing ain't nothing short of murder like he says. It must of been a panic come over me to even give it consideration, and I was all of a sudden ashamed. You can argue a way around it if you got a way with words, but murder is murder however. If it hadn't of been for Jim I would of gone ahead and allowed Grace to get struck down by the hex and have to live with it the rest of my life. It was a mighty narrow escape.

We dug up the doll and wondered what to do with it. If we stomped on it a wagon might tip over onto Grace and squash her flat, and if we pulled it apart she might fall off a mountain and be shattered all to flinders. Finally we figured we'd let it stay where it is and let the sun and rain break it down gradual. It give me a good feeling to know we spared her life like that, and I pulled out the needle to give Grace relief from the belly pain she reckoned I give her. I felt right noble over the whole thing. There's still the problem of her treating me like a nigger, but I'd give it some ponderation and figure out a way to make her quit without a need for hexing or murder.

We started back to the wagons, then Jim grabbed my arm and pulled me down onto the ground and whispers:

"Someone comin', Huck."

We lay there like logs and along come two people talking low, a man and a woman, and when they was close enough I heard it's Grace herself. They strolled by just a short piece away and we could hear every word.

"You know I'm just seventeen, Hewley," says Grace. "It's awful young to be wed."

"That's no answer," says Hewley. "My own mother was married at fifteen and never regretted it."

"It makes me nervous just to think of," says Grace. "At the orphanage they taught me to lead a life of the spirit, not of the flesh. I never once thought I'd be faced with such a choice as this."

"You mean . . . children?"

"Yes . . ." she says, all modest and shy.

"But that's nothing to be afraid of, Grace. I've been watching you, and in my opinion your hips are made for childbearing."

"Oh really?" she says, going prim. "I'll thank you not to look at my person with such lewdness in your head, Hewley Peterson. I find myself distressed by your unseemly attitude, I really do."

"Please forgive me, Grace," begs Hewley. "I never meant to give offense. I'd sooner bite my tongue off than cause you grief, you know that."

"Well, maybe just this once I'll forgive you, only never let me hear such talk from you again. I was raised to be of delicate disposition with regard to marriage and . . . and things."

"I won't ever mention it again, Grace, only promise me you'll think on what I asked."

"What was it you asked again, Hewley? It's flown right out of my head."

"Don't tease, Grace. I mean about wanting you to marry me. I don't expect an answer straight off, but maybe by the time we reach Fort Kearney you'll make a decision."

"I'll think about it, and that's all I'm promising," she says. "Now you can escort me back."

And away they went. It was hard to credit, and I give my ears a rub to make sure they was still working normal. I got two hot ears and a helping of perplexion out of it.

"Jim," says I, "what kind of game do you reckon Grace is playing at?"

"I don' know, Huck. 'Pears to me she stringin' dat boy along for de pleasure she kin get outer tellin' him no."

"Where's the pleasure in that?"

"Some women likes to do it, Huck. Dey jest loves to get a man all fired up so's dey kin pour ice water on him. Dere ain't no reason for it I kin figure, only devilment an' tricksiness."

Now at least I knowed who her new friend is, and next day rode along with Thaddeus and asked if he heard of someone in the train called Hewley Peterson.

"Peterson," he says, and sucked his teeth some. "There's Petersons I recall on the colonel's list. Father and two sons. Your Hewley might be among 'em."

"Which wagon is theirs?"

"I disremember. Ask the colonel."

So I done just that, and the colonel wants to know why I want to know.

"My Ma's folks was called Peterson," says I. "I just wondered if we're related."

That satisfied him and he says they're somewhere halfway along the train. I rode along and asked at a few wagons and finally hit the right one. There's a man on the seat with a boy around twenty beside him.

"Would you be Mr. Peterson?" I ask.

"I am," he says.

"From Evanstown, Illinois?"

"No, we're from Ohio."

"Oh, I just wondered if you might be related to my Ma's folks."

"Not if she came from anywhere but Ohio. Us Petersons have lived there two generations."

"Then I reckon it's a different family. Evanstown was started by her grandpa on her mother's side, Hewley Evans, and she lived there all her life."

"Hewley, did you say? Why, that's a coincidence. My boy here is called Hewley, but we never heard of Evanstown so that's all it is, coincidence."

"Well, never mind. Thank you, sir."

I only went to all that trouble so's I know what Hewley looks like. Off I rode, and when I passed the Shaughnessy wagon I seen Grace sat on the tailboard with her legs swinging free so you can see her ankles right up to her knees, and there's a man on horseback riding alongside talking to her. They was both smiling at each other and the man give her ankles a look every now and then. Grace seen me and waved so I rode over and joined them, curious as a cat.

"Hello, Jeff," she says, like I'm her favorite brother.

"Hello yourself, Grace," says I with a smile and waited for an introduction, but when it come I had to grab hard with both legs to keep from falling off my horse.

"Jeff, this is a friend of mine, Mr. Peterson."

"Peterson?"

"Duane," he says, and reaches over to shake my hand. The resemblance was there but Duane is bigger and stronger-looking than Hewley, meaner too. I could tell he wanted me to backpaddle and leave them alone but I stayed there trying to figure out what Grace is up to, just jawing about how many miles we come and such, till Grace got impatient and says:

"You run along now, Jeff. Duane and I are talking grownup talk."

"Oh, pardon me, Grace, I never realized. I'll run right along directly."

I told Jim abut it that night and he warn't approving.

"Dat girl runnin' aroun' wid *two* brothers. You reckon dey knows 'bout de other, Huck?"

"I guess not. The Petersons has got just one horse apart from their team and I reckon one or other rides it turn and turn about, and whichever one is on it goes straight to Grace and jaws away, and next day it's his brother that does it, both of them thinking he's the only one she's giving the glad-eye to."

"She cain't keep it goin' forever, Huck. Sooner or later she goin' to make a slip an' de boys come face to face wid Grace in between. Den what she goin' to say?"

"Being acquainted with Grace like I am, I reckon she'll find a way to make out like she's innocent. But wait on, Jim. If she's playing them both against the other, it's something she'll want to keep secret, just like I want her to keep my name secret."

Jim got excited and says:

"Das it, Huck! You kin trade off wid Grace, her secret for your'n! Ain't no way she goin' to blab wid you knowin' 'bout de brothers. Maybe now we kin rest easy."

I hunted up Grace that night to play at being her lapdog like always, but she warn't hardly interested in me no more, so I started spying on her from behind wagons, keeping track of her. It was worth it too, on account of she's romancing both Petersons away from the firelight where no one can see them, only never at the same time. I got to admit I was kind of impressed at the brassy way she done it. She had two kinds of acting, one for each. With Hewley she's a lilywhite maiden that don't piss nothing but springwater and with Duane she let her natural self come up for air, not fornicatering or nothing, but she let him squeeze her real hard and kiss her on the lips. It was downright deceitful but awful clever, like watching a show with actors.

I got my clothes good and dirty sneaking along through the grass to spy on them night after night and Mrs. Ambrose made me stay in the wagon one time while she washed my shirt and britches out, so

I had to stay naked in a blanket till morning and never seen what happened, but it was Hewley's turn.

The days rolled on by and after you got used to the plains the scenery would send you to sleep faster than a Sunday sermon. There warn't nothing to look at but little critturs that lived in holes and would duck out of sight whenever you come near, and what they are is gophers, cute to look at, but once you seen a few hundred you just wanted them to stay in their holes permanent. Thaddeus says they're pesky on account of a horse can put its hoof down a gopher hole and break a leg, but I never seen it happen. And still no Injuns neither. Thaddeus says to me:

"They likely know we're here. Any day now they'll want payment for crossing their land."

"What kind of payment?"

"Just the usual trinkets. They ain't discovered money yet. When they do the price'll go up, you can bet. Injuns always cotton onto white ways in the end, even when it don't do 'em a lick of good. All I ever seen 'em get is hard liquor and pox, and neither one makes an Injun look pretty. But they won't stay away from whites, not by a long haul. A trading post works on 'em like a candle to moths. They'll come from miles around to get them beads and mirrors and such truck, and later on it's whiskey. If they don't have the pelts to pay for it, why, they'll tell their wives to shuck off their clothes and go behind a bush with you. There ain't no shame attached to it for Injuns, but it eats away gradual at a tribe till they're all doing it insteader huntin' and trappin', and pretty soon all the women is whores and the men drunks, and that's the finish of that particular tribe."

"Ain't there a way to stop it?"

"Not unless every white man west of the Missouri goes back home, and that ain't about to happen. Fur trappers opened up the way, and settlers followed on. Now it's forty-niners, and you can't turn back a crowd that's got gold fever. The Injuns' days is numbered for sure. I seen the writing on the wall."

"Does it give you the miseries, Thaddeus?"

He chewed on that awhile, then says:

"I reckon so. Injuns is just as decent as whites, maybe more so, but once they get white ways they ain't Injun no more nor white neither, and they just die. But it ain't just a matter of dead Injuns.

It's the prairie and the mountains too. I ain't a religious man but the hand of God must of made 'em, they're so big, and they warn't ever intended to have humans crawling all over 'em. I seen the land when it was wide open and free just a dozen years back, and already it's ending. They'll dig up the mountains for gold and plow the plains for corn, and pretty soon there'll just be the desert left for a man to find himself in. I hope I die before that time comes around."

He can be mighty grim sometimes, can Thaddeus, but I always come away from him feeling respect. I had it for Colonel Naismith too, but his was the kind that got bred into him from the day he's born and warn't earned like Thaddeus's wisdom which come from experience of life lived way out yonder under the big sky. If I had to take after one or the other I reckon it'd be Thaddeus. He told me about a place in California that's got trees three hundred feet tall and as big around as a house. I never believed him at first but he swore it's so, and after that whenever Thaddeus passed through my mind I seen the trees too, till I never thought of one without the other.

Two days later the Injuns showed, and it was me that seen them first just before noon. I rode up onto a rise ahead of the train and seen them waiting a mile ahead, maybe fifty or more all mounted on ponies. I raced down and give the word to Thaddeus and the colonel. They stopped the train and told everyone to wait right there while they went ahead to powwow, but first they got out a big chest and loaded it onto a pack mule to take with them. They set off and I begged to come along too.

"No, Jeff," says the colonel. "I admire your spirit, but a boy has no place parleying with redskins. Stay here with the rest."

Thaddeus give a sort of cough and says:

"Well now, Colonel, it mayn't be such a bad idea to have the boy along. It ain't expected, and Injuns has got admiration for any kind of gumption we care to show. I reckon it'll do us a power of good to have a young'un along to show we ain't afraid. It's the way their minds work."

The colonel tugged his mustache some, then says:

"Very well. You may accompany us, Jeff, but make no sudden movements, especially with your rifle."

"Yessir. Thank you."

And off we rode with me leading the pack mule. The Injuns was waiting same as I first seen them and never moved a muscle when we come near, just sat on their ponies and watched us till we come right up close. They all looked mighty fine with black hair long as a woman's, braided and tricked out with feathers, and their clothes was buckskin all beaded and fringed. Every one of them rode bareback or with a little blanket, and their horses never had nothing but a rope through the mouth for a bridle and had feathers in their manes and tails and here and there a painted circle around the eye or a colored handprint on the rump. They looked just like I always wanted Injuns to look, proud and handsome and free.

Thaddeus told me and the colonel to stay back while he rode up in front of an Injun older than the rest with a feather bonnet reaching clear down his back, so he must be the chief. They grunted at each other some, then Thaddeus says:

"Lay out the goods, but only a third. Leave the rest in the chest."

We wrestled it onto the ground and opened it and an Injun spread a blanket. I started taking out all kinds of bright things, necklaces mostly and mirrors and a few frying pans, even a couple rolls of red cloth.

"That's enough," says Thaddeus.

The chief got down off his horse and sat on the blanket so's he can see it all, then him and Thaddeus done some more grunting with chopped-down little words and Thaddeus says to the colonel:

"He says it ain't enough. He wants more."

"Is that usual?" asks the colonel.

"Just regular bargaining. Jeff, haul out a hatchet and lay it down."

I fetched out a brand-new one from the bottom of the chest. All the other Injuns was off their horses by now and crowding around to see what else I had in there.

"Close it and sit on it," says Thaddeus.

I done it and the Injuns looked peevish at me, but I just give them a smile and a "How do."

"He likes the hatchet," says Thaddeus after more Injun talk, "but he wants cattle too, Colonel. He figures we're pioneers like them that come through eight year ago with plenty of livestock in tow."

"Explain to him that we are not farmers and only have sufficient animals to pull our wagons."

Thaddeus done it and says:

"He's agreeable, but now he wants more trinkets instead."

"What would you advise?"

"Don't give him no more'n what he's got. He knows we got to pass through other tribes' territory and need the rest of that stuff in reserve."

There's more talk, then Thaddeus says:

"It's a standoff. He says we ain't given him enough so we can't go through."

"Then why not give him more? We have plenty left."

"That ain't the point, Colonel. If we do that he'll have no respect for us. He'll let us through, sure, but the next train that happens along'll get charged twice as much, and if they give in the one after'll get walloped for twice as much again. These Pawnee are great bluffers, but they can't abide weakness. I already told him no, so if we give in now he'll figure we're cowards, and rightly so."

"Is there no way around the problem?"

"Bound to be, but it's the chief here who'll come up with it. He's got all the cards right now and he'll take his time about showing his hand."

Nothing happened for awhile and I fetched out my pipe to pass the time. The Injun next to me was mighty interested.

"Why's he watching me so, Thaddeus; Injuns smoke, don't they?"

"Not on such an itty bitty pipe as your'n. Theirs are longer'n your arm."

I puffed away some then offered it to the Injun, and he was all set to take it when the chief barks something and he pulled his hand back quick. The chief and Thaddeus talked some more and he says:

"Now he's pertending he's real upset by Jeff smoking a pipe before we got things settled. They generally smoke after."

"I'm sorry, Thaddeus," says I. "I never knowed."

"He ain't truly upset, just trying to make us scared. Keep on smoking or he'll figure we are."

So I smoked on, and when I finished it I fixed another pipe and lit that too, even if my mouth is getting kind of dry. Finally the chief grunted some more and Thaddeus says:

"He reckons he's sorely grieved at the lack of respect Jeff's gone and showed, and he says he'll have to make up for it."

"He only did as you suggested," says the colonel, looking angry. "What kind of situation have you got us into, Mr. Winterbough?"

"Keep your hair on, Colonel, and let's see what he wants exactly."

After more talk he says:

"Jeff, I figure you're the kind with steady nerves. Is it so?"

"Steady enough, I reckon."

"The chief wants his best bowman to shoot something off the top of your head. Can you stand hard and let him do it?"

"This is foolhardy," says the colonel. "We cannot expect young Jeff to make such a sacrifice."

"It won't be no sacrifice. The Pawnee are mighty handy with bow and arrer. They don't aim to kill no one, just not lose face in front of us. Jeff, it's up to you I reckon."

"My boy," says the colonel, "I apologize to you for my folly in allowing you to accompany us. You are under no obligation to submit to this ordeal."

"I ain't scared," says I, only my voice is pitched higher than usual.

"Go stand over there," says Thaddeus, and I took up position thirty yards off. An Injun come across and put a kind of fur and bead topknot on my head and tied it down with thongs under my chin. It made me squirm to think I look like Becky Thatcher in her Sunday bonnet. Then out of the crowd steps a tall Injun with a bow, and he nocked an arrow to the string and smiled at me friendly-like. I showed him some teeth and wished my knees would quit knocking and my belly quit churning. The Injun pulled back his bow and I held my breath, then I seen the arrow coming, the tail end wobbling some and making a kind of whiffling noise through the air, then it's torn into the topknot and only the feathers kept it from going straight through.

The Injuns give out a roar and the colonel rushed over and says I'm his brave boy and such, and I went back to where the chief is all beaming and happy. I figured it was all over, but then Thaddeus says:

"Fact is, it can't end there."

"What do you mean?" says the colonel. "Matters seem to have been concluded to everyone's satisfaction."

"I ain't denyin' it," says Thaddeus, "only we give 'em the last laugh which means we lost a fair amount of face, even if Jeff showed he's got gumption."

"I'm afraid I don't follow you, Mr. Winterbough."

"What we got to do now is show 'em we can do the same thing. That way we get our face back without them losing theirs."

"The same thing?"

"With a rifle this time, and a whole lot further off."

"I absolutely forbid it," says the colonel. "It makes no sense whatsoever. The Pawnee seem perfectly happy with what has already taken place."

"They're laughing up their sleeves. We got to give it a try, Colonel, just to show 'em we ain't weak. I know Injuns and I know what they like to see."

"Absolutely not. I respect your knowledge of these things, but Jeff must not be subjected to any further danger."

Thaddeus turns to me and says:

"Jeff, you know a Hawken shoots straight and true. Will you trust me to do what that Injun done?"

"How far off do you want me?" says I.

"A couple hundred yards," says he, and I give serious consideration to jumping on my horse and hightailing it away from there, but I already told him I trusted him. The colonel says:

"I have grave misgivings."

Thinks I, likewise and double. But the die was cast, as they say, and Thaddeus told the chief what he aims to do and the Injuns got even happier, thinking to see my brains splattered all over, and tied another topknot onto me. Thaddeus says:

"Jeff, your rifle belonged to my friend Jed Frazer and shot the truest ball of any gun I come across. I'd be obliged if you'd let me use her now."

"If it'll help any you can have her and welcome."

I handed it over, hoping he don't figure that's my last will and testament I give him; it might confuse his aim some, being sentimental like he is about Jed Frazer's gun. Then I walked away, wondering if there's a life after death the way the preachers tell. When I got a considerable distance off I turned around, but Thaddeus waved me off further yet, and while I tramped I figured it'll proberly be the Widow Douglas waiting for me by the Pearly Gates, all gussied up as usual and combing her wings out neat, and she'll stare at me and say:

"Why, Huckleberry, just look at you with your brains hanging out, you untidy child. Go and get cleaned up this instant or you won't get a harp to play with."

I was practickly back to the train before Thaddeus give a holler and I turned again. His horse is lying on the ground and he's lying behind it with my Hawken over the pommel to give it steadiness, and all of it is miles away and tiny. I closed my eyes and waited for the widow to start nagging, then I heard the shot and at the same time felt a little tug at the topknot. When I opened up my eyes there's Thaddeus still behind his horse with a puff of smoke drifting away. The widow never showed. I tore off the topknot and there's a little hole drilled clean through it. I waved it around some to let them know he done it then started back. Thaddeus reloaded my gun for me and says:

"Know how I done it? I seen that target on your head as the heart of the Crow that killed old Jed and stole his rifle. After that it was right simple to put a ball through it."

The Injuns got out a pipe long as my arm, like Thaddeus says, and half a dozen sat in a circle with me and the colonel and Thaddeus. The chief set fire to it and it got passed to me. Now, I've smoked considerable for my age, but I never before smoked on nothing more disgusting than that Injun tobacco. It tasted like a dead dog that's been pissed on by bats, and I had a heap of trouble holding back my breakfast. The colonel turned kind of green after one little puff and passed it on to Thaddeus, who took it casual and even blowed a smoke ring. That impressed the chief and he tried it himself, only he never got the hang of it and sat looking miserable till we loaded the chest back on the mule and headed for the train.

By the time the wagons got moving and we passed the place where it all happened, the Pawnee was gone, and we never seen them again.

That night everyone was calling me a valiant hero and such and clapping me on the back and saying if they ever have sons they'll call them Jeff. It was mortifying having all that attention shoved down my throat and I snuck off soon as I could to get some peace and quiet, only I run smack into Grace behind a wagon, and for once there ain't a Peterson joined onto her.

"Well," she says. "Hail to the hero I don't think."

"Hello, Grace," says I.

"I guess you're feeling mighty smart after this morning. Wouldn't they be surprised to know you're nothing but a murderer underneath."

"You know I ain't at all, Grace."

"I know nothing of the kind, and if you think this changes things between us you can just think again."

Well, I judged that means open war, so I let fly with a broadside.

"I reckon Hewley and Duane would give a lot to know about each other."

"What do you mean?"

"What I mean is, I bet they ain't acquainted with the fact that you're canoodling with the both of them."

"I am not! How dare you say such a thing, you little stupid!"

"Names won't stop me telling, Grace, not unless you promise to keep our secret."

"I won't even listen to this. Of course I know both the Peterson boys. I talk with whichever one happens to be riding by, anyone knows that."

"That's in daylight. Nighttime is different."

"Have you been spying on me, you little sneak? I'll box your ears for you. . . ."

"Hold hard, Grace. Your beaux ain't none of my concern and my preference is to keep things that way. What I'm saying is, don't you say nothing and I won't neither."

"I don't make trade with murderers," she says, all grand and majestical.

"No more than I do with whores, Grace, but we got to reach agreement anyhow. I reckon the Petersons won't want no truck with a whore."

I never would of had the grit to say it, if it warn't for twice coming close to meeting the widow that day. A double brush with heaven like that makes you kind of carefree and loose-tongued, and it done the trick all right. Grace just stared at me like I slapped her in the face, then she done something I never expected; she burst out crying, the tears running down like rain and her sobs getting louder and louder. It was pitiful to see, but it's too late now to take it back.

"I'm sorry, Grace, I only wanted you to quit grinding me under like you been doing."

But she blubbered on, real tears, not playacting, and if I had a handkerchief I would of handed it over, but I never had one so she got dampish. Then she turned off the waterfall and just says:

"Go away. . . ."

I done it, and found Jim and told him everything.

"I reckon you kin rest easy now, Huck," he says. "You done pull de sting outer her tail. She ain't goin' to risk dem boys findin' out she bin a whore."

"I ain't so sure, Jim. She's awful pretty. I seen the way men look at her, and it's the kind of look that'll just ignore the whoring part and forgive anything if she just smiles nice and bats her eyes some."

"Ain't no use in worryin', Huck," he says.

But I did anyhow.

✦ 13 ✦

Brotherly Love—An Oath of Friendship—Pistols at

Dawn—Sad Sights at Fort Kearney—A Peculiar Promise

Now the train was only one day away from Fort Kearney, which is alongside the Platte River. Thaddeus says we'll follow the Platte west for close on three hundred miles to South Pass, the gateway through the Rockies and halfway to California. There was considerable excitement at being so close to sivilization, even if it's only a small-sized military fort, and everyone was impatient to get there quick.

That night there was a fistfight between the Peterson brothers and Hewley come out of it worst, being smaller, and when the colonel and Mr. Peterson wanted to know what it's about they never spoke a word, just glared at each other. The colonel made them shake hands, but after they done it they flung each other's hands away and wiped their mitts on their shirts to let folks know they ain't neither of them in no forgiving mood. There was some that guessed the reason on account of seeing Grace talking with both boys from the back of the Shaughnessy wagon, but they never had all the facts like me. After the fight got broke up I figured Grace might reckon it was me that told Duane about Hewley and likewise backwards, so I set out deliberate to find her and say it ain't so. I found her after a heap of hunting and spoke my piece, and she give me a mournful look and says:

"It was Mr. Shaughnessy told them. He's jealous. You're too young to understand."

"Just so long as you know it warn't me, Grace."

"I know you wouldn't tell on me, Huckleberry," she says. "You're not that kind, and you're not a murderer neither. I know I've been awful to you these last weeks and I'm truly sorry. It's like another person inside me making me do and say things I don't really mean.

Is it too late to be friends again? You're the only person in the whole world I can trust, really you are. Everyone else is sly and mean and lying. Don't you want to be friends again, Huckleberry?"

I allowed I'm agreeable and she brightened up and give me a scorching kiss between the eyes, then she took ahold of my hands and squeezed them tight and says:

"Let's bury the hatchet and swear undying friendship."

Just yesterday the only place she would of buried a hatchet is in my skull, but it don't do no good to live in the past, so I say:

"Well all right then, Grace, if the mood's on you, but to make it truly binding we got to mingle blood."

"Blood?"

"It's simple. You just open a little cut in your hand and shake on it and say a few words. I disremember the ones me and my friend Tom Sawyer used, but we can think up some more."

"I don't like that idea," she says. "It's better if we just touch each other's hearts and say the words. Think of some."

I turned my brain over and out come a perfect oath with poetry in it too:

"How's this'n, Grace: Us two friends will always last/In summer's heat and winter's blast."

"It's pretty," she admits, "but is it long enough? Do another couple of lines."

I churned my brain again and come up with this: "And if the oath is ever busted/We both of us'll be disgusted."

"It's not so poetical as the first," says Grace, "but it'll do. Now put your hand on my heart and I'll put mine on yours."

We done it, and I never felt nothing softer than Grace's heart, just like the little velvet cushion the widow used to stick her pins and needles in, only a mite bigger.

"Why, Huckleberry, your heart's beating away like anything. Are you feeling poorly?"

"Kind of giddy, but I reckon it'll pass."

"Say the words again."

I done it and she says them back to me, then we dropped our hands, only Grace dropped hers faster than me.

"That's that," she says, looking cheery. "Now my only problem is the Petersons. They're so stupid, both of them. I'm just so angry at the way they made a public display like that. Why, anyone would think I was in love with one or other of them."

"Well ain't you?"

"I should say not. Hewley's like a rabbit and Duane's like a bull. They're just too stupid for words. I hope neither of them comes near me again. I wash my hands of them both forever and ever. Who wants men when all you truly need is a loyal friend?"

"Me, Grace?"

"Of course. The Petersons can go hang for all I care."

"Why was it you took up with them in the first place?"

"Practice," she says.

"Pardon me?"

"A piano player has got to practice, hasn't he? Well, so do I if I'm going to marry a rich man. The Petersons are what's called five-finger exercises."

I figured the drift of it and was troubled by the don't-care way she ditched Duane and Hewley like that, but it ain't none of my business so I give Grace a goodnight and went back to Mrs. Ambrose's wagon.

Jim was mighty glad me and Grace has patched things up like we done, but he says she's the kind of female that likes to stir up trouble no matter what, only when the mud starts to fly she'll be sure and not get her own dress dirty if she can help it.

That night I dreamed about Grace dodging mud slung at her by the Petersons, then the whole train joined in till there's a regular mud shower coming down on her, but she never got a speck on her dress, just kept saying over and over "You can all go hang. . . . You can all go hang. . . ." Then she changes and says "Except Huckleberry. . . . Huckleberry. . . . Huckleberry. . . ."

I woke up and Grace is shaking my arm and hissing my name soft.

"Get up quick!" she says.

"What for? . . ." says I, half asleep still.

"Something awful is going to happen. Hurry! Don't make any noise."

I put on my boots and hat without waking Jim and follow her through the camp. It's just before sunup and there ain't a soul stirring yet, and the one guard we seen when we left the wagons behind was asleep, propped up by his rifle.

"We're out of ear-reach now, Grace. What's all the fuss?"

"It's Hewley and Duane. They're going to fight a duel."

"A duel? Where'd they get the swords?"

"It's a pistol duel."

"How do you know about it?"

"Hewley woke me up to say goodbye. He knows Duane's a better shot, but he says his honor's at risk. You've got to stop them."

"Me? You should of gone to the colonel. He'll stop them all right."

"I don't want anyone knowing about it, no one important I mean, so I came to you, Huckleberry."

She could hand you a real compliment, could Grace.

We come to a little hollow in the prairie and Hewley and Duane was both there with a pistol apiece, checking the load and aiming at rocks and such. They weren't none too happy to see us, especially Duane. He says:

"Who told you?"

"I did," says Hewley. "It was the proper thing to do."

"That's typical of you, you lily-livered squirt. You always were the kind that runs to a woman to cry all over her skirts."

"He did nothing of the kind," says Grace. "Now stop this nonsense!"

"It's too late," says Duane. "Just you two stand back and keep out of it."

"Goodbye again, Grace," says Hewley, his voice gone all shaky.

"Stop it, both of you! Don't you understand? I don't want either of you! I hate the sight of you both, you stupid blockheads!"

"It's no use, Grace," says Duane. "I know you're only tarring me with the same brush to spare poor little Hewley's feelings."

"No! I hate you *both*, you ignorant peabrains!"

But they warn't inclined to stop for nothing so simple as the truth, and stood back to back with pistols raised, then Duane says:

"We forgot something, brother. Who's going to do the counting off?"

"You can do it," says Hewley. "I don't mind."

"You can't trust me," says Duane. "I might say the last number faster than the rest and turn and fire before you had a chance to."

"It's all right, I trust you," says Hewley, close to tears.

"No it ain't all right. These things have got to be done the right way."

"Well, I'll do it then."

"No you danged well won't, you little snake in the grass! Think I'd trust you, the sneak that tried to take my girl away?"

"She was never your girl, Duane, she was mine."

"You just won't see the facts, will you, not even when they're staring you in the face. She was never interested in you."

"She was too! I asked her to marry me!"

"You asked her all right, but did she say yes? No, she never did."

They argued back and forth and I whispered to Grace:

"Go fetch the colonel. He's got to be told."

Off she run and they was so busy shouting at each other through the backs of their heads they never even noticed. Finally Duane says:

"Wait on, the problem's easy fixed. The boy can do the counting."

"I'm agreeable," says Hewley.

"Boy, can you count up to ten?" asks Duane.

"No, I never learned. My brother Cecil never learned neither, but he only had nine fingers on account of he was born with two joined together. If you like I'll go fetch someone who can count."

"Don't you move from there. . . . Where's Grace?"

"Gone away to puke," says I. "She's awful upset. Why don't you give it another try tomorrow? Maybe you'll find someone that can count meantime."

"I'll do it myself," says Duane. "All right by you, brother?"

"I reckon so, but can we drop our arms a minute? Mine's gone to sleep."

They lowered their pistols and rubbed their arms awhile then took up position again.

"Hold on," says I. "It ain't fair on Hewley if you do the counting, I heard you say it yourself."

"There ain't no helping it," says Duane, "not if you can't count."

"It's all coming back to me now. . . . Just run through them for me and I'll remember."

Duane counted up to ten and says:

"Can you remember that?"

"It's easy," says I.

"Well, don't do it too fast. Keep them spaced out regular. Ready, Hewley?"

"Ready. . . ."

"Start counting, boy."

"One . . . two . . . three . . ."

They started off in different directions, lifting their feet and planting them like the colonel's thoroughbred.

"Four . . . five . . ."

Hewley was shaking some, but Duane looks solid as a rock.

"Six . . . eight . . ."

They both got confused and missed the step. Hewley practickly fell over, and Duane hollers:

"Six, *seven*, eight! Say it the same as I told you!"

"I'm real sorry," says I.

"Well you should be. Now we have to do it again."

And back they come to start all over from scratch.

"Start counting."

"One . . . two . . . three . . . four . . . six . . ."

This time Hewley sunk to his knees and give a kind of sob, and Duane was fit to be tied.

"What kind of idiot are you, boy! Four, *five*, six! You got that part right last time."

"I must of got confused. I'll do it straight through now."

"You'd just better. Hewley, get up and come back here."

Hewley drug himself over and Duane slapped him in the face.

"Quit that blubbering and act like a man for once!"

"I'm sorry . . ." says Hewley. "I'm ready now."

"You're sure you don't want to admit she's mine?"

"Never!" bawls Hewley, and throwed his shoulders back.

"It's your funeral," says Duane, and they got back to back again.

"If you don't do it the right way this time, boy, I'm doing it myself."

"Yessir. It's clear in my mind now. Are you both ready?"

They was, so I started off again.

"One . . . two . . . three . . . four . . ."

Both of them look mighty grim and determined now.

"Five . . . six . . . seven . . ."

I seen they truly mean to do it.

"Eight . . . nine . . ."

Thinks I, Where's Grace and the colonel?

"Nine and a half . . ."

Duane throwed his gun down in disgust and come running at me.
I seen the look in his eye and turned tail and hared back toward the
train, and just when I cleared the lip of the hollow here comes the
colonel and Grace. Duane seen them and slowed to a stop, then
Hewley joined him and they both looked like considerable fools,
which suited them perfect, I reckon. The colonel give them his spe-
cialty, namely a mountain of scornful talk that made both Petersons
hang their heads. But he never stopped there, and turned on Grace
and called her a heartless, scheming, conniving, mendacious two-
faced minx that ought to be on the painful end of a thrashing. Grace
took it calm and kind of tossed her curls to show she ain't frightened, and when he was done we all went back to the wagons for
breakfast, but not before the colonel made us promise not to tell any
of it for the sake of morale, which he says is important in wagon
trains. But I told Jim anyway.

In the late afternoon we come in sight of the Platte River and next
to it Fort Kearney, and if it hadn't of been the only building in sight I
reckon I wouldn't of been impressed. It's only small and built from
wood, and off to one side was Injun tepees by the score, only the
Injuns never got excited when we come in sight, just stood looking
bored. The colonel had everyone make camp nearby then went
along to pay his respects at the fort. Thaddeus got left in charge of
the train but there warn't much he had to do so he mostly sat and
smoked, looking west across the plains. I went and joined him and
we sat watching the sun slide down across the sky and aim at the
horizon. The clouds turned purple and gold, real pretty to see. I
could of waited till Gabriel blowed his horn before Thaddeus begun
a conversation, so I say:

"You're awful quiet, Thaddeus. Are you thinking on how far we
got to go still?"

"Nope."

"On how many dangersome Injuns there is ahead of us?"

"Nope."

"Well maybe you're thinking on how we're going to get through
the mountains."

"I reckon not."

"Gold?"

"Got no use for it."

"Times gone by?"

"I ain't sentimental."

"Then you're appreciating the sunset."

"Never noticed it."

"Well you must be thinking on *some*thing, dang it."

He turned slow and looked at me, and there's a kind of pain in his eyes and a faraway look, like he never even seen me and was staring across years and miles, gathering them in, the good parts and the bad, and running it all together in his head to make a memory that's beyond ordinary words, too wide and huge to tell of. Then he raised himself up a little and leaned over to one side and broke wind, the longest I ever had the experience of. When it finally tailed off into nothing he says:

"Been trying to pass that all day. Now, what was you saying?"

But I never felt much like talking after that and drifted off. The fires was lit by now and some of the Injuns come among the train. Poorly looking they was, nothing like them we met on the trail; this bunch was sickly and dirty and drunk. They brung their wives along and I soon seen why. The squaws was all whores that flashed their teeth if they had any left and lifted their skirts to show their scabby knees and laughed loud and bumped into men deliberate by way of introducing theirselfs. I seen the Peterson boys go off into the dark with a couple in tow, so they must of mended the feud between them and forgot all about Grace. They warn't the only ones that done it neither. Most of the men in the train never had wives or sweethearts along and the squaws must of looked right handsome to them, but I never seen the attraction myself. Soon they was everywhere in the camp, the Injun men waving bottles and babbling and the squaws getting into wagons without no invitation to rustle up customers. It made the McSweens' outfit look decent and respectable. Mr. Connelly come up to me with his busted arm in a sling and says:

"Did you ever in your born days see the like? It's Sodom and Gomorrah reborn in the west. Where is the colonel? Why does he allow this kind of disgrace to go on under the noses of Christians? Look at these degenerate heathen scum. . . . Their bodies are putrid with drink and lust. Man is but a beast. The proof is here before us. . . ."

Off he stamped to look for more proof, talking to himself and shaking his head. The musical ones in the train dug out their insterments and tuned up and a dance got started, but the handful of white women stayed away on account of the Injun whores. The music was right lively and the Injuns done a dance that had a lot of falling over in it and a heap of screaming and laughing too. I found Jim wandering around seeing the sights and he says:

"Dere be a heaper trouble 'fore too long, Huck. I kin feel it comin'. You bes' be on de lookout so's you don' get mix up in it. I'se goin' to get me some sleep if'n I can wid all dis blim-blammin' goin' on."

He took himself off under the wagon and rolled up in his blankets and pulled his hat down over his ears to keep out the noise. I warn't sleepy and the music and hollering was kind of exciting, so I roamed on watching it all. I seen a man punch an Injun that's asking for money after his wife went in the man's wagon, but the Injun never seemed to mind the unfairness of it, just tilted his bottle and drug his squaw along to find someone else that'll play square on the deal. I seen other stuff that's similar, and got to feeling squeamish and wished I had the same sensibleness as Jim.

Then an Injun girl around twelve or thirteen come running from fire to fire like she's looking for someone, her Ma and Pa most likely, only she never found them and had a fretful look on her face, which is prettier than the rest on account of she's too young for drinking and whoring. A man from the train grabbed her by the braids as she went by and says:

"You lost, little girl? Whyn't you come along with me and I'll give you a present."

His friends give a laugh, all of them drunk, and the girl tried to pull away but he never allowed it. He says:

"No, no, you ain't runnin' off yet. Come and sit on my knee and sing me an Injun song."

She started yelling and he still held on, laughing like it's the best joke in the world to upset her that way. Then a squaw come flying at him with a knife in her hand, only she's too drunk to use it correct and only give him a little cut on the arm. He hollered and let the girl loose to grab at the cut, then he punched the squaw full in the face, the way I only ever seen men do to each other. She fell down poleaxed and lay in a heap and there was quiet for a second or three, then the cut man says:

"Injun bitch! See what she done!"

"Did you kill her?" asks one of his friends, not real concerned about it if he did.

"I should of done. Injun slut. . . . Lookit this blood!"

They stood around grumbling and cussing and the Injun girl come back with her Pa staggering along behind, drunk as all the rest, and he never understood what it's all about till he seen his wife on the ground. That sobered him some and he went over and lifted her head, which has got a busted flat nose on it now with blood all over her mouth and chin, and he looked up at the men still stood around watching.

"Well," says the cut man. "What're you aimin' to do about it, Injun?"

What he done was a big surprise to everyone. He started to sob and bawl and his little girl joined in too, and the men got embarrassed and disgusted and walked away. The squaw opened her eyes and the Injun and girl took her away with them, still crying. Mr. Connelly was right; the colonel should of been there.

I went looking for Thaddeus and found him after considerable searching down by the riverbank, just staring across the water.

"Got a bellyache, Thaddeus?" I ask.

"Heartache," he says after awhile.

"Why so?"

"You're still awake so you know why. Anyone get killed back there yet?"

"No, but if someone does it'll be an Injun."

"Always is," he says.

"It's like you told me, Thaddeus. I reckon you warned me what to expect when Injuns take up liquor."

"They only take up what's offered 'em," he says. "I reckon I'm ashamed."

"What of?"

"Being a white man. Bringing more whites west. It'll sit on my shoulders till I drop. I want you to make me a promise. I don't ask promises from no one as a rule, but I want you to make this'n for me."

"What is it?"

"Don't ever grow up to be a white man," he says. "Now leave me be. I'm talkin' with Jed."

It's the strangest promise, but I told him yes anyway. It sounded like something important to him. He never spoke again so I left him there talking silent to a dead mountain man. I figured he has words with Jed Frazer whenever he's got to unburden his mind, the way them with religion talks to God.

Things had gotten quieter in the camp by now and I was glad of it. I wanted to sleep and just forget all I seen, but sleep never come. I lay there beside Jim and worried over all kinds of things, then I heard voices and two sets of boots stopped right by me. I reckernized the colonel's voice right off, even if it's a little slurred from drinking.

"All seems quiet," he says.

"They've likely whored their bodies to sleep," says the other.

"You're a great cynic, Colonel Tranter, but I'll allow your table is more than adequate for these far-flung regions."

So it's the colonel in charge of the fort that owns the other boots. I can see the yeller stripe on his britches now. He says:

"For that you can thank the Platte and the boats that ply her. We're totally dependent upon shallow-draft steamers for almost everything, from horseshoes to foodstuffs. And drink, as you've discovered."

They both give a hearty laugh and a lucifer was struck and I smelled cigar smoke. Colonel Tranter goes on:

"We're expecting a shipment of supplies any day. The steamboats are merely under contract to the army and are always late arriving. I personally believe the government should have its own river fleet instead of relying on private companies. They're far too unreliable for such work. I've papered many a wastebasket in Washington with the idea."

"I know what you mean," says Colonel Naismith. "My own experience in the military left me sadder but wiser. Unfortunately civilian life proved equally unrewarding, in both senses of the word, which accounts for my presence here as wagonmaster."

"How long will you stay?" asks Colonel Tranter.

"We set off the morning after tomorrow. A longer respite is out of the question. I find myself disturbed by these tales of cholera in our wake. How will you handle the following trains if they prove to be infected?"

"By closing the gates. There is no other way. They must simply keep their distance and move on. Our medical supplies will be made available, but contact must be kept to a minimum. I can't have my troopers stricken by disease."

"I agree. Well, Colonel, my thanks again for your hospitality, and for the personal escort."

"Not at all. It is pleasant to stroll beyond the perimeter on occasion. Goodnight to you, sir, and call upon me for any reason while you remain here."

"I shall. Goodnight, Colonel."

Both sets of boots went off in different directions and the last thing that come into my head before I slid away to Nod is I'm mighty glad we ain't got no cholera in our train.

Steamboat a-Comin'!—Unwanted Passengers—The Bulldog Bites—A Prisoner in the Fort—A Question of Costume—Prairie Storm

There was plenty of hungover men in the camp next morning and not an Injun to be seen. They all went back around the other side of the fort to their tepees and never come near us. I seen Grace and she says last night was so horrible and vile she hid herself away in the Shaughnessys' wagon not to see it, only after Mrs. Shaughnessy fell asleep Mr. Shaughnessy tried to climb back into Grace's part of the wagon and she had to persuade him out again with her boot, so it was nearly Sodom and Gomorrah in there too.

Around midmorning I heard a sound I never counted on hearing way out here on the plains—a steamboat whistle! It blowed a time or three and straightaway folks started running down to the river. The fort's gates opened and out trooped a bunch of soldiers that went down to the bank too, which is where I already am, busting to see the steamboat. You could see the smoke long before she come around the bend, and when she done it I seen she's smallish against the Mississippi kind but built the same with three decks and two chimneys, only with two side-paddles not a sternwheel. Everyone that's waiting give out a cheer and flung their hats in the air, and a sergeant told the soldiers to keep them back and make room for the wagons that come down from the fort to haul the supplies back. There was Injuns there too now and the crowd was hundreds strong, all of them talking loud. The steamboat blowed her whistle without let-up and the sound whipped everyone into exciteration, and when she got closer I can see the name painted on her wheelhouse: *Nicobar*.

The paddles quit turning and she nudged inshore. The deck-

170

hands throwed ropes to them that's on the bank and the soldiers tied them to iron pegs hammered in the ground seeing there ain't no trees or wharf to hitch onto. Then they run the gangplank onto the shore and the sergeant went up it.

There was plenty aboard her, passengers by the score that lined up along the deckrails and shouted to the crowd ashore and pointed at the Injuns. The deckhands offloaded the cargo real quick and the soldiers loaded it into the wagons and took it up to the fort then come back for more. The sergeant come ashore again and I heard him say to a corporal that the *Nicobar* ain't going back downstream like she usually done, but further up into the headwaters of the Platte. It's on account of the passengers, the first ones ever on this run, who are all forty-niners on their way west to California.

"The captain's got to be a fool," says the corporal. "Don't he know there ain't but a spoonful of water left upstream after the thaw?"

"He says they'll make it to the end before she runs dry. Myself, I disbelieve it. They'll get halfway up and run onto a sandbar and be stuck there all summer. He's a pure idiot, but the boat's his to wreck if he wants. Did you ever see deckhands work so fast? They're in a godawful rush to shove off."

"He just better hope his paddles can walk her over them bars, the lamebrain."

None of the passengers got off even for a minute, and when the cargo was all unloaded the gangplank was hauled in and the *Nicobar* got poled away from the bank so her wheels won't hit the mud when they started. They finally got churning when she's a healthy step from the shore and everyone raised a cheer.

I'm watching the passengers on the main deck as she backed off when I seen two faces I reckernized: big Morg with the beard and Pap! I never believed it momentarily, but when I blinked and looked again they're still there, and it's Pap and Morg for sure. I pulled my hat down low and they never seen me. The *Nicobar* backpaddled further out to midstream and I felt safe enough to lift my head, then she swung around and headed upriver with her paddles thrashing. The crowd broke up and drifted off, but I stayed right there rooted to the ground, hardly believing it even yet. Pap and Morg must of throwed in their hand as thieves and murderers and joined up with all the rest that's after gold. Pap must of believed them stories about picking up nuggets off the ground easy and simple because he ain't the kind to drain his strength digging holes.

It shook me down to my boots. Just when I figured the past is getting left behind here's Pap gone and catched up with me, ahead of me even, if the *Nicobar* makes it safe all the way upriver. It was worrisome. There's a fair to middling chance I'll meet up with him someplace west, and that set the fan-tods loose inside of me. I would of rather met the widow in heaven than Pap on earth.

I went and told Jim and the news got him considerable edgy too. He says:

"We bes' be hopin' de trail dey takin' don' cross our'n, Huck. Dere's a heaper space out dere an' it ain't so easy to go bumpin' into folks jest like dat, I reckon. Ain't no use worryin' your head down to de bone on it."

But I done just that, all day and into the evening too. I never had no appetite come mealtime and Mrs. Ambrose says:

"You're looking poorly again, Jeff Trueblood. One minute you're healthy as a pup, then you're just the sickliest creature that ever was."

"I ain't sick, ma'am."

"Well don't do your moping around me. I can't abide mopishness."

So I went away to the edge of the camp and sat and smoked awhile. The air was heavy and still the way it is before a storm, which never helped me settle down at all. I was looking east, staring at nothing in particular, just the plains we come across, big and wide and empty-looking in the last light before dusk when I seen a rider coming. There's just him and his horse and a pack horse, and I figured he's another forty-niner that don't want to travel slow with a train, but more foolish than most on account of not having a friend or two along for company and protection.

He seen the glow from my pipe and steered over to me. His horses was both good and his clothes cut like a regular citizen, all of it from the same cloth, and his hat looked like it come straight off the block in spite of being all over dust. He's tall with a dark mustache that snuck around and joined in with his side levers so his face is in two halves with a long chin poking out below and a nose that done likewise above. He says:

"Good evening."

"I reckon it is."

"I'm in search of the Naismith train. Is that it camped over yonder?"

"That's her."

"What's your name, boy?"

"Jeff Trueblood, sir."

"Well, Jeff Trueblood, I'd deem it a favor if you took me along to Colonel Naismith. I have business to discuss with him."

I knocked out my pipe and led the way. Says I:

"Did you come all this way alone?"

"For the most part," he says. "I did team up with some others for a short while but found their company undesirable."

"Warn't you afraid of Injuns?"

"Luckily, I met none. I shared the trail with gophers and buzzards. Is there disease among your train?"

"Not yet, but the colonel's a mite worried it'll catch up."

"He has cause to worry. The trains behind yours are decimated."

We twisted and turned through the camp and got to the little tent the colonel lives in at night, and there's a lamp burning inside throwing the colonel's shadow on the canvas. I shook the flap and say:

"Colonel, can I come in?"

"Certainly you may, Jeff," he says, and in I go. He's sat at a little table with folding legs writing in his journal, and he looks up and says:

"Do you have a problem?"

I had a heap, but they ain't for telling, so I say:

"No, sir. There's a man wanting to see you. He's fresh off the trail so I reckon it's got to be important."

"Send him in, please."

The stranger was easing down from the saddle and I told him to go right in, then I offered to hold his horse, the reason being so's I can maybe overhear what the important business is.

"No thank you," he says. "He's trained to stay where he is when the reins are dropped."

He went into the tent and I went off to do some more moping. The stars was coming out now, littering the sky and winking. I figure there must be a heap of wind way up high where they are to make them flicker so. The Injuns still kept away so the camp was quiet, with most of the men checking their harness and wagons, getting ready to pull out in the morning. I never wanted conversation with no one so I took myself down to the Platte and looked at the spot where the *Nicobar* pulled in, and all that's left to show she was there is the bank all churned with boot-marks and the anchoring pegs. I smoked another pipe and tried to ease up on the worrying. Jim says worry only makes a body old before his time, so I just smoked my pipe and tried to stay young. All the while the air got thicker and clouds come sliding across the sky, hiding the stars and looking threatsome. Thinks I, there's a storm brewing for sure.

I must of been there some considerable time, because Thaddeus come along and says he's been looking all over for me.

"Why?" I ask.

"The colonel wants to see you."

"What about?"

"He never told."

I bet the stranger's horse wandered off and he figures I done it. Some folks has got real suspicious minds. I went along with Thaddeus to the colonel's tent, but the horse was still outside same as before and the pack horse too, so that ain't the reason. We went inside and the colonel is looking mighty discomforted. He says to Thaddeus:

"Fetch the nigger too."

"What's all this fetching about?" says Thaddeus.

"That will become apparent shortly. Just find him and bring him here if you please, Mr. Winterbough."

"I warn't hired for no fetching, Colonel. If it's all the same I'd prefer to get told now."

"Kindly do not question my authority, Mr. Winterbough. You are in my employ and will carry out any orders I care to give you."

"I reckon not," says Thaddeus. "No disrespect, Colonel, but the folks in the train hired me with their money and Jeff's among 'em, so I'll get told the reason directly, if you don't mind."

The colonel bristled some, not being used to people talking back that way, and for a moment him and Thaddeus just glared, then the stranger says:

"Pardon me, Colonel, but Mr. Winterbough does have a right to know what we are about."

"Very well," says the colonel, keeping his voice under tight rein. "Explain the situation if you wish."

"Thank you," says the stranger, and turns to Thaddeus. "Allow me to introduce myself. I am Chauncey Thermopylae Barrett. I am a detective contracted to pursue a criminal by the name of Huckleberry Finn."

"Never heard of you nor him," says Thaddeus.

My knees buckled some but to hide it I say:

"You must of heard of Finn, Thaddeus. He's the famous judge-killer from Missouri. Don't you read the wanted posters and newspapers?"

"Not generally."

"Well, I do," says I, acting all excited. "I read all about it back in St. Joe. Mr. Barrett, sir, it's a mighty big pleasure to meet you personal like this and the biggest thing that ever happened in my short life so far."

"That will be quite enough," snaps the colonel. "Mr. Barrett has been in pursuit of you for some time now and has traced your path to Fort Kearney. What do you have to say for yourself?"

"Me, Colonel? Why, nothing I reckon. I guess I ain't following the conversation too good."

"Are you or are you not Huckleberry Finn, and is or is not the nigger whom you call Goliath in actual fact named Jim?"

"Me and Goliath? I reckon you've left me way behind, Colonel. I just can't figure none of this at all."

"Now you see what I mean," says Barrett. "The boy has a reputation as an accomplished liar."

"I swear I don't know what you mean, Mr. Barrett, sir. I'm Jeff Trueblood from Illinois."

"Can you name the capital city of that state?" says Barrett.

"Well . . . uh . . . it's . . . on the end of my tongue. I never had much schooling, but I do know Paris is the main town in France."

There's a silence, then Thaddeus says:

"You want the nigger now, Colonel?"

"If you don't mind, Mr. Winterbough."

He went out and there's just me to face them.

"I admire your spirit, Finn," says Barrett. "You've come a long way from St. Petersburg, but not far enough."

"I wish you'd quit calling me Finn, Mr. Barrett, sir. It feels awful to have that name tagged onto me. It's plain you got the wrong man for once. If you'll excuse me now I got to feed a mule."

I got as far as the tent flap before Barrett grabbed me by the collar and hauled me back.

"He'll deny it till kingdom come," he says to the colonel. "It's the measure of his cunning that he never gives a thing away. No doubt he'll insist he's Jeff Trueblood on the gallows itself."

"Gallows?" says I, looking terrified, only half acting. "You wouldn't go and hang an innocent boy, would you?"

"Hanging is not my profession, apprehending criminals and es-capees is. Miss Becky Thatcher will be pleased to identify you for certain."

"Becky Thatcher? Why, who's she if she ain't the cat's mother?"

"You're denying too much now, Finn. If you read about me in St. Joseph as you say then you'll be aware that Miss Thatcher is the daughter of the murdered man. Even such cunning as you have thus far displayed must have its limits. You're only a boy after all."

"I'm Jeff Trueblood, and if my Pap was here he'd punch you on the nose for saying I ain't!"

"Your father is dead, Finn, you know that as well as I."

Thinks I to myself, if only you knowed he's just half a day's steaming away. But he never would of believed it, so I put a lock on my lip and never spoke another word till Thaddeus come back. He's alone and he says:

"The nigger's gone."

"Gone?" says the colonel.

"Flew the coop. I reckon he must of seen the boy get brung in here and figured the rest. He's likely miles away by now. Colonel, I'd like to check out the teams and see if he stole a horse."

"Excellent thinking, Mr. Winterbough. Please do so."

"As for this murdering little snot," says Thaddeus, turning to me, "I reckon he oughter be hanged from the nearest tree, only they're in short supply hereabouts."

His face was away from them while he spoke, and even when them hurtful words was coming from his mouth he give me a slow wink so I knowed Jim is safe, and if there ain't no horses missing from the team enclosure there surely will be by the time Thaddeus gets through investigatering there.

"That will do, Mr. Winterbough," says the colonel. "Bringing Finn to justice will be Mr. Barrett's job."

"And a darned good one too," says Thaddeus and shook Barrett's hand, then slipped me another wink before he went out. The colonel give a sigh and rubbed his brow and says:

"I'm sorely disappointed in you, my boy. I had you pegged as the kind of youth this nation needs to build itself in the eyes of the world, yet now you stand before me revealed in your true colors. I will not forgive myself for having allowed your air of worldly innocence to dupe me. I see now that your bravery is mere recklessness and your seemingly friendly nature just a cunning ploy, the better to insinuate yourself into decent human society."

"Any hunted animal will do the same, Colonel," says Barrett. "The smart ones blend into the scenery so well the hunter passes them by."

I never expected any different from Barrett, but the colonel's words hit hard. I liked him up till now, but I seen he's like all the rest, ready and eager to believe the worst. If he's disappointed in me I reckon I'm double disappointed in him. It's only because I knowed Thaddeus is still on my side I never give them the satisfaction of owning up and saying I'm Huck Finn, and even Thaddeus had me wondering which way he'd jump before I got that wink. With him I had a card up my sleeve, but it'll have to turn into a handful of aces if I aim to get out of the tight corner I'm in.

Barrett looked at me the same way I seen people look at a dead baby with two heads in a bottle at a circus, like I ain't the same as ordinary folk, just some kind of bug he's looked hard for and finally got ahold of and now it's got to be stomped on for the sake of the entire world. I never should of fooled myself I'm safe after we passed St. Joe. He's a bulldog all right, even if he looks more like a fox with that snout. When I come to consider it, this must be the baddest luck day in my life. First it's Pap, then it's Chauncey Barrett, both men I counted on leaving behind, and the first one'll kill me if he gets the chance and the second one is trying to hang me, and the first one is the one the second one truly wants if only he knowed it, but he don't, so like I say it's a bad luck day for yours truly, and there's worse to come. Says Barrett:

"Finn is also wanted for forgery. He obtained two thousand dollars by fraud from a bank in St. Petersburg. It's likely the money is on him yet. May I search the prisoner, Colonel?"

"Of course."

It took him two seconds to find the money belt and he whipped it out and laid it on the colonel's table then counted the cash.

"He has spent a considerable sum already, but Miss Thatcher will be delighted to receive the balance."

I could of told him it's my own money, not the judge's, but he proberly knowed that already and was just trying to make me say something that'll prove I'm Huck Finn, so I say:

"That's the profits from Pap's farm getting sold."

"See how he persists with his pathetic fantasy no matter how the evidence mounts? Many criminals have just such a stubborn streak."

He come over and starts feeling my head with his fingers.

"I'm a student of phrenology," he says to the colonel. "There is a school of thought which postulates the existence of a basic shape to the cranium which houses the criminal mind. Ah, yes, the occipital ridge is heavily pronounced and the obligata definitely conforms to the standard degenerate pattern. The boy is a perfect example, in fact. I have a friend at Harvard who would be extremely interested in this skull."

Well, the Widow Douglas always wanted me to go to Harvard, but I bet she never figured on it happening like that.

"Tell me," says the bulldog, "were you ever dropped upon your head when very young?"

"I disremember. Is it important?"

"Yes indeed. I detect an unusual bone formation at the apex of the crown."

Likely it's where the widow used to crack me over the head with her thimble when I never learned my schooling to suit her.

"Are you quite sure you have never suffered a cranial accident?"

"Not as I recall. But wait on. . . . There was the time Pap Trueblood built a new outhouse and he never had a hammer, so he made me drive the nails in with my nose."

"The boy's an idiot," he says. "This is unusual in one who has demonstrated ample cunning in eluding the law."

I squeezed my brain for a way out, but nothing come of it, just a feeling of desperateness that wound me up tighter than a watch spring even if I never showed it. Then the bulldog starts bragging how he followed my trail from the Aintree farm. It's all that mare's fault, the one we took with us that broke her halter and got away. She went straight back home and Mr. Aintree seen her coming along the road from the west. It never took Barrett much figuring to see me and Jim was hoping to join in with the crowd heading for California, so he just followed along asking in different towns if anyone seen a boy and a nigger, and when he got to Torrence the sheriff there recollected us being with the McSweens, so then he was hot on the trail that brung him direct to St. Joe, and there he checked out all the different wagonmasters' listings until he come across wagon sixty-seven in the Naismith train; Mrs. Hortense Ambrose plus one boy plus one nigger. After that he just followed on till he catched us up here at the fort. I got to give him credit, he done the job good. He knows it too, and that's why he don't take no notice when I say I'm Jeff Trueblood.

After awhile Thaddeus come back and says there's two horses gone along with the saddles me and Jim had in Mrs. Ambrose's wagon. He says:

"Looks like he took along a spare so's to ride hard and fast. I found tracks leading away south, two horses, one with a rider, both shod so it warn't Injun ponies. I reckon he's hightailed it for Texas."

"Mr. Barrett," says the colonel, "what are your plans?"

"My main task is to return Finn to St. Petersburg. Miss Thatcher's terms of contract do not mention this Jim, but he is wanted by the state as an accessory to jailbreak, therefore I consider it my duty as a citizen to bring him back also."

"Then you better get after him now," says Thaddeus. "A trail can get mighty cold if you leave it till morning."

"I am not a native, Mr. Winterbough. I do not have the ability to track by moonlight."

"You don't? Then I'll go along with you. I got eyes like a hawk, even in the dark."

"Your job is to guide the train, Mr. Winterbough," says the colonel, "not assist in the capture of runaway niggers. We are pulling out at first light."

"We'll be back by then. He ain't got but a half-hour's start on us. How does it suit you, Barrett?"

"I accept, thank you."

"Well straddle your nag and let's go."

"One moment. First I must place Finn under guard. Colonel, will the officer in charge of the fort cooperate in this?"

"I believe he will, yes," says the colonel.

"Very well. Will you accompany me while I deliver Finn into the hands of the military?"

"I will, and gladly. We have no facilities for detention in the train."

"Then I suggest we do it immediately. Mr. Winterbough, would you kindly wait for me with both our horses at the fort gates. I will be inside for as brief a time as possible."

"I'll be waiting," says Thaddeus.

So the colonel and Bulldog Barrett marched me along to the fort and hammered on the gate good and loud, and the sentry hollers down:

"Who goes there?"

"Colonel Naismith and Chauncey Barrett with a prisoner."

"What prisoner?" the sentry asks.

"An escaped murderer from Missouri," says Barrett.

"Is he an Injun?" the sentry wants to know.

"No, white."

"Well, all right then. Bring him in, only we don't allow Injuns in after dark."

The gates got hauled open and they marched me across the quadrangle between them and told a soldier they wanted to see Colonel Tranter urgent. I got took into the colonel's office and Barrett give him the story and was backed up by Colonel Naismith, and Colonel Tranter says it's fine with him if they want to put me in the guardhouse, which is what they call a prison cell in the army.

It turned out to be a little log cabin set off in a corner of the fort walls, and they put me in and padlocked the door then went away. It was discouraging. There's a bunk and I sat on it to do some figuring. Thaddeus was fixing to take the bulldog on a wild goose chase south for most of the night, but I'm danged if I can see how it's going to get me out of here. Maybe Thaddeus reckoned Colonel Naismith would just keep me in his tent till they get back, and never figured on them putting me inside the fort. Well, he done his best. At least Jim got away. That was kind of worrisome too, on account of Jim was never before on his own out in the wilderness, and he's proberly right this minute wondering what to do next. A nigger on his own ain't like a white man the same way, because wherever he goes and whoever he tries to team up with they won't want him along, not a nigger. It was stretching fancy to believe he'd make it to California without me, and pretty soon I got more worried about Jim than me, which ain't sensible, so I turned my head onto my own problem, namely how to get out.

The guardhouse was built solid and the door padlocked like I say. Making a hole in the roof slates was a possible, but there ain't any way I can reach up that high. There's no windows and no lamp to set fire to the place, so I'm stranded in there.

About an hour went by, then the padlock rattled and the door opened and in come Grace carrying a lighted candle. I never reckernized her at first on account of the scoop shovel bonnet she's got on, which hid her face inside a kind of cloth tube poking out front. A soldier with her says:

"Five minutes, miss."

"Thank you," she says, and when she heard his footsteps go away she tore off the bonnet and looked her old self again. But she never stopped there; next thing I seen she's popping her buttons and wriggling out of her dress like there's ants in her bloomers.

"Quick!" she says. "Change clothes with me!"

"What for, Grace?"

"So you'll look like me, addle-pate. Hurry!"

"But I feel right at home inside britches, Grace. I'd feel foolish with a dress around me."

"It's so you can escape, stupid," she says. "With the bonnet on they'll never see it's you and you can just walk out the gate free."

"Escape?" says I. "You're fixing to help me escape?"

"It's obvious to anyone but a halfwit. Get out of those pants directly."

I turned my back and was soon just in my long johns, and Grace flung the dress over me and crammed the bonnet on my head and tied it under my chin, all the while stood there in front of me in just her unmentionables. They was all over frills and ribbons, and never covered her arms at all. I seen them from fingers to shoulders, and they're white and soft-looking and kind of shapely. I never pay no attention to arms generally, but Grace's just begged to be stared at, and while I stared she fetched a couple of pairs of socks out of her pockets, all folded and bundled, and stuffed them down my chest to make me look womanish. It was mighty embarrassing I can tell you. Then I seen the flaw in the plan.

"Wait on, Grace, when they come to get me they'll find you here and know you made a swap with me of your own free choosing without I tie you up, and there ain't no rope in here. They won't like it, Grace."

"Do you think I'd do this without a good plan?" she says, pulling on my shirt and britches. "I'll give myself a knock on the head against the wall, just enough to raise a bruise, then after a half-hour or so I'll start to scream and yell until the soldiers come running and I'll say you made a vicious attack and hit me unconscious and traded clothes to escape. That way I'm just another victim of the mean and desperate Huck Finn and they'll all feel sorry for me."

"It's a dandy plan, Grace, and I'm obliged forever."

"Fiddle-de-dee," she says, tucking her hair up under my hat so she'll look like me. In daylight it never would of worked, but that candle only give off a feeble glow so there's a chance the plan will get me free. Says Grace:

"Jim is waiting for you down on the riverbank where the steamboat was this morning. He has horses and supplies thanks to your friend Mr. Winterbough."

"I reckon I'm grateful to Thaddeus too, but you're the one that's taking the biggest risk, Grace."

"We swore an oath of eternal friendship just the other day," she says, sitting on the bunk. "What good is an eternal friend if he's hanging on a rope?"

"That's true, Grace, but how did you get in to see me?"

"It was simple. All I had to do was go to the man in charge of the fort and beg to see my little friend Jeff Trueblood and say goodbye.

He wouldn't let me at first, but I cried all over his desk and he changed his mind. It's so easy to make men do what I want."

I reckon Colonel Tranter would of give any other woman a handkerchief and showed her the door, but not Grace. She could twist a man around her finger without hardly trying. Says I:

"Was it Thaddeus told you what happened?"

"No, it was Jim. He came to me and . . . Here comes the guard!" she hisses. "Act like you're me, and lift the hem when you walk so you don't trip over."

"I ain't ever going to be able to repay you, Grace. . . ."

"Shhhhh. . . ."

The padlock rattled and Grace lay on the bunk with her face to the wall like she's asleep. The door opened and the soldier poked his head in.

"Time's up, miss," he says to me.

"Thank you," says I all squeaky voiced, and picked up the candle and took a last look at Grace. The soldier says:

"Ain't he in a talking mood?"

"No," squeaks I. "He's got a fit of the sulks and won't speak a word after I went to all this trouble."

"Well, that's murderers for you. If it's any comfort to you we never gave him no supper."

"I'm gratified to hear it. I never should of bothered to come see him, but a girl hates to have her friends took away without a goodbye. I guess I'm just a sentimentalist."

"A pretty gal like you oughtn't to waste her feelings on trash like that," he says.

"Well I reckon I've learned a lesson," says I, and walked out the door. Soon as I'm outside I blowed out the candle to be safe and the soldier fixed the padlock then started walking me to the gate. It was troublesome to see where I'm going with all that bonnet stood out ahead of me, like looking down a tunnel, but it hid my face good, which means the soldier is only hopeful when he calls me pretty. He says:

"It's the first time we ever had a murderer in the guardhouse, miss. Mostly it's insubordination and such, and not all that often, neither."

"This will be a night for you to remember, sir," squeaks I.

"That it is," he says, and when we got to the gate he unbarred it and swung it open all on his own to show me how strong he is.

"Will you be wanting an escort back to your wagon, miss?" he says, full of expecteration.

"I reckon not, but thank you kindly anyway. May I ask your name?"

"Corporal McIntyre, miss."

"Well I'll be mentioning your name to Colonel Tranter if I see him again to tell how much of a gentleman you are."

"It ain't necessary, miss. I'm just doing a soldier's job. You sure about not wanting no escort?"

"It's just a step away," says I. "Thank you and goodnight."

"Goodnight, miss," he says, none too happy, and I stepped through the gate free and he slammed it behind me. Just in case the sentry is watching from above I set off for the train, but when I figured I'm out of eye-reach I doubled back around the fort till I hit the Platte and worked my way along the bank to where Jim's waiting with the horses. He give me my rifle and says:

"We ain't got time for talkin', Huck. Thaddeus say we got to cross de river an' go north. What you reckon on it?"

"It's as good a plan as any right now, Jim," says I, and hitched up my skirts and clumb aboard. We edged the horses into the shallows, then into deeper water till they started swimming. We slid out of the saddles and hung onto their manes, me with my Hawken held over my head to keep it dry, which is some trick and mighty straining, then we're into the shallows on the far shore and mounted up again. The air was thick as molasses by now and way off yonder there's a rumbling and a grumbling of thunder and sometimes a flash of lightning.

We aimed due north and started riding, slow at first so no one at the fort suspicioned galloping hoofs, then cantering when we're a mile or so from the river. The country was wide open ahead of us and big enough to lose a hundred armies in, so we dug in our heels and headed into it, just eating up the miles till the horses got winded and we had to slow down, which give us the chance to talk. Jim told how Thaddeus warned him and helped him steal the horses, and how when he learned I'm in the fort guardhouse he figured there's only one person to help get me out, which is Grace.

Trading clothes was her idea and it put her in the Tom Sawyer class for smartness. I told how I lost the money belt, so now all we got is my rifle and the horses. Jim felt bad about stealing them but I reckon the colonel will pay the owner out of my money belt fair and square.

"Thaddeus say de bes' plan is headin' up to Canada."

"Canada? Why, that's an awful cold place to be, Jim. That ain't going to suit us at all."

"Where else we goin' to go, Huck? We cain't go back east, das for sure, an' de bulldog gone south to get me back, an' he knows we was headed west befo' he catched up. North de onliest place lef' as I can see."

"I'll give it some considering. For now we can just keep headed the way we are."

So that's what we done, and all the while the storm come rolling our way from up ahead, stirring the air and moving it against our faces. It swallered the stars with black thunderheads all twisting and changing shape around the edges like ink poured across the sky till there warn't nothing overhead but darkness and thunder that boomed and crashed, one boom sliding right into another continual, and along with it come lightning bolts tearing out of the clouds and jabbing down at the plains, so bright it hurt your eyes like the thunder hurt your ears, flicker flashing and crookedy and lighting up the country for miles around.

Then come the rain, and it rained rivers. I never seen the like of it, just pouring down solid as a waterfall till we was both soaked to the skin. I knowed my Hawken warn't nothing but a lightning rod in my hand, all that iron just begging to get struck by lightning, but I warn't about to leave it behind so I held on and run the risk, and the dangersomeness and the noise and flashing light and being free again give me a sudden rush of blood to the head and I let out a whoop and went tearing across the plains howling like a dog with a crawfish on his tail. My horse got crazed witless by it all and tore along like a cannonball with me hanging on for life and my skirts streaming out behind and snapping in the wind like a flag in a gale. Jim must of figured I went mad and come thundering along behind bawling out my name and hollering to slow down, but I never wanted to, not with the wind whipping my bonnet back and my heartbeat pounding in my head along with galloping hoofs and crashing thunder and lashing rain and death reaching out for me every time lightning come snaking down from above. It was the excitingest thing I ever had the experience of, and when the horses got winded and slowed up I could feel the thrill of it slipping away fast till it's just a trickle, then nothing.

The thunder and lightning passed us by but the rain stayed, hours of it bucketing down on our heads. All we could do is plod along through it, cold and hungry and miserable, drawing a smidgin of comfort from knowing at least our tracks has been washed away behind us. Finally the rainclouds passed and the stars come out again. We watched them turn above us, whole clusters moving slow and majestical as the hours rolled by, then they faded away as the sky got pale and we seen the eastern horizon stretched away on our right, wide and flat and going on forever. It got lighter and lighter and the sun come up real slow, piece by piece till it's all showing and warn't we just grateful for the warmth. Along about midmorning we was near enough dried out to quit shivering and decide what to do. Says I:

"Jim, I been thinking considerable hard and I made a choice. We're going on to California."

"You addled, Huck? Das perzacly where de bulldog goin' to be lookin'."

"Maybe not. Chances are he'll figure we done just what we're doing and head north looking for us. He's a smart man and plenty educated, only he thinks I ain't nothing but an animal fit to be hunted. Well, I aim to prove he's wrong on that. If we do what he reckons is the last thing we'd do we'll get away and he can chase his nose clear to Canada."

"I ain't so sure 'bout dat, Huck. An' don' forget your Pap is somewheres ahead of us if'n we goes west. You don' wanter go bumpin' into him, I reckon."

"There's a heap of space out there that makes bumping into folks hard, so I figure we can take a chance on Pap. Lookit, Jim, we both of us are criminals, like it or not, and criminals leads poorly lives unless they're rich, and seeing as the only way for us to get rich that ain't unlegal is finding gold then that's what we got to do. I made up my mind on it. You can come along or not."

We rode on awhile, then he says:

"I ain't happy wid dis, Huck, but I reckon I'm comin' too."

"Well I'm glad. It wouldn't turn out half so adventuresome without a friend along."

So we turned the horses and headed them west with the sun behind us and was California-bound still, bulldog or not.

✦ 15 ✦

*Captured by Injuns—Amazing Revelations—Hunger and
Madness—Miracle in a Tepee—The Buffalo Hunt—An
Unfortunate Encounter*

The Platte don't run directly east-
west but meanders north some and we run up against it on the third
day. It was too close to the wagon route on the far side so we shied
away from it and kept it a day's ride off after that. The weather stayed
clear and fine and we ambled along easy. We never had no supplies
but I brung down rabbits and birds with the Hawken so we never
starved. We was happy being alone together again just like old times,
and we went on like that for six days. On the seventh day God rested,
but me and Jim run into Injuns.

There was five of them camped down in a little creek that run
south to join the Platte. We never seen them hid among the willow
trees till we got close, then they come dashing at us on their ponies.
They rode around us in circles a time or two then edged in close.
Jim says:

"What we goin' to do, Huck? Dey lookin' mighty interested."

"Just keep still and look friendly."

They never had no guns, just bows and lances, and they eyed my
rifle greedy-like. I could see they was wary too, scared I might use it,
but I warn't about to, not being the hostile kind. I would of got
riddled with arrows after one shot anyway. They talked Injun talk
among theirselfs and pointed at my dress, likely wondering what a
woman is doing with a gun, but they pointed at Jim even more and
it's clear they never seen a nigger before. Finally one of them got the
gumption to reach out and touch him to see if he's real, and when it
turned out he is the whole bunch commenced to touching his face
and hands and hair, looking perplexified about it. We never told

them it ain't polite to behave that way and they got up boldness. One of them snatched my Hawken out of my hand before I could stop him, so then we was helpless. They talked some more then grabbed our reins and took us along with them at a fast gallop across the plains, and there warn't a thing we could do about it.

In the afternoon they brung us to a shallow dip in the land and there's a whole Injun village laid out there with tepees by the dozen and Injuns by the hundred. The leader of them that captured us led the way in, singing some kind of song loud as he can to make folks take notice. The racket he made would of drove away a dog, but it must of sounded better to Injuns than it done to me because a heap of them gathered around and pointed. The women and babies was all mighty frightened of Jim and some even hollered out loud when they laid eyes on him. He says:

"What dey screamin' at, Huck? I ain't growed two noses or nothin'."

"They can't figure why you ain't brown or white, Jim. I reckon they don't mean no harm by it."

We come to a stop outside a tepee all covered in drawings with a mess of scalps hanging off a pole frame outside, some still with the ears on, which was discomforting to see. A man come out that looked stern and old, so he must be the chief. He never batted an eye when he seen Jim, just walked around him and give him a casual poke in the leg to see if he's flesh and blood. The crowd was all silent and respectful while he done it, then he made a sign for us to get down, which we done. He sat on the ground outside his tepee flap then pointed at a spot directly in front of him and we sat down too. He give an order to a squaw and she untied my bonnet and pulled it off. I never had my hair cut since before winter on account of it comes in right handy as a head warmer, so it's plenty long enough to make me look girlish. The chief give me a disinterested look then went straight back to staring at Jim again, so I reckon Injuns don't set much store by females and don't hardly rate them worth a second look.

After awhile he had a squaw bring out a pipe. He lit it and took a puff then handed it to Jim. Says I:

"Better get prepared, Jim. I already sampled Injun tobacco and it ain't the pleasantest."

He puffed on it just once then snorted it out again.

"Das de worstes' I ever had," he says. "Ain't dey got no regular kind?"

"I reckon not. When you're in Rome you got to smoke what the Romans smoke, Jim. Take another mouthful or they'll likely get offended."

He done it and handed the pipe to me, and soon as I took it in my hand the Injuns let out a howl and it got snatched away. The chief never looked pleased at all, and points at me and says a few words to Jim.

"What he sayin', Huck?"

"It's a puzzlement without knowing the language, Jim, but I reckon ladies ain't supposed to smoke, same as back home."

"He lookin' perty mean, Huck. You bes' be showin' you ain't a woman 'spiter de dress."

I still had Grace's two pairs of socks stuffed right where she put them; the top of a dress comes in handy for carrying things if you ain't female. So I opened a few buttons and reached inside and pulled out my bosoms. Them socks was white wool and it must of looked like I tore two chunks of myself out with my bare hands, because the Injuns let out another howl and stepped back a pace or three. Even the chief got alarmed at the casual way I done it, and I seen now was the time to make a lasting impression, as they say. Before they looked close and figured the bosoms was only socks I stood up and went to the nearest fire and flung them in, which set the crowd back another pace, all agasp at what I done. I dusted my hands off like bosom burning is all in a day's work to me, then sat back down with Jim and the chief, who give another order to the squaw. She come up to me fearful-like and patted me on the chest then stepped away again, talking all agitated. After that the chief offered me the pipe, which warn't what I wanted at all, but it's Roman tobacco after all, so best be polite.

Next the chief give another order and a little fat squaw with a baby under her arm come forward, and after listening to the chief she turns to me and says:

"He wants to know how you done it."

It was the surprisingest thing hearing American come out of her face.

"You can talk the same as me . . ." says I.

"Of course I can, and I know what rolled up socks are too, so don't think you got *everyone* fooled."

"Well . . . uh . . . could you keep it hushed, please? He ain't going to be happy if he finds out it's just a trick."

"Are your folks farmers?" she says.

"No, ma'am. Pap was just a drunk."

"Good, because I hate farmers. Seeing as you ain't from farming stock I won't tell what you done, and I won't tell them the nigger's just an ordinary nigger neither, but if it turns out you ain't likable I'll tell, so you just better be someone I can like."

"Yes, ma'am. Most folks say I'm the likablest boy they ever met."

"Well you just prove it to me and you'll be safe."

"Yes, ma'am. Pardon me, ma'am, are you a white lady?"

Her hair was brownish, not black like the Injuns, but I never would of noticed if she hadn't of spoke up like she done.

"No I ain't," she says. "I got born white but now I'm Injun. What do you want me to tell him?"

"Tell who about what, ma'am?"

"The chief about your titties, stupid. He's getting all impatient."

"Tell him . . . uh . . . I'll grow a new pair next year."

She told the chief and he nodded and spoke and she says:

"Now he wants to know why the nigger's black."

This time I'm ready, so I say:

"His ma got awful burned in a fire and he got born directly after and was black from it."

The chief swallered it and looked at Jim like he's the president, and ordered some food dished up to feed us, which went down welcome. Then there's more talk and the fat squaw says:

"Chief Standing Tall says you can stay here long as you like. He's awful proud of meeting a woman that can pull her titties off and a man that got burned inside his ma. He ain't come across no one like you two before so it makes him better than any chief of any other tribe in the Sioux nation. He's given you names, too."

"What names?"

"The nigger's called Burnt Man and you're Burnt Man's Wife."

"Now hold on, I ain't a woman, titties or not. Jim's the bestest friend I got, but I ain't about to marry him."

"Well it's too late now. If you tell him you got a toby between your legs like a regular boy he'll get all confused and upset, and it don't pay to upset the chief. You'll just have to keep on pretending to be a girl I reckon."

I never had no choice. Pretty soon the Injuns got bored with staring at us and wandered off to do whatever Injuns do and Jim and me went for a walk with Fatty. She says she used to be called Hepzibah when she lived with white folks but now she's called Little Dove. A dove that size never would of left the ground. She's just as wide as she's tall like a punkin on legs, and them legs was the stumpy kind that never would of reached the floor if she sat on a rocking horse. She says:

"I used to be an orphan in St. Louis, then the orphanage sent me out to work for a farmer and his wife in upstate Missouri. They made me work like a nigger. I had to get up before the sun come up and milk the cows and chop wood and hoe corn and do all kinds of stuff a girl shouldn't ought to do and never got a word of thanks for none of it. Their own daughter never done nothing around the house except for crocheting and such and they treated her like she's a princess or something. Mrs. Cleavon, that's their name, she was the meanest woman in creation and never give me enough to eat. I was thin as a broomstick, just a skellington. All the Cleavons et plenty, but not me on account of not being family. I just hated that place and everyone in it and was making secret plans to run off, then Mr. Cleavon says they're going to sell the farm and go to Oregon in a wagon along with a bunch of other farmers, and he says I'm coming too.

"They started off, then when they got onto the plains the Sioux attacked them and killed everyone except me. I seen all the Cleavons get killed and I felt real good about it. That's why the Injuns never killed me too, because I kind of laughed when they done it and they figured I'm crazy, which Injuns has got respect for, so they took me along with them. When they seen I warn't truly mad I got married to Running Horse, that's him over there with the big nose, and we had babies. Now I can have all the food I want and I ain't never going back to whites. Whites is just trash."

She was around fifteen when she got captured so she's a full-growed woman now, only she talks like a little girl on account of not speaking American all these years. She says:

"How did you come to be wearing a dress?"

I give her the story considerable pared down, making out like me and Jim run off from my cruel Uncle Silas that worked us both like horses and fed us like squirrels, and how someone in the wagon train reckernized me so I had to get away in disguise. Hepzibah says most whites is poor and miserable except them that's got slaves, and we're a heap better off out here with the Sioux. She was sympathetical and I felt safe, only I knowed I'll have to keep her sweet the way I done with Grace before we made friends again, and I wondered if all females has got to be kept buttered up like that or if there's ones that are different and you can just talk to them normal like I done with Jim.

We went to Hepzibah's tepee and Running Horse was real honored to have us inside. He drunk in every word while we jawed with her, even if he never understood none of it, then Hepzibah undone her dress and brung out a bosom big as a watermelon to give the baby some milk without no shyness at all. There's little Injuns there too, a boy around seven years and a girl sixish and another boy three or four. The baby was a boy too, and Hepzibah says Running Horse is proud of her for making mostly sons, which Injuns prefers to daughters, same as white folks.

Later on we went outside again and Hepzibah showed us how you cure a buffalo hide stretched on a pole frame, and what you do is scrape the flesh from the underside till it's clean, a real boring chore. She talked while she scraped, all about how the Cleavons never fed her enough and how she had to sleep in the barn with the cows and how awful the orphanage was before that and how much fairer Injuns is when it comes to sharing out food, on and on three times over, just jawing away like her lips will seal if she lets her mouth close for more than two seconds. I figured she's making up for not talking to whites all this time and was getting relief from it, so I listened patient and tried not to fall asleep.

When evening come we et some more and I seen why Hepzibah is so fat. Her and the other squaws had to wait till the men had their fill, which is the Injun way, then the women set to and munched away, only Hepzibah done more grabbing and munching than most, like she's afraid the Cleavons are going to show up and feed her on dog rations again. Then everyone gathered around to hear them that brung us in this morning tell the whole story again, acting out the parts real clever. I reckon they must of stretched the

yarn considerable though, because it lasted hours. They could of
brung us back from China in all that time. Then the Injuns started
drifting off to their tepees for shuteye. Hepzibah says Running
Horse would be obliged if Jim and me would sleep in their tepee,
which means he can brag on it to the rest about having such important guests. In we trooped, and if you don't believe eight people can
fit in one tepee let me tell you they can, but some of them has got to
be only part growed. We got parceled out around the floor and Jim
and me wrapped ourselfs in animal hide blankets and got set to
snore. Then I seen Running Horse watching us close by the light of
the little fire burning in the middle of the floor, watching like he's
waiting for something, and I ask Hepzibah who's next to him what
he's doing. She says:

"He wants to see how Burnt Man makes babies with his wife
that's got no titties."

"Well tell him we ain't going to do nothing of the kind till I grow
me a new pair."

Running Horse looked real disappointed when she told him and
turned his back on us. It warn't a restful night, what with the baby
squawling every once in a while for milk, and it made me wonder
why folks go to all the bother of having them when they could just
as easy go to an orphanage and get one growed up past the crying
stage for free, and could sleep peaceful of a night.

Jim and me was real popular and couldn't go nowhere without a
heap of little Injuns on our heels, which got to be pesky after awhile.
I figured part of the attraction is me in my dress, so I ask Hepzibah
if she can't rustle up some old Injun duds for me to wear. She says
Injuns ain't partial to hand-me-downs and always make new clothes
when their old ones start letting the breeze in. She don't mind
stitching me up some, but it won't look right on account of I'm
supposed to be female. That was a problem, but I truly wanted to get
out of Grace's dress, so I talked it over with Jim and Hepzibah and
worked out a plan. Hepzibah went to Chief Standing Tall and says
Burnt Man's Wife is fixing to grow a toby to match up with being
flat-chested. The chief says he wants to be there when it happens,
so I say I'll do it that very night.

Jim and me went to the chief's tepee after it got dark, and all the
important men in the tribe was there to see me change from a
woman into a man. When everyone got settled I sung a few hymns

to pass the time, then rambled on about how me and Tom Sawyer found Injun Joe's gold, then I done another few hymns. Hepzibah told me Injuns ain't impressed by nothing that happens too quick, which they'll reckon is a cheat, so I have to spin it out long as I can. I told a few Bible stories and throwed in a joke or three for good measure, then got down to the transmogrification proper. I lay on the floor and started squirming around and grabbing between my legs like I'm in mortal pain, and Jim pranced about babbling non-sense and wiggling his fingers at me while the Injuns looked on all boggle-eyed. I never had to show them beforehand that I'm a woman, Injuns being surprising modest about showing their private parts, so when I give a final yell and stood up they just naturally accepted it was all over and now I'm a man. Some must of been doubting Thomases though, because when I stepped outside for a leak they followed me out and watched, nodding their heads solemn-like. When we went back in they told what they seen and a pipe got passed around to celebrate the miracle. I reckon they liked me better now that I'm a man like them, women generally being left out of things.

Next day Hepzibah measured me with a rawhide thong, making knots in it to show how long my legs and arms is. Then she got a deerhide and hacked away at it to cut out a pattern, then punched holes for the thread, rawhide again, and in a couple of days it was done. She made me wait awhile longer while she sewed on beads and such and made moccasins to go with the rest of the outfit. Finally she braided my hair in two ratty little pigtails and I put on the Injun clothes all swishing with fringes down the arms and legs. I stepped outside looking just like Thaddeus only younger, and felt like the King of the Plains, especially when I got on my horse and rode around with my rifle, which got give back to me now I ain't female no more. I never felt more like my own natural self than inside them Injun clothes, and wouldn't of traded them for a gold crown and satin cloak and buckle boots.

My new outfit made a difference to Jim too. Now that I'm a man he ain't got no wife, and all the Injun girls that warn't married started making eyes at him and following him around till he never had a moment's peace. Then one night he never showed up in Running Horse's tepee at all, and next morning he walked with a kind of swagger in his step and et more than usual so I figured he's found himself a sweetheart. He says to me:

"Huck, I ain't had no lovin' from a woman in a heaper time an' I'm mighty glad I ain't forgot how. See dat gal over dere wid de smile? Das de one dat 'minded me how good lovin' kin be. She de cutes' thing I ever seen wid no dress on, an' mighty strong an' wriggle-some 'spiter her littleness I kin tell you. I got aches all over on ac-counter de way she rassled me las' night. Dese Injun gals ain't got no kinder shame when de sun go down."

And he squints up at the sky to see how much longer he's got to wait till sundown. Well, anything that makes Jim happy makes me happy too, and it means there's more room in Running Horse's tepee.

Living with Injuns is real lazyfying if you're a guest, and after awhile I got restless. It's sometime in May by now, and I recalled how Thaddeus told me you got to get through the Sierras before winter sets in, and it's still a powerful long way from here to there. The trouble as I seen it was Hepzibah. She got mighty fond of hav-ing me around so she can talk and talk and talk, none of it worth hearing, and I reckoned if I told her we wanted to leave she'd get upset and tell the chief we ain't special at all, just a boy and nigger, and more time got lost while I done my best to figure a way out of it. Just running off never would of worked. Thaddeus told me Injuns can track a grasshopper over running water their eyes is so keen, so we would of got catched and brung back. It was like being in a real friendly wide-open prison.

Every day was the same, with Jim eating like a horse to keep up strength for his sweetheart and me sitting with Hepzibah while she done her chores and talked and talked till my ears come close to dropping off from weariness. Running Horse never got jealous of the time I spent with her, proberly because it give him the chance to let his own ears cool. Jim and me warn't so interesting to the Injuns as we first was, and the men ignored us seeing as we never done brave deeds and hunted and such, the kind of thing men is sup-posed to do. They looked at me like I still had Grace's dress on.

Then Hepzibah give me some news, and it's this; the tribe is packing up their tepees and heading west for buffalo, which means Jim and me will get that much closer to where we want to go before we have to think on leaving the Injuns and going our own way again. I found Jim and woke him up and shared the news, and he says:

"Das good, Huck," and dropped off to sleep again. Having a sweetheart must be a mighty tiring business.

They got started the very next day, and it don't take hardly no time at all to strip the skin off a tepee and roll it up and collapse the pole frame and bundle it all together. The whole village come down in an hour and there was hustle and bustle everywhere with horses being loaded with goods and having poles tied to them to drag along the ground with little platforms between them to stack things on, not so practical as wheels but they done the job. Chief Standing Tall rode out front and the rest followed along behind, the men riding and the women and children mostly walking. It felt good to be west-bound again and double good to be at a distance from where Hepzibah was trudging along, walking her fat off and looking miserable. The silence was a true blessing and give me new heart for the trail ahead.

On the fourth day a scout come riding full pelt from up ahead all excited like he's seen something mighty interesting, so when a parcel of men set off in the direction he come from I rode along too. When we come to the crest of a rise a few mile away, I seen a genuine wonderment. The whole plain just as far as you could see was covered with buffalo like a lumpy brown carpet. The nearest ones was a quarter mile off, front heavy with shaggy humpbacks and big heads with goatee beards, and their little whippy tails never stopped switching flies away. There must of been millions of them all moving along peaceful together.

The Injuns walked their horses real slow down the slope toward them, nocking arrows in their bowstrings and getting their lances ready. The buffalo never even noticed till the wind shifted and give them the scent, then they whirled about and started pressing back into the rest of the herd to get away, and panic run right through all of them and the whole carpet just turned tail and run. The Injuns let out a whoop and dug in their heels and galloped away after them, and I done it too. Horses is faster than buffalo and the lead riders catched up right quick with the tailenders and dropped their reins and begun pouring arrows into them just behind the hump, loading and reloading on the fly and guiding the horses with their knees. I seen one buffalo barreling along with maybe a dozen arrows in him but still going strong, then he swerved sideways and brung down the horse and rider alongside of him. They never got hurt somehow and the Injun sprung back onto his horse and kept right on chasing the same buffalo, which was staggering some now with blood pouring out along his sides. Then his legs never worked no more and the front ones buckled under him and he done a somersault and plowed along the ground and lay dying. Them with lances done the bravest thing, riding up real close and shoving the point in deep behind the hump, just like pictures I seen of men killing whales, and the buffalo that got that treatment died soonest. The chase went on mile after mile with the air full of dust and the ground rumbling and shaking under all them hoofs and the Injuns whooping every time they brung down another.

I rode along with the blood rushing in my head and my eyes and nose full of dust and my ears full of noise. It was as dangersome and thrilling as the thunderstorm, and I whooped along with the Injuns a considerable distance before I recollected I got a rifle slung over my shoulder that ain't earning its keep. I dropped my reins like the Sioux done and swung the Hawken up to my shoulder to draw a bead on a big shaggy bull thundering along maybe three yards off, only my horse ain't trained to run without a tight rein like Injun ponies and he sheered off, so I lost the chance. But I never give up. I steered him back on course and tried it again with another buffalo, but soon as I dropped them reins to bring up the rifle he took a new direction and I lost the chance again. I seen I ain't going to kill no buffalo from a moving horse; I could of tried shooting with one hand but a Hawken has got a powerful kick and it would of jumped right out of my mitt if I done it, so I never.

I reined in to one side and brung my horse to a halt. The herd was still streaming past but thinning out now, so I put the Hawken to my shoulder and tried to pick a likely one to drop. Then I seen a horse put his leg in a gopher hole and go crashing down. The rider went flying through the air and rolled along the ground, but he ain't hurt by a miracle and picked himself up before he even quit rolling, only now there's a huge big bull rushing down on him and likely to grind him under without even stopping. I swung the Hawken and aimed square at his spine behind the head and squeezed the trigger. The Hawken bucked and the bull kind of slid forward through the dust on his knees like a steamboat running full speed onto a sandbar. His head fell to one side and he's dead, just a leg away from the Injun which I see now is Running Horse. Another Injun come along and scooped him up behind at full gallop and took him out of harm's way, and he give me a wave to show he ain't hurt none.

The last few buffalo run by panting like old boilers with their purple tongues lolling out of their heads and the herd rolled away over a rise out of eye-reach. When the dust settled I counted up ten dead along with the one I shot, which is a heap of meat. Running Horse's pony was lying with his leg snapped below the knee, whinnying pitiful. I reloaded and was just about to put a ball in his head when Running Horse come up and stopped me. What he done next come unexpected, because he hacks a chunk out of the horse's neck with his tomahawk so the blood come frothing out, then he made a bowl of his hands and let the blood spurt in to fill it. Then he drunk it! I never seen nothing so awful and disgusting. The horse kicked feeble and there's a pool of blood growing around him. Running Horse smeared his face and chest with it and finally the horse give up the ghost. Buffalo hunting is thirsty work, but there warn't no need I could see to drink no horse blood. It was a puzzlement, but later on Hepzibah told me it's a sign of respect for the horse from the owner, and that way the horse is going to be waiting for him after Running Horse dies too, and they can ride across the sky together chasing moonbeams.

The women come along and started hacking at the dead buffalo, peeling off the hide and cutting off chunks of meat for cooking, and the job took all day. The men done the exciting part of hunting and the women done all the boring dirty work, but they laughed and sung while they done it and when night come down there was a feast that everyone joined in, just stuffing buffalo hump inside of them till their bellies swelled and they can't hardly walk.

The hunters sung songs about how brave they are and Running Horse sung about how I shot the buffalo that was set to squash him. Hepzibah says I got to give the story all over again too, so I got up and done a mime of riding along and everything and they just killed theirselfs laughing when I come to the part about the horse swerving away whenever I dropped the reins to take aim, so I had to do that part about five times more than it really happened. When I finally done the buffalo skidding to a stop they practickly busted a gut and I had to do that part over considerable too, which layered me in dust, but it's worth it to be popular like that. I ain't a notice-grabber by nature, but after I done what I done that day the men never looked at me like I'm wearing a dress no more, which made life easier. They give me official reckernition too; the chief had me come over and he tied a knot of my hair around a long eagle feather as a reward for saving one of his warriors. Tom Sawyer would of envied all the attention I got.

Then Standing Tall started in with a song of his own about hunting in days gone by when he was younger, and about a battle with another tribe when he got an arrow in the arm and ripped it right out and kept on fighting. Everyone just loved it even if they must of heard it a hundred times before. Hepzibah says Standing Tall is real popular and how when a chief dies the whole tribe goes into mourning straight off, even if they're in the middle of something important like a battle. When a chief dies it's like the heart of all of them is gone for a day or two, which shows how much respect they got for their leader. The tale-telling and singing went on all night, then everyone drug theirselfs off to bed and never got up till late next day, which suited me fine.

A few days later we swung south and come to the Platte, and I seen how the water level has dropped plenty since we crossed it at Fort Kearney. We followed it for a week, maybe a hundred and fifty mile, and one afternoon come around a bend and there in front of us is the *Nicobar*. She was stranded high and dry on a sandbar with the bottoms of her paddles sunk inches deep in it, and she'll be part of the scenery hereabouts till the winter rains lift her clear. There was a whole section of her upper deck missing, which is strange, and she's a tragical sight to see all butchered like that. I looked for Pap but he warn't in sight. There's only three or four men around her digging with shovels and trying to make a channel that'll let the water either side of the bar reach the *Nicobar*'s hull, but I could tell just by looking it ain't going to work on account of the level warn't high enough anyway.

When they seen us they dropped their shovels and scrambled on board. The women and children was a little way behind, and Standing Tall and his men lined up along the bank, curious-like. They never seen a steamboat before and was mighty impressed by the size of her. Then I seen the men on board was gathered on the main deck just behind the capstan where there's a brass cannon, which I never noticed when she stopped at the fort. It's aimed at the shore and I seen a wisp of smoke and yelled at everyone to scatter, but they never understood and was staring at me in perplexion when there come a roaring boom and the Injuns and horses a few yards from me got tore to pieces with chain shot. It just mowed them down like a scythe and there was screaming and panic and chunks of men and horses lying all around, and while the Sioux was still wondering what hit them the cannon got reloaded and fired again. This time it whistled overhead, but the damage was already done.

The second blast sent them galloping over the rise away from the river and Jim and me went along too. I never seen such a waste of life. The Injuns was only curious, not warlike, but them on the *Nicobar* must of panicked when they seen so many. The rest of the tribe come running after the riders and they all got assembled a half mile off. The women set up a wailing and moaning over them that was killed. I hoped Running Horse ain't among them or Hepzibah would likely get Jim and me killed too out of revenge, and we shook like scared dogs waiting to see what happens next. Then I seen Running Horse with all his arms and legs and felt reliefed, but not for long because here comes Hepzibah with thunder on her face and she spit on my moccasins.

"See?" she says, all shivering with rage. "That's whites for you! They're going to pay for it, just wait and see! We'll get them and make them sorry! They'll wish they was never born before we finish, and you just better keep out of things if you don't want the same!"

"It warn't our fault, Hepzibah. . . ."

"I don't care!" she screams, and stamped away. Jim says:

"We walkin' on mighty thin ice wid dat gal, Huck. She ain't white no mo', jest Injun. Dese here Sioux is her own folks for sure. You reckon we oughter get away?"

"Too risky, Jim. If she sees we're gone she'll blab on us definite and the whole tribe'll come after us."

"Maybe dey be too busy wid de boat to give us no mind. Dey got de dander up good an' hot an' wants blood I reckon."

"Well, I prefer it ain't ours. We'll just stay out of the way like Hepzibah says and hope they forget about us till they get cooled off."

So that's what we done, sticking to the shadows when night come

down and fires got lit. The men held a big powwow and talked loud
and dramatic, then a dozen or so went down to the river and brung
back the dead under cover of darkness. There was more weeping
and wailing from the women when they seen the awful damage the
chain shot done and the men looked mighty grim. Then they got out
drums and commenced banging on them and shuffling in a circle
around the main fire, chanting a song all deep and terrible sounding, enough to make your hair stand on end. Hepzibah come up to
me with a smug look and says they aim to attack the *Nicobar* just
after dawn and lift the hair off them that's aboard, only first they'll
have some fun out of them. She never explained the fun part, just
says we'll see what she means tomorrow, then she went back to the
women. I done some brain churning and say:

"Jim, them on board done the wrong thing, but it ain't right they
should all get scalped for what a handful done with the cannon, not
even Pap."

"Ain't nothin' we kin do, Huck."

"I got intentions to warn them."

"You cain't, Huck. Dey goin' to figure you an Injun dress' like you
is."

"Not if I talk to them before they see me. I got to do it or feel
ashamed forever."

"If'n Hepzibah fin' out, you goin' to get killed by Injuns. She don'
like us no mo', Huck."

"I'll only be gone a little while. So long as she sees you're still
around she'll likely figure I'm here too."

"I wish you wouldn', Huck."

"Well, I am."

I snuck away from the camp and heeled it for the river. The
Nicobar was all in darkness without no lamps burning, and I hollered across the water to let them know I ain't no war party.

"Hello aboard the *Nicobar*! Can you hear me?"

"Who is it?" says a voice.

"A white man," says I. "I'm coming out, so don't shoot, please."

There's a mumble of low talking on board, then another voice
says:

"Come on, then, but make noise so's we know where you are."

"I'm coming now. Don't shoot."

I waded in and headed for the steamer. The water never come past my waist in the deepest parts and I crossed the sandbar she's stranded on, whistling all the while like they wanted. I reached her and swung aboard and got grabbed by two men and had my Hawken took away.

"Why, it's an Injun after all," says one. "It's a trick!"

"Nossir, I ain't no Injun. I'm Daniel McPhee from Illinois."

"He sounds white," says the other.

"Bring him along," says the first, and I seen he's wearing a gold ear-ring like a pirate, so he's a riverman for sure. They held me tight by the arms and marched me along to the main cabin where there's two other men, one of them a sight older than the rest with a captain's cap on his head. There's a smidgin of moonlight coming through the shutters and I seen Pap ain't there.

"Who are you?" says the captain.

"Daniel McPhee, sir."

"How come you're dressed like an Injun?"

"My folks was pioneers, sir. They got killed by the Sioux and I got brung up Injun style."

"Well, which are you, Injun or white?"

"I reckon I'm white. I come to warn you about the attack that's going to happen tomorrow morning."

"It's a trick," says the ear-ring.

"Hold your water," says the captain. "Let's hear him out. Are you sure it's tomorrow, not tonight?"

"Yessir, straight after dawn."

"He's lying. They'll come while it's dark," says the other one.

"It's the truth," says I. "You best get armed and ready for when they come or take the dinghy and head downriver right now."

The captain give a feeble kind of laugh and says:

"The dinghy's gone and the longboat too. When we got stuck here some took the boats and pulled upriver to reach Fort Laramie and the rest tore the hurricane deck to pieces and floated rafts back down to Fort Kearney. There's only us four left."

So Pap warn't on board after all. Says I:

"Pardon me, Cap'n, but with only four men you can't win, not even with a cannon. There's upwards of a hundred warriors getting ready to scalp you."

The one that ain't spoke a word so far give a moan. He's tall and lanky and don't look hardly tough enough to be a forty-niner, but there's them that'd say the same about me so I can't judge. He looked awful scared and was practickly shivering out of his socks while he done the moaning.

"Stow that racket," says the captain and turns back to me.

"Listen, boy, you know the Injuns and you can see the trouble we're in here. Is there a way out?"

"Not as I can see, Cap'n. I figured on there being around fifty men with guns at least."

He sucked his teeth and furrowed his brow some, pondering. Says I:

"There's maybe one way, but it's slenderish."

"Spit it out, boy. We're desperate men."

"Can all you men ride?"

It turns out they all can except the moaner, who moaned even louder when I told the plan.

"I can snitch horses from the Sioux and bring them back for a getaway. They're kind of busy singing and dancing right now so I reckon I can do it without getting seen, but I ain't about to put money on it."

"I can't ride . . ." moans the moaner.

"Quit that godawful mewling," sneers the ear-ring. "I can't stand to see a growed man take on so."

The one beside him says:

"I come near to crying myself when I think on how you started the whole thing, Rufus. If you had of aimed that first shot over their heads none of this would of happened, you peabrain."

"Who are you calling a peabrain, you dirty eggsucker!"

"Belay that!" roars the captain.

I seen it was bound to be uphill work rescuing men so full of argumentiveness, and there warn't all that much time left neither.

"Pardon me, sirs," says I, "I reckon you best save all the jawing and give me a yes or no on the plan."

"The boy's right," says the captain. "Give him back his gun and let him do it."

"I still ain't sure we can trust him," says Rufus.

"We don't have a choice in it. This way there's maybe a chance for us. Boy, do you remember any Bible lessons from before you got captured by them heathens?"

"Yessir, Cap'n, mostly about begatting and such. The Israelites done a fair amount of it when they warn't praying."

"Good," he says, and goes and fetches back a biggish book and holds it up for me to see. "This here's the ship's log, only you've got to pretend it's a Bible. I want you to put your hand upon it and swear before Almighty God you ain't about to trick us."

It would of wasted more time pointing out the foolishness of it all so I laid my paw on the log and say:

"I swear on the holy book I ain't fixing no trap or trick or not doing nothing that can't be called a genuine dyed-in-the-wool certified grade-A rescue, and may I be struck down by lightning and dwell forever in the hot place if it ain't true, so help me."

That made them rest easy and the captain claps me on the back and says:

"Our lives are in your hands, son. I reckon you're a real white man under them buckskins."

"Here's your gun, boy," says Rufus. "Now get, and don't come back without no horses."

"I'll do what I can. Wait for me on the far bank. If I don't show up inside an hour I guess you better run for it."

It never took long to get back to the camp and I never had trouble finding it neither. Only a deaf person would of missed them drums beating away and all the whooping too. I hunted around for Jim and told all, and he shook his head worried-like.

"De Injuns ain't goin' to b'lieve de men on de boat snuck dem horses away wid no help, Huck. Dey goin' to figure we done it."

"That's right, Jim, so we're going along too. I don't rate our chances too high anyway if the men get away and we're the only whites left around to scalp."

"I knows it, Huck. Dat Hepzibah, she'd have 'em lif' our hair befo' breakfas' an' eat like a horse after. If she ain't red den I ain't black."

He went off to get six horses ready while I strolled into the fire-light to give Hepzibah a look at me so she don't figure I run off or nothing. The men was all painted up by now with stripes and zig-zags all over theirselfs and looking mighty frightening the way they jumped around the fire, slashing the air with their tomahawks and

shooting arrows in the air, which I reckon is a waste if you're fixing
to have a battle next day, but proberly the squaws had the job of
picking them all up again at first light. It give me the shudders to
hear the bloodcurdling yells they give out, and they never looked
like the same men I admirated on the buffalo hunt. Watching a
bunch of folk get ready for fighting is just the fearfullest, ugliest
sight, and I never wanted to see more of it than I seen already, so I
slipped away to join Jim. There warn't no guards on the horses like I
counted on and we led them away into the dark, three apiece. We
never had time to collect our saddles, so all six of us will have to ride
bareback. When we got a fair step beyond the camp we mounted up
and led the rest on a fast gallop to the river and splashed across past
the *Nicobar* to the other side where the men was waiting.

"God bless you, boy," says the captain, then he catches sight of
Jim.

"Who's that?"

"That's Ben."

"He's a nigger, ain't he? What's a nigger doing out here?"

"He got captured by the Sioux too."

"What would they want with a nigger?" says Rufus.

"Oh, they put him to work fetching water and such."

That unsuspicioned them and they got on the horses, then the
moaner fell off and we had to help him aboard again with the others
cussing him plenty. Finally we was all set and rode up the bank to
level ground on the south side of the Platte. The moaner fell off
again soon as we started to gallop and we had to stop and set him on
his horse again. His legs and arms was all gone to jelly and he can't
hardly hold the reins, so I led his horse and told him to just hang
tight onto the mane and grip with his legs and we started off again.

We headed west along the bank fast as the horses would go for a
little while, then slacked off so they never got winded. We trotted
awhile, then galloped, then walked, and kept it up till daybreak,
when we had to stop a spell or bust the horses' lungs. The captain
says:

"We're mighty obliged to you, son. What was your name again?"

"Daniel McPhee, sir."

"Well, Daniel McPhee, you're an angel of mercy that's come to us
in our hour of need and I'm proud to know you. I'm Captain Jack

Banning and these two boys are Rufus Hoyt and Eben Woolcott, deckhands both. That there's Andrew Collins," he says, meaning the sobber and moaner, then he adds, "He's just a passenger," to explain why he ain't been acting manly, and behind his hand he says scornful, "Used to be a shoe clerk in St. Louis," which settled things once and for all.

✦ 16 ✦

A Daring Rescue—The Tables Turned—The Poet

of the Plains—Betrayed!—Revenge

of the Sioux

hen the sun come up full and
strong we rode fast again, nervous now that the Sioux must of found
the boat empty and be hot on our trail. I figured they'll likely catch up
around noon if they take along fresh horses to use. I was forever looking back over my shoulder and the others done the same. Mr. Collins
still moaned occasional but stuck to his horse and never let himself be
last in line. When we was on a slow trot Captain Jack says:

"What do you reckon, Daniel, will they catch us up?"

"They got to, or else lose face for letting us get away. Injuns is
awful proud."

"What kind of punishment do these redskins hand out?"

"It depends. They're partial to peeling your skin off in strips then
tying you onto an anthill, and cutting open your belly and showing
you your own steaming insides is popular too. Then again maybe
they'll just break all the bones in your body with a rock and let you
die slow that way, hung upside down as a rule. Seeing as they like
variety I reckon they'll do something different to all of us, but there's
none of it that's pleasurable. I recollect they captured a white man
and made him eat his own toes, chopped them off and boiled them
up right in front of him, then after he et them they done the same to
his fingers. Then they told him he can go free if he can run from one
end of the village to the other playing a flute, which was unfair in
my judgment. When he never managed it they cut off his ears and
nose and made him eat them too, even if he never had no appetite
after all them fingers and toes. They seen he had trouble cramming
it all in his mouth and done him a favor by cutting his tongue out to

make room, only he had to eat that too. Injuns is opposed to food wastage."

"Great God Almighty. . . . What happened then?"

"He died pretty soon after from overeating."

"I don't believe a word of it," says Rufus.

"That's up to you, Mr. Hoyt, only don't blame me if you can't play the flute after today."

"Ain't there any chance they'll just forget us?" asks Eben.

"I reckon not. The only chance we got is if the chief drops dead."

"That won't stop the rest."

"It surely will. When the chief dies the whole tribe downs tools and don't do another lick that day no matter what. It's the custom."

"You ever see such a thing while you was with them?"

"No, but I got told, and I believe it."

We kept going right on past noon without a break, not even to let Mr. Collins get down and clean his britches, which he filled from nerves and too much bouncing up and down. He stunk considerable and the others made him be last in line. He warn't happy about it but it turned out to be the safest place, because the Sioux showed up in midafternoon, only ahead of us instead of behind. Don't ask me how they done it; maybe they knowed the twists and turns of the river better and stuck to the north bank till they figured they was ahead of us then crossed over to wait. Anyway, there they was, a hundred strong, just sat on their ponies when we come over a rise and met face to face. Mr. Collins let out a groan and slid off his horse and started praying so fast he run through the Lord's Prayer in around fifteen seconds. The rest of us stopped dead. There warn't no use in trying to run; the horses was winded and there's nowhere to run to anyhow.

"This is it, boys," says the captain. "We're dead men for sure."

"Dang it!" says Rufus. "Now we won't ever get to see that cathouse in New Orleans you heard tell of, Eben."

"Furthest thing from my mind right now," says Eben, and puked all down his horse.

The Sioux was maybe thirty yards away, not moving, just watching us trembling and helpless. Chief Standing Tall was out front in a long war bonnet and a breastplate made out of little bones stitched onto rawhide. He raised his lance up and throwed it point first into the ground, which I figure is like declaring war. We already knowed that was the case, but Injuns has got the habit of doing these things formal, same as whites.

"Say, boy," says Rufus, "did you tell the truth about the chief?"

"Pardon me?"

"When he dies they all quit work, ain't that it?"

"But he *ain't* dead. That's him out front."

"Well, ain't that handy," he says, and leaned over and grabbed my Hawken and cocked it, aimed and fired, all in one go. It was the fastest piece of shooting I ever seen, and it never harmed his aim neither, because there's Standing Tall falling backwards off his horse. When I seen it I felt ashamed. He never done me no harm, but it's my gun and me telling about the custom that got him shot. Some of the warriors got down and lifted him up and I seen his breastplate is all splintered open and covered in blood, so he's dead.

They lifted him onto his horse and tied his ankles together underneath and let his head fall onto the mane, then they led him away toward the river. The rest of them never moved a muscle nor made a sound, just turned their horses and set off walking in a bunch behind. They crossed the riverbed and passed us on the other side, never once even looking over, and in a little while was out of sight.

"Well I'll be damned," says the captain. "You were right, boy! By God, Rufus, that was the finest shot a man ever made!"

"I reckon someone had to do it," says Rufus, handing back my gun. "The boy here warn't about to fire on his own kin."

"Leave him be, Rufus. It's thanks to him we're here and not butchered back at the *Nicobar*."

"Someone kick that Collins," says Eben. "He don't even know they're gone."

Mr. Collins was still on his knees praying silent, but he quit when he heard his name and looked around for the Injuns, which give the rest something to laugh at. We all got down to stretch and rest the horses, and Jim and me walked off a little way. Jim says:

"I knows what you mus' be feelin', Huck, but we come out alive. Das de thing you got to hold onter. It don' make no kinder sense, what de Injuns done jest now. I figure one dead man is a heap better'n six, 'specially if'n we's among de six. De killin' bin done now, an' you cain't change nothin'."

He talked sense, but I just never got over the feeling that we don't deserve to be alive seeing as it was Rufus that started everything by firing the cannon, but at the same time it's Rufus that saved us. How can you figure a situation like that and understand if it's right or wrong? There's got to be a deep thinker somewhere that knows the answer, but he warn't on the plains that day so I'll never know what it is.

Mr. Collins took his britches down to the river to wash them out and by the time they was dry it's time to move on again, only now it's a nice easy walk. No one talked much, likely thinking hard on how good it feels to be living and not dead, and the afternoon wore away like that.

Toward evening we seen something in the distance rising up from the land around and I reckernized it from a map Thaddeus showed me. It's Chimney Rock, and Fort Laramie is only eighty or so mile beyond it, which give our spirits a lift. Night come down before we got anywhere near and we spent it in the open, not too cold without blankets till the small hours of the morning when we all woke up shivering and hungry. Captain Jack says there ain't no point in waiting around shaking the flesh off our bones so we got mounted and set off before dawn, which is when I seen a kind of little deer with pronged horns and shot it, so we had breakfast in style and reached the rock in the afternoon.

It was mighty impressive up close, maybe four or five hundred feet high with a wide round base sloping up to the chimney part, which is shaped like a column with a broke-off jagged top, and we all gazed at it till our necks got stiff. On the north side right close to the rock we found wagon tracks, hundreds of ruts all jumbled together. It was reliefsome to know we ain't far from other white folks and it give us fresh heart to move on.

Next day I seen that Captain Jack ain't looking none too well, his face all gray and his eyes squinted with pain. He says:

"It's nothing to worry on, just indigestion. I reckon I must of swallered the ball you put in that deer."

He tried to laugh but it come out all wrong, more like a grunt, and he quit and rubbed his chest some. That kind of man don't like to be fussed over so I let him alone and we rode on. Then in the afternoon I heard a thump and turned around and there's the captain on the

ground next to his horse, and he's twitching and kicking at the air
with his feet. Rufus and Eben got to him before me and when I
kneeled down to see what's wrong he was already still and dead, his
eyes wide open and staring.

"I reckon it was his heart give out," says Rufus.

Mr. Collins got down and says:

"Is he really dead?"

"No he ain't dead, you idiot, just admiring the clouds."

"He was a decent man," says Eben, "and a better'n average river
cap'n. I guess it was losing the *Nicobar* that done it, just broke his
heart."

Rufus pulled the captain's cap down over them staring eyes and
we buried him in sandy soil off the trail. Mr. Collins done the Lord's
Prayer over him and we set off again. I felt sad about losing Captain
Jack's company because apart from him being a decent man it
means Rufus is the leader now on account of he's bigger and
tougher and louder than the rest, and I never trusted him all that
much. Rufus and Eben rode a little way ahead, talking low and
acting secretive, but I figured they're just recollecting old times
with the captain and regretting that he's dead, which is their private
business so I left them to it and got talking with Mr. Collins to pass
the time, Jim on one side and me on the other.

He wanted to know all about life with the Injuns and I spun him a
yarn that would take a whole separate book to put down on paper,
and he drunk it all in wide-eyed and open-mouthed like it's the most
wonderful story he ever heard. Jim was the same, and I got to admit
I was danged impressed with the tale myself by the time I got finished with it, especially the part about getting adopted as the chief's
son after I saved his life in a big battle with another tribe. I reckon if
I had of stretched the truth any more than I done it would of died of
thinness.

When I run out of lies he started in on his own story, and we
learned that he's thirty years old and been a shoe clerk since he's
fifteen and got unhappy bending over smelly feet all day and mea-
suring them and climbing up and down shelfs to find a pair of boots
that fit and generally getting treated like a nigger by even the meanest kind of trash that come in to buy. He used to lie awake of a night
dreaming about grand adventure all around the world, but the only

thing that happened was he got engaged to the daughter of the landlady at his boarding house, mainly on account of she proposed in a leap year. The engagement lasted a fair number of years, then the girl got peevish about the way he kept putting the wedding off and off, and in the end she turned around and married someone else, which give Mr. Collins a power of relief. Shoe clerking was getting him down after so many years of it and when he read about the gold strike in California he fitted his last shoe and quit his job and got on a riverboat up the Missouri and along the Platte. The rest we knowed, except for the part about him being a poet, which took considerable digging out because of shyness and getting laughed at by other men over it. He says:

"Are you acquainted with Lord Byron's *Childe Harold?*"

"I never met him nor his boy," says I.

"No, Daniel, it's a collection of poems written by Byron depicting his journeyings across Europe. It is my intention to do much the same thing, only based upon my journey across America. It will be an epic saga, filled with the spirit of a new and untamed land, raw and wild and virginal, and will include word portraits of the various characters I meet along the way, persons such as yourself."

"Me? You aim to write a poem about me, Mr. Collins?"

"Please call me Andrew. Yes, you are without doubt the most interesting of the personages I have thus far encountered and will merit at least a dozen verses."

"Care to rattle off a few just so's I get the feel of it?"

"I have not composed them as yet, but I do have some lines committed to memory which portray some of the men from the *Nicobar.*" Would you care to hear them?"

"Fire away, Andrew."

He give his throat a good clearing out and says:

> *"Two men together came aboard*
> *To join the teeming, anxious horde,*
> *One broad of shoulder, vastly tall,*
> *The other slender, even small.*
> *The first was bearded, big and strong,*
> *The second sickly, with hair worn long.*
> *Both men silent as the grave,*

The first a master, the second his slave.
Two men bound by bonds hid deep,
The smaller one cried in his sleep,
Tormented man, he frets and curses
Words too strong for published verses.
His tall companion offers aid,
A backhand slap three times he made
Upon the stricken dreamer's head,
Who woke up screaming, filled with dread
And babbled at a rate increasing
Of death and sin, his voice ne'er ceasing,
Till came the friend's restraining hand
Around his throat like iron band.
'Be silent, partner, stay your breath,
Or at my hands you'll meet your death.
Yonder passengers are sleeping,
Not one is roundabout a-creeping.
No one has heard your sad confession
Nor heeds your criminal profession.
None here cares for days gone by,
They yearn for freedom's open sky
And we, like they, will leave behind
Our past transgressions; west we'll find
A land forgiving, ever new,
Where such as we are far and few.
West is where the future lies,
So stay your tears and hurtful cries.
Let sleep o'ercome and purge your mind
Of deeds long done, of dreams unkind.'
Mysterious, this band of two
As dawn revealed the river view.

"Of course it requires polish, but there you have the gist of it."

Well, I never needed a picture to know he's writ a poem about Pap and Morg, even if he had them talking fancy like that. Says I:

"Andrew, these two men in the poem, did they go back to Fort Kearney on the rafts or take the boats up ahead to Fort Laramie?"

"I believe they went with the boats, but I can't be sure. Were the lines not to your liking?"

"Oh, it's mighty fine, I reckon. You surely do have the poetical touch, Andrew. Did you do a verse on Cap'n Jack?"

"I did. Perhaps you'd offer your opinion.

> *"The skipper of this noble ship*
> *Was full of beard, thin of lip.*
> *Upon his head a captain's hat,*
> *His figure lean and far from fat.*
> *Upon his brow a worried frown*
> *As on the flood the ice came down,*
> *But when the foaming waters cleared*
> *He gave a tug upon his beard*
> *And gave another on the whistle,*
> *The grandest sound in this epistle.*
> *'Hurrah!' we cried as paddles churned*
> *'We're off to where our hearts have yearned!'*
> *Westward-ho and feed the fire*
> *That takes us to our heart's desire.*
> *Three cheers for our gallant crew*
> *And three cheers for the captain too,*
> *For his keen eye and steady hand*
> *Will steer us to the promised land.*
> *Set forth upon the sweeping flood,*
> *Inflame the soul and stir the blood.*
> *For bold adventure's in the air*
> *And Captain Jack will take us there.*

"Those were the last lines I composed aboard the *Nicobar*. Now, of course, I have a shipwreck, bloody carnage and a thrilling chase to compose. I'll begin at once."

And he kind of squinted his eyes and nodded his head up and down in time with the verses that come rushing into his brain. It's the first time I ever seen a poem made in front of me, and we kept hush out of respect for the brain squeezing he needed to make all the tail-end words match up.

Rufus and Eben kept ahead of us, still talking and now and then turning around to see if we're still there, which we was so they done more jawing, and that's how the day passed. We still had meat left over from the deer and et our fill gathered around the fire that night.

Andrew kept right on poeming and me and Jim stayed quiet for it, doing our piece for artisticalness. The other two had the sulks over something and never opened their mouths except to put more food in, and it warn't long before we was all asleep.

What woke me up was the barrel of my Hawken poking in my ribs. Rufus was at the other end of it with Eben stood beside him.

"Get up," he says.

"Is something wrong, Mr. Hoyt?"

"You bet there is, and you're it. You and the nigger are just about the wrongest thing I ever come across. Now get up and wake the rest."

I done it and they made Jim and me stand over by a big rock so's he could cover us with my rifle. Andrew says:

"What in the world has come over you men? What does this mean?"

"I'll tell you, Mr. Poet, it's them two there. Me and Eben reckon they ain't who they say they are."

"What do you mean?"

"I mean they're Huckleberry Finn and Nigger Jim. There's a reward out on them for murder back in Missouri, and we aim to claim on it."

"I'm Daniel McPhee, honest," says I, "and this here's Ben, truly he is. . . ."

"And I'm the president," says Rufus. "Eben seen posters in St. Louis and St. Joe, and they give a description of you two plain as day. It won't do no good to deny it, we made up our minds on that money."

"This is outrageous," says Andrew, hopping from one foot to the other all anxious. "The boy has saved us from horrible torture and certain death. You can't repay him in this fashion. Even if he is who you say, what does it matter? Surely by his actions in rescuing us he has compensated for whatever misdeeds he may have done. . . ."

"We don't see it that way, poet," says Eben. "These two are worth a thousand dollars, maybe more by now, and that's the kind of money me and Rufus need to get to California. We lost our jobs thanks to the cap'n and his crazy scheme to run the Platte, so now we aim to be forty-niners. The reward'll be a grubstake for us, so don't go getting in the way."

"I must express my deep disappointment in your behavior. I have never before witnessed such ingratitude. . . ."

"Button your lip and get over there with them if you're that full of sympathy for murderers."

"Very well, if that's what I must do to express my contempt."

And he done it, too. Rufus says:

"I guess it sticks in your craw the way you got this far and then got captured, Finn."

"I reckon I'm a mite upset by it."

"Well it's no more'n you deserve, you little . . ."

He had to stop talking there on account of the arrow that's gone through his neck from one side clear out the other, and he's got a startled look on his face when he dropped the Hawken and crumpled on the ground. Eben's mouth hung open in surprise, so he never got the chance to say nothing before he got an arrow too, square in the chest. It only took but a moment. Andrew clapped a hand over his mouth and stood there looking horrified, then out from cover stepped Running Horse and two more Injuns. They never spoke a word, just scalped Rufus and Eben, making sure they got the ears and ear-rings on Rufus's scalp, then one of them went over to Andrew and got set to lift his hair as well.

"No!" I hollered, and he stopped. "Not that one! He ain't to blame! It was Rufus fired the cannon and you killed him already! Please don't go hurting no one else. . . ."

I got down on my knees in front of Running Horse and done the speech over again. He never understood a word, but the message must of been plain because they left Andrew alone and Running Horse give a speech, maybe telling how after mourning for a dead chief the warriors can go back to what they was doing before they got interrupted, or maybe telling us never to show our faces in Sioux territory again, I can't tell, but when he finished him and the others just melted back into cover and we three was left alone. Andrew says:

"This is a nuisance. I've already composed at least fifty lines describing your capture by natives as a child, and now I know it to be untrue all my efforts have been wasted."

"I'm sorry, Andrew, truly I am, but you can see why I done the lying."

"Yes indeed. I'm being foolish," he says, and took a look at the scalped bodies and fainted.

He looked kind of peaceful there on the ground so we left him reposed with his mouth open while we covered Rufus and Eben with rocks and got ready to leave. I can't say I'm sorry they was dead, which is natural considering the mean-hearted way they repaid what I done for them both, but the thing that bothers me is I never had hardly no feelings at all except maybe relief. Just a few months back seeing them peeled heads would of turned my belly and made me puke for a week, but now I ain't the same person no more, which is worrisome. A body that can't feel no sense of regret when he sees something like that ain't a complete and entire person without he's made of wood. Judge Thatcher told me once that all is flux, which means moving all the time like quicksilver, and time and change will make a man different no matter how hard he tries to hold back, so I reckon that's what must of happened to me, only the inside part of me ain't getting bigger with the change, only smaller. It's a puzzlement.

Andrew come around near the end of the job and I told him the whole truth about Jim and me and made him promise never to tell no one nothing, which he done willing and I believed him. He warn't a strong man but he's honest, and we could of done worse than have him along for company.

We got on the horses, of which there's only three left since Running Horse and his friends took the rest, and kept on following the wagon tracks leading to Fort Laramie. Along toward the end of the afternoon Andrew says:

"I have a few more lines for your consideration, Huckleberry."

"Let's hear 'em then."

> *"Outcast orphan, victim of Fate,*
> *Young Finn did all but hesitate,*
> *Accused of murder, set free from jail,*
> *He cast his lot beyond the pale*
> *And set off with his trusty friend,*
> *His hopeful journeyings to end*
> *In western lands where all are free*
> *To bathe in radiant Liberty.*
> *But Fate was not content to let*

Our unsung hero get there yet,
For on his trail the hounds did bay,
Reminding him of yesterday
While fleeing for his very life
To seek a haven free of strife.
Pursued across the trackless waste
Oft times slowly, oft in haste,
He crossed the daunting wilderness
With Christian charity unblessed.
Befriended by the savage Sioux,
A wordless bond between them grew.
That bond was burst asunder when
There came a ship of foolish men
Who witlessly grew scared and slew
A bevy of the noble Sioux,
A slaughter witnessed by young Huck
Who realized his run of luck
Had trickled off to well nigh naught;
'Gainst fickle Fate he'd so long fought
And now his dream of peace had gone,
Blasted to oblivion
By craven men of Finn's own hue,
Yet to his race he still held true
And chose to risk both life and limb
By saving souls unknown to him.
In darkness came the gallant Huck
With quiet display of youthful pluck
And won the trust of these few men
Who scarce believed their fortune when
He spirited them safe away
Before the dawning of the day.

"The chase and its outcome will follow on, naturally, but for the moment I feel quite drained by creative effort."

"Well I ain't surprised. You must of wrung your brain like a dish rag to strain out all that rhyming. How is it you ain't famous for being the greatest poet in the world?"

"I once tried to have some of my work published. The editor told me he had never in all his life come across such unmitigated doggerel."

"I guess he must of been impressed, and I don't blame him for it."

"I . . . I'm grateful for your appreciation," he says, blushing like a girl. He's modest too, is Andrew.

✦ 17 ✦

Invitation to a Wedding—A Stern Warning—The Woman

in Black—The Bride Unveiled—A Question of Color—

Declarations in the Hay

Two days later we reached Fort Laramie. It's bigger than Fort Kearney, built partly in mud brick and partly in wood, and there's the usual Injun tepees all around but no wagons, so whichever train come this way recent has gone again, heading for South Pass and the Rockies. We reined in a mile or so from the fort and run over the plan we come up with for safekeeping, the main part of which means Jim has to stay in hiding while me and Andrew go into the fort and buy supplies with Andrew's money and hear the news and see if Bulldog Barrett is sniffing around and if Pap's there. In my buckskins I look like an Injun, but with Jim alongside we still look like desperado Finn and his Nigger accomplice. So we found a place for Jim to hide away in a little ravine that never had tracks around it so no one ever went there, and promised to get back soon as we can. Then Andrew and me rode up to the fort, which is considerable bigger up close than she looks from a distance.

Inside there's hustle and bustle with soldiers and other whites all milling around and Injuns propped up against walls or sat crosslegged smoking pipes. There was stables and a blacksmith shop and a store set up in a corner of the quadrangle with a sign outside: PETTIFER'S STORE.

We went in and there's everything you could want to buy, and the storekeeper come up and says he's John Pettifer himself, around fifty with a friendly face. Andrew never had much idea what kind of supplies we needed so I give him a list before we went inside. Part of the plan is for me to act like I can't talk, just in case someone who speaks Injun tries to get jawing, which would of give the game away. Andrew

221

ordered what I listed and paid for it out of a little purse like women
carry and we put it all in sacks. Then he asks where can he buy saddles, seeing as how we're all of us tired of riding bareback, which
makes your legs itchy and mighty odorsome too. Mr. Pettifer took us to
another part of the store and showed a collection of saddles and harness, some of it new but mostly second-hand. Andrew never had good
judgment for it so I pointed out the ones we wanted, battered some but
still good, and the whole shebang come to a hundred and twenty-eight
dollars. Andrew broke out in a sweat at that, but he paid up and looked
at the money that's left in his purse with a mournful eye. It was a fat
purse before and slimmed down some now, but we needed what we
got so there ain't no helping it. Mr. Pettifer says:

"Who's the Injun?"

"His name is Turtle. He's my guide, dumb, poor fellow, but absolutely loyal to me."

"If there's just him and you how come you need three saddles?"

But I already had Andrew primed for that one and he says:

"We will use it for trade with redskins while passing through the
Rockies. Turtle tells me they prize saddles greatly."

"How could he tell you that if he's dumb?"

"I . . . uh . . ."

I seen the danger and started doing sign language in the air with my
fingers, darting them rapid this way and that, and Andrew says:

"Sign language. We communicate by sign language."

"I know Injun sign talk myself, Sioux, Shoshone, a little Cheyenne,
but I can't make head nor tail of what he's saying."

"That is because he's using white sign language, sir. In the east I
tutored deaf and dumb children and found it necessary to perfect a
means of communication with them. I have employed the same lessons with Turtle, rather than subject myself to the inconvenience of
learning native signs."

"That's right smart of you," says Mr. Pettifer. "Did you report to
Colonel Beckwith yet?"

"Colonel Beckwith?"

"He's in charge here. He takes down the names of anyone that
passes through, on their own or with a train. You'd best get on over
and give him the details. He's a stickler for the rules and likes things
sewed up neat."

"I'll do so immediately. May we leave our purchases here for the
moment?"

"Sure you can. I'll keep 'em behind the counter till you get back. You can put your horses in the stable for fifty cents a day. How long do you plan on stopping over?"

"Not long, I think. I'm impatient to reach California."

"Why don't you stay around for a few days? There'll be another train along any day now and you could ride along with them for company. There's a wedding this afternoon, too, and just take a guess who the lucky bridegroom is—yours truly. You wouldn't want to miss that, would you?"

"Indeed not. It's a comfort to find such civilized institutions operating out here. Goodbye until later."

We stabled the horses then walked across the quadrangle where a bunch of soldiers was marching back and forth, back and forth, raising dust and going nowhere, and Andrew asks someone where he can find Colonel Beckwith. We got pointed the way to his office, which is raised up behind some steps and a wide porch to keep the sun off the windows. I waited outside and smoked my pipe like all the other Injuns stood around and a minute later Andrew come out and says the colonel wants to see me too, so I went in.

The colonel's office ain't all that big but it's got the same kind of air the judge's office used to have. There must be something about important folk that rubs off on the walls. The colonel was sat behind a desk all covered in paper and had bushy sidewhiskers that stuck out like little wings on his face, and I figured he growed them to make up for having a baldy head. His nose was beaky and his eyes set close, and he give me a long looking over, more than most whites do when they see an Injun. I got to worrying on them eyes and hoped there's enough sun and dirt on my face to turn me Injun colored.

"What's his name?" asks the colonel.

"He calls himself Turtle."

"He's not full-blooded, his face and hair are all wrong."

"I . . . believe he's a half-caste."

"What tribe?"

"The Sioux."

"Just so. His shirt has the Sioux markings. You say he's mute?"

"Completely. He has a tongue but cannot make a sound. I suspect a damaged larynx, possibly a childhood accident or birth defect."

"Hmmmm. . . . Now then, Mr. Collins, you say you've come all the way from St. Joseph alone?"

"Until I met Turtle, yes."

"That's the foolhardiest thing I've ever heard! You're a greenhorn, Mr. Collins, and you just don't know what you're up against out here. You can consider yourself lucky to be alive. I daresay it's your friend here that's kept you that way."

"I acknowledge Turtle's importance in surviving the journey."

"The only safe way across country like this is by wagon train. A few weeks ago we had a handful of men stagger in here from a steamboat wreck back down the Platte. I ask you, who but a fool would book passage on a dry river like the Platte? They were lucky to be alive too, but did they stop to consider their situation? No sir, they did not, just bought horses from the local redskins and kept going west. I'm growing heartily sick of all you easterners swarming across the plains, ill prepared for what you find. The small parties who want to travel fast are the worst. They're just asking to get scalped. For my own peace of mind and your own safety I want you to join up with an incoming train, Mr. Collins. I can't make you do it, but if you take my advice your chances of reaching California will increase tenfold, that I guarantee."

"I'll give the matter my earnest consideration, Colonel."

"Do more than that, mister, or you'll more than likely wind up as buzzard food. Once you're with a train I also advise you to part company with the half breed. They're even less popular then full-bloods and you'll have trouble on your hands. You won't need a personal guide when you're part of a train. Just give him some rations and gee-gaws and he'll be happy to go back to the Sioux."

"Yes, Colonel."

"Another thing. Have you seen any sign of a boy about the same age as this one along with a tall nigger?"

"No, Colonel, I can't say I have. Are they lost?"

"The boy's wanted for murder and other crimes in Missouri and was last seen at Fort Kearney. A detective called Barrett tracked him there but the little snake slipped away and disappeared along with the nigger. His chances of survival are slim, but he's cunning. How he got that far I'll never know. Anyway, if you catch sight of him keep away or you'll have your head blown off. He's armed with a Hawken rifle like the one your guide has there and he's highly dangerous."

"I see. Is the detective still in pursuit?"

"He came through some weeks back, found the boy and nigger were not here and decided they must have slipped around the fort without leaving their calling card. He took off for the mountains to catch them and I've heard nothing since."

"I'll keep a sharp lookout for the boy, Colonel. What is his name?"

"Blueberry Finn. No, wait . . . I'm confusing him with the pie of the same name. . . . Huckleberry, that's it. Well, as I say, steer clear and tell someone with experience so they can either capture or shoot him."

Andrew knowed the colonel is saying he don't look like the kind that's tough enough to get mixed up in dangersome business and his neck turned pinkish, but he kept on smiling civil, proberly used to getting talked to that way. Then the colonel says:

"We're having a wedding this afternoon and a reception for the happy couple in the evening. You're welcome to attend. There'll be plenty to eat and a bowl of punch, just the thing to cut the trail dust in your throat."

"I'll certainly be there. Thank you, Colonel."

We went outside again and awhile later I took some of the supplies outside the fort to the hideaway so Jim can feed himself. I explanated how things was, mainly that Pap and the bulldog has both come and gone, and he says:

"We cain't join wid no train, Huck. You a passable Injun but I reckon I ain't never goin' to look like nothin' 'cept what I am, an' give us away."

"Don't worry on it. Andrew just agreed about the train to keep the colonel sweet. We'll be heading off directly come morning, just the three of us. We'll likely sleep inside the fort so don't expect us back before sunup, and if you light a fire keep it hid so no one comes poking around."

"I be waitin', Huck. Don' you go turnin' inter no drunk Injun at de weddin'."

"Injuns ain't invited," says I, and set off back to the fort.

Halfway there I heard galloping hoofs behind me and turned and seen a woman on horseback come flying along toward me with two giant dogs running alongside, practickly big as the horse and mighty savage-looking too with their tongues lolling out over their fangs. The woman was dressed all in black with a man's hat and long hair trailing behind in the wind. She's wearing a split skirt, not riding sidesaddle like most women do, and her horse was a black thoroughbred, the kind that don't like to go slow. She sat on him like a soldier with a rifle across the pommel and come thundering down on me like the angel of death. I had to make my horse sidestep or get run down. She flashed past without even looking at me and I seen a handsome face under the hat with a strong jaw like a man's, then she's gone by and streaking for the fort gates, riding full pelt right up to them and through, which must of made people jump that's inside.

I followed along slow and when I got inside there's the horse, a stallion I see now, and he's got a soldier leading him away to the stables, and there's the two dogs flopped on the porch outside Colonel Beckwith's office. They was just the biggest dogs I ever seen, with spiky gray hair all over and long snouts and legs and tails. Both has got fancy leather collars and are the kind you'd have set beside the throne if you was king. They had their eyes closed except when a fly landed on their nose and they snapped kind of lazy at it and dozed off again, looking peaceful but I kept a fair distance off anyway.

Then the woman come out of the colonel's office. She's tall and straight with considerable bosom out front, only the femaleness of it don't match up with her face, which is mannish like I told. There's two red patches on her cheeks and her eyes is flashing like she's riled over something. She stood on the top step and the dogs come to life and jumped up and licked her hand, but she warn't in the mood for affection and just ignored them, then come down the steps stamping hard with her boots, real riding boots for high-class riders. Then she seen me and stops dead.

"You," she says, pointing. "Do you speak English?"

I nodded yes before I can recollect if Andrew and me decided if I could understand English or only Sioux, but too late. She come over and says:

"Go to the cookhouse and fetch back meat for the dogs, and tell them if I shoot a wolf on Monday I expect it to be ready on Tuesday. Do you understand?"

I nod again and she says:

"Well don't just stand there like a post, do as I say."

So I went to the cookhouse, which I reckernized by the smoke coming out of a stovepipe chimney, and a man in a sweaty apron says:

"Well, what are you sniffing around for—scalps? I just cooked up the last one."

Him and two other men there laughed fit to bust, then he asks again what I want. If you ever tried to get across a message without using no words you know the kind of trouble I had. First I got down on all fours like a dog, then I held up two fingers to show there's two of them, then I gobbled air to show feeding, and when they just looked at me blank I done a lady's walk, only straighter and stiffer and the aproned one seen what I'm saying.

"The colonel's wife? She wants food for them dogs?"

I give a nod and he says:

"It's out back. You wait here."

So I did, and he come back with a couple big hunks of red meat all dripping in blood and give them to me. He says:

"You take that to Mrs. Beckwith, Injun, and tell her I'm sorry it warn't ready on time, but when you got to skin it and gut it and all the service can't be regular as she'd like. Go on."

Out I went with the meat leaking blood down my shirt and went over to the colonel's office, only she ain't there no more, nor the dogs neither. There's a soldier standing by a hitching rail and he seen me looking around and says:

"Hey, redbelly, you lookin' for them dawgser Miz Beckwith's?"

I nod and he says:

"Well, you just take that hunker meat aroun' the corner there and you'll see a house with curtains in the winders. That's where they're gonna be."

I done it and seen the curtains and knocked on the door. Mrs. Beckwith opened it and says:

"About time too. Bring it in and follow me."

She led me through to the back and there's a little yard there with a bush growed in a tub and a big bowl of water and the dogs, which when they seen the meat they flew at me like hairy eagles. I dropped it and stepped back quick before they tore me to pieces in mistake for the meat, which got ripped and bit and swallered in around half a minute.

"Come inside," she says.

So back through the house we went. This time I seen it proper, and even if it's small it's awful neat with furniture like in a regular home and a stretch of carpet on the floor and a whole wall full of shelfs groaning under books, just like the judge's library back in St. Petersburg. Mrs. Beckwith went to a bureau and took out a jar and opened it and it's crammed with candy all done up in little colored wrappers, and she stuck it under my nose and says:

"You may take one."

Which I done, and it's marzipan, mighty sweet. I never tasted nothing more delicious ever, and it seemed like no time at all before it melted away on my tongue.

"Well?" she says. "Don't you know how to say thank you?"

I pointed at my throat and shook my head and opened and shut my mouth a time or three, looking plaintive and sad while I done it and she says:

"Are you mute? You are? My gracious, how sad for you. Here, have another. Take two."

Them marzipans slid down easy and left me craving more, but she put the jar away and sat herself down on a fine-looking chair and stared at me with a finger on her chin awhile, then says:

"You are obviously not a full-blooded redskin. Was it your mother who was white? I thought so. Raped, I don't doubt. Has she survived until now? Well, perhaps it's a mercy. You were raised by savages? But now you have attached yourself to whites? Very good. There is hope for you. Can you read? You can? How amazing. And write? I find this hard to believe. Come over here."

We went over to a desk and she fetched out a pen and ink and paper and says:

"Write something for me."

I picked up the pen and dipped it and covered the paper with my arm so she can't see, and when I was all done she picked up the paper and give a loud laugh, because I drawed little stick pictures like the ones on Chief Standing Tall's tepee.

"Thank you," she says. "That's the first time I've laughed in months. Of course you can't read or write English. It was foolish of me to imagine you could. What a shame you're mute. I should like to know your story, young man."

Thinks I, not so much as your husband would, lady. She says:

"What is your name, can you tell me?"

I done another picture and she says:

"A turtle. Your name is Turtle. That's all? How touching. A turtle is separated from the world by its shell, just as you are separated by your silence. Poor boy. If you were not dressed in such a fashion I daresay you could almost pass for white. Yes, without the hair and feathers you would indeed. Why have I not seen you around the fort before, or have you just arrived? You have? With whom, more forty-niners? Just one? My husband will not be pleased. He deplores risk-taking of any kind. Do you wish to be a white man or a red man? No, don't shrug your shoulders, it is a choice you will someday have to make. Your unfortunate ancestry might perhaps be forgotten in the bosom of some worthy family, but not around here. Oh no, on the frontier red is red, and so too is half red. You may go now."

She's a peculiar person, the colonel's wife, kind of wild and free outside the fort with her horse and hounds, but uppity and school-marmish like the Widow Douglas inside, a contrary mixture I reckon.

After I left there I seen Andrew talking to a soldier over by the gates. I never wanted to disturb him in case he was fixing to make up a poem about the soldier so I wandered off to where there's a little room done out like a church with the doors open so I can see inside. It looks like this is where the wedding is going to be on account of there's raggy colored paper streamers strung hither and yon above the pews and lots of little flowers stuck in vases roundabout and a preacher pushing a broom across the floor. I poked my head in for a better look and he catched sight of my outfit and come storming at me, waving his arms like a windmill.

"Out! Out of here, you limb of Satan! Go back to your own kind and dance around buffalo skulls!"

I warn't about to argue none over it and ducked away before he aimed the broom at me. Andrew seen me and come over and says:

"What a remarkable man."

"Who is?"

"The soldier I was speaking with. Do you know, he cheerfully admits killing two men in Tennessee. He says they insulted his sister so he simply killed them. He wasn't even arrested for it. Such things are apparently commonplace in his region. Remarkable."

"Andrew, I been thinking how maybe it ain't such a good idea to wait around for the wedding. We got all the supplies we need. There ain't nothing to stop us going right now and saving a day."

"I see your point, Huckleberry, but Colonel Beckwith expects to see me at the ceremony and will be annoyed if he learns we have gone without waiting for the wagon train as he advised. I think it unwise to draw attention down upon us at this stage, don't you?"

"Well, maybe. I just don't like it here."

"My boy, there's blood on your shirt. . . ."

"It ain't mine. The colonel's wife shot a wolf yesterday to feed her dogs. I reckon they could of got it on their own without no help. Are you sure we got to stay?"

"I believe it's in our best interest to do so. Don't be made nervous by all this activity and population. Your native disguise is totally convincing. That reminds me, in future when we converse we must speak softly and use sign language in case anyone is watching. Never forget you're a mute."

"I won't."

So we stayed, and later on in the afternoon I wished we hadn't of because of what happened at the wedding. It started off simple enough with everyone in the fort gathered outside the church and the lucky ones inside. Being an Injun I just naturally warn't among them. A woman started pumping away on a pedal organ which give out a bleat like a calf with its leg getting chewed off by a crocodile. Somewhere in among the noise there's a hymn, but hid so clever you had to listen close to pick it out, which some done and sung along. It was just as different from McSween at the calliope with the virtues throating away as a mountain is different from a pancake, but no one shot the woman so it must of sounded fine to them.

From where I'm stood on the edge of things I seen the bride come across the quadrangle all done up in virgin white which has got to be a lie because she's got knuckles like walnuts wrapped around a bunch of flowers, which puts her past her prime. I can't see just how old she is on account of the veil that's over her face, but I reckon if the face matched the knuckles that veil was a real blessing. She's got Colonel Beckwith on her arm to give her away and he's tricked out in a uniform with gold braid snaking all over the cuffs and on his cap, which he took off before going in the church. The organist must of got the nod they're coming and hauled that calf away from the crocodile and proceeded to squash him in a cotton press instead, which is supposed to be "Here Comes the Bride." After that things quieted down for awhile and I could hear the preacher inside sounding stern while they done the will you's and I do's, but I never catched the names.

When they was hitched they come outside where the crowd is all set to dump little white flowers over them, but when Mr. Pettifer and his blushing bride come out into the sunlight I got one of them sick-in-the-gut feelings. The bride's got her veil up and she ain't none other than Mrs. Ambrose! She's all gussied up and clean-looking, but it's her all right, so she never had to go as far as California to get hitched after all. My legs wanted to run, only I told myself she ain't about to reckernize me under buckskin and feathers, not even if she got up close, which I aim not to let her anyway. So I got my legs under control and watched her and the eager groom go off under a shower of petals. Before they went inside Mr. Pettifer's store which is going to be the honeymoon cottage Mrs. Ambrose turned and put her arm back to throw the bunch of flowers. There was a considerable number of females all stomping on each other's toes to be the one that catched it, but Mrs. Ambrose put a heap of muscle into making that posy fly, and high up and over their squealing heads it went with a little pink ribbon trailing behind. And landed right in the crook of my arm where my Hawken is cradled.

A thousand eyes must of followed it there, and when they seen an Injun with them flowers there's a silence, then the females screamed and a man come over and grabbed the flowers and give me a shove backwards before he throwed the thing where it's intended to go. A skinny woman in spectacles hooked it and never knowed if to throw it away again seeing as it's been touched by an Injun or fill her pants because she's going to be the next that's wed. She was mighty plain and done the sensible thing, but spirits was considerable wetted down after that and I figured it's smart to make myself scarce. I slunk off to the stables and watched a soldier boy not much older than me groom Mrs. Beckwith's stallion. He seen me watching and says:

"Hey, Injun, bet you wished you had a horse like this'n."

I moved in closer and he talked on. I reckon he figured I never had the grip of what he's saying, so it's like talking to himself only not so lonesome. He says:

"Injun, this here's the finest horse west of the Missouri. Jupiter's what he's called and he goes like the wind. He'd leave them itty-bitty Injun ponies eating dust. You should see the colonel's wife up on him with her hair flying. She's a sight to see, you bet. And them dogs, they're special too. Romulus and Remus she calls 'em. Now me, I'd call the horse Thunderbolt and the dogs Tiger and Grizzly. They deserve better'n them nigger names they got. That Mrs. Beckwith, she's some kinder woman. Sergeant Hollander says she's one of them Amazons that cut their right titty off so's they can aim their bows better. He says one of these nights he aims to find out for sure if she's got the full pair or not. I'd sure like to see that myself. Sergeant Hollander, he'll do it, too. He's what they call a ladies' man, and Mrs. Beckwith, she don't see eye to eye with the colonel, no sir, not by a long streak. You can always tell when they had an argument. Out she goes with Jupiter and the dogs, and she don't come back happy less'n she's killed something. One time she stayed out all night, says she never wanted to come back empty-handed. The colonel was good and mad over that. Say, I bet you wished you was white."

I give him a smile to show I never understood and he looked at me scornful and says:

"Now I come to look at you I reckon you got white blood anyway. You're one of them halfbreeds, ain't you. I reckon that's what you are, you sorry-lookin' piece of trash. I wouldn't be no halfbreed for a hundred dollars. Bet your Ma was a whore that opened her legs willing to Injuns. I just bet she was. You stink, you halfbreed Injun. You're just about the smellingest thing I ever come across that warn't scraped off a boot."

Hearing him talk was strange, like I really *am* a halfbreed. I got all fluttery in the chest and angersome at the way he treated me, and at the same time I wanted to tell him I'm white like him, practickly apologize for looking like I do. But it weren't advisable so I stayed shut, just trembling all over with ragefulness and shame, and it come to me that Jim has got to tolerate feelings like this every time he come across ignorant sap-heads like the one in front of me. How he done it without killing someone or throwing himself in a river from the shame of it I can't figure at all.

I went out of the stable all dazed, like something awful just happened and there ain't a thing I can do about it, not even truly understand the way of it, just suffer the miserablest feelings, helpless and forlorn. Jim was the best kind of man you could of found if you looked for a lifetime across the world. He never had no selfishness and was a true friend that made himself a criminal on my account without even giving it consideration beforehand, and how many friends would do that? He never had no book learning so some might call him empty-headed, but it ain't so. He's got to be brave and strong like a hero just to get through everyday living without turning a hair, all because he ain't colored white, which he never had the choice of in the first place. Why, adding it all up Jim is about the noblest man I ever met, and I wished he was there so I can tell him face to face, but he's hid in a ravine outside the fort, making a sacrifice of comfort so's to make things safe for me, Huck Finn. It almost made me cry, the nobleness of it all, and I figured if Jim can handle it with dignification then so can I. I'd be proud to get called a halfbreed,and the whole trick is to take it with a face that don't give nothing away and a heart that stays calm, not fluttery and hurt. But I can understand how a red or black man might someday hit back at them that torments him so.

Nothing happened all the rest of the afternoon. Some Injuns tried talking to me or using sign language but I just shook my head, which give puzzlement to some and made others spit, so I was feeling kind of desperate by the time sundown come. They whipped the paper streamers out of the church and strung them up again in a big room in the officers' compound and got ready for the reception. I seen soldiers taking music insterments in there too, so it's going to be a regular wing-ding. Andrew never showed for hours and I got to worrying maybe he's in trouble, but I never should of bothered, because here he comes with a smile on his face. He seen me and come over and says:

"What an amazing woman, truly stupendous!"

"Who is?"

"Why, Mrs. Beckwith of course. Lydia. . . ."

The way he spoke her name set off a little tingle of alarm in my head.

"What's so special about her?"

"You were in her home, you saw the books. Huckleberry . . . She reads poetry. . . . She even *writes* it!"

"So?"

"But don't you see? She's a woman of great culture, a rose struggling to survive in a desert of thorns, a lonely bird in a forest of silence, a questing mind bound by fetters of ignorance. Her husband . . . what an oaf!"

"Hold hard there, Andrew. How come you know so much about her?"

"We met at the wedding. She asked my name and when she heard my story and realized I am your employer she invited me to her home for afternoon tea. She drinks *tea*, Huckleberry, can you imagine it? Delicate china cups in this far-flung outpost of civilization. We talked for hours. I admitted my predilection for the muse and she confessed also, and then . . . we exchanged verses! She has talent in abundance.

I have one of her recent efforts here. You must hear it."

He drug a piece of paper out of his pocket and tilted it so light from a window shone on it and commenced to read.

"ODE TO A DEAD WOLF

I gaze upon your shaggy form
That lieth dead upon the ground
With lips drawn back and eyes forlorn,
Already flies do swarm around
To feast upon your noble frame
And slake their thirst upon your blood
That floweth freely without shame
In copious torrents, nay, a flood
Of crimson wine that stains the earth
On which you lie, oh mighty lord
Of prairie wilds, I am not worth
Your proud disdain, yet with my sword
Have lately slain a precious thing.
Fleet and free, unfettered Lupus, lordly beast
So cruelly slaughtered, fallen king,
For easy sport and canine feast.
Forgive me, let my spirit fly
With yours away from here, my liege,
To lands less harsh where you and I
May run together 'neath the trees
In forests of Elysium, there to dwell
In harmony, set free from care,
Far removed from tolling knell
Of death, we'll linger there.

"Sublime, such beauty of expression, such limpid poignancy, don't you agree?"

"It's powerful stuff all right, but I reckon she used a rifle, not a sword."

"Poetic license, Huckleberry. These subtleties are perhaps beyond your understanding. What a cruel waste."

"The wolf? I reckon he got et, every scrap. Them dogs has got appetites."

"Lydia," he says, impatient. "To think she must forswear the culture and comforts of polite society in order to be with . . . *him* in this crude place. Fate has treated her unkindly, I fear. Colonel Beckwith has no appreciation of her poetical accomplishments. He dismisses the outpourings of her soul as mere word rhymings, the plaything of children. He is unlettered and boorish. A soaring dove has been chained to a grunting hog. Her spirit is waning, I can tell. Without nourishment it will fade and die."

I can't hardly see a woman like Mrs. Beckwith fading and dying, not without a fight, but Andrew had the bit between his teeth now and rattled on about nourishment and enrichment and food for thought, which got my belly growling so I munched on some dried meat I kept in my pouch along with rifle balls and such and he finally talked himself out, which give me the chance to slip a word in edgewise.

"We got to leave tomorrow definite, Andrew, wagon train or no. There's a woman here that knows my face."

"What woman?"

"The one that got married today, Mrs. Ambrose."

"You mean Mrs. Pettifer. How can she possibly know you?"

I told him and he says:

"I shouldn't worry. In that costume she won't give you a second glance. We must stay here until the wagons arrive."

"But we can't join up with them, not with Jim along, and I ain't going nowhere without him."

"Yes, yes, I realize that, but it's essential we at least give the appearance of having joined, for Colonel Beckwith's satisfaction. We'll consider ways around the problem of Jim when the time comes. For the moment we must simply relax."

It was easy enough for him to say, getting invited to the reception dance like he was, but I had to do my relaxing somewheres else. By the time all the guests arrived and the music got started I found the right place, up in the hayloft in the stables.

I tried getting some shuteye but the music come drifting across and kept me wakeful. I had a bad feeling inside of me, not the gut-rumbles from eating too fast, something else, a kind of fear that warn't directed toward no particular thing, just squirmed around inside me looking for something to latch onto. I got drowsy halfway through a waltz and slumbered off awhile and dreamed about the *Injun Princess* sailing across the ocean with all sails set and me at the wheel with spray flying over me and whales leaping out of the water alongside. It was the best kind of dream and I warn't happy to leave it, but voices below woke me up, and they ain't unfamiliar.

"Are you sure we won't be missed?" says Andrew, sounding drunk.

"And if we are, Mr. Collins, what of it?" says Mrs. Beckwith. "Does the prospect of an angry husband frighten you?"

"Indeed no, I was merely concerned for your obligations as garrison hostess."

"My obligations can jump into deep water and stay there. Not one of those present is of any interest to me except yourself, Mr. Collins, and I find it impossible to hold a coherent conversation amid such babbling as the rest are given to. They talk of nothing but the heat, and in winter of nothing but the cold. The unfortunates who married today will be discussed until Christmas, and God knows there is nothing about them worthy of discussion."

"You must find conditions here intolerable, Mrs. Beckwith."

I eased over to the edge of the loft and peeked down. They was right below me, stood a little apart. Mrs. Beckwith says:

"I hope you do not find me forward or outspoken for having opened my heart to you on so brief an acquaintance."

"Not at all. I am honored to be the recipient of such intimate outpourings, hence my reciprocation."

"You must understand that Fort Laramie is not often blessed with the presence of gentlemen of your breeding and sensitivity, Mr. Collins."

"I appreciate your candor, Mrs. Beckwith. Kindred spirits will always attract each other as if by magnetism."

"Just so. I have great sympathy for your own plight. It was surely a bitter experience to be banished from the family estate as you were."

Andrew heaves a sigh and says:

"Father simply could not understand my infatuation with the muse. He wished only for a son content to inherit and expand the family business, but control of a vast merchandizing empire spelled only boredom and spiritual poverty for me. We quarreled endlessly, and Father altered his will in favor of my younger brother, upon whose shoulders the burden must now rest. He will make an ideal worshiper at the altar of Mammon. As for me, no task lures me other than the scaling of Parnassus, there to acquire riches of the soul rather than the purse."

"A noble endeavor," she says, all gushing, and I seen he spun her a pack of lies that never had a word about being a St. Louis shoe clerk in them. She goes on:

"But we did not come here for this. You intimated there was a special purpose in our being alone."

"Indeed there is, Mrs. Beckwith."

"Please call me Lydia, and I shall call you Andrew. Formality is redundant between such as we."

"Of course . . . Lydia."

And they looked at each other awhile, then she says:

"The purpose?"

"Ah yes, forgive me dear lady. Your gaze held such fascination I temporarily forgot myself. I have composed a verse in your honor, and rather than risk compromising you by committing it to paper which might later be found and read by a certain person, I will deliver it here and now orally, with your permission."

"I await with expectation," she says, and he cleared his throat.

"ODE TO A LADY

Far out beyond the Great Divide
Where eagles soar and Injuns ride
There dwells a flower of rarest kind
A-blooming in the sun and wind.
More beautiful, this lovely flower
Than ever grew in castle bower,
Alone, untouched among the weeds
She thrives among the centipedes
With ne'er a drop of water clear
To slake her thirst, this flower dear,
Surrounded by a bramble wall
That someday soon perchance may fall
And set her free to spread apart
The luscious petals of her heart.
For flowers that come late to bloom
Are sturdier, and need more room

To spread and grow, freed from restraint.
Whose portrait do I herein paint?
Lovely lady, it is you
Who from this flawless flower grew."

It's hard to credit he's the same man that filled his pants when we was escaping from the Sioux, but there he is, spouting away full of confidence and poems right below me, and it shows how folks can have different sides you never would of guessed was there without you seen it with your own eyes. But maybe it's just the drink inside of him.

"Oh, Andrew," says Mrs. Beckwith. "That was so . . . wonderful. Is there more?"

"Alas, not as yet, but fear not, there will be stanzas abounding dedicated to you in the completed epic."

"I am honored," says she, and I reckon she means it.

"And deserving of it," says he, and he ain't fooling neither, because all of a sudden they flung their arms around each other, only she's stronger and heavier than him and put a mite too much effort into the clinch and they went over backwards into an empty stall. There's a thud as Andrew's head connected with the wall on the way down and Mrs. Beckwith got all anxious.

"Andrew, Andrew. . . . Speak to me, Andrew. . . . What have I done? . . ."

Then come a voice at the stable door, and it's the colonel.

"Lydia, is that you in there?"

"Yes, Horace," she says, jumping up and brushing straw off her dress.

"What are you doing here? There are guests to attend to."

"I was checking on Jupiter," she says, coming forward before the colonel can get a look at Andrew's feet poking out of the stall.

"You spend more time with that horse than you do with me," says the colonel.

"Only because I find his company more congenial, Horace," she says.

"And what's that supposed to mean?" he snaps.

"Nothing, dear. Shall we rejoin the party?"

Away they went with the colonel mumbling and grumbling. I

clumb down the ladder and throwed a bucket of water over Andrew and he hauled himself onto his feet.

"Huckleberry. . . . What are you doing here?"

"Trying to get some sleep, but it's hard going. How's the wing-ding?"

"Awful. Those officers are so smug. They spoke to me as if I were a child. I believe I'll go back and tell them exactly what I think."

"I reckon you been sucking up the punch, Andrew."

"A glass or two, no more."

"Was they bucket-sized or what?"

"Perhaps I did overindulge. My head is giving me pain . . ."

"Can you climb to the loft?"

"Why would I wish to? Please don't bother me with foolish questions. My head . . ."

"You can't sleep down here, you'll get stomped on by horses. Put your foot on the rung, that's it, now put the other foot on the next one up, then the first one on the next one. . . . No, Andrew, you got to hold onto the ladder with your hands too or you'll fall down again. Give it another try. First foot on first rung . . ."

I got him up there, but it took a heap of time and sweat. He sunk into the hay and was asleep before it quit rustling, and I joined him pretty soon after. The last thing I seen was a star winking at me through a gap in the roof slats.

◆ 18 ◆

Friends Fall Out—A Necessary Note—Harmless

Entertainment—The Disguise Fails—Faith Rekindled

Next morning Andrew was tetchy and warn't in the mood for talk, so I let him be and walked out to see Jim. He was mighty glad to see me but wants to know where the horses and Andrew is.

"There's been a change of plan, Jim. We ain't going till the wagons get here so the colonel don't get riled about us going off alone. He's a believer in safety in numbers, so we got to hang on awhile yet."

"I don' like it, Huck."

"Me neither, but we need Andrew. I reckon it'll only be a day or two."

"Say, Huck, kin you hear horses?"

"Get down, Jim," says I. "Someone's coming!"

We ducked down under the lip of the ravine, which ain't wide nor deep, and heard the hoofbeats get louder, two horses I reckon. I could feel the ground shake they're so close, then they went sailing across over our heads and kept going away from the fort. I peeked over the lip and it's Mrs. Beckwith with Andrew. They headed over a rise out of eye-reach with just Romulus and Remus for chaperons.

"Jim," says I, "I reckon we got a problem."

"Warn't dat Andrew?"

"It was, and the lady with him is the colonel's wife, and worse yet, Jim, she writes poetry. That's the problem."

"He sparkin' wid her, Huck?"

"It's got all the earmarks of a full-blowed romance far as I can tell. Dang it, he ain't ever going to want to leave now, not with her talking poems in his ear."

We put our heads together and come up with a plan, then I went

240

back to the fort to wait for Andrew. I got mighty fretful just ambling around without nothing to do but worry. One time I seen Mrs. Ambrose go strolling across the quadrangle; I never reckernized her straight off on account of the smile she's got on her face, so I figure married life agrees with her. She looked at me once and stopped and the smile slipped some, then she shook her head and walked on, so my disguise is good and my heart quit hammering.

Andrew and Mrs. Beckwith got back in the late afternoon, both of them looking happy. The horses got led away to the stables and I followed them to Mrs. Beckwith's place and seen them go inside, which ain't so good.He come out after awhile and I collared him and say:

"You got to quit sparking with Mrs. Beckwith."

"I beg your pardon?"

"If you don't you'll land us in a heap of trouble. I want to leave right now, and so does Jim."

"But the wagons have not arrived."

"Never mind no wagons and never mind what the colonel wants. We got to go *now*."

"Don't be foolish, Huckleberry. There is no cause for alarm."

"There surely is. You don't eat the lion's food if you're in the lion's den."

"Meaning?" he says, looking down his nose at me.

"You know what I mean. She's the colonel's wife, dang it. Ain't you got no sense at all?"

"I thought we were friends."

"It's so, but you ain't acting like one, not risking everything this way. When you play with fire I reckon you got to expect burnt fingers."

"How many more homespun homilies are you going to bludgeon me with? I assure you there is nothing to worry about, and I resent your intrusion into my private life. Now if you'll excuse me I have verses to prepare in commemoration of the day's events."

And off he went all stiff and offended. There warn't nothing else for it, I had to use the plan. I went and knocked on Mrs. Beckwith's door and she opened it.

"Why, Turtle, what a surprise. What is it you require?"

I pointed away off somewheres and she says:

"Is it Andrew? What does he want? Oh, of course, you can't tell me."

I run off quick around the corner and hid behind a barrel. She come after me looking real worried but never seen me there.

"Drat the boy," she says, and went off to look for Andrew. Soon as she's gone I went back to her door and let myself in when there warn't no one looking, then went to the writing desk and put pen to paper.

> Your wife is sparking with a person that ain't you and acting
> like Jezebel so you better put a fence around her quick
>
> A Friend

It's a lowdown trick that don't do me no credit, but I'm a desperate man. I folded the note and shoved it in my waistband then put the pen back the way it was and slid out the door breathing, fast. A genuine criminal would of stole them marzipans too.

There's a fair number of people walking around in front of the colonel's office so I'll have to wait till dark to push the note under his door. That's what I figured, but fickle fate never wanted it to be that way, because just before sundown a wagon train rolled up to the gates and there was noise and bustle and confusement. There was maybe thirty wagons and the wagonmaster come in to meet the colonel. I'm curious, so I hunkered down under the side window of the colonel's office which is open on account of the heat and spread my ears. The wagonmaster introduced himself as Mr. Berringer and after considerable jawing about the trip he says:

"A couple of days past Chimney Rock we found two graves that struck us as strange. We've seen plenty of graves along the way where cholera victims have been buried, but they always had a cross planted on them. All these had were rocks piled atop the corpses, so we opened them up and found two white men, both scalped, both with arrows still in them which our guide identified as Sioux. There's something mysterious in the way these two were laid out, Colonel. I don't believe Injuns are in the habit of even piling a few rocks over their victims for decency, but then whites don't go scalping each other, so it looks as if they were killed by redskins and buried by whites, and not too long ago, maybe four or five days."

"Those are indeed peculiar circumstances, Mr. Berringer," says the colonel. "There have been no recent incidents involving the

Sioux, but if they have begun to pick off stray travelers they must be taught a lesson. I'll send out a patrol to find and question the Sioux tomorrow, in fact I'll lead the expedition myself and take whatever action I deem necessary if they are responsible for the deaths of these men. Meanwhile I suggest you take your train over to the west side of the fort and make camp. You'll find plenty of grass for your teams there."

"Thank you, Colonel. We'll only stop over for one day."

I never waited around to hear no more but went looking for Andrew, only it was him that found me and he's looking real vexated. He says:

"Huckleberry, what kind of game are you playing? Lydia has informed me you brought her a silent message from me, a message I did not send. Explain yourself, please."

"She must of got me mixed up with some other Injun. There ain't time to argue on it. There's a wagon train just arrived, so now you got no excuse for not leaving the day after tomorrow when they go."

"Yes. . . . Well . . ." he says.

"If you don't then me and Jim ain't going to wait around no more."

"You wouldn't abandon a friend would you, Huckleberry? Please try to understand my situation. Lydia is the woman I've been searching for all my life. To leave without her is . . . unthinkable."

"Well, you got to. She ain't about to set up house with no shoe clerk."

"I have not mentioned that aspect of my past to her as yet," he says, squirming some.

"And I just bet you ain't going to neither. She'll find out sooner or later, Andrew, you know she will, and then she'll fling you out the window or shoot you."

"Lydia is the gentlest creature on the face of the earth."

"You can believe it if you want, but I reckon she's a wolf inside sheep's wool, so don't blame me if you get bit."

"I respect your concern for my welfare, Huckleberry, and will make my decision tonight. The Beckwiths have asked me to dine with them."

"Then you'll likely get told news I already heard, namely Rufus and Eben got dug up and the arrows in them reckernized for Sioux, so the colonel aims to go out tomorrow and find them and ask a few hard questions."

"He'll be absent from the fort?"

"Him and a parcel of troopers."

"Hmmmm . . ." he says and turns on his heel, and we went our different ways.

I went outside the fort to watch the train get pulled into the spot the colonel told them and set up camp. It was just like when the Naismith train reached Fort Kearney, with Injuns swooping down on them selling their women for whiskey and trade goods. It's dark by now and there's people red and white around the campfires and plenty of noise. Then I heard a bell ringing and pretty soon seen Mr. Pettifer and Mrs. Ambrose coming through the crowd with her swinging a hand bell and him bawling out at the top of his voice:

"Come to the store first thing in the morning, folks! Everything you could want! Hardware, harness, drapery, firearms, all kinds of supplies at a reasonable price! Just inside the main gates, folks! Look for the sign! Pettifer's Store! You won't find another before you get to California so take this chance to buy what you need first thing tomorrow! Pettifer's Store is where to go to get all the things you need! Quality goods at fair prices for one and all!"

When they passed me by Mrs. Ambrose give me a look then turned away, the second time that day she come close to suspicioning me for Huck Finn, but she kept on going and swinging that bell. The camp warn't a pretty sight, so I left and legged it to Jim's hideout and give him the news, and he says:

"'Pears to me you ain't usin' de big stick on Andrew like you oughter, Huck."

"What big stick?"

"He's mighty scareder de colonel's wife findin' out he ain't no genulman. You got to tell him you goin' to spill de beans on it if'n he don' promise to leave when you say."

"It's a mean trick to play, but no meaner than slipping the colonel a note about his wife, safer too. I reckon you're right, Jim. If the carrot don't work you got to use cunning, the big stick kind."

We talked awhile longer then I strolled through the train on my way back to the fort. There was still plenty of drinking and whoring going on and I never seen one white woman around, so they either shut theirselfs away in the wagons to ignore the sights or else it's a train of only men, two of which was stood watching a squaw get throwed out of a wagon after she's been used. She drug herself away half drunk to find another customer, pitiful and dirty and sad.

"Look at that," the first man says. "Did you ever see a more disgusting sight? These redskins must be the most degenerate beings in creation. They have not one whit of modesty or decency or cleanliness."

"Morally bankrupt," says the second, and points at me. "Look at that, for example. Only a boy, yet here he is with the rest of them, most likely trying to sell his mother or sister. Obviously not enough to eat either, look how skinny he is. Dead before he's twenty-five I'll bet."

The first is short and potbellied and the second tall and smoking a cigar, both of them dressed neat for forty-niners; you could tell they ain't farmers or rivermen, nothing like that. They talked near as good as Andrew. The first one says:

"Looking at a specimen like that makes you laugh at the theory that redskins are one of the seven lost tribes of Israel."

"If that were so the Jews would turn Catholic," says the second.

That give them both a laugh, then they seen I'm still there staring at them, and what I'm doing is testing myself to see if I can take a heap of scornful talk and still walk away proud to be a halfbreed.

"What do you think he's after, money? He appears not to be selling anything."

"Could be drunk, I guess. Very little expression on the features, you'll notice."

"Rather like a nigger in that regard."

"Exactly. He's a red nigger."

They surely knowed how to crack a joke, them two, and I laughed along with them, kind of curious to hear what else they come out with. The potbellied one crooked a finger at me and I went over. "What is your name?" he asks.

I never give no sign I understood American and he says: "Tell me, young savage, are you aware that you are the lowest form of life?"

I give a nod and a grin, which made them laugh all over again, then he says:

"And is it true you take pleasure in fornicating with your own mothers?"

Another nod had them practickly in stitches. He says:

"But best of all, I'm told, is the custom whereby the men abuse each other while standing in a circle under the full moon. Is that correct?"

I nodded again and they had to hold each other up. Potbelly barely manages to talk around his tears when he says:

"We must not, of course, forget the redskins' supreme delight, which is the buggering of buffalo. I'm right aren't I, Injun?"

"Almost," says I, "but it's a heap more fun to listen in on talking jackasses. We don't get the chance too often, so thank you and goodnight, gents."

And off I went with them staring after me, not making a sound. I was walking tall all the way across to the fort, only the gates had been closed for the night, which took some of the starch out of me. I never wanted to sleep on the ground, not with a hayloft waiting for me inside, so I knocked hard on the gates. A couple of sentries poked their heads over the wall and looked down at me.

"Go take a squat," says one. "No Injuns allowed in after dark."

"Wait on," says the other. "Ain't that the Injun that's with the feller Miz Beckwith went ridin' out with?"

"How kin you tell? They all look the same."

"See that long rifle? That's how. Better let him in or there'll be complaints. I ain't pullin' no extra guard duty, not if I kin help it."

So they let me in, and it means they had to come all the way down off the sentry platform and slide back a heavy log to do it, which put them in a mean temper. When I come through they give me a boot in the rear that sprawled me in the dust, but it made them laugh so they never done nothing more to me. Staying proud when you ain't white is a mighty hard thing to do. I picked myself up and headed for the stables, but when I passed the store porch a voice come from the shadows.

"It's you, ain't it, Jeff Trueblood, or should I say Huck Finn?"

I looked close and seen Mrs. Ambrose in a rocking chair.

"Yes, ma'am," says I.

"Come up here where I can see you."

I went up on the porch and stood beside her and she looked me up and down, rocking herself gentle all the while.

"I wouldn't hardly of reckernized you in that Injun rig-out, but when I seen you a time or three it started me thinking, and I figured where I seen that face before. You created an almighty fuss when you busted out of Fort Kearney. The whole train talked on it all the way across the plains. It was just awful the way you treated that poor girl that went to give you comfort, knocking her on the head that way and stealing her clothes, downright indecent. What have you got to say for yourself?"

"Nothing, I guess."

I wanted to make myself more righteous in her eyes, but it would of meant saying Grace done a crime to help me escape, and I never wanted to get her in trouble over it. Mrs. Ambrose says:

"Did you do all them things they say you done back in Missouri?"

"No, ma'am, Mrs. Ambrose."

"I'm Mrs. Pettifer now, since yesterday. You seen the wedding. Why, you even got the bouquet," she says, and laughs, which made me rest a mite easier, then she says:

"Are you saying you're innocent, first, last and always?"

"Yes, ma'am. Hope to die if it ain't true. I been hounded all this way for nothing, only I can't prove it."

"How am I supposed to believe that when you can do a thing like you done to that poor girl? Answer me that."

Well, I can't, not without hurting Grace. Mrs. Ambrose says:

"Are you denying you done what she says you done to get away?"

"I ain't saying nothing, ma'am."

"You ain't even going to try and convince me you ain't a liar?"

"No, ma'am. You can believe or disbelieve it, but I ain't saying nothing. Are you aiming to tell the colonel about me?"

"Do you reckon I should?"

"No, ma'am. If I was you I'd turn a blind eye and let an innocent man go free, I truly would."

"Do you know what I think, Huckleberry Finn?"

"No, ma'am."

"I reckon that girl was a friend of yours. Would I be right?"

"I ain't saying."

"Well I ain't going to press you on it if you're protecting her. How did you come to be dressed that way?"

"Disguise, ma'am. They're all looking for a white boy, not an Injun."

"That's mighty clever of you. You're a mighty smart child. That detective with the highfalutin' manner looked silly as a clown when you got free. Funniest thing I ever seen was his face when he got the news. You brung him down a peg that night. But you watch out, he's the kind that never lets up."

"I know it, ma'am."

"What are you fixing to do now?"

I trusted her somehow, so I say:

"Same as before, ma'am, go to California."

"That's your dream, I reckon."

"Yes, ma'am."

"Well, it was my dream too for awhile, but I only got this far. You're proberly thinking I mellowed some since you last seen me."

"Yes, ma'am. You was right waspish before, if you'll pardon me."

"I know, I was a regular cross-patch, but a grieving widow gets that way. Now I'm married again to a good man I look at things different. That's what marriage is for, to make you see things different. If you don't get yourself hanged in the meantime I hope you'll one day find a nice girl and get married."

"Yes, ma'am."

"Only not with that Grace girl. She's too flighty."

"No, ma'am. She's older'n me anyway. Are you going to tell on me?"

"You're wanting a straight yes or no?"

"I'd appreciate it, ma'am."

"And if I say yes are you going to kill me?"

"You know I ain't."

"That's right, Huck Finn, I know you ain't going to kill, and never did no killing, and you can take that for a no."

"Thank you, Mrs. Amb . . . Pettifer. I'm grateful."

The door behind her opened and out come Mr. Pettifer.

"Not coming to bed, dear?" he asks, then he seen me. "Why, what's the Injun doing here?"

"Just passing the time of night with conversation," she says, and to me, "Go along now, Injun. You'd talk the leg off a chair."

So I kind of nodded and backed off and headed for the stables again, and behind me I hear Mr. Pettifer say:

"Talk? But he's a mute. The man he's with told me so. They use sign language."

"Is that so?" she says. "Well to be truthful it was me that done most of the talking. I wondered why he never held up his end of the conversation."

I slipped into the stables and up into the loft. Andrew warn't there, so I figured the Beckwiths must of put him up at their place, and I hoped Mrs. Beckwith has got more sense than to go walking in her sleep and falling on top of him accidental-like. I got snugged in and settled down for sleep. It was just dandy the way Mrs. Ambrose never wanted to turn me in, and it give me a warm feeling to know there's people that are decent and clear-headed in spite of all, which is a comfort. If I had of been the prayerful kind I would of done a prayer for that woman, but I ain't so I never, and just hoped she knows how grateful I am for being give a helping hand for once and not the back of one.

Then I recollected the note I got stashed in my britches. It's the perfect time to slip it under the colonel's door while everyone is sleeping, but I turned it over in my head and reckoned I'd let it slide. With the colonel heading off into the wild blue yonder tomorrow Andrew can't say he won't leave ahead of the train on account of it'll upset the colonel's notion of what's safe and what ain't. No colonel means no argument, but there's still the problem about Lydia. Well, if he never had the strength to drag himself away from her there's always Jim's big-stick plan to hit him over the head with. A lady like that won't want no truck with no shoe clerk. I got myself satisfied on that line of thinking, then tore up the note seeing as I won't be needing it no more. Tom Sawyer would of et it. Then I fell asleep.

✦ 19 ✦

A Change of Plan—Restless Nights—A Wayfarer's Grave—

Gateway to the Rockies—New Arrivals—

Bearmeat and Misery

Come daybreak there's a powerful din below with horses being saddled up and led out into the quadrangle. I slid down the ladder after most of the stalls was emptied and watched the troopers mount up and form ranks facing the colonel's office. He come out onto the porch wearing field uniform with a pair of fancy buckskin gloves tucked in his belt and made a speech.

"Men," he says, "word has reached me that the Sioux have murdered two white men in cold blood. It's my intention to find out the truth on this matter. I will leave no stone unturned in my efforts to find the facts. You know the Sioux. They have a nasty reputation. But you know me as well, if not better, and you know that I never flinch from doing my duty, no matter what the consequences."

A trooper near me kind of laughed in his nose, and it was catching and run up and down the ranks till half the company was doing it. They kept it up till a captain give them a dirty look, but the colonel never heard it or else just ignored it. He goes on:

"We may face danger out there, but we are well equipped for action."

"Hope he brings along a pot to shit in when he sees them Injuns," says a trooper out the side of his mouth.

"No need," says another, talking soft. "He'll make sure we never come in sniffin' distance of 'em."

"This will be a seven-day foray, maybe longer," says the colonel. "It will be hard on man and beast alike. . . ."

"How about colonels? They ain't neither," whispers the trooper, and a couple more tittered.

". . . But with superior weaponry and tactical judgment we will prevail." He give a nod to the captain who give a nod to a lieutenant who give a nod to a sergeant who hollers:

"Move out!"

Which they done, with the colonel mounted up and in the lead. The whole caboodle went once around the quadrangle then out the gates and off over the horizon in a cloud of dust. Andrew come up to me and says:

"What a stirring sight, men at arms galloping off to make war with the enemy in his lair."

"I hope they don't find Standing Tall's tribe. They never done nothing that warn't justificated."

"Fear not for your noble red friends, Huckleberry. Colonel Beckwith has a reputation for steering a wide path around any kind of trouble."

"You mean if bravery was dollars he'd be the poorest man in town?"

"I mean precisely that. I have it from the horse's mouth, if Lydia will pardon the equine metaphor."

"*She* told you?"

"Indeed yes."

"She don't set much store by the colonel, do she?"

"Naturally. She is a woman who demands the utmost from life and from men. The colonel lacks the former and barely qualifies as the latter."

"You mean . . ."

"I mean, Huckleberry, if potency were water the colonel would be a desert."

"Did you make up your mind about things?"

"I have, and you'll be happy to learn we're leaving this very morning."

"You ain't joshing me are you, Andrew?"

"Not I, young friend. Here, take these to Jim."

He give me a little bag and inside there's a shaving mug and a canteen of water that's warm to the touch and soap and a razor and a mirror.

"What's all this for?" says I.

"What it appears to be for, shaving. Jim must shave his beard completely, but his hair must be left long."

"Why?"

"Never mind why. Saddle up your horse and take Jim's along too. I'll join you presently."

"You got some kind of plan, Andrew, I can tell."

"I have, and all will be revealed when I join you. Now run along."

I warn't none too happy with the arrangement but I done it anyway, hoping it ain't going to be something harebrained and foolish. I took the horses and went out to Jim and he used the shaving stuff till his face was smooth and black as marble. All through it he asked questions but I never give him no answers, not having none.

Then come the sound of horses getting nearer and I figured Andrew must of brung along a spare, but when he come in sight I seen he's brung along a pack horse loaded with supplies all right, but he's brung along Lydia and Jupiter and Romulus and Remus as well. It's too late for Jim to hide so we just stood there not believing what we seen, and I give Andrew a silent cussing with the briskest kind of language I can lay hands on.

"Dis parter de plan, Huck?" asks Jim.

"I reckon so, and I ain't disposed to like it."

They reined in and got down off their horses and the dogs come sniffing around me and Jim friendly-like and poking their noses between our legs.

Mrs. Beckwith says:

"Good morning, Huckleberry. Good morning, Jim."

Jim give a strangled kind of grunt. I never made a sound, too busy trying to figure out how I can best kill Andrew.

"Well, no doubt you're both surprised by all this," he says, smiling.

"You could put it stronger than that," says I.

"Huckleberry, Mrs. Beckwith is an essential part of the plan. Without her it will not work. I *had* to reveal your secret to her. It would not have been fair to include her in our party otherwise."

She give me a smile and says:

"May I say, Huckleberry, that I believe wholeheartedly in your innocence. Andrew has told me of your efforts to save those aboard the *Nicobar,* and I would consider it an honor if you were to regard me as your friend."

"Thank you, ma'am," says I to her, and to Andrew, "What plan?"

"It's quite simple. Lydia must be given the credit for it. Jim, please retire behind cover and put this on."

He hauled a dress and bonnet out of a sack and handed them over. Jim looked at the dress, then at me. Lydia says:

"If Jim passes himself off as my nigger maid no one will question his presence. He will be as invisible to your pursuers as you, Huckleberry, in your Sioux costume."

"I got to put de dress on, Huck?"

"It ain't a bad idea at that, Jim."

He took himself away with his bottom lip stuck out to show he ain't happy. Andrew says:

"I take it, then, that you have fallen in with our scheme?"

"Drug in is more like it. Ma'am, are you headed for California too, I mean, all the way?"

"I am. I trust you do not object to the presence of a woman among your party, young man."

"I ain't particular, just so long as we move fast."

"Neither I nor Jupiter will hold you back."

"Well, all right then, but we're in deep trouble when the colonel gets back and finds you ain't here no more."

"We will have one week's start on any pursuit party, quite enough in my opinion."

"If you say so, ma'am."

"I do," she says, final-like.

Jim come back and stuffed his britches in his saddlebag. He's the biggest nigger maid I ever seen, and he can't button the dress up the back on account of he's too wide in the shoulder and deep in the chest, so Lydia give him a shawl to hide the big split down his back. He had to keep his own boots on too, which looked peculiar, but there ain't a way around it when you got feet that big. We mounted up and started off in a wide circle that takes us around the Injun camp and the wagon train and the fort so no one can be a witness to the direction we took, and an hour later we're following wagon ruts a few weeks' old west toward the Rockies.

Andrew and Lydia rode in the lead with me and Jim a little way behind, and them two looked across at each other so much I seen more of the sides of their heads than the backs, and they laughed and carried on and was forever reaching across to touch each other.

Romance is powerful stuff if it makes full-growed people act that way, and I'm glad I ain't inclined to get mixed up in such foolishness, not now or ever. Jim stayed grumpish all through the afternoon and never spoke a word, just pushed that lip out and kept it there, and I see he's humilerated to be wearing a dress.

"It ain't nothing to be ashamed of, Jim," says I. "Did you forget how I wore a dress after Fort Kearney?"

"You only wore dat dress a week, Huck. I got to tol'rate this'n till we gets to Californy, an' das a long ways off yet."

"It ain't nothing new for men to wear dresses. Why, look at all them folk in the Bible, they never wore no britches for thousands of years. I seen a Bible with pictures in it and the men wore dresses same as the women. Even Jesus wore a dress, Jim. Remember that picture of him on the side of the McSweens' wagon? What was that he had on if it warn't a dress?"

"It were a man's nightshirt, Huck. Dere's a heaper diff'rence."

"Well, I reckon you're just going to have to put up with it, or else stand out like a naked man in church and get us both captured."

"I ain't sayin' I won' do it, Huck, I'se jest sayin' I ain't about to get no pleasure from it."

"No one's asking you to do that, Jim, and I appreciate the sacrifice you're making."

But he never come out with another word that day, and when we made camp for the night he stayed quiet so I let him be. Wearing ladies' duds takes a heap of adjustment. The lovebirds was billing and cooing away in the firelight and it's enough to make you sick, all them words and looks thick as molasses and sweet as honey. When they ain't looking adoring at each other they're spouting poems by the yard and jawing about how Andrew is going to make his fortune with his book of poetry which he aims to call *In Search of El Dorado*. Lydia says she'll be so proud and maybe she'll put out what she calls a slim volume of her own spouting, and it'll be called *Leaves from the Woods of Remembrance—A Collection of Poems and Essays from the Pen of a Frontierswoman,* a fair mouthful, I reckon.

When it come time to sleep they started yawning and Andrew says:

"I believe I'll turn in. It's been a fatiguing day."

"I agree," says Lydia. "The smell of freedom is heady wine to the newly initiated. I feel quite drowsy in fact."

"Huckleberry, perhaps you and Jim would care to place your blankets on the far side of the fire, over by that rock, for example."

"What rock?"

"That one over there. It's enormous. You must be able to see it against the stars."

That's the only way you could of seen it, because it's so far away the firelight don't reach it.

"We'll be cold way over there," says I.

"Nonsense, it's a warm night, and I've been told it is common practice among trappers and so forth to sleep as far from the fire as possible to present a less visible target to prowling marauders."

I ain't a moron. I seen what he wanted and why, so Jim and me took our blankets right around the other side of the rock to give them all the privateness they needed, but even that distance never stopped them keeping us awake with all kinds of moaning and yelping. Jim says:

"Cain't she bite a stick or somethin'? I'se gettin' mighty res'less, Huck. De noise puts me in minder dat Injun gal I had back wid de Sioux."

"You never told me much about that at the time, Jim."

"You kinder young to be knowin' 'bout dat stuff, Huck, but dere's a hunker advice I kin give an' dis here's it. When de time come for you to get close wid a woman jest make sure an' not marry no one till you at leas' twenny-five. I ain't sayin' it hurts to tie de knot, but it means you got to give up a whole heaper freedom, in fac' thirty-five be closer to de mark lessen de woman starts gettin' fat in de belly, den you ain't got no choice, not lessen you wants to run."

I told him I warn't attracted to fat ladies anyway, and we went to sleep, but not before Andrew and Lydia quit racketing.

The night after was the same, and the night after that and so on. Jim and me took to sleeping further and further from the fire just to get a full night's sleep. I had dark circles under my eyes and I reckon Jim had them too, only on him it's hard to tell. He says:

"Dey ain't goin' to keep it up much longer, Huck. De human body kin stan' jest so much den it gets tuckered out an' exhausterated, 'specially a man, an' dat Andrew, he's kinder skinny an' puny lookin' so he ain't goin' to las' de distance."

But he did, and Jim and me practickly had to set up a separate camp each night. The plains was well behind us now. The country around is hilly and there's some pine and cedar, mighty reliefsome to the eye after all that rolling flatness since Missouri. We had to cross over the Platte where it turns south to the headwaters, and it's running swift here on account of the narrowness. We all of us had to get wet by crossing over hanging onto the horses' tails. The dogs swum it easy under their own steam but the pack horse had trouble with all that load on his back and was almost swept away, but he landed safe further down and I rounded him up. We had the flour and such on top of the load so there's only a little of it spoiled by water, and we aimed to eat them portions first before it rotted anyway.

We stripped off to dry out, Jim and me in one place and the love-birds in another, and we heard noises that warn't birdcalls coming from their direction so they never got bored while their clothes dried. I done some wandering through the trees with Romulus and Remus, stark naked except for the rattlesnake charm around my ankle. I come across a little grave dug by the river and there's a moldering wood cross stuck in one end with words burned on it that reads:

Here lyes Otis Buchanan
age 14 yrs 11 mths
Drownded in river
June 12, 1841
RIP

I squatted down next to it, feeling sad. He must of been with the pioneers and come all this way full of the adventure spirit, and then he drowned when he's near the same age as me. I felt like it's Huck Finn under that cross, just a skellington by now, with a family far off in California or maybe Oregon that still remembers me. I could feel Otis Buchanan's ghost beside me all mournful and forlorn on account of missing out on a whole life. I got the shivers, or maybe it's just water drying on my skin, but I left there in a hurry and never told the others what I seen. It's just between me and Otis and the dogs.

Jim and me figured seeing as the lovebirds had a pecking match in daytime they'd be quieter come nightfall, but no such luck. I reckon you could spend a peacefuller night lying in a pond with a million bullfrogs, so next morning I warn't in the right temper to see what I seen, which is a hoofprint a little ways off the trail next to a pile of turds. The print has got a cross on the heel so it's Pap's, and likely the turds too.

I never told no one about that neither, but I spent considerable time wondering just how far ahead him and Morg is, and if there's a chance us four is going to catch them up. When we left Fort Laramie I was in a powerful rush, but not now.

Two days later we come to Independence Rock, which is biggish and stands out some, but not so much as Chimney Rock back on the plains. It's covered in scrawl with names and messages from pioneers and forty-niners, writ in tar or chipped right into the rock. We stayed awhile to look them over and I seen three names I knowed from the Naismith train. The first two is Duane and Hewley Peterson and the third is Grace, writ neat with chalk, so it ain't going to last longer than the next rain. It brung back memories of how we was friends, then enemies, then friends again, and how she got me free that time. I had a mind to put my name next to hers, but it ain't wise, not if your name's Huck Finn and you're wanted for murder, so I never done it. Andrew and Lydia was all for chipping a poem in the rock but we never had no chisel, only my knife and I warn't about to get it busted on such a useless thing, so Independence Rock got left the way we found it.

A few mile on we come to what Lydia's map that she stole out of the colonel's desk calls Devil's Gate, and it's where the Sweetwater River goes churning through a gorge heading east to meet up with the Platte. We stayed awhile there too, just admiring the grandness of it. The sun got low and we made camp above the gorge, and the river made so much noise me and Jim never heard the lovebirds and slept like drunks, which was a tonic.

Further on up the trail the cliffs give way to a valley and we followed it another three days, the ground rising steady all the time and the hills turning gradual to low mountains, the first I ever seen, till finally we come to South Pass in the Wind River Range, the easternmost part of the Rockies. I was kind of expecting a narrow little gap with sides that run straight up and down, but it warn't nothing like that, just a wide valley real nice to look at. Beyond the pass we seen real mountains, tall and grand and awesome. Andrew run out a poem to celebrate, spouting it out from the saddle loud and clear.

> *"Glad of heart, intrepid bands*
> *Of pioneers from eastern lands*
> *Have passed this way with heads held high*
> *Beneath the all-encircling sky,*
> *For here revealed before their gaze*
> *Is meadowland where wild things graze*
> *Upon the slopes that greet the eye*
> *With gently rising majesty,*
> *A prelude to the peaks beyond,*
> *United there in rocky bond,*
> *A sweeping vista, rugged, bold,*
> *The contours of these mountains old,*
> *Standing mighty, proud, serene,*
> *Like landscape dwelt upon in dream,*
> *Enchanting with their distant crowns*
> *The ondrawn traveler; hope abounds*
> *Within his breast and carefree heart,*
> *Halfway to rest from journey's start.*
> *Forward, let the wagons roll*
> *Into this land that stirs the soul*
> *Of all who see her silhouette*
> *Of lofty peaks; the journey yet*
> *To come will weeks entail, but see!*
> *Ahead's the trail of destiny!"*

Lydia give him a round of applause and Jupiter lifted his tail to leave his mark on the enchanting landscape. Romulus and Remus nosed it to make sure it's the right kind of mark and give it their approval by lifting their legs and we set off into the Rocky Mountains.

The going was easy for a day or two seeing as we're on horseback, but it warn't no picnic for them ahead of us with wagons on account of it's all uphill. We come across the proof of it in piles of stuff throwed out to make them lighter, stoves and trunks and tables and chairs and even a patent gold-washing machine like the ones I seen them selling back in St. Joe. We followed a river called the Big

Sandy on Lydia's map, and the higher we went the colder it got, even if it's summer. There was lashing rain on the third day that soaked us through and washed all the poetry and caterwauling out of Andrew and Lydia, which was the only comfort it brung. We made camp that night under a rocky bluff with plenty of trees around and done our best to dry out, but it was miserable and we never slept. In the morning Andrew started sneezing and says he's catched cold, so no poems today neither I reckon, but I would of listened to a whole bookful in preferment to what happened around midmorning.

We was ambling along easy when we hear a shout behind us, and turned and seen four men on horseback and a pack horse coming along behind.

"No . . ." says Lydia, looking scared for the first time, but it warn't the colonel or no one military so she relaxed and passed the worry on to me, because when they got closer I seen that two of them is the two from the Berringer train that give me scornful talk back at Fort Laramie when they reckoned I warn't nothing but an Injun, and seeing as I give them some backtalk at the time they ain't going to believe I'm a mute. I told the others fast what happened and Lydia says it's a pity I give them lip that way because being silent give me that Injun look, taciturn is what she calls it, but there ain't no help for it now. Jim says he wants to be mute this time so's he don't have to talk with no squeaky voice, which would of been the full limit far as he's concerned, and Lydia says yes, it's safer that way. Then the riders reined in alongside us. The first two was still dressed natty and the other two was normal, both with long rifles. One of the natties says:

"Good morning to you. Mr. Collins and Mrs. Beckwith, I presume?"

"What makes you think so?" says Andrew, trying to look tough and dangersome, but spoiling it with a whole slew of sneezing.

"You two are the talk of Fort Laramie. There has not been such drama since Romeo absconded with Juliet. Before you become angry, may I point out that I and my companions do not sit in judgment upon you. Your choice to cut and run is strictly your own business, but it would be needlessly embarrassing for us all if you were to adopt false identities for our sake."

"Such a thought would never have entered our heads," says Lydia.

"A sensible outlook if I may say so, Mrs. Beckwith. Permit me to introduce us. I am Randolph Squires, and this is my cousin Bertram. The two gentlemen accompanying us are Mr. Bob Raffe and Mr. Jesse Drummond."

Those last two was both mean-looking men with full beards and knee boots and looked like they done outdoor work before they was forty-niners. Andrew wipes his nose and says:

"Mrs. Beckwith and I appreciate your candor, Mr. Squires. Such welcome lack of rectitude is uncommon out here, but of course you are both men of intelligence. All four of you, I mean."

He never meant that at all, and Bob and Jesse give each other a look that says they know, but they ain't bothered. Men that tough don't let no one skinny as Andrew bother them unless they get insulted direct, then they generally hammer the one that insulted them into the ground with their chins. Lydia says:

"Were you not with the wagon train which arrived at the fort prior to our departure?"

"We were, ma'am, but the day after your leavetaking cholera broke out among us. In the absence of your husband chaos reigned supreme. The redskins took down their tepees and departed en masse, and all from the train were forbidden entry to the fort upon pain of shooting. We four were unburdened by wagons, having joined the train only a hundred miles or so back along the trail. We therefore decided to resume our journey unaccompanied rather than wait with the rest and risk contamination. That was more than a week ago and we have developed no signs of the disease, so you may rest easy in our presence. May I suggest we ride along with your party? We all bear arms and I see only yourself and the redskin have taken similar precautions. We must not forget the presence of his tinted brethren around us. Together we present a formidable array of weaponry that should deter would-be scalpers."

I never trusted none of them, and I seen Andrew and Lydia warn't none too happy neither, but he's talking sense so they give their agreement and we got moving again with Bob and Jesse at the rear, which give me an uneasy feeling. Randolph talked breezy and confident, telling how him and Bertram, who's the potbellied one, was bored with St. Louis and decided to head west for the rush, but he never give out what kind of work they done there. Andrew asks Bob and Jesse what they done before they was forty-niners.

"Farmin'," says Bob.

"The same," says Jesse.

But I never believed it. They never had that wore-down tired look farmers has got, and I figured them for roughneck rivermen, but it ain't wise to say such things out loud, not if you're Injun like me.

"That's the biggest nigger woman I've ever laid eyes on," says Bertram, meaning Jim.

"Hannah has been with me for some years now," lies Lydia, never batting an eye.

"She must be the progeny of giants," he says. "Why, the father alone must have been over seven feet tall to sire a female that size. How tall was your father, Hannah?"

Jim just give him a sideways glare and Lydia says:

"Hannah is a mute. She is also short-tempered, so I advise you not to trifle with her in any way."

"'Perish the thought," says Bertram, looking at Jim's big meaty hands, then Randolph says to Andrew:

"Your Injun friend intrigues me. We encountered him once outside the fort and were amazed to find he speaks fluent English."

"Turtle was raised by missionaries and taught all that a white child knows, isn't that so, Turtle."

"That's right, Mr. Collins, sir," says I. "They brung me up by the Book since I was just a sprout some squaw dropped on their doorstep. I'm half-white and half-Injun and proud of it."

Behind me Bob and Jesse give a laugh.

"Dirt on its own's a mighty good thing," says Jesse, "and water on its own is mighty good too, but when you mix 'em together you get mud, and that's the closest thing to shit I know."

"Would you mind not using such language!" snaps Lydia, and Jesse sweeps off his hat and bows in the saddle, mocking-like, and says:

"Fifty thousand pardons, ma'am. Momentarily I forgot we're keepin' company with a genuine *lady.*"

The way him and Bob laughed made it clear they reckon a woman who runs off from her husband ain't no kind of lady, then Randolph turns around on them and says sternish but quiet:

"Both of you keep civil tongues in your heads or you'll answer to me."

They scowled some but never answered back, so Randolph has got their respect even if he's dressed fancy. I seen he's the leader and made up my mind to keep a close watch on him. He's a handsomer man than the rest and he give Lydia a look every now and then, admiring, and she seen it even if she pretended she never. Andrew seen it too and got upset, but tried not to show it. The whole situation was primed for trouble and we only just now got acquainted, so I warn't too hopeful about our chances of sticking together all the way to California. Randolph took over that party the minute he rode up, and he acted like it's the most natural thing in the world for him to ride alongside Lydia and Andrew, all three in the lead, with Bertram and Jim and me next and Bob and Jesse last.

All through the afternoon Randolph talked on this and that, but not idle tonguewagging, sensible talk on weighty subjects like the way the gold rush is likely going to change the face of the nation and such, and every so often he'd throw in something lightweight for variety and ended up with a joke that had Lydia almost out of her saddle with laughing. Andrew tried to laugh too, but it come out more like a croak. Randolph decided it's time to include him in the conversation and in about five seconds found out Andrew's a poet, and he asks him to do some of his stuff. Andrew done it, but halfhearted, not like his usual arm-waving self, and the results was dismal listening. I seen Lydia was disappointed at the poor showing he made in front of strangers and she never spoke to him hardly at all the rest of the day.

We made camp and Jim and me got to sleep closer to the fire on account of the others being there put a stop to the lovebirds' billing and cooing, and next morning you never seen a more woeful face than Andrew's. Lydia still warn't giving him no more than the time of day so he got to sulking and let Randolph do all the talking while we rode, which only made things worse.

In late afternoon Romulus and Remus flushed a bear out of hiding and it come blundering into the open ahead of us with the dogs nipping his heels.

"Don't shoot!" yells Lydia, meaning we might hit the dogs.

The bear got mad and swung around and swiped at them, lightning fast for a crittur that size, and Romulus went bowling head over heels and yipping with pain. Remus kept right on rushing at the bear and trying to reach the neck with his fangs, hard to do when there ain't much neck to get hold of and all of that under fat and fur, but he kept on anyway and had that bear turning in circles till he must of got dizzy with it, then when Remus was around the other side of him pulling on his snout Lydia whipped up her rifle and planted a shot right behind the bear's shoulder. The ball went straight through into his heart and he fell dead. We rode up and Remus was stood over it wagging his tail proud like he done it all himself, but Romulus was in a sorry way, his belly all tore open by them long claws and his innards poking out. He was alive yet, and give his tail a feeble wag when Lydia kneeled down by him with tears running down her face.

"Romulus . . ." she says. "Romulus . . . my poor friend. . . ."

It was real sad. There warn't no way to save him, and Lydia reloaded and put a ball in his head herself, then went away into the trees to be on her own a little while. Me and Bob and Jesse set to skinning the bear and cutting off the best chunks of meat. Andrew drug Romulus away and buried him with a shovel from the Squires' pack horse and the Squires both stood around smoking cigars and saying how the bear's head would look dandy mounted on a wall in the Serenity Club, which must be some place in St. Louis they knowed of. It took so long to work on the bear we made camp on the spot, and it warn't till the sky was dark and the fire lit that Lydia come back to join us.

I wondered who she'll go to for comfort, Andrew or Randolph, but she stayed away from both of them and made up her bed early. With her gone the men felt more relaxed and told hot yarns about women they knowed. Andrew never had much to tell of before Lydia so he stayed quiet, sometimes looking over at where she's sleeping under a tree, or pretending to. Bob and Jesse done the most talking and they was the disgustingest stories. I never believed most of them, and it's plain bad manners to be talking that way in front of a nigger maid like Jim, even if she's mute and can't say she's offended by all the brisk language.

After awhile Jim had enough and walked off into the woods, and pretty soon after Jesse went off in the same direction. Thinks I to myself, here comes trouble. Bob talked on, all about this woman he knowed with no teeth in her head but she's popular, why I don't know, a toothless woman don't have no kind of appeal I can see. Then there's a howling from the trees and Jesse come back with blood pouring out his nose and down his shirt, and a minute later Jim come stomping back to the fire rubbing his knuckles and looking put out.

"That nigger bitch!" says Jesse. "I never done nothin' 'cept sneak up on her and give her a fright."

"Is that right, Hannah?" says I.

Jim shook his head and picked up his blanket to go sleep way over yonder before a real argument starts up.

"I killed men for less'n that," says Jesse, leaking more blood.

"You must of asked for it," says I, and Bob turned on me and says:

"You keep your mouth shut, Injun, or I'll shut it for you."

"There's no need for any of this," says Andrew.

"And keep your's shut too, you lily-livered pansy."

"I don't believe insults are called for. . . ."

"Awww, go write a poem about it, mamma's boy."

The Squires never put in a word, just sat there watching it all. That bear made mighty fine eating, but the meal left a bad taste in my mouth, and I figure I ain't tasted nothing yet.

Next day it drizzled rain for hours. You couldn't hardly see the trail for mist, and Andrew says we're so high up we're traveling right through low clouds, and I reckon it's so because we never seen one mountain peak all day, just cottony whiteness all around, and there warn't much talking done. We kept our blankets around us for dryness and our eyes on the ground to follow the wagon ruts. More stuff was throwed out by the trains hereabouts it's so steep and we come across a pedal organ and a commode with a lid over the bowl and armrests, for them that takes their time or falls asleep over their function. Lydia was still grieving over Romulus and Andrew seen it but had the sense to stay quiet. The rain eased up some but the mist thickened even more. It's mighty mysterious to go plodding through it and never see nothing past your horse's head. Seeing as there ain't no talk getting done we never kept bunched up but separated a ways and after awhile got strung out in a line so you never seen who's in front of you and who's behind. Now and then you heard a bird call way off somewheres sounding lost and alone in all the whiteness, same as you.

It was the perfect time to do some considering, and what I turned over was a long scramble of people I knowed and things that happened to me and what it all means, which I never got the answer of. It's like a mirror that's all smashed to flinders; you pick up all the pieces you can find and fit them back together, only you missed some and there's gaps, and even them pieces you found don't fit together true, so when you look at yourself you got one eye higher than the other and two mouths and a nose that belongs in a hogpen, so you don't get the entire picture at all. That's what it's like trying to figure how it come about that I'm crossing the Rockies with a murdering Pap and a famous detective up ahead of me and a whole stretch of country behind me I can't go back to no more. Only one thing come through clear, and it's this: I got to keep going, like a stick in a current that don't have the chance to get ashore. I got to follow where it takes me and just hope there ain't rapids and waterfalls up ahead that can crush me to nothing, which is a fate I reckon I don't deserve.

There ain't nothing like deep thinking to give you the need to piss so I pulled off the trail and got down and done it, and while I'm getting mounted again Bob and Jesse went by. They never seen me and I never seen them, but I heard plenty.

"It ain't right," Jesse says. "When I snuck up on her she warn't squatting like a woman does, she's stood up like a man and pissing over a log. I ask you, how can a woman do that?"

"You must of made a mistake. Maybe she warn't pissing at all."

"I heard enough piss hit the ground in my life to reckernize the sound. She was pissing stood up, I swear. That nigger ain't no female, she's a man. Lookit the size of it. You ever see a woman that big? She's a man, and it's mightly queer the way that bunch is hiding it by putting skirts on him, mighty queer."

Then they was too far away and their voices got muffled in the mist so I never heard no more, but I already heard enough to give me the fan-tods. Now that they suspicioned Jim they ain't going to let up till they figure out the meaning. I never got no enjoyment from the mist after that and kept behind them so they won't guess I overheard what they was talking about. I stayed that way till it got dark and the tailenders catched up with the leaders and we made camp.

I snuck word to Jim that he's been suspicioned and he says it had to come sooner or later even if he's been getting up before the rest of a morning and shaving himself in secret to keep the ruse going long as he can, but he's doubtful if that'll be much longer now Bob and Jesse smelled a rat.

There warn't no joy to be got around the fire that night. The cold and damp had got in our bones and made us shiver and creak like oldtimers with the rheumatiz, so we just et bear meat and stoked up the flames and huddled under our blankets. Lydia was best off with Remus to hug close and get warmth from. Andrew would of give his arm to trade with that dog, but Lydia and him still ain't on regular speaking terms. Up till the time Randolph and the rest joined us the lovebirds was pesky with their noise but happy together, which rubbed off some on Jim and me and was tolerable mainly in daylight. But now the spark has gone out between them and it's all the fault of the new bunch that's gone and shoved a wedge between them, specially Randolph, who's got the kind of manly looks I reckon Andrew wished he had himself, so his confidence is gone just when he needs it most. A poem ain't beans against a profile, not if you're a hot-blooded woman which is Lydia's kind I reckon. But it ain't my problem, thinks I, and nodded off.

✦ 20 ✦

Death in the Mist—A Haven of Safety—A Philosophical

Poem—A Nasty Surprise—Unseemly Laughter

It's a week now since we come
through South Pass and Lydia says we must be getting near Fort
Bridger, which is named for the famous mountain man. Thaddeus
knowed Jim Bridger one time and told me there warn't a tougher man
alive, but decent too. Why, he'd say a prayer over every Injun he shot
and begged pardon off all the beaver he skinned and never done killing
on a Sunday, just a little maiming to keep his hand in, and was fair-
minded as well.

There was the time him and Thaddeus got snowed in among the
mountains and there warn't no game around so they was mighty
pleased to find a dead Injun that froze in the snow, and Jim Bridger
reckoned they'd have to eat him to stay alive. Thaddeus was agreeable and they argued over which was the best part to take along
with them, and after considerable jawing they settled on the legs,
which has got meat on them but ain't too hard to carry seeing as you
can sling one over your shoulder. But when they cut the Injun's
legs off they found one was shorter than the other on account of the
Injun was born and raised on a hillside, Thaddeus says, and Jim
Bridger done the gentlemanly thing and says Thaddeus can have
the longer one. Thaddeus reckoned it warn't right for one man to
have more than his partner so he hacked the toes off his Injun leg
and give them to Jim to even things up, and Jim crunched them up
like pecan nuts and says he got more pleasure from the bones and
toenails than the flesh, which is kind of rubbery if it's et uncooked.
That's what Thaddeus told me. I disbelieved some parts but it's a
good yarn. Tom Sawyer would of loved it.

We went all day without catching sight of no fort, just more mist
swirling around, and we strung out same as before and plodded

along. Without no scenery to catch my eye I got mighty bored, and seeing as I never got my share of sleep last night I slid away into Nod for awhile. When I woke up my horse has wandered away from the wagon ruts and gone among the trees and I don't even know where I am.

Then the horse stopped dead and laid his ears back. I figured he's got the scent of a bear or mountain lion and I cocked my Hawken just in case, but never heard nothing, just sat waiting for I don't know what. Then I hear a twig snap, and out of the trees and mist come an Injun with his hair all spiked out with porcupine quills. He was just as surprised as me and we looked each other over for the flicker of an eye, then he ducks back out of sight and I turned tail and galloped off the other way. It never took long to break free of the trees and reach open ground, and I slowed down and pretty soon come across the wagon ruts, only I don't know which way is east and which is west.

I fired a shot in the air and it echoed around through the mist and mountains. A shot come back in answer and I headed for it, but them echoes had me fooled good because after I followed the ruts maybe five minutes there come another shot and it's way off behind me, so back I went at a gallop and finally come across the others all bunched together.

"Was it you who fired the first shot?" says Randolph.

"I got lost, then I seen an Injun."

"You can't see nothin' in all this," says Jesse, disbelieving.

"I went off the trail and seen him in the trees," says I.

"Just the one?" Andrew wants to know.

"I never seen no more, but they could easy be around."

Everyone looked out into the mist nervous-like, then Lydia says:

"Mr. Squires, where is your cousin?"

Bertram warn't there, and when Randolph give a shout for him there warn't no answer. He shouted again and it echoed round-about. Still no answer, and Randolph says:

"He must have heard. . . ."

"Maybe the Injun's right," says Bob. "There's Injuns out there and they got him."

"Spread out and find him," says Randolph, "but keep your guns at the ready."

"I reckon we oughter stick together," says Jesse. "If we go traipsin' around on our own they can pick us off easy. I'm for lookin' in a bunch."

"Me too," agrees Bob.

"Are you men cowards?" says Randolph, getting his dander up.

"They have a point," puts in Lydia. "We must stay together. Separated we will become lost as Turtle did. Your cousin may have simply fallen from his horse and hit his head, but we must not rule out the possibility of hostiles."

"Very well," says Randolph. "Let's begin."

We rode back along the trail calling out Bertram's name but he never answered, so we spread out just a little so each of us can see at least one other and covered the same ground again. It was Jesse that found him and give a holler, and we all gathered. Bertram was on the ground with an arrow in the hip and another in his chest. He must of died quick because no one heard nothing. His horse warn't around that we could see and was proberly took by the Injuns. His pistol and hat and boots was gone too, and his scalp likewise.

"Murderin' sonsabitches!" says Bob, and him and Jesse glared at me like it's my fault even if whoever done it ain't even my tribe, but to men like them Injuns is Injuns and all tarred with the same brush.

"May I say how truly sorry we are, Mr. Squires," says Lydia. "This is an awful moment for you."

"Thank you," says he, tight-lipped.

We buried Bertram by the trailside and Andrew done the Lord's Prayer like he done over Captain Jack and we rode on, bunched up tight with the woods hid behind the mist, more scarifying than if we could of seen them plain. No one spoke a word for fear of Injuns roundabout hearing it. We kept on going long past nightfall, just wanting to get clear of that part of the trail, and was all dog tired and saddle sore when we smelled woodsmoke. Lydia reckoned it must be Fort Bridger at last and we searched around, but you can't see past your hand in the mist and dark and the fort warn't showing no lights. Randolph says we got to yell and get their attention, which we done full strength, and when our throats was getting sore from it a voice come out of the dark.

"Who's that makin' all the ruckus?" it says.

"A party of travelers," says Lydia. "Are we near Fort Bridger?"

"Just a hop and a step," says the voice, and a man come into sight with a rifle and an Injun with him. He's around fifty with a heavy gut and beard and he says:

"Foller me, folks."

We done it and the fort warn't more than a little way off like he says. It's small stood next to Fort Laramie or Fort Kearney, with a log wall all around but tumbledown and sagging and moss-covered. We got led through a gate that got closed after us and come to a halt in a yard with log cabins and huts around, none of them new looking. There's a forge over in the corner with the coals still aglow but no one working it now.

"I'm Linus Walker," says the man. "Put your horses in the stable and come on inside."

The stabling job got give to me and it took awhile to unsling the packs and unsaddle the horses and get them fed and rubbed down. They was all damp and steaming after the long haul and I done the work proper. Dumb animals has got plenty to put up with and deserve to get looked after, I reckon. It took me an hour and more to do and when I finished I went over to the forge and pumped the bellows to blow the coals into life and warmed myself some, then went inside the main cabin.

There's one big room with tables and chairs all made from split logs and shelfs of trade goods around the walls and a plank bar down one end with jars of liquor behind it, all lit by a fire in a stone fireplace and a lamp or three hung from the ceiling. Our bunch was around the fire eating off tin plates and throwing scraps to Remus. There's a big cook pot hung over the flames and a squaw even bigger ladled out a mess of stew onto a plate and give it to me, and it went down so fast the plate's still hot when I finished. There was other people in there too, mostly Injuns, but there's a raggedy-looking white man with a beard away in a corner nursing a whiskey jug. Him and Linus Walker was the only whites I seen, and Mr. Walker is listening to how Bertram died while he collected payment for the meal.

"I'm mighty sorry about your cousin," he says, "but there ain't much I can do about it. This here ain't a military fort, more like a trading post and way station, so there's no soldiers you can turn to for help. There's Shoshoni in the mountains hereabouts and some are peaceful and some ain't. You just run into the wrong kind."

Randolph listened calm and never looked like he's burning for revenge or nothing and I figure him and Bertram warn't all that close, not like brothers. There ain't nothing he could do anyhow, and the conversation got turned around to the gold rush and the people swarming through the Rockies heading for California. Mr. Walker says:

"Getting halfway there most of 'em reckon the worst is over, but it ain't so. The real trouble starts when you get down into the desert. That's a place that'll knock the spirit out of man and beast. You folks are better off without no wagon, but you ain't going to find it easy, I'm tellin' you straight. I been there."

"Thank you for the warning," says Randolph, then pulls out a pack of cards and lays them on the table. Everyone looked at them like they was something they never seen before, and he says:

"Would anyone care to while away the hours with a game of chance?"

"You'd play cards on the day your cousin died, Mr. Squires?" asks Lydia.

"Indeed I would, ma'am. No action of mine will return him to the land of the living. Do not misunderstand me, the loss of Bertram has not left me unmoved, but I have encountered death before and know that a man must be philosophical. Some mourn by keening and wailing, others by the application of sackcloth and ashes. I console myself with cards. Do I have any takers?"

"Deal me in," says Bob.

"And me," says Jesse.

Lydia was disgusted and took herself off to a chair by the fire where Jim was sat and Andrew joined them, only not too close.

"Mr. Walker," says Randolph, "are you interested?"

"I reckon I am," he says. "I ain't played a hand since Methuselah was in diapers. Wait on while I get a cloth. Just a plain old tabletop ain't right for a gentleman's game."

He went across to the shelfs and took down a shawl and spread it over the table and smoothed it out. Randolph give him a dollar for a jug and when it was brung over he asks for glasses, but Mr. Walker says he ain't seen none since Methuselah's grandma was in diapers, so they had to pull on the jug with it slung over their shoulders riverman style. Bob and Jesse looked like they was born with jugs on their shoulders. Randolph turned to the raggedy man in the corner and says:

"How about you, sir? Are you a gambling man?"

But he just shook his head without lifting it out of his jug, so they put their stakes on the table and started without him. The Injuns warn't invited to join in but they stood around watching, curious what kind of game could be got out of little pieces of cardboard. Randolph mixed all the cards up right quick and spun them out to the others real fast, and I knowed then what his kind of work is. I should of guessed before that he's a gambler from his hands, which is white and smooth with no dirt under the nails. I watched for awhile along with the other Injuns but never understood the rules and finally went over by the fire.

There warn't none of us happy. Jim is miserable on account of he has to wear a dress, Andrew is miserable because of Lydia and Lydia's in mourning for Romulus still. I reckon I'm the only one there that ain't hangdog to look at, and I got more reason to be miserable than all of them. But there warn't nothing else to do except pull up a chair and look at the fire and smoke my pipe. After awhile Andrew says:

"I have composed a short piece. Would anyone care to hear it?"

Jim and Lydia just nodded polite, not really caring, and Andrew's face got longer so I say:

"I'll be right glad to hear it, Andrew. I reckon you got the poet's touch with words and it's been too long since you give out with a verse or three. I'm disposed to hear what you got and I hope it's a long'un."

"Thank you, Turtle," he says. "All too often I must cast my seed upon barren ground."

He stood up and put himself in front of the fire and grabbed his lapels and after considerable throat clearing got down to business.

"IN PRAISE OF LIFE'S INIQUITY

> *What chance have we as mortal men*
> *To steer our course through life's great maze?*
> *For ladies Luck and Bountiful are there*
> *At birth and through the days*
> *Of shaping firm the swaddling babe,*
> *Withholding much or giving all,*
> *Dispensing, blessing, oft neglecting,*

All of us are in their thrall.
From cradle rock'd to grave dug deep
They play with us as queens at chess,
Manipulating us at whim,
These ladies without due redress
Dictate our paths across the board
Where some grow strong and some are lost,
Swept aside, their hopes and dreams
Mere nothings, corks on oceans toss'd.
Yet make a stand as men we must
Or yield all will, for trusting Fate
Alone to guide us through the maze
Is weak; such vaporings innate
In craven cowards renders hope
Of thrusting forth with will and pride
A chimera, receding far
Beyond our grasp; the weak will hide
Behind the myth these ladies plant
In shrinking breast to bind them down
Upon the board; bereft of heart
Or sustenance their dreams will drown
Amid the slough imposed upon
Their timid souls by self-laid hand.
So perish those without the strength
To cast aside those ladies grand
And search the maze, undaunted, free.
Bedeviled by sad circumstance,
Their heads unbowed, they find the path
Toward the gate that offers chance
Of rich reward, kudos for those
Who learn the simple truth and laugh;
Cruel Fate is but the wind that winnows
Sturdy wheat from fragile chaff."

When he finished there's a silence. The card players was stopped and all heads turned. Bob says:

"That's mighty fine versifyin', Collins. I ain't heard the like outside of church."

"What's it mean?" asks Jesse, and Bob give him a scornful look.

"What's it mean? Why, you danged jackass, it's poetry. It don't have to mean nothin', just sound complicated is all, and I never follered a word of that'n."

"Thank you, sir," says Andrew. "Your appreciation is welcome."

"No charge," says Bob, and the cards started flying again.

Lydia warn't the same as she was before the poem. There's a kind of light in her face and she's staring at Andrew like a Bible picture I seen once of Mary Magdalene looking at Jesus. When he seen the look he went straight over and sat beside her and they never spoke a word, just reached out and grabbed ahold of their hands and give each other's eyes a close looking over. I figure things is all patched up between them again on account of the poem, which is nice, but it'll mean more sleepless nights for the rest of us.

The raggedy man in the corner come alive and stood up like he's going to come over and shake Andrew's hand for being such a genius poet, but he went right by and come over to me and laid a hand on my shoulder and pulled a pistol from his belt and stuck it in the side of my head and says:

"Huckleberry Finn, I arrest you for murder."

He's gone and changed himself considerable with disguise but I reckernized the voice, and it's Bulldog Barrett.

"What is the meaning of this!" snaps Lydia, and stood up sharpish.

The card players quit and everyone in the room turns my way.

"Be calm, ma'am, I have the situation under control. I am Chauncey Thermopylae Barrett of Boston. This boy is a wanted criminal and I have been waiting for him to pass this way."

"Don't be absurd," she says. "That boy is a Sioux."

"No, ma'am, I beg to differ, and the nigger in the dress is his accomplice."

"See?" says Jesse to Bob. "I told you he warn't no female."

"Kindly explain yourself, sir," says Randolph.

"I am a detective in the employ of Miss Becky Thatcher of St. Petersburg, Missouri, contracted to apprehend the murderer of her father, Judge Caleb Thatcher. This boy is the guilty party."

"Him?" says Bob. "That runty little halfbreed a murderer? Your brains must of leaked out your ears, mister."

"I have the proof here," says Barrett, and pulled out a wanted poster and tossed it to him.

"I demand that you release our guide immediately," says Lydia.

"He's no guide, ma'am, and no Injun. He's Huckleberry Finn."

"Sure looks like him," says Jesse, eyeing the poster, and I see it's one that's got drawings of Jim and me, not just words, and he held it up so's I can take a good look. I never seen no likeness of myself before except in a mirror and it's real insulting what they done to us both. Jim ain't got no forehead and he's got a scowl on him that scares me to look at, and the artist ain't done me no justice neither, putting my eyes close together and making my teeth all snaggled that way. Says I:

"There ain't no resemblance at all, and I ain't surprised seeing as I ain't no Huckleberry Finn. And I bet Hannah's offended at the way you called her a man, ain't it so, Hannah?"

"I reckon I am," squeaks Jim, disremembering he's supposed to be mute.

"Your disguise is clever, Finn, but not good enough. This time there will be no mistakes. You'll come back with me to Missouri, and the nigger too."

"Pardon me, Mr. Barrett," says Andrew, "but you have confused this boy with another. He has been with me on my journey across the plains."

"You've been deceived, sir, like so many before you."

"But I owe my life to him."

"That is of no account to me. He's wanted for murder and will stand trial in Missouri."

"I got my doubts on that, mister," says Bob.

"I beg your pardon, sir?"

"Missouri's a long ride from here. How you reckon on takin' a boy and a nigger all that way?"

"In chains if necessary," says the bulldog. "The authorities at Fort Laramie will assist me."

"Even that's a fair step, must be close on four hundred mile."

"Attend to your business, sir, and I'll attend to mine."

"This *is* our business, Mr. Barrett," says Andrew. "Turtle is our guide and we have no intention of losing him to become lost ourselves in consequence."

"A praiseworthy attempt," says Barrett, "but I am not a fool. If the boy is a Sioux as you say, he'll know nothing of the land west of the plains. He is therefore no loss. Put down that gun!!"

That was on account of Bob reached for his rifle, but he pulled his hand back quick when Barrett cocked the pistol jammed in my head.

"If anyone makes another move like that the boy's brains will be strewn over the floor. My arrangement with Miss Thatcher includes the option of death if apprehension proves impossible, and the reward offered by the state makes no distinction between a criminal living and a criminal dead."

"You vile, odious, disgusting . . . man-hunter!" hisses Lydia.

"No, ma'am, I'm a detective, and take no pleasure in killing, but if need be I'll shoot this boy rather than allow him to escape me a second time."

"Got away from you once already, has he?" sneers Jesse.

"I reckon he ain't so smart, for a detective," says Bob.

That got the bulldog mad and he says:

"What is the matter with you people? This boy has murdered! He must be brought to justice. You, sir," he says to Randolph, "and you, and you, ma'am," to Andrew and Lydia. "You all appear intelligent. Surely you don't wish to prevent the law taking its course? Have you been so long away from civilization you would hinder me in my task? I cannot believe honest Americans are capable of such misguided sympathy. Do not allow his appearance to deceive you. A criminal is a blight upon the landscape no matter what his age."

"I have already pointed out my obligation to the boy," says Andrew. "If he *has* murdered, and I don't for one minute believe him capable of such a deed, he has set the balance straight by saving not only myself but three others from certain death at the hands of the Sioux. Does this not affect your position? 'The quality of mercy is not strained, but droppeth as the gentle rain from heaven.'"

"The Bard was never in Missouri, sir. The state demands its pound of flesh and will get it."

"You do not represent the state," says Lydia. "You are a private operative without the weight of elected office behind you. I demand that you release Huckleberry immediately."

"Aha! You confirm my suspicions. Your readiness to use his true name reveals acquaintance with his history. Be thankful, ma'am, that I do not report your name to the military authorities at Fort Laramie as an accessory in crime. I'm sure Colonel Beckwith would appreciate such information."

Bulldog passed through Fort Laramie so fast he never got to meet the colonel's wife, so now he can't understand why everyone started laughing. It's the catching kind that builds and builds till folks fall off chairs and get pained in the chest from cackling so. He just stared at them in puzzlement, and when they kept it up he got mad all over again.

"What is the meaning of this?" he says, getting red in the face.

That just made things worse. Even the Injuns was laughing now. Bulldog practickly twitched his mustache off his lips he's squirming so much with the insultingness of it all.

"Be quiet!" he roars. "Are you human beings or hyenas?"

They set out to prove they're hyenas, and sure enough, down went a couple of Injuns off their chairs. Even Lydia was giving out a real unladylike noise. The pistol barrel got pulled out of my ear and fired into the roof, then there's a thump behind me and Chauncey Thermopylae Barrett slid to the floor like a sack of grain. I turned around and seen Mr. Walker has snuck up behind the bulldog while he's watching everyone laugh and brained him with a whiskey jug.

"Never liked him from the time he walked in," he says. "I figured he's somethin' strange when he wanted his horse stabled separate from the rest. I reckon it's so the boy here never suspicioned it when he got to stabling his own."

"Thank you, Mr. Walker," says Andrew. "You have prevented a gross injustice from taking place."

"My pleasure. What do you figure on doing with him now?"

"Put a ball in the sonovabitch's head," says Bob, hiccuping from laughing too much.

"A more practical step would be to tie him up before he revives," says Randolph. "Mr. Walker, do you have a rope?"

"I surely do," he says, and went to fetch it.

When Bulldog was all trussed up we propped him over by the fire next to Remus, who laid his head on his lap real comfortable. Then we figured on what to do next. I warn't about to put no ball in his head, which Bob and Jesse reckon is the only permanent way out, then Lydia says:

"We will leave tomorrow morning, but Mr. Barrett must be delayed for as long as possible. We must have ample time to place distance between our party and him."

"Good thinkin' there, Mrs. Beckwith," says Jesse. "The best way to give a man delayment is break his leg I reckon."

"I would prefer that we do him no physical injury."

"How about a broke foot? That ain't much."

"He could still ride," puts in Bob. "Boy, you got to steal his horse so's he can't foller on, not without he wants to leg it to California."

Everyone give out an idea on what to do, and it was gratifying the way they was all on my side, just as different as can be from the way folks in a town would of acted. It seems like out here you get judged by the way people take a shine to you, not by who and what you was back east. It made a difference to Bob and Jesse now they knowed I ain't no Injun, not even a halfbreed, which is kind of two-faced and one-eyed, but better than having them for enemies.

Finally we come up with a plan, and it's this: Mr. Walker is going to keep the bulldog tied up, but he'll keep him drunk too so's he won't get discomforted, and he'll keep him that way till the next wagon train comes through then turn him loose. If the bulldog is sober enough to start accusing him in front of folks he'll just deny all of it and say Bulldog ain't nothing but a pathetical drunk, and would the train kindly take him away with them on account of he's just a blamed nuisance around the fort. If the wagonmaster says yes he'll have to travel along slow with them because I aim to take Bob's advice and steal his horse. It's a crime, but I ain't got no choice. The others reckoned it's only a little crime anyway, and we started the plan there and then by pouring whiskey down the bulldog's throat before he come to and pretty soon he commenced to snore.

The card players went back to their game and Jim went outside and come back dressed in his usual shirt and britches. Everyone give him a cheer and Jesse says he ain't going to give him no trouble over the way Jim bloodied his nose that time, and even says Jim's a good nigger, which shows how drunk he is because nobody changes their mind on Injuns and niggers that quick, not unless they been sucking goodwill out of a jug. But, like I say, it's better than being enemies.

Mr. Walker give Andrew and Lydia a little cabin outside to bed down in and when they went out the door Bob and Jesse give them a serenade of whistles and off-color remarks, but they never minded. I seen Randolph looking kind of sour and I figure he's jealous at the way the lovebirds has made up together. After that he gambled fast and grim and took a heap of money off the others, but when he seen they warn't too happy about losing to a gambler by trade he let them win it all back again. It was the gambling for itself he wanted that night, not cash profit. After that him and Mr. Walker put their heads together over a map Randolph has got and talked awhile. Randolph drawed some lines on it but I never took all that much notice, being halfway drunk myself. When they finished we was all tired from the long day. The Injuns left and we bedded down beside the fire, but not before Bulldog Barrett got give another slug of whiskey. His face is smiling now, but it never made him look more pleasant.

Westward Again—The Dread Disease—A Band Divided—
Bravery and Sacrifice—The Nature of Reality

The horses was saddled up at first light and I got on board Barrett's gelding, a mighty tall horse almost as good as Jupiter. The bulldog was snoring the last I seen and Mr. Walker says he'll feed him some so he don't die, but mainly he'll get whiskey till a train comes along. I give him a handshake and we started off. The lovebirds was kind of peaky looking from not enough sleep and the rest of us hung over from liquor, but me and Jim felt spry in spite of it, me with my tall horse and him with his britches.

The mist was thinner and finally got burned away by the sun around noon so we can see the mountains again. We followed the trail southwest for two days without nothing happening that's worth setting down except maybe about Randolph being real quiet on account of watching Andrew and Lydia riding side by side all the time. We never seen no more Injuns and the land started downhill again, still rough but easier on wagons I reckon, and by and by we come to a canyon with steep walls that give off an echo for every sound you made. We had a fine old time the first hour, singing and shouting and poetrying and hearing it all come back to us four and five times over, all excepting for Randolph who's quiet like I say.

Bob was singing "Oh! Susanna" when I heard another voice mixing in with his that warn't none of us, and when Lydia heard it too she told Bob to hush. We could all hear the other voice plain now, and it's weak and calling for help, only we can't tell where it's coming from so we split up to search among the rocks. Sometimes it was stronger, then it got weak again, maybe a trick of the echo or else the person that's doing it is tired. We searched an hour and more before Jim give a shout and we all come over to him, and there's a woman lying between some rocks in a little shallow space with a dead man and boy beside her. She's skinny and her clothes all covered in dust and she never even had the strength to sit up, so Andrew got down and lifted her and give her water from his canteen, but she never drunk it, just looked in his face and slumped back, dead right there in his arms.

Randolph looked the other two over and says:

"There are no wounds."

"Must of been thirst," says Jesse.

"No it warn't," says Bob, and picked up a water flask and sloshed it to show it ain't empty, then he pulls a few cans and sacks out of a cleft in the rock. "There's food here too, so they never starved."

The same idea hit us all at once.

"Cholera," says Randolph, and everyone took a step back. Andrew had the decentness not to just drop the woman and laid her down gentle, but he backed off sharp after he done it. He says:

"Poor souls, abandoned by a train to spend their last days alone. Man's inhumanity to man is boundless."

"We got to get away from here right now," says Bob, sounding shaky.

"He's right," says Randolph. "We can't risk contagion by even stopping to bury them."

"Is there nothing we can do?" asks Lydia, real upset. "It seems so heartless, simply leaving them for the vultures."

"They will feel nothing," says Andrew, and went over to put an arm around her for comfort.

"Get away from her!" yells Randolph. "That woman breathed directly into your face. You may already have been contaminated."

All eyes was on the lovebirds. Lydia never stepped away from Andrew, just stayed right where she was to show she ain't afraid, which is brave or foolish depending on how you look at it. Randolph and the others headed for their horses and mounted up.

"Come, my dear," says Andrew. "There is nothing we can do here."

So we all moved on, and further along the canyon we seen abandoned wagons but never dared look in them for fear of what's inside. There was a smell on the breeze that filled our noses, partly dead men and women and partly burnt wood, because some of the wagons was set alight to burn out the cholera the owners fell sick to. The wrecks was cold ashes now with just the iron hoops and wheel

rims left in the piles of dead embers, which ain't a cheerful sight.
The whole canyon was littered with wagons burned or still standing
with their canvas flapping gentle in the breeze. Twenty-three I
counted, and there's proberly more I never seen, burned down behind boulders and hid from sight unless you looked, but we never
felt like looking.

It took all that day and part of the night to get out of that place.
We never stopped to make camp till them echoing walls flattened
out into open country, and even here there's a wagon now and then,
but the horses was tired so we had to stop.

Bob and Jesse set up their own campfire away from us and never
come near Andrew, who done a poem about it.

> *There once were two men from the east*
> *Afraid of not man or beast*
> *But when they espied*
> *A woman who died*
> *They moved like lightning that's greased.*

Lydia laughed, but it sounded kind of hollow. Randolph excused
himself after we et and went over to join Bob and Jesse, but they
never let him near now that he's been with us and even aimed their
guns at him to make him get away, so he had to come back to us and
looked considerable annoyed over it. There warn't no friendly talk
and we bedded down.

It was a short night for sleeping on account of traveling partway
through the dark, but we got fed and mounted up soon as it was
light, wanting to put distance between us and that canyon, and
when the range it's in was miles behind things got relaxed a little,
but Bob and Jesse rode way ahead still. Then in the afternoon
Andrew started to sweat even if we're too high up in the mountains
still for the air to be warm. He sweated a river and drenched his
clothes and went red in the face. Lydia made him get off his horse
and lie down, and Bob and Jesse come back to see what's wrong.
Andrew brung up his breakfast and they took one look and Bob
says:

"We'll be taking our share of supplies and moving ahead."

"It may be something else," says Lydia.

"Nope. We seen the cholera back in the Berringer train. He's got it for sure. He'll last a day or two at most. I'm real sorry, but we ain't goin' to stay around and get catched too."

"I understand."

They drawed the rations and loaded them on a pack horse and was ready to go right quick. They never went over to say goodbye to Lydia or Andrew, just asked Randolph if he's coming too.

"No," he says, "I believe I'll linger on awhile."

"She ain't ever goin' to be your'n," says Jesse, "not even when he's dead."

It warn't a tactful thing to say and Randolph knocked him down for it.

"Get out, you gutless scum!" he says, furious, and they never stopped to argue, just clumb aboard and headed west.

"Good riddance," says Randolph.

Andrew was in terrible pain now, twitching and sweating and shuddering, and just this morning he was fine. Cholera is the suddenest sickness there is, and it was pitiful to see his face all clenched with agony so bad he let out a cry that squeezed your heart to hear. There's a wind whipping along the ground and Lydia says we got to get Andrew under cover, so I scouted around on horseback and found a wagon a little way along the trail and held my breath and looked inside. There ain't no dead people, just a few bits and pieces left behind. I went back and told of it and Lydia got Andrew on his horse all by herself, not letting no one else near. When we got to the wagon she got him bedded down inside with a heap of blankets to keep him warm. It took all the water in all our canteens to keep him from catching fire from the fever, so while there's still light I done some more scouting and come across a little spring a few miles away and refilled all the canteens and brung them back.

It's night by then and Lydia lit a lamp that's in the wagon and wetted cloths ripped off her own petticoats and bathed Andrew's brow to cool it, and when he never had no more to puke up and started running at the other end she ripped off more petticoat and cleaned him, never once letting me or Jim or Randolph near. We built a fire a little way off and every now and then Lydia called and I went over with a long stick and she wrapped the messed cloth around the end, which I took back and dumped in the flames. Andrew cried out regular with the pain inside him and it was awful to hear. Randolph laid out cards on his handkerchief and played a game by himself in the firelight while Jim and me took turns with the stick.

No one got no sleep till near dawn, and then only because Andrew went quiet. I went over to the wagon to see why, hoping he ain't dead.

"Mrs. Beckwith, is he all right still?"

She never showed her face through the flaps, just spoke to me, and her voice was tired and weary.

"Andrew is alive, Huckleberry, but fading fast. He is unconscious, which may be a blessing. I will not need your help for some little while. You must sleep."

"I ain't tired, ma'am, and I reckon you must be awful hungry by now. Can I fix you something?"

"Thank you, but I have no appetite."

"It ain't no trouble. Please, Mrs. Beckwith, you done all the hard work. . . ."

"Very well. Coffee, no more."

"I'll fetch it along directly."

Which I done, and left the cup nearby so she can climb down and get it. She never wanted me to touch no part of the wagon. I seen her face in the early light and she's a changed woman, her skin pale and her eyes sunk deep with weariness.

"Thank you," she says, and tried to raise a smile, but it's crooked and sad. Says I:

"Ain't there nothing else I can do?"

"I think not. You have been a great help. Now all we can do is pray."

She clumb back inside and I went over and put more wood on the fire. The sun come up over the mountains and the light was chilly and cold as the wind moaning across the land. Rufus prowled around, restless and whining.

"How is he?" asks Randolph, still slapping down cards.

"Dying, I reckon."

He just give a nod and kept on playing, never even looked up. He's got to be the coldest man I ever met. I slept for awhile, then heard Lydia calling my name. I went over and she's stood on the tailboard and looking like her own mother she's so wore out.

"Andrew has gone," she says real soft, and I looked at her and she looked at me and we never spoke for a minute. Jim and Randolph come over and I told them and they took off their hats.

"Mrs. Beckwith," says Randolph, "you have my deepest sympathy. Mr. Collins was a gifted artist and a man to be admired."

"Thank you, Mr. Squires," she says, and he goes on:

"But now you must think of yourself. Allow me to help you down," he says, and took a step forward and lifted his arms.

"Stop!" she says, and swayed some with the effort of talking so loud, and had to grab the canvas to keep from falling. He stopped and she lifted her chin and says:

"I shall not be leaving the wagon. I have the disease."

None of us spoke a word. I reckon we all knowed it was bound to happen, her nursing Andrew close that way. She must of knowed it too, but it never stopped her.

"In what way may we assist you, ma'am?" says Randolph, and his voice was choked, so he ain't so hardbitten as he likes to give out.

"There is nothing," she says, and turns to me. "Huckleberry, you and Jim must make all speed. You have lost a day already. Mr. Barrett may already be on your trail. I beg of you, take Jupiter and flee."

"You can't be sure you got it, Mrs. Beckwith. Maybe you're just tired is all. . . ."

"I have the symptoms. Please do not argue. Now I wish to be alone."

She stepped back into the wagon and pulled the flaps closed, and we went back to the fire and smoked awhile as the sun crawled higher.

"She's right," says Randolph. "You'd best be moving if you want to stay free."

"I ain't going," says I.

I never planned on saying it, the words just come out of me in a rush, but I knowed they was the right ones. Even if there ain't a way to save Lydia I can't just leave the way Bob and Jesse done, not if I aim to hold my head up the rest of my life.

"I ain't goin' neither," says Jim.

Randolph stared at the fire till his cigar was just a stub then throwed it in and stood up. He turned to the wagon and took off his hat again and says:

"I salute a queen among women. We will not meet her like again."

Then he went and drawed his fair portion of supplies and loaded up one of the pack horses and saddled his own horse and one of the others for a spare, then says:

"May God or the devil be with you, boy, and you too, nigger. You'll be needing help from one or the other."

And he rode off slow and never looked back.

Me and Jim never spoke much all morning, just fed and watered the horses and ourselfs. I warn't bothered about the bulldog. I never felt nothing except sad and puzzled. Here's two of the finest people you could find ever, and they both was in love and looking for adventure together and now Andrew is dead and Lydia ain't far behind. What does anything mean if people like that can die and simple-minded trash like Bob and Jesse can ride away without no harm? After I got accused of murdering the judge I wondered if there's natural balance and justice in the world, but that's personal, and a body can't trust his own feelings when it comes to figuring his own situation. Then I turned Injun and seen how the color you are makes injustice get heaped on you even if you done nothing wrong, and now my friends is dead and dying right over there in the wagon and they never deserved it.

So now I know for sure there ain't no justice or balance to things, and that the world is topsy-turvy and jumbled and confused, which is the natural way it's meant to be. Them that says God is watching and listening and knows all that's happening down here is talking the sorriest kind of excuses for the way things is, just turning their backs on the confusion and injustice like a man that looks at a tornado tearing toward him and says it's a tree, because a tree is something that don't bother him, and a tornado is too wild and huge and cruel to feel easy about, so it's a tree. Only it comes along and kills him anyway. It give me a calm feeling to know the sky is empty and there ain't no one watching and scribbling down everything with a golden pen. It's like I'm in a house full of people and I'm the only one that sees the roof ain't there, but all the rest says it is and draws comfort from knowing the roof that ain't there is going to keep the cold rain off them. They keep on thinking the same even when the rain comes down and soaks them, and they chatter to each other about how nice and dry things is under the roof, and after awhile I stop worrying about them because they're happy that way, and I ask myself why should I worry about being the only one that sees there ain't a roof? Why *should* there be a roof? There ain't no law that says a house has got to have one, it's just that you expect to see a roof there to finish things off. Well, there ain't one, and that suits me fine.

Around noon Lydia looked out and seen we're still there and called us over. Her face looks like a shiny skull with her eyes darkened all around and her cheekbones and forehead wet with sweat.

"Huckleberry, why have you and Jim not gone with Mr. Squires?"

"I reckon we felt like staying here, Mrs. Beckwith."

"Please . . . you must both leave."

"No, ma'am, we're staying put."

"You're being foolish. . . ."

"Yes, ma'am. We both of us been called idiots in our time, but it don't bother us none so we're staying."

She give us a weak smile and says:

"Huckleberry . . . Jim. . . . Whatever happens . . . you must not touch the wagon or enter it. When the time comes you must set it alight. Do you understand?"

"Yes, ma'am. We'll do it. Can we fetch you some more water?"

"I am beyond any further needs, thank you. Huckleberry, in my saddle bags there are some trinkets I have kept for some time. They have no great value, but they may be of some use to you."

"Thank you. I'm obliged."

She let the flap down and we shuffled back to the fire. Any time now she'd start to get pain like Andrew done and I warn't looking forward to hearing her cry out, but maybe she's so brave she won't make a sound. It give me the trembles to consider the way she's suffering and going to suffer even worse another day at least. But Lydia had another kind of bravery. A little later there come a shot from inside the wagon and me and Jim just looked at each other kind of shocked, then Jim says:

"She ain't in torment no mo', Huck, an' I reckon she done what she done for two reasons. De firs' one on accounter de pain she be gettin', but de secon' to set us free. She don' want us waitin' aroun' for de bulldog to show up, so she up an' took away de onliest reason we stayin' here for. Das some kinder woman in dere, Huck, jest de fines'."

There warn't nothing I could of added to what he says, so we got busy piling brush and dead wood under the wagon and set alight to it and stood back to watch it burn. The flames catched fast and pretty soon was licking up around the wheels and frame. The canvas went up with a whoosh and left the hoops behind all blackened and charred, then the fire got a true hold and burned fierce till every part of the wagon was ablaze and the hotness made us stand off further, watching the smoke roll into the sky. When the spokes burned through the wagon bed dropped but kept on burning, and there warn't a need to stay around.

I looked inside Jupiter's saddlebags and there's the trinkets, a couple necklaces, one silver and one gold, and some ear-rings and a brooch and a ring or three all in a little velvet bag. I would of handed over a mountain of gold and a lake of pearls if the lovebirds could be brung back, but it's childish thinking, and I ain't a child no more. I whistled Remus and we mounted and rode away, and I never needed to see the smoke still curling up behind us to know a part of me is burned away forever, and good riddance too. Whatever part it was I can get along without it.

✦ 22 ✦

City in the Wilderness—A Bargain Struck—The Rewards

of Enterprise—Castles and Kings—A Chance Reunion

We had Jupiter and the bulldog's horse and two others besides for spare, and we swapped around so none of them got overworked in the days that followed. We never done much talking. Maybe Jim had the same kind of things running through his head as me, I can't tell. We slept and et and rode on through rough country with sometimes a grave beside the wagon trail with a sorry little cross stuck in it, but we never catched up with no trains or with Randolph, and the bulldog never showed. Near dusk one day we come through a pass and seen a city laid out below on a wide flat plain with mountains all around like it's been picked up out of the east and hauled across the sky and set down gentle in the middle of noplace. There was hundreds of houses and wide streets laid out square and fields outside town with crops growing. Lydia's map says it's Salt Lake City, and the big lake northwest of it says so too.

"Das a mighty fine sight way out here," says Jim.

"The Mormons built it, Jim. They're real industrious I heard tell, and work like beavers from dawn till dusk except on Sundays, which is when they throw their muscle into prayer."

"What kinder folks is Mormons, Huck?"

"It's a religion far as I can make out, kind of like regular Christianism only more serious minded. Most folks don't get along with Mormons on account of they reckon they're God's chosen people like the Israelites used to say about theirselfs."

"You don' reckon dey's God's chosen?"

"I reckon we best treat 'em polite and not get talking about religion so's we don't give no offense. See them trees over yonder laid out neat? I bet it's a fruit orchard, and I'd purely love to bite an apple after all this time."

289

"I knows how you feel, Huck. If'n I hafter chew jest one more hunker sourdough wid jerked meat I'se goin' to heave it up."

We started along the last stretch of trail that winds down to the valley floor, thinking on apples and oranges, maybe even grapes, just drooling for fruit to sink our fangs in. By the time we come to the outskirts of town it's dark and there's lights in the windows and mothers was calling children indoors for supper. A dog come yapping around the horses' hoofs but Remus run him off right quick. Riding slow along a street made me feel humble and afraid, like we're beggars, and maybe it's so seeing as we ain't got no money. Jim and me planned on selling the spare horses along with their saddles for cash to get fresh supplies, only it's too dark now and the city too big to go finding stockyards or livery stables. I done the only thing we could of done and that's knock on the door of a brick house like the rest with a garden out front. It got opened by a woman around forty and she's kind of startled to see an Injun on her doorstep.

"Yes?" she says.

"Pardon me, ma'am, I'm wondering where I can sell a couple of horses."

"You're selling horses?"

"Yes, ma'am, I mean I ain't no horse trader by profession, just a mite short on cash momentarily."

"Are you an Injun?"

"No, ma'am, I got captured by the Sioux and then escaped. I'm white as flour."

"Who's that by the gate?"

"That's Ben, ma'am. He's a real nigger."

"Well come inside the both of you. Just leave your horses tied to the fence."

"Both of us, ma'am?"

"Of course both of you. Ben's hungry as you I'll bet."

"I reckon so, ma'am. Thank you kindly."

"Who is it, Hester?" calls a man's voice from inside.

"A white Injun boy and a black negro man," she says.

Jim tied the horses and come up the garden walk and she stood aside to let us through. The house never had wallpaper or nothing inside, just brick painted over with whitewash and hung with pictures and shelfs and such, but no mirrors, all of it clean as clean.

She led us into a room and there must of been twelve or thirteen people sat around a big table with carved legs, all of them looking our way. There's a man with bushy hair and a beard and a watch chain across his vest at the head of the table and he never looked too pleased to see us.

"Who are you?" he says direct.

"Newton Boggs, sir, and this here's Ben."

"Are you traveling to California?"

"Yessir, we are."

"Welcome to my home," he says, still sounding peeved. "Agatha, Millicent, fetch chairs for our guests."

Two girls went out to another room and brung back chairs and me and Jim fronted up to the table with the rest. It's the first time ever that Jim sat with white folks at mealtime in his whole life, and he never looked at ease and never spoke a word. The bushy man says:

"I am Nathaniel Weber. This is my family."

He spun off their names so fast I never catched most of them till he come to the end and says:

"And these are my wives, Hester, Judith and Bathsheba."

I reckoned I must of misheard, but he seen my face and says:

"Yes, young man. Three. We Mormons believe the Lord intended man as well as the beasts to go forth and multiply."

"I can't think of no faster way, Mr. Weber, sir."

Food got dished up and plenty of it too, and after we finished they started in with questions about how we come to be there, and I lied myself empty. There was four boys and they was real interested in life among the Injuns so I give them a heaped helping of the biggest lies in creation, which they just lapped up and wanted more. The five girls never took their eyes off me in my Injun clothes and loved the parts where I told about brave deeds and adventures. They kept on filling my cup with coffee and I churned out words like a printing press for close on two hours without saying nothing twice, and at the end Mr. Weber says:

"Son, you have journeyed far and suffered great privation, as did we on our flight from the Gentiles in eighteen forty-six. Your lust for gold is misconceived, that substance being fit only for paving streets, but if there is any way in which we may assist you speak it now."

So I told about wanting to sell the horses, but he says the Mormons has got all the horses they need and sells them and cattle as well to forty-niners passing through with broken-down teams and no fresh meat, so they ain't in the market for no more. Also he says we should keep them for carrying extra water across the desert west of here which is a terrible place where there ain't nothing living nor growing. It's good advice but it don't help us none seeing as we can't pay for no water barrels.

"Do you have nothing other than horses with which to trade?" he says.

That's when I recollected Lydia's jewels and went and fetched them in. The women give them the big eye when I laid the stuff on the table, but Mr. Weber just barely looked and says:

"We have no need of trinkets and gee-gaws. Our women do not decorate their persons with symbols of vanity."

"There ain't nothing else we got," says I, "excepting a dog."

"A dog!" squeals Millicent. "Oh, Papa, mayn't we have a dog?"

"Oh, please, Papa," puts in Christobel or Agatha or one of them. "We haven't had a dog since we left Missouri. Oh, mayn't we please?"

All the other girls joined in and the two youngest boys till you couldn't of heard a bugle blowed in there, and Papa raised up his hands and slammed them down hard on the table, which made the cutlery jump and everyone hush.

"We are a hardworking people," he says, sternish. "We have no need of animals which do not contribute to the furtherance of our industry and farming, and we already have a sufficiency of such. A spaniel is the plaything of Gentiles, not Mormons. I will hear no more of it."

"Pardon me, Mr. Weber, sir, but Remus ain't no lapdog. He's so big I reckon you could hitch him to a plow and turn over ten acres before sundown."

They never believed me so I went out and whistled him and Remus come galloping up the street with a dead chicken from someone's yard in his mouth. I made him give it to me and throwed it away and drug him inside to show off. You never heard such a gasping nor seen such gawping when I hauled him into the room. Even Mr. Weber was considerable impressed.

"What kind of beast is it?" he asks.

"Irish wolfhound, sir," says I, which is what Lydia told me.

"Is it a freakish product of mischance?" asks one of the wives, Bathsheba I reckon, or maybe it was Judith.

"No, ma'am, he's a special breed from Ireland. There used to be wolves running underfoot up and down the country and you couldn't hardly step out the door without getting your leg bit off, then they bred these here wolfhounds and in no time at all there warn't no more wolves left in Ireland. They still had snakes, but St. Patrick got called in to get rid of them."

"Oh, Husband," says Hester, "remember the trouble last winter when wolves came down from the mountains and ran through the streets. Why, the little Wister girl got savaged in her own yard on the way to the outhouse and was never the same again, poor thing. It may even happen to your own children."

Husband hemmed and hawed and I kept a grip on Remus's collar with both hands to keep him from jumping on the table or putting his nose between someone's legs. He whipped up a breeze with his tail in the exciteration and noise and looked real friendly. Finally Husband says:

"He's a massive size, but seems too good-natured to be a guard dog."

I stepped on Remus's paw and he let out a snarl and the girls backed off squealing.

"Oh, my," says Bathsheba or Judith. "Mayn't he be too savage to have around the place?"

So I tickled his ears and Remus lolled his tongue and slitted his eyes and flopped on the floor to have his belly rubbed, which tipped over two chairs the girls rushed out of when he snarled. When they seen him like that with his paws brushing the ceiling they oohed and aahed like he's a little lamb or something and started in pestering Papa again, and Amos and Jeremiah, or maybe it's Joel and Nehemiah was brave enough to get down and rub him till he practickly purred, then they each give him a pat or a stroke, wives and all, and Papa would of been lynched if he told them no. He says:

"The Lord has seen fit to deliver into our hands an answer to the four-legged predators which plague us in time of famine. So be it. I will accept this beast in exchange for a reasonable amount of whatever you require, but that can wait till tomorrow. We have lingered too long through the evening and must be up early to fulfill our appointed tasks. Amos, show our guests the stable and assist them in the foddering of their horses. The rest of you, to bed."

They all give us a goodnight, happy they got their way, and awhile later Jim and me was lying in warm hay with the horses chomping oats below. Jim says:

"Mighty nice folks, dese Mormons, but how come dey got so many women? It parter de religion?"

"Must be, Jim. I can't see why a man would want to saddle himself with more than one wife without the church rules say he's got to."

"It mus' be awful hard on a man listenin' to de wives complainin' 'bout dis an' dat all de time an' gettin' jealous over de lovin' he parcels out. Dat kinder life got to be a worriment to him from mornin' till night wid no let up. How do a man sleep wid all dem problermations on his min', Huck?"

"In a mighty big bed I reckon, Jim."

Next morning Jeremiah or Nehemiah or one of them woke us up before the sun come over the mountains and Hester and Esther give us breakfast. Afterwards Mr. Weber took us to the middle of town where there's a big open space with a brick foundation laid out and scaffolding and such and he says it's going to be the Mormon Temple, the grandest church west of the Mississippi, then he hustled us along to the flour mill he's in charge of and showed us how it's all done with power from a water wheel that's fed from a ditch dug all the way to the mountains so there's always water running along it, which is how they can raise crops in the middle of a desert too. He was awful proud of the setup and we done the polite thing and praised it to the skies, then he took us to a store and got us the supplies we wanted, then says:

"I have been considering the baubles you offered me yester-eve and have decided they may prove handy at some later date when we begin trading with the Gentile world on a regular basis. For suitable compensation I will purchase four small water barrels to be affixed to the saddles of your spare horses. I do not make the offer for profit, but because it would distress me to think I had not done the Lord's will by you both and allowed you to venture into the inferno beyond the mountains without adequate preparation."

He wants both necklaces for the four barrels, which he got from a cooper, plus rope, and then he says if I throw in the brooch he'll get all our horses reshod at the blacksmith's. I give their hoofs a looking over same as he must of done while we was having breakfast and he's right; they're thin as paper, so I done the deal with him. Mormons is nice people, but they surely drive a hard bargain.

Back at the Weber place me and Jim lashed the barrels to both sides of the saddles and filled them with water and tied the lids down. They was heavy so we slung the rest of the supplies across Jupiter and Jim's horse and was all set to go when Hester come running out of the house with a bundle of clothes which she give to me.

"Take them," she says. "Now you're no longer a captive of the Sioux you need not wear their heathen apparel."

"That's real kind of you, ma'am, but I can't take no clothes off Amos and Jeremiah and Joel and Nehemiah."

"It's all old and growed out of," she says. "Please take it."

So I slung the bundle over the pommel along with the rest and the entire family lined up to say goodbye, also the neighbors. Remus wanted to come along too so he had to be locked in the stable, then we give them all a wave and rode off down the street to the edge of town then out past the orchards and fields with the sun behind us to where it gets desolate again. Jim says:

"Say, Huck, what kinder crittur's a Gentile?"

"Near as I can figure it's anyone that ain't a Mormon, but it ain't intended to be insulting. I reckon Injuns and niggers don't count anyhow."

For the next few days we went around the south shore of the Great Salt Lake and aimed for the Cedar Mountains, munching on fruit till we got belly cramp. The wagon trail turned north to go around the mountains and we followed along with the peaks rising up beside us, mighty rugged, so it's easy to see why the wagons took the long way around and never tried crossing over. It was sunny days and I was tolerable happy for the first time since the lovebirds died. That was only a week back but I already quit grieving, which made me feel considerable guilty first off, then I figured it's best after all; if a body done nothing but grieve, he'd grieve himself right into his own grave, and I ain't nearly old enough to be dead yet. Jim was in fair spirits too and sung songs along the way, which is something I ain't heard him do in a long time.

"Jim," says I, "did you ever consider how important songs is to folks?"

"I reckon so, Huck. When I gets to singin' it mean I'se feelin' perty good. I don' rec'llect no time I ever done no singin' when de blue devils insider me."

"It's been a well knowed fact down through history, Jim, but songs ain't only for happy times."

"Dey ain't?"

"Sometimes they come in right handy for other things too. You take King Richard now, he had a favorite song he always liked to hear and it practickly saved his life one time."

"Dis de same king dat went lookin' for de Holy Grail, Huck?"

"The very one, Jim, and when he never found it in the Holy Land he got disgusted and figured he may as well go on home to England, but the trouble was he spent all his money on looking for the Grail and when he opened the royal purse to fetch out a few dollars' ticket money there warn't nothing in it but moth holes, so he never had the coin to go back by ship and had to traipse all the way across Europe with just his horse for company."

"Where de singin' come into de story?"

"I'm getting to that. King Richard was passing through one of them itty-bitty European countries which is all mountains and forests and castles, and the king of that country reckernized him and pulled him off his horse and shut him away in the highest tower of his castle and sent a message to England that says he's got their king and if they want him back they better dig deep in the royal coffins and send the cash right quick."

"Why dey keep de royal cash in coffins, Huck?"

"I disremember the reason, Jim, but it's what they done. Most likely they buried it underground for safekeeping. Anyway, while King Richard was away in the Holy Land all them years his brother John got his turn on the throne and he liked the feel of it, so when he got the message he let out that the royal coffins was empty and he can't pay the ransom. It warn't nothing short of a dirty lie, but he's the king and no one called him a sneaking lying brother-hater to his face or he would of got his head cut off and throwed in the dungeon, so King John figured he's safe to rule England for another ninety-nine years at least with the real king rotting away in Europe.

But he never knowed that Richard has got a faithful singer by name of Blondel on account of his yeller hair, and when Blondel heard the news he packed his harp and jumped on his horse and rode across to Europe, and every castle he come to he strummed and plucked and sung King Richard's favorite song which is called 'Greensleeves' after the king's Sunday best jacket, and he traveled all over Europe for years just playin' this one song under the castle walls."

"How come he never got sick'n'tireder playin' de same song all de time?"

"Earplugs, Jim. It was the only way to keep from driving himself crazy from hearing 'Greensleeves' about ninety million times. There was a heap of castles in them days. Anyway, he finally come to the right castle and sung the song same as usual, and King Richard was still up in the tower after all this time and when he heard it he says to himself, 'That's "Greensleeves," by jiminy. How come I hear it way out here?' And he went to the window and looked out and there's Blondel plucking and strumming and hollering and the king yells out 'You remembered!' meaning he figured Blondel would of forgot his favorite song after all this time, but Blondel never heard him on account of the earplugs, see. Blondel was the most wonderful singer in the world, but not too bright. The king seen the way of it and flung a stone at him but he missed, so he emptied a jug of drinking water over him and that made Blondel look up to see if it's raining, and he seen the king waving at the window and whipped out the earplugs, which is lucky because the next thing the king would of emptied over him was a chamber pot.

"Blondel was real happy to find the king at last on account of it means he don't have to sing 'Greensleeves' no more, and he asks how he can get the king out of the tower. He's got a rope with him along with the harp but he can't throw it up that high, and the king yells down to hold on and then starts feeding his hair out the window. Them Europeans was awful mean to him and never once give him a haircut in all them years so his hair was yards and yards long, awful dirty by now but enough of it to reach the ground easy. He would of clumb down it long before, but it ain't possible for a body to climb down his own hair. Maybe you could climb up it, but that warn't the problem; he's in a tower, not a cellar, so down it all went to the ground with the king leaning out the window, and Blondel reckoned he understood the plan and jumped off his horse and started climbing up King Richard's hair with the rope slung over his shoulder to deliver it, but that ain't what the king planned at all, and he screams 'You're pulling the hair out of my skull, you danged fool! Just tie the rope around the end of it and I'll haul it up!' So Blondel clumb down again full of apologizing and done what the king says, and the rope got hauled up and tied around a bedpost and King Richard slid down it quick before someone come along and seen what they're doing, but he's too late.

"A guard give the alarm and the drawbridge come crashing down and all the soldiers in the castle come thundering across to stop them getting away. King Richard says, 'Quick, gimme your sword so's I can cut off this pesky hair.' Blondel's horse never could of carried him and the king and all that hair too, but Blondel says, 'I ain't got no sword. Why would a singer have a sword?' And Richard cussed him something awful and says, 'Well ain't you even got a pocket knife to trim your toenails?' Blondel had one of them all right and the king sawed off his hair right quick and they galloped away, and when the soldiers come to the spot their legs got all tangled up in the hair lying around and they fell over one on top of the other, and the king and Blondel got clean away."

"What de king do when he gets home, Huck?"

"He was mighty sore at brother John for what he done and marched into the throne room and flung him to the floor in front of all the lords and ladies and sat on his head til he hollered ''Nuff!' then banished him out of the kingdom forever."

"How 'bout de singer?"

"He deserved to get rewarded, Jim, but what happened was King Richard wanted to hear 'Greensleeves' again to celebrate being back on the throne, and when Blondel heard the order he throwed himself in the castle moat and drowned in preferment to singing it even one more time, and the moral of the story is: enough is enough."

"It don' pay to mess wid kings, Huck."

Next day the trail turned west again where the mountains petered out and in the afternoon we seen the awfullest sight ahead which the map calls the Great Salt Desert, flat as a pancake and white with salt and not a blade of grass or nothing far as you could see. We figured we'd wait till night and get as far across as we can in the cool, and maybe reach the far side before nightfall tomorrow. While we was figuring we seen a little stand of trees half a mile off at the base of the mountains and headed for it hoping there's a spring we can refill our barrels from.

The spring was there sure enough, and so was Randolph and Bob and Jesse.

23

Sun and Salt—Trouble and Tribulation—Separate

Paths—Injuns Again—Mission of Mercy

---

ell, well," says Bob. "Look what the net hauled up. How's it with you, Injun?"

"Fine, I reckon."

"Seen that idiot detective?" asks Jesse.

"No I ain't."

We got down and led the horses to the water, which they drunk deep of.

"I see the Mormons have persuaded you to buy barrels also," says Randolph, and I seen their pack horses is barrel-slung too. Says I:

"Are you waiting for night to start across?"

"We are. You may as well join up with us again."

"I reckon we will."

I would of rather not but there ain't no way around it, so we loosened the saddle girths and the horses cropped at the patches of brush hereabouts and we smoked our pipes in the shade, resting up before nightfall. Bob and Jesse fell asleep and Randolph come over to me and says:

"How was it at the end?"

"I don't reckon you got the right to know, Mr. Squires, but if it's all that important I'll tell you. She shot herself, then we burned the wagon. I reckon I'm tired now."

I turned away from him and pretended to sleep. He went away and never asked nothing more about it, proberly feeling guilty, it's hard to tell with Randolph. I never disliked him outright, just never warmed to him the way you can with some folks. Then I truly fell asleep.

Jim woke me when the sun was down and all of us filled our barrels brimful of water and started out. The wagon ruts was easy seen when the moon come up a little later, stretching out straight as an arrow for the far side of the desert. The air was cool and we went on hour after hour just listening to the jingle of harness and hoofs crunching into the salt, considerable noisy when you got ten horses in all. The desert was pale and our shadows stood out sharp in the moonlight. There's stars scattered all across the sky, winking and blinking even brighter than over the plains. They was kind of beautiful and made you forget who you are and where you're headed if you looked at them long enough. No one talked, but it warn't a companionable silence like Jim and me had when we ain't got nothing to say, more like ignoring each other, but I never let it bother me. We went on and on but never seemed to get nowhere. There ain't no trees or rocks or nothing to see up ahead, nothing but salt desert, flat and running away beyond eye-reach.

It took forever till dawn come up behind us and the desert turned pink for a little while, then white again as the sun clumb higher and beat on our backs. Before it got too hot we stopped and watered the horses and rested awhile, then started off again. By midmorning the air was like an oven door that's opened full in your face, hot enough to melt your brain. I wrapped one of Amos or Nehemiah's shirts around my head for a hat and let the tail hang down over my neck to keep from getting sunsick. The horses plodded on, their legs all caked in salt dust. By noon it's so hot it parched your throat just to breathe. I done a heap of drinking from my canteen to get relief and it come flooding out in sweat a minute later, but before it even got my shirt wet it got sucked away by the air and I'm hot as ever.

"I reckon I'll go to heaven when I die," croaks Jesse. "I already seen hell."

The horses was leg weary now and their heads hung low. We stopped again to let them drink then went on again. It took strength just to keep sat in the saddle, and there's a kind of ringing in my ears. Jim says he hears the same thing and Bob says it's a heavenly chorus getting us set for dying, and laughed. Now the sun was ahead of us, too bright to look at, and our heads bowed low like the horses to shade our eyes. Then Randolph seen something up ahead, not big but easy picked out on account of there ain't nothing else around, and when we come nearer parts of it broke off and flapped up into the sky—three buzzards. When we come to the spot we seen a dead man lying by the trail with his skin all puckered and blistered and his belly tore open by the buzzards. I never felt nothing looking at him, just curious maybe, and we moved on without even getting off the horses. He warn't no one I knowed.

On and on we went never-ending. My eyes was gritty and hard to blink so I kept them shut and trusted Jupiter to follow along with the rest. But that made me start to fall asleep, so I opened them again and seen trees kind of dancing along the horizon, rippling like reeds under water. I opened my mouth to tell the others but only croaked. Randolph seen what I'm pointing at and says:

"Mirage. There's nothing there, only more desert."

"Wait on," says Bob. "Look beyond. . . . Ain't they mountains?"

They was there all right, a powerful distance off, but at least we know the desert ends someplace. I kept my eyes on them mountains, wispy blue is their color, but they never seemed to get no closer, just shimmered behind the dancing trees that ain't there.

"Huck," says Jim, "now I knows how Shadrach, Meshach an' Abednego feel when dey's throwed in de fiery furnace. I reckon I'der bowed down an' worship' de golden idol like de king wanted if'n dat furnace jest half de hotness dis place got. I'se jest burnin' up."

"Ain't we all, nigger," says Jesse.

"Quit calling Jim nigger," says I. "He's got a name same as you."

"You talkin' to me, Injun?"

"And you can quit calling me Injun too."

"Can I now, you little piss-ant. Come over here and I'll knock you off your horse, you talk to me that way. Goddamn, it's a fine day when a man can't call a nigger a nigger and gets backtalk from a boy that's done murder."

"If you truly believed I done it you would of handed me over to Bulldog Barrett," says I, and he says:

"I don't like no law officers and detectives and suchlike trash is all. If you was the biggest killer in the country I never would of lifted a finger to see you brung in, but I reckon you ain't so lily-white as you try and make out, boy. Nobody gets chased this far if he ain't done nothing wrong."

It warn't no use to argue. Jesse's the kind with a mean streak that don't allow for friendliness and he'll pick a quarrel deliberate if he wants to so I never answered back, just let Jupiter carry me on across the burning salt. The sun got lower and still we went on, mile after mile, and the mountains quit shimmering and settled down but still never seemed all that much closer. It was weary and dispiriting. Finally the sun turned from white to gold and later on to red just before it sunk behind the mountains, and we stopped and set the barrels down again for the horses to drink. I laid out a blanket and spilled a sack of oats on it for them so they won't lick up desert salt too and make theirselfs thirstier, then we all lay down for a couple hours to rest.

Jesse woke me up with his boot and we got moving again. It's hard on the horses after all they done for a night and a day, but it's smarter to push them through another night when it's cool than have them suffer another day like today. It was the same thing again as last night, only this time the stars never looked beautiful, just cold and not caring and far away. I fell asleep in the saddle and come near to falling off a couple or three times but jerked up straight each time. I seen the others do the same, but Bob done it one time too many and fell right off and cussed a blue streak. He warn't hurt but no one laughed. We was all weak and wore out, and when the dawn finally come along we stopped. The horses sucked the last drop out of the barrels and our canteens was near empty too, but the mountains was much closer now and brown, not blue no more. The desert was changed too, from white to yeller brown and there's scrubby little sagebrushes here and there getting thicker the further we go on. The sun crawled up behind us and I seen a wispy little cloud overhead which I begged to come between me and the sun, but it never. There was buzzards aplenty up there to keep it company, flying around and around without ever flapping their wings.

"Lookit them bastards," says Bob. "They're just waiting for us to drop, the stinkin' sonsabitches."

And he aimed his rifle and fired at them, which never upset the buzzards at all, but Bob felt a mite better for it. Soon we come across a wagon with the back axle busted. There warn't nothing inside it so we kept on and soon was off the salt desert at last, but the regular desert ain't no friendlier. By and by my head started in banging like a big drum and I wanted to puke, only there ain't nothing in me to bring up so I stayed feeling sick as a dog all through the morning. It was so bad I come near to whimpering with the pain of it, and my head hung heavy like a cannonball and finally dragged my whole self off Jupiter. I never even knowed I was falling till I hit the ground. I give a shout with the surprise of it but no sound come out. Then Jim is bending over me and trickling water into my mouth from his canteen.

"Drink it, Huck," he says, "I got more. You in perty bad shape I reckon."

I still can't talk and he says:

"Kin you sit on de horse awhile longer, Huck?"

I give a nod and he lifted me onto Jupiter and give me the reins.

"If'n you goin' to fall again jest you grab onto de saddle horn an' hang on tight. We almos' in de mountains now, Huck. Dey lookin' mighty shady from here."

He got back on his own horse and we started forward. The others never even stopped when I fell so now we're last in line. I looked ahead and Jim's right; the mountains ain't more than a few hours off so I gritted my teeth and held on. It took forever to reach them, and when we done it them mountains warn't so shady as they looked from a distance. Jim rode ahead and come back later and says he found a spring further up the trail, and he's brung back a full canteen to prove it. He come over and give it to me, but before I even got a mouthful inside of me Bob says:

"Grown men first. Bring that water over here. I'm bone dry."

"You drink it, Huck," says Jim.

"Are you deaf, nigger?" says Jesse. "You heard him, now bring it here."

And he aimed his rifle at Jim's back. When I seen that I run the canteen directly over to Bob, but Jesse warn't through yet.

"You dumb nigger," he says. "Ain't you learned how to take orders from a white man? What kinder slave are you, you turd-eatin' black sonovabitch?"

"I ain't no slave," says Jim. "I been a free man dis las' year."

"There ain't no such thing as a free nigger, nigger, and don't you forget it again or I'll blow your head clean off. You hear me, nigger?"

"I ain't deef," says Jim, not bowing his head like a nigger is supposed to when he gets shouted at by a white man. Jesse never believed his eyes the way Jim looked straight into them, and I reckon he would of pulled the trigger if Bob hadn't of throwed the canteen across to him. Jim walked away while Jesse gargled water and got back on his horse. I looked over at Randolph, wondering how come he's so quiet, and seen that even if he ain't facing Bob and Jesse the barrel of his pistol is poking out from under his elbow and he's got his head turned just enough so's he can aim if he wanted to shoot, which he don't need to now the argument is ended, and the barrel vanished even while I'm looking. Randolph has got a cool head for sure, and I bet he never really wanted to get into no fight with Bob and Jesse over a nigger and a canteen of water. It ain't like he looked on Jim as a friend, even called him nigger like the others, so maybe he would of shot Jesse purely on account of he don't like white trash that ain't high-toned like himself. It's a puzzlement the way he acts and I can't figure which side he's on.

When we got to the spring there's a little grass for the horses so we rested there all the afternoon and night. Jim and me kept away from the rest and there warn't no more trouble, and next day we followed the trail twisting along through the mountains, real rugged country with buzzards and eagles always in the sky. When we was halfway through on the second day Randolph looked at his map and says he ain't going to follow the wagon ruts through to Humboldt Wells but go catty-corner across country along what Mr. Walker back at Fort Bridger told him is called the Clyman Route of eighteen forty-six and hit the Humboldt River further down, which he says will save us a couple of days travel. We was all agreeable and left the wagon trail for a little valley heading due west, and followed it along another day and come out the other side where it's flat desert again all covered in sagebrush, which made good burning for the fire that night.

Trouble come when Jesse started staring at Jim, not saying nothing, just staring. Jim seen it but kept right on eating, and finally Jesse says:

"Nigger, you eat more'n a horse. You better quit stealin' our supplies or I ain't answerable."

"I ain't stealin' nothin'," says Jim. "We got our own supplies."

"The way you fill your belly you ain't going to have none left pretty soon, and when that happens you better not come near ours or I ain't answerable, I mean it."

It was just ridickerless what he's saying, and I never held back I'm so fired up over the stupidness of it and got on my feet.

"You quit! You done nothing but pick trouble all along, and if you don't quit we ain't going no further with you!"

It give him a surprise the way I yelled, but he just laughed it off.

"Lookit you," he says, "the great mankiller himself. You oughter watch your tongue, small fry, or I might cut it outer your Injun head."

"Just you try it!" says I, squeaking all high pitched I'm so mad. "You try and I'll lift the hair off your idiot head!"

"Idiot, am I?" he snarls, and got on his feet with his eyes all narrowed down to slits. I seen he's in a mean mood and was just waiting for me or Jim to talk back so's he can start a fight.

"You better get set for dying, boy," he says, and whips out his knife. "Say them prayers, Injun. I had about enougher you and the nigger both."

I don't know nothing about knife fighting so I left mine in my belt and backed away, scared now I seen he ain't fooling.

"Come on, boy. Where's your guts? Ain't you the little coward, backin' off that way. Come on and get acquainted with a steely gent name of Bowie, or else get on your knees and apologize. What's it gonna to be, Injun?"

"I ain't apologizing to you, you peabrain sap-head idiot!" says I, still stepping backwards. "You got to be the pathetickest idiot brain I ever met! You ain't got no more control than a baby that messes his crib!"

His face twisted out of shape and he run at me with his knife raised. I froze on the spot, too scared to pull my own knife or even turn tail and run, and I figured I'm good as dead. But when Jesse went charging past Randolph to get at me Randolph's boot got in the way of his legs and he come crashing down so close to the fire his sleeve catched alight and he squealed and slapped the flames out directly. He warn't hurt none but was still plenty mad, and he looked around for his knife that he dropped but Jim already grabbed it. Then Bob picks up his rifle and aims it at Jim.

"Drop that knife, nigger," he says, and Jim tossed it over his shoulder away into the dark where no one ain't going to find it without a heap of looking.

"Shoot him!" yells Jesse.

"I reckon I just might," says Bob, and cocked the hammer.

"Put that rifle down, Raffe," says Randolph, and he's got his pistol pointed at Bob's heart. Bob let the hammer down easy and laid his gun on the ground.

"Drummond," says Randolph, "get your knife, then sit down and act like a human being."

"I don't take no orders from no one!" yells Jesse.

Randolph put a shot past his ear and Jesse hunted around for the knife then sat down quiet. Says Randolph:

"Now listen to me all of you. We are five men in a wilderness. Only our own good sense will bring us through to California, and I've seen nothing that looks like good sense tonight. It's my aim to get where I'm going in one piece, and that means traveling with others for protection against redskins so I'm stuck with you. But mark my words, gentlemen, if any man upsets the delicate balance of our happy band and jeopardizes our chances of survival I will be angry, and I will kill that man without hesitation."

"Lessen he kills you first," grumbles Jesse.

"That's right, he who shoots first also shoots last. I sleep with one eye open, Drummond, so don't try it. And leave the nigger alone, he's done you no harm."

"Maybe," says Jesse.

"No maybe—you *do* it."

I reckon if Randolph warn't a gambler he would of been a sea captain or in the army. When he talked like that you never had no doubt he means it, and Jesse and Bob settled down to smoke their pipes and Jim and me done the same. Randolph joined in with a cigar and we sent up enough smoke to get seen miles around if it was daylight, then we rolled in our blankets and slept.

I got woke by a kind of grunting, and it's Jim getting attacked by Jesse. They was thrashing around in the dust with Jim underneath and he's got his fingers around Jesse's wrist to stop the knife coming down into his heart. I kicked my blanket away and picked up a rock and smashed it against Jesse's head and he sagged limp and Jim pushed him away. The others was awake now and I grabbed my Hawken and aimed at Bob.

"Don't you move," says I. "Jim, get our horses ready."

"What's your plan, boy?" asks Randolph.

"We're leaving you three before someone gets killed. That Jesse's a lunatic and there ain't no reasoning with him, so Jim and me are going to make our own way from now on."

"We ain't stopping you," says Bob. "The sooner you get the better, but if you went and killed Jesse I'm comin' after you."

"He ain't dead, but I wish he was and I ain't ashamed to say it."

Jesse give a groan and I yelled at him to get over with the others. When he seen my rifle he done it, but on hands and knees. His hair's all bloody and he puked a couple times on the way, but I never felt sorry for him. I would of been more sympathetical to a sick dog than Jesse. It took Jim awhile to get things fixed up working in the dark and the Hawken got mighty weighty in my hands, but I never let the barrel drop. Finally Jim says the horses is ready. He led Jupiter over to me and I mounted up while Jim held the rifle, then I took it back while he got mounted and led our pack horses off into the dark. When he was a fair distance off I turned Jupiter and dug in my heels and went after him.

A mile or two away we stopped and listened but never heard nobody coming after us so I reckon we're rid of them, which is reliefsome. We kept on at a walk and a few mile further on stopped again.

"Jim," says I, "we got to plan out how not to run into that bunch again. I can't take no more muleheadedness from idiots that won't even try to be friendly. We got problems enough without idiots on top of everything else."

"How we goin' to do it, Huck? Dey be follerin' on direc'ly come mornin'."

"Then we'll just hide ourselfs someplace till they go by, and so long as we don't travel too fast they'll get way ahead and we won't ever meet up with them no more. See them rocks? If we camp in among them till daybreak we'll be able to spy the others go past without them catching a look at us."

And that's what we done. We never lit no fire, just hobbled the horses and bedded down for the few hours left till dawn. When the sun come up we kept a watch lying flat on top of a boulder, and sure enough here comes Randolph and Bob and Jesse. They never once looked over at where we are and rode on by, but just when I figured the plan worked dandy we seen a bunch of Injuns on horseback come down from a rocky ridge a half mile or so off and head for Randolph and the rest, maybe a dozen in all.

They rode up slow and stopped real close to the three, which are stopped too. It looks like they're having some kind of powwow, then all of a sudden there's gunfire and three Injuns fell to the ground and the rest galloped off. When the Injuns was out of sight Randolph and them whipped up their horses and hared off in a cloud of dust, and when it settled they was out of eye-reach. The empty Injun horses has run off too, most likely headed for home behind the rest. Says I:

"Jim, I reckon we'll stay put here awhile in case them Injuns has gone to fetch their big brothers to ride after Randolph and them. I got no intention to get mixed up in it. I just bet it was Jesse that fired first."

Jim allowed it's the safest thing so we waited hid in the rocks for hours with one or other of us keeping watch. The Injuns never showed, so if they was aiming to ambush Randolph they must be fixing to do it further down the trail. But the time we spent hid warn't wasted, because around noon Jim give a hiss to get my notice and points across the sage. I slid up alongside of him and looked where he's pointing and my heart give a little jump. It's Bulldog, and he's got an Injun with him bending low in the saddle to read signs on the ground.

"How he know we took de shortcut?" whispers Jim.

"The Injun. Thaddeus told me they can practickly track a bird through the air. He must of seen where we branched off the wagon route and followed along."

"If'n he be dat good he goin' to see where we turned off an' hid over here, Huck."

"I know it. Dang that bulldog. Why'd he have to get smart and hire a tracker?"

Barrett and the Injun was moving along slow and I fretted plenty when they come to the spot where me and Jim changed course for the rocks, and sure enough, the Injun points at the ground and says something to the bulldog. We was close enough to get the noise but not the words.

"Dey be headin' dis way anytime now, Huck. You goin' to shoot him?"

"Shoot him? Why, that'd make me worse'n Jesse, specially if I done it from behind cover. No, I reckon we'll have to run for it."

The Injun was riding in tight circles now and pointing at stuff on the ground. Says I:

"Stay here and keep watch, Jim. I'll get the horses ready."

I crawled away on my belly and tightened up all the saddle girths and took off the hobbles, then Jim signaled me and I slithered back over. The Injun is still riding in circles, but it never should of took him all this time to see where we turned off. The answer come to me.

"Jim, it's the same spot where Randolph and them killed the Injuns! It's the bodies they're looking at, not our tracks."

"He still lookin' mighty close at de groun'. If'n he got eagle eyes like you say den he goin' to find 'em for sure, Huck."

The Injun and Bulldog was talking now, maybe trying to put the story of the massacre together. The Injun pointed up at the ridge where the Injuns come from, then straight at our rocks.

"He's suspicioned it, Jim. . . ."

"Maybe not. Dey's argumentin' 'bout somethin'."

The Injun kept pointing over at us, but Bulldog was pointing the way Randolph and the others went. Their voices got louder but we still never heard them clear, then the Injun reached into his pocket and pulled out something small. First off I figured it's a pistol, but he put it to his mouth and I seen it's a bottle. Bulldog talked even louder and slapped the bottle out of the Injun's hand. It smashed on the ground and the Injun started talking real loud too, and Bulldog give as good as he got.

"That's why he don't believe the Injun about us being over here, Jim. He's a whiskey Injun."

For a little while longer it looked like the bulldog is going to get his way, then the Injun turned his horse and come directly for us. I reckon his pride must of been hurt and he aims to prove he's right, drunk or not. The bulldog give one last cuss and come along behind. Says I:

"Our luck just run out, Jim."

I started to slide away but Jim grabbed my arm.

"Wait on, Huck. . . . De Injuns is back!"

I looked and he's right. They come pouring over the ridge, maybe twenty this time, and when they seen Barrett and the tracker they let out a whoop and come thundering over. The tracker wheeled his horse and made a run for it but some of the Injuns split off and chased him and I seen him fall with two arrows in his back. He died without ever finding out if he's right, but at least he died drunk. The bulldog never tried the same thing, just sat on his horse and got surrounded. Maybe he figures he only has to tell them he's Chauncey Thermopylae Barrett and they'll all fall down and lick his boots, but what they done is knock him off his horse and ride around him in circles, laughing at him. The ones that split off come back with the tracker's scalp and tossed it around and waved it in front of Bulldog's face to get him scared, then they all had a powwow with a lot of pointing along Randolph's trail and in the end must of decided that the ones that done the killing was too well armed and too far away by now and they was content with a scalp and a prisoner that both come easy. They tied Bulldog to his saddle and done the same with their three dead brothers, then the whole bunch headed up and over the ridge and out of sight. Jim says:

"Ain't it funny de way it work out, Huck. If Jesse hadn'ter been so mean we would of been with 'em still an' had a heaper Injuns on our trail. Now we ain't even got de bulldog to worry on no mo'."

He's right, but I warn't happy. The bulldog hounded me halfway across the country and I disliked him for it, but he never killed no Injuns, and for me to ride off knowing he'll be staked out on an anthill or get his skin peeled off or something ain't the kind of thing that sits easy on a body's conscience. There's plenty that would judge me in the clear if I let the Injuns do to him what Injuns does, but that don't help none.

"Jim," says I, "we'll have to rescue him."

"You got de sun insider yo' head again, Huck? Das de bulldog dey done took outer yo' hair. He ain't no friender your'n."

"I know it, but we can't just let him get tortured and killed. It ain't right, Jim. Could you live with a thing like that hexing you night and day the rest of your life?"

"I reckon I could give it a try."

"Well, I can't. It ain't fair for Bulldog to get butchered for something he never done."

"You gone crazy for sure, Huck. I disbelieve what my ears is hearin'."

"Look at it this way, if we rescue him he'll be so danged grateful he won't chase after us no more."

"He ain't chasin' after you *now*. He goin' off to get hisself butchered."

"I can't let it happen, Jim, not even to the bulldog."

We argued on it awhile before Jim give in, then we got mounted up and followed the Injuns' trail over the ridge. Two different bunches of them come and went this way four times in all, so even if we never had eagle eyes it warn't hard to follow the trail all them ponies left behind. They was way ahead of us, just a dust cloud miles away now, and we trailed them at a steady lick till late afternoon when we seen smoke from their campfires, then we hid among rocks in case they got lookouts posted and waited for dark. Jim was sulking and never talked to me, but it give me the time to ponder what it is I'm aiming to do.

Ever since we started west little pieces has got whittled off the inside part of me that makes me Huck Finn, all the killing and death I seen carving off another piece till I don't hardly reckernize my old self no more. I could feel it getting smaller and smaller inside me, that part I can't describe. It's the part you take for granted, the good part I reckon, and I used to wonder how come men like Pap and Morg and Rufus and Eben and Bob and Jesse don't have none of it, and now I know it's on account of having it whittled away by the things they done that they shouldn't of and the things they never done that they should of. There ain't no escaping it. If you disbelieve in judgment from above then you got to make up your own mind on what things is good and what's bad. Leaving the bulldog to die is bad, even if I don't like him. I never wanted to feel another piece whittled off me. Maybe there's just so much of it inside you and no more, so you got to be careful how much you let slip away. If you pull out a hair it'll grow right back, but just try the same thing with a tooth, or chop off your hand and see what happens. So I ain't doing it for the bulldog so much as for my own self, and if it ain't possible to rescue him at least I'll know I give it a try. I ain't preaching, it's just how I feel.

We waited till after sundown. I made Jim stay with the horses and

left my Hawken there too. I never wanted to kill no one, just get
Bulldog free. When it was truly dark I legged it for where we seen
the smoke, maybe a half mile away. I hunted around awhile before I
found the camp on account of it's hid down in a little ravine, and it
warn't much to look at neither, just scrappy-looking huts made from
skins laid across bent-over poles, not so big as the tepees the plains
Injuns uses. There was maybe twenty scattered along the ravine
and when I snuck down to them a dog come at me barking, but I
planned for that and throwed him some jerked meat which he et
quiet-like. I tippy-toed through the village, listening close at every
hut for the sound of sobbing or praying, but all I got was snores. The
dog come along with me whining for more, so I give him the last of
it to keep him hushed and hoped there ain't no other mutts around,
but it looks like it's just a one-dog village.

Then I seen the bulldog. He's tied to a pole frame that's got scalps
dangling off it and he's stood up but spreadeagled, tied by his wrists
and ankles, and his head is drooped forward. There warn't no one on
guard so I slid up to him and whisper:

"Bulldog. . . . Are you alive?"

His head jerked up and I put a hand over his mouth to stop him
yelling. There's blood on his face but far as I can tell he ain't been
tortured and was still dressed except for his hat.

"It's me, Bulldog. . . . Huck Finn."

"Phinnph? . . ." he says.

"Just hold still while I get you untied and don't make no noise."

I went to work on the knots, but untying them was a problem in
the dark.

"Stop wasting time," he hisses. "Cut them!"

"That ain't the way I got it planned, now hush up."

It took awhile but I finally got him loose, then I say:

"Take off all your clothes."

"What?"

"Take off everything, every last stitch."

"What for, you fool?"

"Listen, Bulldog, it's the only way to stop them coming after us. If
they figure you just got free they'll chase after you and likely get us
all, but if they figure you got away by magic they'll be too scared to. I

lived with Injuns so I know. Get them clothes off, we ain't got time to argue."

He done it reluctant, but he done it, and after he took out his wallet to keep I fixed up his clothes and boots in a loose pile and retied all the ropes with open loops where his wrists and ankles was, then pulled the eagle feather out of my hair and stuck it inside his crumpled jacket.

"What are you doing, Finn?" he hisses.

"Making it look like you turned yourself into an eagle and flew off. They'll talk about it for the next fifty years I reckon."

"Ingenious," he says. "You have cloaked the commonplace in the trappings of mystery."

"This way," says I, and we snuck back through the village with the dog keeping us company till we was a fair ways beyond. The bulldog give out a cuss whenever he set his feet down on sharp rocks or thorns and it was a slow haul back to Jim and the horses. Bulldog wanted me to tell him how come I knowed the Injuns had him, but I just cloaked it all in the trappings of mystery and told him not to make so much noise. Jim was waiting for us and all set for the getaway. He's put all the water we got left into two barrels and dumped the other two so Barrett has got a horse. We mounted up and walked the horses away so's not to make noise by galloping, not till we was miles off.

It must of been the easiest escape in history. Tom Sawyer would of been disgusted and called it a cheat on account of I never let the Injuns know ahead of time I planned on getting the bulldog free and never done it around noon so they can see it happen. He would of left a note to tell which way we're headed too, just to put ginger in the whole adventure, and I'm mighty glad he ain't here to snag up things with his cleverness.

When we got far enough away I say:

"Bulldog, get off that horse if you don't mind."

"Why?" he says.

"Just do it, please."

"You're going to kill me, aren't you."

"I could of let the Injuns do that."

He got down and stood there all white and naked in the moon-light. Says I:

"Bulldog, you been after me some considerable time now, and

seeing as I never done the murder I'm getting mighty irritated by the way you keep hounding me. What I done tonight is save your pesky life, so I reckon you owe me a favor and I aim to claim it right now. You got to quit keeping after me this way. You got to go back to Missouri and tell them you never found me, or found me and killed me or anything you want, but don't let me catch you on my trail again. I want a new life without no clouds hanging over it, which means you."

"Finn," he says, "I'm obliged to you for your timely and audacious rescue, and when we reach Missouri you may rest assured I will tell the story in court as proof that you are not entirely an animal. Your sentence will no doubt be reduced from hanging to life imprisonment as a direct result of my testimony, you have my word."

There's gratitude for you. He's just the most muleheaded person I ever come across, acting like he owns the world even when he's stark naked in the desert with no horse and no gun.

"See here, Bulldog, if you don't promise to quit chasing me I'll have to put a ball into you," says I, lying.

"I am prepared for death," he says, "but not for defeat. I have never failed to catch my man and will not do so in the case of a mere boy. I may die in this forsaken place, but my reputation will remain unsullied by failure."

He's a lunatic, definite, and there ain't no point in arguing on it.

"Barrett, see that bluff over yonder that comes to a twin peak? We'll leave a horse there for you. I reckon it'll take you all night to reach, and that'll give me and Jim a chance to put distance between us and you. If you got any kind of sense you'll head back east, because if I see you ever again I'll kill you for sure," says I, lying still.

"I accept your terms, Finn. Wherever you go, always look over your shoulder for me."

"Jim," says I, "have you still got the dress Mrs. Beckwith give you?"

He pulled it out of his saddlebag along with the bonnet and I flung them to the bulldog.

"That's to keep the sun from burning you. We ain't got no spare boots so you'll just have to get along without none."

"You won't deter me with humiliation, Finn. I am made from stronger stuff than that."

"Suit yourself, Bulldog. We'll leave the horse where you can find it easy."

And we rode off. I figured he'd be more inclined to put the dress on once we was out of sight. Desert nights is surprising chilly. Later on we tethered the horse under the twin peaks then set off north and west to hit the Humboldt River and get back on the California Trail.

24

Samaritans—Two for the Price of One—Hard Times—

Snakemeat and Swampwater—Hardest Time of All

We got lost. Lydia's map told where all the mountains and deserts and such is, but it never told where *we* was. We never had no compass and wandered off course a couple or three times, once deliberate when we seen a bunch of Injuns way off in the distance from high ground, and it was four days till we come to the Humboldt and seen wagon ruts running alongside the river. The Humboldt don't have the sweetest water I ever tasted, but our barrels was empty so we're obliged to drink it.

A few days along the trail we come across a four-horse team and a wagon that's leaned over with a busted wheel, and when we rode up a man in a suit of clothes that seen better days rushes out and says:

"Welcome, friends, welcome! I have glad tidings for you. The person you seek is but two days ahead of this place where we presently stand."

"Who might that be?" I ask, wondering if he's another lunatic, which I had considerable acquaintance with by now.

"The lady . . . or gentleman did not say, but he . . . she gave an exact word portrait of you both and seemed anxious to meet up with you again."

"Was it a lady on a brown and white horse with a beard?"

"The lady was bearded, the horse was not."

So the bulldog was still after us. Well, it come as no surprise, and now everyone we never wanted to bump into is ahead of us, and I reckon it's better that way than behind. Says I:

"That's my Uncle Silas. He ain't peculiar or nothing, it's just that our family has got a custom that says all the men has got to wear a costume all the time on account of the family home in St. Louis got burned down in the middle of a costume ball and we never saved

nothing but for the clothes on our backs, and we all of us made a
vow we'd always wear some kind of costume till the time we get our
fortune back again. That's how come I'm dressed like an Injun. Me
and Uncle Silas is on our way to California to get rich so's we can
dress like normal folks again. We're good and tired of getting stared
at in the street."

"A fascinating story," he says. "My name is Obadiah Jennings."

"I'm Jeff Wilson and this here's Goliath."

Mr. Jennings ain't a young man no more, around forty-five
maybe, but with only half his hair. He says:

"Are you perchance familiar with the fixing of wheels in a state of
bustedness?"

I went over and give it a look. It's the spokes that broke and
they're hard to fix without you got all the right tools. Says I:

"The easiest thing is to get a whole wheel off a wagon that's been
left behind and fit it on."

"Alas, young Jeff, my hands are unsuited to such labors, being as
you see of artistical configuration."

And he waggled them at me so's I can see how long and skinny
his fingers is, and his wrists too. He says:

"When the unfortunate accident happenstanced I was pitched
from my seat into the dust of the trail and well nigh squashed by
oncoming teams, a terrifying moment which will loom large in the
corridors of memory-keeping. Only my fleetness of foot saved me.
Why, I hear you ask, did my fellow travelers not come to my aid in
the matter pertaining to wheel fixation? Because, young friend, I
was unloved by that ill-natured throng of gold lusters, a thorn in
their miserable sides accounted for by my sensitivity of nature and
ill-endowment with the brawny flesh to which all such aspire and
are measured against. They went by with not a backward glance to
the rear, content if not joyous to leave me stranded in these wilder-
nessy regions frequented by savage redskins. Was ever man more
cruel to man? And now here I wait for the arrival of one, or even
two, possessed of the samaritan mode of expression, that they might
offer assistance renderable without recompense, yours truly being
blighted by poverty as well as a busted wheel."

We got ourselfs in a peck of trouble helping the McSweens with
their wagon that time, but they say lightning don't strike the same
thing two times so me and Jim rode back a few mile to where we

seen an empty wagon and pulled a wheel off it and brung it back. We jacked up the wagon end with rocks and fitted the new wheel and Obadiah done a little dance for joy. He smelled of whiskey and I reckon he had a jolt while we was away.

"Thank you, thank you." He smiles, showing off his yeller teeth. "I am much in your debt and appreciable of the time you have spent in this worthy cause. I presume you will not be wending your way west to waylay Uncle Silas."

I warn't about to go wending nowhere near him. Says I:

"Me and Uncle Silas ain't on good terms right now, so I reckon we'll travel along with you if you ain't indisposed to the idea."

"Indeed not, young Jeff. Two days spent in the company of my own self have taught me the burden of lonesomeness, and there is none greater."

So we unloaded our barrels and supplies into the wagon and hitched the pack horse behind and rode alongside. Obadiah was starved for talk and rattled on all afternoon, most of it the kind of conversation you take in through one ear and let out of the other without troubling your brain in between. He drunk considerable too, reaching behind him now and then for a bottle and gargling on it, but it never made him talk cockeyed or nothing so I reckon he's used to it. When he drained that bottle dry he flung it aside and struck up a friendship with another, so he's got a regular supply of drinking partners stashed away in the wagon. Whiskey never brung out meanness in him like it done with Pap. Friendly and cheerful is what whiskey makes Obadiah, only by sundown I kind of wished he's a mite more quiet and moody like the general kind of drunk that's poured that much inside of him; my ears was wore out with all that talk, talk, talk.

We made camp and built a fire and et, and afterwards Obadiah offered me and Jim a drink, the first white man that ever done that to Jim except me, and we both drunk deep. Obadiah says:

"My profession back in Springfield, Illinois, was the most fraughtsome and difficult upon the face of the earth, namely and to be specific, intermediary between this world and the next. I consigned the sad deceased that are dead and gone from carefree day to endless night, there hopefully to find rest eternal and not pay rent nor suffer the indignities that are heaped upon us one and all in this life we struggle through."

"You was a preacher?"

"No indeed, an undertaker."

"I never met one before," says I.

"We are a lonely breed, young Jeff, and must endure the separateness that is our daily lot. No man, given the preferment, will take an undertaker as his bosom friend, yet when there is death in the family to whom does he rush with flying feet? Why, to me, and upon my shoulders falls the burdensome and thankless task of laying out the dear departed and wiring up jaws left agape in dastardly death. The undertaker plows a distant furrow and carves a lonely turkey unless he takes unto himself a wife of female characteristic for solace and to keep him from abuse of his mortal coil, but alas, it was my misfortune never to meet such an angel of mercy."

Me and Jim listened awhile longer to stories about what happens to dead folks before they get shoveled under, real hair-raising stuff, then Obadiah says:

"I feel tired . . ."

And he keeled over on his back directly. Lucky he was sitting down or he could of done himself serious hurt. Says I:

"Do you reckon he's sick, Jim?"

"Naw, jest drunk is all, lessen his jaw tuckered de rester him out."

We put him in the wagon and left him snoring and done some of the same.

Obadiah warn't inclined to wake up next morning so we hitched the team and drove along with him still snoring in the back, and we went along like that all day till it's time to make camp again. He opened his eyes then and come out of the wagon and says:

"Who are you?"

"Jeff Wilson and Goliath, Mr. Jennings. Don't you recollect us from yesterday?"

"Yesterday?" he says. "Ah yes, but surely that was today."

"It was yesterday, honest. You had yourself a heap of sleep."

"Nonsense," he says, snappish, and never spoke another word till after we et. Says I:

"You must of been starved for food I reckon, Obadiah."

"My name is Frank," he says.

"But you told us you was called Obadiah."

"No, no, you mistake me for my brother of that name, a name

seldom if ever mentioned within the family circle. Into every generation is born a black sheep, and Obadiah has long been the bane of my existence, a sour and withered fruit upon the family tree. Pray do not mention him to me again, as his name causes indigestion."

Jim give me a look and scratched his head to show we got to be careful with a lunatic around, and I say:

"Well why don't you tell us about yourself instead, Frank?"

And he did. He says he's an inventor that ain't been give the reckernition he deserves on account of his plans was all stole by Obadiah and burned in a fire out of jealousy of his smartness. He reckons his greatest invention is something he calls the Earth Trumpet or Soul Detector, and he drawed a picture of it in the dust, like one of them horns deaf folk stick in their ears for you to holler into. Says I:

"How does it work?"

"The operation of the device is so simple a child of three, or even yourself could use it, but first the theory. When the dead are buried what becomes of their souls?"

"I don't rightly know. Most folks reckon they go up to heaven, but I disbelieve it myself."

"Rightly so. The soul remains with the body below ground, and the earth trumpet is designed to receive such ghostly messages as the deceased wish to pass on to us, the living. You simply invert the trumpet, resting the broad end on the ground, and apply the ear to the small end."

"Then what?"

"You wait for the messages. The dead are bored, you see, and will talk for hours, grateful for a listening ear. I have had many a stimulating conversation with corpses, and also many a dull one. The soul retains the intelligence it possessed when the physical body lived, therefore a dead farmer will wish to discuss crop prices and the weather, an army officer will talk of military strategy and an enlisted man will complain of bad food and blistered feet. A professor, of course, will lecture endlessly on his particular field of learning, which is stimulating in the extreme. The sad fact is, a dullard remains so even after death, while the superior brain such as my own continues to function on the higher plane of learning."

So you can see just how mad he is. He never spoke another word after that, just went to the wagon and come back with a book that ain't got no words in it and covered the pages with pencil drawings by the light of the fire, inventions proberly, but I never liked to ask. It's a puzzlement which one is the real person, Obadiah or Frank. If I had the choosing of it I reckon I'd pick Obadiah for company seeing as he talks friendly, even if too much.

It turned out we got both. The next two days and nights he stayed Frank and never touched a drop of whiskey nor spoke to us except to give orders about hitching the team and building fires and fixing food and such, but then he started drinking again and for three days was Obadiah till he passed out from it same as before, and when he woke up he's Frank again, which give our ears a rest. A couple or three days on he got thirsty and drunk himself into Obadiah's boots again, and this time when he quit talking for two seconds to catch his breath I ask him about Frank.

"Frank?" he says, and looks around. "Is Frank here? That would be unfortunate indeed. . . . We do not love each other as brothers should. . . ."

And he jumps off the wagon and looks underneath for him, all twitching and trembling till I set his mind to rest.

"No, he ain't here. You just talked about him in your sleep is all."

"Thank the Lord," he says, and wipes his brow on his sleeve. "Frank cannot abide the sight of me, nor indeed the sound, in fact he has sworn to kill me if I so much as cross his shadow."

"Well he ain't hereabouts so his shadow ain't neither. I reckon it must of been a nightmare that made you shout his name like you done."

"Haply so, young Jeff," he says, climbing back aboard, and we went on.

We was following the trail along the Humboldt River, which has got mountains all around and runs through hard country with only sand and sagebrush and some willows here and there along the banks with maybe a little grass alongside for the horses. The water got lower in the riverbed day by day and tasted worse every mile. It run east to west then bended down in a loop till it's headed southwest, losing heart as it goes.

All along the way we seen stuff throwed out of wagons. Back in the mountains it was steepness made them do it, but here it's because the teams was dying from not enough food or good water. There was dead animals every step of the way practickly, horses and oxen both, with buzzards ripping them open, and more wagons left too where the whole team has died off. It warn't just the grass and water that's problemating things, it's Injuns too. We seen more and more carcasses with arrows in them. I could understand Injuns killing cattle for food and running off horses to use for riding, but them animals was killed for mischief I reckon, or because the Injuns ain't pleased to see so many whites traipsing across their territory. Anyway, it's a shameful waste for all that good meat to be rotting away under the sun with flies crawling over every inch that ain't got a buzzard claw dug into it, and the stink in the air matched up with the taste of the river perfect.

Jim and me figured it ain't going to be long before we come in for our share of Injun trouble. We come nearly two hundred mile along the Humboldt without none so far, which is just a miracle when we seen the way other forty-niners has been bothered, and miracles is one thing I ain't inclined to set much store by no more, not full time anyway. So we stood guard of a night in turns, only Frank reckoned it's work that ain't suited to big brains like he's got and never done a lick of it. He just sat by the fire every night drawing inventions in his book, and when Obadiah was around he warn't sober enough to be no good as a guard so it's just Jim and me. It made us weary in the day for lack of sleep and we took it in turns to catnap in the wagon while she rolled.

It never done no good. One morning after I've been on watch there's two of the horses gone. It happened without me hearing a single sound. Frank give me a good cussing then went off to draw up plans for a new kind of cannon to scare the Injuns off, not the helpfullest way to fix the problem. We put Jim's horse and the pack horse into harness and kept going, and two nights later it happened again. They never got Jupiter, but another two team horses went. This time it's Obadiah that got the news, and he took it calm and says with only three horses left there ain't nothing for it but to leave the wagon behind, so we done it.

Obadiah loaded his saddlebags with all the whiskey he's got left, just a few bottles now, and I done some figuring. Without the wagon we'll travel faster and maybe catch up with them that's ahead. The bulldog proberly told hundreds of people by now to watch out for an Injun boy that's Huck Finn in disguise, so I took off my Injun clothes and had Jim chop my hair short with his knife. He done a terrible job and my head felt like a field that's got mowed close with only stubble left behind, but when I put on the clothes Hester Weber give me I looked white again. So it's a worthwhile sacrifice, as they say, but I reckon I ain't ever going to be so comfortable as I was in them buckskins.

We rode off feeling freer now we're traveling light, but trouble come the very next day when Frank found out Obadiah never brung his invention book along and we had to tie him up to keep him from going back for it. He ranted considerable but was too weak to give us any real fight over it. All that drinking Obadiah done was making both of them thin and fidgety and feeble, and we wondered if maybe we should throw the bottles that's left away before the whiskey does a double murder, but then we seen that without no whiskey Obadiah won't come around no more and we'd be stuck with just Frank, which ain't our idea of good company so we let the bottles stay.

We made twenty mile and more on horseback that day, but when I woke up next morning I seen Frank has gone, and it never took much figuring to work out where. We saddled up quick and rode after him and catched up maybe five mile back along the trail. We tied him up again but lost time because of what he done, so when night come we got him drunk and next morning Obadiah was back. He stayed with us two days till the whiskey run out, then Frank come storming along and cussed us for the way we stopped him fetching his book, but it's too far back now even for him. He reckons we're teamed up with Obadiah to make him miserable, and says if he catches sight of him he'll kill him, so it's lucky we got no mirrors along with us. Just to keep Frank happy I looked in every wagon we passed that's been left by the trail till I found one with a beat-up old diary in it with only half the paper used and give it to him. He tore out all the used part and was happier now he can scribble and draw again, and even told us about his newest invention which is a boat for rowing under the water, so it's clear he ain't getting no better in the head.

All of us got sick. The river turned a kind of yeller green from alkali in it and warn't fit to drink. We seen cattle dead on the bank from having tried it, so we found a cook pot that got throwed away and boiled the water before we give it a try. It never killed us but give us the squirts, so even if we had of et three times a day we would of lost it all by nightfall. Our supplies was down to a peck of flour and that's all. The horses got thin from no grass and never touched the brush hereabouts; proberly they knowed with horse sense it would of poisoned them. Our eyes got hollow and our cheekbones stood out some and it was tiresome just keeping sat in the saddle and not falling off from weakness. Sores come up on our bodies and faces, and teeth come loose in our heads. One of my front ones come right out when I give it a little tug, but it never hurt all that much and there warn't hardly no blood at all. Sometimes I got dizzy spells, and Jim got them too. Frank was worse off than us on account of he needed whiskey, or Obadiah needed it, and now there ain't none left he got crazy and raved and fell off his horse ten times a day. I seen it all before when Pap had to give up drinking one time when he never even had a cent to buy a drop with. It ain't a pretty sight and cost us more time and strength wasted getting him back in the saddle, but we never could of just left him there to go crazy all the way and die.

Then one day we seen something we never would of believed if it hadn't of been right there in front of us. The river quit moving at all and just turned into a swamp right there in the middle of the desert, with nothing but rushes and the disgustingest stink you ever smelled, mile after mile of it. Frank give up and fell off his horse again and we figured here's as good a spot as any to rest up awhile and see if we can't find a taste of food. Water rats is what I reckoned on catching in a swamp, and I waded in knee deep among the rushes to look for them, but they was keeping out of sight. All I seen was moskeeters and one time a snake, but he lit out fast for cover before I could shoot him. You got to be mighty hungry to want to eat snake, and that's what we was. Jim rigged up a little shelter made of rushes to keep the sun off Frank, who's raving in his sleep now, sometimes talking cockeyed like Obadiah and sometimes straight and nasty like Frank, all of it jumbled together and making no kind of sense. I went back in the swamp to try again, and this time come across a dead man all rotted away. I come out fast and when I took off my britches to dry my legs was covered in leeches, thirty or more. It made me want to puke and I even started blubbering I'm so disgusted. Jim whipped up a fire and burned them off with a hot stick, but they left holes in my legs that dribbled blood.

We was never in such bad trouble before, and I wondered to myself if maybe we're going to die. Then I got mad at myself for blubbering over them leeches and put my britches on and went into the swamp again, and I warn't aiming to come out till I had something for us to chew on. I waded and waded with my Hawken at the ready but never seen nothing except stinking water and mud and rushes, and got half bit to death by moskeeters. I never felt the leeches but knowed they was there, burrowing into my legs and sucking the blood out. Then I seen another snake and blowed his head off and headed back, only I got lost and slopped along another hour, going in circles I reckon. Finally I seen the smoke from Jim's fire and headed for it. He burned the leeches off me again then boiled up some swamp water to wash my legs down, but it never done much good. I felt sick as can be and crawled under the shelter with Frank to rest up while Jim skinned the snake and cooked it. I tasted worse things.

Toward sundown we drug ourselfs away from the swamp on account of the moskeeters and scooped holes like shallow graves in the sand. Then we wrapped up in our blankets and piled sand over us to keep out the nighttime cold. Frank was babbling again and thrashing around and we had to tie him before we covered him over. I slept on and off till dawn with bad dreams in my head, then Jim started another fire and we et the rest of the snake. Frank was considerable better than yesterday, which means he ain't exactly dead or raving.

We went back to the swamp and boiled up water to fill our canteens and boiled up more and let it cool for the horses, then done another couple for them till they drunk their fill. Then we mounted up. My legs was sore from being covered in scabs, but it's easier to ride than walk. The end of the swamp come in sight after noon with a flat desert after it stretching way off yonder. We made camp in the middle of noplace that night and never even had the comfort of a fire; there just ain't enough brush around to build one, same as on the salt desert. We drunk only a morsel of water each and the horses got none, then we done the same trick with the blankets and sand and in the morning went on. The ground got more sprinkled with sagebrush gradual and there's other runty little bushes too, but the end of it warn't in sight. It stretched and stretched away south and west with mountains all around, and the wagon ruts headed out into the middle so we followed on.

It was the worst part yet, worser even than the salt desert. At least there we had them water barrels; here we got just a few mouthfuls each. There warn't nothing to do but keep going and hope there's a spring up ahead somewheres. The sun come down on our backs and heads like a heavy weight it's so hot, enough to give a body dizzy spells. We seen plenty of wagons and dead teams only they never had no arrows in them now, just plain died of thirst I reckon, and there's dead people too, not even buried decent. Jim took a hat off a dead man and says I got to wear it or get my brain cooked, so I done it and the shade give me relief, but not near enough. I drunk the last of my water and was ashamed because Jim had the will not to do the same. Frank drunk all his too. We kept on and on till Jim's horse kind of crumpled under him. Jim warn't hurt but the horse never wanted to get up again, so I shot it and we carved off hunks of meat to cook later on. Jim and me took turns on Jupiter all that afternoon, and when night come we et horseflesh for the first time ever. It warn't too bad, better than snake, and we got back a little strength from it and slept easier.

When the dawn come we still never seen no end to the desert, just the trail stretching ahead with more wagons left by the side and buzzards with their heads stuck inside the teams. I counted twenty-seven wagons in the morning for something to do while we dragged along, then lost count and was too tired to start again. Jim was counting dead men and he made it sixteen and one woman, but there could of been more off in the brush that he never seen. Around noon Jim shared out the last of his water, just a couple spoonfuls each, then it's all gone. In the afternoon Frank's horse sunk down and never got up again so we killed it and cut off more meat to keep us fed, then Frank rode Jupiter with Jim and me hang-ing on to the stirrups to keep from falling over with tiredness.

All that day I never had a single thought in my head. Most times if you ain't doing nothing in particular you get a headful of pictures and recollections without hardly trying, but that day I never thought nothing. Every time I seen a little picture start to happen I shut it off because I never had the strength to make the next little picture that would of come along after it, nor the one after that the way it always happens. I never wanted to think. I never wanted nothing but water. The hot air going up my nose give me a headache and every step took made my brain jolt. I never had the strength to complain, just give silent groans inside of me, and when evening come I sunk down like a dying horse right beside Jupiter.

Jim covered me with a blanket and lifted Frank down and done the same for him, then got a fire started and cooked up horseflesh. The smell made me hungry, but just you try eating meat without no water to wash it down. It ain't easy. Our tongues was swole up inside our mouths like leather, so big and dry we couldn't hardly talk around them, but we never felt like talking anyhow and pretty soon was drowsy. Jim says we should keep going by night when it's cool and I agreed, but fell asleep halfway through saying it so we stayed there.

In the morning I tried to get up but never budged an inch I'm so weak and feeble. I kind of screamed at myself inside my head and finally come to life, and when I got on my feet I seen Jim has already saddled Jupiter and was putting Frank on him and tying him to the saddle so's he won't fall off. We started moving, then Jim says I left my Hawken behind. I never cared, but Jim went back and got it and carried it the rest of the day. I had my hand wedged tight inside Jupiter's girth strap so I never had to grip with my fingers, which I never could of done, and my legs stumped along like a doll Becky Thatcher showed me once with legs that moved from the hip, left, right, left, right, mile after mile till a picture snuck into my head of me being nothing but a big doll marching along all stiff-legged and pretending to be a human person. It's so funny I got to giggling and warn't able to quit, only it ain't normal sounding, more like a croak. Jim asks if I'm all right and that struck me even funnier so I croaked and croaked till I would of cried if there was any water in me. Then it hurt to laugh and I quit. It hurt my throat and my head, even my legs. Everything hurt. I seen my hand stuck in the girth strap and the skin is wore off it and bleeding some but I never even knowed, and I kind of cranked my head around to face frontwards again to keep from being sick. Frank was slumped with his face in Jupiter's mane, and Jupiter warn't looking too spry himself with his head drooped and his hoofs plodding heavy and slow, not picking them up spirited like he generally does, but he ain't had no water in two days now and has got to carry a rider too. There ain't a handful of horses in the world could of done it I reckon.

On and on we went with the sun beating down hard and the buzzards flapping on top of carcasses, watching us go by then back to supper. Forty-nine was a good year for buzzards. There warn't no clouds up above, the sky just as blue as blue, turning yeller white where the sun is, too bright to look. Then there's a pain in my knees and my hand and I'm kneeling next to Jupiter with my fingers still stuck behind the girth. He must of stopped so he don't drag me along the ground, or maybe he never had the strength left to drag me. Jim come around and set me on my feet again and tries to say something only his tongue is swole up so bad now he can't make a sound. I give him a nod to say I ain't hurt and we staggered on.

There's ringing inside my head and I wonder how long it's been there, maybe hours, but I never took no heed till now. The desert kept leaning sideways and back again and the dead people got up and waved at me but never spoke. There's the Widow Douglas with a little raggy handkerchief waving, and over there is Tom Sawyer and Becky with the judge stood behind them, all smiling, and sneaking behind a wagon is Pap, who don't want me to catch sight of him. Then I seen Thaddeus and he give me a nod casual-like, and after him come two people arm in arm with the sun so bright I can't see who, then they waved and it's Andrew and Lydia. I waved back, only my arm never moved. Then all of them laid down and was dead again and I wished I was too, dead and buried under cold dirt where the sun can't reach and the water trickles down cool when it rains and Frank can come along with his trumpet and listen to me tell how I ain't guilty, only it ain't Frank that's listening, it's the bulldog, and he shakes his head like he don't believe me no matter how I holler and plead, and he drags me to the witness stand and tells all the dead people in the jury box he's got the proof that says I done it. I looked at the judge and it's Judge Thatcher, but he shook his head sorrowful and says he can't give no evidence for me seeing as he's dead, so they took me to the gallows and when the rope got put around my neck I turned and seen the hangman is Pap. He's looking mighty guilty but he goes to the trip lever and pulls it anyway and down I fell off the mainmast of the *Injun Princess* onto the deck, only I ain't hurt and the crew give me a cheer when I picked myself up. The sea wind is cool and the sails full and the deck going up and down with the waves, and Jim gives me a holler from the wheel and says to take over and keep her three points to starboard, which I done and sailed her across all the oceans of the world while the crew sung songs. We seen islands and reefs go by, dozens of them, then mermaids come up to join in the singing and it's all the seven virtues. Grace is the prettiest one same as usual and she give me a smile and a wave and Chastity blowed bubbles like a fish, then along come a big fat face with puffed-out cheeks and streaming hair like I seen on the map in the judge's office and blowed up a storm. We got lashed by the waves that come tumbling over the decks right up to the wheel and come near to drowning me, and Jim grabs me and says to drink. I try to tell him I ain't about to drink no salt water, then I swallered some and it's sweet, so I drunk some more and the waves died away to little ripples and Jim says in a croaky voice:

"Don' take in so much, Huck. You get mighty sick dat way. . . ."

And he's right. I puked up the water and rolled over. I'm on a riverbank down in the shallows with Jupiter's head right beside me guzzling up buckets of cool water and blowing little ripples through his nose. Jim untied Frank and laid him on the bank and fetched water in his hat to trickle in his mouth a little at a time, and I drug myself up onto the bank next to them and passed out.

25

Taking Things Slow—A Golden Fable—A Helping

Hand—No Longer Alone—Along the Carson—

A Tight Corner

We stayed there a week, just resting up and getting fat on fish catched in a trap Jim made from twigs and rushes, the kind with a wide neck that narrows down and the fish ain't got brains enough to back out. There was a fair number of trees and plenty of grass for Jupiter, and that stretch of water was like heaven must be after you come through the hot place, which is pretty much what we done. Lydia's map says it's the Carson River, and it come from the Sierra Nevada mountains over the other side of which is California. It was kind of like being back home, lazying the days away doing nothing but feed ourselfs from time to time and sleep in the shade peaceful, and I never give no time to thinking on the past and all the awful things I seen. Jim fixed up a little shelter from branches, but on the third day I done some walking and found a little dry cave a quarter mile east along the bank so we moved in there. We recollected the cave back on Jackson's Island when we was both escaping that time, only we got Frank with us now. He looked like he was fixing to die for awhile, then he come around and was soon feeding himself regular and scribbling in his book and not talking to us like we was used to.

One morning I'm sat on a rock with my bare feet in the water when along come Jim and he's looking fretsome.

"Huck," he says, "we got some figurin' to do."

"About what?" says I.

" 'Bout what we goin' to do nex'. We cain't jest sit aroun' here de rester our lifes."

"I warn't planning on it. We'll leave just as soon as we're fit to travel."

"What you aimin' to do wid Frank'n'Obadiah?"

"Take 'em along too, I reckon."

"We takin' on a heaper trouble totin' a crazy man, Huck."

"We ain't got no choice, Jim. Frank can't look after himself, nor Obadiah neither. I reckon we'll have to let the both of them string along with us till they ain't crazy no more. They ain't harmful to no one. Obadiah's preferable for company but he don't put in no appearances without whiskey to get him primed so we're likely stuck with Frank till we get to California. They got to have whiskey for sale there, and maybe a doctor that'll set him straight."

"Maybe so, but we ain't got de cash for no whiskey an' doctorin'. We ain't got two cents, Huck."

"There's still a piece or three of Lydia's jewels left."

"Dey ain't worth beans, Huck, you knows it. We got to buy us a pick an' shovel an' such if'n we plans on diggin' for gold."

"First things first, Jim. We ain't even in California yet."

"An' how we goin' to get dere wid jest one horse 'tween all?"

"We'll take turns riding. It ain't so far now to walk part of the way. How come you're so restless and fidgetsome, Jim?"

"I cain't figure it myself, Huck. I jest cain't come to rest on nothin' but I'se up again an' movin' like a bee wid sore feets."

"It's gold fever for sure. Maybe you can smell them nuggets from here."

"I cain't smell nothin', I jest wants to move on an' start diggin' dat yeller stuff outer de groun'."

"You've got it bad I reckon, but listen, Jim, don't you know that gold never made no one happy on its own?"

"How dat be, Huck? Wid a heaper gold in your han' you got to be jumpin' wid joy. It ain't natural not to."

"It ain't so, Jim, and history proves it. Did you ever hear of King Midas?"

"I reckon not."

"Well he's another of them ancient kings I read about, and he was rich as rich on account of everything he touched turned to gold."

"How come he kin do dat?"

"I disremember, but that's how things was. He touched his palace and it turned to gold, and he touched all the trees in the garden and they done the same, and he petted his tame monkey and it turned into a gold statue, and that's when he knowed he's got a problem."

"What kinder problem?"

"Well, he touched one of his wives and she turned into gold too, and he touched another and she done likewise. A gold wife looks mighty grand stood in the hall for visitors to gawp at but she ain't no good for nothing else in the way of wifely comforts, and King Midas went through the entire harem touching left and right to find a wife that never turned to gold so's he could get some comfort, but all he got was a harem full of gold statues. Then he went to lunch, but soon as he put his hand on a chicken leg or piece of pie it turned straightaway to gold, so he can't even get fed, which is worse yet than not getting comfort from his wives, and he got mad and hit one of the servants and then another, and pretty soon the king was all alone in his gold palace with nothing but gold statues for company. He was the miserablest man alive, but his problem got fixed that same day."

"How dat happen?"

"He went for a leak and soon as he touched his pecker he turned to gold himself."

Jim warn't satisfied with the story and reckons it won't stop him trying to dig up a mess of gold. I give some pondering to the situation and it's true, I ain't truly considered the gold-digging part since we left Missouri, just counted on California being so far away I won't get stretched for the judge's murder. But now we're practickly there it's discomforting to figure on how we aim to get tools and supplies when we ain't got no cash like Jim says. We could sell Jupiter for a good price on account of he's a horse and a half, but I never wanted to do it. He's all I got left apart from Lydia's rings and ear-rings to remember the lovebirds by, and I'm powerful fond of Jupiter anyway. I never come up with no answers and reckoned I'd give my brain another squeezing on it later on. There ain't no particular rush.

Next day I seen Frank prowling around the trees with my Hawken. I ask him if he's hunting, talking gentle so he never got the jumps and drilled me with my own gun.

"Yes," he says. "I am hunting Obadiah. I feel his presence nearby and am determined to rid myself of his odious influence once and for all. Have you seen him?"

"Why, Frank," says I, "don't you recollect how Obadiah died back in the desert? He just got weaker and weaker and give up the ghost. You warn't so dandy yourself at the time so I guess you disremember us burying him."

"Is it true? . . . Is he genuinely deceased? . . ."

He looked real happy about it, his own brother. Lunatics got no sense of kinship.

"Dead as a wedge," says I. "You ain't ever going to see him again, now how about you and me go hunting for some red meat? Fish is fine for awhile, but I got a hankering for real game."

"Very well," he says, and give me back the Hawken and we went tramping off. It's just as well I never truly had a notion to hunt because Frank would of scared away any game with his jabbering, and what he's jawing about is my Hawken.

"A fine weapon in its day," he says, "but now somewhat antiquated. Why did you not avail yourself of a more recent model?"

"This'n was a darn sight cheaper, that's why, and it's a good gun anyhow," says I, feeling mighty put out by his tone. Then he stops all of a sudden with his hand on his head and says:

"Of course! . . . Why not combine the ball, the powder and the percussion cap all in one projectile? . . . Think how much faster one could reload! Why, it's the next obvious step in firearms manufacture! Why has no one thought of this before? Why have *I* not thought of it before? I must set to work without delay. . . . Which way is the cave?"

"Back yonder. Don't burn up the page with scribbling."

And off he run to do some more inventing. It ain't such a bad idea at that, much more practical than a trumpet for listening to corpses. I figured I may as well do some serious hunting now that I started and worked my way west along the river past the point where we first come across it after the desert crossing. I went on a mile or two further and finally seen two deer and shot one, then slung it over my shoulders and headed back to the cave. When I'm still a ways upstream of it I heard whips cracking and voices, and snuck along through the brush till I seen three wagons aiming for the river. The men was trying to keep the oxen from rushing down the bank and into the water and was cracking whips to turn them off before they hauled everything into the drink. There was maybe twenty people staggering along behind, and mighty poorly they looked too, limping dogtired and falling down in the rush to water. The oxen got let loose from their harness while the wagons was still moving and waded straight in and sunk their muzzles deep, and the people walked and crawled in after them and flopped in the shallows and drunk and puked and thanked the Lord for delivering them out of the desert at last. I reckon they should of thanked them oxen for smelling it at a distance and leading the way straight to it, but then I ain't got religion.

I stayed hid and watched all of them suck up water like a blotting paper sucks up ink. They was raggedy and thin and pitiful, and when I seen two women lifted down from the wagons half dead I knowed I got to show myself and give them food. I never wanted to on account of they might suspicion who I am, but they was so poorly I reckoned they won't be doing no hunting for theirselfs a few days yet at least. So I come out of hiding and a couple seen me and give me a look like I got two heads or something, which is worrisome, then I figured it's because they never expected to find no one else around, and with a fresh-killed deer too. I dumped it on the ground and says:

"Afternoon to you. I reckon you'll be needing this."

"God bless you, boy," croaks one. "We have nothing left but moldering flour."

"Well, if you get a fire started I'll skin her and cook her for you."

Others come over when they seen me and they was so weak they never showed no curiosity with questions on who I am or nothing, just stared at the deer while I gutted and skinned it. When the fire was ready I cut up chunks of meat and skewered them on sticks over the flames and their mouths just watered. They would of et it half raw if I never warned them against it, and while they drooled and waited for the deer to cook I went off and emptied two big trout from out of Jim's fish traps and brung them back and got them ready for eating too.

Them folks et like they was starving, which they was. There warn't a morsel left but bones by the time sundown come, and once their bellies was full they got curious like I figured they would, so I told them I come across the desert same as them and me and Uncle Frank is camped down the river a little way and my name is Walt Purnell. A tall man with a beard says:

"We're beholden to you, Walt Purnell. I'm Matthew Berringer, and was wagonmaster when we had thirty-three wagons. You can see we've had a peck of trouble along the way."

And he goes on to say how most of them died of cholera, and them that was left got sick later on past Salt Lake City when their food and water got low and their teams got stole or butchered by Injuns, which accounted for three human killings by arrows too. While he talked I recollected his name from that time I squatted under Colonel Beckwith's window when Mr. Berringer was telling him about finding Rufus and Eben with no scalps and Sioux arrows in them. It's a fair bet he's heard tell of Huck Finn along the trail so I can't let him and the rest see Jim or they'll likely connect it all up and figure who we are. It's a real shame. There ain't nothing like being an outlaw to give you a need for human company that ain't part of your desperate band, and even if I was never what you might call the sociable kind, nowadays I'd give a barrel of gold eagles to tell them I'm Huckleberry Finn, who they ain't ever heard of on account of he ain't no one special. Well, I can't do it, not with famousness and a reward tied onto my name, so I says to Mr. Berringer I'll come back and see them tomorrow, and heeled it for the cave.

Jim had got mighty anxious while I was gone, and his mood never showed improvement when I give him the news about the Berringer party. He says:

"You reckon dey suspicion you, Huck?"

"I reckon not, but we got to go careful and make sure they never set eyes on you, Jim. Just me alone'll fool them easy. We best sneak past them one night pretty soon and get ahead again. They'll be laid up here a week at least."

We was talking low so Frank won't hear. He's curled up by the fire with his head under the blanket, so I reckon he never catched none of it.

"Dat Frank a consid'able burden to us, Huck. If'n he goes talkin' wid dem folks dey goin' to fin' out he livin' here wid a nigger, not jest you, den dey suspicion us for sure."

"It's a problem, Jim, but there's always an answer. All we got to do is figure a way to keep him away from them wagons."

"How we goin' to do it?"

"I reckon the best way is to tell him they're crawling with cholera. That'll scare him off for sure when he hears. He's a lunatic but he ain't no fool."

Jim says it's a good plan and we turned in feeling safe.

They say honest men and idiots sleep safe, and Jim and me cussed ourselfs for idiots next morning when we seen Frank is up and gone before we got the chance to tell him the cholera lie. Jim stayed in the cave and I hunted around for Frank to catch him before he come across the wagons. He warn't nowhere nearby and I run along the bank cussing still, but when I reached the wagons it's too late, because there's Frank already jawing with Mr. Berringer. I slowed up and was about to turn tail when Mr. Berringer seen me and calls me over. There warn't no way out now, and I just hope Frank never spilled no beans. Well, he spilled a whole parcel. First thing Mr. Berringer says is:

"Good morning to you, Walt."

"His name is not Walt," says Frank. "I have already told you his name is Jeff Wilson and the darkie is called Goliath."

Mr. Berringer give us both a queer look and says:

"I reckon I'll take the name a man gives me himself, so it's Walt Purnell far as I'm concerned."

"The boy is lying to you for some reason," says Frank, "but I will not concern myself with it further. There is none lower than a person who pretends to be another. There is a distinct odor of mendacity here."

And off he walked with his nose in the air, proberly scooping up all the mendacity. Says I:

"Mr. Berringer, you maybe figured it already, but Uncle Frank ain't exactly the normalest man you could meet. He gets things awful mixed up. Why, sometimes he even forgets his own name and says he's his brother Obadiah, who's my Pap that died, but he mostly does it when he's liquored up. He's been kind of strange ever since he fell out of a pear tree when he was just eleven years old and landed directly on his head. He's real clever now and then but stuff like names kind of leaks out of his brain. He don't ever admit to it, so it's best to agree with the things he says or he gets terrible upset and cries like a baby. Except for that he's a real nice man that I'm proud to have for an uncle, but it ain't easy explaining him to strangers."

"I appreciate your problem, Walt," he says, "and will give his stories no credence in future. Now you tell me he does have a kind of lunatic air about him. It must be hard work caring for that type."

"Yessir. Me and Goliath got to watch over him night and day."

"So there *is* a nigger with you," he says.

I could of kicked myself for letting it out, but I'm considerable rattled by the whole thing so it's understandable, and there ain't nothing for it but to steam ahead.

"He got that part right, yessir. Uncle Frank gets at least one thing right every day, sometimes two, but it's rare."

He swallered it easy and says:

"How long will you remain here before moving on?"

"Well . . . uh . . . we figured to get back on the trail any day now, Mr. Berringer. We're all rested up and raring to find gold."

"Why not wait awhile longer and travel along with us, Walt? California is near, but there are still hostile redskins betwixt here and there. You've been a power of help to us and I can't say I'd sleep of a night wondering if you're in trouble. Talk it over with your uncle. Seeing as he's peculiar I guess the decision will be yours, but take my advice and throw in your lot with us. It would be folly to continue alone, burdened as you are by a lunatic."

"I'll give it consideration, Mr. Berringer."

"Do that, Walt. Your party is more than welcome to join us."

I done more hunting that day and shot a wildcat. Most of it went to Mr. Berringer's people but I took a portion back to the cave. Jim warn't happy they knowed about him, but the way I seen it there ain't no point in hiding out in the cave no more, so we best take up the offer and join them. If we never done it they would of suspicioned us for sure, and if the bulldog is waiting for us somewhere up ahead he won't ever look for us in a bunch of men and wagons, more likely he'll be expecting us to pass by on our own, so that's another reason we got to do it. Jim grumbled some but finally seen sense and says he's agreeable, but when Frank come back to the cave he warn't so eager on it.

"I have spent the greater part of the day with that crowd," he says, "and there is not one intelligent being among them. You will no doubt find yourself at home in their midst but I will not, no indeed."

That's real dandy coming from the one that spilled the beans in the first place, and I got warm under the collar over it and give him a lecture on how a body can't be standoffish out here, and if he don't want to come along he can stay put and just see if he's got the brains to keep himself alive. That shook him some I reckon, and he went away and sulked. Later on he says he'll come along but he ain't happy to do it, and went off and scribbled some more inventions for comfort.

So we stayed another week while the people in the train got theirselfs mended. I done their hunting till the men was able to do it and got to be right popular with all of them. Jim showed his face a time or three but no one started hollering for a sheriff to arrest us so they never guessed our true names. Frank stayed by himself most of the time and never bothered no one except on the night he woke up and shot my Hawken off in the cave on account of he seen Obadiah's ghost standing over him. The noise echoed some and woke everyone in the train and they primed their guns for an Injun attack. I near got my head blowed off when I went along to say it's a false alarm, and slept with the Hawken under me after that.

Folks called me Walt and I learned their names too, and they told all the things that happened to them since they left St. Joe, most of it regular stuff about cholera and dying and leaving their wagons and such, but my ears stood out when one of them told how there was a big conbobberation when Colonel Beckwith got back to Fort Laramie after the expedition against the Sioux (which was never even catched sight of the whole ten days the soldiers was looking for them) and found his wife upped and run off with a stranger. He done considerable rug chewing over it and got drunk five whole days and nights. The forty-niners weren't allowed in the fort after the cholera broke out and only knowed what happened from sentries that talked friendly-like over the walls. They was all disgusted over the way the colonel never done no coloneling, just upended bottle after bottle and left the running of things to a captain, and in the end the captain read out from the army book of rules the part about when a commander is out of his head it's all right for the next in line to take over the job official, which is what happened just before the train pulled out. I reckon the colonel must of been in love with Lydia to let himself go to pieces and put himself in the way of disgrace like that, and I kind of felt sorry for him.

Finally the time come when the wagons and us moved out, and it felt good to be rolling along with folks again and be treated like a friend. We followed the river west for ten days without no trouble from Injuns or Frank, who was busy inventing a giant steam shovel for digging tunnels through mountains so you never had to climb over them. He got all excited when he done the final drawing and showed everyone. They was polite and smiling about it or called him a danged fool to his face, which got him considerable peeved and he never showed them the other drawings like the underwater boat and the earth trumpet, which is just as well because most folks ain't inclined to listen to a madman tolerant.

When we come in eye-reach of the Sierra Nevadas everyone was mightly impressed at how grand they looked, but the closer we got the more we changed our tune. If you ever seen them mountains you know why. They was big and awesome like the Rockies, only steeper and more fearsome looking with jaggedy peaks reaching up at the sky, so high only an eagle could of gone over easy, but on the other side is California, and that give us fresh heart.

We made camp hard up against where the mountains start getting steep and there was singing and dancing around the fire that night with a jew's-harp and a flute, the only insterments light enough not to have got throwed away on the trail. It's all to celebrate that we ain't got far to go and make everyone less afraid of the last stretch, which looks to be mighty tough going like I say. It was cheering the way folks jumped and stomped around, whooping and laughing and enjoying theirselfs and leaving the bad times behind. Then Mr. Berringer give a speech when things quieted down for a spell so's you could catch your breath.

"Friends," he says, "we have journeyed far together across prairie and mountains and desert and lost dear ones along the way. Only a handful remain of those who began, but few though we may be, not one need feel ashamed for having lived when others died, for there has not once in all these miles been an act of cowardice or meanness among the members present and departed of our band. The last hurdle is before us and we will strive to overcome it as we have done those that came before, and we will win through, of that I am sure. But now I ask you to bow your heads in silent prayer for those lost to us, that we may remember their sacrifice and draw strength from their memory and be grateful for the mercy God has bestowed upon we who remain."

They all took off their hats and bowed their heads and I done the same so as not to give no offense. I owed them it for treating Jim and me decent. They never knowed we're wanted men so maybe things would of been different if they was acquainted with the facts, but I reckon I got to give them the doubtful benefit as they say. When the prayer was over they started up the dancing again and I went down to the river to be on my own awhile. It was peaceful there with the music off yonder through the trees and the frogs croaking and the water sliding by. I sat on a rock and smoked my pipe, just watching the river all sparkling in the moonlight and hearing the night birds, real restful to the ear. It was so relaxsome I never jumped when footsteps come up behind me, just turned slow, figuring it's someone from the train come looking for restfulness same as me. But it ain't. It's Chauncey Thermopylae Barrett, and he's got Bob and Jesse with him.

"Good evening, Finn," he says. "I see you have survived the desert crossing in good health."

He ain't in a dress no more and got himself a pistol from somewhere that's pointed right at me. I near choked on my pipe with the shock of it, but I warn't about to let them see me scared even if I'm sick to my belly.

"Evening, Bulldog," says I. "How goes it?"

"I have never had affection for that name," he says. "In future kindly call me Mr. Barrett."

Jesse give a laugh, it's so ridickerless the way Bulldog acts, and got give a look to keep him quiet. Says I:

"Evening to you too, gents. I'm considerable surprised you teamed up with Bulldog here. I recollect you saying you never liked him awhile back."

"We need a grubstake, boy," says Bob, "and you're it. No hard feelings."

"I don't ever let hard feelings come between me and other folks, Bob, but you and Jesse ain't folks, just cockroaches."

"Snippy, ain't he," says Jesse, grinning.

"I reckon he'll sound different with a rope around his scrawny neck," says Bob.

"These gentlemen are now in my employ," says Bulldog. "We chanced upon each other and have agreed to forget past differences and join forces."

"Well, I ain't surprised to hear it," says I. "You made a jackass of yourself so many times trying to catch me on your own I reckon you must be too mortified to try it again without help."

"Insults are never the bravest of words, Finn. You have led me a

long hard chase and demonstrated a degree of cleverness I found
challenging, but your time of freedom is now over."

"Where's Randolph?" says I to Bob, ignoring Barrett deliberate so
he'll figure I ain't afraid.

"We got split up in the desert. Maybe he's alive and maybe he
ain't. It don't matter beans to you no more."

"Have trouble finding me?" asks I of Bulldog.

"It was simply a matter of waiting and watching from a vantage
point above the trail. If you were not defeated by the desert I knew
you would one day pass by. This is the day. You have been under
observation since noon."

"How come you never went into the camp to arrest me?"

"You have the knack of surrounding yourself with friends, Finn. I
swore I would never again underestimate your ability to ingratiate
yourself among protectors, and so waited until dark." Then he looks
at Bob and Jesse and says: "Ironically, your erstwhile friends are
now with me."

"Ain't life peculiar," says I.

"Keep that lip on a tight rein, boy," says Jesse. "I ain't forgot the
way you tried to kill me that time."

"There ain't nothing surprising in that, rabbit-brain. When you
see a cockroach you just naturally want to take a rock to it."

Jesse made to come at me but Bob held him back. Says I:

"What's your plan, Bulldog? Are you counting on them two to get
me back to Missouri, or do the safe thing and shoot me?"

"Neither. There is law of a kind in San Francisco. You'll be taken
there to stand trial or possibly sent back east by way of Cape Horn if
that is the wish of the authorities. Once you have been imprisoned
my responsibility in the matter ends. The law takes its own course
without my aid."

"That's real kind. I always wanted to go on a sea trip. I reckon this
must be your way of repaying the debt."

"What debt?" he says.

"Mean to say you forgot already? Why, Bulldog, you got the short-
est memory in history. Don't you recollect how the Injuns got ahold
of you and I set you free? I even give you a nice dress to wear
afterwards."

"Dress?" says Jesse. "What's he talkin' about?"

"Nothing," says the bulldog, looking a mite upset.

"You ain't told them the story?" says I, and proceeded to do it for him while he chewed his mustache and fumed some. Bob and Jesse laughed and he told them to quit. He's awful proud and don't like to look a fool, and I seen it's a way to give me and Jim a chance. Says I:

"You must be the woefullest detective in creation, Bulldog. You done all the wrong things ever since you started after me, and you can't even take me in without two others to help. It's a mighty poor showing, and on top of it you ain't even got the decency to give me a chance after I went and saved your ungrateful hide from Injuns. I reckon it's downright feeble and it shows you ain't got no kind of confidence to do the job. Well, I ain't blaming you. If I was in your boots I'd proberly do the same as you and squash the voice inside of you that says you ain't got the nerve to give me a chance by way of repayment. Once the story gets around I bet you won't get another job detecting, not after you lose your reputation. Folks say you're smart and a gentleman too, but it ain't so, not if you don't give me and Jim a chance."

"What kind of chance?" he says, and I seen he's took the bait.

"The time from now till daylight to get away without you following."

"Don't be absurd, Finn," he says.

"See? I knowed you're too scared to do it. It's a shame I got to be brung in by a poor loser. I figure I deserve better'n that on account of being famous. I always reckoned you was a coward, Bulldog, and when the newspapers ask me how I feel about things you can bet I'll give 'em the straight facts about that rescue I done for you. Folks'll read a story like that ten times over."

"Take that back," he says, grinding his teeth. "No man calls me a coward."

"I ain't no man, just a boy you never repayed for saving your life."

He grinded his teeth some more then says:

"Very well. You have until sunrise."

"What?" says Bob. "You aim to let him go?"

"He has challenged my integrity. I have no option."

"We're workin' for a fool," says Jesse to Bob. "We don't aim to lose that reward money, Barrett, not now we got it in grabbin' distance. He ain't about to get free, not while I got this rifle on him, the little sass-mouth."

"You'll do as I say," says Bulldog, and he's got his pistol on them to make them do it. "Put down those rifles."

"This don't make a grain of sense," says Bob. "You let him go and we ain't workin' for you no more."

"That is your choice."

"There's one thing more before you and me got a deal, Bulldog," says I. "Jim needs a horse. It ain't fair if we only got one between us. If you don't give us another it shows you ain't a square dealer and the repayment ain't true."

"Very well. Drummond, you'll give him your horse."

"Danged if I will!" yells Jesse. "Give him yours if you got a mind to, but you ain't gettin' mine!"

"Mine neither," says Bob, and they ain't bluffing, I can tell.

The bulldog chewed his lip awhile then says:

"So be it. Finn, you will take my horse for the nigger."

"I reckon it's a fair trade," says I, and they marched me a little ways off to where their horses are hid and I got on Bulldog's while he kept his eye and pistol on Bob and Jesse, both of them cussing and itching to put a ball in me.

"The debt is repaid, Finn," says Bulldog. "From this moment on I will have no mercy, be sure of that."

"I never expected none, and you won't get it from me neither, nor will you two," says I to Bob and Jesse. "I got my Hawken still and can pick the legs off a fly at fifty yards so you better not get close. I got no friendliness for neither of you."

It's a big lie about the fly legs, but it don't do no harm to throw a scare into them, which they hid with more cussing or else never believed me. Says I:

"Goodbye, and I hope we never meet up again ever."

"Rest assured we will," says Bulldog, and the others say the same in the briskest language, half for me and half for Bulldog, and I rode for the camp.

When I found Jim and told what happened his face dropped, but he never wasted no time with questions. We got Jupiter saddled and flung some supplies in a bag and I fetched my Hawken. No one seen us with the music and dancing still going on and we was just about set to leave when Mr. Berringer come along and seen the horses saddled.

"Are you leaving us, Walt?" he asks, all puzzled.

"We got to, Mr. Berringer. I can't explain nothing about why, just thank you for the kindness you and the others give us."

"There must be a reason for this. . . ."

"There is, but I can't say. Goodbye, Mr. Berringer."

"Wait! Are you being . . . hunted?"

"I can't tell. Please don't ask no more."

"You're Huckleberry Finn, I guess," he says. "And you're Jim."

I could of lied, but there ain't no point now.

"I reckon so. I never wanted to get in no trouble with you over it so I never told you."

"There's no need for apology, my boy. I guessed who you are from the moment I saw the two of you together."

"Does anyone else know?"

"There are some, but they have promised me never to speak of it out of gratitude for your kindness back along the river. There's no need for you to run off."

"I reckon there is, sir."

I told him about Bulldog and the others and the deal I made and he says:

"This is foolish. If you remain with us Barrett and his men can do you no harm. You're among friends now, Huckleberry, armed friends. Do not put yourself at risk by leaving."

"If we stuck with you all the way to California the bulldog'd just string along behind and wait for the train to break up when you come to the end of the trail. He'll know exactly where we're at all the time and grab us when there ain't no bunch of people around to stop him. We got to go now and count on giving him the cold shake in the mountains. I appreciate the offer, Mr. Berringer, but it ain't no good staying around."

He tugs his beard, all vexed over the situation and says:

"I see you won't be persuaded. Do you have everything you need?"

"I can't think of nothing else except maybe a heap of luck."

"Then goodbye and may God protect you both."

"Thank you, sir. I hope you and the rest all get to California safe and find a mess of gold."

We shook hands. He even done it with Jim. Then we rode off.

✦ 26 ✦

Hard Riding—A Bad Luck Meeting—Strong Words and
Apologies—A Parting Shot—Journey's End

It was a shame to leave decent folk behind, specially now I knowed they suspicioned me all along but never breathed a word, real hospitality I call it, and it give me another reason for hating the bulldog. One of these days I reckon it'll come to a showdown between him and me. I never wanted him dead, just off my back, but he ain't ever going to be content while I'm free and I ain't ever going to be truly free while he's on my trail, I seen that clear as day. It's one of them problems that ain't got no ready-made answer to it. You just got to see how the wind blows and bend this way and that to stay footstood long as you can. Maybe Bob and Jesse will kill Bulldog on their own account they're so mad at the way he let me go for honor's sake, but it's a mite too much to hope for.

We left the camp at a full gallop and made plenty of noise deliberate so if the bulldog and them hear it they'll figure we headed due west like I want them to. After a mile or two we turned south and crossed the river, freezing cold, and shivered our way alongside the mountains till dawn, then stopped awhile to dry out. When the sun come up we headed west again and started up into the Sierras through a pass with steep sides covered in trees and rocks, grand-looking but we never had time to admire no scenery and pressed on till noon, then rested again and let the horses feed. Jim says:

"De bulldog ain't goin' to fin' us hereabouts, Huck, not lessen he gets real lucky. All dese mountains jumbled up de perfec' hidin' place."

He ain't wrong, but I got something else on my mind. Says I:

"Dang it, we clean disremembered Frank. We never even got to tell him goodbye. Still, I reckon he won't miss us none, not so long as he's got a book to scribble inventions in."

"You right dere, Huck. He ain't nothin' but a spoil' chile moster de time an' bein' crazy don' worry him none. Anyways, we got our own selfs to worry on wid de bulldog snappin' at our britches."

I never wasted no more regretfulness over Frank. We rode on all afternoon and passed from one valley to another, heading mainly west till dusk. We rested and et but never lit no fire, and next day followed the valley up and up into the range, so high the air turned cold. That night we had a fire under a deep ledge where no one can see it that ain't right on top of it, and in the morning there's a mist that slowed us considerable. We never knowed which way is west, just followed our noses till it burned away under the sun, and pretty soon after we come to a high pass where two valleys joined and rode over the ridge and seen a lake stretched out below us, real big with mountains snugged up close around it.

It took all morning to pick our way down to it and when we got there the easiest thing was to follow the shoreline for awhile, looking at the peaks stood upside-down in the lake and the clouds drifting across the water. An hour or two later we seen two men camped on the shore with a small fire and two horses tethered nearby. It ain't them that's after us, but we never wanted to risk getting seen by no one and was just turning away from the lake to go around them through the trees when they seen us. We kept on heading for them so they won't suspicion we're scared and a minute later come up to them. Then I wished it had of been Bulldog, because it's Pap and Morg.

Pap never reckernized me till I'm right up close, then his eyes got wide and he took a step or three back away from me.

"Noooooo . . ." he says, kind of moaning.

"What's ailing you?" says Morg, then he looks at Jim and me again and his whole body kind of drawed up tall and he says:

"It ain't *them* is it? . . ."

Pap never answered, just stared at me like I'm a ghost.

"Afternoon, Pap," says I, and he sat on the ground and put his head in his hands and moaned some more.

"Hell's fire," says Morg. "It ain't possible. . . . Are you truly his boy?"

"The one and only, and this here's Jim."

"You better get down and see to your Pap," he says.

I done it and laid a hand on Pap's shoulder. He give a horrible cry and shook free without daring to look at me, guilt I reckon, for all he knowed he's put me through.

"Where'd you spring from?" says Morg, and I seen he's scared too, even if he's a big man. Says I:

"We was with a bunch of wagons but had to leave it fast on account of there's a detective on our trail. He's got a notion I killed Judge Thatcher back in St. Petersburg, but I reckon you two won't know nothing about that, being law-abiding both."

Morg give Pap a look, but Pap warn't in no shape for talking.

"Why should we know about it?" says Morg, trying to look innocent but it never worked. A dog with a stole pie in his mouth would of looked more innocent than Morg—handsomer too.

"On account of I seen Pap's hoofprint on the judge's doorstep in the snow is why!"

My voice is kind of high with strong feelings that rushed over me all of a sudden, surprise at meeting up with Pap after all this time, and temper because he got me in trouble and never tried to get me out and also, real strange, I'm glad he got this far without getting scalped or dead of thirst or nothing. How can you figure a jumble of feelings like that? I'm twitching like a fly in a spider web I'm so jumbled up over it, and I turn on Pap and screech:

"You done it and let me take the blame! Why'd you do it! I never done you no harm! You're my own Pap and you would of let me hang! And you burned the widow's house down too, you trashpile!"

I took off my hat and swiped his bowed head with it till my arm got tired, and when I quit there's tears on my face, real mortifying in the company of growed men but I can't help it. Pap never looked up once, still with his face hid in his hands and his long hair spilled over his knuckles. Then his back started to shake and out from that mess of greasy hair come a sobbing that quivered and jerked like a nervous mule. I wanted to push him over with my boot and pat him comforting on the shoulder both at the same time, mighty confusing for a growing boy, so I made up my mind and pushed him over. He give a thin little scream and huddled there on his hands and knees still shaking and sobbing, the pitifullest thing you ever seen. Morg says:

"Hold on there. . . . That ain't no way for a boy to treat his Pap."

"You shuddup!" I holler at him. "He ain't no Pap of mine, not after what he done! There's people dead on account of him!"

"You just hush and show some respect!" yells Morg back at me. "He's been on the downhill slope ever since we left Missouri, so just treat him gentle."

"I'll treat him!" says I. "I'll treat him the way he deserves!"

And I pounded Pap's back with both fists till they was sore from hitting against his knobbly backbone and ribs, he's so skinny. It made me ashamed even while I'm doing it to be whaling a skinny man like that but I can't stop I'm so filled with jumble. Then Jim come over and grabbed hold of my hands and hauled me away.

"It ain't no good to whomp him, Huck," he says.

He let me go gradual and I stood shaking like a leaf in a storm with the teeth chattering in my head even if I ain't cold. Morg kind of shuffled from one foot to the other and frowned plenty, not sure what he's supposed to do. Then Pap come to life and looked up with both eyes ablaze and points a trembling finger at Morg.

"He done it!" he screams. "He done the judge! I never! I told him not to but he done it!"

"Who done the fire!" yells Morg back at him. "Who done the fire that took a woman's life! It was you, you house-burnin' woman-killer!"

Then he turns to me and says:

"I never even met up with him before then! I ain't no house-burner, and it was accidental with the judge, I swear!"

"Liar!" shouts Pap, still on his knees. "Liar! Liar! You opened his throat when he never told where the safe is! You done it deliberate! I never wanted to burn the widow, just her house to pay her back!"

"Whose idea was it to get money off the judge, answer me that! Who told he's got a safe full of money in his office! You, that's who, and there warn't even no safe there, you danged idiot fool!"

"I never killed him!" screeches Pap. "I never killed no one deliberate!"

I could feel Jim trembling next to me, shaking all over, and he says real quiet:

"You burned my fambly even if you never intentioned it. You burned 'em to cinders. I got no kin on accounter you."

"Who says you can butt in, nigger!" yells Morg. "You get back in your place!"

"You shuddup and leave him alone!" yells I. "He's worth a million of you!"

"Why, you little squirter. . . . I'll tan the hide off you for that!"

"You better not try or I'll kill you!"

Morg boggled his eyes and open and shut his mouth then come at me, only Jim knocked him down before he got close, which come as a mighty big shock to a white man.

"You . . . you nigger! . . . I'll kill you for that!" he says, and picks himself up ready to fight. I lifted my Hawken but Jim pushed it away and let Morg come at him. He never got no closer than Jim's fist at full stretch and went down again and was disinclined to get up this time. Pap watched it all with a gleam in his eye, glad to see someone bigger than him knock Morg down, and I seen there ain't no love lost between them, only guilt and scaredness to keep them together. Then Jim points at Pap and says:

"Say you sorry for what you done."

Pap never understood, just stared at him, and Jim took the Hawken off me and aimed at Pap. I knowed he won't truly use it, but it give me a queer feeling to see him aim at my own Pap. I never stopped him though. Jim says:

"Say you sorry for de way you burned my woman an' chillern, an' say it loud."

"I won't . . ." he says.

"Dang that nigger," says Morg. "He reckons he's white. . . ."

"Say it," says Jim between his teeth, and I wonder if maybe he'll use the gun after all if Pap don't do it, but I still never stopped him.

"I ain't apologizing to no nigger," says Pap, but he don't sound too certain on it.

Jim cocked the hammer and Pap scuttled backwards like a crawfish. Jim's face was real grim. I never seen him like this before, full of rage and deadliness.

"I ain't about to tell you again," he says.

"I never wanted to kill no one," mumbles Pap.

"But you done it anyhow, so now you got to say you sorry for it."

"Well all right . . . ." he mumbles, "I reckon I'm sorry."

"Don' say it to de groun'! De groun' don' care! You say it to me!" yells Jim, and he took a few steps forward and practickly poked the barrel in Pap's eye.

"I'm sorry!" bawls Pap, frightened for sure now.

"Say it again an' lookit me when you says it."

So Pap done it, then bowed his head, ashamed for apologizing to a nigger. Morg looked at him like he's dirt, for the same reason I guess. Both of them never felt as bad about the murders as they done about getting knocked down and stood over by a nigger. Jim says:

"You want de big one to 'pologize for gettin' you in trouble, Huck?"

"I reckon not. He'd likely say it, but he won't mean a word of it, just saving his hide. There ain't no point."

"What you wanter do wid both of 'em?"

"If we was near sivilization I'd haul Morg to town and make him confess he done it, but we ain't, and even if we was he'd only do it with a gun at his head and that kind of confession don't count in the eyes of the law."

"Maybe yo Pap'd tell de way it happen."

"If he did then Morg'd just tell about the house-burning. Pap'd likely hang for that, so they ain't neither of them going to tell nothing."

"That's right, boy," says Morg, grinning. "You're over a barrel."

It's like he says. There ain't a way I can ever get free of the murder charge now. Even if I made them put a confession on paper it ain't no proof they writ it with their own hands and not me forging again, so it won't mean nothing whichever way. I'm barrelized definite, and it's like a bitter cold wind whispering through me, blowing away all the hopes I been keeping stashed away in the back of my head till there ain't no hopes left, not a one, and no chance ever for a peaceful life without no sword over me, as they say. But it's mighty strange how you get to feeling calm when that last piece of hope is gone, and looking at Morg and Pap now I seen them for the pathetic kind they both is and never wanted to spend no more time in sight of them than we already done. I took the Hawken off Jim and say:

"We ain't in California yet."

We went to the horses and mounted up, and Pap and Morg got on their feet again, glad we ain't going to kill them or nothing. Says I:

"Don't neither of you come near us again ever."

We rode by and kept on along the lake shore, and a minute later there's a bang! and a ball went whistling by. We turned and seen the two of them wrestling over a rifle, but can't tell which one done the shooting. It don't make no difference now; they're both of them trash past caring. Jim and me rode on and there warn't no more shooting while we're still in rifle-reach nor after, so they never shot each other. I reckon they been leaning one on the other ever since the judge got murdered, telling theirselfs they're both good as the next man, only secretly disbelieving it and feeling the truth gnaw away inside of them like a grub in rotten wood.

Three days more is what it took to clear the Sierras. There's snow atop the highest peaks now so it must be early fall. The trains still moving west better move fast or else get trapped in the mountains when the real snowfall starts. Nights was already chilly up here and we traveled quick as we can from sunup till dusk, and like I say, three days done the trick. One morning we rode up a ridge and looked over and seen a big wide stretch of land below, and I never needed no sign to know it's California.

"Jim," says I, "this is the place."

"You sure, Huck?"

"Positive certain. That there's what we come all this way for."

We looked a long time at that country rolling away into the distance. There's clouds drifting along here and there sending shadows rippling over the ground like you see fish do in shallow water, and way off to the north there's a storm with a gray curtain of rain hanging underneath moving along slow. To the south it's clear and bright with sunshine, and in between there's three different rainbows, which is a lucky number.

We rode on down out of the mountains with our heads full of golden dreams. Brass colored is how we should of seen them, but we never knowed it then. It was fine country all right, forest and hills with game running around, and creeks and open land and birds crowding in the air. I brung down two ducks and we et like kings on our first night in California, and afterwards we sat smoking our pipes and looking up at them California stars.

✦ 27 ✦

The Jumping-off Place—A Race for Gold—The Smiling

Winner—Spaniard Hospitality—An Expensive Surprise

Next day we come across a road and followed it west and joined up with a bunch of wagons and men on foot headed for the goldfields. They never give us no suspicioning looks so we figured it's safe and got into place behind the last wagon, which is full of forty-niners. A man on the tailboard yells:

"You headed for the diggings?"

"Yessir. We aim to get gold rich," says I.

"It'll happen! It'll happen!" he hollers, twitching all over he's so excited. "We're practickly there! Did you know it? Practickly right there, and there's gold enough for everyone!"

"That's a comfort," says I, polite.

"Comfort?" he says. "That's what you get in a featherbed full of virgins! That's what I'm getting myself pretty soon now, a feather-bed with all them virgins in it! That's real comfortable I reckon!"

He screeched on about how rich he'll be this time next week till someone else in the wagon told him to quit hollering or he'll tie up his jaw, but it never stopped him and a half mile down the road they pushed him out and flung his bag out after him. He never minded none, too full of exciteration to care, and he run down the road faster than the wagons to get there ahead of them. One of the men that pushed him out says to me:

"There goes a pure-born peabrain. This time next week he'll be crying his eyes out because he never turned over no nuggets with the first spadeful of dirt. Where are you from?"

"Ohio, sir."

"Don't call me sir. You don't sound like an Ohian to me, more like a Missourian."

"We moved to Missouri when I was still kind of small."

"That nigger belong to you?"

"He's a free nigger."

"Is that so? Well you'll be needing a strong back like he's got on him. Only fools reckon you can get rich in one day. I don't believe none of them stories. If the Lord wanted us to get rich in one day he would of put gold under every rock in the land. You got to work for riches, that's a fact."

"I reckon so."

"You lose anyone on the way across, boy?"

"All my kin, Pap and brother Bob, both dead of cholera."

"Happened to my partner. There proberly ain't a soul come through without they lost someone. That's another price the Lord asks for riches, the misery you got to feel beforehand."

"Amen," says I.

"Are you making fun of me, boy?"

"No, sir . . . mister, I'm just the religious type. Pap was a preacher and I sung gospel before I could talk even."

"Well, you set that nigger to work and you'll maybe strike it rich for the glory of the Lord."

He told us more about what God wants before he'll let us be happy, all of it miserable, and the others told him to quiet down with his religion or they'll throw him out too. He called them all sinners and blasphemers then filled his mouth with a wad of tobacco and never told all the other things God let him in on. A few mile further on we seen the screecher sat by the side of the road looking real sad, so God must of give him the word too. The men let him come aboard again, but only if he'll keep his mouth shut, and we rode along all afternoon with nothing but dust around our ears.

The road never led to the diggings at all. Just before sundown we come to a town, and the sign outside says: SACRAMENTO

It's a big town, big as St. Joe, with trees in the streets and buildings all new with no paint on most of them yet, so they must of been built around the trees that was already there. There's a light in every window and people crammed on the sidewalks rushing along like they got to get somewhere fast, saloons mostly. There's teams and wagons wheel to wheel everywhere and arguments about who backs up for who and more noise all over than I heard since the buffalo hunt.

Jim and me rode around town till it's truly dark, just drinking in the bustle and confusement. We seen a river right up close to the last buildings on the west side of town, so deep it's got three-masted ships and even a sidewheel steamer anchored there that must of come upriver from San Francisco.

"What we goin' to do now, Huck?" asks Jim.

"What we ain't going to do is put ourselfs up in a hotel and the horses in a livery stable. We ain't got no cash for it. Let's keep on going out the other side of town and find somewhere quiet we can make camp."

That's what we done, only we had to go a considerable way to get past the tent city that's around Sacramento. Finally we went in among a stand of trees way off from other people and made a fire and et and slept, but it warn't easy after all that exciteration.

Next morning we swallered the last of our supplies, which reminded me we not only got to get more food but also mining tools and such, none of which can be got by the power of prayer.

"Jim," says I, "you stay here and mind things while I go back to town and figure a way to get us some dollars. I reckon it's best if we don't get noticed together too much with so many people around. There's bound to be some that seen them wanted posters sometime or other."

He's agreeable so I saddled up Jupiter and rode back into Sacramento, which is even more crowded by day and twice as noisy. I never knowed where to start, just pushed along through the streets looking for hardware stores. There warn't more than about one every ten yards, so the goods we need is all there for the buying, but no dollars to buy with. Finally I figured the only way is to sell the rest of Lydia's jewels, so I went into a half dozen stores but they warn't interested except the last one, where the storekeeper looked at me sorrowful and offered five dollars, which is just insulting, so I never sold them.

I watched men buying supplies. You never needed dollars so long as you had gold dust that got weighed out right there on the counter, but I ain't got no gold dust neither. It was worrisome, and all the shouting and laughing and jawing flying around give me a headache, which is proberly why my brain never give me no answer on the problem of cash. I ask the nearest miner how I can raise a grubstake from nothing at all and he says there ain't no way unless I wash dishes in a hotel or eating house. I never wanted to do nothing like that, too proud I reckon. Famous outlaws don't do no humble work.

I soldiered on around town trying to figure a way and come to a street that's blocked off at one end with a big crowd of men all jumping up and down and standing on wagons and other men's shoulders and rooftops and hanging out of windows to see something special. It got me curious, so I rode up close and stood in the saddle to get a look. The whole street was empty except for the sidewalks which is packed both sides, and the other end was blocked with people too. Then I seen why. A pistol fired and two horses with riders started off at full gallop from this end and charged along the street till they got to the far end, and the air was full of cheering and yelling from the crowd. When the horses was reined in some men hollered for joy and some cussed, so it's a horserace with betting. I pushed in closer and ask a man if they always run races like this and he tells me only on Sundays, which is today. Then he says:

"That's a powerful-looking animal you got under you. Fixing to race him, boy?"

"I reckon I am," says I, not even stopping to give it consideration.

"Well get in there and make your pitch," he says. "I'll bet a couple ounces on that black crittur. He looks like a real mile-eater."

I pushed Jupiter through by telling the crowd I aim to race so's they'll let us by, and when I come into the open street another race just finished and cheers and groans went up and little bags of gold changed hands. Then a man with a big hat and a red flannel shirt hollers:

"Who's next?"

Up rides a man on a bay horse and dropped a little bag into Redshirt's hand. Redshirt bounced it up and down a time or three, weighing it right there in his hand.

"Five hundred," says the rider, and Redshirt give him a nod and hollers:

"Who'll take on this noble beast and nobler rider for a purse of five hundred dollars?"

"Me!" says I, loud as I can.

"Where's your bet?" he says. "Let's see the weight of your pouch."

"Pardon me?"

He rolled his eyes and the men around him give a laugh, and he says weary-like:

"Show the color of your dust, boy. You can't make a bet without putting up a stake."

"I ain't got one," says I, feeling foolish.

"Then step aside for someone who has, and don't waste no more valuable time."

"What if I bet my saddle?" says I.

"That's no good. We race for big money here, boy. Go play somewhere else and leave men's business to men."

"How about if I throw in my rifle too?"

"That? Why, it looks older'n my granny," he says, and got another laugh, which got me angersome.

"All right then," says I, "I'll throw in my horse too."

"Now you're talking like a man," he says, and turns to the crowd and yells:

"Place your bets! The bay versus the black!"

There's a delay for a minute or two while bets got made up and down the street. I give my Hawken to Redshirt for safekeeping then me and the other rider lined up together. He's on a fine horse, but not so good as Jupiter so I warn't worried.

"Are you ready?" asks Redshirt with his pistol raised.

"Ready," says both of us.

He fired and we thundered away up the street, less than a quarter mile. It warn't no contest. Jupiter and me come in way ahead without no bother and trotted back to collect our winnings.

"Care to do it again?" says Redshirt.

"Ain't no reason why not," says I. "Jupiter can run all day."

Redshirt bawled for runners but no one brung his horse forward. They seen the way I won so easy, and I wished I had of held Jupiter back some so's it would of looked like a harder race, but too late now.

"Is there no one with a horse to match the black cannonball?" hollers Redshirt.

There warn't, and he says:

"Sorry, boy, you'll have to step down for other riders."

"One moment, if you please," calls a voice, and the crowd at the end of the street parted to let a man through. When he come into the open he's the handsomest person I ever seen, with light brown skin and long black hair and a fine mustache, Spaniard I reckon. He's got on tight black britches with silver buttons up the sides and a short black jacket and a flat-brimmed hat the same, and he's toting a pearl-handled silver pistol across his belly. His saddle is just littered with silver stars and shapes all over, even the bridle and stirrups, but best of all is his horse, pale yeller-brown with a white mane and tail and socks and face. I only ever seen that kind of color on a rocking horse before. They rode up with the horse picking up his hoofs real dainty, prancing almost, and the Spaniard was sat on him like a king, all noble and majestical and proud. There's a heap of muttering run through the crowd when they seen him, but it ain't the kind of sound that says they're impressed like I am, more like they ain't partial to him, which is a puzzlement on account of he don't look mean or nothing. He prances up to me and says:

"Señor, will you do me the honor of contesting with my poor beast?"

"I reckon I will, thank you," says I, being polite in return.

"Make your bets," says Redshirt, only he sounds kind of sour now.

"I will match the five hundred dollars the young señor has this moment won," says the Spaniard.

"I'm agreeable," says I, and he give Redshirt a little clinking bag to hold, coins, not dust, and I done the same with mine.

"Get back to Mexico, greaser!" shouts a man, and the Spaniard turned to him, smiling with all his teeth, white and flashing like snow.

"Señor," he says, real pleasant-like. "I have never seen Mexico, nor has my father. I am a Californio."

"You're a goddamn greaser!" shouts the man.

"I would not think to disagree with a man of your breeding, señor," he says, still smiling, then he turns to me and says:

"We begin, yes?"

"Yessir," says I.

He's the elegantest-spoke person I ever heard. The man in the crowd warn't finished yet though.

"Goddamn greaser!" he shouts again, but some others told him to quit so's they can lay their bets. They was real excited about seeing a race between two real good horses. Then the Spaniard says to Redshirt and me:

"Señors, two horses such as these should I think prove their spirit in a race worthy of them. The street is too short, no? Beyond Sacramento perhaps one mile in the direction we face there is a large rock standing alone. To this rock and return is a true test, you agree?"

Everyone liked the plan and the end of the street got cleared. Someone rode out to the rock to make sure we both go around and not turn short of it. When he's ready he's supposed to fire a pistol to let us know, only he's so far away no one heard it if he done it. Redshirt reckoned he's had plenty of time to get there so me and the Spaniard lined up. He tips his hat to me and says:

"May the best horse win, señor."

I tipped mine back to him and we waited with my heart hammering real hard on account of I ain't so sure of winning this time. Redshirt fired and we shot away like lead from a barrel. Jupiter run like the wind all the way along the street and out past the edge of town on a road heading south, but that yeller horse kept up easy with his white mane flying, and the Spaniard laughed over them pounding hoofs, just for the joy of it I reckon. I ducked my head behind Jupiter's neck and hunched low, trying to see the big rock through all that black mane in my eyes, and there it is way up ahead with a man and horse stood in front of it.

We streaked for it side by side and swung around back of it without hardly slowing down, me on the inside so I got a little way ahead, but not for long because here comes the Spaniard and we're neck and neck again, pounding along back to town through our own dust. I drummed my heels into Jupiter and he give me all he could, but it ain't enough to pull ahead. Now I can hear the crowd hollering we're so close, then we're thundering up the street for the finish. The Spaniard give another laugh and pulled ahead till I'm back by his tail, and I larruped Jupiter some across the shoulders with the reins, which I never done before but I hated to see him beat. He sprung ahead till we're side by side again but it ain't no use, because just before we shot across the finish line drawed across the street the Spaniard pulled ahead by a clear neck and won. I had to comfort myself thinking Jupiter would of done it if he hadn't of been in another race just before.

We pulled up sharp to keep from running into the crowd at the end of the street and went over to Redshirt with the horses blowing hard and the crowd yelling fit to bust.

"Here you are, boy," says Redshirt, and handed me both pouches.

"But I never won it," says I, and made to hand them over to the Spaniard, but Redshirt says:

"Yes you did, boy. You won by a head and there's not a man here that'll say different."

The men around him all agreed. I looked at the Spaniard and he's just smiling. Says I:

"You won fair and square. The money ain't mine, it's yours."

When I tried to give it to him all the men set up a commotion and the one that yelled "Greaser!" before started up again. The others joined in and pretty soon everyone was yelling it. I tried to give him the pouches anyway but he just smiled and waved them away. He even had the gumption to tip his hat to the crowd, which only made them madder, then he made his horse go down on one knee and give them a bow from the saddle, done real mocking with his teeth showing all the while, and when he finished the show he turned his horse and rode through the crowd real slow. They kept on yelling at him but let him by, and he never even looked at them, just ambled through like he's all alone out on the plains looking at the horizon or something.

The whole thing made me disgusted it's so mean-minded. I grabbed my Hawken off Redshirt and rode after the Spaniard and catched him up. He's got another man with him now, a Spaniard too but not so fancy dressed.

"Pardon me, sir . . . señor, you got this money coming to you I reckon."

"You have heard your fellow Americans grant you the prize. Why do you not agree with them?"

"They never seen it straight. You won easy and the money's yours, so take it."

"I will accept my own, but you will keep yours," he says.

"But you won it."

"I do not wish to have it. Keep your American gold dust."

He sounded kind of snotty now, so what happened back at the race must of upset him even if he never let them know out of proudness.

"There ain't no need to say it like that," says I, giving him his own pouch. "I never agreed with them."

"That is true," he says. "It is hard to see a small bird among vultures. You will accept my apology, but you will keep your gold dust. Your clothing tells me you are not wealthy."

"Not till I won the first race I warn't, but I'm rich now."

He turned to the other Spaniard and says a few words and they both laughed like it's a big joke, then he says to me:

"Our pardon, señor, but five hundred dollars does not make a man rich."

"Well it's a heap more'n I had before today."

"You are a gold miner from the east?"

"I aim to be. I just got here yesterday."

"What is your name?"

"John Hawken."

"I am Don Esteban Hernando Rodrigo Alonso Vicente Miguel Luis Espinoza de Villamarga," he says.

"Pleased to make your acquaintance," says I, looking around for all the rest, but it's only him he's talking about. With a name like that it's a wonderment his horse can carry him. He says:

"You have much to learn in California, Juan Hawken. Much you learn will make you sad, but you are young and sadness will fall from your shoulders like rain from the leaves. You will take food with us, yes?"

"Thank you kindly. I ain't had a morsel since breakfast time."

We pushed along through the streets to the river road and followed it south out of town to where it's quiet and peaceful. Esteban says:

"My compadre is called Ramon."

"How do, Ramon," says I, but he only nodded a fraction, not familiar with the language I reckon.

"How does a man who is not rich come to own such a horse as yours?" asks Esteban.

"My Pap won him in a card game, then he died of cholera."

"That is unfortunate," he says, only I can tell he don't give a can of beans what happened, but then why should he?

"Perhaps that was the first of the sad things you must learn in California," he says.

"It does not matter. You were journeying to California with hope in your heart. If not for that hope you would not have been in the mountains and your father would never have died of disease. California is a beautiful woman who lures men on to fortune and death. Never let yourself fall into her arms, Juan Hawken, or she will crush you with love and feast upon your flesh."

"I reckon I'll keep a sharp lookout," says I, considerable surprised there's cannibal women in the state. Says I:

"Don't you do nothing but race your horse for a living?"

Esteban turned it into Spaniard for Ramon and they both laughed, then Esteban says:

"I am the son of a grandee."

"Is that good?"

"It is better to be the son of a grandee than the son of a peon."

I never liked to ask, but I reckon peon must be Spaniard talk for trash the way he spits it out, which makes me wonder why he's talking to me. He goes on:

"My father has an estancia in the south. There are kings who have less. My father's house is called Casa Grande. There is no finer house in California. On my father's land are more cattle than can be gathered in one place. There the sun always shines upon us. Here in the north it is cold. I do not like it."

"How come you're here then, Esteban?"

"Call me please *Don* Esteban."

"Excuse me, I never intentioned no offense."

"You are an ignorant American, but your heart is true. For this reason I forgive you."

"Thank you kindly."

He talked on about the way things is down south, kind of arrogant like his family invited God to dinner every week regular, and he says the estancia uses Injuns like the cotton plantations down the Mississippi uses niggers.

"You mean they're slaves?" says I.

"Yes, slaves. The Indios are fit for nothing else."

The way the racing crowd treated him on account of him being a Spaniard ain't teached him no lesson like wearing Injun clothes teached me, and I figured rich people only learn the kind of lessons they want to. Esteban says he made the trip north out of curiousness to see what Americans look like. His Pap warn't happy when

Mexico sold California to America about a year and a half back, and when gold got found after the sale went through him and a heap of other Spaniards and Mexicans chewed the rug over their bad luck. Esteban come up for a looksee to find what kind of changes the new government and the gold rush is making, and he ain't impressed. He's already been north of Sacramento where most of the diggings is and he reckons the miners is generally lower than hogs. Peons is what he calls Americans, and I can see why after what happened in town, but it ain't hardly fair to tar us all with the same brush and I told him so, but he just laughed.

"You are proud, Juan Hawken, but you will one day see your countrymen as I do. This will surely happen if you find much gold, for with riches comes a new way of seeing the world."

"Well I ain't about to let it change me. I got five hundred dollars today and I don't feel no different than yesterday."

That give them another laugh, and around that time we come to a gap in the trees off the road with the river nearby, and in the open space is a fancy coach with a little picture on the door of crossed swords and a cow's head, only with real long horns. There's twenty or so horses tethered to one side and maybe six or eight Spaniard men stood around and two women in bright red and green dresses. They all shouted and waved when we rode up and Esteban says:

"These are more of my traveling compadres. Now there will be fiesta."

Which means a whole lot of food got hauled out of the coach and spread on blankets on the ground. Two men started playing fandango music on guitars and the two women stamped all around the place with their hands over their heads, squashing bugs I reckon so the picnic don't get spoiled, but doing it to music so it don't seem like hard work. They was all real friendly to me, but only Esteban speaks American so there warn't much talking in my direction. After they et a heap of food the two women got up and started stamping bugs again. I bet no bugs ever get closer than a hundred yards to Casa Grande without women leaping out and squashing them. There was wine, which I never tasted before, cherry colored but not tasting nothing like it, but I drunk a bottle anyway out of politeness and et everything that got put in front of me. It's hot Spaniard food that I ain't familiar with nor partial to, but it never mattered so long as I drunk enough of that wine to cool my mouth.

"Pardon me, Don Esteban," says I. "Are them two ladies your sisters?"

"They? No," he says, and shouts something to the rest and they all laughed. The women come over and patted me on the head like a dog, real mortifying, and it took more wine to cool off my blushing. They was both pretty with dark eyes, and they showed a considerable amount of shoulder and chest and ankle to what I seen other women showing. The Widow Douglas would of called them loose women. Esteban seen me looking close at them and laughs and says:

"You must find your own women, Juan, or I will have to challenge you to a duel over these two. You devour them with your eyes."

He reckoned it's so funny he fell back laughing, which makes him a different person to when he's arrogant and prideful. I liked him better like that, same as I liked everything that afternoon, all down to them wine bottles I figure. I must of been there hours, because all of a sudden I seen the sun is sliding down the sky and I ain't even got supplies yet and Jim's waiting for me. I got up in a rush and fell down again and got on my feet the second try, then walked all tanglefooted over to Jupiter. I got the last little pieces of Lydia's jewels out of the saddlebag and give the two women a ring and pair of ear-rings apiece, which made them kiss me a time or three while everyone cheered, real grade-A mortification for yours truly, then I done my goodbyes and thank you's to Esteban and he says:

"If you are ever to the south, young Juan, we will fight a duel, for you have made me jealous with your gifts."

"Well, all right," says I. "We'll throw grapes at each other from fifty paces."

He laughed and shook my hand real warm and friendly and says:

"Goodbye, my friend. Never gamble away your horse. He is one among many. Adios, and God go with you."

"Thank you for the hospitality," says I, after trying a couple of times to get it out correct, then I got aboard Jupiter. They all give me a wave and the women blowed kisses. I turned Jupiter and we set off up the road back to Sacramento with just a stop or two along the way to drain the wine out of me.

It was dark when I got there but all the stores was still open so I done some buying. Apart from food and such I got two gold-washing pans, and when the storekeeper added up the cost he tells me:

"Ninety-three dollars and fifty cents."

I figured I must still be drunk from the wine and went outside and put my head in a horse trough, then come back into the store.

"How much was that again?"

It's still the same, and I say:

"It can't be. . . ."

"You go to any store in town and you'll find the same prices," he says. "This stuff come around the Horn and upriver from Frisco, and all that transportation means you have to pay more."

So I had to hand over my gold dust and he weighed out a portion and give me back the rest, then I loaded up Jupiter and had to walk him all the way out to our camp, the saddle is so crowded with supplies. Jim warn't happy when I got there on account of not having no food all day, so I fried him up eggs and bacon and bread and opened a can of preserves to get him friendly again and told all about what happened to me. By the time I finished he warn't so snippy, and he says:

"You ask which way de diggin's be, Huck?"

"I clean disremembered, but we'll find out first thing tomorrow."

✦ 28 ✦

A Familiar Face—To the Goldfields—Hard Work for No

Profit—Unfriendly Neighbors—First Strike—A Mean Trick

I figured the way to do it is just mingle in with men from the tent city outside town and wait for a bunch to head for where the gold is. Sacramento is right handy as a jumping-off place for them that's come overland like Jim and me and for them that's come upriver from San Francisco too. Everyone gathered hereabouts before they headed for the gold. It's all hustle and bustle and confusement when we come along early next morning, with men packing up their tents and supplies and loading everything in wagons or on horses or their own backs, and I ask a dozen different ones which way they're going and got as many different answers. A heap was aiming for the creeks along the American River that runs into the Sacramento River just north of town, and others was headed further north up to the Feather River and the Yuba. We never knowed which one to pick, they was all brimming over with gold so the stories go, but finally we figured we may as well try the American seeing as it's closest. We was just about to join in with a band headed that way when I heard a voice holler:

"You! Jeff Wilson!"

I turned around and there's Frank charging through the crowd with a big smile creasing his face and a bottle in his fist and two more poking out his pockets. He come up and fell right by Jupiter's hoofs then picked himself up again and says:

"My dear young friend! How gratifying to feast my eyes upon your face again as before. Why did you abandon me without word of goodbye or farewell? My puzzlement was boundless and immeasurable when I learned of your leavetaking."

The bottles should of warned me it ain't Frank at all, it's Obadiah, drunk as a skunk for the first time since way back along the Hum-

366

boldt. He's covered in dust and dirt but happy as a hog in mud and real excited to see us, grinning away with them yeller teeth.

"What joy!" he says. "What merciful happenstance to come upon you this way by sheerest coincidence without warning! How long have you been in this locality?"

"Only a day or two, and we're leaving right now."

"Leaving? In the manner of departure? But where?"

"We ain't exactly sure, but them ahead reckon they know a place so we'll just follow on."

"Ahh, yes, I behold mining utensils among your baggage. I will accompany you."

"But you ain't got no supplies or nothing, Obadiah."

"This statement is without error. I have spent my last dime on whiskey, of which I have a plentiful supply about my person. When that has been drunk to emptitude I am at the mercy of Fate. May I not find companionableness with you until that awful hour which fast approacheth?"

I never wanted him along. Jim and me got problems enough without no lunatic drunk to watch out for, but leaving him behind ain't charitable on account of he'll wind up in the gutter like a sick dog, which is a situation I'd prefer not to have the responsibleness of. I looked at Jim and he give a shrug, so I say:

"All right then, but when you run out of liquor I ain't answerable for it."

"Indeed no, young Jeff. You need have no fear for my safety."

I judged we was landed with just that, but there ain't no going back now. He walked alongside us for a mile or three at the tail end of the line, but after awhile the liquor took his legs away and he fell down in the road, so we hoisted him onto Jupiter and Jim and me took turns walking.

The road we're on run east from Sacramento along the American, and a few miles out I seen a big building close by with thick clay walls like a fort.

"What's that place?" says I to a man driving a wagon.

"Sutter's Fort," he says. "Colonel Sutter's a mighty big man hereabouts. He's the one that owns the sawmill where the gold first got seen in forty-eight. It's up the road a piece yet. You headed for the upper field or the lower?"

"I don't rightly know which is which," says I.

"The lower diggings is where the river forks, maybe twenty-five mile from here, and the upper's along the south fork another twenty-five mile or so. You take my advice and keep going to the furthest one. The lower field's staked out from here to Sunday with claims already. I got a store there I run with a partner, so I know. All this here in the wagon is supplies. I done some mining but seen right off the fastest way to make money is selling goods to miners, easier too. You take my advice and be a storekeeper."

"I ain't got the temperament for it, I reckon."

"Looks to me like you ain't got the muscle for a miner neither. It's cruel hard work, boy. Don't let no one tell you different."

We seen the sawmill awhile later but there ain't nobody working it, and the storekeeper says:

"Poor old Sutter. Opens a sawmill and gold gets found in the mill-race. Now he can't get a single man to work here. Everyone and his brother wants to be a miner and get rich fast. They'll learn. I learned and so'll they, you take my word."

We reached the lower diggings next day. Half the men stayed there and the rest marched on along the south fork of the river, Jim and me and Obadiah included. Most drunks generally got no appetite for nothing that don't come out of a bottle, but Obadiah warn't that kind and et his fill out of our supplies like he's been starved for food a year or so. There ain't no use complaining on it. I reckon the food is all that's keeping him off Death's doorstep, with Death peeking through the keyhole and tapping his foot impatient-like. When he warn't babbling nonsense he stayed silent as the grave, just sucking on his bottles till they run out. Sometimes he sung songs with a voice like a rusty file rubbing on a tin can. Them times was the worst, and the men along with us made it clear they ain't happy about Obadiah. Says one:

"If you don't keep that mush-head quiet I'll ram a sock down his throat."

"Make it a pair, and follow up with a couple of shirts too," says another.

By the time we got to the upper field we was mighty unpopular and split off from the rest soon as we could. There was hundreds of men here already, maybe thousands, all of them panning gravel without no let-up, eager for a streak of color in their pans. They warn't just along the American neither, but down every little creek that run into it, and we got to wondering if there's a place left that ain't been claimed yet. There's a kind of town there with six or eight big tents all close together and a couple of log cabins and some that's partly both, with wood walls and canvas roofs, but the biggest one is the store. We went on up the river another half mile then turned down along a shallow creek where the miners ain't exactly rubbing shoulders together, and a quarter mile along there's a spot where no one staked a claim yet, with a gravelly bank either side of the water and wooded hills roundabout, real pretty.

"Jim," says I, "I reckon this here's as good a place to start as any."

So we done it, and offloaded the supplies and Obadiah, snoring drunk. He got propped against a tree to sleep it off and I started panning for gold straight off. Jim figured he better build us a shelter to make it clear this stretch of creek is our claim and set to work on it. I panned and panned for an hour but never seen no gold, so I figured I must be doing it wrong and went down the creek a little ways and watched how some others done it. I seen I had way too much gravel and sand in my pan; you got to take it a smidgen at a time and slosh the water round and around with the pan tilted over so the water slops over the rim and takes the sand with it and the gold and gravel get left behind on account of being heavier. I went back and started over, doing it the way I seen, but there still warn't no shiny specks in the pan and I got disgusted as well as stiff with backache from stooping and squatting all that time, and my fingers was froze too from the water. It was real discouraging, but I figured we'll maybe have to tolerate no luck for a day or two till we strike it rich. But I ain't so excited about it now.

Jim got the shelter fixed up and got busy with the other pan after I showed him how, and we panned and panned all day with the birds singing and Obadiah snoring and every now and then the sound of other miners down the creek brung to us on the breeze. It was companionable work with Jim next to me, and I took new heart, but it never made no gold show up. When sundown come we went over to the shelter all crookedy-backed, so it never mattered if the roof ain't high.

"Huck," says Jim, "dis here pannin' de hardes' work I ever done, worse'n choppin' a whole mountainer wood. I cain't straighten up nohow."

"It's the price you got to pay for being a miner, Jim. Mostly they wind up humpbacked permanent."

"I hopes you joshin' me 'bout dat, Huck. A man cain't do hardly nothin' wid a humpback."

"It ain't so bad as you might reckon, Jim. There was an English king that was humpbacked, and from gold too."

"How dat be?"

"It was the crown that done it. He was kind of spindly and the crown was solid gold, so heavy it bowed him over and he stayed that way. He could of took it off and stood up normal if he had a mind to, but he kept that crown on his head to let folks know he's the king out of pure cussedness. It stooped him lower and lower till he could of shoveled up dust with his chin, but he kept on wearing that gold crown anyhow, which is what's called the burden of state."

Obadiah woke up in time for supper but his appetite was gone along with the last of his whiskey, the exact turnaround of a normal drunk that will eat like a horse when the drinking stops, but then Obadiah ain't no normal drunk so you can't expect him to act like it. Only it means come morning when he's sobered up enough to use his tongue he won't be Obadiah no more, he'll be Frank again, which ain't good news. Jim and me talked it over after he snoozed off again and decided if Frank gets too snotnosed to be tolerable we'll just get him some whiskey and bring Obadiah back. Whichever way we're bound to get a fair amount of trouble and pain from the situation, but samaritans is supposed to handle that stuff easy, and we asked for it bringing Obadiah along like we done so there ain't no use in complaining.

Before we turned in I checked the horses was picketed safe then walked along the creek to the river to get my back unhumped, and once I got that far it seemed like a good idea to walk on to where the store is, so I done it. The store was still open but not doing half the business the tent next door done. It's a saloon, with miners crammed in there singing and hollering and spilling out the door flap to puke and piss. There's a man on his knees and when he seen me watching he says:

"Drinkther on me, young 'un! Come on inthide an' thwaller thummer that forty-rod juith."

He never had no teeth in front, proberly wore away on bottle necks, and his face was red and whiskery in the lamplight with his eyes all bugged out like marbles. He says:

"Drinkther on me, yeth thir. I thweated an' panned like a nigger fifty-theven dayth without no lucky thtreak, an' today I thtruck it rich. Jutht dug me a hole to thit in an' there it wath, the biggeth nugget thith thonovabith ever theen. Weighed her in at thirty-thikth ounceth. How'th that for luckineth, hey?"

"That's real nice for you, mister," says I, feeling sore it warn't me that done it.

"Well have a thnorter whithkey inthide. I'm payin'."

He stood up and tried to go back in the tent, only he got all snaggle-footed and fell against the canvas walls. It never stopped him getting in though; he just out with his knife and slit a new door in the canvas and crawled inside laughing and coughing, never even thinking how he might of stabbed someone on the other side using his knife that way.

"Drink up, boyth!" he hollers, and everyone roared and the tent walls shook and heaved. Someone come tumbling out the new door and lay there where he fell, dead drunk. He had long hair and I wondered if it's Pap, but when I got up close I see it ain't, which is reliefsome.

I headed back to the claim with a head full of problemation. If Pap and Morg got out of the mountains safe they're likely around Sacramento someplace by now, and when they head for the diggings they might just pick the same as we done and one of these days come face to face with me and Jim. Maybe we'd just pretend we never seen each other and go our different ways, but that's mighty wishful. And there's Bulldog Barrett too. He'll be going from camp to camp till he finds me I reckon, but it'll take him awhile, there's so many, and maybe me and Jim will strike it rich and be on our way someplace else by the time he reaches hereabouts. Jim and Obadiah was both asleep when I got back and I rolled up in my blanket and done the same, but it was hours till I got my brain cleared and was able to sleep.

Sure enough, Frank was with us come morning, but so sick he never had the strength to be waspish, just nursed his head all day while Jim and me panned and panned and growed our humps all over again. Then around evening Frank got well enough to be cranky.

"Why am I here?" he wants to know. "You two have abducted me again, have you not?"

We warn't in no mood for argument, both in considerable torment like we are, so I launched a broadside, as they say.

"No we never, and if you don't like it here you can go drown yourself, you danged ungrateful useless sap-head!"

"What's that you say? . . ."

"You heard it de firs' time," says Jim. "You ain't nothin' but a millstone aroun' our necks, so you jest better watch out or we ain't feedin' you no mo' an' pickin' you off'n de groun' like we done till now."

"What's that? . . . What! . . . How dare you address me that way, you darkie, you! . . . I am Frank Jennings of Springfield, Illinois. . . ."

"We know it, and it's a shame we do," says I. "You been nothing but trouble to us ever since we run into you and you ain't showed no gratitude for it even once, just all the time complain and sulk like a baby and complain some more, and before you ask where's your invention book we ain't got it, and you ain't got it neither on account of you proberly lost it last time you got drunk, so don't you go telling us we stole it or we'll put your fool head under the creek and keep it there till you get some sense inside of you!"

He looked at us like we just cut his nose off or something, then he kind of slumped inside his clothes, just shrunk away into a skinny little man with a baldy head and yeller teeth and starts to cry. I disbelieved it first off and figured he's just after sympathetical treatment, but them tears was the genuine thing and got bigger and heavier and rolled down his face in floods, cleaning it some. He sobbed and sobbed and never seen fit to quit till we talked gentle to him and fetched some food over. Feeding and sobbing together give him the hiccups and he never shook them all night. Just when me and Jim was sliding into the land of Nod there comes another hiccup from Frank and we're back in California, weary and wore out. In the end we made him take his blanket and go sleep under a tree, which got him upset again but he done it and we got some rest. It's a pesky business being a samaritan.

We panned three days more and washed every inch of the bank on our side, then seeing there ain't no one staked a claim on the other side yet we done that too, and near killed ourselfs for nothing. Frank give us a hand when the mood come on him, which ain't often, but it don't matter how many hands you got if there ain't no gold on your claim. One night we talked it over and figured we may as well try somewhere else. Frank says:

"Thus far you have only worked the banks of the creek."

"Well that's where you find gold," says I. "Everyone knows that."

"An educated mind would ask how the gold came to be there in the first place," he says, "but since I possess the only mind of such type here I must answer the question for you. The gold is washed by erosion from further up the slopes which confine the creek to its course."

"You mean there's gold up the hill?"

"Possibly. I suggest you find out before you desert the claim."

"Wait on," says Jim. "How we goin' to wash de dirt if'n it halfway up de hill?"

"You must dig it out and bring it down to the creek for washing. I further suggest you purchase a cradle for this purpose. A pan holds too little soil and is too slow, in addition to which a cradle can be operated from an upright position."

That last part was all it took to make us change our way of doing things. Next day I went to the store and laid out fifty dollars each for a pick and shovel that ordinarily would of cost five, and a hundred dollars for a wheelbarrow that should of cost ten to take the dirt down to the creek, and another hundred and fifty for a cradle, and it ain't nothing but a fancy wooden box! Including the money I paid for supplies it means my race winnings is practickly gone, so Frank better be right with his notion or we're busted.

If you never done no cradling I best tell you how it works. There's the box, around the same size and shape as a baby's cradle and with rockers underneath, and on top of that you got a littler box with holes in the bottom and no top on it which is called a hopper, and it's got a handle on one side which you grab to rock it back and forth. But before you start rocking you fill the hopper with dirt and pour water over it, and as it gets washed through the holes the rocks and such get catched and the rest slops along the bottom of the cradle where there's little wood slats called riffles that snag the nuggets and let the sand and water flow out the front. It's real clever, but it ain't worth no hundred and fifty dollars, not unless you get one with gold already in it.

We started using it next day. Jim dug out a pile of dirt from the hill behind the shelter and I brung it down to the creek in the wheelbarrow and emptied it into the hopper a little at a time. Frank used a pan to slop water over it and while he done that I rocked the cradle. The water and dirt run through all right but never left no nuggets behind. It took awhile to wash that first load and I seen we had to speed things up some if Jim ain't going to lean on his pick most of the day waiting for us to catch up. We traded jobs now and then but it never made much difference; working a cradle is a two-man job. Whichever Frank was doing, digging or hauling or dumping or rocking, he done it slow and made things worse. He says he ain't got the brawn to do muscle work, but I reckon he's disinclined to anyway. It was real annoying, but what can you do with a lunatic?

In the afternoon two men come along and staked the other side of the creek then went away a little while and come back again with their tools.

"Pardon me, gents," says I. "We already panned that side and there warn't no gold."

"You done what?" says one with a ginger beard.

"We already panned along that side twenty yards and more."

The other one puts his hands on his hips and says:

"I suppose you done it before you moved over yonder."

"No, sir, we done it after, then come back here."

"You was still living over that side when you worked this side?"

"Yessir. It never seemed worthwhile to shift the shelter when all you need to do is jump across the creek."

They looked at each other and the ginger one says:

"Don't you know you ain't supposed to occupy more'n one claim at a time?"

"Why not?" says I.

"Why not! It's against the rules, that's why not! You can only work one claim at one time, jackass!"

"Oh. Well we never knowed that rule, honest. I reckon it's just as well we never struck no gold over there."

Ginger turns to the other one and says:

"Do you believe anyone could be so dangblasted stupid?"

"No I don't," says number two. "I bet he ain't half so stupid as he looks. It's all acting, that's what I reckon. Their side's a no-gooder and they was fixing to jump across here and give this side a try. Well we ain't stupid neither. This side's ours now so just you keep your boots over there. We catch you trying to sneak over here and you'll get a shovel across your head, you hear me, boy?"

"I ain't acting."

"The hell you ain't, you little claim jumper. What's your name?"

"Jeff Wilson."

"You try any fancy tricks and we'll give your name to the mining office and they'll run you clear across the Sierras."

"That's if they don't lynch you first," says Ginger.

"Mining office?" says I, and they looked at each other again, then back at me.

"You mean you ain't registered your claim?"

"I never knowed you have to."

"I was wrong," says number two. "He's even stupider than he looks."

"You better get yourself down there right now, boy," says Ginger. "You ain't got no legal claim to that ground you're stood on."

"Thank you, sir," says I. "I'll do it this minute. Where's the mining office located?"

"Sacramento," he says.

"But that's two days' ride away."

"Well you should of done the right thing before you come all this way. You better get, boy."

"Yessir," says I, but I knowed they're trying to fool me because how can you register a claim in Sacramento before you even get out to the diggings and stake one. Says I:

"Is that where you gents registered yours?"

"That's right, boy. We always do the right thing."

"Thank you for setting me straight, sirs."

I saddled up Jupiter real fast and pretended I never seen them both laughing behind their hands. Jim and Frank heard the whole thing and stopped work to tell me what I already guessed, namely that the mining office must be where the store and saloon is, because Ginger and his partner warn't gone all that long between staking the claim and coming back with their tools. I whispered for them to play along and they done it, and I rode off along the creek looking real worried.

When I got to the store I seen a sign outside a tent a little way off and give myself a kick for never paying it no mind before this. It says clear and simple:

MINING OFFICE
Register Your Claim Here

I went in and done it and paid five dollars. On the front page of the register book is the name of our creek, Sandy Creek, which is something else I never knowed, and just above my name is the names of the two jokers, Jake Wells and Patrick Riley. I bet Riley is the one with ginger hair. I got give a sheet of regulations, printed in a rush so the letters is smudged and the readableness just awful, but I ciphered it out on the way back to the claim. Most of it is about only having one claim like the jokers told and not jumping no one else's or taking up more than thirty yards of creek, and down at the bottom it says you ain't allowed to kill no one to get their claim neither.

When they seen me coming Wells and Riley fell over theirselfs laughing, and Riley says:

"What's the matter, boy, lose your way?"

"No, sir," says I, all innocent, "but they must of set up a local mining office just recent. It's downstream with the store and saloon and such."

"Well, ain't that handy," he says, grinning.

"Are you gentlemen Mr. Wells and Mr. Riley?" I ask.

"What if we are?"

"The man in the mining office says can you go see him real quick, sir. He says he put you down for Juniper Creek by mistake, not Sandy Creek, so you ain't truly registered. He's real upset over it."

"Hell," says Riley. "I figured that dangblasted bookkeeper for a fool soon as I laid eyes on him. We better go see what he done to us."

"I'll stay here," says Wells. "I don't trust them over there not to jump our claim while we're gone."

"They can't do nothing while we got our stuff lying around, that's the rules. You hear that, boy? No claim jumping while there's tools lying around."

"Yessir, I hear you, only please hurry. You ain't got no legal right to be where you are."

They both legged it downstream and I unsaddled Jupiter and told Jim and Frank the joke, only Frank never seen the funny side of it, not even when I went over the creek and hid their cradle and pans and shovels under some bushes. When they come back they looked mean and all set to argue with me over the time they wasted, then they seen their tools is all gone.

"Holy Mother!" screeches Riley. "They've stole our stuff! . . ."

"It warn't us, sirs," says I. "It was a little old lady come along and says she's Mr. Riley's mother and she ain't ever seen such untidiness on the ground since little Patrick was crawling around the house creating mess and disruption underfoot."

Riley started across the creek with blood in his eye and I waved the regulation sheet at him.

"Don't do it, Mr. Riley. It says here you can't set foot on another claim without you been invited, and you ain't. I don't want to report you to the mining office for breaking no rules, but I reckon they was drawed up to get kept."

He stopped in midstream with water running into his boots and I say:

"That's a certain way to catch your death of pneumonia, Mr. Riley."

His ginger beard kind of bristled and practickly catched fire he's so angersome, then Frank says:

"I believe you will find your implements beneath yonder bushes."

Riley turned around and they set up their camp without even looking at us the rest of the day. After supper Frank give me a lecture.

"Never antagonize men of inferior intellect," he says. "They will invariably respond in a violent manner."

"Well, I reckon you should know," says I. "You get folks' backs up every time you open your mouth, you and Obadiah both."

"Obadiah? . . . I have told you never to mention that name in my presence," he says, getting all fidgety. "You know it causes me distress, yet you continue to persecute me. Why, *why* do you do it? Am I not your friend? Are my hands not blistered? Have I not toiled alongside you in sweaty partnership?"

"If you reckon the amount of work you done so far is what part-nership is all about then we ain't even barely acquainted," says I. "You can just quit all that heartbreak stuff with me. It don't work no more, and it won't ever do till you work hard as me and Jim . . . I mean Goliath, and don't bother crying none neither; we got all the water we need right handy."

He looked at me for a moment then stood up and walked away into the dark. We never tried to stop him, but after he went Jim says:

"Huck, you a diff'rent man, das a fac', an' I ain't so sure you changin' for de betterment."

"I ain't in no mood for riddles," says I, real snippy.

"Den I reckon to tell it simple. You gettin' de hard shell aroun' you like a turtle, an' I means de snappin' kind. You ain't de man I knowed when we's on de raft las' year, not nohow."

"I reckon a body can change in a year. There ain't no law against it."

"Dere's changes an' changes, Huck. You actin' mighty tough jest recent."

"Well, so have you. You even held a rifle to my own Pap's head awhile back. What's that if it ain't acting tough?"

"I ain't denyin' I done it, but I come over wid pure shame later on jest recollectin' what I done. I never had de right, not wid yo' Pap de way he be. He ain't a regular man no mo', if'n he ever was after hittin' de bottle all dem years back. Now he jest be a sad pathetical man like Frank'n'Obadiah, only not so smart talkin'. I shoulder jest let him be. All dat wid de rifle never fixed nothin'. My ol' woman an' de chillern ain't goin' to come back on accounter what I done. You keep up de backtalkin' wid Frank an' one day you goin' to say some-thin' you wished you never had of. I reckon he went off to where dey sellin' liquor, an if'n he don' come home drunk an' turn hisself into dat crazy brother by mornin' you kin whomp me wid de shovel. I knows we figured on givin' him whiskey if'n Frank wore out de welcome, but dat man drunk a whole river of de stuff in his life an' one more drop kin maybe kill him. Lessen we wants to take de blame for it we got to keep him happy an' sober."

"Keep him happy? I recollect you told him he ain't nothing but a millstone around our necks just a little while back."

"I knows it, an' I regrets it even if'n he needed de tellin' den on accounter bein' uppity wid us, but he been mighty polite lately an' don' need no tonguewhippin' like you give him jest now."

I stuck out my lip so he'll see I ain't happy to get criticalized that way, but only for show. Deep down I knowed he's right. I seen the same things in myself he's talking about, but it ain't a situation you can set on the table and work out, too complexified I reckon, so I just say:

"He ain't got no money for whiskey."

"Huck, you knows dere's always someone das free wid money dat'll buy a sad face' man a drink. Whyn't you go fetch him back befo' it happen?"

"I ain't his nursemaid. He's three times older'n me," says I, getting peevish out of guilt. "And you ain't my nursemaid neither."

He give me a long look that spoke books, as they say, then he says:

"How come you took de risk on rescuin' de bulldog das out to get you hanged an' you don' even wanter get on yo' feet for de saker Frank das in needer lookin' after? Dat don' make no kinder sense, Huck."

It's a good question but I ain't got no answer. Like Jim says, all I got to do is go fetch him back and apologize, but I never done it, I don't know why. Says I:

"If you don't want him to get drunk you can go fetch him yourself."

"I'se wastin' my time conversifyin' wid you," says Jim. "Dere ain't a body alive das closer'n you to me, Huck, an' I jest don' like to see you gettin' change for de worse, das all. I ain't about to say no mo' on it."

And he walked off a little way and sat and smoked his pipe. Seeing him there by the creek with his back to me give me the double guilts and I went over and says:

"Jim, mind the store while I go get Frank."

"I reckon I ain't goin' nowheres," he says.

I legged it downstream to catch up but never seen Frank all the way to the saloon, so he must of legged it pretty fast himself to get here ahead of me. There's noise by the bucket coming out of the big tent and I never wanted to go inside, but if I go back without Frank, Jim won't believe I done my best, so I pulled open the flap and slid inside. The floor ain't nothing but dirt with sawdust sprinkled around to soak up the puke and there's a lamp or three hung from the long ridgepole. Down one side there's a plank bar with bottles and barrels and jugs and bartenders taking gold dust off miners, who was all in high spirits, shouting and jawing and cackling like birds gathered in a tree at dusk. I pushed through the drinkers looking for Frank, but he warn't there. I ask the bartenders if they seen a little baldy man with yeller teeth but they never, so I reckon Frank must of got sidetracked on his way here, or was maybe taking a leak behind a tree when I run past. I went outside again where you can breathe the air without getting drunk and waited, but he never showed. I waited and waited; even a snail would of got here by now.

Then I see there's a new tent over yonder that warn't there even this afternoon when I come in to register the claim, and a man come out of it buckling his belt and says over his shoulder:

"Next time I reckon I'll waste my gold at a saloon."

"I reckon you already went," says a woman's voice, so it's a whore's tent and the customer ain't satisfied. Maybe Frank went in there while I was in the saloon, or he seen me waiting outside and snuck in to hide. Well, I had to know, so I marched over and give a knock on the tent pole and the woman hollers:

"Don't stand on ceremony, come on in!"

I done it, and she's real big, not small big like Hepzibah, just the biggest, fattest woman I ever seen, about the size of a cotton bale but maybe heavier. She says:

"Are you a midget or lookin' for your Pap?"

"My Uncle Frank, ma'am. He's kind of skinny with a baldy head and yeller teeth and talks educated."

"I ain't seen him. I would of remembered someone booklearned. Them around here is ignorant as pigs, and smellier too."

"Yes, ma'am. Sorry to take up your time, ma'am."

"If you find him tell him Bella only costs a pinch of dust."

"Yes, ma'am, I'll tell him directly I find him."

There warn't no use in waiting around no more so I lit out for the claim, and when I got back there's Frank snoring in the shelter. Jim says:

"He come back jest after you lef', Huck. 'Pears to me he jest wandered aroun' de trees some den got tired an' come back."

"There," says I, "I never even should of bothered."

"Maybe so," says Jim, but I seen he's glad I done it anyway, and I reckon that's worth all the legging I done that night. I smoked my pipe awhile with him to show we're friends again and then we done the same as Frank.

Matters got considerable worsened with Riley and Wells. They panned and cradled the same stretch we already done and when they never seen a trace of color they got mad. To cover up the way they felt about things they took to poking fun at us. Riley says:

"What the dangblast are you tearing down the hill for? Near water's where you find gold, not halfway to heaven."

"We reckon different, Mr. Riley. A claim don't just run along the creek bed, it runs back away from it too, so the hill's part of it."

"Maybe so, but you ain't going to find no gold there. Only a jack-ass would waste his time that way."

"What kind of jackass would that be, Mr. Riley, the kind that does a thing nobody else figured out on account of he's got fresh ideas, or the kind that washes the same stretch of creek twice?"

"Boy," he says, "one day you and me'll meet up when you ain't stood on your claim, and when it happens I aim to lift you by the ears."

"That's a right kindly offer, Mr. Riley, but folks tell me my flaps already stick out a mite too far. Maybe you can find a real jackass to do it to, seeing as they got plenty of ear to grab hold of, but don't go reaching for no looking glass by mistake."

I reckon he would of splashed across the creek and killed me if Jim hadn't of come down and took over the cradle so I can't sass Riley no more, and he give me a lecture about it later on. But I never wanted to quit. It's only fair for me to sass them in return for the way they keep on insulting us. I figure both of us done it for the same reason, namely to hide the frustrativeness of finding no gold. Jim and me started wondering if Frank had such a good idea after all, but Frank reckons we should let ourselfs get guided by his wisdom and knowledgment. "The moth does not question the ways of the eagle," is how he puts it. So we kept on, and one night he says to us:

"I have an announcement to make."

"Well don't let it get stale," says I.

"Before I reveal my news I must warn you not to make any noise."

"What kinder noise?" says Jim.

"Cries of jubilation and the like," says Frank, real smug. "We have found gold."

"Who has?" I ask.

"To be precise, *I* have, this very afternoon."

"Where?" says I, disbelieving it.

"Why, in the cradle, where else?"

"But you never told us. . . ."

"Of course not. I had no wish to alert our neighbors across the water. They already hate us because of your senseless taunting. If they learn that we have made a strike their jealousy will overcome such control as they have thus far shown and we will certainly be murdered in our sleep."

"They ain't no murderers, just idiots," says I. "And where's this gold?"

He took out his handkerchief and opened it, and in the firelight we seen five lumpy little pebbles the size of lemon seeds, only yeller.

"Are you sure?" says I.

"Positive."

I rubbed one against my teeth like I heard is a good test, and sure enough it feels smooth.

"Frank," says I, "you ain't wrong."

"No exultation, please," he says, looking across at Wells and Riley's fire. "I found them in the last load to be washed before dark, so the chances are excellent that tomorrow we will wash out a bonanza if we dig from the same spot we finished at today. But we must remain secretive. I do not trust any of the yokels in these diggings."

"Frank," says I, taking off my hat to him, "if that's how you want it I reckon we owe you the favor of doing it out of gratefulness for the fact you figured out the whole thing and was the first to find nuggets. Me and Goliath won't say nothing to no one."

"It de smartes' way," says Jim, staring at the gold. "My, my, don't it shine. . . ."

Come morning it's the way Frank says, with gold in the very first load we washed and almost every load that come after. Whichever of us that's working the cradle took the nuggets out from the riffle slats without giving no sign Wells and Riley can pick up on, just slipping them casual into our pockets, and at the end of the day we got a heaped handful of nuggets and grains. Frank reckons he should keep it in his handkerchief seeing as it's all because of him, but he's a lunatic still and Jim and me figured the safest thing is to keep it hid in the shelter. Frank got peeved but done what we wanted when we told him he can keep them first five nuggets in his pocket for a good luck charm.

For five more days we dug and washed and found about the same each time. Riley and Wells kept on laughing at us, but by now they was all through with washing creek gravel and started digging a hole instead after they heard about a man over on Juniper Creek that done it and found a whole bushel of nuggets. They dug down fifteen feet and more but still never found nothing, and the madder they got about it the more they laughed at us.

"I never seen such a team before," says Wells. "Just look at you, a boy and a nigger and a candy-ass greenhorn. Why don't you just give up and go home? You ain't going to find nothing."

"I reckon our luck's no badder than yours, Mr. Wells," says I. "I ain't seen you jumping for joy over no strike."

"Hole mining," he says. "That's the answer, none of that hill grubbing like you morons are doing. We'll hit pay dirt anytime now, you can bet on it."

"I ain't a betting man," says I.

"You ain't even a man," he sneers.

Well, you can take just so much from a sap-head, then comes a time you got to fight back. It ain't no use sassing them; they got used to it and nowadays just ignore any smart lip I give them, so I give the problem considerable brain squeezing and come up with the answer. I never told Jim and Frank about it because it means I got to borrow a little of our gold, just a nugget or three. I snitched them next time I warn't in eye-reach of no one and when night come and everyone was asleep I snuck across the creek and pushed one of the nuggets into the pile of dirt they dug up from their hole and dumped over by the cradle ready for washing next day.

It worked perfect. Around midmorning Riley give a whoop and held up the nugget and danced around the cradle. Wells heard the ruckus and hauled himself up the windlass rope from down in the hole, and when he got showed the nugget him and Riley danced around together till they fell in the creek, then Riley holds up the nugget and says:

"See that, boy? That's what you ain't ever going to dig out! If you wasn't so idiot-headed you'd dig a hole same as us and maybe get rich!"

"I'm real happy for you, Mr. Riley," says I, "but I reckon it's a mighty small nugget to get excited over."

"It's only the first," he says. "The first of a haul like no one else found ever!"

"I surely hope so," says I.

"Don't you go acting all friendly with us, Wilson," says Wells. "You're green with envy, I can see it plain as day."

"No, sir, that's just the grass we been eating lately on account of we can't afford no proper food."

"Boy, before you and them others is through you'll look back on grass eating as the best time in your life."

After they finished laughing they went back to work and beavered away till sundown. They never found no more seeing as I only put the one nugget in their pile, but it never stopped them going downstream to the saloon to celebrate after dark, and maybe to visit Bella. While they was gone I went over and stuck another little nugget in their fresh dirt pile same as before, only this time Jim seen me and says:

"What you doin' over dere, Huck? Dey open yo' head wid a shovel if'n dey catches you messin' wid de claim."

"I warn't doing nothing, Jim, honest, just touched their pile for luck."

"We don' need no luck, you knows dat. We gettin' perty rich now."

"Well, I done it anyhow."

Next day it's the same thing over again when they found the nugget, and again the day after that when I hid the third one in their dirt. They was strutting around like roosters now and talking big and never even looked our way seeing as we ain't nothing but poor miners, not rich as kings like them. That night I done the next part of the trick. A few days back I went for fresh supplies and changed a little of our gold at the mining office for coin money, and now I stuck a twenty-dollar gold eagle in their pile like I done before with nuggets, and never slept much for thinking on how their faces is going to look in the morning when they find it.

I give myself the cradle job deliberate so's I can be close and worked with one eye on Riley, rocking hard as he can and checking the riffles for new nuggets, only the gold eagle is too big to go through the holes in the bottom of the hopper so that's where he found it after the dirt got washed away. I seen his jaw drop when he picked it up and he stared and stared, then I see he's looking over at me suspicious-like, and I say:

"Find another nugget, Mr. Riley? My, but that's a big 'un all right. . . . Why, hold hard, Mr. Riley, I believe you got a coin there! They don't get made underground by nature as a rule so I reckon you must of hit buried treasure! Ain't it exciting! I never knowed pirates come this far inland to bury their loot! Is it just the one?"

He give a nod, kind of confused, and put it in his pocket and kept on washing the rest of the dirt, but all through the day he never had that eager look on his face like before.

That night I pushed something else into their pile, and it got found on schedule next morning. Says I:

"What is it, Mr. Riley, more treasure?"

"No," he says, and wipes dirt off the piece of paper and unfolds it and reads what I writ, namely:

We never minded you taking them three pesky little nuggets, but it ain't right when you steal our treasure money too, so put it right back where you found it or your family and friends will get kidnapped and their heads sawed off with blunt cutlasses.

signed,
THE PIRATES

He must of read it right quick because he flung it down and come charging across the creek at me. I let the cradle do its own rocking and headed for the trees, cowardish but smart I reckon. He chased and chased but he never catched me, which is why I'm alive to tell the tale, and I never showed my face at the claim all the rest of that day. When I figured he's had enough time to cool down I went back, and both Wells and Riley was gone, along with their tent and tools.

"Dey jest packed up an' lef'," says Jim. "Dey was both lookin' real sheepish 'bout somethin', but dey never tol' what, jest upped an' lef'."

"I daresay you are somehow the cause," says Frank, looking at me down his nose, but I'm all wide-eyed innocence and confusement.

"It can't be on account of me, Frank. I ain't done nothing. Mr. Riley just went mad and chased me for no good reason as I can see.

Proberly he's one of them lunatics that only cuts loose and foams at the mouth occasional, not full time."

Next day some men come along and took over the claim. They done the same as us and mined the hillside and started pulling nuggets out of their cradle a couple of days later, so if Wells and Riley had of done it too and not wasted their time laughing at us they would of ended up rich, which is what they call a moral.

Golden Harvest—Rough Justice—A Roof Overhead—The

Grim Reaper—A Friendship Renewed—Goodbye, Diggings

We mined on and practickly dug away the hill behind the shelter. The gold slacked off some for awhile and we figured our lucky streak run out, but then we hit another pocket and got as much as we done before.

Then fall come down around us and the air turned chilly. When we woke up in the morning there's mist in the trees and our bodies was full of aches, so Jim reckons it's time to build a cabin if we aim to stay here and keep mining. We chopped down trees and worked hard laying out a log cabin like Pap's back in Missouri, and the walls got raised up one log higher every day. While we worked the weather got colder and the shelter warn't good enough no more, so we got ourselfs a tent to live in till the cabin is ready. Some days it rained down hard and we stayed in the tent, keeping dry. Jim and me smoked and yarned the time away and Frank weighed up the gold we got so far. He counted up little rows of numbers on a sheet and figures we own around sixteen thousand dollars' worth! Nowadays it's all kept in little bags stashed in a special hole in the tent floor that's covered by a hunk of wood with dirt sprinkled on top. There warn't no banks around so all the miners kept ahold of their gold like we done or else went down to San Francisco to spend it all on a wing-ding. It never worried us to keep it stashed on account of everyone hereabouts is honest and no one got robbed or murdered, at least not till October.

I rode to the store for supplies and seen a big crowd outside the saloon, which has got turned into a two-story wood building just recent and called the El Dorado. There's hundreds all gathered around a man without no hat and blood on his face. When I ask someone what happened I got told the bloodied man was catched after murdering his partner, and they rushed him into the mining office and give him a trial, three minutes, and judged him guilty and now he's got to get hanged. They marched him over to a tree and flung a rope over a bough and put the noose around his neck, then the man that runs the mining office got up on a box and stuck his arms out for quiet, which was a considerable time coming because the crowd is so excited and gingered up waiting for the lynching.

"Men," he says, "we are from all walks of life! We came by land and sea from near and far, but wherever we came from there were laws to uphold the two things that make this nation great: democracy and justice! We have democratically judged this man guilty and now, in the absence of any official law enforcement agency, we are going to see justice done!"

They give a roar that shows they're all behind him, and he turns to the murderer and says:

"Prisoner, do you have any last words?"

"I was drunk, . . ." he sobs. "I never meant to do it. . . . He was my partner. . . ."

"Anything else? Make up your mind, it's starting to rain."

The murderer looks up at the sky all dark and gray and feels the drops of rain coming down on his face and closes his eyes.

"Well?" says the mining officer, getting impatient.

"I reckon not, . . ." he snuffles, and brung his gaze down from the clouds and looked straight across at me where I'm sat on Jupiter with a clear view over all them hats. It's Jesse. He reckernized me the exact same time I done the same to him, and his eyes opened wide and he points at me and screams:

"It's him! . . . He's a murderer! Catch him quick!"

All them hats turned into faces when everyone looked around to see who he's pointing at, but all they seen is a boy on a horse, which ain't how you generally picture a murderer. Someone yells:

"He's goin' crazy! String him up while he's still in his right mind!"

"Listen to me! . . ." squeals Jesse. "It's him! . . . He's a wanted man! It's Huck . . ."

But he never finished. They hauled on the rope and Jesse went up in the air with his boots kicking hard and his eyes bugging out. He swung and jerked and danced in the air maybe two minutes, awful long minutes, with his face turning blue and his tongue stuck out all thick and purple like a buffalo's. Then he quit kicking and just hung there with his rained-on hair hanging in his eyes, still open and staring directly at me. It give me the shivers to see. The end of the rope got tied around the tree trunk so he'll hang there awhile to make an example to recollect if you ever get the urge to do murder, and the crowd got bored with looking at a dead man and drifted away under cover from the rain, mostly into the saloon. There ain't nothing like a hanging to give a body a thirst, they say. I got down off Jupiter and went over to the mining officer.

"Pardon me, sir," says I. "Was he from hereabouts?"

"No, son," says he. "Him and his partner had a claim up on Little Deer Creek. He did the murder two days back and was stupid enough to stay around the camps when he should of run for the mountains or Frisco. Two men from Little Deer in here for supplies spotted him and made an arrest. It's a damn shame it had to happen. Up till now it's been mighty law-abiding right across the diggings. They say him and his partner argued over a bottle of whiskey. Some men are born fools."

He looked up past Jesse to the skies all heavy with rain then stamped off through the mud to the saloon. It's a fair guess that the partner which got murdered is Bob, so I reckon they must of quit keeping company with the bulldog after he give me a chance to slide away back behind the Sierras. Well, they ain't going to do me no harm now. I watched Jesse's boots swing back and forth slow in the wind with raindrops falling off his toecaps and heels, then I got my supplies and went back to the claim. It ain't no surprise to me that Jesse done what he done. If ever a man wanted to do hurt to someone it's him, so I never shed no tears, and when I told Jim he feels the same.

We kept working steady on the cabin and the walls got higher day by day, only the rain slowed us some. We got the ridgepole up and fitted snug with a little help off the men from the claim across the creek in return for helping them build a cabin too. There's plenty more doing the same all over now that winter's coming. When the roof is done we aim to fix up a stable for the horses so they got a roof over their heads and don't have to stand under the trees for shelter.

We was real proud of what we done so far, but Frank got a chill and had to stay in the tent while we raised up the roof beams, working fast as we can so Frank can have someplace warm to rest up in and get his strength back.

We never had no proper shingles so we bought planks brung up-river from Sacramento and used them, with canvas stretched over the top and tarred for rainproofing. We never had no time nor bricks for a fireplace but got a stove from the store that done just fine for warming the place and a bed too, and we figured Frank has got to get better tucked up snug inside. But he never. He started to cough, and the coughing got worse and he brung up yeller stuff, real thick, then brown, and Jim says in a whisper:

"He ain't goin' to get no better, Huck, I kin feel it. My own Ma dieder lung fever de same way."

"Maybe if we fetched in a doctor. . . ."

"Dere ain't no doc, Huck, lessen it be some horse doc callin' his-self de genuine kin'. Dere ain't nothin' we kin do 'cept keep him warm an' fed I reckon."

We kept the stove roaring hot and fed him soup and broth seeing as he ain't got the strength no more to chew on nothing solid. His face was red and sweaty and he got skinnier every time we looked, but he never complained like you would of expected Frank to do. And here's a strange thing; we seen he ain't always Frank no more by the way he talks, sometimes like Obadiah even if he ain't had no liquor to make the change, and that's when we knowed he's fixing to die. On Thanksgiving the men from the other claim invited us over to celebrate with a turkey and drinking in their cabin which they just finished, but Jim says he'll stay with Frank. I never et my fill and never got drunk neither, and left early which they was un-derstanding about. I got Frank a book of empty paper and some pens and ink for a present to distractify him from the pain he's in, and when I handed it all over he says:

"Is it Christmas already as I speak?"

"Well, near enough, Obadiah," says I, reckernizing his way of talking.

"But I have no present for you, not one," he says, and coughed awhile. "You have done me proud without thought for cost notwithstanding. I thank you profusely with an abundance of plenitude. I must put this to some good use. . . ."

"You could write a letter, if you got folks back east I mean."

"There is no one, only Frank and myself, and I do not know his whereabouts, nor indeed his location."

"I reckon Frank would of drawed another invention," says I.

"Perchance haply so, but I am no mean hand at sketching myself."

"If you like you can do a picture of me. I ain't never been drawed."

It ain't exactly true, seeing as I got my face on them wanted posters, but Frank and Obadiah don't even know who me and Jim truly are, so I ain't about to get catched out on the lie.

"An excellent idea," he says. "Sit where I can see you."

I got him propped up so's he can rest the book on his knees and sat myself on a barrel because we ain't got no chairs yet and he got started. Jim sat quiet and smoked and I stayed still as I can, just listening to the rain hammer down hard on the roof and Obadiah breathing in and out real fast, like his chest has only got room for a cupful of air. There warn't no other sounds, just him and the rain and the fire crackling soft in the stove. I sat there still as a stump with my eyes on him but he never once looked at me, which is a peculiar way to do a body's picture, but I never mentioned it and kind of drifted off inside my head.

A year ago Jim and me was in Pap's cabin back home, listening to the stove and feeling glad we ain't out in the snow. Now we're two thousand mile away in another cabin and I'm a wanted man with my share of sixteen thousand dollars buried under the floor and getting my picture drawed by two men in the same person that ain't got much longer to live. I run over all that happened in the past year piece by piece right up till now, just like a storybook, and it's hard to figure how all of it happened to me, one little piece of the story stuck onto the next and the next, getting more and more complexified along the way. When I done my best to make sense of it the only fact I'm certain sure of is the story ain't ended yet. I would of give anything if I could just close up the book and rest easy awhile till I got everything figured out, then I can open it again and go on, but it ain't possible. Them pages keep on getting turned anyhow.

Finally Obadiah says:

"It is finished to completion."

I got off the barrel, my legs and back considerable stiffened by now from all that stillness, and he showed me what he done. It ain't a picture of me at all, just some kind of contraption with rods and levers like Frank was forever drawing. Says I:

"It's a real fine likeness. I'd be proud if you put your name on it for me."

"My name? Yes, the patent office will require it. This design will not fall into unscrupulous hands that may steal its originality of concept for their own enrichment at my expense. That has happened many times before without number."

I can't figure if he's Frank or Obadiah, but he warn't bothered none himself so it ain't important. He says:

"This will make my fortune. Nothing resembling its likeness has ever been seen in the civilized world."

"I reckon you're right," says I, "but I ain't exactly sure which part is which. Maybe you could explanate it for me."

"Certainly," he says. "You know, do you not, that my previous profession was that of undertaker?"

"You told me a long time back."

"Yes, indeed, and that I am also an inventor of devices of a mechanical nature?"

"I recollect that too," says I.

"Well then, this before you is the perfect blending of these two influences."

"It is? I mean, sure it is, only what is it?"

He lifts his chin kind of proud and says:

"It is the very first valve-operated air-pressure device for coffin descent."

"That's what I figured," says I.

"Have you ever witnessed a funeral, young Jeff?"

"I seen a couple or three."

"And how was the deceased lowered to eternal rest on these sad occasions?"

"The usual way, with ropes."

"Exactly. Since time immemorial and possibly longer man has lowered his dear departed by means of muscle and sinew. Now, for the first time in history science will come to our aid. Do you see this metal flask? It is a chamber for the containment of air at high pressure, and to it are affixed these hollow metal rods which will stand upright in the four corners of the open grave. A platform between them will support the coffin at ground level, its position maintained by air pressure within the rods and chamber. These will have been filled with air from a detachable set of bellows before the mourners arrive at the graveside. When the service has been concluded this lever is pulled, releasing air slowly from the chamber through a hole of mere pinprick dimensions, thus ensuring a steady descent of the coffin platform. The rods are then withdrawn for further use with the chamber."

All that talk was too much for him and he coughed and spit awhile, then wants to know what I think.

"I reckon it's the cleverest thing I ever seen. Jim, come and see what Mr. Jennings done."

He come over and I told how it works and he declared it's the fanciest machine he ever seen a drawing of, then Obadiah done a whole string of coughs and had to lie back down, and when his chest let him he says:

"Jeff, you will make sure my design is shown to important people, will you not?"

"I surely will. First chance I get I'll send it to the president, and when dead folks all over the country is getting lowered into their graves with your contraption I bet they put up a statue in Washington so the whole world knows who invented it."

He fell asleep after that, tired out I guess, and he laid there with his breath rasping and bubbling and the sweat pouring off him. It ain't respectful to say it, I know, but he smelled like a dead dog, and Jim and me had to step outside once in awhile to get a sniff of fresh air. We slept on and off, catnapping, and got woke by Obadiah calling out.

"Mother, . . ." he calls, "are you there? . . ."

I went over and he looks at me and says:

"Mother? . . ."

"Well . . . all right," says I.

"The front window needs fixing, I fear," he wheezes. "I can hear it rattling . . . or is someone knocking? . . ."

"There ain't no one there, only the wind. I'll fix it directly."

"One thing more . . ." he says.

"What might that be?" says I, but he never told, just give a sigh and closed his eyes. After awhile I got up bravery and touched him on the forehead where he's got this vein that kind of throbs, only it ain't throbbing now. Jim says:

"He ain't here no mo', Huck."

You can't sleep with a dead man in the room so we used up the rest of the night stitching him in a blanket, and come the dawn Jim dug a grave away in the trees. We never had no air-pressure machine so Jim lifted him down without no help from science and we both done the spadework burying him. Jim says:

"Dere ain't no preacher, Huck. You reckon you kin say de words?"

"I'll give it a try," says I, and cleared my throat some.

"This here is Obadiah or Frank, one or other of 'em or maybe both. It don't hardly matter which, only that they're dead with just us to be sorry over it. But I reckon two friends that's sad is better than nothing. Amen."

We planted a cross too. It seemed like the right thing to do.

The weeks run by swift after that but we never counted them up on no calendar. No one done much mining on account of the weather. It never snowed or nothing, but outdoors work ain't easy in pouring rain and mist and cold. Jim and me never felt no obligation to do more toiling than we felt inclined to, which ain't much, except when the sky fined up every few days. Even then all we done was finish off the stable. There ain't nothing like bags of gold hid under the floor to make you feel lazified and easy. Then come a day just before Christmas when there's a knocking on the door and it's one of them from the claim across the creek.

"I just come from the store," he says. "There's a feller there asking after you."

"After me?" says I.

"Says he's looking for a boy called Jeff and a nigger."

"Did he give his name?"

"He never offered it and I never asked."

"Well how does he look?"

"Like anyone else I reckon. I told him where you're located so he'll likely be along anytime. He kin of yours?"

"Proberly so," says I. "Thank you kindly."

"Merry Christmas," he says, and squelched away through the mud.

Jim heard it all and says:

"What you reckon, Huck, de bulldog?"

"It's got to be. There ain't no one else looking for us."

"We goin' to run or fight?"

"Dangblast it, why don't he just go home or fall off his horse and break his head?"

"He ain't about to do nothin' you wants him to, Huck. Lessen you aim to kill him we got to run."

I ain't no killer, so we got all our totables together in a rush and I primed my Hawken just in case Bulldog is in a fighting mood. Jim dug up the gold and I went out to saddle the horses, only I never got the job finished. There's a heavy mist hiding everything except for a few trees close by, and I heard a horse splashing across the creek and heading up the slope toward the cabin. Then I seen him. I can't tell if it's the bulldog or not, but I ain't taking no chances. I put the saddle I got in my hands down gentle so he never heard and picked up the Hawken which I brung outside with me. He got down off his horse and knocked on the cabin door, and I snuck up behind him and put the gun to my shoulder and say:

"Don't you move, Bulldog. I got my rifle aimed square at you."

He never turned, just says:

"I been called a bobcat and a squawman and a liar, but I ain't ever been called a bulldog before."

He ain't wearing his buckskins no more and he's sawed his Injun braids off, but I reckernized his voice even from behind.

"Thaddeus? . . ."

"I been called that too. Reckon I can turn around now?"

The door opened real quick and Jim's stood there with a hatchet in his hand and a surprised look on his face.

"Afternoon, Jim," says Thaddeus. "You two must be fixing to start a war hereabouts."

I put down my rifle and we shook hands and danced around in

the mud awhile, then I brung the saddles back inside and stabled Thaddeus's horse. He set a bottle of whiskey on the table and me and Jim cooked up a meal and the cabin never knowed a minute's quiet all the rest of the day and halfway into the night. I told Thaddeus everything that happened since I busted out of Fort Kearney, only I left out the part about Pap and Morg. When I finished he told how the Naismith train suffered terrible across the desert and was whittled down considerable by cholera too, which killed Colonel Naismith and plenty more. Thaddeus got elected leader and brung all them that was left across the Sierras and into California safe.

"When we got to Sacramento the train split up in just one day," he says. "Some went north and some went south to the diggin's down along the San Joaquin and Stanislaus. I figured I may as well turn my hand to mining myself and went up around the Yuba. Had a peck of luck too, after I tried three different claims, then I got into argument with my partners and seen it's time I moved on. I ain't never wanted no big house or nothin', just so's I got enough not to die like a dog. So I headed south and got a notion to ask after you two along the way seeing as I ain't in no hurry. I was mighty curious to see if you come all the way to California like you wanted. I must of asked around a thousand times if anyone seen you, but no one had, only I ain't the only one that's been asking. Three times along the Feather River I got told someone else is lookin' for you, and I reckon it's got to be your bulldog friend. Seems to me he ain't the kind to give up easy. He's moving north to south goin' through all the diggin's with a fine-tooth comb. If I found you just by askin' around the general store you can bet he won't have no trouble locating your door same as I done. You boys best be figuring on whether to fight or run I reckon."

That's two times in one day I got handed the same choice, and like it or not we got to decide, only this time there ain't no panic. Says I:

"We got to run. I ain't about to shoot Bulldog even if he's begging for it, only I just know he'll follow on wherever we go. I'm wanted clear across the country now and he's got the law on his side."

"There's only one answer," says Thaddeus. "You got to leave the country. Outside of America you ain't done no crimes and there ain't nothin' Bulldog could do even if he catched you up."

"It's a good plan I guess, only where? Mexico maybe?"

"Too close and too hot," he says. "Also they got terrible food down there that don't give your bowels no peace. You got to plan bigger'n that if you aim to get free of persecution. How much gold you got, if it ain't a personal question?"

"Around sixteen thousand dollars, we figure."

"Well you got to pardon me for never dusting the floor with my beard. I never knowed I'm in the company of rich men. You boys has had better luck than most. I reckon not one in a thousand has struck it rich, so you can be gratified at what you got even if the rest of the news is bad. Why, with that kind of money you can go anywhere in the whole wide world and live like kings if you got a mind to. All you need to do is go to Frisco and pay your passage on a ship to any place that takes your fancy. There ain't no problem to it."

"Well all right, but where?"

He give it some hard thinking, then he says:

"Boys, the answer has come to me as if from above. I met a sailor up on the Yuba and he worked on whalers before he jumped ship in Frisco. He told me the beautifulest place he ever seen is one of them islands out in the middle of the Pacific by name of Oahu. He says the sun shines all year and them brown-skinned native women is real friendly, and all you got to do when you're hungry is climb a tree and get yourself one of them big nuts to eat, which comes provided with a drink inside of it too, so when you drunk the drink you kind of eat the bottle. A body can't ask for no more'n that I reckon."

"Has dey got sher'ffs an' such?" asks Jim.

"Not by what this sailor told. He says there's a town called Honnylulu that's wide open. That's what he called it, wide open, but you don't have to live in no town if you ain't got a mind to. You can have a grass shack right by the shore and get lullabyed to sleep by the waves."

It sounded mighty fine to me, and Jim agreed. Says I:

"Why don't you come too, Thaddeus? You ain't never been on no sea trip, same as us, so it'll be real adventuresome."

"Not me," he says. "I got no urge for it. I figure there's still room enough here to find me a quiet spot without I got to cross no ocean. What I aim to do is go south away from the cold and see that valley full of tall trees I told you about."

"You reckoned they was the tallest in the world."

"Well I warn't stretchin' the facts none, I can tell you. The only thing taller than them trees is the sky. When I see them one more time I'm headin' for a piece of country I can get some quiet in, someplace between here and Texas, I ain't exactly sure whereabouts yet. It's got to be someplace real lonesome so's I don't get no disturbance from no one. I seen enough of people in my time to know most of 'em ain't worth a pinch of dog turd. You two ain't included in that, but most is, and now we got the rest of our lives figured out neat there ain't nothin' I want more'n to sleep. I come a long ways today."

Thaddeus got the bed seeing as he's our guest. We was all considerable drunk by then. Thaddeus give out more words today than he give all the way from St. Joe to Fort Kearney, which is the proof that liquor loosens tongues. We bedded down but I'm too drunk and excited to sleep, with all kinds of pictures in my head keeping my eyes wide, big oceans and ships and islands with bottlenuts in the trees and me and Jim in a grass shack by the sea, fishing and smoking the way we like to do. It's a shame we got to leave our cabin after all the work we put into it, but with the bulldog sniffing closer day by day we got to move, and San Francisco is where it all begins. Says I in a whisper:

"Thaddeus, are you asleep?"

"Nope," he says. "I'm in the saddle still. Danged if I can get used to this here bed. Care to trade for some floor? I'd be a sight more comfortable down there."

We traded over and I say:

"Thaddeus, what happened to Grace after Sacramento?"

"I ain't sure. I seen her just one time down by the river lookin' at them ships tied up there, but after that she never showed again. You sweet on her still?"

"I warn't ever sweet on her, just grateful is all. She's the one that got me free that time and I hope she ain't fell on no hard times."

"Women like her, they're like cats. You drop 'em in any kind of place without a nickel or a friend and they'll land feet first. You ain't got no need to worry, not for a gal that's got her looks. She's likely married off by now to some miner that made a strike."

"You reckon she'd marry a rich man?"

"It's a sure bet. It ain't just on account of she's pretty, it's a need she's got inside of her to be belle of the ball. A need like that's just got to be satisfied, and the only way to do it is marry money. I ain't sure where that gal come from, but I got a strong hunch she aims to put it behind her. You can't see no valley floor from the mountain-top, which is where she aims to be. If I was you I'd put her out of my mind."

"She ain't in my mind, honest."

"No? Well it must of been Jim that wanted to know what become of her. I swear he sounded just like you. Now let a man rest."

He started in to snore pretty soon after and I followed on and dreamed the night away, bad dreams about the bulldog sinking his teeth in my leg and Pap groveling on the ground saying he never wanted to kill no one, but he'll surely give it a try next time he sees me or else see ghosts as long as I'm alive to put him in mind of what he done.

It was reliefsome to get shook awake next morning. We never wasted no time, just had a bite to eat and saddled up the horses and loaded the saddlebags with our gold and put our supplies in sacks. Then I went over to the other claim and give my goodbyes to the men there. One of them says:

"But why leave now? There's bound to be more gold on your claim."

"We ain't felt the same about it since Mr. Jennings died. I reckon we'll head north and try the Feather River or the Yuba. We can't take the wheelbarrow or cradle so you're welcome to them, and the cabin too if you got a mind to separate and have two claims between you."

"That's right generous," he says, and the others agreed and never let me go till they give me a good few ounces of gold for payment. They promised they'd tend Obadiah's grave too. I never liked to lie to them that way, but if the bulldog asks them where we went they'll lay a false trail for us without even knowing it.

After a final goodbye I went back to our cabin. Jim and Thaddeus buried our picks and shovels and pans, which we would of took with us if we was truly headed for the northern diggings, then we mounted up and rode away. We lived three months and more on that claim and it give me the miseries to leave, but a wanted man ain't got no choice. We got all the gold we needed and there's more adventure to come, so I never looked back. It would of been wasted time anyway on account of the mist, real thick again the way it is most mornings nowadays. We rode slow but steady along the creek to where it joins the river and then along to the store and saloon, which has got such a collection of wood buildings roundabout they finally called it a town, Forty-Rod by name, the kind of whiskey they mostly drink hereabouts. Thaddeus says whenever a place gets populated and permanent enough to get made into a town and give a name it's time to move on, definite.

✦ 30 ✦

---

*Downriver—Merry Christmas—A Close Shave—Fond
Farewells—The Price of Pies—Welcome to San Francisco*

We reached the lower diggings
along the American on Christmas Day. There warn't no mining getting done at all, just celebrating, which means a whole heap of drinking. There was drunks everywhere you looked, rolling around in the
mud and loving it. Music got played and men stood around big fires
singing till their throats was sore, which give them a reason for drinking more till they fell down in the mud along with the rest. I seen a piss
pot get emptied out of a cabin, just throwed straight out the door all
over a drunk that's sat there, but it warn't deliberate.

We seen our first Chinaman too, little and brown-skinned, not
yeller like they say, and he's got baggy pants and a baggy jacket that
looks like it's made out of a bed quilt, and a little cap without no
brim or peak on his head with a long braid of hair coming out from
under it and down his back. He's kind of trotting along the main
street with his arms stuck up inside his sleeves and looking down at
the ground so's he don't step on no drunks or fall in a mudhole and
drown, and when he went past a saloon one of the men outside with
a stovepipe hat and a bottle in his hand hollers:

"Hey, you! Chinky-chink!"

The Chinaman never stopped or turned his head and Stovepipe
got all fired up over it.

"You!" he hollers. "You! Chinaman! You pay heed when you're
spoke to!"

But he never wanted to and trotted faster, which got Stovepipe
mad and he run after him and grabbed him by the pigtail and jerked
hard.

"Wait on there, Chinaman," he says. "I got a question for you.
What's a heathen Chinee do on Christmas Day? Answer me that."

The Chinaman just stood there looking at the ground, like he's waiting for Stovepipe to get bored and go away, but he warn't about to now he sees there's a bunch of men gathered around to see what he does next. He says:

"I'll tell you what a Chinaman does on Christmas Day. Nothin'. That's what he does, except for smokin' opium and climbin' on his little yeller Chinawoman. I ask you, is it Christian?" he says to the crowd, and they hollered back that it ain't.

"Well, then," he says, "I reckon we oughter show this here China-man how he oughter be acting on a holy day like today is, ain't that so?"

They all reckoned it was, and Stovepipe pulled the Chinaman in close and says:

"First off, you got to get on your knees and pray to God and apolo-gize for gettin' born a yeller Chinee and not a Christian white man. Down on your knees, you heathen yeller dog."

And he pushed him down hard in the mud. The Chinaman must of figured he done enough polite listening to words he don't even understand and tried to get up again, but Stovepipe shoved him back down and says:

"Now you got to put your hands together and pray, like this, see?"

He showed how to do it but the Chinaman never done it, and Stovepipe got hold of his pigtail again and wrapped it two times around his neck and hauled hard from behind with his knee in the Chinaman's back. He kind of gurgled and put his hands up to his throat and Stovepipe says:

"That's it, that's where they go, only flat together."

He eased off the pressure a little and the crowd all laughed. They showed the Chinaman what he's supposed to be doing, and he fi-nally seen the light and joined his hands in prayer.

"There now," says Stovepipe. "You should of done it when I wanted. Now you got to hand over a Christmas present. That's what us Christians do this time of year. I reckon this hunk of rope'll do fine."

And he got out his knife and lopped off the Chinaman's pigtail and held it up so's everyone can see, and they all cheered. The Chinaman give a screech and yelled a lot of Chinaman talk and Stovepipe give him a shove that sent him face down in the mud with his rear end in the air, which Stovepipe reckoned is an invitation so he kicked it hard and now all of the Chinaman is in the mud. Everyone figured it's mighty funny and slapped each other on the back, only one man done it too hard and give his neighbor a slap that would of made a humpback stand up straight and got a punch in the jaw by way of thank you. Soon as the rest seen them start to fight they done the same, not wanting to feel left out. There must of been fifty men fighting, and the Chinaman seen his chance and run off, but was knocked down a couple more times before he got clear.

"Peace on Earth," says Thaddeus to no one in particular, and we rode on.

When we got to Sacramento late next day the town was filled with men just arrived and raring to get to the diggings, and more that just come from there, some with gold but mostly without. The streets was crowded sidewalk to sidewalk, same as when we come through the first time. We never stayed longer than it took to pass through and get onto the road that follows the Sacramento River down to San Francisco Bay. We had to ride in single file along the edge of the road on account of all the thousands headed upriver, anxious to try their hand at mining. I reckon if the gold holds out California is bound to get overcrowded in a year or so. There was camps all along the road when it got dark and only the eagerest ones kept on marching. Mighty cold and miserable they was too, rained on from dusk till dawn, and next day it rained some more. We seen a man selling rain slickers from the back of a wagon and got one each, and soon as we paid out the money it quit raining. Thaddeus says it's worth it to get a dry spell and be able to breathe air and not water for a change.

From Sacramento to the bay is only a two-day ride, and on the second night along the road we stopped at a camp to get warm over a fire. The men there seen us come off the road from the north and wanted to know how things is at the diggings and which places is richest. Thaddeus done the talking and give them a true picture of how hard work is what they can count on a whole lot more than luck, which warn't what they wanted to hear at all. He says:

"Boys, I could spin you a yarn about gold mountains with rivers of gold dust pouring out of them, but it ain't the way I seen things. You can't hardly pan color out of the creeks no more, it's all been took before you got here. The kind of gold you can still get is under the ground and in the hillsides, but you got to dig plenty for it. I ain't saying it ain't possible to find some, but it don't happen every day, so don't go expectin' too much and you won't be disappointed."

"How'd you make your strike?" asks a man.

"Me? I dug and dug down into the ground, and every shovel load I dug I figured to find gold in, but there never was none. I dug and dug and when I got around five mile down I reckoned I'm in the wrong place, so I clumb up the shaft toward the little-bitty piece of sunlight at the top. I started climbing on a Tuesday and on Sunday I got there. Well, after all that sweat and strain for nothin' you can guess the amount of disgustment I had inside of me, so I killed a grizzly bear for supper and after I finished pickin' my teeth with his claws I figured I may as well pack my tent and go look for gold somewheres else. I yanked on the tent pegs to get them up, only I been so long under the ground them pegs has sprouted roots, real deep ones, and I had to chop them out with a pick, and when I got a few yards down I seen the roots is all clustered around a pocket of gold, and that's how I made my strike. There's some that's called me a liar for that story, but they warn't gentlemen like you boys."

They appreciated the story but still never believed him about the hard work, and he started on another tale so tall you would of needed a ladder to get over it, and when he finished he started another, the one about him and Jim Bridger and the Injun's leg. I already heard it before so Jim and me took a stroll around the camp from fire to fire, and when we got near the edge Jim points and says:

"Looky dere, Huck. I ain't de onlies' nigger in Californy."

I looked and there's six niggers sat by a fire with one white man, and we got curious and went over. They was just as surprised to see Jim, and the white man says:

"You and me got the right idea, boy. Digging ain't white man's work, so bring the niggers in, that's the smart thing to do. You just got the one?"

"He's a free nigger," says I.

"A what? Where the hell are you from, boy, one of them abolitionist states? Don't you know niggers can't do nothing without they got a white man to tell them? What the hell use is a free nigger? These here six is all slaves the way God intended, and I aim to put 'em to good use. I laid out plenty for 'em and by God I'll get it back ten times over."

"Dis here ain't no slave state," says Jim.

"What's that? . . . Did you say something, nigger?"

"I'se sayin' dere ain't no slaves in Californy."

The man's cheeks blowed out and he stared Jim up and down and says:

"No nigger talks to a white man like that, not where I come from. . . ."

"You ain't there no more," says I, wishing Jim had of stayed quiet, but it's too late now and you can't let a friend get in trouble without giving no help. The man's real angry now and says:

"And little piss-ants like you don't give no lip to their elders neither."

Getting called names made me kind of reckless, which I ain't as a rule, and I got my dander up.

"And out here fatbelly gnat-brains like you ain't worth a hair off a dead dog's ballbag," says I.

He got on his feet all shaking with angriness, and Jim says to the niggers:

"Ain't nothin' to stop you walkin' away lessen you likes bein' slaves. If'n you digs up gold you ain't goin' to get none of it, jest food, das all he goin' to give you, an' a mean kickin' if'n you don' fin' none."

They all looked at each other and at the man, and he says:

"Don't none of you listen to no abolitionist talk or I'll take the hide off you. I paid good money in Louisiana and you niggers are mine by law. I got the paper that says so."

They never opened their mouths, just looked real uncomfortable.

"He cain't own no slaves out here," says Jim to them. "Ain't nothin' stoppin' you from doin' jest what you want."

"One more word out of you, nigger, and I ain't answerable," says the man, and pulled a pistol from his belt. He's good and mad and it's a real dangersome situation. I got my Hawken with me out of habit but it ain't cocked, and it's too heavy to swing around on him while he's got that pistol pointed. I ain't even rightly sure a bill of sale from Louisiana ain't legal in California or not, and I seen the niggers is too scared to do nothing anyhow. I reckon being a slave must squeeze all the spirit and fire out of you and leave you fearful of any different kind of life if slavery is all you ever knowed from getting birthed onwards.

"Leave it, Jim" says I. "It ain't no good to argue."

"It ain't right," he says. "He ain't allowed no slaves out here."

"Maybe so, and if it's true he'll get told by others and be obliged to set them free."

"Ain't no white man goin' to care if'n dis one totin' slaves," says Jim. "Ain't no white man goin' to care nothin' 'bout no niggers nohow. Niggers an' Injuns an' Chinamen ain't nothin' to no white man, jest trash, an' it ain't ever goin' to be no diff'rent, not lessen you niggers light out for de hills de firs' chance you gets. Ain't no use you fixin' to stay aroun' no gold diggin's lessen you's white. You jest get stomped on."

"How come you never done it?" asks one of the niggers, and the man give him a sharp look for speaking out.

"On accounter I got me a frien' das white, das how come I got by," says Jim. "Das de onlies' reason I ain't got stepped on an' squash' by no whites. You ain't got no white frien's, jest dis here master, so if'n you runs off you better watch out."

The man seen Jim has gone and argued himself into a corner, and he lowers his pistol and says to the niggers:

"There, you see? Without me you boys'd be lost. Thanks, nigger," he says to Jim. "You pointed it out real good."

Jim give him a disgusted look, but I seen he's disgusted at himself too for telling the niggers to get free and then saying freedom ain't no better if you're a nigger anyhow. That's the true way of it. A nigger that ain't a slave is still a nigger, just like Injuns and Chinamen, and no better off for freedom even if he gets it. There ain't no way around it. Jim turned away and went off into the dark and the man laughed after him and says:

"Boy, you got one ornery nigger there. He's kin to Nat Turner I bet. One of these days he'll murder some white folks in their beds."

"Well I reckon they'll deserve it if they're kin of yours," says I.

"I ain't about to forget your face, boy, you and the nigger both. Abolitionist sonsabitches like you two are just bound to brush with the law one of these days, and when you do I'll come to the hanging and bring my boys along too, just so's they don't think they can backtalk a white man and get away with it. . . . ."

He stopped right there and I seen his face change, just staring at me, and I got a big dose of the fan-tods, because it's the kind of look you get when you all of a sudden see a thing that's been in front of you all along and you only just now reckernized it.

"You're Huck Finn, ain't you? . . ." he says.

I reckon it's that talk of hanging that's made him figure it out, but I ain't going to give him no satisfaction.

"Who?" says I.

"Huckleberry Finn," he says, "the one that killed some judge up in Missouri. . . . Hell on earth, I got Huckleberry Finn! . . ."

He's kind of amazified that he's the one that'll bring me to justice and get his name put in the newspapers and collect the reward, already counting the dollars I bet, but he ain't lifted the pistol again on account of the surprise, so I swung my Hawken to the side of his head. I never even planned it that way, just done it out of scaredness, and he went down like a clubbed hog. A Hawken is a heavy gun and I near filled my britches wondering if I killed him, but he's breathing still so I ain't. No one else around seen it happen and the niggers never moved. Maybe they heard of me too and figured I'm a natural-born murderer that aims to kill them if they raise a holler. I reckon I could of bluffed them with some threatsome talking, but it don't come natural to me, not with niggers that done me no harm, so I say:

"Please don't make no noise, not till he's awake. You can run for freedom or stay, only please don't make no noise. . . ."

Then I run off after Jim. He's back with Thaddeus, and the men that was listening to him yarn-spinning has drifted off. I give them the facts real fast and they never spoke a word, just got the horses saddled up again faster than a fox making for cover. A man seen us doing it and come over.

"Leaving?" he says.

"Itchy feet," says I. "I reckon we'll move on before the rain comes back."

We rode out of the camp slow and went a little way down the road before we even dared to breathe normal.

"He'll raise a holler anytime now," says Thaddeus. "Listen out for horses coming up fast from behind and we'll get off the road and let 'em by."

But we never heard none all night long. Maybe the slaves run off and the owner's got his hands full trying to round them up, but proberly he's just feeling mighty poorly with a sore head and reckons it ain't worthwhile backtracking down the road for no miserable thousand dollars' reward, not when there's millions up ahead waiting to be dug out of the ground. Once a miner gets headed for the diggings it takes a twenty-mule team to drag him back the other way, so we're saved by gold fever.

"You boys got to keep your heads down," says Thaddeus. "You ain't in no position to be preachifyin' about freedom and such. It just makes you stand out like a Bible in a whorehouse. From now on don't pay no mind to nothin' except getting yourselfs on a ship out to sea. You boys ain't behaving sensible at all. Up on the Yuba I seen a Spaniard get lynched for cutting a man that insulted his wife. He never killed him, but he got lynched anyway. Did I get up and make a speech about injustice? No, sir, I would of got lynched myself. Peacemakers and philosophers got no place here, not yet. Maybe their time'll come later, but you and me ain't going to see it."

Toward dawn the road got filled again and we rode on against the tide and come to San Francisco Bay around noon. There's a ferry steamboat pulling in at a log pier just a little way from where the Sacramento runs into the bay, a sidewheeler with high-standing sides, not flat like a Mississippi steamer. The paddles backed and churned the water as she slid alongside the pier and the deckhands throwed ropes to them that's ashore. Soon as she's docked and the gangplank was down off come the miners in a stampede, like ants swarming out of a smashed anthill, and they run along the pier to reach the road and start walking. They was in such a rush two fell in the water and would of drowned under the weight of the picks and shovels strapped across their backs if a couple of deckhands hadn't of jumped in and saved them. The other miners never even stopped to see if they was rescued they're so eager to get north, and when I seen it I'm glad we left mining behind. There ain't no dignification to be had from a bunch of men like that. Thaddeus says:

"I reckon this is where we part company."

We kind of looked at each other, gone all tongue-tied. I got admiration and respect by the bushel for Thaddeus. Next to Jim I figure he's the decentest man I ever met, only it's mighty hard to tell him so, and I say:

"Thaddeus, why don't you come to San Francisco with Jim and me, just for a little while till we find a ship. It's something you ain't ever seen before."

"I thank you for the invite," he says, "but I already seen a city one time, St. Louis, and never hankered to see another. You boys better get your tickets before she pulls out again."

"We don't need our horses no more," says I. "Take Jupiter. He's the best horse in California. He'll take you wherever you want."

"Well, I don't know . . . I ain't had the ownership of no thoroughbred before."

"Please take him, Thaddeus. If you don't all I can do is sell him to some miner that don't know him and'll maybe treat him bad. I got nothing else to give."

"I'll do it," he says, and we got dismounted and me and Jim handed over our reins and untied our saddlebags with the gold in them. I run over to a little cabin and got two tickets, twenty dollars each, then run back. Thaddeus is up on Jupiter and looked like he growed there, and he reaches down to shake our hands real solemn and says:

"Huckleberry, Jim, I ain't about to forget neither of you."

"Same here, Thaddeus," says I.

"You watch out when you get in the city. It's likely full of thieves and murderers."

"We won't get in no trouble."

The steamer blowed her whistle and the men that's been waiting to board started up the gangplank. Thaddeus says:

"Go on now or you'll be stuck here till the next one."

"Thaddeus, when you get to where them tall trees grow will you do me the favor of carving my name on one? I reckon I won't ever get to see them now."

"You got my word, and I'll put Jim's name there too. Now I ain't wastin' no more daylight gabbin' with you both. Get on that steamer directly."

The whistle blowed a second time and we shook hands all over again, then Jim and me run down the pier, hard work when you got bags of gold over your shoulders, and we staggered up the gangplank just before they run it inboard and the paddles started churning. She backed away from the pier real slow then swung about and headed out into the bay. We waved and Thaddeus waved back, and I watched till he turned Jupiter and rode south along the shoreline leading the other horses behind. Then he went behind some trees and out of eye-reach. I watched them trees till they was far off and blurred, but I never seen him again. Jim put his hand on my shoulder and says:

"Ain't no sense in grievin', Huck. Least he ain't dead like Andrew an' Miz Beckwith an' Frank."

"I ain't grieving, just sad is all. He's one of a kind I reckon."

"Das so, Huck. We kin be proud to of knowed him."

There ain't nothing so mournful as being stood at the end of a boat looking back, so we went to the bows and waited to see San Francisco, but it never showed. A deckhand come by and I say:

"Pardon me, I can't see the city."

"She's likely burned down again," he says. "She burns down just about every other week. The last time was Christmas Eve but the fire never done a total job, just a block or three."

"But where is it?"

"You won't catch sight for hours yet. We have to go all the way down this bay to where it turns into another bay, then we go across that till we reach the third one, which is where San Francisco is. It'll be long gone dark before we dock."

We stayed on deck till it come on to rain again. We was hungry by then and went below to where they had food for sale. There warn't hardly no one there, and I seen the reason when I paid eight dollars for just two little pies. There's a man next to me dressed neat with a brass stickpin in his necktie, and he says:

"Savor every morsel, youngster. That's the most expensive pie you'll ever have."

"How come it costs so much?"

"This is California," he says. "We must pay for the privilege of being here."

Then a man in a uniform come along and says:

"Only whites allowed below. Niggers and chinks on deck."

He's a skinny little weasel that only reckons he's big on account of the uniform, and Jim turned around slow and kind of leaned over him with a big smile on his face.

"'Scuse my askin'," he says, real polite. "Was dat niggers an' chinks you was tellin' about?"

"That's right," says the uniform, leaning over backwards away from Jim's smile, and Jim says:

"Das mighty reliefsome. I ain't no Chinaman an' it's kinder cold out dere."

"But . . . you're a nigger. You have to go out," he says.

"Is dat in de rules? Maybe you got it writ out somewheres an' my frien' here kin read it to me."

"It's . . . just a rule," he stammers. "No . . . niggers and chinks."

"I always tries to go by de rules," says Jim, still smiling, "only it's cold like I say."

"Well . . . I can't help that. Rules are rules. . . ."

I seen Jim ain't learned a lesson from last night, so I reached in my pocket and brung out twenty dollars and give it to the uniform. Says I:

"It's awful rainy out."

He looked down at the money then up at Jim and says:

"All right then, just till the rain stops."

"Thank you kindly. We appreciate it," says I, the words kind of sticking in my craw, but we can't afford no trouble. He went away and the man with the stickpin says:

"Well, turn me over and call me a pancake. That's a sight I never expected to see, not even in dreams. You boys are regular rascals, but don't wait around to see if your bribe worked. He'll be back with a few friends to throw you out, twenty dollars or not."

He's right, but I practickly had to drag Jim out on deck. We squatted under an awning out of the rain and I say:

"Jim, you're forever telling me I changed since we started out, but I reckon you're the one that's changed. You know we got to be quiet and not bring no trouble down on us."

"I knows it, Huck, but I cain't help de feelin's I gets insider me. All my life I bin steppin' off de sidewalk for white folks, an' I hates de feelin' it give me. I bin alive maybe thirty years, an' de feelin's bin kinder stackin' up insider me all dat time, an' now dey so high I cain't hardly see over de top no mo'. It ain't right what dey do, Huck. I ain't de proudes' man in de worl' but I figure I got rights. I ain't no slave. I ain't beholden to no one, jest my own self. I reckon even when we cashes in de gold I ain't goin' to be nothin' but a nigger. It don' matter if'n I'se rich, I'se jest a nigger still, an' it burns me up inside de way I gets treated. I figure de onlies' way I'se goin' to get smooth' down is way off where Thaddeus tol' us, dat islan' wid brownskin' women. Maybe dey ain't so partic'lar 'bout niggers dere."

"I know it ain't right, Jim, but there ain't nothing we can do."

"My granpap come from Africa," he says. "He tol' me de whole place got nothin' but niggers in it. He tol' me dey got nigger kings even, but I ain't incline' to b'lieve it. How kin a nigger ever get to be king?"

"I reckon it must be true, Jim. The Widow Douglas told me about how when she was a girl she went on vacation to St. Louis and seen one of them theater plays with actors and costumes, and she give me the story of it. I disremember what it's called, but the hero is a nigger king and the queen is a white girl called Mona."

"Das de mos' ridickerless thing I ever heard. Ain't no white gal goin' to marry no nigger. Ain't no one'd talk to her if'n she done it, mos' likely run her outer town an' lynch de nigger."

"Maybe the play was in Africa, but the king's a nigger, definite."

"What he do?"

"Just the usual king stuff I reckon. The story's mainly about him and Mona in the palace, and how they was real in love till the day come when she lost her handkerchief. The king give it to her special and was mighty sore about her losing it, and strangled her."

"Jest on accounter de hanky?"

"I reckon he had a mean temper."

"Soun's to me like he warn't no better'n a white man."

"Well he warn't all bad. Afterwards when he seen what he done he felt real guilty and strangled himself too for atonement. It's a real sad story. The widow reckoned it just goes to show you can't mix black and white."

We stayed sat there watching rain fall into the bay, then along come Stickpin. He seen us and come over and says:

"Discretion is the better part of valor, or to put it another way, prudence before provocation."

"Proberly so," says I, wanting to sound polite.

He come under the awning without no invite and goes on:

"You'll find San Francisco is a tolerant town in all regards but one. Men may shoot each other and beat their women, consort with whores and charge outrageous prices for pies, but nowhere is a nigger sold a drink or asked to linger, not even in the lowest waterfront bar. We San Franciscans are a new breed of American, with wilderness on one side and ocean on the other, perforce isolating us from the rest of the nation. Thus we have evolved our own characteristic style of living which might be termed nonvirtuous, nonabstemious and nonstop, but never nonprofitable. We are a society without mor-

als, but as you have seen we do maintain all the standard prej-
udices. We are a melting pot. In San Francisco can be found
Americans, Englishmen, French, Spanish, German and Dutch,
Peruvians, Pacific Islanders, Chinese and Australians. With such a
heady brew of cultures you must expect some racial discord. Every
day hundreds arrive and leave again for the diggings. We are a city
in flux, young man, a social stew unlike any other in the world, and
we have only just begun. Your bags appear heavy. I presume you
have come from the upper reaches of the Sacramento burdened
with the spoils of your labor."

"Kind of," says I, wanting him to go away.

"Are you alone?" he wants to know.

"Pap and Uncle Silas is both aboard."

"Why do they leave such valuable cargo in the care of a boy and a
nigger?"

"They're down below getting drunk already, so it's safer this way.
They aim to go on a real spree when we hit town."

"They have come to the right place. The city offers delights to
tempt all appetites. My name is Orville Treece."

"I'm Jack Winterbough and this here's Ben."

"And how did you enjoy mining, Jack?"

"It ain't easy."

"Nothing is when a man is poor, but with gold in your pockets
you'll find out how easy life can be."

"Is that what happened to you?"

"I have never been closer to the diggings than the ferry disem-
barkation point. I take the trip once in a while for fresh air, but
today's trip is business. I am a correspondent for the *Bulletin*.
Would you be interested in discussing your experiences upcountry
with me? If the story is interesting it will find its way onto the pages
of that worthy sheet. Wouldn't you like to see your names in print?"

We already seen them on wanted posters, so I say:

"We ain't got no interesting stories. It was real boring, just hard
work and rain."

"Now there's a pity. My editor sent me out here to bring back
stories on the rags-to-riches theme, and you boys are well freighted
with precious metal."

"Well, we're kind of shy."

"You're not Huckleberry Finn are you, by any chance? Now *there* would be a story."

"No I ain't," says I, acting offended. "Me and Ben is plain sick and tired of getting asked that. It ain't our fault if we look like Finn and his nigger. If we never had Pap and Uncle Silas along with us we would of been lynched by now, and if you figure that'd make an interesting story you can just figure again, because we're sick of it like I say, so don't you go putting nothing in print or Pap and Uncle Silas'll come around and smash your press. They're both mighty big men and powerful mean when they get drunk."

"No offense," he says. "Enjoy your stay in our fair town."

And off he went, holding his hat to keep the wind from blowing it overboard. When he turned a corner Jim says:

"You reckon he suspicioned us, Huck?"

"Maybe. If he don't bring back a bunch of men and arrest us in the next ten minutes I reckon we can count ourselfs safe, but when we get off in San Francisco let's make sure he don't follow us, just in case."

Them minutes passed awful slow, but no one come near us so it looks like he swallered the lie, and we relaxed some. It quit raining after awhile and we stretched our legs again. The ferry went through a channel into the next bay and we seen another steamer coming in the other direction, which passed us pretty close with a heap of whistle blowing. The same deckhand as before seen us watching her slide by and says:

"That's the *Mirabelle*. She goes all the way up to Sacramento. We just do the short haul to the end of the bay for those that don't have the cash to go the whole route in comfort."

"You must make a heap of money on it," says I.

"Not me, friend, the owner. Mr. Wyeth, he's the one that cashes in. They say he's the richest man in Frisco. Owns the Cornucopia Mercantile Company, biggest on the coast. Anything you want to buy, he can sell, from ferry passage to a hand-carved bed. He's got a finger in every pie in town."

"I reckon that includes the ones we just lately et," says I.

He laughed and went away to coil ropes and other deckhand stuff. There's a patch of light low in the sky where the sun is, and we watched it slide down behind the brownish hills. The sky and water got grayer and darker while we're watching and the wind come blowing even harder across the bay, so cold we felt it even through our rain slickers. It was miserable to watch the light die away so we walked around and around the deck just keeping warm, and by the time we come through another channel into the third bay it's night, and way over yonder we seen the lights of San Francisco winking and blinking and looking mighty welcome in all that darkness.

"There she is, Jim, the city that's got streets paved with gold."

"Das somethin' I got to see befo' I b'lieves it."

"You and me both. It's most likely pure exaggerment, but it'll be kind of exciting to see anyhow."

When we come closer we seen the reason for the lights blinking that way, and it's a whole forest of masts and crosstrees on ships in the bay, hundreds of them I reckon, all riding at anchor without even a masthead light burning so's you don't run smack into them. The masts and such kind of swayed on the swell and blocked off the city lights behind for just a fraction of time then swayed back again, so the lights twinkled like stars. I never seen a true sailing ship before in my life and now there's more than I can count, just black shadows on the water. Some was a considerable size but even the biggest ain't got no lights burning, not at the portholes or bow or stern, not nowhere. When the ferry slowed down and nosed in among them it give me the strangest feeling, like being in a graveyard at night. Says I:

"Jim, there ain't no one aboard all them ships. They're deserted, each and every one. . . ."

"How dat be, you reckon?"

"It do beat all. . . . There ain't even no night watchmen as I can see, not a soul. They're ghost ships."

It give me a shiver to watch them all sliding by, big and silent and dark, and then the answer come to me.

"Jim, you remember that sailor that Thaddeus told of, the one that's been to the islands? Well he jumped ship here, and it looks like he warn't the only one. All the crews has gone to the diggings. . . . There ain't no one to sail the ships out to sea again. . . ."

"Den how we goin' to get away on one of 'em?"

"I reckon we ain't," says I, and got that old familiar feeling I get when a situation I figured is going to be fine and dandy turns around and bites me, kind of like a lead weight sinking down through my belly. All them ships could of took us away to freedom, and all the sailors has gone ashore to dig for gold and left them to rot. It's a bitter pill, as they say. If it was gold fever that saved us from getting chased last night it's gold fever that's sunk our hopes tonight, which is what the judge would of called a double-edged sword that cuts both ways.

We felt forlorn and hopeless while the ferry slid along through that floating graveyard, and when we come to the dock and tied up it warn't so exciting as I figured to walk down the gangplank and set foot on land. There's a fair crowd on the wharf waiting, most of them women with bright colored dresses and painted faces and showing a lot of their chests even in winter, so they're whores. We seen Orville Treece go down the plank first, and he just pushed straight through the women like they ain't there and headed off down the wharf, so we fooled him definite. But it ain't much consolation.

The men in front of us got argued over an account of there's more whores than miners, but some men showed the wisdom of Solomon and quieted things down by marching off with whores on both arms. When Jim and me come down the plank there's just three or four left. They warn't about to sell theirselfs to no nigger, but they flapped around me like buzzards fixing to tear me open.

"Hello, little miner," says one with a mouthful of rotten teeth. "I've been waiting all day for you. Let's go to a place I know and you can tell me all about it."

"All about what?"

"Anything at all. Ain't you lonely for company?"

"No, ma'am, thank you anyway."

She kind of hisses at me and says a few things I ain't about to repeat and the others joined in, talking the disgustingest kind of language. We pushed through with their smell thick in our nostrils, paint and powder and perfume enough to make you puke, and was soon free of them. They stayed by the plank, waiting for the deckhands to finish work proberly, and we come to the end of the wharf where it joins onto a street with buildings two and three stories high along it. There warn't too many people around when we set off down that street and there ain't no lights so it's considerable gloomy in between them high walls. We was halfway along when a woman come rushing up, not a whore I judged, and she's real upset and says:

"Please help me! My little girl is under a box that fell on her! I can't lift it off! Please come and help!"

"Yes, ma'am," says I. "Where is she?"

"Down here. . . . Oh, please hurry!"

She rushed down a little alley and we followed on. She says over her shoulder:

"I told her not to play here after dark, but she never listens. . . . Oh, pray God she won't die. . . ."

We turned a corner and something come down hard on my head from behind. I felt Jim fall against me on his way to the ground and I followed him down with a crash. There's footsteps and voices, the woman and a couple of men, then nothing at all for a little while. Then Jim is shaking me by the shoulder.

"Huck . . ." he says, "Huck . . . we bin robbed."

✦ 31 ✦

Roughing It—Work for Idle Hands—A Small World—

Whiskey by the Bay—Shady Business—No Help Wanted

They took everything except our clothes. The gold was gone and my Hawken too, so even if the ships in the bay warn't deserted we never could of paid for tickets now. It's fickle fate again. We come all this way and worked hard for our gold, but at the end of the rainbow there's just sore heads and the cozy fact that we're stuck in a city where a pie costs a week's wages and we ain't got a cent between us. If I never had of give a bribe to the uniform on the ferry we would of at least had twenty dollars still, but I did so we ain't. It's enough to make a growed man cry, but we never, just picked ourselfs up and walked back along the alley to the street.

"Jim," says I, "from now on we don't trust no one."

"Dat goes double for me."

We wandered around town, and if you ain't ever been there let me tell you San Francisco is a big place, with tall buildings that's even made of brick, some of them, and a heap of streets that ain't paved with gold after all, only mud. We got muddied up to our knees, mighty discomforting, and was hungry as wolves in winter. There was plenty of people around, and more women than I seen since Missouri, whores mostly, but still outnumbered ten to one by men. There was Chinamen too, and we heard all kinds of foreign talk like Orville Treece told us we would, but after awhile we had trouble hearing it over the grumbling in our bellies. Says I:

"Jim, there ain't nothing else for it. We got to beg."

We warn't neither of us happy to do it, but Jim seen the sense in swallering pride so's we can swaller food straight after. We agreed it's best if I done the begging; a skinny boy is more pitiful than a big nigger, so Jim stood off to one side and I went up to a drunk that's got new clothes on, a lucky miner I reckon.

"Pardon me, sir," says I. "Could you spare a dollar for a starving orphan that ain't et in three days?"

"A dollar?" he says, looking me up and down. "What kind of piker do you take me for, you little squirt? Here's ten."

He slapped a coin in my hand and went off, but he must of been drunker than I figured because it's a twenty-dollar gold eagle. I done it plenty more times for an hour or so. Some men give me a good cussing but most give me money, and we ended up with forty-seven dollars. Maybe that sounds a lot for just an hour's begging, but when we went into an eating house that's packed and noisy with men and et our fill we come out again with four dollars seventy cents. I seen that the generousness I got ain't such a big thing as I figured in a place like this, and I got begging again so's we can get a bed for the night.

San Francisco don't close down after midnight like most towns, just keeps on riproaring along with the streets jammed and all the lights on and music coming out of saloons and plenty of laughing and drinking and brawling going on all around. Maybe folks sleep in the daytime when there ain't so much racket. I collected fifty-three dollars but got discouraged when a man never liked my face and pushed me off the sidewalk into the mud. I sunk in so deep Jim had to haul me out. I reckon there's worse mud in the country, but it's all under the Mississippi. I got cleaned off the best I can and we went into a hotel that ain't too grand looking, but soon as we walked in the lobby the clerk says:

"No niggers."

So we walked out again and tried another place next door, but they never liked niggers neither, and the other four we tried along the street was the same. Both of us was considerable wearied by now, and we finally drug ourselfs behind a big brick warehouse that's got empty crates and cases stacked around in a yard and crawled inside the driest. Back home I slept in a hogshead barrel in summertime, but warn't fool enough to try it through winter. We shivered and shaked the whole night long and never got three winks of sleep, never mind forty, and in the morning crawled out again feeling like life ain't worth the living. Jim says:

"Huck, dis kinder setup goin' to kill us for sure."

"I know it. We got to get some real money and buy horses and maybe catch up with Thaddeus. Wait on. . . . If them ships in the

bay is crying out for sailors I reckon we can get work on board one or
other of them. I bet there's captains that'll give us a heap of money
to help them sail away out of here. It don't matter if they ain't going
to no islands, just so long as we get clear of San Francisco before the
bulldog catches us up."

"You reckon he ain't goin' to be fool' by de lies you tol' back at de
diggin's?"

"We can't afford to take no chance on it. He's a smart detective, I
got to admit it, and he ain't going to quit till he sniffs us out."

We had a simple breakfast for thirty-six dollars then headed for
the waterfront. There's a place there with a sign out front that says:
SHIPPING OFFICE.

We went in but there warn't no one around except for a clerk with
his feet on the desk and his nose in a newspaper. He give us a look
and says:

"Well?"

"Pardon me, we was wondering if there's a ship we can sign on
for sailoring."

"New in town?" he asks.

"Just yesterday."

"Well, the shipping hereabouts is one-way. They come in and
don't go out again. Take a look out the window and you'll see what I
mean."

"We seen it already, thank you. Ain't there no ships at all that's
leaving? Ain't there captains by the score hollering for men to splice
the capstan and luff the buntline and such?"

"The captains are all at the diggings, the same as the men. Try
again in a month or two, but things will still be the same."

"Thank you," says I.

"You're welcome," says he.

We went out and wandered the streets again, not knowing what
else to do. We seen a place called Portsmouth Square that's got one
side burned down, which must of been the Christmas Eve fire the
ferryman told of. They never wasted no time in building it up again
and most of the frontage is already filled with wood frames for new
buildings.

"Jim," says I, "maybe we can earn our keep without begging after
all."

I ask one of the builders which one is the foreman and got pointed

to a big man in a derby hat with a cigar in his mouth. Me and Jim
went over and waited till he finished hollering at someone about
nails, then I say:

"Pardon us, sir, but we need a job."

"Ever done carpentering?" he says.

"Not for a living."

"Bricklaying?"

"Well . . . no."

"The nigger can haul bricks and mortar for the laying team and
you can haul planks. Fifty dollars a day for you and thirty for the
nigger."

"That ain't fair. He can do three times more'n me with one hand
behind him."

"All right then," he says. "Forty."

"We'll take it."

"Albie!" he hollers. "Two new men for you!"

A man about twenty-three or -four come up on the trot and got
give orders about us and set us to work. It warn't easy hauling that
lumber without no sleep the night before, but I soldiered on and Jim
done the same with barrowloads of bricks. At the end of the day we
lined up with the rest of the men for our wages. We never done a
full day's work so I only got forty and Jim got thirty. Albie come over
and seen what we got and says:

"You'll get more tomorrow, only you got to turn up at eight o'clock
sharp to get a full day's pay. After a few days you can get even
more."

"How so?"

"Workers is the rarest birds in town right now with everyone haring off to the diggings. Any man that stays put can earn good
money, even if he's just a dishwasher. You let Herb get used to your
face for a couple of days and work hard then ask him for a hundred
dollars a day, which is what the rest of us is getting."

"How come Herb never told us that?"

"On account of he'll mark you down on the pay sheet for a hundred and pocket what he don't pay you. He's a sonovabitch, but if
you say you'll quit if you don't get full wages he'll pay up. Like I say,
it ain't easy to find men that's willing to do laboring."

"Thank you for the facts. Ain't you got gold fever your own self?"

"I done a spell of mining," he says, "but never had no luck. I reckon I'll give it another try when I get enough saved for a grub-stake. Building work ain't so bad, not as bad as farmwork. You ever done that?"

"No, we done deckhanding on riverboats."

"Say, are you from Missouri? You got that kind of sound, same as me."

"Well . . . I got brung up there, but I got born in Illinois."

"What's your name?" he says. "Mine's Albie Aintree."

I near fell over when he told it, but I can't rightly tell him I et food at his folks' farm and told his Ma a slew of lies and tied up his Pa and stole their horse. Ain't it peculiar the way you can meet up with someone you heard about two thousand mile away? Says I:

"I'm Jack Winterbough and this here's Ben."

He shook hands with us, even with Jim, which is mighty strange for a Missourian, then says why don't we go and get fed a meal someplace. We done it and while we et he told all about how he hated working on his Pa's farm just outside of St. Petersburg, which is a little river town we maybe heard of, being rivermen, and how he left home after his Pa called him a lazy dog. He got a steamboat down to New Orleans and worked his way on a ship down to Pan-ama then rode muleback over the skinny stretch of land that keeps the Pacific out of the Atlantic and get et alive by moskeeters on the way. Then he worked on another ship up to San Francisco and walked to the diggings from there and walked all the way back again when he never struck it rich. It's a mighty interesting story, but I never got the chance to tell him the usual lies about how Jim and me got here because the owner of the eating house says we got to leave and make room for them that's waiting for a meal. We went outside and Albie says:

"Where are you staying?"

"Oh . . . we got a place a few blocks over yonder."

"You're mighty lucky. The boarding house I'm at is the cheapest in town and they don't take no niggers."

"We had to search around awhile to find this'n," says I.

"Well," he says, "I reckon I'd invite you back to my place for a snort, but I need all the sleep I can get, working like I do. You both better catch plenty too if you want to be on time tomorrow."

We give our goodnights and me and Jim wandered off into the streets, just as tired as tired can be. I done some more begging to keep my hand in just in case the building job don't work out, and I must of looked truly pathetical; I got sixty-eight dollars and a gold nugget without hardly trying. After that we went back to the warehouse yard and this time got some boxes fixed up so the wind don't come through so much and even found a heap of straw packing that's dry to fill a crate with so it's middling comfortable, then dropped asleep.

When we woke up it's hard to tell what time it is seeing as we ain't got no pocket watch, and we never wanted to be late. Soon as we got on the street I ask the time off a man and got ten dollars too. It ain't even half-past seven yet so we filled up with breakfast then strolled around to Portsmouth Square. We worked hard all day, but it's easier than yesterday with a good sleep behind us, and when we collected our money Herb the foreman says:

"I want every man here tomorrow same as usual. There's a fifty dollar bonus."

"What for?" says I.

"What for?" he says, and all the others laughed. "What for? Tomorrow's New Year's Day, muttonhead!"

It come as a big surprise to me and it must of showed, because they laughed plenty, then Herb says:

"But we got to finish this job fast, so it ain't going to be no vacation for no one here. You want me to say it all again, bonehead?"

"No I don't," says I. "I ain't deaf."

"Maybe not," he says, "but you sure are dumb."

That got another big laugh, and he says:

"I bet you don't even know what year it'll be tomorrow, do you?"

"This year plus one," says I, and got laughs on my side this time, which Herb never liked.

"You take care of your health, boy," he says. "Carrying around a heavy brain like yours must be an awful strain."

"Not so big a strain as carrying yours must be. Keeping your head straight so your brain don't rattle around inside is a mighty hard trick."

They all laughed, but quit when they seen Herb ain't amused. He says:

"Boy, you just backtalked your way out of a job."

"Ain't you got no sense of humor?" says I.

He just shook his head, smiling, and Albie says:

"Don't fire him, Herb. Him and Ben is good workers both."

"We don't need no smart-talking snotnose around here," says Herb, "but the nigger can stay."

"I ain't stayin'," says Jim.

"No, Ben," says I. "You got to. Ma and Sis got to have their medicine and you know how much we got to pay for every bottle. The doc says if they don't get it regular both of them'll die spitting blood. You got to stay on and work, Ben."

"Hear that, Herb?" says Albie. "You're killing a helpless woman and girl. The nigger don't earn enough on his own to buy no medicine. How much was it you was telling me the stuff cost, Jack?"

"Fifty dollars a bottle," says I, snuffling, "and they both got to drink three bottles a week each just to stay alive. It's only Doc Sawyer's Elixir that's keeping Ma and Sis out of the grave."

The other men set up a sympathetical racket and Herb seen the way of it.

"All right," he says, holding out his hands for quiet, "the bonehead can stay on too, only he's got to keep a civil tongue in his head."

"Oh, it'll be real sivilized, Herb," says I.

"Well make sure it is. I don't want no one starting the new year on the wrong foot," he says, and turned away quick so's to have the last word, only he never watched where he stepped and put his foot through a gap in the floor planking and fell down hard, which give us all a good long laugh.

"Must of been the right foot but the wrong leg, Herb," says one of the carpenters, and the laughing doubled.

But we had to stop when Herb hollered at us to pull him out, and when he's laid out on the planks, Albie looked at his leg and touched it and says the bottom half is broke. The carpenters fixed him up with splints right quick, being handy with wood, and his leg got wrapped tight with sackcloth. Albie done most of it seeing as he done the same for a dog once.

"Don't worry, Herb," he says, "that dog walked again. Mind you, he never catched another rabbit in his life."

Someone give Herb a snort from a bottle of whiskey to ease the pain, then we lifted him onto a lumber wagon and took him to the hotel he's got a room at and hauled him up the stairs and into bed, by which time he was considerable drunk. He says:

"Albie, you got to keep the boys working hard. When the contractor comes around with the wages you got to hand them out and keep things running smooth. Don't let nothing get in the way of finishing that job."

"Don't you worry, I know how to be a foreman," says Albie.

"Talk loud and smoke a cigar," says someone, but we never laughed out of respect for Herb's busted leg. Albie told the woman that runs the place Herb has got to have his meals brung upstairs and his chamber pot emptied till his leg gets mended and he can move around again. She never took the news with a smile so we all give a little donation to sweeten her, which Albie calls the Pisspot Fund. Then we left to celebrate New Year's Eve, all eight of us in the wagon.

I never would of believed it if I never seen it myself, but San Francisco was even livelier that night than usual. It's only early evening yet but the streets was packed so tight the buildings got their paint wore off. It warn't possible to take the wagon nowhere in all that mud and crush so we drawed straws to see who has to take it back to the livery stable where it belongs, but then we seen it's a waste of time and the team got hitched to a post and left right there while we looked for a saloon. The closest was just across the street, but it may as well of been across a river. There's duckboards laid across the mud to cross over on, but every man that used them figures he's got the right of way, and men coming from both directions got into arguments and one or both of them ended up in the mud. I swear I seen one man vanish clean out of sight in the ooze, but I could of been wrong. Albie says:

"Men, we need to get across somehow, and I figures it ain't right if all of us has to get muddied. If four of us carries the other four over that leaves half of us clean and decent to face the world. How about it?"

"Which four gets carried?" asks a carpenter.

"The first four to clap hands, . . ." says Albie, and straightaway everyone except Albie, me and Jim clapped hands and looked mighty smug.

". . . is the ones that'll do the carrying," he says. "You should of waited till I finished, boys. Henry, you was a mite slow to clap so you get carried. All right, men, mount up!"

"Hold on there, Albie. It ain't fair, . . ." says a bricklayer.

"Tell me something that is, but do it bent over so's I can climb aboard."

"I ain't totin' no nigger," says another, and Albie give him a vexed look and says:

"Zachary, you're just the pigheadedest man I come across. Don't go getting fractious on the last day of the year."

"Well I ain't," says Zachary, poking out his chin.

"Me neither," says someone else. "Not for no nigger."

"I'm takin' the boardwalk," says a third, and in the end we all done it, and Zachary and a couple more got pushed off before we even got halfway, which I'm glad about. But the real trouble come almost at the other side when a real big man with bushy whiskers come face to face with Jim.

"Step off this walk, nigger," he says. "I aim to pass."

"Dere's room to get by if'n we both squeezes," says Jim.

"There ain't. The only thing I aim to squeeze tonight is a woman, so get them nigger feet over the side."

"I ain't partial to mud," says Jim, and the bushy man pulled a pistol from his belt and pointed the barrel square at Jim's belly. The men pushing and shoving along the walk stopped when they seen it and that part of the street got mighty still.

"Off, nigger," says the bushy man, smiling.

There's a long spell of quiet, then Jim done it, and stepped into mud way over his knees. The man give a big laugh and put his pistol away.

"White men before niggers, nigger," he says.

He took a couple or three steps, real pleased with himself till I put my leg between his and tripped him. He went into the mud head first, so deep here only his legs stayed above it. The crowd give a cheer, not on account of sympathy for Jim, just because them legs looked mighty funny waving in the air. Then someone hollers:

"He'll drown! Get him out!"

Jim was closest, just a few feet off, but he never made no effort to pull the bushy man out. He just climbed back onto the boards and left that man to drown, and I can't say I would of done different. He got saved anyway when a couple of men that's already been pushed off waded over and hauled him up by the belt, and the first thing he done is puke up mud and supper. All of us was across by now and Jim says quiet to me:

"Das de las' time, Huck. I ain't steppin' down no mo'."

Albie and the rest pushed their way into the saloon, but Jim never moved.

"I ain't goin' in, Huck. If 'n I don' get sold no liquor I'se goin' to bust a few heads, I kin feel it. You go on in if 'n you wants to."

"Naw, I reckon I'll let it pass by. Liquor ain't good for you anyhow."

Albie comes out again and says:

"You boys the slow mail or what?"

"We ain't going in, Albie," says I.

"Why not? I'll buy Ben a drink. He don't have to get served."

"I ain't goin' in," says Jim.

"Maybe if we do like Albie says there won't be no trouble."

"You go on in, Huck. I ain't goin' to."

"What'd he call you?" says Albie.

"Just a pet name my Ma give me. Tucker's my middle name, see, and she used to call me Tuck all the time, not Jack like I wanted her to."

"Well come on in, the both of you. It ain't in the rules to greet the new year sober."

Jim give a sigh and we went in, and him and me wedged ourselfs in a corner while Albie went for a bottle I give him the cash for. Jim shouts above the noise and conbobberation:

"I shoulder kep' shut! You reckon he figured it out?"

"He ain't got nothing on his mind but drinking! It don't matter!"

We waited and waited, then Albie come back with a bottle.

"I'll be over there with the rest!" he says, pointing across the room into all the smoke and confusement. "Come on over when you feel like it!"

It's real considerate of him the way he knows we ain't truly a part of the bunch he's with and never forced us to join him once we're inside, but he ain't about to let no problemation spoil his fun and went off again. Jim and me swigged from the bottle awhile but never got comfortable in there with all the shouting and laughter. Somehow it hit the wrong note after all that's happened to us this past year, and we figured we may as well leave, which we done gradual on account of the crush.

Once we got outside we pushed our way through the crowds and worked our way to the edge of the city and up over a hill to where we

can see the bay. It's a real sight even at night, with the sky clear for
a change and moonlight sparkling on the water. We went down to
the shore where there ain't no houses and it's quiet, with just the
waves lapping soft and soothing, and found a sheltered spot and sat
there passing the bottle back and forth, sipping and smoking our
pipes.

"It ain't much, Huck," says Jim.

"What ain't?"

"De lives we's livin'."

"It ain't so bad now we got a little spending money."

"I ain't talkin' cash, I'se talkin' life. You rec'llect what we was
sayin' all de way back in Missouri after you got busted outer jail?"

"I disremember exactly."

"We was talkin' 'bout po'try an' de Holy Grail an' such."

"Well, maybe so. What's your point?"

"We ain't foun' none of it, das de point. You still a wanted man an'
I'se still a nigger, an' we ain't nothin' but trash to de rester de worl'."

"Who cares what they think? The rest of the world can go hang."

"I reckon I don' care 'bout de worl' so much, Huck, but de worl'
don' wanter let me be. I'se peaceable, you knows dat, but de worl'
jest keeps on jabbin' at me wid a stick, tryin' to rile me, an' someday
I'se goin' to turn aroun' an' bust dat stick over whoever doin' de
jabbin'. I been holdin' on ever since we lef' de diggin's, jest hopin'
de plan 'bout de ship an' de islan's work out de way we want, but it
never, an' when de gol' got stole I come near to givin' up."

"I kind of felt that way myself, but it don't do to weaken, not after
all we been through. I reckon we just got to look on it like it's an
adventure in a book. You don't put down no book without you read
to the end and see how things pan out for the hero."

"I cain't read, an' I ain't no hero."

"You surely are, Jim. I got to beg to differ there. Why, look at the
way you busted me out of Sheriff Bottoms's jailhouse. I bet that's
permanent history in St. Petersburg now. I'd be a rotting corpse
with maggots coming out of my eyes if you hadn't of done it. And
look what you done in the desert. You saved Frank and me both
from getting parched to death. If that ain't a heroical deed I don't
know what is."

He stayed quiet for awhile, then says:

"If'n you says so, Huck."

"Well, I do."

By and by we heard a scattering of gunfire over the hill from the city, so it must be midnight. It died away after awhile and we drunk up the rest of the bottle slow and easy and shared out more tobacco. Says I:

"I reckon New Year's Eve has got to be the disappointingest time of year."

"Why's dat?"

"Well, I never yet felt different on the far side of midnight to the side just gone. Everything is still the same after you hear them twelve licks on the clock as it was before. I reckon a new year is something that don't exist except on calendar paper."

"You proberly right 'bout dat, Huck, an' Cris'mastime too. Ain't nobody'd know it's Cris'mas Day without other folks tol 'em so."

""I reckon you and me need a special day that don't mean nothing to no one else but us, Jim."

"You means like a birthday?"

"Kind of, but that's a day that gets handed to you by fate. What we need is a day that's ours just because we picked it ourselfs."

"What we goin' to call it?"

"Huck'n'Jim Day is the best-suited name. It's got the right ring to it."

"Soun's perty good to me. What day it happen on?"

"Somewhere in summertime I figure, so we get good weather for it. But not too close to July fourth. We don't want Huck'n'Jim Day to get confused with no other holiday."

"How 'bout de las' day in July? Das still high summer."

"July thirty-first is still a mite close to July fourth," says I. "How about the first day of August?"

"I never like de sounder August. Puts me in mind of a woman I knowed befo' I'se married, Augustine. She give me a hard time, dat woman."

"Then we'll split the difference and make it July thirty-second."

"Das fine by me, Huck. It feel mighty good to know we got ourselfs a special day ain't nobody else goin' to know 'bout."

We finished off the bottle and both blowed a wish into it then throwed it into the bay, only we forgot to put the cork in on account of being drunk so I reckon it must of sunk. Then we headed for our crate and 1850.

There ain't nothing like a bottle to make you sleep snug, but I got woke up while it's still dark by a power of banging and crashing and clopping hoofs and grinding wheels. When I poked my head out of the crate I seen that two big doors in back of the warehouse has been opened and four or five wagons with canvas-covered loads is being emptied by a couple dozen men. They worked real fast with trolleys and such and got them wagons unloaded in maybe half an hour by lamplight, boxes and crates mostly. One got dropped accidental and busted open and it's full of cans, preserves most likely. They never seen me watching from the dark, and when the job's done they closed them big doors and fitted a padlock or three and lined up to get wages for what they done, then went off in different directions without much talking. When the last two got paid there's an argument, and they got mad and talked loud enough for me to hear.

"It ain't fair," says one. "We're ten dollars short."

"You broke a case," says the one handing out the money. "You don't expect to be rewarded for carelessness do you?"

"It slipped," says the third one, smaller and whinier, and I got a chill down my back.

"It slipped because you're drunk, both of you. If you want to keep working for the company just sober up in working hours."

"I ain't drunk," whines the little one, and now I knowed for sure. It's Pap, and the big one has got to be Morg. He says:

"I reckon we should get the same as the rest. Hell, it's New Year's Day."

"That's right, not Christmas, so no presents," says the money man. "Take what's offered and keep your mouths shut."

He walked off to put an end to the argument. Pap and Morg grumbled some more then went off down an alley to the street. Jim's still snoring, drunker than me, so I never disturbed him and followed after them. They walked slow and stumbled some, but the streets was full of drunks even if it's near dawn by now, and I kept close without getting seen. Finally they come to a hotel on Montgomery Street and went inside. I give them a minute then went up to it. There's a sign out front that reckons it's the Ophir Hotel, but the building has got flophouse writ all over it, dirty and neglectable even if it's a new place. I went in and there's a clerk half asleep behind the desk with a bottle for company.

"Happy New Year," says I.

"Nnnnngh," says he.

"Pardon me for bothering your celebration, but I think I just seen my uncle come in here with another man. I ain't seen him since back in Ohio, and I wondered if you can maybe tell me if it's him, if it ain't too much trouble that is."

"I never seen 'em."

"You must of. They come in just this minute, a big man and a little man with long hair."

"I know 'em," he says, and fumbles with the register book awhile and says:

"Oliver Twine and Casey Holbrook. Room twenty-seven."

"Thank you. I reckon I'll go up and surprise them."

He slumped down in his chair again and I clumb the stairs and found number twenty-seven down the hall at the back. There ain't no one in the hallway so I kneeled by the keyhole and spied through. There ain't much to see, just Morg's back where he's sat at a table, but I can hear them pretty clear.

"One of these days I aim to stomp on that sonovabitch," says Morg.

"He deserves it," says Pap, "takin' our hard-earned money that way."

"You never helped none smashing that case."

"It was both of us had hold of it," whines Pap. "You can't blame just me."

"I can and do. You let your end go like it was red hot. Next time I ain't letting you drink before we go out."

"You warn't sober neither."

"On me it don't show, but on you it does. Take a look at yourself. Anytime you ain't got a bottle in your hand you shake like a god-damn leaf. I ain't going to be answerable when you die of it."

"Don't say that!" squeals Pap. "I ain't poorly, just tired. . . ."

"You're drinkin' yourself into the grave, Finn. You ain't got the strength to quit now. It's bound to happen."

"It ain't! Don't tell me what ain't!"

Morg give a disgusted kind of sound and stood.

"I'm for resting up," he says, and went out of eye-reach. I heard the bed creak when he flopped down, then snores. Pap stayed sat at the other side of the table so I never seen him, but he's sobbing quiet to himself. It almost made me take pity, that sound, but I recollected too many bad things about Pap to let myself sentimentalize. My legs was cramped by now and when I tried to stand up I fell hard against the door.

"Who's that?" hollers Pap, startled I guess, and I heard his boots come clumping across the floor. Quick as can be I tucked my legs under me and bowed my head just when he yanks the door open.

"Whater you want?" he says, looking down at the top of my hat.

"Spare a dollar for a poor cripple, sir?" says I in the differentest voice I can do.

"I ain't got no dollar," he says, and slams the door. Pap's the kind that won't piss on you if you're burning to death, just the meanest man there is. I shuffled along down the hall dragging my knees so he don't suspicion me and went downstairs, stood upright now. The clerk never even looked at me when I went by, so I reckon he won't be asking Oliver Twine or Casey Holbrook if he had a nice reunion with his nephew from Ohio.

I heeled it back to the warehouse yard and got back in the crate with Jim, still snoring, but I can't sleep no more, and when it's full day I woke him and we went for some breakfast. I told him everything I seen and he says it's all mighty mysterious.

When we showed up for work we got another surprise.

"Boys," says Albie, "I don't rightly know how to tell you, but the rest of the crew ain't none too happy."

"About what?" says I.

"Well . . . uh . . . about you two I reckon," he says, shifting on his feet and looking at the ground.

"What'd we do to make 'em unhappy?"

"Nothing special. It's just. . . . Dang it, Jack, this ain't none of my doing. I got to do it or they say they won't do no work, and we got a schedule to keep. Things is hard enough with Herb's broke leg. . . ."

"You mean they don't want to work with a nigger no more."

"Not exactly. . . . It's just . . . they reckon you and Ben don't fit in. We're kind of a team here, and if the team gets upset the work goes all to hell. It's the foreman's job to see that it don't, and I'm the new foreman. I'm directly answerable to the contractor that's paying our wages, and if Mr. Wyeth finds out I ain't getting the work done on schedule he'll fire me. I got to have this job, Jack. . . . It ain't nothing personal. . . ."

"Mr. Wyeth? The one that owns the Corneycopey Mercantile Company and the ferry steamer?"

"That's the one. He's a mighty big man in town and I can't afford to get on the wrong side of him."

"So we ain't working here no more."

"I reckon not. I'm real sorry, honest."

"Well, we was getting tired of it anyway."

"You ain't going to hold it against me, are you?"

"You ain't answerable to me, Albie, just to Mr. Wyeth."

Jim and me walked away then, so I had the last word. Halfway across Portsmouth Square Jim says:

"Happy New Year, Huck."

"Happy New Year, Jim."

Huck'n'Jim Day seemed like a long ways off.

✦ 32 ✦

The Price of Fame—The Facts Fancified—

A Renewed Acquaintance—Food and Water—

Cash and Promises

We had money enough to keep us fed a few days more so it ain't all that worrisome, but it means we got to find more work, so we went around every building site in town. They was all the same. No niggers. I could of got a job on any of them, but I never wanted to on account of principle. Jim's as good a man as me, proberly better, and if he ain't working then I ain't neither. It's the kind of thinking that makes you walk tall, but it don't do nothing for your pocket. At the end of the day we was both footsore and weary and maybe just a little discouraged, so after we et I come up with a mighty fine idea.

"Jim," says I, "did you ever go to the theater?"

"I never did, Huck."

"Well, neither did I, so tonight we're going to see a show, and it don't matter what it costs. We need a helping of cheer."

Jim's agreeable so we hauled ourselfs around all the theaters and looked at the billboards outside to see which one we figure we'll like best. They all looked considerable bright and cheery, with pictures of ladies in frilly little dresses that showed off their legs, but the doormen always says I'm too young to see them shows, so we moved on to a theater down the end of Dupont Street for a looksee there. I reckon we warn't ready for the billboard they got outside, and I had to read it twice over before I believed it.

FINN THE RED HANDED
by
New York City's most renowned playwright
Auberon Clitheroe
Three (3) Complete Acts!
SEE
the Juvenile Murderer of Missouri
commit his Dastardly Deed
Before Your Eyes!
THRILL
to the excitement of the
Famous Jailbreak!
WITNESS
HUCKLEBERRY FINN'S
Desperate Journey across the
Trackless Prairies & Rocky Mountains
with his companion in blood
the fearsome
NIGGER JIM
featuring
Quentin d'Arcy as Huck Finn
Ambrose Hearn as Jim
Matthew Prine as Bulldog Barrett
Kenneth Montcalme as Tom Sawyer
and
Miss Grace Gentle as Becky Thatcher

When I read it out to Jim he never believed it neither, so we just
naturally had to go inside and see. The tickets was ten dollars each,
and it's me that laid out the money just in case they don't like niggers. But there warn't no trouble once we're inside. There's a big
crowd all jammed in a room with red walls and paintings and a bar
up one end, and they warn't all dressed special or nothing, mostly in
muddy boots with their hats still on and jawing and smoking so
hard you can't hear or see nothing across the other side. Then a
man come through a door and bangs a little brass dish with a stick
and everyone swallered their drinks and grabbed hold of bottles to
take into the part where the seats is, real big and high with balconies around the walls. There's a curtain hanging down one end

with a big eagle painted on it, only it looks more like a buzzard so it warn't done by no famous artist. There must of been hundreds of people already sat down waiting for the show to start, but not like in church where they're all sat quiet. This bunch was liquored up and let the world know it, leaning over the backs of their seats and shooting the breeze with them that's sat behind, and swigging from bottles and flasks and laughing fit to bust, and the men warn't no better behaved neither. There was every kind of person there, in dirty clothes and fancy clothes and all kinds in between, but all the women was dressed like queens, whores proberly. Up front just below the stage there's an orchestra kind of twiddling and fiddling and tootling and plinking and scraping to get their insterments warm, a real racket.

Me and Jim sat about halfway down next to the aisle and got our toes squashed a couple dozen times by folks passing along the row. There ain't much light except for lamps along the walls and a string of lamps along the stage, pointed inward so's we can see the buzzard clear. I got hit by a hunk of orange peel that come from one of the balconies and looked up, but can't see who flung it. There's dozens of legs stuck out over the edge and every now and then fruit and scrunched up paper bags and nuts come flying out. Someone upset a bottle that's balanced on a balcony and it poured out onto someone's head that's below, and he hollered up at them that he don't appreciate a drink that don't come inside of a bottle, so they flung the bottle down at him too. He still warn't happy and pulled a pistol and shot the heel off a boot that's hung over the edge, which was a bad mistake because he got buried under a pile of stuff before he can even get off another shot, and finally went and got a safer seat somewhere else.

By and by the crowd got restless waiting for the show to get started and hollered for the curtain to go up, but it stayed down so they tried stamping their feet. It catched on and everyone done it till it sounds like a marching army, and this time a man in fancy duds come onto the stage from the side and the orchestra give out a kind of braying and blaring for a second or three. He holds up his hands till the crowd simmered down and there's quiet, then opened his mouth.

"Ladies and gentlemen . . ." he says.

"Where?" hollers someone, and they all hooted.

"Tonight the Eagle Theater will present for your entertainment and erudition a story of today, a story of passion, a story of cold-blooded murder. You will witness many marvelous effects specially designed by the author of our play, Mr. Auberon Clitheroe himself, some never seen before on any other stage."

"Let's see 'em then!" the same drunk hollers, but the man on stage never paid him no heed and goes on:

"You will experience the thrill of danger as the notorious outlaw Huckleberry Finn is captured and escapes to continue his flight from justice. You will weep with compassion as the luckless waif Becky Thatcher struggles to avenge her father's death. You will cheer the efforts of our hero, the greatest detective in Christendom, Chauncey Thermopylae Barrett, as he grimly seeks out the wrong-doer in the name of retribution, and above all, you will see how crime is rewarded only by punishment in a finale which has not yet taken place outside the precincts of this theater, but which, as surely as there is God above, must happen in the near future. For no man, or indeed boy, may transgress the laws of our great nation and live to profit thereby. This, then, is the essence and moral of our tale."

He ducked a few pieces of fruit that got throwed at him and talks even louder above all the grumbling, flinging his arms wide again.

"Ladies and gentlemen, we proudly present . . . *Finn the Red Handed!*"

They give him a big hand now that he's through and he walked off. The orchestra started up again and hammered away real dramatic, but the curtain never lifted and things got noisy again with more boot stomping and whistling too. Even before it starts I ain't inclined to enjoy the story, not after they give it that name to mean I'm a murderer with blood on my mitts. I only got called Finn the Red Handed by Tom Sawyer when we used to play pirates with Jo Harper and Ben Rogers and the rest, but used like this it sounds real bloodthirsty.

Finally the buzzard lifted in the air and flapped up out of the way and we seen a room that's got a rolltop desk and bookshelfs and a couple chairs. There's a middle-aged man sat at the desk writing something down, and the violins kind of whimpered to let you know he's a goodly kind soul. Then come a knock at the door and he says:

"Come in."

It opens and this dirty-looking boy without no boots come in and sat himself on a corner of the desk when he could of took a chair, and made himself comfortable there while the man give him a mean look, specially when he spit tobacco juice on the floor. Soon as he come in the piano rumbled away dangersome and dark so you know it's the villain, then quit so's you can hear him talk.

"You wanted to see me, Judge?" says the boy, and I see he's meant to be me and the other one is Judge Thatcher. Neither of them looked nothing like the real thing, let me tell you.

"Yes, Huckleberry, I did," says the judge. "And I would appreciate it if you would not sit on my desk like some ruffian. A respectable person sits in a chair in polite company."

"I ain't polite and I ain't respectable," says Huck, and a woman in the front row calls out:

"Shame on you, you brat! Have some respect!"

"Aawww, go drown yourself," says Huck to her and the crowd roars, not disapproving or nothing, just having fun, and the woman never talked back so the story got moving again.

"Well, spit it out, Judge," says Huck. "I ain't got all day to flap my gums. I got important matters to take care of."

"And what might they be?" asks the judge, looking stern.

"Fishin' mostly," says Huck, "and maybe a little smokin' too. Me and Jim got a busy day planned out."

"That is what I wish to talk to you about, young man."

"Fishin'?"

"No, the nigger."

"Well, what about him?"

"It is rumored that you have filled his head with abolitionist trash talk about freedom and equality."

"You heard correct, Judge. I figure a nigger's as good as a white man any day."

The music rumbled and crashed like buildings is falling down and everyone booed fit to raise the roof. Huck just sneered at them and when things got quieted down some the judge says:

"You must mend your ways, my boy. Since the death of your miserable father I have acted as your legal guardian, but you have been a great disappointment to me, nay, a burden upon my good intent and generosity. You must stop filling the darkie's head with nonsense and let him live his days in fruitful labor for those best suited to run the country, namely us. You are playing with fire, and should those flames of freedom ever catch it would be tragical."

"I ain't interested in none of this," says Huck, spitting again.

"Alas," says the judge, looking out past the stage lights and putting his hand on his heart. "I have nurtured a viper in the bosom of my happy home. Is there no hope of mending the boy's devilish ways? Long have I yearned for a son, but remained unblessed till the death of my dear wife. In vain did I hope this errant youth would be that boy I never had, and now look, he talks of niggers as equals, hateful words to my ears, and refuses to conduct himself or dress in a manner befitting the adopted son of a judge. And worse, I fear his influence upon my lovely daughter Becky. Above all else she must be kept free from the impure stain of this boy's godlessness. Would not every father feel this way?"

Everyone agreed it's so and cheered him on, and he points to the door and says:

"Leave my sight, Huckleberry Finn, and do not enter my home again until you have mended your ways!"

"I'll do it, and gladly," says Huck. "I never liked it here anyhow. If there's three things I can't abide it's clean sheets, clean clothes and clean living. It ain't my idea of a good life, no sir. I reckon I'm happier living like a hog and getting drunk and keeping company with a nigger. That's the life for me, and I'm off right now to get me some, so you can just holler up a drainpipe, Judge, for all the good it'll do you."

He went out the door but you can't hear it close behind him on account of the booing, then a moment later it opens again and in comes a girl with yeller hair all done out with ribbons and a frilly white dress. The violins shivered and sobbed way up high to tell you the only thing that's keeping her down here instead of up there with the angels is the weight of her shoes, and she goes over to the judge who's slumped in despair over his desk.

"Papa," she says, "what ails you so? Was it that wretched boy I have just now seen leaving our home? Oh, fie upon him for upsetting my noble parent so. He is a sore trial to us all. Speak to me, Papa."

"I can scarce draw breath, Daughter," says he, "for the stench of dirt and evil left behind by Huck Finn's pernicious presence. You must never go near him again."

"But Papa, I warned you when you took him into the bosom of our happy home that things would turn out this way. You cannot tame a snarling beast to a gentle lamb. I fear your efforts have met with naught but heartbreak for you, my darling Papa. Oh, wretched youth, and to think I once looked upon him as my friend! But no more, for his niggerish ways are loathsome to me. I am glad, glad! that he has at last left our tranquil abode. Without doubt he will return from whence he came, that broken-down cabin out in the woods wherein he lives as does a beast, and that is where he belongs. Good riddance to bad rubbish, I say!"

They all agreed and give her a heap of clapping, and the buzzard come crashing down so we can't see the room no more. When it went up again they got the inside of a log cabin set up on stage, with Huck sat on a rickety table whittling wood and talking to himself, which is something I ain't never done seeing as it's the sign of a fool.

"That danged judge has got me all meaned up," says Huck. "He thinks I ain't nothing but trash, but I reckon I'm worth ten of him. One of these days I'll have my revenge on him for them words he spoke, and my partner Jim will help me."

The cabin door opens and in comes a man with his face and hands all blacked with paint. All the deep-down insterments kind of plodded along like elephants and a lone violin skittered around like a lazy fly that can't figure out where to set down. Jim shambles over to Huck and says:

"Huck, we ain't got nothin' to eat. De fish nebber bit."

"Well what kind of bait was you using, Jim?"

"I put a real nice apple core on de hook, but dey nebber et it."

Everyone laughed at him for being a simple nigger, and Jim says:

"I reckon we got to go hungry now de judge ain't gibbin' you no spendin' money no mo', Huck."

"Jim, I've just now hatched a plan that will get us all the money we need."

"We goin' inter counterfeitin', Huck?" says Jim, and got laughed at again.

"No we ain't. We're going to rob the judge's house and take all the cash he keeps in the safe!"

The music crashed and thundered awhile and the people booed some, then Huck and Jim talked on about how they aim to do it that night, then Huck finishes by standing up and saying:

"Nothing will stop me getting my own back on the man that has spoke harsh words to me. He's the most respected man in town for being decent and honest, and that is reason enough to hate him, for these things do not come natural to me and I just can't abide to see them in others. If I had my way all decent, honest folk would get throwed in jail so's people like you and me could run things, Jim."

"I ain't incline' to do no runnin', Huck. You knows I'se jest de lazies' nigger on de ribber."

When the crowd quit laughing Huck says:

"You leave it to me, Jim. This time tomorrow we'll both be rich and we'll travel away from here to be with our own kind in some thieves' kitchen in New Orleans. Judge Thatcher, beware!"

The orchestra blatted and blared and down come the buzzard, then up again and we're back in the judge's place. He's still scribbling away and in comes Becky with a lamp in her hand. The violins got so high and zinging it sounds like there's about a million moskeeters in there, but Becky and the judge ain't slapping theirselfs so it's just angel music again.

"Papa," she says, "you must not work so late into the night hours. You will tire yourself, and your health has already suffered over the worries Huck Finn has heaped upon you."

"I must finish my work, Daughter dear. You go along to bed and don't bother your pretty head about me."

"I cannot help but worry, Papa. After all, you have all that money in the safe which robbers may try to steal."

"The money was being held in trust for a businessman, my dear, and has this very day been taken off my hands by the gentleman concerned and deposited safely in the bank. You need have no fear on that account."

"That is indeed a relief to hear, and I shall certainly sleep easier for it. Goodnight, darling Papa."

She goes and kisses him and after she's gone out the door he says:

"She is the light of my life. What man could ask for a more loving and dutiful daughter? She is unblemished by evil thought or deed, as pure and pristine as the driven snow. How it gladdens my heart that she will no longer be obliged to endure the company of Huck Finn, who has been such a thorn in my side. Yet she is right, I dwell too hard upon my work, but only that she may someday have a worthwhile dowry to bring to her wedding day. She has not told me so, but I have heard rumor of a heart that beats in unison with hers, the noble heart of a noble youth, Tom Sawyer. It would please me if such a match were to come about, for he, not Finn, is the kind of son I would be proud to have. I pray the romance blossoms without hindrance. Ahhh, me . . . but I am tired at this late hour. I will complete this final task and retire to my bed."

But he never finished the task and fell asleep with his head on the desk, and soon as it happened in comes Huck and Jim with the music tippy-toeing along secretive and sly. I ain't about to give you the whole story, just parts. After Jim and me has threatened to slice the judge's nose off if he don't open the safe he still won't do it so Huck says he'll send Jim upstairs to wake Becky none too gentle if he don't, which gets the crowd practickly tearing their seats off the floor they're so mad, and the music thunders and rolls real alarming. The judge agrees to open the safe but when he does it's empty, and Huck gets so mad he stabs the judge in the chest then Jim cuts his throat to make sure he's dead. Huck tells Jim to go fetch the horses while he looks behind all the books on the shelfs just in case the cash is stashed away secret there, hard to do on account of the books is painted on the wall, but he tries anyway and while he's doing it in comes Becky. She throws up her hands and screams when she sees the judge laid out on the floor and Huck tussles with her to keep her quiet, but by the time he's knocked her to the floor alongside the judge in comes the sheriff and I'm took away to jail. While I'm there Becky gets paid a call by Tom Sawyer who's come to comfort her, which happens in a garden full of flowers even if it all happened in winter. Tom's dressed real neat with a hat on, something he never liked as a rule, and he says:

"Becky, my heart goes out to you on this saddest of days."

"Oh, Tom," she whimpers, and the violins join in. "I knew you would stand by me in my hour of need. You are the sturdy tree upon which this fragile blossom may bloom."

Then they sung a song about hearts and flowers, and done it again so's everyone can sing along with it, which plenty done, then we're down at the jailhouse where Huck is snarling behind bars and foaming at the mouth while the sheriff feeds him off the end of a long pole. Jim comes crashing through the door with a club and lays the sheriff out and they get away, then it's back to the judge's place and along comes a man in a Panama hat and the orchestra puffed and blowed real loud so we knowed he's the hero, namely Bulldog Barrett. Becky says to him:

"I have summoned you here for one reason only, Mr. Barrett, and that is to find and capture the evil wrongdoer that has slain my dear Papa. He has gone to ground no one knows where, for he is cunning as a fox. With all my heart I urge you to seek him out and bring him forth into the light of day that my darling parent shall be avenged."

"Little Miss," says Bulldog, "the moment I laid eyes upon you I knew you to be a maiden of spotless purity, the very last person who should be hurt so cruelly. For that reason, and because you have the most becoming eyes I have ever beheld, I will accept the challenge and pursue Huckleberry Finn though he may run to the ends of the earth. This I swear: that I will not cease in my appointed task till he that has caused you such grievous unhappiness is swinging at the end of a rope."

"Oh, Mr. Barrett," she says, gone all coy and simpering. "I am overpowered by your strength of purpose. . . . It has all been such a strain these last few days . . . I feel faint. . . ."

And she swoons into Bulldog's arms so she don't bang her head on the floor and he looks down at her and says:

"Would that I were swine enough to kiss these chaste, undefended lips while their owner knows not, but no, I am not such a one that would take advantage of a maiden's momentary helplessness."

He dumps her on the sofa, but what he don't know is that Tom Sawyer seen the whole thing through the window, but we seen him see it and knowed from now on Becky's heart is half and halfed over Tom and Bulldog. Now the real excitation begins, with Huck and Jim riding on wooden horses that never budged an inch, but the scenery with trees and mountains painted on it goes sliding past behind them, mounted on rollers I reckon, because the same trees and mountains keep sliding past five times a minute so it looks like we're riding in circles, and the piano gallops along like hoofbeats. Huck says:

"We must ride danged hard, Jim, for the noblest detective of them all is on our trail."

"Reckon dat be him comin' up behin'," says Jim, and the bulldog comes on stage on another wooden horse and creeps up on us gradual, firing his pistol. Huck and Jim fire back but no one gets hit, then later on Bulldog captures us both when we're sat around a campfire and takes us to Fort Kearney. We get throwed in the guardhouse, then along comes Becky to visit Huck, not Grace like it really was, and he don't repent of his sins in front of her like she wants and knocks her over the head instead. When he takes off her dress to make the switch everyone screamed and howled and one woman a few seats off fainted dead away with shock. Then Huck lets Jim free and decoys a guard while Jim sneaks up behind and smashes his head and they're free again. Becky's out west following the bulldog, see, and Tom Sawyer's out there too following Becky on account of what he seen through the window.

There's a whole heap of lies like that and it just made me disgusted, specially the part where Bulldog captures us both at last and we get walked up to the gallows together and Bulldog says:

"Since you have seen fit to live your life with a nigger it is only fitting that you share the same scaffold. Do you have any last words, Finn?"

"I surely do," says Huck. "I'm glad I done it all and I'd do it all over again!"

He got booed and the bulldog pulls a lever and down goes Huck. Then Jim gets asked the same thing and says:

"Lawdy Lawd! If 'n only I nebber hadder listen 'ter dat boy wid his ebil ways an' bin a good hardworkin' darkie dis nebber woulder happen'. I'se jest de mistakenes' nigger in de worl', an' now I gots to pay for de ebil I done. Lawdy Lawd hab mercy on a sinnin' darkie's soul!"

The lever gets pulled again and down he goes. Everyone cheers, then along comes Becky and Tom, and Becky tells Bulldog she made up her mind; it's really Tom she's in love with and Bulldog takes the terrible news like a man and says he's too busy catching outlaws to get married anyhow, and Tom and Becky sing another song about how grand love is and the buzzard come done with a crash. The music played right lively and the crowd hooted and hollered and stamped to show they loved every minute.

Up goes the buzzard again and all the actors lined up and done a bow, only Becky Thatcher's curls fell off when she done it and underneath all that yeller she's dark haired, and I seen who she truly is. The billboard outside says she's Grace Gentle, but it ain't. It's

Grace McSween! She give the wig a wave in the air and got a special cheering, then down come the buzzard for the last time and folks started leaving. Me and Jim kept our heads down and walked a little ways apart so we don't get seen together, but nobody suspicioned us and we got out on the street again without no trouble. Jim says:

"Warn't dat jest de limit, Huck? Ain't one part dat warn't stretch' nine diff'rent ways. It ain't nothin' like what happen."

"I'm mighty sore about it too, Jim, but did you see who was acting Becky?"

"I seen her, an' I reckon she could of put dem others straight on how it truly happen. Dadblame it, Huck, how come she be lettin' folks figure it were Becky dat got de dress switch' on her when Becky ain't even lef' Missouri? An' how come Tom Sawyer gallivantin' aroun' out on de plains? Dat boy back home doin' his schoolin', not figurin' on no marriage wid Becky. Ain't neither of 'em old enough for it."

"They took a power of liberties, Jim, only back home's a long way and I guess they ain't expecting no complaints. But I'm sure surprised at Grace. I reckon I'll ask her why she ain't fixed the story none."

"How you goin' to do dat?"

"Why, I'll go backstage like gentlemen does to give flowers to the ladies that's in the show."

"You ain't got no flowers."

"I reckon she'll see me anyway, but you better not come along, not after all these people been watching you and me cutting up judges on stage. I'll see you back at the crate later on."

We went off separate and I walked around back of the theater. There's a bunch of men with bunches of flowers like I figured there'd be, mostly dressed in new clothes and sporting big rings on their fingers and diamond stickpins and such to let you know they struck it rich. Grace is the only female in the show so they ain't here to pay court to no one else, and they all knowed it too, eyeing each other up and down and sneering and matching up rings and stickpins and flower bunches to see who's got the biggest. Then the stage door opens. It's a little woman that ain't Grace, and she says real sharpish:

"She will not be coming out, gentlemen. I've told all of you and a hundred others besides that Miss Gentle is not in the market for matrimony, or for anything else."

And she slammed the door on them. They cussed considerable and one of them says she proberly ain't worth it anyhow, and after the rest finished stomping him they all went away. That's when I went up to the door and knocked, and after a heap more knocking it got opened by the same woman.

"Well?" she says, wrinkling her nose like I'm a skunk or something.

"Evening, ma'am. Would you kindly tell Grace it's Jeff Trueblood wanting to see her, please."

"I will not," she says.

"It won't cost you nothing to tell her, ma'am. Ain't you curious to see the way she acts when you give her the name?"

"Wait here," she says, and the door slams. She had a long nose, and long-nosed types is generally the curious kind, which is what I counted on and it looks like it worked. A few minutes later the door got flung open again and there's Grace with a robe around her and a big smile on her face.

"Huckleberry! . . ." she says. "Where in the world did you spring from?"

"Please, Grace, call me Jeff if you aim to shout it out loud."

"Oh, fiddlesticks. Come inside out of the cold."

I followed her along a stretch of corridor and into a little room with lots of lights and a nice hot stove in the corner and mirrors and costumes. The long-nosed woman was there too and looked real shook up when I marched in, and real offended when Grace says:

"That will be all for tonight, Rosemary, thank you."

"If you're quite sure? . . ." she says, doubtful.

"I am. Goodnight."

She went out scowling fierce, so I figure I ain't won a friend, then Grace looks at me long and hard in all that bright light and I seen her face fall.

"Huckleberry . . . you're a tramp! Oh, what has happened to you?"

"Nothing special in particular, just a heap of traveling and escaping and mining and other stuff. You look a real picture, Grace."

"You have a tooth missing! Oh, my, I never would of known it's you, you poor lamb. Why, you're skin and bone all the way through. How long is it since you had a meal?"

"Just a few hours, Grace," says I, peeking in a mirror to see what the fuss is all about. A raggedy scarecrow peeked back at me, the sorriest looking thing I ever seen besides Pap. It come as a shock and made me kind of ashamed stood next to Grace, who's just as clean as clean. It was real mortifying. Says I:

"Jim and me seen the show and reckernized you when your hair come off."

"Jim is safe too?"

"That he is. Him and me come to town a few days back."

She starts to sniff and I say:

"Don't cry, Grace. It's real nice to meet up like this but . . ."

"I am not crying, Huckleberry Finn, I'm smelling you. Don't you know you smell like a trash heap?"

"Well . . . uh . . . it ain't been easy finding a bath just recent. . . ."

"We must clean you and feed you," she says, "and afterwards you'll tell me all."

She got a stagehand to rustle up a real live coach with a coachman and horses and everything and poked me inside of it with a little umbrella she's got and made me sit over in the other corner while we bounced and squelched along the streets.

"Is this coach yours, Grace? It's mighty fine."

"It belongs to a friend of mine, but he allows me the regular use of it to get to the theater and home again. San Francisco is not safe for a young girl at night, or even in daylight. Why, as soon as men lay eyes on a female they take her for a whore. Decent respectable women have got to travel by coach."

I seen she wants to forget about the McSween Traveling Church and Whorehouse of Christ the Lamb, so I never mentioned it. Grace kept a handkerchief over her nose most of the time which made it hard to talk anyway. Pretty soon we come to a halt outside one of them big fancy brick hotels which is called the St. James. The coachman hollered to the doorman, who come over and carried Grace across the mud to the front doors and set her down. I figured he ain't going to do the same for me so I clumb down and done the trip under my own steam. Soon as he seen me stood there the doorman yells at me to go find a drain to play in, but Grace says:

"He's with me, George. I feel it is my charitable duty to feed the beggars of town once in awhile."

"That's a noble sentiment, Miss Gentle," says George, but he looks at me like I just got scraped off his boot. I followed Grace inside and up a stack of wide stairs all covered in carpet then along a hall. She opened a door and in we went, and it's like a magic room inside, with carpets thick as spring grass and satin on the walls and mirrors and pictures and velvet curtains big as a ship's sails hung over the windows. Grace went and yanked on a rope that's joined to the ceiling and a door opens and in comes a Spaniard girl.

"Consuela, a bath," says Grace. "A very deep, very hot bath with bath salts."

"Si, señorita," says Consuela, and out she goes again.

"Don't sit down," says Grace.

"Are we going somewheres else?"

"The furniture must not be soiled," she says.

So I stood there while she went off and changed her outfit for another robe that's made of silk with a mixture of colors in it. She seen me looking and kind of twirled around so it flew out and I seen her legs all the way up from ankles to knees, which is where her frilly pantyloons is tied with little pink ribbons to match up with the ones on her slippers.

"This came all the way from China," she says, and flopped onto a real elegant sofa and looks at me with her head on one side and says:

"Time and fate have been unkind to you, Huckleberry. You look like an old man."

"I've had considerable worries, Grace. The bulldog's still hard on my heels and . . . and how come he catches me and hangs me in that danged show? And how come there's Tom Sawyer and Becky Thatcher in it? There ain't a single true fact in the whole story."

"I am an actress, not a writer," she says. "Auberon is the one to complain to, but you can hardly do that, now can you?"

"I reckon not, but it's a danged shame the way he stretched things."

There's a knock on the door and in comes Consuela again with a little smile that's hid behind her hand whenever she looks at me.

"It is ready, señorita."

"While he's in it you can fix up some food for both of us. I'm just starved."

Off she went and Grace showed me through to the bathroom. It's bigger than some houses I seen, with shiny marble everywhere and a bath you could of floated a steamboat in. It never took long to fill because there's gold faucets shaped like fishes that puked all the hot water you need direct from a boiler someplace else in the hotel, Grace says, so you don't have to haul buckets of it upstairs or nothing. She was real proud of that bathroom.

"Get in," she says, "and if you don't get rid of every speck of dirt I'll make you do it again."

"I'll do it proper, Grace," says I, and she left.

I clumb out of my duds, gone kind of stiffish with sweat and dried mud now I come to pay them mind, and dumped them in a heap on the floor. Then I lowered myself gradual into all that steaming water. Apart from when we crossed rivers and such it's the first bath I took since 1848 back when I lived with the Widow Douglas. Hot water ain't all that familiar to me, but it's friendly stuff once you get down into it, and real relaxsome after awhile. There's perfume in it too, which is a first-time experience for yours truly, and a hunk of soap that's shaped like a turtle. That turtle seen every part of me close up, but never got offended by none of it, and when I'm finished in comes Consuela and picks up my clothes on the end of a broomstick and walks out again, giggling all the while. I was too mortified at the way she strolled in to tell her to let them be, and now I'm in confusement with regard to the matter of duds. Then in comes Grace with an armload of clothes and puts them on a chair.

"These should fit you," she says. "They belong to Consuela's little brother. He's the bellboy here. Huckleberry, you're trying my patience something sore."

"What'd I do, Grace?"

"It's what you haven't done. Look at your face! And your hair! You're supposed to wash above the neckline too. Squint your eyes and get under that water this instant."

I had to do it or she would of poked me under with her little umbrella, and when I come up for air she watched over me to make sure I give my headstraw a good sudsing with the turtle, then I ducked under again and when I come up she poured a pitcher of cold water over my head, punishment I reckon. Then she left so's I can get dried and dressed.

The clothes fitted fair and I come out feeling kind of awkward and shy. Grace was sat at a little table piled up with food, and she points to another chair on account of her mouth being full. I sat and et and in between mouthfuls she told me how she left the Naismith train at Sacramento after Mr. Shaughnessy asked her to marry him, seeing as Mrs. Shaughnessy died in the desert. Grace warn't partial to him but says she'll do it if he gets her a ring, which he done, and she went straight back to the store and got the money back on it, just enough for a steamer ticket downriver to San Francisco. When she got here she warn't inclined to wash no dishes or nothing and got work with a bunch of dancing girls, even if she can't dance, and while she's there she met a man that come backstage with a bunch of flowers and a diamond ring, and pretty soon after that she changed her name and started work in what she calls legitimate theater, which means they don't allow no bastards to work there I guess. The Eagle Theater where she does the show is owned by the man with the flowers and diamond ring, who's called Miles, and *Finn the Red Handed* is the successfullest show they ever put on there.

"I earn a thousand dollars a week and I'm happy as can be," she says. "Now tell me what happened to you."

I never let on about Pap and Morg; it's too secret to tell no one except Jim, but I laid on all the rest thick as I can. It took awhile and she listened real close, and when I finished she says:

"Oh, Huckleberry, what an adventure! It puts Auberon's silly story to shame. All he ever had was newspaper clippings to inspire him. If you told him the truth I'm sure he'd rewrite the whole play."

"You told me yourself it ain't possible, not while I'm a wanted man. I don't want to meet him anyway, not someone that reckons I'm a cold-blooded murderer and Jim's a fool. He'd likely turn me in soon as he knowed who I am."

"Well, suit yourself," she says, "but it could give you undying fame, and Auberon would pay you for the story."

"I'd prefer to get forgot."

"You won't be unless you escape from Chauncey Barrett, and you can't do that without money, and you've got none."

"It's a problem, but I reckon me and Jim'll find a way out."

"You're so impractical sometimes you make me want to scream. Did you wash your face?"

"All over, Grace."

"Well, it's still dirty," she says, leaning over the table. "Why, Huckleberry Finn, you've grown whiskers! I never noticed them under all that dirt. We'll have to get you shaved."

It's true what she says. When we was mining I rubbed my chin one day and felt little tickling hairs there, and on my lip too, but I figured it's just as well to let it grow and make me look older, not like Huck Finn no more. But Grace says it looks just awful, what folks call catkin fluff, and she orders me into the bathroom again and sits me in a chair and whips up a bowl of suds in a jiffy, then gets a razor off a shelf and comes at me.

"Grace, I ain't too sure about this. . . ."

"Don't be such a silly. I've shaved men before. Just you sit there and don't move."

I never argued, not while she's got a razor in her fist, and she painted my face with suds and scraped away.

"Don't be so stiff," she says. "I'm not pulling a tooth."

It never took long. She holds up a mirror and says:

"There, now you're the smoothest thing outside of glass."

"Aawww, Grace . . . you've gone and took years off me. Now I look like Huck Finn again. Dang it, I never should of let you."

"You're just the most exasperating person I ever met. I give you a bath and a shave and food and new clothes and what kind of gratitude do I get? None at all."

"Thank you for all of it, Grace. I appreciate what you done."

A clock in the other room bonged midnight and she says:

"You'll have to go soon. He'll be back anytime now."

"Who will?"

"My gentleman friend Miles that owns the theater, puddin'-head."

"I figured this place was yours."

"It is, and his too."

"You mean he lives here?"

"Of course he does. Where would you expect, out in the hall? We've got a bed with a canopy over the top like European royalty sleep in. Do you want to see it? It's the biggest bed in the world."

"No thank you, Grace. I best be getting on back."

"Where are you staying?"

"Oh, a place that ain't nothing like this."

"This is only a hotel. Miles is building a big mansion for me on top of a hill, but it won't be finished for awhile yet. It's going to have fifty rooms and acres of garden and a fountain with statues out front."

"That sounds fine, Grace. I reckon you'll be happy there."

I got up and she followed me through to the other room, but before I can open the door to the hall she grabs me by the arm.

"Huckleberry, you'll come back and see me, won't you?"

"You can't need no more company, Grace, not with the kind of life you got now."

"But I want to see you again. I can talk to you. You understand me. . . . Pretty please, Huckleberry?"

For all that she acts like she's growed up and dignificated I can see there's a whole lot of little girl left inside of Grace still. She's got her face all screwed up with worry that I ain't going to come back, and I seen something for the first time since she let me in the stage door. She ain't happy, not one little bit. Now I come to look at her close there's shadows under her eyes and her mouth is kind of pinched and quivery. She's still the prettiest girl I ever seen, but it's like I can see behind her face, and that ain't pretty at all, just miserable and jumbled and sad. She says:

"If you like I'll talk to Miles and he'll give you and Jim work so you can save money to get away."

"I ain't asking for no favors from a body I ain't even met."

"He'll do it for *me*, not you. He gives me whatever I want, truly. If I ask him he'll fix you both up so you don't have any more worries. . . . Please say you'll come back."

"Well, all right, but not here."

"At the theater? Come by the stage door after the last show and I'll have Rosemary let you in. You won't let me down, will you?"

"I reckon not."

"Wait. . . . I've got something for you," she says, and rushed away and come back with a purse and pulled out a handful of money.

"Here, take this and get Jim some clothes too," she says, shoving it in my pockets.

"I can't take no money off you, Grace. . . ."

"Don't you dare be late tomorrow," she says, and opened the door and shoved me out in the hall and slammed it shut again. I stood there trying to figure if maybe I should slide the money back under the door, then I recollected how raggedy Jim is nowadays and made up my mind. It's a rich man's money anyhow, and most likely plenty more where it come from, so it don't make a grain of sense to feel guiltiness about it. There's folks in the hall that's giving me strange looks just stood there figuring things, so I went downstairs and out in the street and headed for the crate Jim and me calls home.

A Narrow Escape—Chance Meeting—The Seamy Side—
Night Work—Partners in Crime

Next day Jim got new clothes and went in one of them Chinaman bath houses and come out a new man. He even got his hair barbered and his beard shaved. I hardly reckernized him he's so dandified, but he ain't finished yet. He says we both got to get new hats to kind of round things off, so we went in a hatshop where there's all kinds of head warmers. When it come our turn to get served the storeman acted kind of snotty when he sees Jim's a nigger, but he smiled when I let him see the color of our cash. He wanted to serve me first on account of I'm white, but I made him fetch Jim's hat before me. Jim put it on and strutted a little in front of the mirror and says he'll take it, then the storeman wants to know what hat I want.

"The one in the window," says I.

"There are several dozen styles on display," he says, real snippy. "If you would care to step outside perhaps you could point it out."

"I surely will," says I, and went out on the sidewalk. He poked his head in the window from inside and took the one I want off a little stand, and about then I got a kind of tingly feeling down my back and turned around. Right across the street is Bulldog Barrett, and he's looking straight at me! I never stopped to give it no consideration, just run like a rabbit off down the street, switching and dodging through the crowds fast as I can without running into no one that'll grab me and want to know where the fire is. I figured I had a lead on Bulldog seeing as he's got to get across a muddy street before he can follow on, but when I give a fast look over my shoulder I seen he's smarter than I counted on and never bothered with crossing, just run along keeping track of me from the other side. Then the street got crowded with wagons and he can't do that no more, so now he's crossing over, splashing through the mud and ducking under teams and not stopping for nothing. His legs is longer than mine so I got to lose him quick or get catched. I seen an alleyway and pounded along it through the trash and mud and turned left into another big street and hared along it then down another alley into another street that ain't so crowded. Behind me I can hear the bulldog crash through a pile of garbage and cuss something awful. He's real close now and I got to find a place to hide or get chased all around town. If he gets tired he's only got to holler "Stop thief!" and I'll get collared by someone that's law-abiding, which there's got to be a couple of in San Francisco.

Then I seen a fancy coach by the sidewalk just a little way down the street with the driver fitting nosebags on the team, so I run to it and hauled open the door fast but quiet so the driver don't turn around, and clumb in and closed it soft behind me and squatted on the floor in the dark, seeing as the window blinds is drawed. I put a hand over my mouth to make myself quit panting and waited, then heard running footsteps that slowed down gradual and come to a stop right by the coach. Then the bulldog's voice asks the driver if he seen a boy run by, but the driver says he never and Bulldog run on, so it looks like I'm safe.

Ain't it peculiar how when things is happening real fast you can see a thing and at the same time not see it? Now that I can rest easy it come to me all of a sudden that the little picture I seen on the coach door when I opened it is mighty familiar, two crossed swords and a bull's head with long horns. Of all the coaches I could of come across I went and jumped in Don Esteban Hernando Rodrigo and All the Rest's! It's enough to make you wonder if maybe guardian angels watches over us after all. Don Esteban must of took his time about going back south after his trip to the diggings, or maybe he just likes it here in Frisco. But it's strange that the driver never sounded like a Spaniard. Then I hear the bulldog's voice again.

"I've asked up and down the street but no one saw him," he says.

"Well neither did I," says the driver, and he ain't no Spaniard, definite.

"He may have sneaked into your coach. Would you mind if I looked inside?"

"Help yourself. What's he done, stole something?"

"My pocket watch."

The dark inside the coach ain't going to help me none when he opens that door, and I got a dose of the frantics trying to figure a way out. Then I felt a little latch digging in the side of my arm where I'm scrunched on the floor, and what it is give me the answer. It's the latch to a little door under the seat to a stowaway space for traveling rugs and such, and I opened it and squirmed inside and pulled the door shut. There ain't hardly room to breathe in there, and no rugs neither, which is a mercy. I hear the coach door get opened, then Bulldog says:

"No, my mistake. Thank you anyway."

"Maybe he went along the other way," says the driver.

"That is possible. Good day to you."

I stayed where I am for fear of getting in more trouble if I leave. The bulldog'll likely prowl around hereabouts for awhile yet, so I'm safer here, even if I can't feel my legs no more from being cramped up. To take my mind off it I planned on how I'll give Esteban a big surprise when he comes back to the coach from wherever he is, but he better come quick or he'll get surprised by finding me dead of not breathing. I ain't sure how long it took till he clumb inside, but my face must be blue by now. The coach dipped a little with his weight, then the driver slapped the reins and we was off and lurching through the mud. I figured now's as good a time as any to do the surprising and opened the little door, but being cooped up in there has gone and cramped my muscles so bad I can't do no more than that. Then a pistol gets poked in my face and a voice that ain't Esteban's says:

"Come out slowly."

"I ain't able . . . I'm stuck. . . ."

"If you're not out by the count of five you'll also be dead, my friend."

There ain't nothing like fright to make you do things you figured ain't possible. I come wriggling out like a snake and rolled around on the floor with the blood coming back in my legs along with pins and needles. The blinds ain't been opened still and I never seen too much except for the barrel of that pistol held close to my face and a shape behind it with a wide-brimmed hat.

"Pardon me," says I. "You ain't Don Esteban after all. . . ."

"No indeed," he says, "but you're surely Huckleberry Finn."

"No I ain't. I'm Jack Winterbough. . . ."

He took the pistol away and snapped up the blind so I can see, and it's Randolph Squires! If you ever lose a friend or kin just go to San Francisco and you'll find him in around five minutes.

"Well, well," he says, smiling. "So you survived the desert after all."

"And you, Randolph," says I, figuring I ain't about to call him no Mr. Squires. "Ain't it funny the way we keep bumping into each other."

"What brings you to hide in my coach?" he wants to know.

"Bulldog Barrett."

"He's still after you? I saw a show a few nights back that had you hanged by final curtain."

"I seen it too and it ain't nothing but lies. How'd you come to be in Esteban's coach yourself?"

"The coach is now mine. I won it from the Don in a game of poker. The Spaniard was congenial company, but he knows nothing of cards. He was, however, a fine loser."

"He ain't in town no more?"

"He has returned to his hacienda in the south, where his rich daddy will no doubt thrash him for his foolishness. How do you come to know of him?"

I told about the horse race up in Sacramento and whittled down the rest to the part where I got jumped by the bulldog outside the hatshop. He says:

"If you're buying a new hat I guess you struck it rich up north."

"We made a strike all right, but it got stole off us soon as we got here. Grace give me the money for new clothes and such."

"And who might Grace be?"

"She's the one that acts Becky Thatcher in *Finn the Red Handed*. Her and me is old friends."

"Is that so?" he says. "You're keeping high-class company, Huckleberry. What do you and the nigger plan to do now?"

"Get out of town before the bulldog sees us again, I reckon."

"And your friend Grace will render assistance?"

"That's what she told me."

"She must be a girl of sterling character to risk helping a wanted criminal for friendship's sake. I'd count it a favor if you introduced me to the young lady."

"What for?"

"Because my coach has aided your escape. One good turn deserves another."

I can't deny I owe him that much at least, but I never felt good about it. Randolph is kind of flint-hearted under all that charm and handsomeness and he ain't the kind I would of wanted Grace to meet up

with. Even a strong-willed lady like Lydia come close to getting attracted to him and she was awful in love with Andrew at the time. I
just hope Grace is powerful fond of her mansion-building rich man.

Randolph says I can stay at his hotel all day so the bulldog won't spot
me and I'm agreeable, but worried about Jim. He won't know why I
shot away like I done, but I reckon he's smart enough to figure there
ain't but one thing would of made me do it and he'll keep low so's he
don't get spotted neither. When we got to Randolph's place I seen it's
only a block away from where Grace lives, another fancy hotel but not
so grand. When we stepped out of the coach the driver looked considerable surprised to see me, but he never asked how come and Randolph told him to put the coach and team in the stable and have them
ready for tonight so's he can go to the Eagle Theater with me and meet
Grace. He ain't one to waste no time, Randolph. Up in his rooms he
had a bite of food sent in and jawed awhile about how he never bothered with mining, just come straight to San Francisco and started
gambling.

"Why sweat for gold?" he says. "The miners head for Frisco as soon
as they hit pay dirt and scatter their hard-earned nuggets like seed.
Whores, liquor and the gaming tables are the natural resting places of
that golden rain, and I have taken my share."

He don't give a hoot for no one but his own self and I warn't too
comfortable being there with him, but he never talked for long. Gam-
blers generally work all night and sleep in the day, and that's what he
done all through the afternoon. I stayed quiet so I don't wake him and
smoked one of his cigars, then I nodded off too on the sofa. It's full
dark when he come awake and got supper sent up from the kitchen
and we et without talking. There's still hours to go before Grace
finishes the last show but Randolph warn't inclined to wait around.
We got in his coach and bumped and swayed along the streets and
come to a building that ain't showing no lights behind the drapes and
went inside.

I ain't never been inside such a place before but I can reckernize it
from lectures the Widow Douglas give me. This here is a Den of Iniq-
uitousness. There's gambling tables with green cloth under low-hung
lamps and a piano player tinkling soft so's he don't disturb the players
and a bunch of women that must of just this minute got out of bed,
because all they got on is skimpy nightdresses that show off their
shoulders and chest and legs. A big woman in a piled-high wig seen

Randolph come in and throws her arms around him like he's her son that's come back after getting drowned at sea or something.

"Randolph, you devil!" she says. "It's been days. We wondered if some sore loser shot you."

"Maude, you know even death would not keep me away from here."

She laughed and says:

"And who might this whippersnapper be?"

"A friend of mine, Jack Winterbough. Say hello to Maude, Jack."

"Evening, ma'am."

"Why, he's polite. I thought you never moved in polite circles, Randolph."

"I'm cultivating them nowadays in case I decide to become a gentleman. Who's at the tables?"

"Chickens waiting to be plucked," she says, and both of them laughed and started talking low together, so I went over and watched the piano player, a real sad-looking man with long hair. He seen me watching and says:

"Do you have a request?"

"No, sir, I like what you're playing right now."

"Thank you. It is pleasant to meet a music lover of your discernment. See how you like this one."

He done another tune, but before he's finished a lady come up to me and says:

"Are you Jack?"

"Yes, ma'am."

"Well come with me," she says, and grabbed ahold of my hand and hauled me over to the stairs. I seen Randolph sat at one of the tables and he give me a wink when I got drug past.

"Pardon me, ma'am," says I, "but is it something urgent?"

"Not at your age," she says, "but there's no harm in starting early. I did and never regretted it."

She ain't talking about learning to smoke, I can see that, and when we started up them stairs I got panicky, trying to figure if it's best to break loose and run out the door or go on up. If I cut and run I just know Randolph and the rest that's there will laugh and reckon I'm a coward, and I ain't, I know I ain't, but I ain't ready for nothing like this neither. Then we're at the top and I got pulled along a hall and through a door that got locked behind us and it's too late.

"Well now," she says, smiling at me. She's kind of pretty but with a mite too much paint from the neck up, and she's got what Jim calls a womanly figure. There's a hammering in my chest and a shaking in my legs and I'm feeling kind of parched, all at the same time. I should of run when I had a chance. This ain't what I want at all. They say you got to go through the gate sometime, but there ain't a law that says you got to use the first one that happens along, not when so many others went through it before you and practickly swung it off the hinges.

"Well," she says, "are you just going to stand there or what?"

"Thank you, ma'am, I'll take a seat."

There's a chair handy and I perched on it with my knees rattling in my britches, and she says:

"I ain't paid to stand here all night."

"You can have the chair if you want, ma'am."

"You ain't ever done this before, have you?"

"Yes, ma'am, I been sitting on chairs all my life. This here's one of the comfortablest I ever had the experience of."

"Now look," she says, losing her patientness, "Maude says I have to fix you up. Your friend paid for it and I got picked for the job, so you better do it or I'll get in trouble."

"You don't have to do nothing, ma'am. I won't tell. We could just pass the time with a yarn or three if you like."

"Don't you want to do nothing?"

"Not if you don't, ma'am."

"I suppose you think I ain't pretty enough. Well let me tell you there's plenty that think I am. I'm real popular, so don't you tell me I ain't pretty."

"Oh, you're pretty all right, ma'am," says I, and kind of twitched my shoulders and head a little. "I reckon you're downright beautiful now I come to look at you."

"Well I should hope so too," she says.

I give another twitch and my legs shot out straight and my heels drummed on the floor. She looks at me and says:

"Is there something ailing you? . . ."

"No, ma'am, it happens every once in awhile. My Pap was the same, but he mostly done it when there's a full moon. I'll be my regular self momentarily. Just pay no mind to me. It ain't nothing harmful."

I twitched myself clean off the chair and thrashed along the floor and done a few rollovers on the way.

"Ain't the weather been terrible just lately," says I, and chewed a hunk of the bed cover that's hanging in my face, then I twitched over to the bureau and gnawed awhile on the leg, then say:

"But it's accountable this time of year."

She never spoke a word, just watched with her mouth hung open, and I give a few more jerks and then quieted down.

"I reckon that's all just for now. I'm glad you got a carpet in here, ma'am. There's times I done myself harm falling off horses and such."

"You ain't . . . crazy, are you?" she asks.

"No, ma'am. It's a body ailment, the doc says, but it's mortifying when it happens in the street. I reckon I'll get back on the chair now."

I done it and she sat herself on the bed and stared at me, and I knowed she won't come nowhere near me now. I give her a smile and she kind of curled her lip polite, but I figure if I twitch just one more time sudden-like she'll be up and out the door. I stayed still as can be with her watching me like a mouse does a snake, and after awhile I say:

"Well, I reckon I'll be getting along now, ma'am. It's been mighty nice talking with you."

I stood up and she backed off a little, and she's still staring at me when I went out the door. Downstairs Randolph is still gambling and he's got a pile of money in front of him. The others sat around the table was looking mighty miserable on account of it, but Randolph warn't smiling or nothing, just flicking cards left and right and chewing on his cigar. I stayed out of sight while he gambled on another hour or so, then he looked at his pocket watch and stood up and says:

"Gentlemen, it has been a pleasure matching wits with you."

"What's your hurry?" says one. "Afraid your luck'll run out?"

"I'm afraid of nothing more than overburdening my pockets," he says, but they never seen the joke. He spoke a few words to Maude and then we left. Back in the coach again he says:

"How was it?"

"Interesting, thank you. I reckon I must owe you money."

"On the house," he says, and laughs. He can't see inside of me no more than he can see through a brick wall, and we never spoke again all the way to the theater. I still ain't happy with the plan to meet Grace, but he done me a favor this morning and I got to return it honorable.

There's more moonstruck men waiting by the stage door with flowers, and stood back away from them is Jim. I figured he'd be here

seeing as he knowed we got to see Grace tonight and find out if her
rich man has got work to give us, and he's real surprised to find I
brung Randolph along. I told him what happened outside the hatshop
and he says he figured it must of been the bulldog but went looking for
me anyway, then back to the crate when he never found me. I can see
he must of been more worried than he's letting on, but he ain't too
talkative with Randolph there. We went up to the stage door and
knocked and got let in by Rosemary. She warn't happy to see there's
two more besides me, which is all Grace must of told her is coming,
but Randolph sweet-talked her and in we went, which give them that's
left outside plenty to howl about.

I knowed the way to Grace's dressing room and went in first, and
there's Grace and there's her rich man. He's around fifty or so and kind
of thick around the waist, but it's his face that grabs your eye, strong
and hard-looking with black muttonchop whiskers either side. Grace
opened her mouth to do the introductions but he never give her the
chance.

"Good evening," he says. "I am Miles Wyeth."

I reckon it come as no big surprise to me that he's the one we
already heard so much about, what with sailing into town on his
ferryboat and working on his building site and seeing a play about
ourselfs in his theater.

"Good evening too," says I. "I'm Jack Winterbough, and these here
are two friends of mine, Ben Rogers and Randolph Squires."

"Of course," he says, but his mouth has got a crooked smile that says
he don't believe me. He never made no effort to introduce Grace so I
done it for him. He's rich, but he ain't got no manners.

"Randolph," says I, "you proberly reckernize Miss Grace Gentle, but
if you don't, well, this here's her."

"Indeed I do," he says, and kisses her hand gentlemanly-like. "I
have been three times to see your play and was more impressed each
time."

"Thank you, Mr. Squires," she says, looking down at the floor all
modest.

"I believe I've seen your face in the Crystal Saloon, Mr. Squires,"
says Miles. "My manager there has pointed you out to me as an invet-
erate winner at my tables."

"He does not exaggerate, sir, but now that we are acquainted I will
be less severe upon your hardworking dealers."

Miles give a short laugh and says:

"Play as you will, Mr. Squires, my bank can hold out against your best efforts."

"That sounds uncommonly like a challenge, Mr. Wyeth, and that is something no gambler can resist."

"Take it as such by all means," says Wyeth, but he ain't laughing now and they kind of looked at each other a heartbeat or so without no one making a sound, then Grace says:

"Miles, we'll be late, I fear."

It ain't her regular way of talking, but I guess she figures rich men's ladies is supposed to talk snooty that way. Says Miles:

"Miss Gentle and I are attending a social gathering at Governor Burnett's home this evening. Maybe you'd like to come along, Mr. Squires. The governor is an informal man and will accept a guest invited by myself."

"A great honor, sir," says Randolph. "I accept with thanks."

"My dear," says Miles to Grace, "would you accompany Mr. Squires to the coach while I discuss business matters with our young friend here?"

"Certainly, Miles," she says, and her and Randolph went out. Soon as they're gone Miles put a less friendly look on his face.

"I know who you are, Finn," he says, "but do not worry. I have no argument with you and no interest in your past."

"Did Grace tell you?"

"Of course. She knows the reward on your head and the nigger's is too small to tempt me. I'm prepared to do you both a favor for Grace's sake. Work for me and you'll earn good money. It's night work, which will keep you off the streets. I happen to know that a famous gentleman by the name of Barrett is in town looking for you, so it will be to your advantage."

"We'll take it."

"What is the nature of your friendship with Mr. Squires?" he asks.

"Him and some others got me and Jim out of a tight corner with Bulldog Barrett back in the Rockies."

"So he knows who you are?"

"He ain't tempted by no puny thousand dollars neither."

"Good. It's as well to know who your real friends are. You'll start work tonight, but mark my words, I expect hard labor from you both. I never grant favors for nothing. No businessman does."

"I reckon we can oblige you," says I.

He give me a long look then says:

"Very well. Outside with you both."

We went around the side of the theater where Randolph is talking with Grace by his coach, and they quit jawing when we come up.

"Ahh, yes," says Miles, "the famous de Villamarga coach. The whole town talked of that game, Mr. Squires, and now I see why. It's a finely crafted vehicle to be sure."

"I'd be honored if Miss Gentle and yourself would allow me to convey you to the governor's house, Mr. Wyeth," says Randolph.

"A generous offer, sir. I accept. Allow me just one moment to send my own away."

He give me and Jim a sign to follow him, and when we got to his coach a little way off he whispered a few words to a man sat inside then says:

"Get in. Mr. Portiss will give you your instructions."

He went back to Randolph's coach and we got inside of his. Mr. Portiss ain't a handsome man, big and deep-chested with a scar down his cheek and dressed in rough clothes. The coach started off and he says:

"Mr. Wyeth don't like people that's got loose lips. You got loose lips?"

"No," says I.

"How about you, nigger?"

"I reckon not," says Jim.

"That's good. Loose lips ain't healthy. You can even die from it, know what I mean?"

"I guess we do."

But we never, not then anyway. I figured Portiss is just trying to let us know who's boss the way some men always got to do, even when it's just a boy and a nigger they're telling.

"What kind of work is it?" I ask.

"You'll find out," he says.

The coach jerked along the streets awhile without no more talk inside and then stopped.

"Out," says Portiss.

We done it and seen we're stood right by the exact same warehouse around back of which is the empty crate we slept in, the place I seen Pap and Morg taking stuff into in the early morning hours.

"Pardon me," says I. "Would this place be the Corneycopey Mercantile Company's warehouse?"

"This is it all right," says Portiss.

"There ain't no sign that says so."

"Maybe that's on account of it'd bring thieves," he says, and give a laugh that ain't got a smidgen of humorousness in it. "Get around the back."

We marched along the alley and there's all the crates same as usual, only there's a half dozen wagons too and a bunch of men waiting around. I got a notion to run off before I seen their faces up close, but Portiss is right behind us. Says I:

"Mr. Portiss, sir, me and my partner has decided we ain't partial to Mr. Wyeth's offer after all, so we'll just be strolling along."

"You stroll straight ahead or I'll break your neck," he says.

"Well, all right then, if you need us that bad."

He marched us into the bunch and says a few words to the same man that was handing out money a few nights back, then bawls out:

"Get in the wagons!"

Five or six got in each wagon and they pulled out in line and headed south, near as I can figure. I kept my head low and peeked at the men that's with us, but none of them is Pap or Morg. It never took long to leave the city behind, then we turned east for the bay and after awhile the wagons stopped and everyone got out. There's thick fog rolling around, soft and white and making the waves a little way off kind of muffled. I had a mind to slide off into the fog with Jim but Portiss kept too close a watch on us, so we was obliged to go down to the water with the rest. There's seven longboats drawed up on the shore and the men got in and unshipped the oars. Says I:

"Mr. Portiss, sir, we both get awful seasick on water. . . ."

"Get in," he says.

And we done it. You don't give no argument to a man that's got a face like Portiss.

"Shove off," he says, and all the boats got pushed off and the oars was dipped into water black as molasses. They got strung into a line and slid along quiet on account of the oarlocks is wrapped in cloth, and when I seen that I knowed for sure we ain't bound for no legal work. Jim and me was in the lead boat along with Portiss. He's got a compass and a piece of paper in his hand that he looks at real close

every now and then by the light of a lamp with a shutter he opens just
for a second or three then closes again. The paper must be a map I
reckon, but how can you have a map of water? Pretty soon we heard a
bonging sound, real mysterious till I figured it ain't nothing but a
marker buoy with a bell. Portiss steered us for it and the other boats
come along behind without no one talking, and there's the buoy poking out of the water like a dead tree in a swamp.

Portiss steered us to port and we rowed on with the oars creaking
just a little and the waves lapping soft against the bows and the bell
fading away behind. Portiss looks at his compass and paper all the time
now, and he's got a pocket watch too, marking off the minutes since
we left the buoy. Then he alters course and I seen three masts poking
out of the water where a ship has sunk at anchor, real dismal looking.
We rowed around it and then we're on the edge of the floating graveyard. Them deserted ships was shadows in all that swirling fog, riding
the water like big sleeping birds. Portiss guided the longboats from one
ship to the next, and I reckon his map shows where every one is anchored. They're so crowded together we ain't ever out of sight of one at
least, and Portiss was mighty clever the way he steered through to
where they're crowded like hogs in a pen. We rowed by so close I seen
their names on the bows: *Patagonia, Baltic Queen, Venturer,* all of
them quiet as can be. Then Portiss says to ship oars and we slid alongside a big clipper, the *Prometheus.* There's a rope ladder been left
hung over the side and one of the men clumb aboard and got throwed
a line to secure. The men on the other boats throwed lines too, and
soon as they was all tied fast everyone swarmed aboard the clipper. It
was ghostly and strange to be stood on deck with just the rigging
blocks creaking and the fog rolling around, and the men all felt it and
kept herded together.

Portiss went to the for'ard hatch and took a hammer out of his jacket
and knocked out the clips so's the hatch can be took off. They lifted it
clear and I seen the cargo hold is filled with boxes and suchlike,
which I never expected on a ship that ain't even guarded, and now
I knowed what we come here for, which is robbing. A rope got tied
to a cleat and throwed down and Portiss points to Jim and me
and says:

"Get down there."

We slid down into the hold and a dozen more followed, along with a
big rope net. Lamps got lit so's we can see to steal better, then Portiss

come down too and took out a bunch of papers. He looked at them and then at the crates and started marking different ones with an X in chalk, so I reckon what he's got there is a cargo manifest and he's figuring out the best things to take away. Soon as he X'd a box the men drug it over to the net and it got hauled up on deck. They was real expert and done it quick without no fuss, and me and Jim never had no choice but to do our part, and sweatful work it was too. The air down there must of been fresh back in New York or China or wherever the *Prometheus* come from, but it ain't improved with the voyage. Injun Joe's cave back home smelled sweeter, and that's with Injun Joe dead in it awhile. I sneaked a peek at all the men that's down there and none of them is Pap or Morg, but there's plenty more on deck that's swinging the goods over the side on a boom that I ain't seen the faces of yet, and more again down in the longboats stowing everything away. We worked steady and fast, even moving crates that ain't X'd to get to them that's underneath, so Portiss's manifest must be real exact to show him right where all the best stuff is.

It must of took hours till someone whispers down that the boats can't hold no more, but Portiss made us dig out three more crates anyway before he's satisfied we got the cream of the cargo. The lamps got blowed out and we clumb up on deck, then the hatch got fitted back in place and the clips fixed like they was before. The longboats was all piled high with crates and boxes and bales so there ain't hardly room enough for us, but everyone squeezed onto a seat and untied the lines then pushed off with the oars till we was clear, then started rowing.

Portiss guided us back the way we come with his map and compass and watch and the keels grinded onto the shore just before dawn. But the work ain't finished yet. We had to take all them stolen goods out of the boats and load them in the wagons, and it's on my fifth trip from the boats that I seen Pap the same time as he seen me. He give a shout and fell down, and a man come up to see what's wrong and it's Morg, but all Pap can do is point. When Morg seen me he gaped his mouth and says:

"What in hell are you doin' here? . . ."

"Stealing, same as you," says I.

"But . . . hell, it ain't possible . . . not two times. . . ."

"Ain't life strange. Is Pap dead of shock or what?"

"It ain't you. . . ." says Pap, so he's alive still. "It just can't be. . . ."

"I reckon it is, Pap."

"Get away from me!" he hollers. "Get away! . . ."

It warn't a happy reunion, but it's a noisy one, and it brung Portiss down on us right quick.

"What in thunder's all this racket?" he hisses, then he sees Pap on the ground and says:

"Holbrook, are you drunk again?"

"He ain't drunk," says Morg. "He just fell down."

I slid away before I get mixed up in it too and kept on working, but I can hear Portiss and Morg hissing at each other like snakes and Pap moaning some. Jim brushed past me and whispers:

"What happen, Huck?"

"It's Pap and Morg after all. They seen me."

Portiss come stamping along and says:

"Quit jawing and work."

The last crates got loaded and the wagons started back to San Francisco, and on the way I had a considerable amount to ponder over. I never would of figured a rich man like Miles Wyeth is a thief, but it's so, and right now he's in the governor's house drinking his liquor and most likely the governor reckons he's a decent man. I seen that it ain't always hard work that gets a man rich, just two-facedness and hiring others to do the stealing for you. It's real disgusting, and I aim to tell Grace the first chance I get so's she'll know just what kind of double-dealing trash she's got herself mixed up with. She'll be gratified to know the truth and thank me for it I reckon. Then there's Pap and Morg. They ain't in this wagon but they're in one of them, and after we're all through unloading at the warehouse I aim to sneak away with Jim without getting spotted by them. I ain't happy about us meeting up again and they ain't neither, but Jim and me got no intentions of working for Miles Wyeth after tonight so Pap and Morg'll be able to breathe easy again without having us around.

It never worked out like that. We unloaded and stowed all the cargo in the warehouse along with big piles of other stuff that must of come off practickly every ship in the bay, then got paid, but Portiss tells me and Jim and Pap and Morg to stay behind.

"You two," he says, meaning Pap and Morg, "this is your last chance. If I catch you drunk one more time you won't work here no more, understand?"

They both looked real scared and never spoke, then he turns to me and Jim.

"How do you like your new job?" he asks.

"We don't," says I, "and we quit."

He give a soft laugh and shook his head like I'm an idiot or something.

"Boy, there's one thing you got to learn. When you work for the Cornucopia Mercantile Company you don't ever quit, not till you're dead. It's in the contract, and no one ever broke it yet."

"If that's so how come you told Pap . . . these two here they got to sober up or get showed the door?"

"I never mentioned no door. If they finish working here they ain't going to be working nowhere else, know what I mean?"

"No, and we never signed no contract neither."

"It's the kind that don't get signed, just agreed on."

"Well I reckon we're disagreeable."

"Boy, a month back we had a man that never wanted to keep working for the company. He was real bull-headed about it and never listened to reason. We was real sad to let him go, and sadder yet when we heard the news he got found in the bay with his throat cut. If he had of honored the contract he never would of died, see? It was real unfortunate. You don't want nothing like that to happen to you, I reckon."

"No, sir, Mr. Portiss. We figure the Corneycopey Mercantile Company is just the best company in the world to work for and we're real proud to be a part of it."

"That's the kind of thinking we like," he says. "You keep thinking that way and you'll stay healthy to spend all the dollars you earn. There's arrangements been made for you to stay at a hotel that's company owned, the same one that these two here and some others live at. We like to keep our boys together so's we can keep a fatherly eye on them, see?"

"It ain't necessary, Mr. Portiss, sir. We already got a nice place. . . ."

"No you ain't. You're at the Ophir Hotel like the rest. Where are you?"

"The Ophir Hotel. Thank you for fixing it, sir."

"My pleasure," he says. "Now get out of my sight."

The four of us went away and soon as we're out on the street Pap says:

"Don't you come nowhere near me. . . . Don't you dare. . . ."

"Maybe you never heard it clear, Pap. Me and Jim is going to be under the same roof as you two, like it or not."

"Just don't talk to us," says Morg. "You keep in your room and we'll keep in ours and all of us'll keep our mouths shut."

"About stealing for the Corneycopey Company or about you both being murderers?"

"I ain't no murderer! . . ." bawls Pap, and Morg clapped a hand over his mouth. He says:

"We don't talk about nothin', not ever."

"Ain't you disgusted to be thiefs now as well as murderers?" says I.

"It ain't stealing," says Morg, "not regular stealing anyhow. Them ships ain't got no one to unload them. Why, all them cargoes'd sink to the bottom if we never brung 'em into the light of day. It's a shameful waste to let it all rot out there on the water. I reckon we're doing this town a power of good letting folks get the stuff they need."

"Just don't come nowhere near me. . . ." says Pap, who ain't following the conversation at all.

"We got no plans to come near no murderers," says I, "so quit beating your gums on it."

"I never murdered no one," he says, whining pitiful, and Morg give him a punch in the neck to make him act more manly, then had to pick him up off the sidewalk. I seen that Pap has gone so far downhill he's crossed the valley floor and started up the other side, and even if I hated him for what he done it give me a pang to see him drunker and dirtier even than he used to be. Morg says:

"Don't you pay no mind to what Portiss says. It's only bluff. They can't stop you quittin' if you want. There ain't nothin' to stop you doing it right now, so why don't you?"

"We need the money," says I, which ain't no lie, but I reckon Portiss warn't bluffing and Morg just wants to see us floating in the bay with our throats cut so him and Pap don't need to worry no more about me turning them in. Well I ain't falling for it.

We got to the hotel and Morg hauled Pap straight upstairs. The same clerk as before when I come here says:

"No niggers."

"We was told arrangements got made to put us up here, so if you got any objections you can tell them to Mr. Wyeth."

"Sign here," he says, and give me the register book and a pen. "Any old name'll do."

So I signed us in as Richard Lionheart and Blondel.

"Room twenty-four," he says, and give me a key.

We went up and locked ourselfs in and talked awhile, but never seen no way out of the situation. Says I:

"We'll just have to keep on being thiefs, and after we got enough cash we'll light out for someplace so far away the Corneycopey Company won't ever find us. It ain't like we're robbing houses or nothing, just cargo that got left to rot like Morg says."

"Dat don' make it right, Huck," says Jim.

"Well, I know that, but I don't aim to get my throat cut yet awhile, so for now we just got to turn a blind eye."

Jim seen I'm right and we flopped on the beds and slept all day.

✦ 34 ✦

The Painful Truth—A Hot Landscape—Resting Up—The

Robbers Robbed—The Finger Pointed—An Appeal Refused

In the evening I went to see Grace. The show ain't started yet and I got let in to see her backstage without no trouble seeing as I'm a familiar face around here nowadays. She's in the middle of painting her face in front of a mirror when I come in, but real pleased to see me.

"Huckleberry, such excitement! The whole town is talking about what happened at the governor's last night!"

"I had a little excitement myself," says I, but she warn't about to let me get in ahead of her.

"Guess who was there," she says.

"The president?"

"No, silly, Bulldog Barrett. He got invited because he's famous, and guess what happened."

"He arrested a sofa for being Huck Finn in disguise."

"Stupid. He saw Mr. Squires and accused him in front of everyone of helping you and Jim escape him in the Rocky Mountains. Is it true?"

"I recollect telling you about it, Grace."

"But you never told me Mr. Squires was the one. My, but that was a gallant deed, to risk his life saving you."

"He never exactly saved me, just sat there and never lifted a finger to stop someone else braining the bulldog with a whiskey jug. He warn't interested one way or the other at the time."

"Oh, Huckleberry, how can you say such a thing? I never thought you could show such ingratitude. If it was the way you say then Barrett would never have accused him."

I reckon Bulldog would accuse water of running downhill if it

472

suited him, but Grace never wanted to hear nothing that don't make Randolph out a hero.

"Mr. Squires denied everything," she says, "but I know he only did it to protect you. It was the noblest thing I ever saw, and when the bulldog kept on at him Randolph . . . I mean Mr. Squires challenged him to a duel to settle the matter like gentlemen."

"Did Bulldog say yes?" I ask, hoping Randolph is as good a shot as he is a card player.

"Everyone was watching by then, and Governor Burnett himself stepped up and told them that dueling is forbidden in California by law, so Mr. Squires apologized to the governor for causing any upset, which is more than Bulldog did. He told Randolph he'd find evidence against him before too long, and he did. He left straight after the argument and when he did he saw Randolph's coach and asked who it belonged to and came straight back in again and told everyone how he chased Huckleberry Finn just yesterday and lost him near that very coach. Then Randolph made him admit he looked inside the coach and it was empty, and the bulldog lost his temper and called him a scheming southern degenerate, and Randolph called him a Yankee dog that only captured so many criminals because it takes one dog to sniff out another. After that they had to be held apart. It was like something in a play. Then Randolph took Miles and me home."

"That's real interesting, Grace, but I got some news for you on Miles, and it ain't what you'd call good."

"What news?" she says, putting on her yeller Becky Thatcher wig.

"Well . . . uh . . . he ain't honest. That job he give Jim and me out of his generous heart is stealing cargo off ships in the bay, and we can't quit neither or we'll get our throats cut."

"Huckleberry, you're spinning lies again, I can tell. That's just typical of you, to bite the hand that feeds. I bet the work was too hard for your lazy bones so you don't want it. Well, I did my best for you and Miles did too, so don't expect me to believe any such fantastical tales. Why, Miles wouldn't hurt a fly. He's a gentleman, not so much a one as Mr. Squires, but not the kind to cut people's throats. It's just foolish talk and I won't listen to any more of it."

Her voice got high and she kept getting the wig put on wrong, and I seen that however much she don't want to hear the truth it's been brung to her ears before this. If she truly believed I'm lying she would of acted snooty and scornful, not upset and nervous like she is. I argued with her awhile but she never listened, not wanting her rich man that give her everything she wanted to be showed up for what he is, namely a thief and liar. Then when she's practickly tore her wig to shreds trying to put it on right it's time for her to go on stage, so I left and went back to the hotel.

There warn't no ship robbing to be done that night and Jim and me got awful bored just sat around on our beds staring at the walls, then come a screaming from down the hall. I reckernized Pap's voice and run along to see what happened. His door warn't locked so I went in, and there's Pap sprawled across his bed with a turned-over bottle gurgling whiskey onto the floor, and he's staring at a jug and bowl on the washstand like it's got snakes wrapped around it. Morg warn't there to look after him so I figured it's only decent for me to tend him when he's crazed like now.

"What is it, Pap?" says I.

"The face . . ." he says, and points at the jug, which ain't got no face, just little pink and blue flowers on it. "That awful . . . awful . . . face."

"There ain't no face there, Pap. It's just a jug."

But he warn't hearing me, just kept looking at the jug with his eyes bugged out and his lips twitching some.

"Who's face is it, Pap?"

"*His* . . . the devil. . . ."

"Well, he ain't registered here so he's got no business being in your room," says I, and took Pap's jacket and draped it over the jug and bowl like you do with a parrot's cage. I never expected it to work, but soon as the jug got covered Pap slumped back with a reliefsome groan and stared at the ceiling awhile. I reckon he never even knowed I'm there he's so still, hardly breathing even.

"Pap, are you all right?"

He turned his head slow and looked at me and says:

"It warn't the devil first off. . . . There was other faces before. . . ."

"Who was it, Alexander the Great or Christopher Columbus?"

"The Widow Douglas," he says, just whispering, "and before that . . . your Ma. . . ."

"Did she say anything, or just stare?"

"She . . . she told me it ain't long now. . . ."

"What ain't?"

"Till she sees me . . . after I'm dead. . . ."

"That don't make no kind of sense, Pap. You always reckoned Ma was a good woman that died young on account of you. If she's like you say then she's in heaven, and there ain't no chance of you joining up with her there, not after the sinning life you had. Why, you'll be so deep in hell she won't be able to see you even from way up on high. You must of imagined it all out of a bottle."

"I never . . . I seen her and heard her too. . . . I ain't long for this world. . . ."

"Well, if it's true I best get the stove stoked up so's you can get used to the kind of weather they got down below. I heard tell it's so hot they fry eggs on their heads, only they ain't allowed to eat 'em as part of the punishment. Some poor souls down there figure the only relief they can get from the hotness is by jumping in the river of blood, but that's always on the boil so they don't get no comfort from it at all, and when they haul theirselfs out demons give them a heap of poking with pitchforks to let them know the mistake they made, then they got to swaller down a bucket of hot coals for supper. It's a cruelty what they make you do. They got lakes of brimstone full of snapping turtles that's always hungry, and you got to swim naked, and if that ain't enough you got to spend ten hours a day stood up to your neck in pits full of maggots that's plenty hungry too, but no matter how much of you gets snapped off or et all of it grows back again like magic so's you can do the punishments over and over again forever. Just think, Pap, if you had of led a decent life you could of got wings and a harp and flitted from cloud to cloud nice and cool and drunk rainwater out of a gold cup whenever you want. But no such luck, not for you. It's down to the hot place where the flesh melts off your bones and . . ."

"Stop!" he yells, and claps his hands over his ears. "It ain't right to torture me so! I'm your own Pap that give you life, you danged ungrateful dog! I got respect comin' to me on account of it, so just you keep hush about hell and damnation!"

"Hell ain't no more'n you deserve, you murdering coward drunk, and it's a shame there ain't no such place, because I'd surely like to know you're there!"

"Wash your mouth out, boy," he says. "Ain't you kept up with your Sunday schoolin'? Don't you dare doubt there's a heaven and hell! Why, that's blasphemy! My own boy that I brung up to be a Christian, a blasphemer. . . . Ain't you ashamed? Your Ma would of whaled you with a switch if she could of heard you talk that way."

"She's likely inside the jug listening to every word."

"You little sass-mouth!" he hollers. "Don't you go funnin' your own Ma that died young and gentle! I'll break you in two! . . ."

He tried to grab me but ain't got the strength to do no more than flop around on the bed like a stranded fish, and pretty soon he's puffing for air.

"Whiskey . . ." he says.

There's still some left in the turned-over bottle and I give it to him. He drunk it down like it's mother's milk and let the bottle drop on the floor again. His scrawny chest heaved in and out frantic then slowed down some, and I reckon he's right on one thing; he ain't got long now. I seen dead men that looked healthier than Pap. After awhile he says:

"I wasted it all . . . every minute and day. . . . Now it's too late and my own boy is bound down that same road."

"Only on account of you, you wore-out bag of bones. I could of stayed in Missouri and not got chased by the law if you hadn't of done what you done."

"It warn't me. . . . Morg done it, I told you that . . . and don't go bad-mouthing your Pap or I'll tan your hide, you ungrateful pup! I done my best to bring you up right. I could of done it too if it hadn't of been for liquor. Promise me you won't ever drink, boy."

"I promise I'll drink a jug a day to show how much admiration I got for you, Pap. Every boy wants to be like his old man and I ain't no different. I reckon I'll be half dead by the time I'm twenty, and proberly burned down a house or three meantime, but only if they got people inside. I ain't burning down no houses that's empty."

"No . . . no . . ." he groans, and tears of whiskey dribbled out his eyes. "You got to be decent and law-abiding. . . ."

"It's too late now, Pap. I just hope you're satisfied."

"It ain't my fault," he blubbers, real pathetic, then the whiskey took ahold of him and he started snoring. I stayed there awhile just looking at him and trying to feel sorry, but I ain't. He dug his own grave, as they say, and done his best to drag me down into it along-side him. I ain't in no forgiving mood. I got all squirming and tight inside just recollecting what he put me and Jim through, but when it passed there's just a hollow place in my belly that don't feel nothing at all, so I laid a blanket over him and went back to Jim.

A week run along and we robbed two more ships same as before. I never seen Grace or Randolph or no one, not even Pap just down the hall, and him and me give each other plenty of distance when we was robbing and never rode in the same wagon or longboat. It was the miserablest week I ever had, and there's a whole tribe of blue devils camped on my shoulders all the time.

Jim warn't none too happy neither, and when we ain't robbing or sleeping I read him book stories to give us both some cheer. There was one I got and it's called "The Little Toiler or Virtue Rewarded" by Mrs. Olive Clemence Simpson, and it told how this girl in London lived real poor with her Ma in a house that leaked rain all the time, and her Ma is forever jawing about how she used to live in a big house with servants and such but her wicked brother took it all away with a forged will that left everything to him. So they lived poor as fleas with the mother taking in washing that split her hands open and the girl, Maisie by name, doing sewing for pennies, until one day she finds a purse full of money in the street with an address inside. There's hundreds of pounds there, which is what dollars is called in England, but this idiot-brain Maisie goes and takes it back to the man that was fool enough to lose it, and he's mighty impressed with her being so honest and all. When he finds out how poor her and her Ma is he's real shocked and says he'll fix things for them, and even invites them to come and live in his house permanent, which they done. The purse-dropper's a lawyer, and he does some detective work and finds out how to prove the wicked brother forged the will and has him put in jail for it. Meantime Maisie has gone and fell in love with the lawyer's son called Frederic and it's plain they'll get hitched one of these days, so the story ends full of happiness and roses. It give me such a pain I flung it across the room and it fell in pieces, which we burned in the stove.

Then come a night we went out in the boats again and tied up to a schooner called the *Antelope*. We started robbing the usual way and was already sending up the first boxes when footsteps come pounding along the deck overhead and there's shouts and thumping. Portiss went up the rope like a monkey and hollered for the rest of us to come up too. When I got my head above deck I seen a heap of men

with clubs and knives laying into our bunch and there's more coming over the sides. Soon as I seen it I give a yelp like I got my skull
clubbed and dropped back in the hold and lay still. The rest all
swarmed up the rope except Jim.

"You hurt bad, Huck?" he says, all worried.

"I ain't hurt at all, and I don't aim to be. Don't go up there, Jim.
There's a bunch of other robbers fixing to take the cargo off us and
they ain't in no mood for argument."

The noise on deck was real loud with all them drumming feet and
falling bodies, and they was yelling plenty whenever they got hit or
stabbed. A considerable number got throwed overboard or else
jumped by the splashing we heard, and Jim and me made up our
minds to hide. We blowed out our lamp and went over in the darkest
corner of the hold and squeezed ourselfs behind some bales till the
ruckus died down. We ain't sure who won so we stayed right there
till someone come down the rope with a lamp and says:

"Anyone there?"

We never budged or spoke. Others come down too and they got
started on the cargo. I never heard no familiar voices so I reckon
Portiss and the rest is dead or throwed overboard. This bunch
worked fast but never done it the same as us, just grabbed whatever
is nearest and hauled it up till their boats was full. Me and Jim
warn't in no danger of getting found, not hid way back in the shadows like we are. When the job got finished they went up the rope
and hauled it up after them and fitted the hatch cover back. We
heard them clump across the deck, then there's oars creaking and
voices talking, getting fainter and fainter till they're gone, and it
come to us we're stuck down here without no way to get out.

I got out my lucifers and lit the lamp and seen that from the top of
the hatch to the cargo deck where they cleared away all the crates is
maybe twenty feet. There ain't nothing for it but to drag boxes over
and pile them up till we can climb up and see if the hatch is clipped,
and if it is we're dead men, because there ain't no one going to hear
us out here no matter how hard we holler. It cost us a heap of sweat
and took hours, but finally we got a pointed pile like them old Egyp-
tians used to make and Jim clumb up it and balanced on the top and
pushed up against the hatch. It's one of them times you don't hardly
dare to breathe, but they must of left in a hurry because the hatch
ain't got no clips fastened. It shifted an inch or so and Jim strained

hard to lift it more and move it sideways. His muscles twitched under his skin it's so heavy, but he done it in the end and rested
awhile, then grabbed the edge and hauled himself up then reached
down for me.

That bay air smelled mighty good after the hold and we sucked it
in by the yard. It's coming on for dawn by now and we seen blood on
the deck and ropes dangling in the water where Portiss and them
must of cut loose quick to get away. We ain't marooned or nothing
because there's the ship's dinghy sat upside down and lashed to the
afterdeck. We got it free and opened the side section where the
gangplank goes for unloading and slid it out through there. The
dinghy hit the bay with a splash and I jumped in before it drifted off.
Jim handed down the oars then lowered himself and we rowed
away. We never bothered going the long way around like when the
longboats is carrying stolen cargo, just headed straight for the waterfront and tied up at the wharf. The ferry steamer that brung us to
San Francisco was docking at the same time, and plenty of forty-
niners down from the diggings come off her and got met by the
usual bunch of whores. They never took no notice of Jim and me
seeing as we come out of a dinghy, and we walked along the same
street we took that first time when we got robbed. Things ain't improved a whole lot since then, and I say:

"Jim, I'm powerful sick and tired of this town. We got to get out
and soon. It just ain't our kind of country."

"I ain't argumentin' wid you, Huck, but how we goin' to do it
when we ain't got no cash behin' us?"

"I counted up our savings last night and we got over two hundred
dollars."

"Dat don' buy beans here'bouts, Huck."

"Well, we have to figure a way out. I ain't working for Miles
Wyeth no more, and I ain't staying in the same hotel as Pap. I can't
stand it."

"Me neither. I been thinkin' maybe we kin go down to de diggin's
souther here an' try de minin' again."

"You just now brung up the fact we ain't got hardly enough for a
grubstake, Jim, but maybe we could figure out a way to get more on
the way. We got to do something to get away from here, definite."

"You figure we kin leave de Corneycopey gang an' not get our
necks sawed open'?"

That got me thinking hard, and the answer come to me in a flash.

"Jim, my brain ain't been working at full pressure these last few hours! We been handed the perfect way to do it and I only just now seen it! Why, they'll figure we got stabbed or drowned in the fight and won't even bother to look for us if we don't show back at the hotel!"

"You forgettin' somethin', Huck. Das where we got our money stash'."

He's right about that, and it kind of throws cold water over the plan. We need that money. It ain't much but it's all we got, hid away under a floorboard in our room. There ain't no fire escape stairs up the back of the building we can sneak up, so we decided the only way is to breeze into the lobby, stroll upstairs casual, hook the loot fast and breeze out again before we get took notice of. I wanted to do it alone, being smaller and not so distinctive looking as Jim, but he says he ain't going to let me risk it on my own in case things don't turn out the way we want and I need a helping hand. I give in and both of us slid in through the front door of the Ophir and never believed our luck when we seen the desk clerk ain't there. We went upstairs without making no noise, and there's no one in the hall so we unlocked our door and went in.

"Good day to you, Finn," says Miles Wyeth.

He's there with Portiss and a couple other men, all big and none of them smiling. Miles points to a chair and says:

"Sit down."

I done it and the men made Jim sit on the bed, then they stood between us and the door so we can't run for it. Miles walked up and down slow with his hands behind his back like a schoolteacher, and talked while he done it.

"What can you tell me of the incident last night, Finn?"

"I never seen much of it. I got hit on the head when I come up out of the hold and fell back in."

"And the nigger?"

"He's real protective. He drug me over in a corner and stayed with me so's I never got hit again."

Miles give a nod to Portiss and he come over and felt my head.

"No bumps," he says.

"Maybe you'd like to change your story," says Miles.

"Yessir, I would. It's awful hard to admit, but I'm the dangdest coward in all creation. Soon as I seen them men fighting I dropped back down and played possum so's not to get hurt. Jim wanted to go up and do his part with the rest but I never let him. I wanted him down there to protectify me."

"Mr. Portiss has formed the opinion that you were hardly surprised by the attack, and I see his point. The coming together of two rival groups, one of them armed for a fight, is no coincidence. They knew in advance which ship we would be visiting and were lying in wait. There is a traitor in our midst, Finn, and you with your general reluctance to join our happy band are a prime suspect."

"I ain't no traitor! I'm just a coward, honest!"

"So you say, but how can I be sure?"

"Hit me and see if I don't scream. I'm the lily-liverdest thing on two legs, but I ain't traitorish."

"You have a reputation for weaseling out of tight corners with your tongue, Finn, so don't try these feeble dramatics with me."

"I never told no one what ship we was going to pirate. How could I? I never knowed till we got there, and neither did the rest except for Mr. Portiss I guess."

"Not so. There were others who knew beforehand, but you and the nigger were deliberately kept in ignorance."

"Well, don't that make me innocent?"

"You may have overheard one of the others mention the *Antelope* and relayed the information to certain of my enemies."

"Well, I never. Why don't you ask all them that knowed about the *Antelope* if they ever spoke it out loud when I'm around to hear it?"

"Unfortunately two of those men have not returned. I greatly fear they are dead, and therefore beyond questioning."

"If Jim and me had of been in cahoots with them enemies how come we got left in the hold?"

"How'd you get out?" says Portiss, and I told him.

"How fortunate they neglected to secure the hatch," says Miles. "It creates a plausible alibi without causing bodily hurt. They seem to have thought of everything, but I am not convinced."

"How many others never come back besides them that knowed about the *Antelope*?"

"Three," he says.

"Then maybe one of them's the traitor."

"Possibly."

"Anyway, you deserve it," says I. "If you ain't the crookedest man in town I'm a prairie dog. All you got was a taste of your own medicine I reckon."

It ain't the smartest thing to say, things being like they was, and it got me a hot ear off Portiss. Miles paced around awhile longer then says:

"You and the nigger will stay here until this mess has been cleared up."

He give a nod to the rest and they trooped out. Soon as their footsteps died away I went along the hall and knocked on Pap's door, wondering if he's one of the missing ones. No answer, but it ain't locked so in I went. Pap's lying on his bed with a bottle like always, but he ain't stinking drunk yet. He give a sneer and says:

"So they never got you."

"They missed you too I reckon. Where's Morg?"

"He never come back. He'll be dead."

"You ain't exactly tearing your hair from grief over it."

"Him and me should of parted company a long while back. He ain't no loss."

"Maybe not to you, but he's the only one can clear me of murdering the judge."

"He never would of owned up anyhow."

"Pap, listen to me. Morg ain't here no more to tell about the house burning. If you went to Bulldog Barrett and told about what happened at the judge's house maybe he'd believe you and quit chasing me."

"Why'n hell would he believe me?"

"On account of you can say you was there and seen it all."

"And get charged with accomplicin'? You can't ask a thing like that of your old man! What kinder son are you?"

"You look like you ain't got long to live anyhow, and this way you can say how-do to St. Peter with a clear conscience and get saved from the hot place. Ain't that a worthwhile reason, Pap?"

"I ain't dead yet!" he hollers. "And I ain't endin' my days on no gallows, not for you or no one!"

"The bulldog'd give you a twenty-four hour start to get away if you confessed, Pap, I just know he would. . . ."

"I ain't confessin' to nothin'! Now you get out!"

"Can't you even do one good thing in your life, Pap?"

"No I can't! You get before I whale you black and blue, you . . . you ingrate!"

It ain't no good. Asking Pap to show his better side is like asking a fish to do arithmetic, so I went back to Jim and we done some talking. We figured we best stay put for now and hope we can sneak out of town in a few days maybe, if they catch the traitor meantime, that is. It ain't hardly what you could call a plan, but it's all we got.

✦ 35 ✦

A Disappearance—Deception and Revelation—A
Leavetaking—Poetic Justice—Out of the Egg—
The Spider's Web

In the evening the door flew open
and Miles is back with his men. He never wasted no time, just says:

"Where is she?"

"Where's who?"

"Grace had disappeared and I advise you to tell me where."

"I ain't seen her in a week. . . ."

Portiss grabbed me and the other two men held Jim so he can't do nothing, then Portiss give me a punch that sent me flying across the room.

"Where is she?" says Miles.

"I dunno, honest! Maybe she don't like you no more and lit out, how should I know!"

Portiss give me some more treatment and I seen little blobs of light dancing around in front of me like fireflies, then I'm looking at the ceiling and the fireflies is gone.

"Where is she, Finn?"

His voice come from a long ways off, too far to bother answering, so I never. Then Jim's voice come to me, real hollow sounding.

"Maybe you should ask Randolph," he says.

"Why him?" says Miles.

"On accounter he de onlies' man we knows dat knows Grace. Jest don' hit de boy no mo'. He don' know nothin'."

"Squires has left his hotel and sold his coach," says Miles.

"If'n you took de trouble to fin' dat out I reckon you must of done de figurin' I jest done. It ain't nothin' to do wid Huck an' me, so I'se askin' you to let him be."

"If you learn anything of her whereabouts you'll bring the information directly to me, understand?"

"I reckon I do," says Jim, and I heard them go out. He picked me up and set me down on my bed and mopped the blood that's running out my nose. It never surprised me about Grace and Randolph. Soon as she quit calling him Mr. Squires I seen which way the wind was blowing, only I never wanted to admit it. She warn't able to see through them good looks I reckon. But I got enough problemation without getting all worried over Grace, and I went all quiet and peaceful inside the way you do when there ain't nothing else can go wrong, and after Jim cleaned me up I say:

"Jim, I reckon it's time we quit hiding under a rock and come out fighting like men is supposed to."

"How you mean, Huck?"

"I ain't sure myself, but I ain't ducking and hiding no more. We never done nobody no harm and it ain't right the way we been hounded all this time. The camel's back has been broke, Jim, and I aim to climb out from under all that straw."

I lay there pondering awhile and at the end still figured the only way to get Bulldog Barrett off my back is make Pap confess about how Morg murdered the judge with Bulldog there to hear it. But Pap'll have to be mighty drunk before he'll agree to do it, and maybe even then he won't. He never wanted to this morning, but he only just started drinking at the time and half his brain must of been working. He's likely been sucking the sauce all day and right about now he'll be in a mellower mood. You don't take no chances when you play for big stakes, so before I went to Pap's room I went out and got a bottle of whiskey. The hopes I got that he'll go along with the plan is thin as paper, but there ain't no other way. I went in and he's slumped over the table with an empty bottle in front of him. I set the full one down where he can see it through them red eyes of his and he come alive slow like a tortoise poking his head out of the shell, blinking and smacking his gums. He looks up at me and says:

"Your face is all swole."

"Portiss give it to me. Him and Wyeth reckon I done the company wrong over what happened last night."

"Ain't he the limit. I never worked for no one so cold-blooded. Soon as I got me a little saved I aim to quit."

"They say anyone that tries gets his throat cut, Pap."

"I disbelieve it. That's just to keep us in line. Anyway, I ain't scared of 'em. Us Finns got grit."

I uncorked the bottle and poured us both a glass, then say:

"Here's to you, Pap, a man that life never give a chance to."

"Changed your tune, ain't you?" he says.

"I surely have, Pap. It's took all this time for me to see how you been mishandled by fate, and seeing as the same thing happened to me I reckon there ain't a need for us to be enemies no more."

"Well, it's about time you seen the light," he says. "You been treating me like trash lately. A boy oughtn't to treat his Pap that way."

"I'm real apologetic over it, Pa, that's why I brung the bottle, which is a gift to mend the bad feeling we got one for the other."

He drunk his glass down and I done the same, then I poured out more, and for the next hour or two I lied like I ain't never lied before, praising Pap to the skies and back again and saying how it's a shame the way we both been treated. He swallered it down along with the whiskey, and I kept his glass filled but only sipped from mine. He got drunk slow, being used to it, but finally he's had enough for me to start talking about how Morg, rest his soul, warn't halfway decent enough to be partners with the likes of Pap, and how I seen the way Morg bullied him and never treated him gentle and sympathetic which a man of Pap's refinement deserves. He agreed with all of it and got to cussing Morg's memory with the briskest kind of language.

"And just think, Pap," says I, "he's gone to his watery grave with folks figuring he's a fine, upright citizen, when you and me know he warn't nothing but a lowdown murderer that led his partner astray. Ain't that shameful?"

"It sure is, boy. He don't deserve no tears wept over him that way."

"The thing to do, Pap, is kind of blacken his reputation now that he ain't around to deny it."

"Blacken? How? I ain't follering you, son."

"Why, tell the world he murdered the judge is how. That'll make folks quit shedding tears over him right quick."

He give me a long look with them beady red eyes from behind his hair, then give a cackle and says:

"I ain't a fool. I already told you I ain't tellin' no one about what happened in St. Petersburg. You can fill me with all the whiskey you want, but I ain't tellin'."

I misjudged him, that's for sure. He's the worst kind of drunk, but he's still got a smidgin of shrewdness left, and that whiskey cost me thirty dollars too. Says I:

"You're too quick in the brain for me, Pap. I guess a young pup can't fool no old dog."

He give a laugh, real pleased with himself, then says:

"I reckon Morg warn't no fool neither, even if he's a sonovabitch. You recollect that time a couple years back when you made folks figure you was murdered and they drug the river and all? Well I got a notion ol' Morg's gone and done the selfsame thing."

"Why, Pap? Ain't he truly dead?"

"No one seen him get knifed or throwed overboard and drown, so maybe he ain't a corpse at all. Maybe he's still alive and kickin'."

"He would of showed up by now if that's so."

"Not if he wants the Corneycopey Company to reckon he's dead."

"Why would he want that?"

"On account of he acted mighty strange the last few days before them danged pirates landed on us."

"What kind of strange?"

"All superior, like he ain't going to be poor much longer, saying he aims to be someone big in town after things has changed."

"What things?"

"He never told, but I reckon he knowed the company was close to gettin' poleaxed by another bunch that's tired of seeing Mr. High-and-Mighty Wyeth run things all his own way. That night we went out to the *Antelope* he told me to be sure and stay in the boats to load the stuff and not go on board to get it outer the hold. He knowed there's a fight bound to happen, that's how I figure it, and while the ruckus is on he kind of slid away so's we'll all figure he's dead."

"But how could he know before it happened?"

Pap tapped his nose and give me a wink and says:

"Know nothin', tell nothin', but if Morg ain't dead he's tucked up cozy with Hattie the Trout right this minute and laughin' at Wyeth and the rest. I reckon that should make you feel better about that swole face you got."

"Who's Hattie the Trout?"

"A whore. Morg got bit by her awhile back and kept on layin' out cash for more. I figure there ain't nothin' more disgustful than a man that goes with a whore regular. You ain't done nothin' like that have you, boy?"

"No, Pap, I ain't partial to whores."

"Well don't ever get that way. I brung you up Christian and don't you forget it."

"I won't, Pap," says I, with a plan hatching slow and steady in my head, but before I can get it figured out perfect there come a knock at the door. I opened it and Jim's there with a Spaniard boy around my age. He says:

"Dis here's Manuel. He sayin' he got to talk wid you."

"Talk away," says I.

"The message is private," says he, speaking real good American.

I took him off down the hall and he give me a scrap of paper. It says:

> Follow this boy
>
> G

"You will come now?" asks Manuel.

"I reckon I will, but wait on a moment."

I told Jim about the message in a whisper so Pap don't hear, and it got Pap peeved to be left out that way.

"What's the greaser want?" he says.

"It ain't your business," says I.

"Oh, ain't it just? You got no right keepin' your business secret from me till you're twenty-one, boy."

Acting nice to Pap this last hour or so ain't left me in a sociable mood, so I say:

"You ain't got no rights over me and you know why, you house-burner."

He got on his feet, swaying from all that whiskey, and I seen he had it in mind to give me a whomping for talking back like I done. But he ain't got the steadiness for it, and when he seen it himself he kind of shrunk inside his clothes and can't look me in the eye no more. Just a few minutes ago he was talking big and acting smart, but now he ain't nothing but a feeble old man, pitiful as usual.

"I run out of tobacco," he mumbles. "Loan me a pinch, boy."

I give him some, then me and Manuel snuck out the back door in case Miles has got men watching the front. We went south through town to where the buildings thinned out and open country starts, with the hills all bare and empty in the moonlight. Manuel never spoke up till now, and he says:

"My clothes look well upon you."

"*Your* clothes?"

"You do not remember? My sister Consuela gave them to you."

"Grace's maid?"

"Señor Wyeth's men have given to her a black face and broken lip, but she told them nothing. When I am older I will kill them all."

"I can understand it, I reckon. Where's Grace now?"

"A little way still. You are Huckleberry Finn the bandit?"

"I wish Grace warn't so free with her mouth."

"It was not her that told me. My sister has long ears."

"Well, I hope she ain't going to tell no one else when her lip gets mended."

"She knows you are the compadre of Grace, who is kind to her. She will tell no one but me. I am honored to meet with a bandit of fame."

"I ain't no bandit. I ain't nothing you'd be proud to know."

"But you are with fame, no?"

"I'd trade places with someone that ain't got none if I could."

He give me a look that says I ain't acting like the heroical type, but I ain't concerned with him, only with Grace. Another half mile on we stopped at a big tree by the road and he give a whistle. Out from cover come Grace and Randolph on horseback, riding side by side. Grace got down and says:

"Your face is all puffed out, Huckleberry."

"Never mind no face, Grace. Wyeth's awful mad at you. If he never had a heap of other worries he'd be turning San Francisco upside down for you right now."

"He can turn all he wants, I won't ever go back. Everything you told me about him is true. Randolph told me the same and after that I believed it. I'm sorry I called you a liar, Huckleberry."

"Most of the town knows about Wyeth," puts in Randolph, "even people in high office. He pays them off and they turn a blind eye."

"That's why we have to leave," says Grace. "We aren't safe here now, but I wanted to say goodbye. I owe you so much. If it wasn't for you I never would of met Randolph. Why, I might have wasted years of my life with that Miles person and never found out the truth."

"Uh . . . Grace, can we talk private?"

"If you want," she says, and we walked a little ways off. "Was it something personal you wanted to ask?"

"I just . . . well, so long as you reckon you're happy, Grace, with Randolph I mean."

"Of course I am. I've been sneaking over to his hotel every day and we went and fell in love."

"He's awful hard-headed, Grace. He ain't the sensitive kind at all."

"He is so too. He's just the kindest, gentlest man in the world, and he's mine. I do believe you're jealous, Huckleberry Finn."

"I ain't no such thing. I just wanted to be sure you ain't doing nothing to regret later on."

"Thank you for worrying," she says, and give me a kiss on the cheek. "You've been a true friend and I won't ever forget you. I know Randolph is what I want. When you're grown up you'll understand."

That's just about the worst thing she could say to me, but I never showed it. Us Finns has got grit.

"Where are you going?" says I.

"Down the coast to a little place Consuela comes from, San Diego. She says boats come in there for fresh water. We'll get on one and go down to Panama then on to New Orleans. Randolph knows plenty of people there. I'll be thinking of you, Huckleberry."

"I ain't about to forget you neither, Grace."

She put out her hand mannish and I shook it, then we went back to the others. Manuel helped Grace into the saddle and Randolph throwed me a little bag that jingles.

"You'll need that, Huckleberry," he says. "Goodbye and good luck."

"And you, Randolph," says I, and they turned their horses onto the road south. I watched them ride away, getting smaller and smaller, and it felt like something inside of me is getting smaller too.

Grace give a final wave then they was gone over a hill and I can't even hear the horses no more.

"She is beautiful, no?" says Manuel. "You regret?"

"I don't regret nothing."

"Randolfo is macho. They will have many sons."

"It ain't none of my concern," says I, and we headed back to town.

"When I am older I will be a bandit like you," says Manuel. "How many Americanos have you killed?"

"Oh, just a couple dozen. They had it coming."

"You showed no mercy?"

"They never expected none so I obliged 'em."

"When will you kill the señor bulldog that chases you? I have seen him. He does not kill easy that one I think."

"I reckon I'll wait till he comes in sniffing distance then put a ball between his eyes. He's been asking for it some considerable time now."

"Will you cut off his head?"

"If I ain't got nothing better to do."

"This I would like to see with my eyes."

"Well I'll let you know beforehand so's you can tell folks how you was there when it happened."

"Thank you. I am proud to be your friend. What has Randolfo given to you?"

"Money I reckon."

"But how much? You must see."

I opened up the bag and we counted out a thousand dollars in gold eagles, but it seems like thirty pieces of silver. I give Manuel twenty dollars for fetching me, but the look he give me made me feel cheap so I made it sixty dollars. Even hotel bellboys has got big expenses in this town. I ain't bothered about money no more because I got that plan hatching in my head, and I'm keeping it warm like a broody hen so's it don't die in the shell.

"Look!" says Manuel.

There's a red glow in the sky up ahead and we run up the last hill to see what it is. When we got to the top San Francisco is spread out below and part of it's on fire, a whole block at least. We hared down the hill and into town, and the streets was jammed with men running the same way. Me and Manuel squeezed along through and the closer we got the sicker I felt, just like that time I seen the fire in St. Petersburg.

It's my street all right, and the Ophir Hotel and all the buildings along that side and back into the block practickly to the next street was just blazing and roaring like the end of the world. There ain't even a bucket brigade on account of the scorching hotness, just hundreds stood around watching the flames thunder up into the sky and shaking their heads regretful. There ain't nothing could of stopped it I reckon, and my belly got knotted up with worry over Jim. I just got to find him, and I searched frantic through the crowds looking for his face. But he ain't nowhere to be seen. I give Manuel the slip, wanting to be alone awhile. I just wanted to lie down and go to sleep I'm so wore out and woeful. Now I ain't got nothing at all, not without Jim. He's the truest friend a body could of had, the best and decentest person I ever met or ever will, and now he's crisped to death same as his family back home. It ain't fair. Them flames burned fierce as ever and roared in my ears like demons laughing, and I can't even cry for the hotness blasting my face. Then a hand come down on my shoulder.

"Huck, chile . . . I been lookin' all over. . . ."

I turned and it's Jim, with his clothes all scorched and his hair and eyebrows frizzled by fire.

"Jim. . . . You ain't hurt are you?"

"Naw, jest baked some. Das some kinder fire."

"Did you see Pap?"

"He never come out, Huck," he says. "I seen de start. It happen right in de hotel down de hall, yo' Pap's room I reckon. Soon's I smell de smoke I open de door an' de ender de hall ain't nothin' but fire. I never coulder got to him, Huck. I jest grab de money we got hid under de flo' an' run down de stairs to git away. Dat fire de hungries' I ever seen, jest leapin' from one place to de nex' while I'se lookin'. I reckon a heaper folks been burned."

There ain't no way I can ever be sure, but I bet Pap stuffed his pipe with the tobacco I give him and lit it then flopped on the bed drunk and fell asleep with it in his hand, so his bed would of been the first thing to catch alight and him too drunk to know. Now I'm an orphan all over again only this time it's true, but I ain't got no tears to shed, not any more.

Me and Jim went away from the fire and rested up in someone's yard till dawn. There's still smoke in the air but when we went back to the fire it ain't nothing but charred bricks and embers with smoke curling out of it, real ugly looking.

"Jim," says I, "you and me are going to pay a visit on Miles Wyeth."

"Wait on, Huck. Now de time to do what we was fixin' to do when we got lef' on de *Ant'lope*. Dey goin' to figure we burned up in de fire. We kin jest skedaddle an' de Corneycopey gang ain't goin' to give us trouble no mo'."

"We ain't running another step, Jim. I got a plan hatched in my head that'll fix things fine."

He's doubtful till I told him the plan, then says maybe it'll work and maybe it won't, but it's worth the risk anyway, and we went directly to the St. James Hotel. I seen Manuel in his bellboy uniform in the lobby and he come hurrying over.

"Why are you here?" he whispers, real anxious.

"To put a ring through the bulldog's nose."

"But he does not stay here."

"I know, but Wyeth does."

"Why do you come to him? He is your enemy also, no?"

"Manuel," says I, "sometimes you got to get friendly with spiders to catch flies."

We went up and I knocked on the door. Portiss opened it and says:

"What brings you here, squirt?"

"I know who done the betraying."

He let us in and went in another room, then come back and showed us through. Miles is in a fancy robe and sat at the same little table where Grace fed me. He's halfway through breakfast and mopping his chin with a napkin, and he come straight to the point.

"Who is it?"

"I ain't telling you till you make a deal with me."

"What kind of deal might that be?"

"The kind that gets Bulldog Barrett off my back once and for all."

"You're talking gibberish, Finn. Tell me the name."

"I ain't going to till you make the deal."

"What does this deal have to do with Barrett?"

"The man that sold you out is the one that done the judge's murder."

He poured himself coffee but never offered us none.

"I'm still listening," he says, sipping dainty. I just don't know how Grace could of stayed with him all that time.

"If I give you the name you got to promise me the bulldog can arrest him for murder and take him for trial and clear my name, and you got to bring in a reporter from the biggest newspaper in town for a witness. I ain't taking no chances."

"Don't talk like a fool. I can't have reporters knowing my business."

"I ain't going to talk about the Corneycopey Company or ship robbing."

"Why should I do this for you, Finn? I don't give a damn if you murdered the judge or not."

"You do what I want and I'll tell you where Grace is."

"I could have Portiss beat the facts from you."

"I reckon you could and would, but if you help Bulldog catch him that's nameless you'll get your name in the papers for being a real solid citizen, and that's something I figure you'd like a whole lot."

He picks up a piece of toast cut three sided and nibbles awhile like a rabbit, then turns to Portiss and says:

"Get Chauncey Barrett and a reporter from the *Bulletin* here. Tell them it's to do with the arrest of Judge . . . what was his name?"

"Thatcher," says I.

"Judge Thatcher's murderer. I want them here in one hour."

It never took that long. They come like bees to honey, and I listened at a keyhole from another room while Miles got them sat down and offered biscuits and coffee, but they ain't interested.

"What is this about, Mr. Wyeth?" says Bulldog. "I hope you don't intend presenting me with yet another sighting of Finn. I receive around twenty a day, placing him anywhere from a hotel around the corner from my own to the North Pole."

"He's in neither of those places, Mr. Barrett, in fact he's in the next room. Come in will you, Huckleberry."

I come through the door with a swagger and the bulldog and the reporter both jumped up like they sat on porcupines, and guess who the reporter is; Orville Treece that we met on Miles's ferry.

"You . . ." he says, but the bulldog elbowed him out of the way.

"Huckleberry Finn, I arrest you for the murder of Judge Caleb Thatcher in Missouri!" he hollers.

"The *Bulletin* will pay you a handsome sum for an interview, Mr. Finn!" gabbles Treece.

"Sit yourselfs back down again, gents," says I, holding up my hands for hush. "I aim to tell you a long story, but while I'm doing it, Mr. Wyeth, sir, I reckon it's a good idea if you send Mr. Portiss to find the whereabouts of a whore called Hattie the Trout."

✦ 36 ✦

Close to the Rug—The Truth Will Out—The Wages of Sin—

Vindication!—Goodbye, America

I got to skip a whole heap of talk
and planning here, but two nights later I'm in a room in a waterfront
whorehouse called Mae's. Hattie the Trout is sat in a chair but I can't
see too much of her on account of I'm on the floor under the bed, and
there's a pistol in my hand. Comes a knock on the door and Hattie got
up to answer it. In come a pair of muddy boots and Morg's voice says:

"What's all this about a message you got for me?"

"Shut the door," she says. "Better lock it too."

He done it and says:

"Well, what's the message, or maybe you just never wanted to
wait for me to come around at the regular time, is that it?"

"There's a message," she says, "but first take a seat."

He done it and she says:

"Are you armed, Morg? You know Mae won't allow guns in the
house."

"No, I ain't. Should I be? Wyeth's men ain't onto me are they?" he
says, sounding alarmful.

"It's nothing to do with them," she says. "The message is something bigger than you could find in this town, so big it could scarce
be contained in all the wide world."

"What the hell are you yapping about? You ain't yourself, Hattie."

"No I'm not," she says. "I am a changed woman, changed
forever."

"You don't look no different to me," he says.

"The change is within me, and can be within you too if only you
will listen to the message, Morg."

"Aawww hell, Hattie, you ain't gone and got religion have you?"

"Verily I have," says she, sounding real holy, "and from this day forth I shall live a life of purity and obedience to the wishes of the Lord."

"I ain't hearing straight . . . I can't be. . . . You ain't truly seen the holy light have you, Hattie? I come here expecting . . . well, the regular. You ain't about to close them pretty legs permanent I hope."

"Alas, you poor sinner, the fleshly appetites still have you in their foul grip. I shall pray for you this instant, for murderers and fornicators must have need of prayer if they are to reach the kingdom of heaven."

"Murderers? . . . Who says I'm a murderer!"

"Deny it not, Morg, for your very soul is at stake."

Hattie told me she always wanted to be an actress but turned to whoring because the wages is better, and I can see she's got a real talent for the stage. Now she's on her knees praying, and Morg says:

"I ain't no murderer! Who told you I'm a murderer! I'll kill him!"

"The truth came to me in a vision," says Hattie, her voice all high and drifting. "I saw you and another man in a room at night, searching for something. A distinguished gentleman found you there and you . . . cut his throat. Oh, Morg, you must repent and be saved!"

"I ain't repentin' nothin'," he says. "Who told you about the judge?"

"Is that what he was, a judge? How could you do such a wicked deed?"

"I never done nothin'," he mumbles, then he stands up. "And I ain't about to believe in no visions neither! Who told you about it? You better tell me quick or by jingo I'll whale the truth out of you! I mean it, Hattie! Quit that danged praying and tell me who told you!"

"I done it!" says I, rolling out from under the bed and pointing the pistol at him. Hattie give a moan and acted a faint, and Morg just stood there with his mouth hung open.

"You . . ." he says.

"No one else," says I.

"How'd you find me? . . ."

"I done some sniffing around for the biggest rat in town and you're it."

He looks down at Hattie, all crumpled in a heap and says:

"She turned me in. . . ."

"No she ain't, Morg, just gone off her head with religion."

"It don't make no sense. . . . How come you're here, you little runt! Did she know you was under that bed?"

"Yes and no. I told her I'm an angel that's come down to make sure she don't do no more sinning and she believed it. Like I say, she's Bible-crazed."

"But . . . how come she knows about the murder?"

"What murder's that, Morg?"

"You know what I'm talkin' about, runt. You told her."

"Only so she had a chance to save your soul, Morg. I would of let her save mine but you and me know I ain't done nothing wrong."

"Hand over that gun," he says.

"I can't do it, Morg. You got to come with me to the governor and confess what you done so I can quit running."

"You ain't serious," he says, smiling.

"I surely am, and don't you make no move to get away or I'll shoot."

"Then you'll be wanted for two murders," he says, smiling wider.

"They can't hang me but once," says I.

"You kill me and they'll surely do it, boy. I'm the only one that knows. I heard the Ophir burned down so I reckon ol' Finn's dead. There ain't no one can clear you now except for me. Ain't that right?"

"I reckon so, and if you got any decency you'll do it."

"Well, I ain't," he says, "and I dare you to pull that trigger. You ain't got the gumption for it."

He took a step toward me and I backed off a little.

"Don't come no closer, Morg. . . ."

"I ain't lettin' you off no hook, boy," he says, still coming. "The whole country figures you killed the judge and that suits me fine. I ain't confessin' to no governor."

"Well, then," says I, sounding afraid, "why don't you confess to me?"

"Why should I do such a damnfool thing? You already know I done it, but it ain't going to do you a peck of good, not even if you shout it from the rooftops."

"That will not be necessary," says Bulldog, stepping out from the wardrobe with his pistol aimed. "I arrest you for the murder of Judge Caleb Thatcher in Missouri."

Orville Treece come out of the wardrobe too and was just about to offer Morg some handsome money for his life story when Morg swung around and flung himself through the window in a shower of glass. Bulldog fired a shot and Hattie screamed and Orville fell over her, then Bulldog's out the window too and firing down the alley at Morg, who's only fading footsteps now. Me and Orville got jammed trying to get through the window together, then we're both outside in the mud and garbage and running along after the bulldog. He turned a corner and we followed around into another alley and seen him down the far end next to a body on the ground, so he must of hit Morg after all.

When we catched him up Bulldog is stood over the body and the legs is still kicking, but Morg ain't fell prey to no pistol; his throat is cut ear to ear and pumping out buckets of blood while we watched. Then he's dead. I reckon Miles must of put his men around Mae's place to get Morg so's he don't do no babbling on the witness stand about the Corneycopey Company. Most likely it's a warning to me too, and I aim to take it. My lips is sealed. Later on Miles wants to know where Grace is like I promised for the deal, so I told him honest and sincere how her and Randolph was in a hotel just down the street from the Ophir on the night of the big blaze and both of them got burned to cinders. I reckon he disbelieved me, but never called me a liar outright and we never come face to face again.

All that happened awhile back now. The story got put in the *Bulletin* and the presses run twenty-four hours a day for three days so all of California knows HUCK FINN IS INNOCENT! Governor Burnett himself invited me and Jim to stay in his home and says he wants a full and entire account of what happened, which is why this book got writ. Mae that runs the whorehouse got two thousand dollars for letting the bulldog set up a trap there and Hattie the Trout got one thousand, all paid by Miles, who's running for Congress nowadays and likely to get there too. Ships is leaving San Francisco regular now with rich forty-niners as passengers and poor forty-niners as deckhands, and they say Bulldog Barrett has took to drink while he waits for a berth on one. He ain't been the same man since he found I'm truly innocent and was obliged to give me an apology in front of the whole world. Proud men like him ain't partial to the taste of humble pie, but for me the look on his face when he done the apology was sweet revenge, as the saying goes. Auberon Clitheroe that done *Finn the Red Handed* has writ another play that tells a heap more truth. It's called *Finn the Fearless or Unjustly Accused*, but it's still full of stuff that never happened, which is another reason I done the book. I ain't stretched nothing, just told the facts the way I seen them. I was there all along so I know, and I want it all set down so's folks can learn what happened, specially Tom Sawyer. He'll be green when he sees all the adventures I had, bigger than anything he ever done.

Living in the governor's house is quiet and peaceful after all we been through and him and his wife treats us both decent, even Jim, but Mrs. Burnett has got me in clothes that fit tight around the neck and boots that pinch my feet considerable, and we're both getting a power of restlessness inside of us. Jim says he wants to go to Africa and see for himself if it's true there's nigger kings there, and I got a yearning for them South Sea islands and howling adventures among the cannibals. When the whalers start coming into San Francisco regular me and him has got a notion to sign on as sailors. Jim reckons he'll be a harpooner and see if them fish is big enough to swaller a man like the Bible says about Jonah.

But while we wait to slide out, I got a heap of time to spend in remindfulness of people and places I knowed. Sometimes I think about Grace, and sometimes about the lovebirds or Frank'n'Obadiah, but mainly it's Thaddeus I got memories of. I hope he found somewhere in the mountains to live the way he wants, and carved Jim's name and mine on one of them giant trees like he promised. Maybe right now he's sat outside a log cabin way out in the lonesome yonder, smoking his pipe and spitting and recollecting me.

Most days we ride out and look at the ocean, which is big and wide and stretches away forever. We aim to be gone by July thirty-second, Huck'n'Jim Day, which ain't far off now, so

Goodbye,
yours truly,
Huck Finn

69